His Sunshine Baby

Silver City Series Book 2

Jenny Fox

ISBN: 978-1-8381097-4-5

Dedication

Pour toutes les femmes fortes et indépendantes.
Pour celle qui a été ma Reagan, ma mamie.

Contents

Acknowledgements

Thanks to my Author friends, especially Mana, for helping me and supporting as I grow as an Author.

Thanks to the kind proofreaders who helped me bring this story from an awkward first online draft to a book I can feel confident publishing: Annie, Jayde, Katie, Lauren, Ludmila, Rebecca, thank you all for your kindness and patience!

Thanks to my friends and family, for being in my life, bringing me so much every day and supporting me in everything I do.

And finally, thanks to you, dear reader, for making this sequel come this far.

Thank you.

Introduction

Elena

I wish I could tell you about him.

I feel the sunshine on my skin, and I breathe in the cold dawn air. Everything is so quiet and peaceful. There are nothing but trees as far as my eyes can see. A wild north forest, surrounded by the morning mist. It's like the middle of nowhere, far away from the world.

I put the thick blanket back around me, and the rocking chair creaks softly. Let's not get cold today, my love. I grab the cup of warm tea and take a sip. You move around a bit. You already like the scent of lemons, don't you? Just like me.

I hope I can meet you soon. I hope you won't mind having a mother like me. I hope you'll forgive not having a father like him.

Nathaniel

Men are idiots.

Men in love are worse. Why is it that I can't forget her? I should throw those memories away. Live my life like always. No lingering feelings, no attachments. Isn't that how it was supposed to be anyway? I don't want to love her. I don't want to miss her.

Yet here I am, like an idiot, shutting everyone that is not her out. I don't want her lies, I don't want to be taken for a fool again. So why do I want to see her so bad? I miss her scent, I miss the soft way she smiles. I'm unconsciously looking for her everywhere I go, thinking about her every second that passes.

I want to see her. I don't care about the lies, I don't care about what's real or not. I just want all of her. Just one more chance.

I'm going crazy.

Part I

Chapter 1

I throw a new punch, hitting my target right in the stomach. He takes a couple of steps back, catches his breath. I don't give him any rest and change position for a side kick. This time, he sees it coming and uses his hands to shield his flank. Never mind, I shift my balance at the last second, and my other foot flies to hit him right in the head. He's sent flying away while I fall back on my feet.

I hear a whistle of admiration but ignore it to walk to my opponent. That last one was a bit too much, I think.

"Are you okay, kid?"

"Yeah, I'm a bit dizzy. You got my jaw, but damn Elena, that was a cool move. You have to teach me that last one."

I can't help but smile. He is a good kid. No matter what, he never complains. I hand him a water bottle while he sits up. We have been at it for twenty minutes at least, that should be enough. I start unwrapping my hand wraps and head to the gym entrance. Daniel is waiting for me on a bench.

"Someone is in top shape today," he says while staring at the teen still in the boxing ring.

"Danny, you know I hate when you whistle while I fight!"

"You were done. And I can't help it, you were smoking hot and fierce. It was so exciting!"

I roll my eyes. He sees me fighting almost every day, how does he not get bored? I grab my Adidas jacket, but just when I am about to head to the shower, I notice a figure entering the gym.

"Damn," I mutter.

"Elena!"

Crap, the Alpha looks angry. I lower my head, waiting for the storm. Danny just froze, too. We already know what he is about to say, but we can't avoid it. My wolf is already on all fours, annoyed, but I must tame her. The Alpha almost runs up to me, furious.

"How many times do I have to tell you? You are supposed to train him, not kick his ass in front of everyone!"

Everyone? There are only half a dozen people in the room! Aside from Daniel, two guys are lifting weights, and a young she-wolf is shadow boxing in the next ring. And none of them cares whether I beat Chris or not. The kid runs up to us as soon as he hears his father's yelling. Despite his swollen cheek, he steps in between his father and me.

"Father, stop it! I asked Elena to do this! Everyone already knows I'm not strong enough, how can I get stronger without getting my ass kicked?" Chris says.

"You're my son! How am I supposed to face the rest of the pack if my own son gets his ass beaten in front of the whole pack!"

Here we go again. The Alpha hates when I show my strength and am stronger than his son. But Chris is four years younger than me, and he doesn't even have an adult body yet. He's good enough for a boy his age.

I have a hard time containing my wolf. I'm not happy about this scolding either, but I don't want to make a scene. The Alpha hates it no matter who I train anyway. Even with the youngsters, I am supposed to train them without fighting or just let them win. I only agreed to fight seriously today because Chris insisted, a lot. Usually, I would only fight other warriors of the pack, and I would still be holding myself back against them. But no one is blind. They all already know I'm way stronger than most. Our Alpha is the only person who wants to keep up appearances.

"I'm sorry, Alpha."

I may as well submit right away. Otherwise, this will go on for hours, and I can't take my shower until then. His father growls, but Chris pushes me to go.

"Father, can I talk to you?"

I gave Chris a silent thanks with a nod. I know his dad will yell at him for being weak, but he is ready to endure it so that I can go. A really good kid. Daniel follows me into the ladies' changing room when the yelling starts again from behind us. We both ignore it.

Daniel waits until the shower is running to talk from behind the curtain, ensuring the Alpha can't hear us.

"Seriously, I have never seen an alpha with such a stupid inferiority complex! Why does he always have to take it out on you?"

"Danny, Chris is the one getting scolded right now. I'm good."

"I don't care, Elena. You or the kid, same thing. Why can't the Alpha leave you alone!"

I leave Daniel to his rambling, ignoring my best friend to focus on the cold water running on my skin. The feeling is amazing. While the water chases the heat and the sweat from my body, I do a quick check-up. I have a bruise on my left side, but that's it. Well, Chris is getting better. A few months ago, he couldn't even hit me. I'm proud of my student.

Danny hands me my towel when I come out. It's still early in the morning, and now that I'm all cleaned up, I'm starving.

"Do we have time for breakfast?" I ask while grabbing the clothes in my bag.

"Let's drop by George's. I can text him our order. What do you want?"

While we argue about what to eat, I put on my baggy jeans, a gray tank top, and a large hoodie. Danny makes an annoyed face.

"What's with the boyish clothes? Why don't you ever show off those curves and abs?"

I ignore him. We have this same argument every day, but no matter how much my best friend hates my style, I ignore it. I like comfy street clothes! And I hate showing off my body. I don't need other people to look at me. The more invisible I am, the better. Daniel keeps complaining until I cut him off.

"Danny, shut up. You'll get to dress me up when we go out, okay? Can we go now?"

He pouts, but at least he is not complaining. Instead of drying my hair, I just put it up with a pin. We are in June anyway; it will dry in no time. We leave the clan's gym and get into Danny's car. It's an old Toyota. He bought it two years ago from one of the old guys from the pack. It was a rubbish car, but Danny managed to make it decent by covering the cigarette burns, adding new tires and a radio, and painting the rusty parts.

I turn on the radio as soon as we are inside. Of course, it's an old Madonna song, Daniel loves her music. He starts humming along with "Holiday" as soon as we depart. I normally don't drive, but I love riding in Danny's car. I stare at the scenery outside. Living in the Arts District is like getting a free art museum tour every day. New waves of graffiti on every wall, weird pipe sculptures from time to time, and colorful houses. An old car was even emptied and transformed into an urban garden, flowers sprouting randomly all over it. I open the window to enjoy the morning breeze and sunshine. Danny is now happily singing "Like a Virgin."

"Okay, let's go out tonight, babe. I feel like dancing."

"What about your exams?" I ask.

His Sunshine Baby

Danny is a nerd 80% of the time and a party animal for the rest of it. He is always the one to insist we go out, but also the first one to complain about his headaches before going to work. He is a biology student, but I bet none of his lab partners know that the lab rat loves going to nightclubs.

"They're still a week away."

I nod. Daniel is a straight-A student anyway, he will probably ace them like he always does whether we go out or not. I peek at my best friend while we are stuck in traffic. Daniel is the skinny type despite his efforts to build some muscle at the gym. But with his blonde hair and gorgeous blue eyes, he is quite popular. I hate when he grows that stupid goatee of his, though. He's too lazy to shave during the week, so he leaves it to grow wild and puts his hair back. He only dresses up for the weekend; otherwise, he picks whatever weird, patterned shirt he can find. Who said gay guys were stylish? Daniel is only good at complaining about my style.

"What is it, mesmerized by this handsome blondie?" he asks when he catches me staring.

"I was wondering when you are going to shave. You look like a caveman."

"And you look like a boy. My sister gave you some actual women's clothing. You know, the kind that is your size and doesn't make you look like you live in a garage."

I roll my eyes. Daniel hates my boyish clothes. I used to be much more feminine, and he misses that part of me. But that part of me is bound by some painful memories I don't want to deal with.

"Okay, you get to dress me up tonight, if you shave off this beard."

He makes a victory sign in the air.

"Moon Goddess, yes! My girl is going to be so hot with her heels, skirt, and makeup! The poor men of Silver City better get ready, I am taking an *anatomic* bomb to the dance floor tonight! We need to show off those killer legs! Come on, Madonna, I need to sing it. Where is that song again?"

I laugh when he starts making ridiculous dance moves to match 'Vogue' 's beat. I love Danny exactly for this. No matter what, my best friend has no sense of shame. He does whatever he wants and doesn't care what other people think, even when he's dancing to some pop music while singing loudly with the car windows down. I keep laughing and start singing my heart out with him.

We act like teenagers until we reach George's restaurant. I can't stop laughing at Danny's singing as we walk in. From behind the counter, George smiles.

"Into the groove so early in the morning? You two are in high spirits!"

"It's Friday, and I am taking this lady dancing tonight," says Daniel.

"Really? You should go to Pepe's club then. It's Pride-themed all month, and he misses you guys."

"Sounds good. And Daniel loves Latinos."

I wink at my best friend, who nods with a sneaky smile. Daniel's favorite type of man is easy to remember. If they are tall, Latino, and muscular, he falls in love within minutes. George takes out two boxes with our order and clicks his tongue.

"Come on, Danny, you should find one for Elena first."

"No, no, George. Dancing is fine, but no guys. I can enjoy myself just fine on my own," I reply.

"Oh, come on, girl. You should give it a try sometime! A guy asked for your number again this week."

"Was he handsome?" Daniel asks.

"Not really. And I already told him you wouldn't be interested, sweetie, don't worry. But if you ever change your mind about the whole I don't need a man thing, let me know! I kept some of the numbers from the cutest guys."

He gives me a wink and turns around to prepare our coffees. Daniel pouts.

"I hate it. Why do I have to be the sexy blonde's friend? Why don't I get phone numbers?"

"First of all, I'm not sexy. Second, George said the guy wasn't that cute. And third, you're blonde and popular too. Who was kissing that hot Brazilian guy last weekend? What happened to him?" I ask.

"Hernando? He's from Mexico, and he wasn't that hot."

That's Daniel for you. He falls out of love just that quickly. Sometimes, I wonder if he doesn't do it on purpose because of me. He knows I don't want a boyfriend, but he wouldn't stick to one-night stands just because of me, right?

We pay and leave with our breakfast to eat in the car. Cinnamon roll for me, veggie bowl for Daniel, and black coffee for the both of us. It's a ten-minute ride to my school, and I'm done way before Daniel drops me off in the parking lot. I grab my bag from the back seat and kiss him on the cheek.

"I can meet you at the lab later. My classes finish at 5 p.m."

"You better bring coffee with you!"

I nod. This is our usual routine. We repeat this conversation every morning. The car starts again, and Daniel heads off to the science university a few streets away. I take my cap out of my bag and put it on as I head to the business school.

Chapter 2

"Will you just stop moving!"

"Seriously, Danny, this is too tight."

"It's not too tight, it fits! This is the feeling of adjusted, well-sized clothes!"

I growl at him, annoyed. Is this supposed to be so revealing, too? This dress doesn't even cover half of my legs!

"Where did you even get this?"

"Don't ask. Come on, don't you like it?" he asks with a smirk.

Well, I can't say I hate it. It's a rose gold sequin dress without sleeves, just thin straps. But it still stops mid-thigh and reveals a lot of cleavage. I don't think I've ever worn something so sexy. I glance at the mirror, but no matter how I look at it, it does go well with my beige skin.

"I know you like it, babe, and it's high time you learn to show off those legs. Come on, just take it as a birthday present from me."

"We decided my birthday was in August. You're two months early, Danny."

"Details. Now stop whining and do your hair."

I roll my eyes. He can be so pushy sometimes! Nonetheless, I grab my comb and start taking care of my wet hair. He's really going all out tonight. It's funny how easily he can totally change his outer appearance. Danny insisted on taking his shower before me and changed into a silver shirt and black jeans. The lab rat turned into a sexy guy within an hour. He even took off his nerdy glasses and put a silver piercing in his ear. Damn, he is hot.

"Here are your shoes," he says while pushing a pair of high heels in front of me.

I finish combing my hair and decide to let it fall naturally on my back.

"Did you go see your dad? How was he?"

"Same as usual. Still not much of a talker," I sigh.

"It's okay, baby. He'll get better."

I nod but don't reply. Daniel asks the same question every day. I wish I had a different answer for once. He checks his hair in the mirror while I step away to put on my heels.

"By the way, Mom wants to see you. You're invited to our next family brunch."

"Your sister is back?"

"Yep! The dress is from her shop."

"I should have known."

Daniel's sister is only a few years older than us, but she already has two clothing stores. She's a hard-working, self-made woman. Most importantly, she loves dressing people up, even more so than her brother. No wonder Daniel picked this dress.

"Come on, let's get going, gorgeous!"

I barely have time to grab my favorite earrings before Daniel pushes me out of our apartment. It takes me a few seconds to adjust to the high heels while we walk to his car, and he chuckles. I ignore him, and once we finally reach his car, I check myself in the mirror. I'm satisfied with the light makeup, but I still can't get used to being half-naked. Why does he care so much about what I wear tonight? Usually, a pair of black pants and a fancy bareback top are enough.

Daniel starts driving, and I notice the direction we're headed is odd. I frown.

"Did you forget the way?"

"Nope. We are not going to Pepe's bar."

"Why not?" I ask, annoyed.

He could have told me before changing our plans!

"You need a break from the clan, baby. The Alpha's been on your back nonstop these days, and he's going to fuss again if someone sees you partying. And you know the guys always talk."

I can't say he's wrong. Last time, a pair of guys told Xavier, and the next morning was hell. He scolded me for hours because I went partying before a training day.

"Those guys were just pissed because I ignored them," I sigh.

"I know, baby, but I'm not letting those idiots be jackasses to you again just because you aren't acknowledging their stupid flirting. I'm taking you somewhere we will be at peace."

I sigh again, but damn, Daniel is right. No matter what, my uncle finds any possible excuse to scold me. Moreover, he always knows when I go out and which clubs I go to. I know this is our territory, but still, sometimes I wish I was part of the main White Moon clan instead of the Opal Moon clan. Clark Hamilton, the White Moon Alpha, treats me way better than my uncle Xavier.

"Alright Danny, where are we going then?"

"A new club! The Rain. Brand new, and anyone can attend."

"I didn't know there was a new nightclub opening. Is it in the Latin district?"

Daniel looks a bit embarrassed and focuses on his driving a bit too much. What is he hiding now? It doesn't look like he's headed to the Latin District or even staying within the White or Opal Moon territories. We're almost at the border!

"Daniel, where are we going?"

He ignores me and starts humming. Is he kidding me? I turn the stereo off, one thing he hates, and glare at him.

"Danny!"

"Fine! It's on the Velvet Moon territory."

"The Velvet— Have you gone mad, Daniel Lewis?"

What is he thinking! This is basically jumping into a whole of problems!

The Velvet Moon belongs to the Black brothers, the most dangerous trio in this city and for miles around it! I've never seen any of the three brothers, but I've heard plenty enough to know this is madness. The eldest of the Black brothers is the King of this city and the most dangerous brother. Not only is he known to be impatient and violent, but the guy also murdered his own father, who was a butcher himself! The second brother is famous too. He is the one meeting the other packs on behalf of his brother and is depicted as cold, ruthless, and unforgiving. "An iron hand in a velvet glove," that's where his pack's name comes from! The youngest brother is somewhat of a mystery, mostly because he's too young for any position.

The Velvet Moon territory, what is he thinking?

"Calm down, baby! It's an open event, anyone can go! And it's super close to our border too. If anything happens, we'll be out of there in a flash. I promise," says Daniel.

"Daniel, if—"

"No, no if, babe. You need this. Some fresh air, outside of the clan. No one to watch you, no one to bother you. You can have your fun for one night."

He puts a hand on my shoulder and gives me a warm smile. Danny may be right; I could use a real night of relaxing. Things have been tense recently, and with my exams due next week, I didn't get any time off either.

"Alright, fine. But promise we will leave when I say we do."

"Promise. You know I'm not leaving my girl alone."

I finally smile and relax a bit. That's true. Daniel is the most reliable friend I could have. No matter how drunk he gets, he's always looking out for me.

He drives a few more minutes, and we enter the Velvet Moon territory, just like that. As he said, no werewolves seem to mind our intrusion when we park right in front of The Rain. The music is already pulsing from the inside of the club, and I can tell it's probably packed with people. Daniel gives me a wink and takes my hand, guiding me to the entrance. A large guy and two wolves are guarding it, but after taking a peek at our IDs, we get in just like that. The bouncer even gives me a smile.

Once we are finally in, I must admit, I'm impressed. It's classy, with velvet sofas, a large bar, and more than enough space to dance in front of the DJ's mixing table. There are lots of different colored lights, but the main display is mostly shades of pink, purple, and white.

Daniel guides me to the middle of the dance floor, already excited. I notice most of the girls barely have any clothes on, and my dress looks just right in here. I feel a lot better, and the rhythm of Ariana Grande's "Into You" starts pulsating loudly. The DJ is quite good; the music's volume is just right. Daniel starts dancing immediately. He smiles like a kid as he enjoys having fun and showing off his dance moves.

I find the right beat and start dancing as well. It feels so great! I just let it all go and let my limbs move on their own. I rotate my hips, shift my weight from side to side, sway my arms, and find any movement that feels good. My rose gold dress is shining brightly under the lights, and I like it. I lip-sync the lyrics without thinking.

'Got everyone watching us, so baby let's keep this secret... A little bit scandalous, but baby, don't let them see it...'

I notice Daniel is singing out loud, though no one can really hear. He's so into it. A girl has started dancing with him, and he lets her without moving away from me. I smile at him and turn around, enjoying myself to the fullest. This is awesome! I keep dancing as the song goes on with its enticing rhythm.

A few songs pass, but I can't stop. Daniel is totally into this, too. Suddenly, the rhythm changes into a new song, something different. Around us, a few girls look a bit confused. Oh, come on, never heard of reggaeton before? Oh right, it's the Velvet Moon. They are probably used to more mainstream stuff. For Danny and I, who enjoy nights in the Latin clubs, this is perfect. My best friend joins me and we start dancing real close. Reggaeton is slower but much more sensual. I move my hips, playing with my legs too. Now I know why Daniel picked this dress.

We keep going without any shame, and I feel several eyes on me. Flirtatious glances, but I ignore them and enjoy myself. The temperature keeps rising with the southern sounds. I flip my hair and raise my eyes. There is a balcony upstairs, running all around the dance floor, with people dancing or chatting with glasses in their hands. Is that a VIP floor or something? Looks like some private party for flashy people.

What is up with that guy? Right in the middle, a man is staring right at me. He's staring so intensely with ice blue eyes. I unconsciously keep staring at him too, while dancing. Damn, he is devilishly handsome and equally as hot. Blondes aren't usually my type, but this one is beyond any criteria. He looks like a devil disguised as an angel. A white silk shirt that's open down his torso, with pale, perfect skin, and features like a Greek sculpture. Fierce looking, with sharp traits, and thin lips. Moon Goddess, I'm going to melt if he keeps staring.

I avert my eyes, trying to focus on something else, but it doesn't change a thing. I can still feel his intense stare on me. My skin is on fire, but this time, the dancing isn't the real cause. I turn my head and find him in the exact same position, still eyeing me. I feel a sudden chill. Think straight, Elena, this smells like a lot of trouble, ignore him.

"Baby?"

"I'm okay, Danny."

"Ahem, I was asking if you want something to drink."

"Oh, a Mojito then."

"Gotcha."

But before Daniel leaves, I shake my head for him to stay and I walk up to the bar. I need a drink, like, right now. Something to calm me down. When I reach the bar, I order our drinks. When I go to pay, the barmaid smiles.

"It's on the house, Miss."

Of course it is. I raise my head and find the guy again with my eyes. He raises his glass to me.

...What does this guy want? We stare at each other while the barmaid is busy preparing our mojitos. Him, from upstairs, leaning nonchalantly on the railing, and me looking up in his direction from the bar. His eyes look so cold, yet I feel myself getting hotter from his gaze. He's an alpha, but which pack? Not one I know. I would never forget a man like him.

I try to ignore him and quickly thank the barmaid when receiving our Mojitos. Now to find Daniel. My best friend joins me first, and we decide to take a break and sit down at the bar. I purposely choose to sit facing the other way so I don't have to look at that guy, but I can feel his burning stare.

"What is it?" asks Daniel.

I decide to talk to him using our mind-link. I hate having to yell over a crowd, and the music is really loud.

"*See that guy behind me? On the second floor, blonde guy.*"

"*Holy Mother Moon Goddess, I do. Are they missing a sculpture at the museum? That guy is hot as f—!*"

"*Is he staring?*"

"*Yep, right at you. Heavens, how do you always attract them? This guy looks like he could be undressing you from where he is!*"

I blush like crazy and slap him on his leg. He is not helpful at all! I take a long sip of my Mojito, trying to think about something else. Daniel is busy eyeing other guys in the bar, but none of them seem to be to his liking because he wants us to go back to dancing as soon as our glasses are empty.

While we head back to the dance floor, I can't help but steal a glance toward the second floor, but this time, he's gone. I try to look for him, but he's nowhere to be found. I feel an ounce of disappointment but try to ignore it.

I want to focus on the music. The DJ makes it louder with a new mix of "Taki Taki," another song we know. Daniel's already dancing, sexy and hot like a pro. Nobody could tell he's a total lab nerd by day. I try to follow the rhythm and chase that unsettling feeling away. I wish I had drunk a bit more, but the music gets to me, and I forget myself again. I move my legs, my hips, my arms, and enjoy myself. The song changes again, and more people come dancing to the now-famous "Cross Your Mind."It's a bit more crowded, but I don't care and keep dancing.

At some point, I realize I've lost Daniel among the people dancing. I'm not so worried, he's a big boy, so I keep dancing and looking for my favorite blondie. While doing so, I suddenly stop. A pair of striking blue eyes got dangerously close.

It's that guy staring straight at me again. He's dancing this time, but his eyes won't leave me. Damn, he even knows how to dance. He's good, too. As we dance, we naturally get closer, attracted like magnets. I can't take my eyes off him. His open shirt showed off his pale skin with a bead of sweat. Daniel's right, guys like that can't be real, can they?

But before I can decide, he's right in front of me, disarming me with a sly smile. Following the flow of the music, he puts his hand on my waist in a very subtle and natural manner. Damn, this guy smells like trouble, yet I can't refuse it. I keep dancing, my skin flirting with his, our bodies in sync with the flow. I've never felt so sexy while dancing, but this guy is raising the temperature through the roof.

The rhythm accelerates, and so does my breathing. I flip my hair, turn and move, and he follows it all without a flinch. His hand is still there, guiding me. He is playing with his fingers around my hips. We're so close, yet that's the only part of him touching me. His face is only a few inches away and I can see every detail of the blue streaks in his eyes reflecting with the lights. I feel his breath caressing my neck, my shoulders. This tension is unreal.

The music changes again, but we don't stop. This time, we're really dancing together, his body against mine, his hands going up and down on my thighs. I feel his torso against my back, and I realize my back is bare against his skin. Yet that doesn't stop me. He puts a hand on my stomach and lets me dance against him, keeping us close together.

I feel guilty for enjoying this so much, but Moon Goddess, I won't stop. It's like I'm trapped in this dance with him, and the music is barely of any importance anymore. We keep going, for I don't know how long. He's maintaining a perfect balance between sexiness, enticement, and respect. His hands never venture too far, yet the desire is real. I can tell from the way he caresses my skin to the burning looks we exchange. His lips get awfully close to my skin a few times and I find myself wanting more.

I find my rhythm within his arms, and without exchanging a word, we enjoy ourselves to the fullest. I smile confidently, yet I also blush a bit. It's a weird sensation, something that burns my skin and tickles my insides. I'm so hot I can barely breathe. I need to get some fresh air outside, yet I keep delaying the moment we will have to stop.

Is he going to dance with another girl if I leave? Is he just playing around? Is he serious? I'm going nuts with wild thoughts. I need to stop.

"Wanna take a break?"

He said it before I stopped. I'm so surprised. I was thinking of walking away, but he stopped dancing first and asked while keeping a hand around me. He doesn't want me to go away. I nod, trying to regain my composure. Yes, I could really use some fresh air.

Before I can say a word, he suddenly grabs my hand and takes me with him. I follow behind, but against my expectations, he doesn't take me outside but up to the second floor where he was a few minutes ago. I realize a guy is guarding the stairs, but he only gives one look to my partner before letting us through. So, he's definitely a VIP here. The second floor is a lot less crowded, but he doesn't stop and takes me through the whole floor. He flips a curtain, still holding my hand tight, and we suddenly arrive on a deserted balcony.

Damn. It's a small space, with only a couple of oriental-style sofas and a tent, but the view is breathtaking. All of Silver City and a bit of the sea behind it. It's gorgeous.

"Incredible," I whisper to myself.

"Glad you like it."

I turn towards him, surprised he heard me. Damn werewolf hearing. He's smiling softly, obviously satisfied. He takes a seat, nonchalantly leaning an arm on the rail. I sit facing him, but I just have to slightly turn my head to enjoy the view. To my surprise, a waitress walks in with two glasses. A new Mojito for me, and a glass of bourbon for him. I thank her and take my drink.

"Thank you for the drink," I tell him before taking a sip.

"Thank you for the dance, Miss…?"

"Elena."

"Elena, nice to meet you. I'm Nate."

Nate? Is that a nickname for Nathan then? Maybe he doesn't use his full name often. I nod and try to distract myself a bit with the view.

"You go dancing often, I would guess? I've never seen you around."

"I'm more used to the Latin district," I answer honestly.

"Oh, that explains how good you are with that kind of music."

"You weren't too bad yourself."

"Thanks," he replies with a smile.

We both stay silent for a while, and the freshness of the night starts to calm me down. It feels so great. Summer is definitely my favorite season, and what I love most are these hot summer nights.

"You're from here?"

He nods.

"The Velvet Moon clan."

Shit. One of the Black brothers' packs. I bite my lip. Judging by his

Alpha Aura he can barely hide, I bet he's a lieutenant, too. I knew this was their nightclub. I can't be too surprised, but I do feel a bit disappointed. Hanging with a guy from a different pack is asking for trouble, even more so if he's related to the Blood Moon clan. And the Velvet Moon is the Blood Moon branch clan. What a mess…

Yet, I glance at him, unwilling to leave. What am I thinking about? I swore I would never get a boyfriend again anyway, so what am I hoping for? Don't be an idiot, Elena, don't!

"Elena?"

"Yes?"

Wow, it feels weird to hear my name from his lips.

"Do you have a boyfriend?"

"No, and I don't want one," I reply mechanically.

"Interesting."

I frown, a bit surprised. What a weird answer, and what does it mean?

"Why are you asking me this?" I ask, curious.

"Because I'm interested in you."

His blunt answer is disarming. I frown. Don't get into this mess, Elena. Don't, don't, don't.

"How so?"

"I'm like you. I'm not interested in getting a girlfriend either. I don't do commitment or long-term relationships."

Well, that's definitely noted. At least I'll be safe in that way. I actually feel myself relaxing a little. So, he's a player. Great, that means no expectations and no disappointment whatsoever for me. No falling in love, either. I nod slowly at his answer, thinking I had fun anyway. And he's honest, too. Now I know what to not expect. I take a new sip from my drink. Maybe he just wanted a nice talk without me getting any ideas, which is understandable. With an appearance like his, girls must be fighting over being his girlfriend.

"But you said you're interested in me."

"Yes. I find you beautiful and attractive, in a physical way."

Oh, so it's about the sex then. Wow, this feels like a 50 Shades scene, aside from the fact that he doesn't look like a sadist and I'm not a clueless virgin. I smile, and I'm about to answer when he opens his mouth first.

"Can I kiss you?"

I stare at his very serious expression, for a while, before I chuckle, not knowing how to react. Who asks that kind of thing? Seriously!

"Is that a joke?" I ask, a bit confused.

Maybe he just said that as a joke, or to ease the atmosphere. Or to test me? However, his expression is clearly anything but funny.

"No, I meant it. I don't make those kinds of jokes, especially about things I want. And I want to kiss you."

His answer agitates me. How can he be so blunt? Isn't he ashamed or embarrassed at all? I don't know how to answer for a few seconds, but he's obviously the type who doesn't know shame, only what he wants. He smiles and suddenly moves towards me, only slowing down a second before he takes that kiss. For a moment I'm too surprised to react.

He's a really good kisser. Moon Goddess, his lips. I don't think before I answer his kiss, totally giving in. I close my eyes. It's been a while since I've felt like this... something delightful in my stomach, and my skin burning up. The butterflies. I take pleasure in it and don't want to think about anything else. He takes his time, playing with my lips, being passionate and gentle at the same time. Time stops around us. I forget the music, the nightclub.

I have no idea how long our kissing lasts. I feel his hand gently caressing my neck, and I have no idea when I grabbed his shirt either. What is it about his smell? My wolf loves it, is it because he's an alpha? Well, who cares? This is just so delightful.

We both slow down, and our lips part. I blush a bit, still feeling hot and overwhelmed. He is still smiling faintly, looking at me with satisfaction. Damn, that man just reduced my whole twenty-one years of experience and self-control to dust. I sigh and run my fingers through my hair, trying to regain my composure. He stopped kissing me, but the tip of his fingers still quietly caresses my leg. It's faint and very natural. Nothing unsettling about it, but I can't pretend he isn't doing anything either.

"I'll assume that you enjoyed it?" he asks.

Of course I did, and he knows it. I sigh and nod, trying to think about what to say next. Moon Goddess yes, the woman in me wants him. Yet, something in the back of my mind is warning me. My wolf senses an Alpha, and I smell a lot of trouble ahead.

"Is that all you want?"

It was almost a whisper, but the question went from my mind to my lips, and I didn't stop it. He looks a bit surprised, and for a second, even seems to hesitate. However, he has that smile on again soon enough.

"Yes. Just one night, between consenting adults. At dawn, we will part ways. No pressure whatsoever. I just hope you'll accept."

Until dawn. I take a sip of my drink, hoping the alcohol would help me calm down a little. What am I hesitating for? This isn't a first for me, and we are both clear on not getting any feelings involved. I have this little voice in my head, telling me this might be dangerous, that it might be a mistake.

"Alright. Just for one night," I hear myself saying.

His face lights up at my answer and my heart skips a beat. He drinks a sip of his whiskey and gives me one of those devilish smiles of his.

"Great," he whispers.

I take another sip, and he suddenly changes seats to take the one next to me. His proximity makes me nervous. He doesn't get too close, however, maintaining a few inches between us.

"Did you come alone?"

"With my friend."

"Will your friend mind if you leave early?"

"No, I can let him know."

"*Danny?*"

"*There you are! Where did you go, babe?*"

"*Upstairs.*"

"*Not alone?*"

"*Not alone. Danny, do you mind if I leave first?*"

"*Moon Goddess, the blonde guy? Go for it, girl! Just mind-link me if you need anything, okay? He better be a gentleman! Velvet Moon or not, don't hold back and kick his ass if he is a douchebag!*"

"*Alright, alright. You be careful too, okay? Text me when you're home!*"

"*You better not be home until morning, have your fun!*"

"*Love ya.*"

"*Love ya too, babe.*"

I end the conversation and turn to Nate. He probably guessed I was busy, because he waited patiently, just finishing his drink.

"Done?" he asks.

"Done."

"Alright. Come."

I finish my Mojito in one go, and he takes my hand as we exit the balcony. I do regret a bit that we are leaving so quickly, I wish I had enjoyed the view a bit longer. I'll have to see if there's a way to get that VIP access if I ever come back with Danny.

Nate doesn't let go of my hand as he guides me to the entrance of the nightclub. Did he come alone? Several people seem to recognize him, but he doesn't talk to anyone as we leave the building. We walk to the parking lot, where he guides me all the way to what looks like a very expensive car. A convertible Mercedes? Handsome and rich, of course.

"Where are we going?" I ask.

"A suite."

Now I wish I hadn't asked. Is he willing to spend money, or just reluctant to take me to his place? Could be both, but I wouldn't ask. Just as I am about to open the door, we both stop.

Some yelling and growling are coming from one side of The Rain nightclub. Is it a back entrance? Nate is frowning and staring in that direction too.

I would usually ignore that kind of thing, but I recognize a couple of the voices. My wolf's instinct is reacting too. Oh, crap.

I let go of his car's handle and head straight for the origin of the voices, hoping I'm wrong. As I get closer, I realize I'm unfortunately right. A couple of bouncers are growling angrily at a small group of teenagers. Half a dozen young werewolves, Moon Goddess, and they belong to the White Moon pack. I can't ignore it.

"*Danny, get your ass outside. We have a problem.*"

"*Wait, what? What problem?*"

But I don't have time to answer. As I get closer to the group, it becomes obvious the youngsters are angry for not being able to enter the place. They are really drunk. The girls are all stumbling in their high heels and party dresses and the guys' shirts are open and messy. Seriously? Why are they causing trouble on another clan's territory!

"Jackie!" I yell at one of the girls I know.

She sees me, as well as the rest of the group. There are three girls and two boys, all familiar faces. The brunette runs to me and I immediately notice how she reeks of cheap vodka.

"Elena! That guy won't let us in! Can you believe that?"

As I walk up to the rest of the group, she keeps clinging onto my arm and complaining. One of the other girls is about to open her mouth and do the same, but I interrupt with my growling.

"Are you kids crazy? This is not our territory!"

The girls stop complaining and look down because of my angry growling. One of the boys, obviously drunk, doesn't care and starts yelling at me.

"They said it's an open invitation! Any wolf! We want to get in and have fun! This is discrimination!"

"Any sober and adult wolf, you brats!"

I growl at him again, but unfortunately, I'm not used to scolding someone so drunk. Nate arrives next to me and glances at the bouncers. They explain themselves before he even asks anything.

"They don't have any ID and are obviously in no state to come in. We asked them to move along but they insisted, sir."

Oh, right, if he's a lieutenant of the Velvet Moon, he probably is responsible for what goes on here too. I turn to him, both embarrassed and annoyed because of the kids.

"Sorry about the commotion. I know these kids, I'll handle them."

Nate looks pissed, but I get the feeling that it's not because of the youngsters' attitude. It's because that means I'm not coming with him. One of the girls suddenly starts crying over absolutely nothing and I sigh before grabbing her arm.

"Enough, Prue! You guys stop it, you're coming with me right now. I'm taking you all home."

"Who do, who do you think you are to give us orders?" one of the boys suddenly yells.

I growl at him. Before I can answer, Daniel suddenly arrives and grabs him by the neck.

"She's your freaking trainer, you idiot! Respect your superiors, you little punk! Eyes down and shut it before I slap your drunk little butt!"

I sigh in relief. I don't know if I could handle five teens alone, but Daniel's arrival saves me a lot of trouble. At least, the boys stop growling and the girls stop whining. I turn to Nate, who is still frowning, and obviously pissed.

"Sorry, I have to take them back home. I'm really sorry."

He takes a while to answer, studying our little group with his cold eyes. Wow, I can feel his wolf's anger from where I stand. Is it that mad that the youngsters caused a commotion? I hope he doesn't tell his boss or something like that, those kids aren't supposed to be here to begin with. Neither are Daniel nor me.

"This is only a postponement. We can catch up later."

I nod without thinking too much about it. I have no intention to keep chatting about our agreement when we are not alone. I already feel Daniel's stare on me.

"Okay, let's go. Come on, get moving," I sigh while dragging the kids along.

This time, the group doesn't resist and starts walking northward,

Daniel leading them. As we walk away, I suddenly hear one of the bouncer's voices.

"Sorry about that, Mr. Black."

Wait a second. What the hell did he call him? I immediately stop, and Daniel does the same, turning to me with big eyes. Holy crap. I turn around to look at Nate once again, completely shocked.

"*What did you say that guy was called?*"

"*He just said to call him Nate…*"

"*You mean Nate, as in Nathaniel freaking Black?!*"

Chapter 3

"Nathaniel Black? Really?"

Daniel keeps repeating this, and it's annoying. It's 2:00 a.m., we just got home, and I'm too exhausted to put up with his nagging now. I take off my heels and throw them across the room, hoping they would land close to the wardrobe.

"Don't throw stuff!"

"Who cares? I'm tired. I will put them back properly tomorrow."

"Anyway, girl, Nathaniel Black is a big no, you know that right? Any member of that family is a no. Actually, anyone from the Blood or Velvet Moon clans is a no!"

I know, I know. I still remember that chill I got when I heard his name. Nathaniel Black. What were the odds? Now that I think about it, there were signs. His acting like he owned the place, how everyone acted around him, his Alpha Aura. I'm so stupid! We get out of our territory once and I meet one of the most dangerous guys out there! I take off my jewelry and dress, then head to the bathroom to remove my makeup. Danny's voice follows me.

"Seriously, how do you always end up attracting those kinds of troublemakers? I know, it's my fault for taking you there, but still, babe! You have rotten luck! Nathaniel Black of all people. This is the last time you see him, you hear me? I'm putting in my best friend veto right here and now, Elena!"

I roll my eyes. Whatever with his veto, I'm probably never going there again anyway. I still feel a bit bitter about it. I was replaying the night again and again while we took the young ones home. Moon Goddess, that kiss. No doubt I would have gone with him if that stupid incident in the parking lot hadn't happened. And then what? He would have taken me to a fancy hotel, and we would have had sex. Then goodbye? He was very blunt and clear about it, yet I keep thinking about his words. And his eyes. He did seem very interested. Was it just physical attraction?

Danny joins me in the bathroom, but I act normal. I wash my face and brush my teeth.

"Let's just go to Pepe's next time. No strangers, no surprises. We should play it safe. I don't want you in any more trouble."

"I'm not in trouble," I sigh.

"You are so in trouble. Your uncle is looking for any reason to scold you every chance he gets. You know that. So let's not give him any for a while. Okay, babe?"

I nod, but Danny is way too optimistic. My uncle probably already knows we went out, and I'll get a scolding tomorrow for sure. It's not that bad though, I'm used to it. I jump into my pajamas and get into bed after saying good night to Danny. Though once I'm there, I can't fall asleep. I'm still thinking about what happened on that balcony and what I felt. He was attractive, for sure, but I've met handsome men before and never felt like that. I thought I had closed my heart, that I would never let my feelings decide for me again. But this guy, Nathaniel. Nate.

I turn around and grab my phone. After hesitating a couple of seconds, I type his name in the search bar. A few local news articles pop up. As usual, his brothers' pictures are unavailable, but Nathaniel seems to be the face of the Black Corporation. No wonder they picked him. He looks good from any angle. Always well dressed in brand-name clothes. Very clean and classy. The pictures show him shaking hands with CEOs, big names of every industry, and even a couple of other packs' Alphas. I find an article with his short biography and scroll down. High-school dropout turned multimillionaire, owns several estates in the leisure industry, as well as a few renowned restaurants and clubs. The guy just turned 22 years old. He's about a year older than me. I keep reading, but we don't have much in common. I'm still a university student, with a big loan, and too many family and pack issues to handle.

I put down my phone. I just dipped a finger in a different world than mine, and that's already way too much for me to handle. Danny is probably right. I should avoid him, avoid trouble, and be grateful I did not cross that line. As I said, it's very unlikely we'll meet again anyway…

My two Mojitos help me find some sleep, but the night is short. My alarm rings at 8 o'clock sharp until I turn it off with a groan. Saturday, here we come.

The apartment is empty. Daniel already left for the university to check his experiments, according to the sticky note on the fridge. Thank Moon

Goddess he made coffee before that because I'm going to need it. A shower and two cups of coffee later, I head off to the dojo. I'm training the young ones and after the mess they got us into last night, I have no intention of going easy on them. I'm already in my workout outfit. A simple sports bra and shorts; it is June after all. I just head straight to the tatami mats.

The first one ready, as usual, is my cousin Iris, Chris' big sister. She is my age, smart, and pretty, yet she barely has any Alpha Aura. I don't know if she conceals it or not, but she looks totally harmless and nice. Which explains why she is so popular among the male wolves of our pack. When I approach, she nods very politely.

"Hello, Elena. You look tired! Rough night?"

"Hi, Iris. Yeah, you could say that. How was your week?"

"Just fine, the usual," she replies with a smile.

Iris is your typical bookworm, a shy but nice girl. However, I can never understand why she decided to dye her hair a lilac shade with such a quiet personality. Figures.

We chit-chat while everyone else gets ready. My cousin and I were never really close; our personalities and interests are just too different, I guess. Though I consider her a friend, we barely ever talk about personal stuff.

Meanwhile, the group slowly gathers. There are about thirty people, mostly teenagers and a few young wolves around my age. In the beginning, I felt a bit uncomfortable teaching people who were about my age or older, but no one ever challenged me. I used to think it was because of my uncle's orders, but later I realized they were actually aware of my strength and Alpha Aura and had no problem acknowledging either of them. Moreover, a few of them did see me fight a couple of times with wolves twice my size and age and win. That's exactly the kind of thing that werewolves respect most, regardless of anything else.

As I give the first exercises, everyone starts running or working out. I do the same with the group. I've always loved exercising and fighting. It might be my wolf side talking, but ever since I was a pup, I've been a fighter. I can't go a day without working out somehow, whether I go running, hit the gym, or do some shadow boxing.

Among the pack, I'm one of the top fighters, though my uncle doesn't let me compete with the others. I only get to fight rogues from time to time. I wish I could have proper matches with my peers, but my uncle just won't let me. So frustrating.

After a few hours, the whole group is exhausted. I help everyone stretch before letting them go. Once again Iris walks up to me, a bit sweaty but smiling. My cousin has remarkable endurance too.

"That felt great! I still have to work on my form though."

"You already look great, Iris."

She sighs. "Not as great as you! Everyone knows Chris and I are way behind you. Especially Dad."

I feel sorry about that, but I can't change my strength, though I do try to keep it concealed. I just nod and grab my towel to wipe off. My cousin is not done talking.

"I heard you and Danny went out of the territory last night. Is it true you went to that new club? The Rain?"

I stop. How did she know? Oh, she probably talked with the other kids that we caught yesterday. I decide to tell her the truth.

"Yeah, Danny wanted to check it out. We didn't stay long though."

"I know. Too bad the others decided to act silly. How was it? I've heard about it, I'm curious!"

Really? Iris doesn't seem like the type to go to nightclubs. I never see her around when Daniel and I go partying; not in the Latin District, at least.

"It was okay. A bit too classy for us, I would say."

"Well, the Velvet Moon tends to be high-end after all. I heard all their establishments are like that."

She's probably right on that one, from what I saw yesterday. Though I like Iris, I don't plan to stay around long enough to run into my uncle. I grab my bag and head to the showers, but Iris follows me.

"I wish I could go to one of those places one day. Do you plan on returning there again?"

I remember Danny's words from last night. At least one person doesn't want me to. But Iris seems interested. Be reasonable, Elena.

"Probably not, Iris. You know your dad wouldn't want me there. I'm probably going to stick around and not cross our border for a while."

Yes, I should do that. Forget about it, not get in trouble. Stick to my daily routine. That shouldn't be too hard, right? Iris looks disappointed, but she doesn't respond to that and we part ways to take our showers.

But my cousin's words gave me food for thought. Would I see him again if I went to The Rain one more time? Danny is right, I have a thing for trouble. Seriously, why am I even thinking about this?

I finish changing and head to the library, trying to fill my mind with something else. I still have a paper to hand in for economics. I immerse myself in studies and caffeine, watching the hours pass. Just when I'm about to be done, my phone vibrates. Probably Danny saying he's done. I take out my smartphone, but the text I received leaves me speechless. An invite for a private event at The Rain?

I stare at that text for a few seconds, a bit distraught. How did they even get my number? We only stayed a few hours and paid in cash. I read it again, but it's short. Just mentioning something about an "invite-only" fancy event on the upper floor.

I can't ignore the idea that this might have come from Nathaniel, but there wasn't any chance for him to get my number. From what I recall, I just gave him my first name! Should I share this text with Daniel? He will probably freak out and tell me not to go. Though I do want to go, I just don't care about the party.

Let's just ignore it for now. I put my phone aside and try to focus on my paper for a couple more hours. It's finally 1:00 p.m. and I leave the library. I get into Danny's car that he left at the university parking lot. Just as I'm about to start the car, Daniel sends me a couple of texts to complain about his morning at the lab and his experiments not going well. I give him a quick message of encouragement, with lots of hearts and the emojis he likes. I don't mention the text I received earlier about the nightclub. I love my best friend, but sometimes, he is a bit too much.

I start the car and drive all the way to the hospital. When I enter, the nurse at the front desk recognizes me.

"Hello, sweetheart. Say hi to your dad for me, will you?"

"Hi, Annie. I will, thanks."

I hop onto the elevator, reaching the fifth floor a few seconds later. I've walked these corridors so often, I could get to my father's room with my eyes closed. He is sharing the room with two other people. As a result, I always go in as quietly as possible and walk straight to his bed. He has the one closest to the window. No one is here today, but I still take small steps for some reason.

The flowers I brought earlier in the week look fine, I may have a couple more days before needing to buy a new bunch. I take a seat next to my dad's bed and put my bag down. My dad looks the same, except that the nurses apparently shaved him earlier. I grab his large, warm hand and press it against my cheek, something he loved to do.

"Hi, Dad."

He stays silent with his eyes closed, as usual. His heart monitor is still giving off a slow, rhythmic beeping.

"How are you today? Are you missing Mom? I miss her a lot. Do you dream of her, Daddy?"

The doctor told me patients in a coma can dream. I wonder what my dad would dream about. He probably misses Mom. And her cooking, he loved her cooking a lot. His motorcycle and his old garage too. He taught me how to ride when I was fourteen, and always said he would buy me my first bike when I turned twenty. Sadly, he didn't get the chance.

I just hope he doesn't dream about their accident. I'd rather think he's just having a long, peaceful sleep.

"I finished my last paper today. Economics. You always said I was too smart for you whenever you saw me doing my algebra when I was a kid. Remember? Now only one year to go with my studies, Dad."

My parents didn't get to go to university, and my dad didn't even finish high school, yet they insisted I do if I could. I always wanted to please them and made sure that I got good grades, although they didn't really care about my grades. They were proud whenever I was studying and consoled me if I was tired or sad about my results.

I always tell my dad about my studies, hoping he's listening and proud of me. When the school topic is over, I tell him about how the pack is doing, about this morning's training, and about Daniel and his experiments that make him crazy.

I get to last night, but I don't tell my dad anything about Nathaniel. I just mention that Daniel and I had fun, and that's it. I don't usually tell Dad anything that might anger or sadden him, only happy things. My father is my only family left, and I'm so scared of losing him. I pray every day that he will wake up.

"You alright sweetie?"

Deborah, another nurse, just walked in. I smile at her. I used to cry every time I came to see my dad, but I'm a lot better now.

"I'm fine Debbie, thanks."

"You're such a good daughter, coming every day. Those two gentlemen's families don't even come once a week to see them. Your daddy is a lucky man, sweetie."

I smile. That is one of the nicest things I've ever heard. All the nurses here are so nice. Deborah checks everyone's vitals in the room before leaving.

Once she's gone, I take out my headphones, give my dad one of the earpieces, and put on his favorite song, *I'm A Believer* by The Monkees. I take the other one to listen to it with him. I love that old song. I smile whenever I listen to it.

Whenever he put it on the old stereo in our house, Dad and I would dance around and sing loudly, making Mom laugh. He loved rock bands mostly but would listen to anything. My mom liked Latin songs more, it reminded her of her roots. Our house was the kind that had music on from sunrise to sunset. I miss the old days. I close my eyes and let my playlist shuffle through the list I made for him.

I doze off while listening to the music, and when I wake up, it's almost 5:00 p.m. Crap, it's that late already. Daniel sent me two texts, letting me know that it looks like he will have to stay at the lab for the night. I feel sorry for him, those experiments are really giving him a hard time lately. I don't really get his biology stuff, but he's so into his research, it's not unusual for him to pull an all-nighter from time to time.

I say goodbye to Dad, taking my time before leaving. I hate leaving him in that hospital room day after day, but I've gotten used to it. When I'm about to start driving, someone suddenly mind-links me.

"*Hey, Elena?*"

"*Chris? Something wrong?*"

"*Yeah. My dad is looking for you, and he's not too happy.*"

"*Crap. Where is he?*"

"*At the Main House. Apparently, he heard about you going out last night. I didn't understand everything, but he looks really angry, Elena.*"

"*I'll be there in a few minutes.*"

"*Okay.*"

How did he learn about our escapade in the Velvet Moon territory? Did the young ones we caught yesterday talk? One of them probably blabbed about it. I growl nervously while driving, and my wolf is annoyed too. As more time passes, I have a hard time controlling her and her alpha instincts against my uncle Xavier. Werewolves are complicated creatures, and our relationships and society are even more complex. Especially between alphas.

I pull over in front of what we call the Main House. My uncle's house is also the main gathering place for our pack. It's a large, old, but richly decorated house. Iris is waiting for me outside, and she runs to me as soon as I get out of my car.

"I'm so sorry, Elena, I think he overheard me talking about the nightclub with Prue on the phone. I tried to calm him down but…"

"It's okay, Iris, it's not your fault."

Though I do feel a bit bitter that she accidentally let my uncle know, I can't really blame her for her dad's temper. I walk past her to enter the house, where a couple of guys I know are standing guard. They both salute me, but their faces show they know what I'm here for and feel sorry about it.

My uncle is in the kitchen, and his expression changes as soon as I enter the room.

"Where the hell have you been?"

"At the hospital, with Dad."

My response surprises him, and for a few seconds, he doesn't know what to say. I don't think my uncle has visited his brother more than a couple of times since the accident, but he knows I go often. He apparently decides to ignore my answer entirely.

"Where were you last night?"

He is growling furiously, and my wolf is ready to growl too. I hold her back, trying to make her act docile, but it's against her nature, and I struggle. I lower my eyes even if I don't have any obligation to and decide to go for the truth.

"I went outside our border to party."

"What the hell were you thinking? Going past our borders? And to the Velvet Moon territory at that! Who the hell do you think you are Elena?"

"Sorry, Uncle."

"I told you not to call me that!"

This time, I glare at him. He doesn't let me call him uncle and doesn't visit my dad in the hospital, how am I supposed to consider him family? He growls even louder, but as usual, that has no effect on me. For a reason I can't understand, my uncle's Alpha Aura is totally harmless to my wolf. Unfortunately, that only angers him more.

"You're supposed to be one of our warriors! How do you dare defy my orders to sneak out like some rogue? Just to go drinking!"

"It wasn't to drink, it was for…"

"Don't talk back to me! I don't want you acting like some whore and showing off!"

"Excuse me?"

This time, my wolf is growling and won't take this insult. How dare he call me that? But he doesn't back off.

"You heard me! Do you feel so great about yourself that you have to show off to everyone in this city? Learn your place! You are not some damn princess! You are a fighter and belong to this pack!"

I growl even louder, furiously. I don't belong to anyone! And I do whatever the hell I want, in this territory or any other! I'm fed up with my uncle restricting me any chance he gets!

"What is so wrong with me? I just do what everyone else does! I'm twenty-one, for Moon Goddess' sake! What do you expect, for me to do nothing but train others and sit around? I'm a wolf! I can't stay still and obedient like a damn dog!"

"You will learn! You are supposed to set an example! Why do you think the kids went out last night? They all want to be like you!"

So the young ones' outing last night is my fault now? What the hell? I only learned about the party ten minutes before going. Why is he pushing all the crap on me?

"Enough! I've had enough of you binding me and restricting me any chance you get! I can't hunt, I can't fight, I can't go out! I'm fed up with this! Stop ordering me around! I'm your niece, not your damn guard dog!"

"You're not my niece! My brother only adopted you, that doesn't make you my family!"

I'm stunned, shocked by his words. How dare he? He would have never said such a thing in front of my dad. Across the room, the other guys are looking at him with disgusted looks too. I growl again.

"Fuck you, Xavier."

I turn around and storm out before he can say a word. I walk past Iris while exiting the room and she looks surprised too. She calls my name but I ignore her and jump in the car.

I'm going home. I drive fast, exceeding the speed limit a few times. I'm so mad and disgusted about what happened, I can't stop. I take the car back home and run up the stairs all the way to our apartment. My phone rings a couple of times, but I ignore it and go straight to the bathroom. I undress quickly and take a cold shower.

Moon Goddess. I hate my uncle and his stupid inferiority complex. He could never swallow that my dad, his little brother, was stronger than him. Now he hates that I'm even stronger. Damn alpha pride. I let the water clear my thoughts. I know what I need to do. Something stupid, something forbidden.

I wash my hair and body then walk to my room, grabbing my denim skirt and a black lace crop top, the one Daniel finds me sexy in, along the way. With black lingerie, it is perfect. I grab some cash from my wallet, my phone, and my ID, then go out again, heels in hand. I take a deep breath and start the car. I take a look at the car's clock. It's almost 8:00 p.m. now. I take the highway, heading for The Rain.

I keep driving, trying to remember the nightclub's location. I have the address from the text I received this morning, but I don't need it. I have a good memory and can find my way back from what I saw yesterday while Danny was taking me there.

This nightclub. I know why I'm going there. I mean, I could have gone to any club on our territory, even another territory, but I chose to go to this one. Half of the reason was to piss off my uncle and go against his stupid order. The other half makes me sigh, and my anger slowly turns into some excitement. I know exactly what, or rather who, I'm going for.

His little number from yesterday hasn't left my mind. I'm curious. I don't really care if it's just about sex, but this attraction I feel towards Nathaniel Black is no joke. I want to see if this is real. Just for once, follow my instinct and let go. I haven't forgotten that spark of his fingers under my skin, when we moved our bodies close, or the feeling of his hands on me. I feel myself getting flushed just thinking about it.

A few minutes more, and I park in front of the nightclub. It's Saturday, but the place doesn't look very crowded. There's only a small queue, not even a dozen people. It is quite early after all. I take a deep breath, and for a few seconds, observe the place. What stupid thing am I about to do? No matter how stupid it is, I'm not about to stop. I need this.

Just like yesterday, I manage to get in quite easily. The bouncer just looks at my ID, but there is no reason for him to refuse a girl by herself. Once I'm inside, I hesitate. There aren't many people on the dance floor yet, but my interest is more on the upper floor, the VIP area. Last night, Nate got us in without an issue. But tonight, I don't know if they would let me go upstairs. I decide to go to the bar, order a honey-flavored whiskey, and observe for a while. Once again, there are very few people, but I don't see Nate.

How stupid! Why did I assume he would come two days in a row? I take a sip and watch the dancers. The music is a more savage, sexy beat. I stay sitting at the bar, watching them absent-mindedly. The barmaid who was wiping glasses comes to me with a smile, as she doesn't look too busy either.

"Waiting for someone?"

"Maybe," I sigh.

"A pretty woman like you won't stay alone too long."

I give her a smile as thanks, but my heart isn't there. I give another glance upstairs.

"He's in the Clouds Area?"

"Clouds Area?"

"That's the name of the upper floor. Do you have an invite to get there?"

"I went just yesterday, but I was with someone. But it's fine, I'll just wait here and see if he comes or not."

"He got a name, honey?"

I hesitate for a second. The name Black is somewhat of a taboo in Silver City. The name of the brothers, the name of a scary king, and a reign of fear. Most people fear that name and for good reasons. The Black brothers aren't known for being nice, either. Yet, here I am, waiting to meet the second of them. What kind of an idiot am I?

Seeing that I'm hesitating to answer, the barmaid goes first.

"I suppose it's not a name you can say out loud then. Just go upstairs, he'll be there soon."

I frown. How did she understand who I meant? And why would she let me go to the Clouds Area without any sort of pass, or even a good reason? She shrugs while I'm still confused and gives me another glass to replace my empty one.

"I have a good memory. I saw you with the boss yesterday, honey. If you're here to meet him again you might as well just go upstairs. And my name is Kylie. Just tell Garry I let you go."

"Okay. Thanks, Kylie."

"Have fun, honey."

I nod and grab my glass to head toward the stairs. The gorilla-looking guy guarding the entrance frowns, but I explain to him Kylie said that it was okay. He looks hesitant, but just one look at the bar seems to be enough. Once Kylie gives him a nod, he steps aside, and I can finally climb those stairs.

Yesterday, Nathaniel took me across the whole floor in a flash, and I barely had any time to look. Now that I'm on my own, I have plenty of time to observe my surroundings, velvet in shades of purple, leather sofas, and fancy glasses. You can tell it's another kind of customer wandering here. Suddenly, my denim skirt seems a bit out of place. Thank God I applied makeup. I quickly put my hair in a bun, hoping that would be enough to avoid the stares.

Since I already have my drink, I pick an empty spot to sit down, my eyes on the dance floor below. Everyone here is in a flirty mood. Mostly women in brand name clothes playing hard to get, while the guys show off their wealth. This is definitely not my world. I don't belong here. I just sip my whiskey, reflecting on what I'm doing here. Something stupid, as I mentioned, and most likely a very bad idea. I take a glance at Kylie, busy pouring drinks downstairs. She said he would come, right?

I want to check what time it is, but I don't have my smartphone! What an idiot! I probably left it in the car, since I came inside in a hurry. I vaguely remember grabbing it when I came down from our apartment. I sigh. Never mind, I can always mind-link Danny if needed, and I don't really feel like talking to anyone else right now.

"Are you alone, Miss?"

I turn my head but face deception. Some tall guy, with a smile worth any toothpaste ad, is beaming at me with confidence. Before I can even answer, he sits in the empty space next to me. I slide a bit away. Why do they have to be so blunt? The guy glances at my drink, obviously looking for any way to engage in a conversation.

"Whiskey. I like a woman with some character!"

So what, we have to drink a "manly" drink to actually have some character? What would he have said if I had been drinking a Mojito? Is it a sexy drink? I ignore him, showing my annoyance, but the guy doesn't get the message.

"Which pack are you from? You have to be someone to come up here. I'm an attorney, Joey, by the way."

"Great. Now instead of just 'I'm not interested,' I can say, 'I'm not interested, Joey,'" I answer.

"Oh, don't worry, I'm fine with just talking! What happened to gentlemen, huh? I know, you must think I'm one of those douchebags who just come to fish out pretty girls. But I–"

"Actually, I think you're one of those men who doesn't get what 'not interested' means. I don't need someone to keep me company, nor a gentleman wannabe. You can move on," I answer with a growl this time.

"Hey, you don't need to be rude! I was just trying to be friendly, yet you won't even give me your name! You think you're some princess, answering me like that? I come with honest thoughts and you…"

I'm growling again, seriously annoyed now, but before he can finish his sentence, someone suddenly grabs his neck and slams his face against the balcony guardrail. Joey, totally confused, struggles to break free, but the man holding him doesn't flinch.

"How about you fuck off and be friendly outside my club before I get mad?" he says in an ice-cold voice.

"What?"

Pearls of sweat run down his temples. Everyone around us stops their conversations to look at the scene. I'm holding my breath. Nathaniel pushes the guy to the stairs with a growl, where the huge guard grabs the poor Joey to take him outside. It's over within half a minute and, like a silent order was given, everyone resumes their conversations.

Nathaniel runs his fingers through his hair, regaining his composure like nothing happened. I notice a black wolf by his side, but he just turns around and leaves us.

"So, you really came back," he says.

He's still standing, tall and handsome right in front of me. I gasp for some air. He's even more tonight. He's wearing a gray silk shirt and black pants. His hair is half-wet like he just got out of the shower. A drop slides from his ear to his chest.

"I needed a drink," I answer.

What a poor response, Elena. I could've done better, but his sudden appearance surprised me a bit too much. I take a new sip of whiskey to give me some more confidence, the sweet taste adding some red to my cheeks and warmth to my body. Nathaniel has a glass too, some translucent liquid.

He finally takes a seat next to me, dangerously close, but I don't back away this time. I'm feeling bold, strong, and defiant. My skin is getting hotter, as he is a few inches away. His face is so close, I can see every detail of his traits.

"Good place to get a drink. I was hoping I'd see you again."

His honesty surprises me, but I don't think twice before giving my response.

"Me too."

He smiles and a chill runs down my spine. Moon Goddess, his sexiness puts me on the fucking edge. My stomach feels as if it is about to burst. Suddenly, his fingers reach for my drink, and he takes it away without a word. I'm about to protest, but before I can, his lips are on mine.

It's a delicious surprise and I answer his kiss without thinking. Just like yesterday, his movements are so precise and measured that I lose myself in his expert moves. I kiss him back, and Moon Goddess, it feels so wrong but so good. I'm aware people might be watching us; we are in a crowded nightclub after all, but I don't give a damn.

I just want his lips on mine, the touch of his tongue, and the fire of his hands caressing my skin. His fingers run over my thighs, my neck, and through my hair. It feels like fire and desire are taking over me. I forget and give up on everything else. I want more, I want to feel this good forever.

It's innocent and sexy. Something half forbidden. I gasp for air and his lips reach out for my neck. Without realizing it, I put a hand on his arm, flirting with his skin too. When we slowly stop, I'm feeling amazing. Shame and hesitation have faded as he smiles at me.

"I take it that you haven't changed your mind," he whispers.

"I haven't."

I reach for my glass and finish my whiskey in one go under his amused eyes. It would take a lot more to get me drunk, but the sweet taste helps in making me feel lighter. He finishes his too, and we get up at the same time. He doesn't take my hand or touch me, just leading the way as we head down the stairs.

One night, he said. One night that I really need. One night when I can be someone else, someone's one-time lover.

Like yesterday, we leave the nightclub in a flash, no one holding us back. He takes my hand when we get outside and leads me to his car. We sit inside, and just before he turns the engine on, he sighs and turns to me with a frown.

"No running away?"

I can't help but laugh. This question is so sudden and random!

"No, not this time," I answer with an amused smile.

"Good," he says with a smile too.

He starts the car, and we head further into the Velvet Moon territory. It's a silent ride, but I don't feel any uneasiness in it. Instead, I'm mesmerized by the scenery as we take the highway. All of Silver City, a glowing nightlife, yellow lights on dark buildings, like some golden glitter on a black curtain. It's the kind of scene you see on a poster, a view you can never get tired of. Nathaniel lit up a cigarette and is enjoying it. I've never been in a convertible. Feeling the night air and summer wind on my skin as he speeds up is awesome.

A night ride with a stranger. Asking for trouble, probably, but Moon Goddess, I don't care. I need one night to be someone else, leave my life behind me for a while. No worries about my duties, my uncle, my life. I take a big leap into the unknown without looking back.

He finally parks in front of some very chic hotel I've never seen before. An incredibly tall building with a fancy entrance and VIP service. Is this really okay? This is way too classy for my means! He notices my expression.

"What is it?"

"A hotel?" I ask, a bit unsure.

But he just shrugs.

"I own it."

He owns a hotel. Am I supposed to act as if this is common? He owns a freaking hotel! Well, I knew the Black brothers were rich. Probably some of the richest people in Silver City, as far as I know. Oh, whatever. It's just for one night anyway. I can play fancy as well, after all. I follow him as he walks across the lobby without stopping, simply nodding at the receptionist. He's walking fast, like he's in a hurry. I silently hate my heels in that moment as I struggle to catch up to him.

He steps into an empty elevator, pushes the button for the highest floor, and I join him before the door closes.

The second the elevator starts moving, he suddenly turns to me and grabs my waist to pull me close to him. I'm pushed against the wall and we stare at each other for a moment before he starts kissing me again. It's more passionate and forceful this time. We are both hungry for each other and our lips get more impatient. I caress his neck and the base of his blonde hair. I feel his hands on my thighs and back, caressing my skin and moving along with our kiss.

What is it about him that makes me forget everything else? I pursue this kiss even more, playing with his tongue. The sound of his breathing makes me forget about gravity. This elevator is getting higher, reaching for the sky, and Moon Goddess, I hope it won't ever stop. My eyes are closed and I feel the heat of another language, something silent we exchange with our fingers. He interrupts our kiss to look at me. I feel like my heart's about to burst out of my chest just looking at his hypnotic blue eyes. He doesn't say a thing as we pant, staring at each other with desire etched on our faces. I'm alone with an angel and his demonic kisses. I don't want to look at the floors scrolling on the screen. I just want to stay trapped in here and exchange the remaining seconds for hours. He smiles, as if he could read my mind, and suddenly goes for my neck, kissing and biting it gently. Oh, Moon Goddess. His hand suddenly ventures under my skirt, and I shiver with desire.

He keeps this torture going, and for a second, I wonder if we can make love right here instead.

A bell suddenly rings, announcing our arrival. 53rd floor? Damn, it's a skyscraper after all, and Mr. Millionaire went for the top floor. I try to catch my breath, but Nate grabs my hand and pulls me behind him across a corridor. We walk by a couple of doors before he stops. He takes a black card from his pocket and opens the door before taking me inside.

Moon Goddess, this is one really impressive suite. A cold marble floor, red cedar on the walls, and gold decorative patterns throughout the room. And that incredible view over the city! I wish I had the time to see it, but for now, all I can focus on is Nathaniel.

As soon as we cross the threshold, his hand reaches for mine, and before the door is even shut, his lips are on mine again.

It's like a sweet drug, something I crave uncontrollably. The taste of him, the manly smell of his skin. I kiss him back fiercely, abandoning myself to desire. I want more, I want this man right now. I'm against the wall again and our bodies are intertwined with each other. His leg is between mine as I feel his desire growing under his pants. Nathaniel kisses me again, a deep, savage kiss. A fire is raging inside me, burning my skin and my senses. I'm so hot. My hand caresses his torso, appreciating the open shirt. I can feel those perfect abs under my fingers, and they are impressive, and make me curious for more. I try to unbutton him despite our wild kissing. I'm so clumsy, it takes forever to get to the last one. He smiles against my lips, and in the next second, the shirt is on the floor, and his torso is fully exposed.

Holy Moon Goddess, even Apollo should be jealous of this man. How do you get a perfect body like his? Or is it just my personal heaven? I gasp as this half-naked man steps back to take off his shoes. I'm still drooling over his perfect muscles when he faces me again, and that makes him smile.

"Enjoying the view?" he asks with an annoying smirk.

I try to ignore him, but I can't, his fingers are already reaching for my top. Taking it off over my head, he throws it across the room too. He doesn't wait though, and his hands get a hold of me again, his lips going for my neck. I'm just as hasty, reaching for his back, caressing his arms as we hold on to each other.

Suddenly, his fingers decide to explore my body some more, and they caress me under my skirt. Oh, Moon Goddess! Is he skilled or am I overexcited? Or both? I tremble from the sensations, but he doesn't stop and starts kissing my chest instead. If I wasn't against the wall, I might have lost my balance already. His fingers keep moving and my voice suddenly comes out in an embarrassing moan that surprises the both of us. I cover my mouth. How did I make such a sound? But after a second of surprise, Nathaniel has this devilish smile on.

"I love your voice. Let me hear it some more."

And with that, he resumes his movements against my panties, his kisses going up and down my neck and chest. He knows what he's doing, and those fingers are driving me crazy! I grab his wrist, but that doesn't stop him. The torture goes on and only stops when he decides so. Damn, my legs feel so numb. Why is he the one with the upper hand? As payback, I kiss him even more fiercely and push him all the way to the large bed.

I can feel his smile under my lips, but I don't care. I get on top of him and bite his shoulder, annoyed. It's childish, but his groan is satisfying enough. I have a little victory over him. It's my turn to smile.

"It hurts," he whispers.

"And I don't care," I answer just as softly.

We stay like this for a few seconds, him under me, staring at each other. I can't tell what he is thinking. His eyes are fixated on me, a bit confused, like he's reevaluating, looking at me differently. The atmosphere between the two of us seems to change slowly. I lean in to kiss him again, and he replies to my lips.

This time, it's different. Our exchange feels much more tender, gentle. His hand caresses my shoulder, and he guides me for a change of position. We don't stop kissing, but our hands are also busy taking our clothes off. It takes a while, but it doesn't matter. We take our time kissing each other, exploring each other's bodies, and playing with our senses. My skin is so hot despite the air conditioning in the room, we are sharing our warmth again and again.

Nate's kisses are addictive. Sometimes gentle, sometimes sultrier, they are unpredictable and I love it. He keeps me on edge every time. I want him, but he still finds a way to make me want him even more. It doesn't feel like a cold, heartless one-night stand, but like a passionate night between two lovers. We kiss, we enjoy ourselves, and we even smile between our kisses and caresses.

But we both know what our bodies are yearning for. After who knows how long, when I can't take it anymore, we finally join our bodies together. Moon Goddess, I can't even describe how perfect this feels. We take a few seconds, and another kiss, to enjoy that sensation of completing each other. He starts moving, slowly at first, and I join him.

Our bodies dance at a perfect, gentle rhythm. He's on top of me, staring at me, watching my every reaction. His intense blue gaze is making me even crazier. He grabs my wrists and pins them against the mattress, and I can't control anything. Neither of us averts our eyes from the other. The movements of his waist are intense and driven by desire. I can't hold my voice, and the sounds of my pleasure echo in the room. He matches his speed to my reactions, and damn, he's good at it. Everything increases:

pleasure, sounds, groans, speed, until I can't control myself anymore.

I let myself drown in intense pleasure, not holding back, and I hear him join me a second later. My own orgasm took me by surprise and Moon Goddess, it's a whirlwind of sensations I was not prepared for. For some long seconds, my body is experiencing heaven and hell, trembling and searing.

When I come back to my senses, I'm still panting, and Nathaniel is in the same state as me. Oh, Moon Goddess, that was intense! I feel like my whole body was just struck by lightning. I close my eyes, in a post-orgasmic daze. To my surprise, his lips come looking for mine again, in another tender kiss, and his hands caress my neck. I don't resist it.

My Moon Goddess, why does this one-night dream have to be so perfect and heavenly?

Chapter 4

That was nothing like I imagined it would be. I thought this would be short, only physical, even cold maybe. But this, this was completely different from what I thought.

Under the shower, I let the water wash away all my confusion, just enjoying those post-sex sensations. Even the cold flow can't appease my burning skin; I still feel all hot, trembling inside. I push my hair over my shoulder and try to look for some shampoo when I realize I'm not alone. Nathaniel is standing against the wall at the entrance, obviously enjoying the view with his little smile.

"Maybe I should warn you, Mr. Black, you have perverts in this hotel."

He scoffs, walks up to me, and puts a hand around my waist. He still smells of cigarettes from smoking on the balcony a few seconds ago.

"Really? We might need tighter security then."

And with those words, he gets closer to me, cornering me with that annoying smirk of his. We are now under the showerhead, the cold water flow drenching us. He doesn't even flinch, his eyes focused on me with this glimmer of lust in them. How can he be so handsome and tempting? His hand caresses my butt and I don't reject it. I put both arms around his neck instead, caressing it with my fingers. His lips come looking for mine. We share a long and passionate, yet gentle kiss.

Once again, I'm losing myself in his embrace, addicted to the taste of his lips and his smell. I just can't seem to reject him, and I have no intention to. My inner wolf is just the same, excited by this Alpha male and this intense night.

Nathaniel's fingers run down my back, caressing my skin, reviving the fire. Desire sparks again between us like it never really left. He swiftly moves his hand to caress my front, taking care of my intimate parts while his lips go down on my breasts. I gasp again, surprised by him. He kisses my neck again, nipping and playing with my skin with his lips, driving me crazy.

"You're wet," he whispers in my ear.

I blush. Even with my eyes closed, I can hear his smile. I know he doesn't obviously mean the water. Why does he have to make this kind of pervy joke? I want to protest, but before I can, he's moving my leg up, and the next second, I feel him in me. A mixture of surprise and pleasure makes me cry out. He chuckles and kisses my neck, moving to my cheek, and finally my lips. After a second of getting used to the sensation, I wrap my leg around him and answer his kiss. He starts moving slowly, and Moon Goddess, it feels so good. I leave Nathaniel to set the pace, too immersed in my own sensations to decide anything for now. Oh, Moon Goddess! I breathe and gasp loudly, unable to hold it. I just can't, this is too much to feel already. My own body is drowning in pleasure, and Nathaniel's movements are keeping me on edge. I hear his loud breathing against my ear, he's feeling it too. Maybe it's because I already orgasmed earlier, but it feels twice as intense this time. I start moaning. I try to put a hand on my mouth to cover it, but Nate grabs my wrists and holds them above my head, against the wall, as he keeps moving vividly.

"I want to hear you. I want to hear your voice…" he whispers as he keeps going.

With no choice, I let it out as he increases his rhythm, unable to hold it. Moon Goddess, my own voice echoes in my ears, and as if it wasn't enough, he starts kissing my neck again. I'm going crazy. It's like he's controlling me, keeping me in this state of insane pleasure. This sweet torture just goes on and on, giving me hell and heaven, and damn, I just wish it doesn't stop.

I wake up, completely confused. Where am I? I look around. A suite? Suddenly, the whole night comes back to me. Oh, Moon Goddess. That was freaking wild and intense. We did it three, no, four times? Seriously, when did I become so sex-crazed? No wonder my whole body feels sore. And this hellish headache, where did that come from? Not from two Mojitos!

"*Elena, you little—!*"

I almost jump, surprised by Daniel's yelling in my head. Great, now at least I know why my head feels like a damn drum. I sit up slowly on the bed, still barely handling my overall soreness. My whole lower region is throbbing, and I blush while remembering why. Holy crap. I look for my panties while Daniel keeps going.

"Are you fucking kidding me? Do you have any idea how worried I was when I came home this morning and you weren't here? And not answering your phone either! I spent two hours trying to mind-link you and call you!"

"Thank you for the headache."

I probably have no right to growl at him now, but I don't care, I'm annoyed by his nagging and can barely think straight. I need to find my clothes. While I turn around to look for them, my eyes fall on Nathaniel, still sleeping in the bed. He's sleeping on his stomach, his face turned toward the window, opposite me. Damn, even like this he looks so handsome. And he's still naked too. That probably doesn't help.

I avert my gaze from his sleeping figure and finally spot my skirt and bra on the floor. Silently, I get dressed, ignoring Daniel at the same time. I have no idea what time it is, it looks like it's barely dawn. I don't even remember falling asleep! The last thing I can remember is our fourth time, on the bed, Nathaniel's kisses on my…

Okay, let's stop thinking about it before I die from embarrassment. Moon Goddess, I'm no virgin. So why do I have to get so red just by thinking about it? Let's just find that damn top. I finally find it and finish getting dressed, except for my heels which I carry in my hand. Is it okay to leave like this? Maybe I should leave a note or something. That feels very cliché though. It might have sounded right in a movie, but not here. Nathaniel did say it was only one night, anyway, so I should probably leave it at that I guess.

I take one last look at the man sleeping alone in that large bed and leave the suite. It was a great night, for sure. I keep reminiscing as the elevator goes all the way down to the lobby. I put my heels back on before it reaches the first floor, but the memories of last night's kisses in this very elevator keep me distracted. It was idiotic and reckless to follow him, but I don't regret it one bit at all. As I walk across the lobby, I actually feel great. It's not about my body, but I do feel a lot lighter. Like this one night of sex washed all my worries away.

"So where are you anyway?"

"On my way home, Danny. I'll be there in a moment, okay?"

I catch a taxi outside and ask him to take me back to the nightclub. It will be a small detour, but I need to retrieve the car, and my phone's in there too.

Half an hour later, I'm finally parking the car in front of our residence. Danny is right there, waiting for me with dark circles under his eyes and an annoyed expression. I sigh and exit the car, ready to face my best friend's anger.

"Hi."

"Hi? Hi? Is that all you have to say? Seriously, Elena, I was freaking out! You go out without even telling me, disappearing to Moon Goddess knows where, and you come back at six in the morning with only a stupid 'Hi'? I really want to spank you right now!"

"I'm sorry, okay? I needed a time out, and I forgot my phone in the car."

"Who gives a damn about the phone? We are freaking telepathically linked! Don't you go with the forgotten phone excuse!"

I understand his anger, but I wish he had waited until we were inside. I feel like we will have a couple of complaints come in if he keeps being so loud at this hour. I quickly walk back to our apartment with Daniel following me closely.

When we're finally inside, I toss my stuff on the sofa and head for the kitchen. I need coffee, or juice, anything that can give me some energy. I feel horribly sluggish, and I probably could use a nap too.

"Okay, you better spill the beans before I bite you, girl. Where have you been?" Daniel growls.

"I went back to The Rain," I sigh while pouring myself a cup.

"To the– I'm pretty sure I mentioned that was a shitty idea, Elena!"

"Well, if it makes you feel any better, I didn't even stay a full hour."

"Why do I feel like I'm not going to like whatever you're about to say next?" he says with a grimace.

He probably won't. But no matter what, Daniel is my best friend, and I hate hiding things from him. I sit on the couch, letting a sigh out before answering.

"I spent the night with Nathaniel Black."

Daniel rolls his eyes and lets himself fall next to me. His reaction wasn't as bad as I thought. He sighs.

"Elena."

"I know you're going to say it was a shitty idea, but it was just a one-night thing, Danny. I'm not seeing him again, and no one knows, except you."

I see him hesitate, but he eventually gets up to pour himself a cup of coffee too. Guess he spent most of his night working at the lab. That also explains why he's not as heated as he could be. When he comes back to sit with me, he looks exhausted but calm.

"Elena, I get you needed to let go and have fun for a night, but I just wish you had done it some other way. That guy is dangerous, babe, and you've had your share of bad boys."

I glare at him. Why did he have to mention that asshole now? I can't believe my best friend. Of all things, why did he choose to remind me of my ex right now? This is so unfair! I throw a cushion at him, annoyed.

"Seriously, Danny? Why do you even have to mention that damn jerk? I just spent one night with a guy, that's it!"

"It's not just a guy, Elena, we're talking about the brother of this city's Alpha King. He's probably just as dangerous," he replies right back, frowning.

This time I'm the one rolling my eyes. Why does he have to act overprotective now?

"I'm never seeing him again Danny, okay? Seriously, it was a one-time thing, that's all it was, we made that clear from the beginning! He could have been any guy in Silver City, it would probably have been the same! And I'm not making the same mistake, Danny. I've learned my lesson, trust me."

He stays silent for a while, staring at me. I'm done mentioning my damn ex, he better not bring it up again!

He takes a long sip and I wish I knew what he's thinking. Daniel is my best friend, but sometimes, I can't decipher him. After a long minute, he sighs and puts his cup down on the table.

"Alright, I get it. A one-night stand. Okay babe, your call. Just promise me you are never seeing Nathaniel Black or going to that nightclub ever again. Promise me you won't go near his territory, babe."

I sigh.

"I won't, Danny, I promise."

I never intended to go there again after that anyway. I know what Danny is scared about, but that just won't happen. A single night between strangers, that is all it was.

"Seems like you had a good time."

I blush. How could he read my mind right now? I growl, annoyed, but he shakes his head.

"Don't get mad at me, you're the one having dirty thoughts so early in the morning! So, you want to tell me about your wild night with blondie?"

"You do know you're blonde too, right?"

We bicker for a few minutes, but I end up telling Daniel everything, well, not the details of course, but just enough for my best friend to have a general idea. He listens to me while preparing some breakfast for the two of us with whatever's in the fridge. I'm not really a good cook, and aside from a few family recipes, I'd rather leave the cooking to Danny.

When I'm at the point of the story where I left the hotel, he brings me a bowl with a mixture of fruits, cereals, and a bit of almond milk.

"You know babe, that sounds like a very good night of sex, but are you sure that's all it was?" he asks while sitting next to me, our knees touching.

"What do you mean?"

He sighs and takes a spoonful of his bowl.

"I've had my share of one-night stands, you know, and this doesn't sound like one. I mean, from my experience, men usually do their business quickly and go, especially those who say they don't want to get attached. But here, your guy took you to a suite, stayed the whole night, asked for seconds, was gentle and all."

"He owned the suite, may I remind you, and not all men are beasts, Danny. Besides, the sex was really good. Doing it more than once was probably just about enjoying it. That's all."

He shrugs and makes a smug face before filling his mouth again.

"Well, you were lucky then. The guy was a gentleman. Never happened to me."

I feel a bit sorry to hear that. Daniel has one-night stands too, but I have never seen him in a relationship that lasted longer than a couple of weeks. Of course, my best friend is the nicest, most adorable guy in Silver City. Sadly, all the guys he ever went out with always turned out to be jerks, stupid boys testing their curiosity, or even married men. Moreover, he's so busy with his studies, except for our Friday nights, he barely has any time to look for a companion. I just wish he would find his own man already, but I feel like he's half-given up. Guess one heart can't take too many bruises.

I put my hand on his knee.

"Come on, Danny, I bet we'll find you a nice man. The nicest, most committed guy in all of Silver City."

He scoffs.

"Thank you, honey, but that only happens in TV shows. Wait until you realize they were just testing the waters with you."

This time, I give him a slap on his leg. He groans, but I don't care. I won't take his pessimism today!

"Don't say that! There's got to be one gay gentleman out there for you, and we are going to find him! Tonight, we are going to Pepe's and you are getting laid!"

He raises an eyebrow.

"Who are you, and what have you done to my babe? Get laid? Girl, one night with Black, and you start talking like me!"

I laugh, well, I do feel like I broke through a few barriers. I feel a lot better, enough to be the optimistic half of our pair for the day.

"You know what? Ditch your work for today. We clear our schedules, and we have fun, just the two of us!"

"Elena, I have to go check on my experiments and you have a whole bunch of bustling teenagers to train."

"You can call and ask for one of your colleagues to take over for one day, Danny. You spent the whole night working your ass off! And the kids won't die from a day without training either. Come on, just for today."

He opens and closes his mouth. I can tell he's tempted, so I bat my eyelashes and act cute while he's still hesitating. After a while, he smiles and takes out his phone. Yes!

"Sylviana? It's Danny. Do you think you could do me a favor and… oh, well, yeah? Really? Are you sure? Thank you, girl! I'll buy you lunch next week. See you."

I have a bright smile on. Danny's off the hook and all mine today! I want to ask him what he wants to do, but before that, he hands me my smartphone.

"You call Chris and tell him to do a self-class with the kids. It's always better than having one of them tell your uncle you never showed up."

I sigh and obey him, calling my cousin. Thankfully, Chris is already more than able to train himself, as are most of my usual trainees. He laughs when I tell him about my plan to just enjoy myself with Danny today.

"I approve of that! Have a good day you two, and don't worry about my dad!"

And with that, he hangs up. I smile at Daniel, but to my surprise, my best friend grabs my hand and takes me to my room. Without a word, he just pushes me onto the bed and lays beside me.

"I'm not going anywhere until I take a long nap," he says before closing his eyes, "and you could use one too."

He's not wrong. I only slept a couple of hours at best last night. I sigh and close my eyes, trying to ignore the floating memories of blue eyes, a warm embrace, and a fancy suite while finding sleep.

A few hours later, as promised, Daniel and I are hanging out without a worry on our minds. We woke up right before lunch and decided to eat at home before heading to the heart of the White Moon territory. It's a beautiful sunny day, which I love, with the sun warming up my skin and shining in my hair. I'm glad I decided to wear my denim shorts and a simple off-the-shoulder white top to enjoy it twice as much.

The Latin neighborhood is as lively as ever. I grew up in these colored streets, hearing the music coming from the windows, and all the *mamás* shouting to one another. Like all the other werewolf pups, I would run on the uneven stone paths to test my speed or escape the baker after we stole a couple of *conchas*. I know by heart all the corners where I could hide as a kid and the shortcuts from one place to another. I could walk around with my eyes closed and recognize each shop only by its smell.

These people adopted me as if I had been born here just like the rest of them. I know all the families that live here, each person by their name. It never mattered where I came from, this was a place of immigrants anyway. Like we say here, your home is the place your heart settles in.

Daniel and I walk around arm in arm, commenting on the shop stalls we love most or what childhood memories we have here and there. I'm trying to leave behind the remnants of last night as I walk with my best friend, but no matter what I do, flashbacks keep coming to me.

The way he touched my skin. His voice in my ear. His warmth. His clear blue eyes fixated on me, burning with desire. I shiver, and I'm not the slightest bit cold. Why am I getting all heated up in broad daylight?

"Elena!"

I turn my head and see Daniel sigh. He's handing me a pretty box full of miniature seashells. I take it, trying to remember what he was saying.

"Uh, thanks," I mutter, a bit ashamed.

We stopped in front of one of those little cheap bazaar shops, where you can find pretty much anything for creation hobbies or kid activities, like paint, colored paper, or glitter.

"You're welcome, but I was just asking if you think my mom could use it for her hobby stuff," he says while rolling his eyes.

Oh, right, his mom makes jewelry out of these. I already have a pair of earrings and necklaces she gave me. I nod, feeling a bit dumb.

"Totally. Didn't she mention she was doing summer-themed ones?"

"She did. Glad you were listening then. Babe, what were you thinking about?"

I mumble something, but my blushing pretty much gives me away.

Danny pinches me, making me squeal loudly.

"Hey, that hurts!"

"I'll do it again if you keep thinking about your dirty you-know-what with you-know-who again, you little pervert!"

Why does he have to blurt this out in the middle of the street? I growl at him, but he ignores me, pretending to pick some other materials. The shop owner Maria, a young woman about our age, obviously heard him and is looking at me with a little smile. Great, the whole street is going to know about my activity last night. Now I'm really embarrassed!

Suddenly, I hear someone's heavy steps running toward us.

"Elena! Elena, this time I'll definitely make you my mate!"

Ugh, Moon Goddess, not this idiot again. He will never learn! Next to me, Daniel whistles.

"Man, you're all fired up today. Like the last twenty-six times you tried, but hey, who's counting?"

Daniel may find this entertaining to watch, but this is really getting old. Will he ever give up with this stupid idea? I turn around to face Eric.

Eric Solace is a big guy, a head taller than me, and muscular with broad shoulders. He is not the handsome type or ugly either, just a regular guy. But he does tend to talk loudly. He could have a grizzly among his ancestors, and I wouldn't be surprised.

I cross my arms, annoyed already.

"Eric, you really need to stop this now."

"Backing off already? I want a proper duel!"

I roll my eyes. Damn, he may not be smart but he sure is one stubborn wolf!

Since we met as teens, Eric had this stupid idea of making me his mate. I've rejected him countless times already, but he just doesn't take no for an answer. I once told him that I would never date a guy weaker than me, hoping that would make him give up considering our strength difference. Not only did it not make him change his mind at all, but now, that idiot is set on the idea of winning a duel against me!

"Eric, seriously drop it. You're a great guy, I don't want to fight you!"

"Not great enough for you to accept me as your mate. I want a duel to prove to you that I can do it!"

"It's not about you, I just don't want a mate! Not you, not anyone! Why are you so set on this stupid idea?"

"I told you, I will make you my partner! You're the only one I will accept as my girlfriend!" he blurts out.

I'm exhausted with him! It's been years since he first spouted out that idiocy, when will he ever learn? Moreover, a few other guys from the pack made up this whole competition thing about whoever will be able to win against me and some are hoping for something not as innocent as dating me as a prize! Not only is this stupid, childish, and annoying, it's also another reason for my uncle to resent me!

"You may as well get this over quickly, babe. You know that moron ain't going to let go," sighs Daniel.

I roll my eyes, but he's right.

"Come on, Elena!" Eric yells, getting impatient.

What an pain. I give up and nod, facing him. I don't even need to shape-shift to take care of this idiot. My inner wolf is annoyed at him too. Who does he think he is? Becoming our mate? Ugh, no way.

Eric jumps at me, but he's big and slow. I step aside at the last second, leaving him to fall face-first against the floor. Around us, some bystanders can't help but laugh at him. Seriously, Eric.

"If you're going to attack, do it seriously," I growl.

He growls back and turns around to jump at me again. Honestly, Eric may be big and tall, but he's slow and attacks blindly. I could leave him to get tired just by ignoring and dodging his attacks like this, but that would take a while. I don't like that so many people are watching and laughing at him. He may not be the smartest of the pack but he's still a good guy. When he attacks for the third time by throwing his fist forward, I bend over. I drop below his shoulder level and throw a rotating kick right to his stomach. He loses his breath and struggles to get up, but I use this moment to get up and give him a punch in the solar plexus. My strength sends him a few steps back, and he collapses on his back, gasping for air. I sigh and walk up to him, crossing my arms. I put my foot on his torso, making sure he stays down.

"Eric, you really lack some basics. Why do you keep doing this? You can't even touch me!"

He suddenly laughs, though his voice is hoarse, due to the pain.

"I know. But at least I make you notice me!"

"You come right to my face to duel with me, how am I supposed to not notice you?"

He keeps laughing again. How can he look happy when I just ridiculed him in the middle of the day? Strange guy. I take my foot off.

"You had enough for today?"

"Yeah, yeah. Damn, that hurts," he whines, palpating his torso.

"Of course, it'll hurt. Just put some ice on it, you'll have a bruise. Go get checked if it still hurts tomorrow."

I sigh and turn around to join Danny, who is shaking his head while looking at Eric.

"Girl, that's why he keeps coming back. You're too nice to that idiot!"

"Eric is a good guy, Daniel, I can at least feel a bit bad for hitting him."

"He asked for it, babe. His problem, not yours."

And with that, Daniel pushes me further down the street, leaving the defeated Eric behind us. If it wasn't such a repetitive scenario, I probably would have felt worse about it. But anyway, he'll get back on his feet soon enough, I guess.

Daniel takes me to a shop where he wants to buy some new CDs. He and I are the old-fashioned type, collecting CDs and vinyl of our favorite bands. The store is small but not empty, a couple of other people are there too. While Daniel goes to the 90's pop section, I decide to wander around the rock one. I like old English bands. Maybe I can find a good one to add to my dad's collection?

"Elena!"

I turn around. Bianca, a young girl from the group I usually train, is walking up to me with a smile.

"Hi, Bianca. What are you doing here?"

She shows me a pile of vinyl she gathered.

"I'm looking for new pieces for my mix."

Oh right, she's an amateur DJ. I've heard her sets a couple of times at Pepe's nightclub. Not bad, though her style might be a bit too futuristic sometimes, well, you can tell she's the new wave kind of girl, with her blue hair and piercings.

"Elena, did you go see Granny Reagan?"

What? I almost drop the CD I was holding to face her.

"Wait, Granny Reagan is back?"

Bianca nods.

"She just came back this morning, I thought you knew!"

"No! Where is she?"

Bianca frowns, trying to think.

"I saw her at the main house this morning, but she didn't stay long. She's probably at the pub, you know, the one that belongs to Henry. She said she wanted to drink."

I can't believe that old hag is here, and no one told me! I thank Bianca quickly and almost run to Daniel across the shop. We almost run into each other, but before he can protest, I yell first.

"Danny, Old Reagan is in town!"

"What? That old hag? Since when?" he asks while putting the records he had in his hands back.

"This morning! Come on!"

We both run out of the shop, and head to the northern part of the territory. Henry's pub is only a few blocks away, I can't believe I almost missed her!

Reagan is an old woman, who left our pack many years ago. She hates to talk about it, so no one but the elders really know what happened for her to leave. The only thing I know is that she had a big fight with the former Alpha, nothing else. Now she leaves on her own, as a wild wolf most of the time. However, she comes back from time to time, when she misses a real bed and food. She's a grumpy old lady that complains a lot and doesn't like anyone. She doesn't have any family left in the pack, and only a couple of friends can endure her constant bad mood.

To me, however, Granny Reagan is much more than that.

She's the one who brought me to Silver City and the White Moon clan, almost eighteen years ago.

I reach the bar after a few minutes of running across the streets, Danny right behind me. When we enter the bar, Henry, the barman and owner, raises his head.

"IDs?"

"Oh, come on Henry, you've known us since we were pups!" sighs Daniel.

Ignoring them, I walk straight to the old woman by the window. She is drinking a pint of local beer. She looks exactly like I remember; disheveled gray hair, worn-out leather clothes, and clear green eyes. When she sees me, she rolls her eyes.

"You again."

"Hi, Granny Reagan," I say while sitting at her table.

"Don't call me that and don't sit here, kid."

I don't move an inch and even better, Daniel comes to sit right next to me. She rolls her eyes and grumbles something before taking a huge gulp of her beer.

"It's been a while," I say. "Why didn't you tell me you had come back?"

"Because if I did, you would come here to bother me with your annoying questions, kid."

I growl. Old hag. Henry brings us two beers, and Daniel hands him a bill, but I really don't care about that for now. I cross my arms, staring right at the old woman.

"You know what I want to know."

"I already told you, I forgot."

"I still don't believe you."

She swears again, pissed.

I don't know why she lies every time about this, but I won't let it go. I come closer to her on the table.

"Why won't you tell me?" I ask.

"I already told you a lot, kid. Now stop asking."

"No, it's not enough. You said you found me and brought me here when I was about three, but you never tell me anything else. Why? I want to know where you found me, Reagan, so I can go there and look for my birth parents."

"I said no, kid. You have parents here."

"My parents had an accident a few months ago, Reagan. Right after the last time you left."

She puts her beer down, looking shocked.

"What?"

"Car accident," explains Daniel. "Elena's mom didn't make it. And…"

"My dad's in a coma, Reagan."

The old woman looks totally surprised, looking at me in disbelief.

"Holy Mother Moon Goddess ," she whispers. "No one told me. I saw your uncle earlier, he didn't tell me."

"Well, he doesn't talk about it at all," says Daniel with a snort.

I stay silent, as Granny Reagan looks sincerely overwhelmed by the information. I'm not even surprised about my uncle not saying anything. He avoids the topic half of the time and pretends he doesn't hear when someone brings it up.

She sighs, scratches her head, and drinks more beer.

"Poor people. Those good kids. I can't believe your uncle! That idiot will hear from me when I get back!"

"Granny Reagan, you can scold uncle all you want but first, answer me, please! You really don't want to tell me anything about my birth parents?"

"You stubborn little punk! I'll keep saying what I said: they are dead!

And I found you in the North, that's all I have to say!"

"You've been living in the wild for years now, don't tell me you can't remember where you found a three-year-old girl, Reagan, you have to know! What is it that you want to hide?" I yell, annoyed.

I've always known that this woman knows a lot more than what she's willing to say. For some reason, I have to argue with her for hours before she ever tells me anything about whatever she knows about me from before she brought me to the pack. Why does she have to make my upbringing such a secret? I know there's a lot more than what she has told me, I heard her talk to my parents! She said they had to hide me no matter what, and never tell me the truth. What truth?

"Why is there always so much foam in this?"

I can't believe she's complaining about her beer in the middle of this! I growl, but Daniel puts his hand on my shoulder, whispering to me to calm down.

"Granny Reagan, Elena's almost twenty-two now. Whatever it is you're hiding from her, isn't it about time she knows? If her dad doesn't survive, you would be the only one left who knows the secrets of her origin. What if you don't come back next time?"

I have a hard time holding back my anger, but Daniel's words might be more effective than mine. For a while, Reagan stays silent, looking at her beer with a strange expression. I exchange a glance with Daniel, hoping this time she will talk.

But after a long wait, Reagan suddenly burps very loudly.

What?

"Damn, I knew this beer was no good," she growls while looking at her cup.

After a second of consternation, I start yelling.

"Are you kidding me? You old hag! Is this a joke to you? We're talking about my family here!"

"They are gone, kid. Now stop yelling, you're going to give me a headache."

"I don't care! All you do is drink all day when you come here! Can't you help me a little? I've spent most of my life trying to figure out who I am! And now, you come here, with all the answers, and burp in my face? You old witch!"

Suddenly, she frowns, looking angry for the first time, and glares right at me.

"Don't you dare call me that, Elena."

"What? Old witch? Is that worse than old hag?"

"You have no idea what witches are, so don't you dare."

"I'll call you old witch if I want to! Old witch!"

"You little runt!"

We keep yelling at each other. Between us, Daniel sighs while looking at his beer.

"The level of this conversation is extremely low and childish, ladies."

"Shut up, Daniel! Elena, come outside with me! You little pest!" suddenly growls Reagan.

"Elena, don't," whispers Daniel.

But it's too late, I'm already pissed and on my feet. I follow her outside, driven by my anger. As Danny said, this is childish and stupid, but I don't give a damn. I'm tired of being in the dark and Reagan is just playing with me.

Once outside, she takes off her worn-out leather jacket. She might be old, but she's still in pretty good shape. Is she fifty, sixty? Hard to tell. Anyway, this won't be a pleasant moment, she looks really pissed now.

After all, she was my teacher.

Half an hour later, I'm exhausted, with a burning cheek and bruises all over. Damn, my whole body is aching. Reagan, however, is still standing there, looking calm now.

"What's this? Is that all you can do?" she sighs.

"You're a monster, Granny. Elena is still the best fighter in our pack," says Daniel, looking sorry for me.

"Then you're a whole bunch of weaklings!"

I knew she's always been crazy strong, but I never thought that old hag could still be good enough to beat me so easily! I wipe off a bit of blood from my lips. The worst thing is, I know she went easy on me. When I was younger, she would make me fight until I couldn't stand up anymore or passed out. Everyone in the pack thought I was naturally strong, but whatever natural skill I had as I child, Reagan sharpened it by teaching me how to fight all those years.

She puts her jacket back on, still grumbling.

"Where is this damn clan going? So weak. Is Clark lazy now? Damn dogs."

"Granny, if the Alpha hears you…" says Daniel.

"So what? Let him come at me! That runt could use a lesson too! He needs to be taught some manners!"

I massage my shoulders. Reagan has always been like this: at war with the whole world, and happy to growl at anyone. She takes out a cigarette and lights it up. Like this, with her long waves of gray hair and her leather outfit, she looks like some biker. I've always admired her, as my mentor, but I still don't know much about the woman who taught me pretty much everything about being a wolf.

Sometimes, I wonder if Reagan only comes back to Silver City because she feels some responsibility toward me. Since the day she brought me here, whenever she comes back, she never looks for me, but we always see each other at least once somehow. I know she used to see my parents a lot when I was young. After that, she sorts of became my mentor, teaching me how to fight, hunt, and become one with my inner wolf. She never acted nice or gentle towards me. There was always this distance between us, so I never considered her as family. Only as my mentor, my teacher.

"Why did you teach me?"

She looks at me, surprised by my question.

"What do you mean?"

"Why did you become my teacher? I could have been raised like the other pups, taught how to fight with the rest of the pack. You could have left me and never come back. But you came back and insisted on being the one to teach me how to do all this, how to be a werewolf. Why?"

She clicks her tongue, something she does when she's annoyed. She takes the cigarette out of her mouth and crushes it under her boot. After looking at me for a while, she sighs.

"I made a promise to watch over you, kid. I'm not one to go back on my word."

"A promise? To whom?"

"Now stop asking questions, I'm done."

She turns around and leaves. I want to ask more, a lot more, but this stubborn woman won't stop, and to be honest, I'm too exhausted to run after her. I sigh.

Daniel walks up to me, giving me a hand to help me up.

"She was almost nice this time. But girl, those bruises will remain for a couple of days."

"Who cares. I can't believe she still won't talk to me."

"Well, at least it's good to know she still comes back. It's been, what, two years since last time?" asks Danny.

"Twenty months or so, yeah," I sigh.

"This promise. She never mentioned it before, did she?"

I shake my head. That one's a first. Question is, who did she promise this to? To my birth parents? Or to the ones who adopted me? Someone else? I sigh while massaging my neck. When will she ever tell me the truth?

Daniel helps me back to the apartment, where I indulge myself in a cold bath. Meanwhile, I keep thinking about this whole secret surrounding my birth. For twenty years, everything I've found out about it comes from Reagan or my adoptive parents, and it's not much. I was found in a forest when I was around three, alone and famished. Reagan brought me to the White Moon clan, where Clark, the Alpha, gave consent for my dad to adopt me. Reagan left right after I came to live with the Whitewoods, and only came back five years later, when she started her ruthless training.

That's it. If that's all of it, why do I remember nothing of this forest? Whenever I try to think about a forest, nothing comes to mind. It just feels wrong. I don't even know how to explain it, I just know this forest thing is a lie. Moreover, when I was around ten, I found a box my mom kept in the bottom of her wardrobe. After asking a lot, she finally revealed this box contained everything I had on me when Reagan found me. The box was almost empty. It only contained two things: a blood-stained child's dress and a necklace.

I get out of the bath, grab a towel, and walk up to my room. Reaching under my bed, I finally put my hands on the tiny box. I took it from my mom's bedroom after the accident, to keep it with me. I take a deep breath and open it.

My old dress is there, as usual. Still white and red. The smell has faded over the years, but anyone could recognize blood. The only thing I could recognize from this dress, even back then, was Reagan's smell. After all, she carried me while I was wearing it. I leave the dress where it is and grab the little box laying on top of it.

It's a simple jewelry box. But when I open it, my most precious belonging is right there, shining as always. A gold necklace, with a thin chain and a unique pendant. It's a golden sun pendant, encrusted with diamonds. But the biggest mystery is the inscription on the back of the sun. It's written so small I had to use a magnifying glass to actually read it.

"To my Sunshine, G."

Who is G? I keep staring at it, as clueless as always. Why did I have this necklace on me? Is it even mine? Who would call me Sunshine? Isn't it odd to even compare a werewolf to the sunshine? We are creatures of the moon!

"…Babe?"

Daniel found me, sitting in the middle of my messy room while staring at this curious necklace. Unlike the dress, the sun necklace feels strangely familiar whenever I look at it, as if I had seen it a lot before.

"What are you thinking about?" he asks.

"That I wish that old hag talked more. I can't believe she still won't say a thing."

Daniel sighs and scratches his goatee. "She probably has her reasons. So did your parents, babe."

"Question is, what was the reason? What did they have to protect me from?"

I keep thinking, but I guess the answer won't just fall from the sky. Gosh, this is so enervating! Daniel puts an arm around my shoulders, comforting me.

"Hey, Elena, you'll find out eventually. Okay, babe? You know, I don't care where you come from, even if you turn out to be some weird alien."

I laugh a bit. Danny and his thing for sci-fi movies.

"Anyway, you're my babe, my bestie, okay? You can always count on me. I'm here for you."

I smile at him. I love my Danny. He's always been there for me. When we were kids, when we were teens, and now. I know he'll never ever let me down. He knows how scared I am for my dad, how badly I want to know who I really am, and how messed up I am inside.

I sigh and hug him back. If it wasn't for Danny, I would be a wreck right now. I might not even be here at all.

"Alright, who was going to take me to Pepe's and get me laid? My turn to get a guy!" says Danny, suddenly excited.

I sigh and show him my arm.

"Danny, I'm covered in bruises. I'm not sure I can go out looking like this."

"To hell with that. Put on your purple jumpsuit, I'll take care of the rest!" he says, then kisses my head and gets up.

I obey and get dressed as he said. Indeed, my legs are completely covered, all the way down to my ankles, but the neckline is still quite low and the purple spots on my arms are still exposed. However, it turns out Daniel has a solution for that too. After a few minutes and with a bit of foundation, most of my bruises have disappeared. Now I just have to make sure not to accidentally stain my jumpsuit with it. I grab a few bracelets that his mom made; the bohemian style compliments my outfit. Daniel is all dressed up too, in a sexy shirt and tight pants that enhance his thin legs.

I slap his butt when he walks past me.

"Hey, nice booty!" I say with a laugh.

"Stop it!"

I laugh at his outraged expression. For someone who always talks so bluntly, Daniel can be such a prude! I love to tease him like this. He doesn't like to let it show, but he's such a romantic at heart. He secretly reads mushy stories and he's the first one to cry when we watch a sappy movie.

Alright, tonight, I'll find a good guy for my Danny! While putting my hair up, I try to think of some mental criteria I should keep in mind. Danny loves tall guys, the muscular hunk type, preferably Latin. He's crazy for Spanish accents.

"You ready, babe?"

I nod, and we exit our apartment and head to Pepe's nightclub. It's small, but the most famous one downtown. Notably, a hotspot for good Latin music and dancing. Daniel and I ventured there before we were even of age and have loved the place since. A lot of the patrons are regulars; hence we see a few familiar faces in the queue. Some friends from our pack come to say hi, but as we enter the nightclub, I suddenly feel a strange sensation of disappointment overcome me.

I know this place almost by heart, so why do I find myself comparing it to The Rain right now? I follow Danny, looking around, looking for someone who has no reason to be here. I'm stupid, alright. There's no way one of the Black brothers would get lost in a small nightclub in the Latin District.

I feel stupid for being so disappointed! What the heck am I thinking right now? This is supposed to be our fun night! I go ahead of Danny to order myself a Cosmopolitan from the barman. Daniel goes for a caipirinha, one of his favorites. By the time our drinks are ready, the crowd has grown rapidly. I don't recognize the DJ, but he looks young, probably a newbie. Pepe lets the young ones start the night, as usual. Daniel is already moving his feet in sync with the music, but I'm not really in the mood yet. I don't even pay attention to the mix playing. I'm just looking around, with that little, silent hope of finding a pair of sky-blue eyes.

"Elena!" Daniel's pinch on my arm makes me jump.

"What?" I ask, a bit ashamed.

"You've got to be kidding me! Really? Snap out of it, girl!"

"I was not–"

"Oh, shut it!"

It's no use lying to Danny, he knows me better than anyone. Instead, I avoid his glare by putting my lips on my glass of Cosmo. I hope I'm not blushing like a tomato. He's right, he's right. I'm stupid and I need to snap out of it, for sure. I sigh.

"Alright, found anyone you fancy?" I ask, in a desperate attempt to change the subject.

"I'll look as soon as I know I can take my eyes off you! Elena, you forget you-know-who right here and now! Come on, the nightclub is full, just go dance with some dude!"

The nightclub is full for sure, but about two-thirds of the venue right now is most likely gay. It's Pride Month, and as George said, Pepe's club is the perfect place for the community to celebrate that. Indeed, I spot a lot of same-sex couples cuddling and rainbows proudly displayed or worn.

But before I can even say a thing, Daniel puts me in the arms of the first person he sees. The guy, a bit surprised, laughs and makes me spin. He's got curly brown hair, round glasses, a cute denim romper, and sure enough, a warm smile. I smile back by reflex and start dancing with him. I see Daniel give me a wink from the bar before he steps off and joins the crowd.

Alright, I should have some fun. Tommy, as my partner introduced himself, is not very good, but he's nice and here to enjoy himself. His boyfriend joins us a couple of minutes later, and we keep having fun a bit longer as more of their friends join our little dance.

I'm having fun and let the beat wash away all thoughts about a certain blondie. The last notes of "*Con Calma*" are mixed with those of a new song, a Latin romantic song, clearly a couples' thing. It's my chance to excuse myself and retreat all the way to the bar and take a break. Moon Goddess, I'm exhausted but feeling alive! Where is Danny?

"Elena!"

I turn around. It's Bianca, the girl from earlier. She's holding a large glass in her hand and I immediately frown. She's freaking underage! But seeing my expression, she shakes her head and offers me her drink to try.

"It's just orange juice. I'm only here to mix, Pepe is letting me do the next set!"

Sure enough, it doesn't smell like alcohol. I nod, and she sighs in relief. I'm still her trainer and older than her, I could have made her exit the club if I decided to. But I'm not the type to be so strict. She takes a sip of her glass and looks around.

"You're alone?" she yells trying to be heard despite the crowd and music.

"Danny is here too, but I don't know where!" I answer.

"Oh, I think I saw him! Dancing! With a big guy!"

Well, that would be good news! I try looking for him again, but with the crowd, and that weird purple lighting, it's hard to tell anyone apart. Bianca puts her fingers on my knee to get my attention.

"By the way, is it true?" she asks.

"What?"

"About the meeting? With the Blood Moon?"

What meeting is she talking about? With the Blood Moon? Why would we even meet with them? Our Alpha and the King, the eldest Black brother, don't even see eye to eye. I shake my head, confused.

"What are you talking about?"

"I heard it just before coming here. Iris said the Black brothers want to meet with Clark!"

Where is this coming from? Bianca, seeing my confusion, shrugs. She just overheard my cousin talking about it at the Main House today. Why now? This timing is so weird! If the Black brothers come here, to our territory, then that means I might see him again!

Moon Goddess, this is only a rumor, right? Iris often overhears stuff like this from my uncle, but that doesn't mean it's true, after all. I empty my glass in one go under Bianca's surprised eyes.

"You okay?" she asks, a bit confused.

"Yeah, yeah. Where is Danny?"

"I saw him near the entrance, on the left side. But, Elena…"

"I'm okay, Bianca. Have fun mixing, I'll be listening!"

She's obviously a bit confused by my attitude, but she just nods obediently. Meanwhile, I get off the chair and try to go in the direction she indicated. It's only a few feet away, but I must walk across the crowd of dancers. The song playing is a bit wilder, so I have to be careful not to get hit by an elbow or a hand.

But honestly, my thoughts are elsewhere. What's wrong with me? I promised Danny! Even if he comes by, that doesn't mean anything! A one-night thing, Elena, one night only! Get your ideas straight, girl! Did I drink too fast? I feel a bit dizzy as I stumble among the dancers.

After a while, I finally spot Daniel, standing against a pillar, and he's not alone. A super tall guy is facing him, but I can't see the guy's face. I suddenly hesitate. Daniel's obviously busy flirting. He's extra close to the tall guy, and I recognize his flirtatious eyes. He's got one hand on the guy's shoulder and the other on his torso. The guy's hand is on his waist, too. Damn, those two look good together, almost like a couple. A couple being flirty! Their faces are so close, from the wrong angle you could think they're kissing!

What do I do now? Daniel didn't notice me, too busy with his current partner to notice anything else. Do I even need to tell him? It's not confirmed yet and, if it turns out to be true, he will probably prevent me from doing something stupid.

Yes, something stupid. Am I overthinking? Probably. Even if I see Nate again, it's nothing! Right? He said one night. It's over! I look around, feeling lost and a bit lonely in this crowd of dancers. I sigh and decide to step out. I don't want to bother Danny with my stupid ideas.

I take a few steps outside, breathing in. I feel better being outside. It's a bit cooler, and there's no crowd either. I look at the line of people waiting to get inside. Everyone's here to have fun, yet here I am, thinking about an impossible scenario. All worked up because of a few words.

"Babe?"

I turn around. Daniel just came out too, followed by his love interest of the night. Damn, the guy is even taller than I thought now that I see him up close, and not Latino either. He looks kind, with big, dark green eyes and a soft smile.

"Sorry, I just needed some fresh air. You should have stayed inside, Danny."

"I was worried, I saw you leave."

"I'm fine, babe."

He doesn't really trust me, making his suspicious face. So I decide to turn my attention to the boy next to him.

"Hi, I'm Elena."

"Boyan. Nice to meet you."

"Boyan?" I repeat.

"Yeah, but you can call me Bobo."

Eventually, Daniel convinced me to have fun. Let it all go, dance until my feet were sore, and let my thoughts drown in a glass of Margarita. Several of them… Enough to explain this morning's mild headache.

I massage my neck, and get up from my bed, grabbing my kimono. It's a fancy and hot pink, but I love the embroidered flowers and the feel of silk on my bare skin. Danny gave it to me for Christmas last year, and I always wear it on the weekends, especially on Sundays. I hear some rummaging in the kitchen. What is he doing? I exit my bedroom and walk barefoot to our kitchen.

To my surprise, it's not Daniel who's being nosy, but a big, dark guy standing in the middle of the room. Oh my gosh, I didn't think his man slept here! I came home early and didn't even hear them come back last night. He spots me, standing like an idiot at the doorway, and smiles.

"Good morning, Elena."

"Ahem, morning."

It would probably be a bit awkward if he didn't have a warm smile. Instead, he is acting natural, walking around in our kitchen as if he'd been here before. I walk up to the kitchen counter and sit on a stool, a bit amused. There are a bunch of new ingredients on our kitchen counter. Did he buy groceries?

"I bought coffee. I didn't know what you guys drank, so I got several."

Really? I take a look at the paper cups. He brought four of them: macchiato, black, latte, and tea. Gosh, we have a coffee maker! So cute though. I grab the macchiato.

"He likes his coffee as dark as possible," I tell him with a smile.

Big boy nods.

"Noted."

I look at him cooking with all those ingredients. I'm not a good cook, so I'm just impressed to see him doing this. There are eggs, milk, sugar. Is he making a cake? I want to ask, but I suddenly realize. What was his name again? Boyan? Oh right, he said to call him Bobo! Even his name is easy and simple to remember. I lean over the counter to take a peek at whatever is on the stove.

"What are you cooking?"

"Crepes. I don't cook much but this recipe is easy. My nieces love it."

"You have nieces?" I ask, interested.

He nods with a smile, still focused on his pan.

"Yes, twins. They are my brother's kids and are four years old."

He seems so genuinely happy while talking about those children, my heart melts. Damn, he cooks breakfast for us, loves kids, is super nice, polite, and he's even good-looking! Danny, you better hold on to this one!

"You have other roommates?"

I take a sip of coffee and answer him, a bit surprised by the question.

"No, just Danny. We started renting this place about two years ago now. Daniel wanted a place quieter than his parent's house and I, well, let's just say it was at a time when I needed a fresh start."

He nods and grabs the butter. I appreciate that he doesn't ask more than that. I wouldn't want someone to get curious about my complicated past.

Now that I think about it, two years have already passed since those events. A shiver runs down my spine. Moon Goddess, I never want to see that guy ever again. Me and my bad judgment. I sigh, and Bobo notices it. With a smile, he doesn't say anything and just hands me a crepe. Surprised, I hesitate a second before taking it. Oh my, this is so good! He just put lemon and sugar on it, but it's deliciously hot, and the lemon's sourness and the sugar's sweetness melt in my mouth.

"Moon Goddess, this is so good! Can I just eat it all before Danny wakes up?" I ask while licking the juice off my fingers.

He laughs.

"I'll make enough for the two of you, don't worry."

Indeed, there is already a good pile! How many is that? Thirty or so? There is enough for the whole floor!

"So, Bobo, what's your story? What pack are you from? I've never seen you around. The Purple Moon?"

He shakes his head and flips another crepe.

"The Blood Moon."

I almost spit out my coffee. Seriously! The Blood Moon? Of all clans, he's from the King's pack? Moon Goddess! That guy's not even supposed to be here!

"You okay?" he asks, seeing me coughing miserably.

"The Blood Moon, seriously? Bobo, you shouldn't be here, what if our pack members find out?"

But he shakes his head, very calm, and hands me a napkin to clean the mess I just made on my chin and the kitchen counter.

"Don't worry, your Alpha allowed me to be here. I came to deliver a message from my boss."

How can he be so calm? His boss is none other than the King! Once I'm done wiping off the coffee from my mouth and chin, I put down my cup and frown.

"Can I ask what message?"

"Nothing big or secret. He wants to meet your Alpha, Clark Hamilton. He's looking for someone."

While saying those last few words, Bobo's green eyes suddenly darkened. The Alpha King is looking for someone? Who could it be?

Judging from Bobo's expression, it's not about just a fight or any simple issue. I wonder what kind of person the King is looking for.

"So, the King wants to come here? Mr. Black?"

It feels odd to call him that. Not only because it's Nathaniel's brother, but because, well, nobody really uses his name. He's just referred to as the King whenever he's mentioned, from what I know. Actually, he's just so feared that most people avoid talking about him altogether. His influence is just that impressive.

But Bobo shakes his head.

"No, not the boss directly. His brothers will come in his stead. He doesn't like to meet people."

I freeze almost immediately. Bobo doesn't notice, but I'm petrified just sitting there, and my mind enters a flurry of emotions. Oh, Moon Goddess. Nathaniel might come here, on our territory. Nate. Here. Those two words put together cause unfathomable confusion. What am I thinking? Once again, I'm flooded with memories of our night together. Don't, don't, don't, Elena. Stop reminiscing, this is stupid! It doesn't mean anything. Just because he's coming to the White Moon territory doesn't mean I'll necessarily meet him again. There is no guarantee.

I breathe in and drink a big mouthful of coffee. I burn the tip of my tongue, but who cares. I need to cool down those thoughts.

"Good morn-'."

Daniel, who was walking in, just spotted Bobo and froze instantly, visibly shocked. I see his eyes go to Bobo, then to me, and to Bobo again. It's like I can hear his brain's breakdown from here. Yep, he had no idea Bobo was, well, still here. Then, after a second of embarrassing silence, Bobo walks up to him with a smile and kisses him like it's totally natural for them. I see Daniel's eyes grow bigger and the next second, he's as red as a tomato.

"Good morning," says Bobo with his disarming smile.

"Go-good mor-morning," stutters Daniel.

I can't help but chuckle behind my cup, and despite my attempt to pass it as a cough, my best friend sends me a deadly glare.

"*Don't. You. Dare.*"

"*Not my fault you two are so cute! Seriously, Danny, if you could see your face right now-*"

"*Shut it!*"

He ignores me and walks very awkwardly to the available stool next to me. Once again, I must repress a laugh. Danny's gait is quite telling; I'm surprised I wasn't alerted to Bobo's being here with how thin the walls are. I can't resist teasing him, and my best friend has to ignore my intense suspicious staring to address Bobo.

"Um. What are you making?"

"Crepes. Here."

He hands a plate to Daniel. His plate is nicely stacked with a little pile of crepes, and he even has a strawberry on top! Moon Goddess, how can he be so adorably cute and obvious! He's even looking at Daniel with those ravishing green eyes. I can see my best friend's ears blushing, while I'm struggling not to gush!

"Thank you."

Daniel's voice is as tiny as a mouse. I finally have some pity for him and hand him the cup of black coffee. Meanwhile, I turn to Bobo with a smile.

"I'll go get changed. Thank you for the crepes, Bobo, loved them!"

"You're welcome. There's more if you want it."

I give him a wink and finally leave them alone, heading for the bathroom. Now that I don't have Daniel's silly embarrassed face to entertain me, I'm suddenly left alone with the news. Nate is coming to our territory. How am I supposed to react to that?

I let the cold water wash away the last effects of alcohol and my thoughts. I shouldn't think about this. Even if we had a great time together, that's it. I shouldn't hope for more. Move on, Elena, don't start making the same mistakes again!

I won't go. I won't be at the meeting, or near the main house. Let's not create occasions, it would only create more confusion, right? I need to be reasonable. Remember what Reagan always taught you: the first thing you need to strengthen is your mind. Don't be stupid, Elena, don't fall for it. Don't make another mistake over feelings.

I walk to my room to change and hear Danny and Bobo casually chatting in the living room. I hope this pair works somehow. I suddenly remember Bobo is from the Blood Moon. Shit, Daniel probably doesn't know either. This will definitely be an issue later, but for now, I want him to enjoy this a bit longer.

I find a pair of shorts and a tank top. I don't intend to wear them long anyway; I need a good run, in my wolf form. I quickly say goodbye to the guys, and leave the apartment. Sunday mornings are usually quiet in our neighborhood. Those who aren't sleeping are enjoying a family breakfast or are at church. I walk down a few empty streets, enjoying the early sunshine. What time is it anyway? Around 9:00 a.m. probably. I regret not taking more of Bobo's crepes; the sweet smells of the Monteiro Bakery wake my wolf's appetite.

I keep walking until I reach the border, where the White Moon territory stops, and the North Forest begins. A vast, dense forest reaching farther than the eye can see. I've always loved running in the forest, running as far as I can.

I take a few steps past the tree line, and take off my clothes, putting them in between a couple of tree branches. Stretching a bit, I shape-shift into my wolf form. An intense feeling of satisfaction runs through my body as I get on all fours. I love being a werewolf.

I start running casually, just heading north as usual. Why am I always so attracted to the North? It's an odd feeling, like something's there, something waiting for me. Something I've forgotten, maybe. I keep running, chasing a few rabbits for play, and climbing and jumping rocks for fun. I come across a couple of wolves, probably lovebirds who spent the night out. Are they hiding their idyll from their packs? I don't recognize them, but they stay away from me anyway. I just keep running my own way.

The feuds between the packs make it so hard to interact nowadays. Silver City is only a few centuries old, but some packs have fought so many times, they just can't see eye-to-eye. So, bonding or marriage between wolves of different packs is always a complicated topic. Sometimes, the lovers are lucky enough that both clans tolerate each other, and one of the two can change their allegiance to join their mate's pack. But I've only heard about this, I've never witnessed it myself.

Having sex with Nate was totally forbidden. If my Alpha heard about it… I don't even want to think about it. Nathaniel is his own Alpha, so he probably would have a different kind of pressure about that. I slow down, I'm on a cliff, with a splendid view of the forest below.

If only we were… No, stop, Elena. No ifs. Just face the reality.

This is never happening again.

Chapter 5

I stay there a long time, thinking about it. I don't know why I'm getting my hopes up all of a sudden, but I just can't. I have enough trouble in my life as it is.

My eyes linger on the horizon, looking for answers. Where did I come from? I was about three years old when Reagan brought me before Clark Hamilton, the new Alpha of the White Moon. He saw me, a strange child who turned out to be an obvious alpha she-wolf, with amber eyes and cream fur. I learned later that it was an unusual combination, something that reminded others of the royal families of the past. The ones no one had seen in a very, very long time. But my fur wasn't completely white like the legends, and I didn't have blue eyes. Mine were amber. Yet, my strange appearance and alpha disposition raised suspicions. I couldn't be raised among normal wolves. So, Clark found a young alpha couple to raise me. My adoptive father, Samuel Whitewood, was the younger brother of Xavier Whitewood, the leader of the Opal Moon, a branch of the White Moon that had just been created. My mother, Ivy Whitewood, was young and pretty but had not been able to conceive children. She was the one who approached Clark, asking the Alpha to let her take me in. He agreed, and the whole pack accepted me as their child.

However, no matter how well the pack treated me, I always felt I was different from my peers.

I was stronger than the kids my age. I was faster. I shape-shifted for the first time when I was five. No one had ever seen shape-shifting at such a young age. I was the best hunter, the best fighter among all the pups of the pack. With my alpha blood and Reagan training me, there was no way anyone else could keep up. Sadly, that also meant I was naturally ostracized by the other pups.

I didn't really mind, though. The others couldn't pick on me, as I was strong and an alpha's daughter. I had Daniel too, the only other kid that didn't blend in.

"*Hey, look who's here.*"

I turn around, surprised to see another wolf here. The dark gray male joins me, playfully pushing my side with his nose.

"*Hi, Levi.*"

"*Long time no see, beautiful. What are you doing here?*"

"*I needed some fresh air. What about you?*"

"*Patrol duty. Where's my little brother?*"

"*He's at home.*"

"*Did he tell you? Our mom wants to see you at brunch.*"

"*Oh right. Yeah, sure, I'll come. I miss her cooking.*"

"*You'd better!*"

We chit-chat for a few minutes. Levi is the oldest of Daniel's siblings, and I consider him my brother too. He's a few years older than me, and one of the only people in the pack strong enough for me to really train with.

"*Levi?*"

"*Hm?*"

"*Have you heard about the Blood Moon coming for a visit?*"

Among the Lewis children, Levi was the only one born with a Beta Aura, which is unusual for a pup born of two regular werewolves. It suits his big brother attitude and personality though. Hence, he became a close aide to the White Moon Beta and might even be a candidate to take over her position someday.

He agitates his ears, looking for something unusual far away. I already know it's not a threat but a couple of deer. After a few seconds, he growls.

"*Yeah. A big guy came yesterday to talk to Clark. They say they just want to visit. Sounds fishy, but our Alpha probably won't refuse. We can't anger them.*"

"*I heard they are looking for someone.*"

He turns to me, surprised.

"*Huh? How do you know that?*"

"*I met the guy last night, at Pepe's. He said the King is looking for someone. I don't think they mean trouble.*"

"*Interesting.*"

"*What did Clark say?*"

Levi shakes his head.

"*You know him. He said he'll think about it. He never makes rash decisions, but Xavier is pushing him to accept.*"

No surprise there. For some reason, my uncle is always willing to find new allies for our clan, though I doubt that's what the Blood Moon is really after.

"*I heard you met with Old Reagan.*"

"*How do you know?*"

"*She made a fuss with Xavier last night. About your dad. That granny is scary when she's mad. Xavier couldn't even talk back to her. I don't see him getting reprimanded like that often. It was funny.*"

"*Well, she's a stray, so she doesn't really care about the Alpha hierarchy I guess.*"

I never thought my uncle Xavier was very imposing to begin with. I can barely feel his Alpha Aura. Compared to a regular alpha like my dad, he is weaker. The only reason Clark chose him to be the Alpha of the Opal Moon instead of my father was that he is the oldest brother. No wonder he always had an inferiority complex.

"*Levi, how far north have you gone?*"

Flustered by my question, he gazes in that direction, sighing.

"*About twenty miles, I'd say. We never crossed the river, even when hunting. Clark won't allow it, and it's too far from our territory. Besides, it's only snow most of the time, nothing much to hunt.*"

I just nod. His answer is as I expected. I've never been past the river, either. In winter, the snow progresses past it and the cold freezes the river enough for someone to cross it, but as Levi said, there probably isn't much life past that border.

"*Still thinking about it, huh?*"

As always, Levi knows what I'm thinking about. He gives me a gentle push with his head against my shoulder.

"*Don't worry, beautiful. One day you'll find your answers. Reagan is just one stubborn old lady. Want to come with me? We could run to the river, see if, well, we find anything.*"

"*Thanks, Levi, but we already did that about ten times, and never found anything. I don't think it's worth the trouble. I just... Reagan is the only one who knows what I should look for. As long as she isn't willing to talk, I have no answers.*"

I sigh, a bit depressed by that thought, but it's the truth. No matter how many times Daniel, his siblings, and I ran through that forest, we never found a single clue about my past. We didn't have any, to begin with. The only thing we ever learned from Reagan was that I came from the North and that was it.

Levi sighs too, next to me.

"I'm sure she's got her reasons, Elena. Reagan is a smart kickass oldie. She'll tell you when the time is right. And anyway, you've got us, okay?"

I nod. I'm so grateful to Daniel's family. Ever since I was young, they treated me like family, all his siblings, and his parents. After my parent's accident, they supported me all the way, even if I was an emotional mess.

Levi pushes me playfully, and I growl back, playing along. We play fight for a few minutes, then we both start running and chasing each other. Our race takes us to another group of patrollers from our pack, and I end up spending the rest of my morning with them, catching up with those I haven't seen in a while, playing tag, or patrolling with them.

When we get back to the White Moon territory, I follow Levi to the main house. It's an old building, sitting on a high hill in the Hispanic neighborhood. The colors on the building have faded away, leaving a reddish clay appearance, though one of the regular punishments for the young ones is to paint the shutters, leaving them always perfectly white. It's a nice contrast and makes the house really visible from anywhere around. When Levi and I step in, back to our human appearances after we fetched our clothes, a teenager is busy painting them again with a grumpy face.

We walk in casually and get a warm welcome from everyone in the room.

"Elena, *mi amor,* it's been a while! You're so pretty, *mi cariña*!"

"Look at her! *Que hermosa eres!* Come here, say hi to this old uncle!"

I hug and say hi to everyone there, mostly adults who saw me grow up, friends or family to the Alpha. I feel a bit guilty for not coming more often, but this warm atmosphere reminds me a lot of my parents, and I feel a bit uncomfortable with it. Thankfully, Levi never leaves my side, even putting an arm casually around my shoulders to take me to the kitchen. There, we come across Ben, another one of the Lewis siblings.

"Hey, Levi, how was patrol? Anything new? Hi, Elena! You coming for brunch?"

"Hi, Ben. Yes, I am! Where is your other half?"

He smiles at me.

"Bonnie's helping mom cook. They are both super excited since Rachel's back. What about Danny?"

"He will probably join us there…"

I hope he does. It would be super awkward to have to explain to his mom and all five of his siblings he's missing their traditional family brunch because of his love interest! But Benjamin doesn't notice my hesitation and starts talking to his brother about his patrol. Meanwhile, I decide to mind-link Daniel, since it's almost noon now.

"*Danny? What about the brunch?*"

"*I'm coming, babe.*"

"*Are you okay?*"

His inner voice seems a bit weaker than usual. Like he's sad or something. But he brushes my question away.

"*I'm fine. See you there.*"

He doesn't sound fine; I know my Danny. Did something happen with Bobo? Everything seemed alright when I left this morning.

"Elena?"

Ben and Levi noticed my expression, and the two redheads are staring at me with worried faces. I try not to give too much away and smile.

"Daniel said he's on his way."

"Oh, yeah! The whole fam in the house!" says Ben, overexcited.

He runs past us to leave the Alpha's house, headed for their home. He shape-shifts as he exits the house, ruining his clothes in the process. Levi growls after the red wolf.

"Seriously, Ben? Mom's going to be mad!"

But his younger brother is already gone. I help him gather the scraps of clothes. Out of the four Lewis boys, Ben is the mischievous one. While Bonnie, his twin sister, is shy and quiet, he's the exact opposite, a real tornado. Levi is grumbling about his brother's carelessness when I suddenly hear someone calling me.

"Look who's here!"

I turn around. Clark! The Alpha himself, smiling at me with his arms wide open. I can't resist and run to him, giving him a big hug. I haven't seen him in days! He laughs and hugs me back, with his arms almost crushing me until he lets go to look at me.

"There she is! How come you never stop by to see your godfather, huh?"

"Sorry."

Here's another reason why Xavier doesn't like me: I'm one of the Alpha's three godchildren, and in our world, that also means I'm a potential successor to be the White Moon clan's leader. Clark's wife died before she could give him any children, and hence, no one can predict who will succeed him.

"Elena, I need you here next Friday."

"Next Friday?"

What is this? Clark never asks me to attend the meetings, I usually just come when I want to or not. I realize one second too late what this is about.

"You may have heard; The Blood Moon's Black brothers will be coming. I want you to be there."

Oh, crap.

"Is there a problem?"

Clark is frowning because of my shocked expression. He can ask me anything but that! Being in the same room as Nate again, I have no idea how I would handle that. But I can't tell him the reason!

"Elena?"

"Sorry, it's… I mean, why do you want me there?"

"Come on, I always take you to important events for the pack, and meeting the Blood Moon, the King's brothers, is one of them. I want them to know the faces of my potential successors."

Moon Goddess, if Clark knew I had sex with one of the King's brothers, I don't know if he would kill me or Nate first! I try to think for a second, but really, I can't tell him any valid reason for me to not be there! I find myself nodding to him.

"Alright, Clark, I'll be there."

"Good!"

And with that, he plants a quick kiss on my forehead and walks away. Gosh, what did I just agree to? I must be going crazy!

"Elena, let's go."

Levi joins me, and I nod before following him out. He puts an arm around my shoulders and starts talking to me, but my mind is elsewhere. I can't believe this. I just freaking agreed to be in the same room as Nathaniel. Again. Next week. Damn it.

This is ridiculous. I should be very composed about this; it's just a meeting and nothing will happen because this is what we agreed on. Right? You're an adult, Elena, you can stay in the same room as him and be chill about it! And it will be with lots of people, absolutely nothing will happen. Nathaniel and his brother will discuss their business with Clark, I'll probably be around somewhere, and that should be it. Let's not dwell on any other thoughts until then.

To try and change the pace, I discuss with Levi all the way to his parents' house. I basically grew up with the Lewis siblings, with their mom inviting me to brunch almost every Sunday. When we arrive, I can already smell apple pie.

"Mom, I brought Elena."

"Oh, welcome, honey! How are you?"

Abigail Lewis hugs me warmly, despite being a head shorter than me. She's a petite, plump, and bright woman. The twins take after her, with their straight ginger hair and freckles, while Danny has her blue eyes. Wearing her usual blue apron, she takes me by the hand and guides me to the salon.

"We've missed you, honey, you should come by more often! You and Danny both! Darling, look who is here!"

When I walk into the main room, four pairs of the same green eyes turn to me: Rachel, Bonnie, and Micah, the rest of Daniel's siblings. Of course, Joseph Lewis, their father, is there too, and the first one to smile at me.

"Elena!"

I feel a big wave of warmth welcoming me. Ahead of his children, Joseph walks up to me, putting his big hands on my shoulders, and giving me a kiss on my forehead.

"Glad to see you, Elena. Abbie is right, you should come over more often, sweetheart."

"Thanks, Joe."

He gives me a warm smile in return. Joseph was the one who helped me after my parents' accident. He filled out all the paperwork, waited hours with me at the hospital, and made sure I was never alone. He even helped me pay some of the medical bills and insisted on having me stay at their house for a few days, which turned into weeks, so I wouldn't be alone.

He's my father's best friend and is always there when I really need him. I love the entire Lewis family, but Joseph's endless support is something I'll never forget. No doubt Daniel takes after him a lot.

He steps aside to let his children welcome me, but winks at me before heading to the kitchen. The first one is Rachel, the energetic eldest sister, then the quiet Bonnie, Ben's twin, and finally Micah, the youngest of the six siblings.

As usual, Micah caresses my face with his fingers instead of hugging me. I guide him to my cheeks, smiling so he can feel it.

"Hi, Elena. You seem happy," he says.

"I am. How are you, Micah?"

"Happy that all of the family is here. And I missed your voice, you know."

Micah lost almost all of his sight to a genetic disease when he was only six. He is seventeen now and got used to it. He has a strange, surprising personality, but not in a bad way. He just acts much more mature than his age at times.

"Is something bothering you?" he suddenly asks.

"Nothing important, Micah."

Sometimes I wish he wasn't so good at reading emotions! I gently grab his fingers to hold his hand instead, and Bonnie takes the other one.

"Is that so? Well, mom's cooking will probably make you feel better."

"Elena! Tell me what you thought of the dress!" suddenly asks Rachel.

Damn, I forgot about that dress and Rachel's enthusiasm. I answer her endless questions while Levi starts talking with his dad, Micah, and the twins while helping their mom in the kitchen. Catching up with Rachel is nice, but she's such a chatterbox! Within half an hour, I already know all her new friends' names, everything she did last week, her entire plan for next year's collection, the latest gossip in the pack, and even her idea for her third store event! At some point, I just let her talk and look across the room to watch Joseph and Levi chatting.

Those two really look alike, well, Levi took almost everything after his dad. They are both a bit darker-skinned than the rest of the family, and very tall with broad shoulders and lean muscles. But Levi, like Danny, has his mother's blue eyes and strawberry blonde hair, making a beautiful contrast.

"*Don't tell me you still have a crush on my brother?*"

"Danny!"

My best friend just walked in, wearing a simple white shirt and a pair of jeans, his hair messy as usual. At least, he shaved before coming. I take this opportunity to escape Rachel's babbling and walk to him. I only meant to welcome him, but he suddenly hugs me like he needed it. I pat his back as I feel his face hidden in my shoulder.

"*Talk later?*"

"*Yes. Please.*"

"*Okay.*"

I know my Danny. If he's like this, he won't want questions in front of his family. Indeed, he lets me go like nothing happened and shows his usual smile to his dad and siblings.

"There he is! Son, you should come more often!"

"Danny, you're late, we're starving! And mom made mashed potatoes!" Ben says.

"Benjamin, stop complaining and go wash your hands! Bonnie, Micah, you too!"

Abigail sends her three youngest away and comes to hug Danny. She pinches his cheek without warning, and Levi and I have to repress a laugh watching his helpless grimace.

"What's this? Daniel Lewis, how come you are so thin? You bookworm, do you even eat at all? Thank Moon Goddess Elena is living with you, or I would come every day to feed you myself, I swear!"

"Mom, that hurts! And yes, I eat! Lots! Ask Elena!"

But she just sighs. Abigail is the typical wolf mom that always finds her children too thin no matter what. Hence, she keeps complaining about Daniel's lifestyle until we are seated all together for brunch.

As per usual, the table is full of homemade dishes Abigail and Bonnie made. I really missed their cooking. Most of it is meat, as one would expect from a werewolf family, but the Lewis mother also made every one of her children's favorite dishes, even my cinnamon rolls. I grab one as everyone starts eating loudly. As usual, Rachel and Ben are leading most of the conversation, but I notice that, next to me, Daniel is unusually quiet. I give him a gentle push with my elbow, but he ignores me and just takes more coffee. He is barely eating, too! I wish we could talk already.

"Dad, did you hear about the Blood Moon brothers coming?" Levi asks suddenly.

Everyone stops talking to look at Joseph, except for Daniel, who turns to me, suspicious.

"*You knew?*"

"*I just learned about it!*"

"Yes, Xavier is quite ecstatic about it."

"Why?" Ben asks. "It's not like it will be any better for him."

"I think he wants to try and introduce Iris to one of them," sighs his mother. "Poor girl. She's so nice but her dad is a bit..."

"Oh please, Mom, this is the twenty-first century," says Rachel, rolling her eyes. "She can meet and date whoever the hell she wants. She's twenty already, and smarter than that!"

Next to Rachel, Bonnie nods, looking very serious.

"Please, not the feminist speech now."Ben mumbles.

"What? Do you think women–" Rachel starts, but her father interrupts her.

"Not now, honey, we get it. And I think your mother's right, Xavier hopes we can form some sort of alliance with the Black brothers."

While they keep talking, I can feel Daniel's eyes piercing me.

"*Tell me you're not going. Tell me you're not even thinking about it, Elena.*"

"*Danny, I already agreed to it.*"

"Are you kidding me?!"

Everyone jumps at Daniel's sudden yelling. That idiot, can't he control his mind-link and actual tongue! The whole family is staring at us now! I grab his arm, trying to get him to sit down again, but instead, he grabs my hand and turns to his parents.

"Sorry, Elena and I need a minute to talk in private."

"Alright, honey."

And with that, Daniel pulls me all the way to his father's study upstairs. How can he make us leave the table like that? And without a proper reason too! Moreover, why is he so angry?

He closes the door behind him, and turns around, glaring like a mom about to scold her pup.

"Are you fucking kidding me, Elena?"

"Don't growl at me, I didn't have a choice! Clark asked, you know I can't refuse him! How would I have explained it?"

"Yeah, I guess he wouldn't like you bedding one of them!"

I roll my eyes. Why are we even having this argument?

"Danny, I get it, it's bad, okay? I did it once, and I'm not going to do it again! I can't say 'no' to the Alpha, but I can just be there and do nothing!"

"Girl, you better not do anything and be as cold as ice to him! I know this kind of guy, Elena, he'll just use you and throw you out the window when he's bored. You don't need that kind of shit!"

"For the last time, Danny, I get it! Okay?"

He's still glaring at me, and I get why he's so anxious and annoyed about all this, but still! I put a hand on my waist, trying to change subjects instead.

"Where is Bobo?"

His face suddenly shifts from anger to surprise. This time, he crosses his arms and avoids my eyes, looking a bit unsure.

"He went back."

"But you'll see him again, won't you?"

"No."

What? Is he kidding me?

"Danny!"

"He belongs to the Blood Moon, Elena! And he's a beta, too! And guess what? He's not even gay to begin with!"

"Wait… What?"

Well, that's new. I stare at Daniel, waiting for more. But my best friend is obviously very uncomfortable with the subject, looking everywhere but my direction. This time I'm the one doing the questioning, for a change.

"Danny, what do you mean?"

"He told me this morning. He had never been with a man before. He only dated girls. You know how those kinds of things end, Elena."

"He is bisexual, so what? This won't necessarily end like you think, Danny. Bobo looked like he was very into you. I don't think this was just a test, or that he'll change his mind like that."

"It's not even a question of sexuality, Elena! This kind of guy ends up with a girl, two or three kids, and a pretty house with a white fence!"

What the heck with the white fence? He's being stupidly stubborn right now! Bobo looked like the perfect gentleman, and super in love with him too!

"Stop being such a chicken, Danny! I know you've had your bad experiences, okay? But this is no reason to give up on a guy like Bobo!"

"Elena, he's not even in the right pack, to begin with! It's the freakin' Blood Moon we're talking about! And he's a beta, too! It's not like he can drop everything to come and cuddle with a nobody from the Opal Moon like me!"

"You know what, I'm done with your excuses! He is the cutest, nicest guy you've met so far. You are just finding excuses not to try it out with him! You don't want me with Black because the guy is not serious. I've got my emotional baggage and all, I get that! But you are a moron for not giving Boyan a chance, I tell you!"

"Stop dreaming, Elena! This is the Blood Moon we're talking about, what more do you need to know? The King's closest people!"

But before he can finish his sentence, Levi suddenly opens the door. Oh, crap, did he hear us? Daniel's older brother looks at both of us with an angry face.

"If you don't want Mom to hear about your passionate sex lives, I would strongly suggest you tone it down. Then you can explain to me what the hell is wrong with you two!"

Chapter 6

I just can't stop playing with my hair, so restless. I'm anxious beyond words, yet I have no idea why exactly. This is stupid. Levi is eyeing me intensely from across the room, but I try my best to ignore him.

It's Friday, the big day, and Moon Goddess, everyone is on edge. About a dozen people are standing in the room, waiting. Clark is talking to his Beta, Isabel, and to a couple of their lieutenants. The rest of us are standing around with nothing to do.

I check the clock again. Only a few minutes left. I shouldn't be so nervous! It's nothing, just a dinner with the Black brothers, maybe a walk around our turf and that's it. I should barely have any reason to talk to Nate, right?

I check the expressions around me. Aside from our Alpha, his Beta, and a handful of lieutenants, there are only me, Levi, my uncle Xavier, my cousins Iris and Chris, and Clark's two godsons, Eric and Orpheus. Everyone looks serious; some impatient, some nervous.

Among them, I notice my cousin Iris looks prettier than ever. Her lavender hair is styled into a complicated braid, and she is wearing an eerie white dress. She's even wearing a pink quartz necklace and matching earrings. I guess the rumors about my uncle wanting to introduce her to the Black brothers were true. Compared to her, my outfit is rather casual. I picked a red leather skirt and a denim shirt, the right balance between properly dressed and not too much. I only hope I won't have to stand for much longer; these damn heels are killing me.

Aside from us, all the guys are wearing shirts and dark pants, which I think is formal enough for a simple dinner. I mean, I do think the whole silverware and large table are a bit too much though.

We finally hear a car stopping in the street, and people coming out.

As they said, a few of their people are in their wolf form. Nothing alarming though, when they come in, I realize their group is smaller than I expected. I count five wolves and six humans.

Of course, I notice Nate right away, leading the group. He only walks a few steps and my heart skips a beat. Damn, why does he have to look so good?

He combed his blonde hair back, showing off his mature traits and mesmerizing blue eyes. A magazine-worthy face, handsome and attractive. He's wearing this terribly tempting white shirt again too, slightly open on his chest. Inevitably, memories of this perfectly sculpted chest under my fingers come back to me. Damn, if only he wore a necktie or something. I try to look away as Clark greets him politely. Right behind him is his younger brother, whom he introduces as Liam Black. The two brothers do have some common features if you look for it, but that's about it. Their faces look different, their stature as well. Liam's hair is pitch black, and his eyes are more of a blue-ish gray. Moreover, the teenager didn't put in as much effort as Nate, wearing only a gray T-shirt and denim pants.

"Welcome, Mr. Black, to our humble turf."

"Your clan is very esteemed and with good reason, Mr. Hamilton. Thank you for having us. I know it was an abrupt request on our part but we deeply appreciate your hospitality," replies Nate with that angelic smile of his.

"Our pleasure. We are not used to having visitors but please make yourselves comfortable. First, let me introduce my Beta, Isabel."

With that, Clark starts introducing the lieutenants one by one to Nathaniel and his entourage. They greet and shake hands; all of this is terribly ceremonial and somewhat awkward, but everyone is going along with it. Behind Nate, no one else is talking. Only one guy behind him is smiling amiably, but everyone else is silent and expressionless so far. I stay as quiet and composed as I can. Clark quickly introduces Xavier as the Opal Moon Alpha, and Iris and Chris as his children then moves on to us.

"And finally, these three are my godchildren. Eric, Isabel's son, Orpheus, our most promising hunter, and Elena, our best fighter."

"Nice to meet you all."

While saying this, Nathaniel's eyes meet Eric's, then Orpheus', and finally mine. For a second, I feel a wave of heat rising in me. Is it just me or did his pupils suddenly get darker? His intense stare on me only lasts a couple of seconds, but he has this slight smile on while looking at me, and all of a sudden, I'm thrown into a flurry of emotions.

Moon Goddess, I try to hide my feelings, but I'm so shaken right now. If it wasn't for all the people currently surrounding us, I might run away! Run away from him, his tempting eyes, and his devilish body! But I don't say a thing and just nod politely. Ignore his eyes, Elena, just ignore them.

"Well, let me introduce my party. As you know, this is my younger brother, Liam. My Beta, Isaac Graves. Those are three of our lieutenants, Joshua Hale, Vanessa Lockwood, and Tonia Mura."

Clark politely salutes them. They have two women accompanying them as well. Both Tonia and Vanessa are obviously fighters, judging by their lean bodies, practical leather outfits, and serious expressions. My inner wolf is curious to see how good they are, though they appear weaker than me. Tonia is a beta and Vanessa is a natural alpha. Now that I observe them more intensely, it appears everyone in their group is either a beta or an alpha, like us. But the King and his Beta are not here, and I can tell Xavier and Clark are a bit disappointed about that.

They keep chatting, some very basic information about the pack hierarchy and turf. Meanwhile, I can't help but notice Nathaniel's eyes sometimes shift from Clark to look over his shoulder, right at me. And every time, I feel my wolf reacting, like a magnetic attraction, some spell I can't help but answer. I try to avoid his stare, but even while looking somewhere else, I feel those two blue eyes piercing a hole through me.

"Well, we have a nice dinner waiting for us! I don't mean to brag, but we have some of the finest cooks and I heard you were quite a gourmet, Mr. Black."

"I plead guilty. And I'm all the more curious about your cuisine, with all the cultures you have mixed here, Clark."

Looks like I missed the moment when he started calling our Alpha by his first name. But Clark doesn't say anything and invites everyone to sit. To our surprise, Liam Black picks the seat right next to Clark, while Nate sits on the opposite side. For a few seconds, no one is sure where to sit, until Tonia suddenly offers me the seat right next to hers.

I would probably have said yes right away if it wasn't also the one right next to Nate. But everyone is watching, and I can't just say no.

Trying to focus my attention on the female warrior, I sit down, and almost immediately, she starts chatting with me about fighting techniques. Apparently, Clark introducing me as the best warrior caught her attention. I'm only too happy to chat with her and do my best to ignore Nate sitting on my left.

Moreover, he is talking about cuisine with Clark and doesn't seem to pay any attention to me. That's alright with me so far!

The starters are served, and Nathaniel exchanges a few comments with Isabel, who did most of the cooking for today. He really is a gourmet as he said, talking about each dish with expertise. He stays surprisingly polite and friendly towards our Beta though, complimenting her menu.

I reach out my hand to help Chris serve wine around us. However, I suddenly freeze halfway. Did he just? I turn towards Nate, but he is still talking with Isabel. I swear I felt his fingers on my leg. Maybe he didn't do it voluntarily? I mean, the seats are quite close to each other. I decide to ignore what just happened and pour a few drinks. When I put down the bottle and reach for my glass, though, I feel it again.

This time I know for sure. His fingers brushed my knee again under the tablecloth, and it can't possibly be by mistake. His whole body is turned towards Isabel! I frown. What the hell is he playing at? There are about twenty people around this table!

But as I look around, it's obvious nobody noticed. Actually, it would be hard to. The table is large and rectangular, with a dark tablecloth, and all of the seats are very close to one another. Even if Nathaniel's hand ventures under the table, it would take someone sitting directly behind us to notice, and there's nothing but a wall and an old chimney. Thank Moon Goddess that everyone is busy with their own conversations. Tonia is talking with one of our lieutenants facing her, and she has no idea. No one does!

I take a large gulp of red wine, hoping to conceal my emotions somehow. But Nathaniel's hand finds my leg again, and I stiffen up a little, anxious. I feel his fingers gently brushing my skin, right where my skirt stops. Why the hell did I choose to wear a skirt? I feel myself blushing while his fingers go back and forth on my inner thigh, tracing invisible lines and making me crazy. He's barely touching me, yet I'm as hot as a furnace. I want to run away, but damn, this is also terribly electrifying. I don't even think of pushing his hand away. I bet he would stop if I did anything. I know I should, but I can't bring myself to do anything.

His full hand is now caressing my thigh, and I don't move an inch of my lower body. I'm so hot. I drink more wine, and suddenly catch Levi's eye. He's in a conversation with Eric, but he just happened to look at me.

"*What is it?*"

"*Nothing.*"

He frowns slightly, but I smile naturally and turn towards Tonia as if I was following their conversation. Moon Goddess, after the scolding Levi gave me and Daniel, if he knew Nate was actually caressing my leg at this very moment… I did notice him frowning when I sat next to him, but Tonia was the one asking, so he couldn't possibly have said a thing. Moreover, technically Nate and I haven't exchanged a word since our introductions.

He resumes his conversation with Eric, and I try to blend in with Tonia and the little group talking with her. Nate has moved on to talking with Orpheus and Clark, but his hand won't leave me. His fingers are playing with the end of my skirt. I want to move, badly, but I'm too afraid I would give anything away. I really, really shouldn't, for Moon Goddess' sake.

"Elena!"

I turn my head and realize Isabel was calling me.

"Sorry, Isa?"

"I was asking if you were okay, sweetie. Is the wine too strong? You're a bit red."

Oh shit. Isa's words suddenly bring me down to earth, and Nate's hand is gone too. I smile at her, looking a bit sorry.

"Can I excuse myself for a second? I want to refresh myself."

"Go ahead, Elena. Can you bring a new bottle on your way back?"

"Sure, Isa."

I try to control my steps and not leave the room too fast. It's so hot in here, and I need to get as far away as I can from Nate and his hands! When I finally reach the bathroom, I rush to splash my face with cold water, clearing up my thoughts. You stupid, stupid girl! What the hell was I thinking?

I catch my breath, looking at myself in the mirror. Calm down, Elena, calm down.

But then I suddenly catch a glimpse of two electric blue eyes in the reflection.

"I really like that skirt."

What the–! What is he doing here? I turn around and walk up to him, pushing him away. Is he crazy?

"What are you thinking? You shouldn't be here!"

"Don't worry, I told them I needed to go to the bathroom too," he answers calmly.

I shake my head. What kind of stupid excuse is that? This guy is way too confident and full of himself! And I hate that stupid grin of his! I look behind his shoulder in the doorway, but I can hear the muffled sounds of the group still discussing. Looks like nobody's paying attention to our absence, for now.

"Seriously, Nate, what if someone sees us?"

He steps aside and closes the door, looking serious.

"I needed to talk to you, alone."

"I can't. I mean, we can't be seen together like this. You're just–"

But before I can finish my sentence, he steps forward, and grabs my waist, pushing me against the wall behind me. I lose my breath under his electric-blue stare, as our faces get dangerously close. My whole body is tensed up by Nate's touch, burning hot already. I gasp, his lips only an inch away from mine. I can't avoid the lusty look he's giving me, I have no choice but to look at him.

"I want more."

His three words make my heart skip a beat. Oh, Moon Goddess. Think rationally, Elena, rationally. But before I can formulate any decent thought, I feel his hand going down my leg, and he starts whispering.

"I mean it. I liked it, and I know you did too. I want to take you again, Elena. And don't you say no."

Why the hell can't I? I glare at him, frustrated. The inner battle is raging inside me, and he has no fucking idea how torn I am right now. I try to think of Danny and every good reason I have to refuse him. And damn I have a lot.

"I don't want to be involved with you. I can't afford it. You're from the Blood Moon, and I'm from the White Moon. Even if this dinner is happening by some miracle, it doesn't change anything."

This time, he looks angry and frowns.

"I don't give a fuck about the packs, or your Alpha. I do whatever the hell I want, Elena, and I don't answer to anyone about who I'm seeing."

"Well, you may not care but I do! If my Alpha finds out about us, I may be punished or banished! Don't you realize I'm the one at risk here?"

His expression softens, and his hand gently caresses my back, venturing under my blouse to give me delicious chills. I can't hold back a shiver, and this fever rising under my skin.

"Is that why you're refusing me? You think I would let you be banished? And your Alpha, no, your clan doesn't need to know in the first place."

Damn him and his overconfidence! Can't he understand the place I'm in right now! But it's even harder to oppose him when his hands are quietly caressing me at the same time, one under my top and the other on my leg, and his whole body is cornering me against the cold wall.

I look for something to say, but his lips suddenly ravage my neck, and my breathing gets more erratic from the kisses he lays there. When did he undo my first button? I put my hand on his chest and, after a second of gathering whatever strength I have left, I push him away, forcing him to look at me.

"Weren't you the one who wanted a one-time thing to begin with? You said we would be done after! One night and that was it, remember?"

He stays silent and expressionless for a second, and in that short while, I have the illusion he might have come back to his senses. But all of a sudden, his hand suddenly ventures under my skirt and I gasp involuntarily, grabbing his wrist by reflex. That doesn't stop him one bit, though, as I feel his fingers roam underneath and start playing with my most vulnerable parts. He smiles upon feeling my moistness, and I blush unconditionally from this sweet torture.

"Who is it that doesn't want more?"

I bite my lip, annoyed at him. How dare he? Of course I would be excited after he played with me like that! But he doesn't care about my frustration, and suddenly starts an intense, deep kiss.

I know I should fight him off, push him and his lips, his fingers away, but I don't. My body isn't acting rationally anymore. I'm overtaken by the pleasure, the sensations this man is giving me. I hold onto him, giving in to my desire and letting him do whatever he wants. Nate just keeps going, both with his devilish kisses and fingers moving actively under my skirt. I feel my legs going numb, and my hand clenching around his wrist. I try to keep up with his intense kiss, his lips playing, his tongue flirting with mine. When he switches from my lips to my neck, I try to catch my breath, but it's erratic and messed up by the pleasure he's giving me.

Moon Goddess, he is insane. I close my eyes, trying to control my voice. But I feel it coming, and soon enough, the movements of his fingers get more intense, driving me crazy. I whisper his name uncontrollably, again and again, like a quiet prayer. When I suddenly feel this familiar heatwave brutally hitting me, my whole body tenses up, and I relish in a muffled cry against his shoulder.

It takes a few seconds for me to get out of this trance and calm down. Nate supports me and my numb legs while I come back to my senses, but neither of us say a thing. I just need to catch my breath, calm down, and realize what the hell just happened. I must be crazy. In a few minutes, maybe five or ten, I let him give me a damn orgasm in the bathroom!

"I hate you," I mutter, with a voice less angry than I would want it to sound.

"Is that a yes?" he asks with a smirk.

"No."

"No to what? My question, or…?"

"I did not say yes."

He sighs and helps me walk to the bathroom sink, as I want to rinse my face, and he washes his hands. I'm still not really thinking straight, half scandalized by what happened, and half lost in a post-orgasmic daze. He crosses his arms, staring at me with a complicated expression.

"What would it take for you to say yes?"

"What would it take for you to give up?" I sigh.

"Oh please, Elena. You liked it. We both enjoy sex with each other, why won't you admit it?"

"I enjoy the sex, alright. What I don't like are all the risks that come with it!"

"What risks? We are not going public or getting into anything serious. Just strangers having fun once in a while. No need to let anyone know what is happening between us. No strings attached, no obligations."

He looks very composed and serious. I sigh. His arguments are starting to get in my head, and I hate that. I have a hundred reasons to say no, yet I can't bring myself to refuse him. How insane is that? I put my hair back and check my appearance in the mirror while he waits. After a while, I just leave the bathroom, with him following right behind me. I walk to the wine cellar, looking for any bottle. But Nathaniel is faster in grabbing one and comes to face me again. My whole body reacts to his proximity again, and I step back.

"So?" he asks, finally getting impatient.

"Let me think about it, okay?" I blurt out.

He frowns, but he seems to accept it.

"How long?"

"What?"

"I'm not as patient as I look. When will you give me an answer?"

"Look, I'm not having this discussion in my clan's basement, okay? Give me time to think about it and–"

"Sunday evening. Dine with me."

This time, I'm the one frowning, a bit surprised by his proposal.

"Dinner?"

"Yes. I'll show you I can respect your privacy and we can discuss this calmly. Isn't that what you wanted?"

"Yes, but–"

"Then it's settled. You'll be free to give me the answer you want, as long as you come to dinner with me the day after tomorrow."

And with that, he turns around and leaves the cellar first. I can't believe it! When did I even agree to that idea of his? This is so frustrating!

I just swallow my anger and follow behind him, trying my best to conceal the hurricane of emotions overtaking me right now. When we walk back to the main room together, Isabel spots us first.

"It took you long enough!"

Crap, I don't know how long we were gone. How do I explain this? But Nathaniel speaks out first, very composed.

"My apologies, I ran into Miss Whitewood as she was going to your wine cellar and my curiosity got the best of me. Quite a nice selection you have down there!"

"Oh, really? Well, I do have a hobby of collecting fine bottles. Do you have a preference, Mr. Black? Personally, I have a soft spot for Portuguese ones."

I can't believe he got away with such a lie! I'll have to remember how good he is at lying, that's for sure! I get back to my seat and decide to ignore him, hoping I don't look odd or anything. Thank Moon Goddess I checked myself in the mirror first. Aside from being a bit red on the cheeks, I should look fine. However, I notice Levi's intense stare from across the table.

"*Was that the truth? You only showed him the cellar?*"

Shit, why does Levi have to be so suspicious now? I try to keep myself as composed as I can. For a second, I wonder what would happen if I told him the truth, if I told him I had five minutes of intense pleasure with Nathaniel in that tiny bathroom. Just thinking about it makes my heart beat faster, so I settle on an answer before it becomes too obvious.

"*That's right. He was just acting curious about Isa's collection.*"

Awesome, now I'm a shameless liar as well. I don't know if Levi believed me or not, but after a minute, he went back to talking with Eric and Orpheus without adding anything. I don't even dare look in Nathaniel's direction after that. Levi already scolded me and Daniel yesterday.

He had heard a bit too much of our conversation, and neither of us felt like lying to him. After all, he was Daniel's older brother, and practically mine too. So we told the truth, or most of it: that Daniel had met and slept with Boyan, one of the Blood Moon members, and that I had sex with Nathaniel Black. Despite the shock, Levi contained most of his anger, but only because the rest of the family was close. Other than that, he still gave us one hell of a scolding. He called us irresponsible and reckless, among other things. He was shocked that I had the nerve to willingly sleep with the King's brother, or that we even ventured outside our borders. Daniel and I didn't get to say a single word to defend ourselves, and I don't think we would have been able to anyway.

Moreover, he reminded us of the risks: if we were discovered to have relationships with people from the Blood Moon pack, we could get punished or worse, banished from the pack. I already knew that, of course, but hearing it from Levi's mouth, a beta close to Clark, made it even scarier.

"Nate, are you going to ask or what?"

Liam Black's voice suddenly brings me back to the present moment. Everyone else, surprised to hear the teenager's voice, stopped talking at the same time. Ask what? Next to me, Nathaniel nods and turns to Clark with a very serious expression.

"We came here with a motive. We are actively looking for someone on behalf of our older brother."

I exchange a glance with Levi. It's exactly as I had told him. Clark frowns, a bit surprised.

"Do you think this someone would be in our pack? Can I ask who it is and why are you looking for them?"

"We cannot give you our reasons. This is our brother's will. But be assured this person is not to be harmed in any way by us. Moreover, we are not in any way sure they might be in your pack, or in any other."

This is so intriguing. If they have no ill intentions toward this person, why are they looking so frantically? And for the King, no less? I look at our Alpha, but Clark is still looking hesitant. Of course, he wouldn't be able to trust them so easily. If the person they are looking for turns out to be from our pack, who can guarantee they won't go back on their word and do anything they want to them?

"Does this mean you plan to visit all the packs? Isn't that unusual for the Blood Moon clan?" Isabel suddenly asks.

"Indeed, but we thought this might be our best way to deal with this. This is an important matter to our brother, and we are running out of options," says Nathaniel.

That's right, both brothers look very serious about this. I wonder what's the real issue here, but they won't give more info. I see Clark hesitate a few more seconds until he sighs.

"Alright. Who are you looking for?"

"A young girl. She should be seventeen now, with black or dark brown hair, and sapphire-blue eyes."

Sapphire-blue eyes? This is rather unusual. So she's most likely a werewolf. Why would the King look for a young woman? Clark looks surprised. As far as I know, no one in our packs matches this description. We do have a lot of dark-haired people, but none with dark blue eyes.

"Most importantly, she should have a large scar on her eye."

"A scar?"

"That's right. Pale-skinned, with dark hair, dark blue eyes, and a scar on her face, around seventeen years old. That's as much information as we have."

"What about a name?" Asks Isabel.

But Nathaniel shakes his head. Wow, it's a lot about her physique, and yet, not much to find someone. No wonder they are desperate. Once he's done, I see Clark's shoulders relax.

"Sorry, but no one from our packs matches that description, either in the White Moon or Opal Moon. Especially not with that kind of scar."

"We thought that might be the case," says Nate.

Both brothers look disappointed.

"Is there anything else we can do for the King?" Xavier suddenly asks.

Both Isabel and Clark glare at him. Why does he have to blurt out that kind of thing? He makes us sound so desperate to please them, it's embarrassing. Liam Black considers him with disdain, and Nathaniel doesn't even respond. But my uncle doesn't even seem to realize how ridiculous he is acting, and this is awkward now.

"Mr. Black, I've heard you are very invested in the catering and leisure businesses. Do you have anything interesting going on these days? Our neighborhood has a few famous places as well, have you heard of them?"

Wow, I'm surprised by Iris. Since when does my cousin know so much about the Black brothers' activities? Did Xavier train her or something ahead of the dinner? Her little brother Chris looks just as surprised as I am. Since we were kids, Iris has always been a discreet and reserved girl, not one to stand out. Suddenly hearing her speak out at this dinner is a bit surprising.

But Nathaniel answers her, and they start having a conversation about the most popular restaurants around. For some unknown reason, I feel very uneasy watching the two of them exchange. Is it because, unlike Isabel, Iris is a young single woman? They talk very politely to each other, but they obviously get along fine and are having a smart and entertaining conversation. I don't feel like butting in, so I just start eating in silence, ignoring my unsettled heart. I drink a new glass of wine, scolding myself for feeling this way.

"*Easy on the wine, kiddo.*"

Clark is looking right at me with a frown, and I immediately put my glass down.

"*Sorry, Clark.*"

"*You okay?*"

"*Yeah.*"

I even make my godfather worry about me. I look around, but Tonia is busy discussing with Eric and Chris, and Nathaniel's conversation with Iris is still going on. I can't even use the bathroom excuse to get out of here. Instead, I eat silently and suddenly decide to mind-link Daniel.

"*What are you up to?*"

"*Catching up on some TV show since my roommate is busy being naughty in the wine cellar with a certain Black.*"

"*Oh please, Levi already snitched to you?*"

"*Yeah, and he is not blind you know. Did you fuck him?*"

"*Daniel!*"

I have a hard time controlling my anger right now. I can't believe him!

"*No, I did not!* "

"*What?*"

"*Wait until I get home. We gotta talk.*"

"*Don't get home late then. I only have half a season left.*"

I sigh and put an end to our mind-linking. This is going to be another dispute again.

The rest of the dinner goes by, and I suddenly learn Tonia is Boyan's older sister! It's a bit tricky to follow the conversation after that since she probably has no idea about her brother's sudden change of tastes. I'll need to let Danny know though, this is such a coincidence that his sister actually attended the dinner.

Suddenly, I feel something brushing my fingers on the table. I look down and realize Nathaniel just discreetly pushed a business card under my napkin. I take it quickly and look under the table. It's his business card, but he marked through the phone number to write a private one. Probably his. I take it and hide it in my skirt's pocket. We don't exchange any words. He just saw me taking it and returned to his conversation with Iris and Clark. Why do I feel a bit better now?

I try to not think about the little piece of paper and spend the rest of the dinner focused on chatting, eating, and behaving normally. My mind doesn't follow and wanders somewhere else. In the memories of a luxury suite, with a view of the city night lights and white silk sheets. I get lost in my thoughts for a while before I realize my wolf is growling internally. When I look around, I suddenly spot my uncle, Xavier, intensely glaring at me. What's wrong with him now? I ignore him, and this time, turn towards Nathaniel who is talking with Isabel and Chris. My cousin catches his father's glare in my direction and frowns. I give him a silent look, and we both ignore him to pursue our conversation.

Like promised, Nate actually acts very normally towards me after that, finally allowing me to relax. We talk and enjoy the dinner, with various guests joining our conversation. It's mostly business and trivial talk, but we can't show we are involved in any way. Anyway, many join our conversation, until the dinner ends.

Around 11:00 p.m., the Black brothers politely decline a tour of our turf, and without too much ceremony, leave our grounds. Our group watches as their car drives away from our streets in silence.

However, as soon as they are out of sight, Clark suddenly turns around and grabs Xavier by the collar, growling with all of his might. Everyone freaks out, and for a second, I think this is about his remarks earlier, until Clark speaks out to my uncle's terrified face.

"This is the last time I ever see you glare at my goddaughter like that again!"

A cold silence falls around us while everyone is shocked by the scene. Clark, still holding Xavier by the throat, is growling like a furious wolf. I get a chill and realize this is because of me, or because of my uncle's attitude towards me. I didn't expect Clark to get so mad.

"I'm fed up with your attitude!" growls my godfather again.

"Uncle Clark," says Chris, a bit scared.

Next to me, Iris looks serious and even a bit annoyed at her dad. Did she notice his glare as well? The only calm one is Isabel. She knows Clark by heart and doesn't look surprised at all. Instead, she turns toward the rest of us.

"Everyone but the Whitewoods, time to go home."

Nobody dares to argue with her and soon enough, I'm left with Isabel, Clark, my cousins, and my uncle in this tense situation. Xavier growls back as a reflex, but there is no way he can oppose Clark. He is the rightful Alpha, while my uncle is only Alpha of a sub-pack, and by his will too. He eventually looks down and stops growling, submissive. But my godfather looks really pissed and only lessens his grip by a bit.

"I'm warning you for the last time. I've had enough of your attitude.

Her father might not be here but damnit, I am, and as long as I am the Alpha of this clan you will not show disrespect to Sam's daughter!"

"I'm sorry."

He can barely talk, but Clark finally lets him go after a while. My uncle massages his neck, still visibly shaken by what just happened. But Iris walks up to him and takes his arm, neither complaisant nor angry.

"Let's just go home, Dad."

My cousin and her father leave without another look. We watch them walk away, Clark still growling. Chris, who stayed behind with us, turns to me and Clark, looking very sorry and uneasy.

"Sorry, Alpha. I don't know what's with my dad. You too, Elena, sorry."

"You're a good kid, Chris. Don't worry. Your father's just a greedy and stupid man," says Isabel, clicking her tongue.

Clark doesn't even look his way, his eyes still glaring in the direction that Iris and Xavier took. I sigh, tired of all this crap and the emotions from tonight.

"All I ask is that he leaves me alone."

"Don't worry, kiddo. If that idiot messes with you again, let me know."

Clark finally seems to relax and ruffles my hair with a gentle look but a bitter smile.

"I miss your dad. Samuel knew how to handle his brother's greed."

"I still think you made a mistake with Xavier," growls Isabel.

Is she talking about how he chose my uncle Xavier instead of my father to be the head of the Opal Moon? But Clark rolls his eyes and ignores her.

"You've said it enough times already, Isa. And I had my reasons. Anyways..."

He massages his shoulders, looking tired. My godfather is already in his fifties, but despite this, he is still a handsome man, with his snow-white hair and beard, deep husky voice, and very muscular body. A lot of single ladies in the pack wish he would pick a new mate, but Clark doesn't show any intent to, not since his wife passed.

"That was an interesting night," he mutters.

"Right. You think they really are looking for someone?" Isabel asks.

"Probably. The description was odd, though. Sapphire-blue eyes. And the scar thing, too. Let's just see if they do the same with the other clans."

"I was surprised you accepted," I say to Clark.

"I was curious to meet them, especially since they reached out to us. The Black brothers may have a shitty reputation, but we have to give it to them, Silver City has never been so peaceful since they got rid of their father."

That's true. I still remember how tense Silver City used to be back then. The Mad King was scaring everyone, and no clan, no territory was safe. He would go on crazy rampages and kill a lot of people. Moon Goddess help those who were at the wrong place at the wrong time. He was strong like no other alpha ever was. Strong enough to chase the remaining vampires of Silver City out. I was younger then, but I still vividly remember the dark days, when we couldn't take a step out of our turf and strictly obeyed the curfew.

"True. They weren't as complacent as I thought."

I let them discuss the brothers' actions a bit longer, but I'm eager to go home. At some point, Clark notices me and Chris standing there and sighs.

"Time to go home, kids."

He walks up to me and gives me a kiss on the forehead, and Chris gets a little pat on his head, making him all proud. We bid them good night and start walking north side by side. Chris looks a bit awkward until he starts speaking.

"Sorry about my dad."

"It's okay, Chris."

"You know, I think he's afraid Clark will name you to replace him. He wants me to be the next Opal Moon Alpha so much."

I had already kind of thought the same too. Xavier's actions are too transparent, especially those towards me. Everyone knows how he felt about my dad too, so it doesn't really come as a surprise that he sees me as a threat to his position.

"I don't really feel like being the Alpha, you know. I know I'm not that strong."

"You would do great, Chris. And you'll keep growing and getting stronger too. Plus, you're understanding and patient. Everyone in the packs likes you."

I can't say the same about his dad. Things would be different if Xavier's jealousy wasn't so obvious. Chris and I chat a bit longer until we finally part ways, him heading to his dad's while I go to my apartment.

When I get there, it's past midnight, the whole place is in the dark, and, as I suspected, Danny is snoring on the couch, the TV still on some sappy telenovela. I try to walk in silently and turn it off, but the sudden absence of sound actually wakes him up.

"Elena?"

"Yeah, I'm here, babe."

He sits up drowsily, obviously still half asleep. I try to get him to go to bed, but Danny insists I tell him about the dinner. Finally, I give up and sit next to him. I tell him about everything the happened, including my time with Nate in the bathroom and Clark and Xavier's dispute. Daniel listens, sleepy but all ears. He only interrupts me a couple of times to ask for details.

When I'm done, he shakes his head, and I'm surprised he's not even mad about what happened with Nate. I realize it's odd that he didn't even react that badly.

"Danny, what is it?"

He sighs.

"Well, I know I should be scolding you, but…"

He suddenly looks for something under our pile of mini cushions, and finally finds his phone for me to take. I immediately see a bunch of notifications. Two missed calls from Boyan, and three times as many unread texts. I turn to him and notice his bitter expression. Oh, Danny.

"You ignored them all?"

"I left the phone there all night and tried to focus on this stupid show."

"I guess it worked?"

"With the Captain's help."

I only now notice the bottle of rum and empty glass on the table. Seems like someone had a difficult time while I was at the dinner. I sigh and extend my legs on the couch, Danny doing the same so his are resting on mine and we are facing each other.

"What about you?" he asks.

"What? I shouldn't go."

"But you want to."

Daniel reads me like an open book. I sigh and nod, unable to lie to him. I grab the bottle and pour myself a glass. I'm not fond of rum, but alcohol is alcohol.

"What about you?"

Daniel sighs.

"Girl, I fell hard. He's a fucking gem. And I'm a boring science nerd."

"Come on, he loves you."

"Yeah, and that's the scariest thing, you know. Having the dream meeting, with a guy who claims he's gay for me, sweet and gentle. And I swear, babe, this guy is so good in bed, he's making me even more gay, if that's possible."

I chuckle. Stupid Danny. He's a down-to-earth guy, never believing in fairy tales, and more often than not, he is right about the douchebags he meets. He takes the glass from me to have a new gulp while I sigh.

"Just go for it, Danny."

In the darkness, I see his blue eyes on me, skeptical.

"Come on, this guy might be the man of your life. I don't want you to stay a boring single lab rat all your life because of a few dumbasses."

"You know this smells like trouble. For you, too."

"I know."

"But I'm more at risk than you."

I frown. Why would he be more at risk than me? Daniel is a regular member of our pack, not a potential successor like me.

"My feelings are on the line. You, on the other end, are negotiating a strictly-sex relationship. If the guy never falls for you, that should do the trick, right? No feelings, no way the past would repeat."

"Danny, you wouldn't be saying this if you were sober."

"Probably, but I mean it. The thing is, can you not fall for Black?"

That's a tough question.

I really thought I was over relationships and the messiness of falling in love with someone. I know I don't love Nathaniel. I feel attracted to him, that's for sure. I want him badly every time I see him, and sex with him is like a drug, plunging me into my desires. So far, it's been physical only. I don't know anything but his name and how we fuck. Until tonight, I didn't even know his brother's name, or what he really does for work. I don't know anything significant about him.

"I don't know," I eventually admit to Danny.

That's the truth. I want to say there's no way I'll fall for Nathaniel, but I know it's not true. I'm not someone who can have sex without feeling attraction, and I've felt this connection to Nathaniel from the start. A passion that can't seem to die out between us.

"I don't want to. I'll run away before I fall for him."

Daniel nods.

"You'd better. I don't want to see your heart broken twice, Elena. That's the kind of pain you never recover from."

"What about you?"

He hands me the glass with a sad expression.

"I don't know. I'm supposed to be the reasonable one in this room, but I want to take this phone and beg him to see me again. I'm an idiot, babe, you know. I want to believe again, to think this is the one and try. I'm just afraid of being wrong one more time."

I finish the rum in one go.

"Let's go for it, babe. In another life, I'd be a virgin and you would be in the closet."

"You mean we would be fifteen years old again."

"Whatever. I know this is wrong, I know this might hurt, but you know what? I don't even care. We can't expect to die without any bruises, right?"

Chapter 7

I'm just five minutes late, yet I'm nervous as heck… Why did I agree to meet him in such a fancy place? This isn't like me. I picked a brown dress that can probably get a pass everywhere as I didn't know what to expect, but now I wonder if I should have picked something fancier. I walk-run into the establishment, hoping he'll overlook my tardiness. Why am I this nervous? This isn't even a real date. I quickly mumble something to the waitress about meeting someone there, give Nathaniel's name, and she gives me a weird look, checking me out from head to toe… What the heck? It's almost reluctantly that she takes me to his table… and then I realize why. He's handsome and half the females around keep eye the very handsome guy alone at his table. They were probably all watching to see who he was waiting for. Well, I'm not sorry. I put on my sexiest smile, and gather my self-confidence to walk up to him, getting rid of that waitress with a wave of my hand.

"Nathaniel?"

He was on his phone, but I'm happy to see a relieved look on his face when he sees me.

"Sorry, a guy from my pack caught me near the border," I explain briefly. "I had to go the long way around. Did you wait long?"

"Not at all, I just got here."

Oh, thank Moon Goddess… I grab the seat next to him at the table before it gets awkward, and the waitress literally jumps across the room as Nathaniel asks for the menu. I'm going to need some drink to start off with… I glance at him over the menu. We don't match; he's wearing a fancy suit that fits this place a lot more. Shit, he noticed my gaze. Play it cool, Elena, at least act the part… Luckily, I'm saved by my cocktail that arrives, and we click glasses to get rid of that awkwardness.

"This one is yours too, I presume?" I glance around the restaurant.

"Yes. How did you know?"

Ah, it matches him perfectly…

"Well, all of the staff is giving you glances every five seconds, and not just the women."

He chuckles; of course he knows he's attractive, and probably used to getting this much attention too.

"First, thank you for coming," he changes the topic. "I just want to discuss the arrangement with you and you're free to go at the end of the dinner if you don't like it."

"Meaning I could also stay."

"Well, I do own the hotel so…"

I don't repress a chuckle. At least he's honest…

"Alright, Mr. Black, let's discuss then," I put my glass down. "What are you expecting of me?"

He frowns and grabs his whiskey.

"Well, if we are going to discuss the possibility of a long-term relationship, Miss Whitewood, maybe we need to know each other a bit better?"

Know each other? This isn't the direction I expected…

"You said long-term relationship, but isn't it just physical? Why would you need to know me any further than that?"

"If that was the case, I could just pick anyone and not bother with a second or third time. But if this is to happen several times, I would want to know what kind of woman I'm dealing with. I think I have a rough idea of who you are. But that doesn't tell me why you are so against relationships, for example, or why I would be certain you will never have deeper feelings for me."

So this is more to double-check…

"You want to know why I can't fall in love anymore?"

"Well…" he seems hesitant.

"It's very common," I shrug. "Heartbreak, and scars that will never heal."

"Well, I guess everyone has–"

"No, I'm talking about actual scars."

I'd rather be honest from the get-go if he wants to know this much, and hopefully, he won't pry too much into my personal matters. I need to set limits right away.

"I really don't want to get into the details, if you don't mind."

"I understand."

… Does he really? That seemed too easy. I do need to make sure he stays out of my personal business, though.

"I just had a really, really bad experience," I say. "It was someone who I trusted and he trampled all over my feelings, so I'm resolute not to make the same mistake twice."

"You intend to remain single?"

"Yes," I nod. "I don't want any children for now either, I'm already busy as it is."

"And what is it that you do then?"

He's more curious than I thought… I take a couple seconds to think about what he is curious about. Oh, well. It can't hurt to let him know a little bit more about me, just the basic stuff, especially if we're going to keep seeing each other.

"I'm a senior, for now, at the Business Management school. I also work as a trainer for my pack and I do odd jobs from time to time… Alright, enough about me, Mr. Black. You are some sort of CEO, right?"

He smiles, as if this was nothing.

"Correct, Miss Whitewood. I represent my brother's company on several levels, but he lets me handle the parts I love most, so I don't complain."

"The restaurant industry, was it?"

"Correct again. I have a thing for cooking, so my favorite aspects of my business are my restaurants. The entire service industry, to be honest. Restaurants, hotels, casinos, resorts, anything related to leisure and entertainment."

"Sounds like a lot for one person," I admit.

He definitely sounds like a hard worker, not a guy who just has a job in name only.

"I'm not alone. I'm just busy enough to have the right balance between office paperwork and fieldwork."

"I would go crazy, locked in an office all day," I groan.

"Didn't you say you were in Business Management?"

We probably have very different ideas about what work should be…

"I don't have plans to work for a company. I want to do my own thing: make enough money to open my own shop, and live a modest life."

I don't see myself as some busy CEO… and I'm fine with that. Will he look down on me for that? Well, I'll see what kind of guy he is. I take a sip of my cocktail to try and stay composed.

"What kind of shop?"

… I'm surprised he's even asking, but I appreciate it.

"A music café," I answer honestly. "I've always dreamed about it. Somewhere people could come to study, relax, or chat with their friends while enjoying a good homemade coffee and listening to new music from all around the world. I want a corner of the cafe to be set up to sell music from both independent and mainstream artists. I even know what I want it to look like."

Crap, I ended up chatting a lot about this… I stop myself and grab my glass again. He probably thinks I'm some dreamer…

"That's one very interesting plan," he smiles, "and a good one."

"Don't you steal it," I chuckle, a bit flattered.

"I wouldn't dare to."

Alright, he is alright so far… and surprisingly amiable. I expected him to be a bit stiff, maybe because of this atmosphere, but he seems relaxed and genuinely listened.

"Shall we have dinner?" he asks.

"Oh. Yes."

A waiter appears out of nowhere to guide us to an elevator… Why did it have to be an elevator? Now I'm having silly thoughts and thinking about a certain memory… Thank Moon Goddess it doesn't last long before we step out.

"Your table, madam, sir."

Wow. Is this a room just for us? So intimate… and stunning. I have to remember to close my mouth as I discover the sun setting on Silver City, the sky in dazzling shades of blue, pink, and orange. Shit, this is beautiful.

"You like it?"

"It's amazing."

Damn, he's good. And I can't help but lower my guard a bit. He did go all out for this… or is this nothing for him? I try to erase that amazed look off my face and walk to our seats, but the sunset is just amazing. I don't really care for the waiter, I bet Nathaniel knows the menu by heart anyway. I just grab one, but there's something odd about it.

"The prices are not on it?"

"Not on yours. It's a European custom that the person invited to the restaurant should not see how much the host is paying. Especially in this situation, where the man invites the woman."

A bit sexist, but I do see why they would think of this…

"I like it. I mean, not the man inviting the woman part, but the host's bill being private. If I'm a guest, I would feel bad ordering a lot or something expensive, but since I have no idea, I can just order anything and you can't resent me for that."

He laughs.

"Are you afraid I'll go bankrupt from treating you once? How much do you eat, exactly?"

"A lot! Daniel says I eat like a baby dinosaur."

"Daniel?"

"My best friend and roommate. My childhood friend. My best for everything really… What do you recommend? I don't know half of the things on here."

He patiently explains it all to me, and I settle for a fish carpaccio to start, while he picks the wine as I'm completely uneducated about it. We go on to chat about my non-existent culinary skills, and I explain my only talent is mixing drinks from my experience as a barmaid a few years ago.

The waiter comes back, and he gives him our orders while I peek at the landscape again. It's so gorgeous… I need to enjoy, who knows when I can enjoy such a view again? I remember to glance back at Nathaniel, but to my surprise, he's been staring at me.

"What is it?"

"I was wondering how can I get this beautiful woman to spend some more nights with me."

Shit. What a flirt… Come on, don't give in too easily.

"Me coming here doesn't mean my answer is yes."

He smiles, and takes his hand off the table. I'm confused for a second as he stays silent, but I suddenly feel his fingers on my leg!

"You—!"

But the waiter comes in at this very moment with our plates, and I have to shut up. He just smiles like a naughty kid while the waiter takes forever introducing our plates, while I glare.

"Do you need anything else?" asks the waiter.

Yes, can he fuck off so I can get mad at Nathaniel?!

"No, we—"

Holy shit, where is he touching! I didn't realize he was close enough to actually touch my underwear!

"Miss?" the waiter asks, confused.

"Did you want anything else, Elena?"

I glare at Nathaniel.

"No, I'm... I'm good."

He keeps playing with my underwear, visibly having way too much fun teasing me!

"You can go," he finally tells the waiter.

"Yes sir. *Bon appetit.*"

The waiter leaves, and I grab his wrist.

"*Stop it!*"

He jerks his hand off, visibly surprised. Crap. I really hadn't planned to show him my ability tonight. Or any other night, for that matter! I just reacted so suddenly I couldn't control my wolf. As the waiter leaves, I still feel Nate's stare on me, and I look away.

"Elena?"

He wants an answer, but I don't know what to say. I sigh.

"Yes, I did mind-link you. Sorry."

"What are you apologizing for? Rather, I'd like to know how you can do that."

"I don't really know. It's been an ability of mine since I was a kid. I can mind-link any other alpha in Silver City whenever I want, whether they are from my pack or not."

There, I said it. How will he react? He won't think I'm a freak, right? I scared a few other people when I was younger and did it unknowingly. I don't know how I would take it if Nate reacted badly too. But instead, he seems… impressed?

"That's… rather unique. Is that the only thing, or do you have any other abilities I should know about?"

What does that mean, that he should know about? It's not like I'm that different. I sigh.

"Not really, other than that, I'm pretty normal. Because of my alpha heritage, I'm strong enough to be a fighter."

No need for him to know more, right? Why does he care, anyway? It's not my wolf side he's interested in. After a few seconds of awkward silence, he suddenly shakes his head, grabbing his fork to start eating. I watch him, a bit surprised.

"I'm not going to insist if you don't want me to. I understand. Feel free to tell me what you want, but I have no intention to pry into your private life any further."

"Really?"

I feel relieved, but also, I can't help but have a hint of doubt. It's not like this would be the first time someone said they would keep it a secret and didn't. Did I become too doubtful over time? While I'm still staring at him in disbelief, Nate puts his fork down to look at me very seriously.

"Elena, even with no strings attached, I'm not the kind of asshole that will spread our private affairs around. Whether it's about you, me, or us, I won't. You can trust me. And you can even consider me an open ear if you want to talk. If we agree on this relationship, it has to be one where we can trust each other, alright?"

I suddenly feel a wave of relief wash over me. Maybe I was waiting for this. For some sort of comfort. A way to confirm if I could trust him or not. It's not as if I would believe him with those few words, no matter how sincere they seem, but the fact that he just thought about it is...

Without thinking, I lean over to kiss him, a brief but deep kiss. When I back away, he's staring at me, half smiling and half confused.

"What was that for, Miss Whitewood?"

I can't help but smile too.

"A thank-you kiss."

"Hm... I don't know what I did right, but I should do it more often."

And with that, he leans over in my direction to kiss me again. It's a longer, deeper kiss than before, one that tastes like sweet whiskey. I like it and answer without thinking at all. It's not an innocent kiss, but a passionate one, and soon enough, I feel his hand on my thigh again. His lips go down to my jaw and my neck as I feel my breathing get a bit more erratic.

"Nate… We're not..."

I struggle to talk, but he doesn't care. His fingers are already venturing under my dress, moving to where they previously had been. This time, however, I can tell he's only teasing me… And it's a bit frustrating. I'm torn between the fact that we are in a classy restaurant, more or less in public, and the fact that I actually want more. I glare at him, but he still has this innocent smile that doesn't match his electric blue eyes with a hint of lust in them.

"You still haven't said yes," he whispers against my ear.

"No."

And with that, I gather my rational self and push his hand away, crossing my legs in the most defiant move I can think of. He pouts a bit but doesn't insist. How surprising, Mr. Black is consistent about obtaining my consent.

I grab a fork and ferociously start eating my starter, while he smiles and takes a sip of that fancy wine he ordered. He is still giving me some glances, but we both start eating in silence, except for a couple of trivial comments about our dishes. I have to admit, it's very good. I understand the concept of putting quality before quantity, but I do hope my main dish will be a bit bigger. I finish my plate in no time.

"So, what exactly are you looking for?" he asks.

"In what?"

"Having sex with me."

I almost spit out my wine. Can't he be a bit less blunt sometimes! I put my glass down.

"You mean, like, conditions?"

He nods and crosses his arms, looking curious.

"I want to know. What is it exactly that you want us to agree on, and what do you need to accept me?"

"I get it! I get it!" I say before he says something embarrassing again. "Alright, we can discuss this."

I try to gather my thoughts for a moment. Truth is, I came here thinking I wanted to agree to it already. After discussing it with Danny, it became clear. Even if this is going against my pack's rules, I'm deeply attracted to Nate. Moreover, having a physical relationship with someone from a different clan has its perks: no gossip in the pack, higher chances to keep this private, and no risk of wanting more either. Neither of us could afford that last one.

"First, I don't want to be at your beck and call only. If I don't feel like seeing you, I won't," I state very bluntly.

"Agreed. I have no intention of insisting if you don't feel like it. Likewise, I might not be available either. I tend to have long days. Are there any times that wouldn't be appropriate?"

"In the mornings, I train the young ones from 8 a.m. to noon. And not on Sundays around lunchtime, I eat with Danny's family or my pack members."

I don't mention it, but the training actually doesn't start until 9 a.m. However, I usually stop by the hospital to see my dad before that, and I don't want to mention that to Nathaniel. He nods.

"Agreed. For me, Mondays are a no-go: it's the busiest day of the week. And I usually see my brothers on Sundays as well."

"Noted."

"Texting and calls are fine?" he asks.

"I prefer texting. And don't nag if I don't answer right away."

He laughs.

"I might be the one not to reply right away, so no worries."

"Good. Also, don't come to my territory again. Where should we meet?"

"I can text you the locations, but mostly in my hotels, so I can control who talks or not."

I notice he doesn't mention going to his own place, but don't say a thing. That is probably not what he wants if he doesn't mention it. Going to hotels feels a bit cold, but I don't think I would want to see Nate at my apartment either. Especially if Daniel starts seeing Boyan, that might be super awkward.

"What about protection?" I ask.

He looks a bit surprised, but shrugs.

"I don't mind using condoms, but I would like it better without."

"We can get tested. I'm on the pill anyway."

"Alright."

Funny he doesn't seem more curious than that about contraception. But then again, we are both adults, and so far, he didn't make any mistakes.

"What about other partners?"

This time, I'm a bit surprised. I decide to answer honestly.

"I probably won't have any if I start seeing you. I have my hands full enough as it is. You?"

I hold my breath, waiting for his answer. Somehow, I know I wouldn't really appreciate being just a name on a list. Did he ask that to see if he can be with other girls? Isn't he used to one-time things?

But to my surprise, he smiles faintly.

"Same for me. Actually, I would like it better that way; I'm not a fan of sharing. But if you do end up seeing someone else, I would appreciate it if you'd tell me. I'll do the same."

Interesting. Why would we need to inform each other? Oh, probably about the safe sex thing. It would become annoying if we start sleeping around. I just nod. It's not like I have anything to say about that anyway. I doubt I'll see anyone else for a while if I'm busy with secret rendezvous with Mr. Black.

"One more thing," says Nate. "I would appreciate it if we could also share more moments like this from time to time."

I frown, a bit confused.

"You mean, like, dates?"

"I wouldn't call it dates. More like dinner between friends, once in a while. I feel like it might get boring to only see each other for sex, and I do appreciate spending time with you so far."

"You do realize our conversations have been mostly about sex, though?"

"I also learned your best friend's name, what you do for a living, and your aspirations for the future. I don't mean to pry, but I would like to have someone to talk to who doesn't actually work for me or my family."

I stay silent for a while. I did not expect that. Wouldn't it become more than just physical, though? What a strange request from him. I think I understand what he means. Not just being sex partners, but sex friends?

The waiter comes back to take our empty plates away, while another one brings in our main dishes half a minute later. My steak looks terribly delicious, but for now, most of my brain is focused on Nate's request. I take my time to think until the waiters are gone again.

"Alright. Actually, I could use someone to talk to as well. But I'm not coming all this way just to chit-chat, okay?"

He smiles like a Cheshire cat.

"Oh, don't worry about that. I have no intention to let you go without touching you."

That pervert. I raise my head and suddenly think about one important thing.

"Then I'll agree."

"Really?" he asks, surprised.

"On one condition."

"What is it?"

"Promise you won't fall in love with me. And I won't fall for you either."

For a second, he looks stunned. He stays speechless for a few seconds, then slowly nods.

"Alright, I promise."

My heart tightens inexplicably for a second, but I take a deep breath in and answer in my calmest voice.

"Thank you," I whisper.

"Then, that's it, right? You accept?"

"Yes."

He puts his fork down.

"Then I want you. Now."

After a second of surprise, I gasp. Here, now? Has he gone crazy? But before I can even formulate any word, Nathaniel suddenly grabs my chair to pull me closer to him. We are now dangerously close to each other, his eyes staring right at me with that mischievous look of his. I blush unconsciously.

"We are in public," I protest again.

"No, we are in a private room."

With that, his lips suddenly start attacking my neck, deliciously nibbling on my skin and giving me hot chills. I feel his hand back under my skirt, playing with my panties and gently pulling on them. I breathe out and relax a bit, but Nate finds his way back to my lips, and his tongue drives me nuts. Moon Goddess, he is so good at kissing. I'm drowning in this sweetness.

I answer his kiss, the last strings of my willpower snapping. He makes me crazy. I don't resist it and grab the collar of his shirt, pulling him closer. I feel his smile against my lips. He likes my willfulness, I know it. Nate's arm grabs my waist, and I move from my chair to his lap. We keep kissing, and it's more intoxicating than that bottle of expensive Bordeaux wine. It's addicting. Our lips collide, play, and mess with each other. I want more, like a junkie. His hands caress my skin. One is on my nape, playing with my hair and grabbing it gently between his fingers. The other is stroking my thigh, going back and forth under the fabric of my dress.

Why did I wear a dress in the first place? I had figured I should somewhat make an effort for this and prepared myself a bit more carefully than usual, but I had no idea things would lead to this so quickly. Yet, Nate is caressing every inch of my skin, ignoring my dress to reach for my panties. I gasp when he gets rid of them in one movement. It's so embarrassing not wearing anything under my dress!

But Nathaniel doesn't give me a second to think. His kisses are all I can focus on for now. Even so, I don't want him to be the one leading the whole time. I reach for the buttons of his shirt and swiftly undo them one after the other, despite my trembling fingers. I love his torso. He obviously works out to have such muscles. Moon Goddess, he looks like a model. And it's all for me to enjoy right now. I caress his chest and pull his shirt until it's completely off. Finally, I have him half-naked in front of me. Or rather, under me. And I can feel the bulge in his pants, right there. His breathing gets shallower, and our eyes meet. Our flaming desire is palpable. I want him so bad.

After a few seconds, our kissing resumes, even more passionate, harder. It's like we are hungry for each other's lips. My hands go down and I undo the button of his pants with shaking hands. Meanwhile, one of Nate's hands is on my lower back, holding me, but the other one is back on my skin, caressing me. I have a hard time concentrating as his fingers dance against my most intimate part. Where the hell did he learn that? I'm already on edge when I finally release his member from his pants. I breathe in before leaning in for a new kiss, Nathaniel's lips welcoming mine unconditionally. I hear something tearing, and after a few seconds, he pulls me closer to him. I can't wait. I gasp and take him in, with a long moan of relief I don't even try to hold.

Moon Goddess, I missed this. I take a second to adjust, indulging myself in this moment of guilt and delight. He completes me perfectly, so perfectly my own body is trembling in pleasure just from being joined with his. I catch my breath, savor this, and put my arms around his neck. Nate, facing me, groans from it too. His eyes are closed, and like me, he takes his time to enjoy this. I smile and plant a kiss on him while he's like this. He smiles and gently pulls me toward him for a new, longer kiss.

Like this, he starts moving. His first back and forth took me by surprise, but when he keeps going, I join him, moving my hips to his rhythm. I don't even need to focus. It comes naturally, the right pace for us. I don't care about anything else but colliding with him at this moment. This is so crazy and erotic. Riding Nate on a chair, in a restaurant. I must be insane. But Moon Goddess, I don't care. All I can think of is this chemistry between us, the tension of his body fiercely stirring mine, the flow of his thrusts inside me. I pant and breathe hard. The sound of our flesh pounding against each other, his breathing against my ear, my own moans. This melody is so obscene, yet so satisfying. I don't control my voice anymore. I can't think straight, not with Nate doing what he is doing to me.

It gets more savage, with both his hands on my hips, guiding me, and the two of us moving faster and harder. I'm panting, lost in a whirlwind of sensations.

"Elena."

Hearing my name from his lips is so unbelievably erotic right now. But he repeats it again and again and again. As his moves get more erratic, unpredictable, and deep, I cry out, unable to hold it. I feel it coming. I hold on to his shoulders, and a couple of thrusts later, a mind-blowing orgasm finally unleashes.

"Hngggh!"

I'm still trembling when I hear Nate groan too, his whole body frozen with pleasure. In this moment where fire meets ice, my mind is totally empty. I'm numb. The fire dies out, while we both slowly regain our senses. I rest my head on his shoulder, still catching my breath. He puts gentle kisses on my neck and caresses my hair.

"You okay?" he whispers against my ear.

"Hmm..."

That's all I can formulate at the moment. Moon Goddess, I could have some of that anytime. I sigh and raise my head to face Nate. He smiles, with that impossibly sweet look. It's a bit strange that instead of feeling awkward, this all feels so tender. He gently pulls me in for a new kiss. When we separate, he chuckles. I frown.

"What is it?"

"Just… Gotcha, Miss Whitewood."

That satisfied expression of his is a bit annoying! But I only roll my eyes, since I'm smiling too. I kiss him, biting his lip a little to be playful. He doesn't even complain and gets back at me with a little slap on my butt.

"Alright, now we should get back to our meal. We have to feed the baby dinosaur."

"Moon Goddess, my steak!"

I totally forgot about it! I get off Nate's lap to look at my plate as if it could have vanished in the meantime. Of course, it's still there, and looking as appetizing as ten minutes ago. Next to me, Nate bursts out in laughter.

"Elena, you look like you haven't eaten meat in ages!"

"Hey, try living with someone who's nearly a vegetarian, and then we'll talk."

"A vegetarian? Seriously?" he asks while picking his shirt up off the floor.

"Yeah, Danny is the kind of weirdo that only eats meat once a week, and I can't cook. But he does some really good veggie stuff."

I put my panties back on, and we get back to our seats. Nate leaves his shirt open, though, and I don't know if he did it on purpose, but it's hard to concentrate.

"Well, it's a trend these days, but I do know of a few vegetarian dishes that are indeed quite good."

"I would still like to eat red meat more than once a week," I sigh.

Especially if it's as good as this steak! It's melting in my mouth, along with the perfect red wine sauce. Gosh. For a while, we eat and chat idly, just like friends would. When the waiter comes back to pour us more wine, I feel a bit ashamed and wonder if he has any idea. I mean, Nate doesn't seem embarrassed by his messy appearance at all. Are they just pretending not to see? When he leaves, Nate wipes his mouth and looks at me with a smile.

"What?"

"Nothing. I'm just… satisfied over winning this."

I scoff.

"You aren't the only winner. It's a win-win situation."

"Obviously."

There he goes again with his Cheshire cat smile. I finish the last delicious piece of steak while we playfully sneak glances at each other.

"Hey babe, how is it going?"

"Great. I officially have a sex friend and I'm literally having the best dinner in town. How's yours?"

"This date is a dream, babe. He took me to the movies. The movies! I mean, I don't really care for The Lion King, *but I like being able to cuddle in the dark."*

"Bobo deserves a top score."

"Oh girl, I'm gonna give it to him as soon as we get home. Any sex on your menu?"

"You bet."

"Atta girl! I want a full report first thing tomorrow."

"Danny!"

"No buts. I get the apartment, you get to stay out. Have fun- but safe-sex!"

I mentally roll my eyes at Danny. I'm glad he is finally having fun. I don't have enough fingers to count how many heartbreaks he's gone through. Sometimes over innocent crushes, sometimes over real relationships he had poured all his trust into. That Bobo guy had better take care of him or, Blood Moon Beta or not, I'll cut him.

"Elena?"

Absorbed with mind-linking my best friend, I didn't hear Nate's question.

"Sorry, you were saying?"

"I was wondering if you wanted some cheese?"

I shake my head. I've never been into dairy products that much; the only time I get cheese is on pasta or pizza.

"No, thanks."

He gives me a smile, and I detect a hint of lust behind it.

"Then, wanna get some dessert upstairs?"

I step out of the shower, letting the steam relax me. Goodness, that was great… again. I wrap myself in the bathrobe and walk out of the bathroom.

"Nate?"

I find him waving at me from the balcony, and I join him. He stares at my legs and wet hair, but I don't say anything, and instead, grab one of the two beers on the table.

"I didn't know you were the kind of man to drink cheap beer," I say while sitting on one of the lounge chairs.

"I wasn't always rich, you know," he smiles, "and I like a cold beer after a hot shower."

So do I! I open it and take a sip, glancing at the view. This is amazing… The moon is beautiful tonight too.

"Why would a she-wolf wear a sun pendant?"

I turn to Nate, his eyes on my necklace.

"It's a memento from my birth parents."

"Birth parents?"

"Yes, I was actually adopted."

He's probably surprised, but politely makes sure not to show it.

"Do you know what happened?"

"I wish," I shake my head, "but there's this big mystery around my adoption that no one in my clan is willing to talk about. I've been searching for answers, but I haven't found any."

He comes to sit on the chair next to mine, grabs the second beer, and takes a sip too.

"I could look into it if you want. I have contacts at the police-"

"No!"

My sudden yell startled him, and I realize I overreacted a second too late… He stares, confused, while I try to regain my composure.

"No, I appreciate it, but I don't want you to look into my past. Please?"

I really don't want Nathaniel to look into my police file. If he found out what's in there… I don't need him judging me for my past too. I have no idea how he'd react. He hesitates for a few seconds before he finally answers.

"Understood. I won't."

… Does he mean that? I shouldn't have overreacted, I'm such an idiot!

"Sorry I yelled," I mumble.

"No, that's okay. There are things about me that I wouldn't want to be made public either."

We stay silent for a few minutes, in a bit of an awkward atmosphere. I hate it… I take out my phone and play some calm music. It's better than this awkward tension between us…

"I've always hated silence," I admit.

"Why?"

"I don't know. Whenever it goes quiet, I have this feeling of fear that overwhelms me. As a kid, I needed a lullaby to fall asleep. Even now, the first thing I do if I'm alone is turn on the radio. At night, if the house is too quiet, I put my headphones on and listen to something like this. I even love the sound of the rain… You're not into music?"

"Not really. Our mother loved a few old classics, but that's it. I let other people handle what we play in the clubs or the restaurants. It's not that I don't like it, I just don't have much taste. The only time I don't listen to the news is when I work out; I just play random playlists instead."

I wonder what his mom was like… Seems like her influence played a huge role in Nate's character today.

"That's good," I say. "I get to choose the music then."

"Whatever you want," he chuckles. "You can educate my poor ears."

"Challenge accepted!"

"And I can teach you how to cook."

"Hell no," I frown. "I don't like cooking. I'm so bad at it, it's dangerous. I'm only allowed to use the microwave!"

He laughs, and we keep chatting and drinking our beers in a lighter mood. After a while of giving him funny recollections of my epic failures, we naturally cease talking and watch the moon together. I start feeling sleepy, but I don't fight it.

Chapter 8

2 months later, end of August.

I slowly wake up, so drowsy it takes me a while to realize where I am. White sheets? I struggle to get up, but there is something. A man's arm around me? That familiar smell of cologne… Oh shit, did I fall asleep in Nate's bed? I remember us coming to the suite last night, having sex, then… Oh Moon Goddess, I really fell asleep right after that. I'm such an idiot!

"Nate. Nate, please move. Nate!"

I hear a groan, and I have to struggle a bit more for him to get off me. Seriously! I finally sit up, and reach out to grab my panties, forgotten at one end of the bed. What time is it? Gosh, I hope it's not late! I can't find my phone, so I just grab Nathaniel's to check the time. I sigh. Not even 8:00 a.m. I hear him move around next to me and he finally turns his head.

"Something wrong, Miss Whitewood?" he asks.

His eyes are still closed but there's a little grin crossing his lips.

"It's not funny. I'm such an idiot. I shouldn't have fallen asleep here."

He stops smiling and sits up to look at me very seriously.

"It's not such a big deal."

"Yes, it is, Nate. We talked about this before, I shouldn't stay overnight," I answer while getting dressed.

"Why not? If we set an alarm, you can leave early enough to not miss training or whatever."

It's not just about being late; I am growing awfully comfortable with falling asleep with Nate. I don't like it. I even have a couple of outfits stored here in the suite. The hotel's staff recognizes me and I have no idea how that happened. The more time we spend together, the more I get attached, and that's just terrifying.

I turn to him, still dazzlingly naked in bed. So handsome, so early.

Nathaniel is frowning, unhappy with my haste.

"I have to go," I blurt out.

"You know you don't, Elena. It's Sunday; you only have brunch with your friend's family at around 11 a.m."

Actually, I don't. I didn't even tell him today's brunch with the Lewis family wasn't happening, and it's not the first time. I've been making excuses to flee lately. Instead of adding to the lies, I just silently put my dress back on, trying to avoid his stare. Where are my shoes now?

"Elena."

His tone is not a good sign. I want to ignore it, but I just sigh and turn to him. Damn, he is still as handsome as the first night we met. His dark blonde hair, his mesmerizing blue eyes. I still can't believe I spend three to five nights a week sleeping with this living god.

I thought the passion of our first meetings would somehow calm down after a few weeks, but as of today, it hasn't. Whenever we meet, it's always the same sparks, the same hunger for the other's heat, and our inner wolves craving each other.

But, more than that, we are definitely getting closer. With time, we have now come to share more and more about our own lives. If we meet on a weekday, Nate will let me know how busy his schedule at work was, and I will naturally talk about training or whatever I did that day with Danny. He even helps me prepare for my upcoming classes in September.

We text a lot too. I wasn't expecting that, but we have gotten very comfortable with sending each other random texts at any time of the day or night. He will let me know when one of his meetings is dragging on and boring him to death, and I complain whenever the kids are acting rudely during training. On nights we can't see each other, we sometimes discuss what we will do the next time we're together, like the restaurant Nate wants to take me to or where we should meet.

Unless we don't have time to meet earlier, we very rarely meet directly at the hotel. Nate likes to invite me for a drink or dinner before, and sometimes we even go dancing together in one of his elite clubs.

It's a strange routine, like I've been experiencing a double life and an even stranger relationship. We are closer than normal friends with benefits, I guess, though we don't cross that thin line that involves our privacy. He still has no idea about my family situation, and he never talks to me about his brothers' lives or pack matters either. I guess there are some boundaries we tacitly do not cross.

"What?" I ask with a sigh.

He grabs my wrist and gently pulls me back to sit on the bed with him.

"Nate."

I want to protest, push him away, and get going, but he suddenly starts kissing me. I can't say no. I'm desperately addicted to this. Nate knows my body and how to caress it by heart. I gasp loudly when he takes off my panties again. Moon Goddess, I wanted to get dressed, not undressed!

"Nate, enough," I sigh, but I know I'm not convincing at all.

"No. I'm not letting you go yet."

Of course, he doesn't listen. He pushes me gently onto the bed, so I'm lying underneath him. I give up and finally answer his kisses. Nate takes my dress off in one movement, bringing me back to square one. But I don't care, I'm burning up and feverish under his hands. He caresses my body here and there. I gasp and try to hold my voice, but he keeps going, and attacks my neck with more kisses and bites.

"Don't. I want to hear your voice, Elena."

I try to hold on some more, but his fingers finally make me cry out in pleasure. He's being a little forceful, a bit controlling, and I like it. Submitting to Nate's lead is easy, like submerging myself in fresh water. I don't have to do anything but let myself go, abandon my restraints. When he positions himself and joins me, I'm already on edge. But he is the one to decide, and I'm not allowed to come yet. He starts moving, without holding back. I'm pinned to the bed and totally helpless, only responding to his speed and strength with my embarrassing voice.

About two hours later, I'm finally on my way home, a bit more tired than I was earlier. He really never gets enough. I sigh and take out my keys. However, when I get to my apartment and open the door, I'm suddenly faced with Boyan, standing fully naked in the middle of our living room.

"Hi."

"Hi..."

Moon Goddess, this is so awkward.

"Boyan, dammit, your clothes!"

Danny's panicked voice came from the kitchen. I do my best to look away while Bobo shape-shifts and my bestie runs in to scold him. I notice Daniel is only wearing his pajama bottoms.

"Daniel, I really don't mind naked men at our place, but I would appreciate it if you could keep it to your bedroom," I sigh.

"Sorry, babe, sorry!" he sighs with a cute pout.

I laugh a bit. I don't really mind, I've seen naked men before. It's just funny to annoy my ever-so-prudish Danny about it. We stay silent for a while. I take off my jacket and heels, and Danny brings me some hot coffee. Outside, a slow summer drizzle starts falling.

"How was it?" asks Daniel.

"Still as incredibly awesome as ever," I sigh.

"You don't seem too happy about it."

He's right. I like those moments with Nate, but the more I see him, the more scared I get. I'm afraid of what's to come, of the two of us betraying our promise to one another. It's not only me; I'm aware that he doesn't act simply as friends with benefits either. I don't know what the exact rules are for these kinds of relationships, but I can tell Nate is going a bit overboard sometimes; it's in the way we talk and how we interact.

And it terrifies me.

"Babe, talk to me," says Danny.

"I'm fine. Things are fine with Nate."

But he doesn't believe me. After a second of hesitating, he finally speaks.

"Elena, I need to know if this is about Black, or…"

"Or what?"

He bites his lip, the same way I do when I am unsure what to say.

"Elena, I know the date is approaching."

Shit, I didn't want to think about that. The mere thought that my ex might come back is enough to drive me nuts. I don't want to think about it. I put my cup down angrily and shake my head.

"Danny, please, don't. I'm over it."

"Elena, I don't think you are. We need a real talk."

"I don't want to."

"Babe."

"Seriously, Danny, I can't! Enough… I'm going to take a shower now."

I'm sorry I yelled at him, but I just can't. I get up and run to my room, closing the door a bit more violently than I intended to. Moon Goddess, I didn't want to think about it. I wanted to forget and pretend it wouldn't possibly happen.

This is driving me mad. I was feeling so good just a while ago in Nate's arms, and now I'm back to thinking about my ex again. Why do I have to feel so helpless? I don't want to fall in love again, and I don't want to reminisce about what happened five years ago either!

Still upset, I grab whatever clothes I can find and hurry into the shower to avoid Daniel. I can hear him talking to Bobo outside, but I don't listen and focus on the hot water. Don't think about it, don't think about it. This is over and he is not coming back.

About fifteen minutes later, I'm getting dressed in a tank top and denim overalls when I hear a soft knocking on my door.

"Babe. It's not about your ex but I need to talk to you about something else. Can you come out? Please? I'm sorry, okay? I promise I won't talk about that matter again."

I sigh. It's not like I can ever stay mad at Danny long anyway.

When I walk out of the bathroom, Danny is waiting for me, with a very sorry look on his face. I feel like I'm about to abandon a puppy.

"Alright, what is it?" I ask with a sigh.

"Come here."

He takes my hand and pulls me to the couch so we can sit down. To my surprise, he takes out his phone, looking for something.

"So, you know how my brother often comes late to the Main House to give his report about the patrol to the Alpha? Well, when he came back last night, Levi heard the Alpha talking with Reagan. They were talking about you. Listen."

What is this about? He plays an audio file, and after a few seconds of silence, I suddenly hear muffled voices. Someone manipulates the phone until we can actually hear properly. I instantly recognize my Alpha's voice.

"... won't be able to protect her, Reagan. I have to make a choice, and she won't understand unless we tell her the truth."

"I already said no, Clark!"

My mentor's angry voice surprises me. I knew Reagan had no problem arguing with the Alpha, but...

"You shouldn't have let her meet with the Blood Moon pack to begin with. I told you, Elena's existence must stay as concealed as possible!"

"She will be twenty-one soon, Reagan! I can't always control what she does! You know how stubborn Elena is. She is strong; if she wants to know the truth..."

"The truth is dangerous," replies Reagan. "She is not ready for it, no one is. Making Elena one of your heirs was stupid to begin with."

"I did it to protect her. Moreover, you know very well she has every right to be. And without Samuel around—"

"You're a bunch of idiots. You and Sam. You think this is just about the White Moon? Did you really forget where that child came from? She is the only survivor, Clark! If they find out she is alive..."

I exchange a shocked look with Daniel. What the hell? Only survivor?

What is Reagan talking about? I thought I was found in a forest! I'm barely breathing, trembling while waiting on every word. Who is the "they" she is talking about?

A long silence follows, but when I'm about to say something, Daniel signals for me to stay quiet. Just then, I hear Clark's voice again.

"You had said she might not be the only one."

"I only said there was a possibility. When I got there, the other child was missing. I have no idea how she could have survived, if she did. Moon Goddess bless her, but I already have my hands full with protecting Elena."

"Reagan, I still think we should talk to her. Elena is—"

A furious growling interrupts him, and I jump in surprise from hearing so much anger. Moon Goddess, is Reagan actually growling at the Alpha?

"Listen to me very carefully, Clark. If you say one word to Elena, I swear you'll regret it. I don't care about Samuel or your pack issues. Nothing matters more than her safety. I made an oath. I took that girl from her dying mother's arms, and I swore to her, and the Moon Goddess, that I would protect her child, even if it's the last thing I do!"

What? She swore to… my mother? I wait for more, holding my breath in anticipation, but the recording ends. Danny is staring at me with worried eyes.

"Babe, are you okay?"

I'm speechless. What the hell was that? Reagan said so many shocking things that I feel like a bomb was just dropped on me. I finally find my voice only to urge Danny to play it again. This time, I take the phone to hold it close while he gets up and makes us some coffee. He probably listened to it several times too.

When the recording ends the second time, I stay stunned, my mind overwhelmed with so many thoughts. I don't even know where to start! Danny comes back to sit next to me, carrying two large cups of coffee.

"I called Levi right away last night. Apparently, they heard him and he couldn't learn anything more."

"Danny, all this is…"

"I know babe, it's a lot."

"Reagan knows my birth mother!"

This is what I'm the most surprised about. She knew! She knew all this time who my mother was and she never said a word about it! Why couldn't she tell me the slightest thing about my real mother? I stand up. I need to talk to her! But before I can take a step, Daniel grabs my wrist and pulls me back onto the couch.

"Hold your horses, babe. I know what you're thinking, but that stubborn old hag won't say a word. Even Clark can't win an argument against her!"

"She has to! Danny, now I know that—!"

"Now you know more than you're supposed to, babe. Elena, think about it. Reagan never, ever agreed to tell you a word about your origins. If you go there and blurt out that you know a bit, how do you think she will react? She will kick your ass and still not say a word!"

Damn, Daniel is right. Worst case scenario, Reagan might even leave Silver City for several months again. When my mentor disappears, there is no guarantee that she will ever come back, and that would only lower my chances to know the truth.

"I know what she said about your birth mother is big news, but did you listen to the rest?"

"Yeah, she said I had survived something."

"I think she was talking about your family, or maybe even your whole pack. More importantly, Elena, whatever killed them might come after you. It has to be serious, babe, if Reagan is this worried…"

Daniel looks very worried, but I am not. I don't feel like any of this is real. Whatever the whole thing about surviving is, it is nothing compared to learning the slightest thing about my birth mother. Reagan said she died with me in her arms. Why can't I remember any of it? How old was I really? Reagan always said she found me when I was very young, but could she have lied about that too? Why?

"You know, I always felt there was something odd about my memories. I can't remember anything before my fifth birthday."

"Most people don't remember their early years."

"But you remember your mom being pregnant with the twins, or when Levi broke his arm. You were only two or three years old, Danny. I don't remember anything at all, not the slightest memory."

He nods with a sigh.

"I know. I don't see how Reagan could be responsible for you losing your memories. Maybe you have some sort of trauma or something."

I wish I knew. But it's a black hole whenever I try to remember anything before my fifth birthday with my adoptive parents. I finally grab that cup of coffee and let out a deep sigh.

"I'm just so tired of all the mysteries, Danny, even if Reagan is trying to protect me from who knows what. This is just a whole mess in my head."

"I understand babe. But I don't think there's anything more we can do for now. Do you wanna search the forest again?"

I shake my head. I already know it's no use, though I appreciate Danny's efforts to comfort me. We searched that forest a thousand times already, and I feel like the answer isn't there anyway. Daniel gets up again to put some music on and prepare brunch, but I stay seated, thinking.

What about that other child she mentioned? Is she from my pack too? Why didn't Reagan know about her situation? And what would have caused my family to die? Something attacked them and might come after me at any moment... What sort of threat could that be? Werewolves have so many enemies: vampires, witches, and even humans… Another pack of werewolves could have been involved. If only Reagan would finally talk. How is not saying anything protecting me? From her conversation with Clark, it even seems as though she is against me taking the position of Alpha. Why is she so insistent on concealing my existence? Is the threat really that serious that I could be hunted all the way here? Is that why she trained me since I was young?

While I'm lost in my thoughts, my phone suddenly vibrates. A text from Nate.

Elena, sorry about this morning. I didn't mean to upset you. You can stay over if you want, but I won't force you.

I can't help but smile. He's as understanding as ever. He never forces me into anything anyway. I think long and hard before answering.

It's okay. Sorry, I lost my cool.

Any plans tonight?

I could use a change of scenery.

I'll be at this address from 6 p.m. onwards. Meet me whenever you want.

It's a location I don't know, on the outskirts of their territory. He sometimes surprises me like this, and it's nice. I already feel a lot better knowing that I'll see Nate later.

Danny brings two vegetarian omelets with potatoes and a new serving of coffee.

"Where is Bobo, by the way?" I ask when he sits down.

"He left. I told him I needed a private talk with my favorite girl, and anyway, he's busy with his pack these days, he can't stay too long."

"Something going on?"

Daniel grabs the TV remote and nods.

"More or less. They are still looking for that girl, remember? The one your man asked Clark about?"

"He is not my man," I automatically reply with an annoyed growl.

"Anyway, it seems like they are still actively looking for her, whoever she is. The King is crazy obsessed about that these days. They have been visiting more packs."

Nathaniel didn't mention anything. He never talks to me about his brothers, either. But I know when he sometimes has to leave abruptly, it's because of one of them. The younger one seems to be a bit of a runaway kid, going off the grid from time to time. The King, however, seems to have another kind of problem. I never see Nate as worried as when he has to go back to see his older brother. He never tells me why, though.

Daniel puts on some TV show he's been watching, but I'm not very into it. Instead, I grab some of my study books to get back on track before I resume classes in a couple of weeks. It's not thrilling, but I just want to stop thinking about those other annoying matters: the mystery around my birth, my asshole ex-boyfriend, and my relationship with Nate. Each and every one of these matters is giving me a headache.

Cold stone, and people screaming. A warm embrace is protecting me, and someone is whispering a prayer. I'm so cold... I want to cry, but somebody's rocking my tiny body, trying to keep me quiet. A warm man's voice says everything will be alright, he will protect us. He loves us. A woman weeps quietly next to my ear. She doesn't want him to go, but there is no choice.

We are left alone. It's suddenly quiet, and very scary. I'm so scared, I'm shaking. A cold voice is talking, but they can't find us. The gentle voice is whispering again. They don't know our secret, it will keep us safe. A violent light appears!

"Elena! Elena, babe! Wake up, babe!"

I finally open my eyes, out of breath. I'm trembling all over, and it takes me a few seconds to recognize Daniel, holding my wrists with panicked eyes.

"Are you okay, babe? Moon Goddess, you scared me!"

"Da… Danny? What happened?"

"I don't know, I think you were panicking. You were crying and shivering. Did you have a nightmare?"

A nightmare? Now that he says it… Something vague is floating in my mind, but I can't remember exactly. What was that about? That dream felt so familiar… and I'm feeling terribly cold and lonely. I grab the blanket laying at one end of the couch and wrap myself in it, under Danny's worried eyes.

"You're cold?" he asks.

He puts a hand on my forehead to check my temperature, frowning.

"How rare… You're never cold, usually. Do you want me to get you some medicine?"

"No, never mind Danny. My period might be coming, that's probably the reason. You know I always get unwell before that."

"What?"

He gets up to check on our calendar hanging in the kitchen, but it's no use, my period is so irregular and unpredictable, any attempt at tracking it has been useless so far. Daniel comes back, looking upset.

"It's been a while… Shit, and I'll be away at that seminar next week too!"

"Seriously, Danny, it's okay. I'll just wait for it to pass."

I grab my phone and text Nate that I can't come tonight. I don't give him any details, and just say that something came up. As usual, he doesn't ask for any more details. Daniel, however, is watching me with his worried expression.

"I don't want to leave you alone when you are like this."

"Danny, I'm going to be fine, stop being such a worrywart. I'll just text Eric to ask him to take over the training for now and stay home until I'm better."

That doesn't take the worried look off his face. I know why he's so worried about me, but I shake my head.

"Danny, I…"

"You should see someone, Elena, to check."

"Daniel, stop it. I'm over what happened back then, okay?"

"Then why are you so afraid to check if you can still have children or not?"

I glare at him.

"We are not talking about it, Danny. I don't want kids anyway."

He sighs.

"Alright… Sorry babe. I'll go check what we have in the medicine cabinet, okay?"

Daniel leaves the room, and a heavy silence falls. I'm so tired… Is it because of the rain or my nightmare? I'm feeling so gloomy suddenly; I'm almost regretting canceling on Nate tonight.

I close my eyes, trying to chase the darkness away.

I'm sorry Angel, but I don't want to think about you right now, it's still too painful…

Chapter 9

No wonder I felt like crap: my period is hitting me full-on. Damn you, Mother Nature… I groan all the way from the bathroom back to the couch, and miserably let myself fall there. That explains the nightmares and all… I notice a missed text on my phone and check the notification. Shit, it's Nate… He probably wants the usual since it's been a few days, but today's just not the day. I send a quick reply, letting him know I'm not well. That should be enough of an explanation… I put my phone aside to curl up on that stupid couch and ruminate about my female condition, but my phone vibrates again just a minute later. Nate again, asking if I'm sick. Ugh, get a clue please… I don't want to give him the details, but he sounds worried and it's making me feel worse about turning him down.

Just as I'm still wondering how to politely answer, the phone rings; he's calling.

"What?" I groan.

"Hi. Sorry, I was just… Are you sick?"

"No, I'm not."

"… Are you mad at me for some reason?"

Of course he'd think that, I must sound like a bear disturbed during its hibernation…

"Why would I be mad at you, Nate?" I sigh. "I'm just having a shitty day. I'm tired, and Mother Nature is reminding me of my female condition with these damn cramps!"

He doesn't answer that… I bet he hadn't thought about me possibly having my period at all. Did he really think I was mad at him? Shit.

"Sorry you thought I was mad at you or something. It's just that it's been a while and I have very nasty ones. I'll be better in a couple of days, okay?"

"… Is it that bad?"

"Seriously, Nate, I'm not discussing my period with you!"

He chuckles, but it's really not funny. I'm dying here and I hate having to even talk about it.

"Alright, alright... Do you need anything?"

"Unless you have some miracle solution to make time pass faster, no. Danny is away at that stupid seminar anyway so I'm just going to wait at home for it to be over."

"Okay. Call me if you need something, alright?"

Shit, he's cute, worrying about me and all... And here I am, almost growling over the phone.

"Yeah, thanks. I'll text you later."

"Bye."

I may have hung up a bit too abruptly... I look at my phone, but Nate doesn't send anything after that. Moon Goddess, I feel like crap. I barely slept last night and today, the pain is killing me. I have no energy and I've been glued to the couch all day. I don't even feel like getting up to eat or to change my clothes.

Moreover, it's dark and pouring outside, as if the day needed to be any gloomier. I don't know what time it is and I don't care. I'm just dozing off and waiting for my hellish period to be over with...

I wake up to faint knocking at the door. What the...? I don't even remember falling asleep, but there's still a downpour outside. Who would possibly come in this weather? They're knocking again. Damn... I get up, only grabbing my kimono to cover myself a bit. It's probably only one of the neighbors anyway.

However, when I finally open the door, I'm shocked to see Nate standing there. Moon Goddess! What the hell? His hair is dripping wet, and he is carrying a backpack and his helmet.

"Nate? What... What are you doing here?"

"I came to see you. Can I come in?"

I grab his wrist and quickly pull him inside. I can't believe his nerve!

"You shouldn't be here! Are you crazy? This is the White Moon territory!" I whisper-yell while closing the door.

"Calm down, no one could have possibly seen or smelled me with this rain. You also don't live that far from the border anyway."

"Still! If anyone had seen you..."

"You would know already, Elena. Calm down."

Moon Goddess, how could he be so reckless... I stare at him, still in shock, and suddenly realize what I must look like. An unsexy mess! I undo my stupid bun and push my hair back, embarrassed. I haven't even taken a shower!

"How are you feeling?"

Nate's gentleness surprises me. He puts his backpack down on the table, and I wonder what is inside. I've never seen him with a bag. He's not wearing a suit today either, just a plain T-shirt and a worn-out pair of jeans, which is quite unusual for him on a weekday. And he's awfully sexy with those wet clothes… I try to organize my thoughts a bit better than that.

"Not the best," I admit.

He just nods while putting his motorcycle helmet in a corner. Damn, and the place is so messy too… I've been too tired to get any cleaning done since Danny left, and my things are all over the place. There are dirty dishes in the sink, a few clothes lying around, and even my study notes I had been meaning to organize are scattered on the table. I would have at least tried to hide the mess if I knew he was coming!

"Nate, what are you doing here?"

"I came for you. I was worried."

He was worried about me? But he already called… I don't even know how to answer that. Nathaniel is disarming me with that honesty of his. But he is acting like usual, looking around and curious about my place.

"Sorry I… I haven't done any cleaning lately," I sigh with embarrassment while trying to gather the clothes.

"Elena, stop, stop."

He takes them out of my hands, and brings me back to the couch, making me sit. I'm so confused, but he just kneels down to my height and smiles gently. Why is he acting like this? This is so troubling! He puts a hand on my forehead, frowning.

"You're feverish… Do you have any medicine here?"

I push his hand away, ignoring his question to address him very seriously.

"Nate, what are you doing?"

He sighs and takes my hand. Again…

"I told you, I was worried. I came to look after you, alright? You didn't sound good over the phone, and I didn't feel good about leaving you alone when you're like this."

"Nate, you don't have to take care of me! This is not what we agreed on…"

Nathaniel rolls his eyes, annoyed at me.

"Elena, stop being so stubborn for once. I came as a friend because I was worried about my friend, all right? 'Friends with benefits' implies some friendship too. Daniel was also worried, so he gave me your address."

"What? You even called Danny?"

"Yes, Boyan gave me his number a while ago."

I'm going to kill Daniel. And Boyan too. Those traitors! Without anything left to protest, I watch Nate take some stuff out of his backpack. Why the hell is he carrying shredded cheese and tomato sauce… He takes it to the kitchen and comes back with a mug full of hot water.

I'm about to protest that I don't drink tea until I recognize the characteristic smell of my favorite flavor. How did he know that lemon tea is the only one I like? Without saying anything, he hands it to me, and leaves the room again, headed for the bathroom this time. When he comes back, he is frowning, holding two boxes.

"Is this one alright for a fever? The other is past its expiration date."

"Yeah…"

He hands me the right box and simply throws the other away before my shocked eyes. He is acting so naturally, and I'm just speechless! He heads off to the kitchen again, and I grab my phone. I send a very rude text to Danny. I need to unleash on someone. But against my expectations, he doesn't read it right away like usual. Oh, right, that stupid seminar! Right as I'm swearing silently, Nathaniel comes back.

"Elena, did you take it?" he asks, pointing at the medicine.

"Uh, no, not yet."

"Well take it now so you can sleep a bit before dinner."

"Nate, how am I supposed to sleep with you here!"

"It's not like I'm going to attack you!" he replies with a laugh.

"You know what I mean!"

"Seriously, Elena, you're making a fuss for nothing. So just take that damn pill and sleep!"

I want to protest again, but he hands me the mug and the pill first. That stubborn man… I swallow it with a frown. I can't believe this man's nerve.

"I am not sleeping."

"Well, you can watch TV then."

Ignoring my grouchy face, he turns the TV on to some stupid show, before leaving the room again. Why the hell is he going to the kitchen?

"Nate, what are you doing?" I ask, exasperated.

"Just making myself a coffee."

I don't believe him. I can hear him rummaging through the fridge and using the sink. What is he doing? I want to check, but I'm too tired to move. That idiot…

I slowly wake up, feeling drowsy. I'm still on the couch… but someone covered me with another thicker blanket. The TV is turned off, and gentle music is echoing through the stereo. I recognize an old jazz classic. Something feels different. I move my head a bit and notice someone cleaned up the mess from earlier. No clothes lying around, and my papers are stacked more orderly on the table. The whole room seems a lot brighter now.

I finally see Nate, actually sitting right beside me but on the carpet, his back resting against the couch. He is working on his laptop, but notices that I'm awake right away. He gives me his gentle smile.

"Hey. How are you feeling?"

"Better… Did I sleep long?"

"Only about an hour or so."

It felt longer than that… The medicine totally knocked me out. I sigh and sit up, keeping the blanket wrapped around me. I feel bad, but not because of my period this time. My crappy attitude with Nate earlier wasn't right at all.

"Sorry about earlier."

He shakes his head.

"It's fine. I was prepared for a lot worse, considering what you're going through."

"Still…"

But Nate leans over to kiss my forehead, putting me at a loss for words. Why does he have to be so painfully gentle…?

"Don't worry. Do you want to sleep more? You still look tired."

"No… I need to go to the bathroom. And I want to change too, I'm all sweaty."

"Okay."

I get up and walk to my room, going through my wardrobe to find something comfortable to wear. After hesitating a few seconds, I pick an oversized top and some cotton leggings. It's not like Nate cares much about what I'm wearing at this point… I also take a few minutes to brush my hair and put it in a proper bun. At least I look a bit better now, despite the eye bags and sickly complexion.

However, when I go back to the bathroom, I'm surprised to see Nate there.

"You prepared me a bath?"

The hot water is still running, but the bathtub is almost full. I can't believe him. Nate turns it off and nods.

"Yeah, I read that it was good for you. You don't want it?"

"No, it's great actually... thanks."

I just don't know how to react! I never imagined Nate would be so… thoughtful and considerate! But again, he just smiles as if it was perfectly normal.

"Good! Take your time then."

And with that, he leaves me alone in the bathroom. I swear, that man has to be from another planet. There's no other explanation. Honestly, I don't care anymore at this point. I get naked and step in with delight. Moon Goddess, it's so hot and good… I haven't taken a bath in ages, I'm usually too impatient or in too much of a hurry. I stay there a while, thinking about Nate's behavior. Why is he acting like this? It's not that he has never been gentle before, but for him to be this considerate… I'm a bit lost. How should I react? It doesn't feel right, but it's agreeable. Should I just treat it as a friendly attitude, like he said?

When I finally get out of the bath, feeling a lot better, I quickly put on the outfit I picked and go back to the living room.

I'm feeling a bit shy towards Nate. We are alone at my place, I'm not dressed with any effort, and he basically came here despite the shitty weather just to take care of me. As a friend, he said.

When I step into my living room, my heart feels a bit heavier than usual. Outside the window, the sky is clouded in a dark gray, with the rain still falling heavily. But in the middle of the room, Nate turned on our string of light bulbs and is on his computer again. Did him coming here cause trouble for his work? However, upon seeing me enter, he immediately turns it off and gets up.

"Hey, how was the bath? Just wait a sec."

He goes to the kitchen, and when he comes back, I'm speechless. He is carrying a plate with a freaking pizza on it! I'm so shocked I can only try to hide my embarrassed laugh behind my hand.

"Moon Goddess, you made me a pizza?"

"Well, to be honest, I had the dough done at the Italian restaurant, and only gathered the ingredients here to cook it."

"You made a freaking pizza!"

I can't believe it! It looks all hot and fresh out of the oven too. He laughs at my shocked expression and puts it down. I look at that pizza again. Mushrooms, onions, chicken, peppers… All my favorites!

"Danny told you?"

He nods.

"I had no idea you could crave stuff like pizzas on your periods."

"Yeah, it's one of the only things I can swallow."

Actually, I'm barely resisting the temptation of jumping on that pizza right now. But the thing is, what I want to jump most isn't the pizza. I'm still dumbfounded by Nate's attitude. All of this is so new and, well, unsettling. A part of me is overwhelmed by his gentleness, and the other part is scared. What is this all supposed to mean? How can I not melt when he does stuff like that?

But how can I tell him? Hey, could you stop being so nice and gentlemanly because I'm freaking out about my feelings for you? Damn, this man is killing me in the softest way possible, and he has no idea. I stare at him for a few seconds, with my heart on the edge of my lips. I can't resist.

I take a few steps and grab his face to kiss him passionately. I don't want to stop. I love the taste of our kisses, how we take it slow but deep. The way Nate always caresses my skin, my hair. He makes me feel different, like something is blooming inside. Something so fragile I had kept it hidden until now. It's a warm and cozy feeling, yet it makes me feel like I'm on the edge. On the edge of a precipice.

I interrupt our kisses, and our eyes meet dangerously close. I can still feel his lingering taste on my lips. This is scary. A part of my heart that I had kept in ice is warming up and I can't control it. It's scary.

I want to step back, regain my senses, but Nate suddenly grabs my waist, pulling me against him, and kisses me again, more forcefully this time. He doesn't want to stop. His tongue is insistent against mine, and his lips won't let me get away. One of his hands is on my ass, fondling me over the thin layer of my leggings, keeping me close. He grabs my hair, just like when he does when he's entranced…

Inevitably, I answer his kiss, completely surrendering to him. Before I know it, he is sitting on the couch with me on top of him, my hands on his shoulders. Moon Goddess, this is so perfect… The uncommon lighting of the rain and the slow jazz music make it more romantic than usual. It's endless, sweet, and delightful. Nate's hands are on me, caressing me, breaking down my barriers one by one. How do I resist this? I just want to get lost in this moment, forget everything else, and kiss him forever. It's not about the sex, it's about us, about the man who has been driving me crazy, and making me lower my defenses day after day. I feel good when

I'm with Nate. I feel safe, confident, happy.

"Elena?"

He stares at me, a bit confused. I'm shaking.

Damn, I can't control it. I get off his lap, trying to calm down. Nathaniel looks worried, he grabs the blanket to cover me with it and waits, rubbing my arms gently.

"Are you okay?"

Stop being so nice and gentle. You make me crazy.

I nod, catching my breath.

"Sorry… Just give me a minute."

"Okay."

He gets up to fill my cup of lemon tea again, and I sigh. I'm slowly calming down. What a mess… When he comes back, I'm breathing a bit better. I take the cup to drink a bit, and Nate waits patiently for me, sitting close.

"… Sorry about that."

"It's fine, but… Elena, what was that?"

"Nothing."

"Nothing? That looked like a small panic attack to me. Did I do this?"

"What? No! It was not a panic attack, Nate."

"Then what was it?"

I sigh and shake my head. Why does he have to be so curious now?

"I was just a bit overwhelmed for a second. I don't… I'm not used to these kinds of things anymore."

He frowns.

"Kissing? I'm pretty sure we do that quite often."

"No, silly. Being so… cared for. I mean, I have Danny, but he's family to me. But you… You fucking scare me, Nate. I don't get why you're so nice, so caring. Even as friends with benefits, you disarm me in a way that's past what I can handle."

"What does that mean? I can't be nice to you?"

"This isn't about being nice, Nate! You're not just being nice, you… you show me you care for me, and…"

"Why is my caring for you so frightening?" he interrupts me. "Yes, I like you a lot, and yes, maybe I overstepped a bit by coming here, but you don't have to back away or freak out because of that, Elena. I'm just doing what I want. I'm not going to lie, and I'm selfish as fuck. If I want to come here and be with you, I'll do it."

I shake my head again. Without me even noticing, he took my hand,

and he's rubbing it gently with his thumb.

"Nate, I can't. I can't be selfish like you, and I can't act as I please. I am so fucking scared of repeating my past mistakes… I don't want to be hurt. I don't want to go through what I went through again."

"Elena, look at me."

He gently raises my chin to have me look at him, his face dangerously close.

"First, I am not going to hurt you, ever. I'll play by your rules and respect your wishes. If you tell me to come, I'll come. If you ask me to back off, I will. I won't be a mistake, or whatever asshole you're thinking about. This is different. I won't be your boyfriend, or marry you, or give you children. I am not that type of man, so you can relax. Take it easy."

I slowly take in his words. He is right. From the start, I knew what this was going to be: a relationship without any promises nor commitment, only that one rule to not fall in love with the other. I don't know if I should be relieved or just sad. I just find it… hard, and straining. I just have to keep my feelings for Nate in check.

I nod, helpless. What can I say? I'm an emotional mess, maybe because of my period. But he smiles gently.

"Really not your day today, hm?"

I sigh and rest my head on his shoulder, closing my eyes. He's probably right. I just needed something to whine about, and some comfort. Nate rubs my back and hugs me, and for a few minutes, we stay like this, with him gently caressing my hair.

"… Do you like cold pizza?"

I chuckle. That idiot. When I lift my head up again, I'm feeling a lot better. Pouring my heart out to Nate a little has done me some good. He gives me a quick kiss on my forehead, and it feels like everything is fine.

Alright, time to eat that pizza.

We share it, critiquing it like we are culinary experts. Well, Nate plays the part better than I do; I'm just stuffing my face. But Moon Goddess, that pizza asked for it, it's delicious! I gulp it down, slice after slice, barely leaving any for him.

"The baby dinosaur is back!" he laughs at me.

"Shut up, I haven't eaten in almost two days."

"What?"

"Well, Danny is away and I hate cooking, so…"

He rolls his eyes.

"I'm pretty sure I saw a microwave and a freezer in that kitchen,

Elena. Even you should be able to use those."

"Well, I usually do, but my cramps were killing me."

He sighs.

"I can't believe you."

"Stop making fun of my poor culinary skills."

"Non-existent, you mean."

I growl at him, a bit annoyed. He is having way too much fun mocking me. I grab another slice of my delicious pizza. Damn, even this cheese is so much better than the one I usually buy! I can't stop eating, but I don't care. My cramps have reduced, and my stomach is very demanding.

"Alright, tell me how you got so good at this. Even chores, you cleaned the whole place in only one hour!"

Which is both annoying and embarrassing, if I am honest. Nathaniel shrugs and grabs his coffee, leaning back on the couch. I put my feet on his lap, ready to listen.

"I used to do the chores for my brothers when we were younger. Our dad was good for nothing at home, leaving us on our own. Damian worked himself to the bone, and Liam was too young, so I started doing most of the chores naturally when our mother fell ill. It was my way of helping Damian, and I liked it. It kept me from thinking of the most annoying things or worrying. I just had to focus on cleaning, washing, etc. It was simple, and I liked cooking from the start anyway. My mom used to teach me when I was a kid. She loved it, especially with her French roots."

"You have French roots?"

Now that I think about it, I did notice he had no problem pronouncing some of those fancy words off menus. He nods.

"From Mom, yeah. She was born and raised in the south of France before she came here to study. She taught us."

"So, do you speak French?"

"*Évidemment.*"

I smile, amused. Damn, he even speaks French, that is so damn sexy. I look around, wondering what I can ask.

"Alright, teach me some French! I mean, I know the basics, *bonjour, merci, bon appetit.*"

"That's a good start, Mademoiselle Whitewood."

"How do you say I'm hungry?"

"J'ai faim."

"I want to eat some pizza?"

"Je veux manger de la pizza."

I chuckle, amused. I'm pretty sure I won't remember any of this, but hearing Nate speak French is so damn cute! I look around, and my eyes end up on my slice.

"How do you say chicken?"

"Poulet."

"Mushrooms?"

"Champignons."

"Cham…Champignons? That one is funny! Cheese is *fromage*, right?"

I remember that from one of his restaurant's menus. He nods, amused to see me so excited.

"How do you say moon?" I ask.

"*La lune*."

"I like that."

"Sun is *soleil*, and stars are called *étoiles*," he continues.

I like that one too. Alright, maybe I'll try to remember some of those. Nathaniel drinks a new cup of coffee.

"What about you?"

"I just know a bit of Spanish. And Danny likes K-pop and cheesy Korean series, so I know a couple of words too."

"K-pop?" he says, frowning.

"Probably not your style, Mr. Black!"

I grab my phone and connect it to the speakers, looking for one song. Nate frowns when some really girly and bubbly song suddenly comes on. His reaction is so funny I laugh a bit. I decide to spare his poor ears and put on a more soothing one.

"I like this one on rainy days," I explain.

"… I like it too. Better than the previous one, that's for sure. What's it called?"

"'*You, Clouds, Rain'* by Heize."

He nods and we listen to the piano and the singer's voice for a while. Nathaniel seems to really like it. I see him check something on his phone.

"Oh… I didn't expect the lyrics to be so sad."

"Really? I think Danny told me it was about love."

"More like a break-up," says Nate. "'For the first time in a while, I thought about you today. I deliberately look for a song we listened to together. My heart says it's okay to be sad or depressed today. It doesn't matter anyway when this night is over. I'll forget you again and live like that for a while, and you'll only live on in my heart.'"

I listen to him reading the translated lyrics, and I must agree. Quite sad, and a bit melancholic too. He gets absorbed in reading for a while until I decide to interrupt him.

"You've had one? A sad break-up like this?" I ask.

I don't know where I got the courage to ask that question, I just blurted it out. Because I wanted to know. He never really gave me a reason for his "no love" rule…

"More like a heartbreak. My first love, I was only seventeen. She was a few years older."

"Like your teacher or something?"

"No, my fated mate."

I almost drop my cup. I feel my heart tighten, and my breathing stops for a couple of seconds. His fated mate. So, Nate had a fated mate. A real one. That sentence alone is kind of hard to swallow. Something inside me resonates a bit.

Finding our fated mate is like a one in a thousand, no, maybe even a one in a million chance. Most werewolves can only dream about it, and a lot of us spend our whole lives looking for it, hoping to find that one person to spend our life with. We are told, while still pups, that our fated mate is someone the Moon Goddess chooses for us, that one individual who is our complete match. A singular connection that can't be misunderstood. The few fated mate couples I know are perfect for each other. Couples that can fight like any other sometimes but feel like two pieces of the same mold. I dreamt of it too, like everyone.

But I never thought that Nate would have found his, and lost her.

I feel a bit uneasy, now, asking about this. Isn't it awkward? But Nate keeps talking without warning.

"It's an old story, Elena. She was older, and already engaged to someone else. She recognized our bond, of course, but she wasn't really interested. Her husband-to-be was loaded, and I was just a nobody, with a crazy Alpha father, a complicated life, and two siblings to watch over."

"You mean she rejected you?"

"Yes," he nods.

I can't believe it. Who would be stupid enough to reject their fated mate? And someone like Nathaniel, to boot!

"Seriously?" I yell, annoyed. "She rejected her own fated mate? Who would be selfish enough to value money or whatever over that?"

"Elena, calm down. She had valid reasons, to be honest, and I don't blame her."

I'm so angry for him! How can he be so calm about this? I hate that woman to the core already. Am I blinded by something else? Probably, but you won't hear me say it, no way. I can't believe someone would willingly reject their own fated mate, it's like our most sacred bond after the one we have with the Moon Goddess!

"Is she still here?" I ask a bit abruptly.

Nate seems surprised by my question.

"No, not that I know of. My brother banished her from our territories. I have no idea where she is nowadays. Last time I saw her, it was years ago, after we took over the Blood Moon clan."

I clench my fist. Moon Goddess, if I meet that woman, I have no idea what I'll do to her. How could she reject Nate?

"Hey, Elena."

I turn to him, unable to hide my anger. He sighs.

"Stop with that grumpy face. I told you, it's history."

"Is it because of her? Your 'no love' rule?"

He hesitates for a second before he answers.

"Mostly, yes. But not only…"

I growl, still annoyed. And I'm even more annoyed that he seems forgiving of that woman.

"Elena, don't sulk."

"I'm not sulking."

"Yes, you are."

I sigh. He's right, I really need to work on controlling my emotions a bit more… I'm so petty sometimes, I have to admit. I roll my eyes.

"Okay, I'm not angry. Let's change subjects?"

"With pleasure."

Indeed, in an attempt to help me change my mood, Nathaniel goes on to teach me some more French. It's amusing, but I really can't tell how much I will be able to remember by tomorrow.

We keep talking, and I keep eating pizza, until late into the night. I'm not that tired, so I eventually end up lazily laying down on the couch, watching TV blankly. Nathaniel is on his computer again, probably catching up on some work. My feet are on his lap, and he sometimes caresses my leg without thinking. We stay silent for a while, with only the downpour in the background. We lit a few candles earlier, so now the room smells like citrus.

I'm finally starting to feel a bit better.

"Elena?"

"Hm?"

"What if I financed it?"

I frown. What is he talking about? He puts down his computer to face me, one of his hands on my leg.

"Your Music Café. What if I financed it?"

"Nate, I don't get what you're talking about."

We talked about my idea a few times before, and I know Nathaniel's always acted interested in it. He asked many questions and raised issues I hadn't thought about before while making plans on my own. But I don't get why he's suddenly bringing this up again?

"Look, the idea is good. All you would need are funds and some professional advice. I can give you both. Isn't that what you want?"

I sit up. What's with him now?

"Nate, you know this is my own dream."

"I know, I'm just saying."

"My own dream means I want to be able to do it on my own, without using someone else's money, or connections."

He stays silent for a second. Nate looks a bit shocked by my words, but I have to be resolute about this. I know his life is different. He isn't limited by money problems or pack issues, but that doesn't mean he can't understand that I am. I sit up and take a deep breath. After everything he said before, I do have to give in a bit to him too.

"Nate, I appreciate what you're trying to do, but that's a no."

"Elena, I don't get it. I'm giving you a chance to realize your dream and-"

"It's not a chance, Nate. For me, it's as if I cheated. Even if you really believe in it, it's not right for me to do this. From the start, this Music Café has been a goal of mine, something I want to work hard for and earn by myself. If I accept your money, I'll be taking a shortcut and betraying the person I want to be."

He is still frowning, and I know he understands what I'm trying to say.

"Nathaniel, even if I had all that money right now, it might not be the right time. It's… complicated with my pack, I have to resume my classes next week, and there's the matter with my dad too."

He suddenly raises his head, surprised. Of course.

"You never told me about your family. Aside from your adoption."

"I know. It's just that there isn't much to say. My mom died in a car accident almost two years ago now, and my dad has been in a coma since that same accident."

"I'm sorry."

I shake my head. I don't feel like I can handle any pity right now.

"… Were you there? In the car?"

"No. I had just moved in with Danny, they were coming to see me. They were super late, and my mom was never late, so I figured something was wrong. They weren't answering our calls or our mind-linking. I called half of the Opal Moon pack to help look for them."

I sigh. I still remember the sight of their wrecked vehicle in the ravine. The horror when I realized what had happened.

We were supposed to celebrate so many things that night: my moving in with Danny, his scholarship, Mom's new job, and my freedom, at long last.

Instead of letting the sorrow sink in, I shake my head and drink a bit of tea. I force myself to smile, even with that bitter taste behind it.

"It's okay, Nate. But, please, understand I can't tell you yes for now. I have so many reasons not to. Moreover, I'm not even sure I could accept so much money from a friend."

I almost said friend with benefits, but that would have been a bit weird in this situation, right? Damn, our relationship is getting stranger day by day. Worst thing is that I don't hate it.

"Alright, I understand. Maybe I compared your situation to mine a bit too much."

"What do you mean?"

"When I was younger, I wanted to have my own restaurant, too… When our father was still here, every day was such a struggle."

I listen to Nate, a bit surprised. He's never said much about their childhood. All I know is from my memories of those years before they took over their father's place and changed a lot of things. It was as if an age of fear had passed. The Black Moon became the Blood Moon, as if their name was cursed. They inherited the King's spot and the fear he had spread among the packs.

"Damian worked himself to the bone so we could eat. I had to take care of the house and we both made sure Liam kept going to school. We lived in fear of our father, even more so than the other packs. If anyone else was scared of seeing him, imagine what it was like for us to live with that monster."

"So you… all three of you hated him?"

"To the core. There wasn't one of us he didn't beat. He sent me to the hospital twice, and almost killed Damian so many times. We barely kept

Liam safe. Yet, he was still injured a few times too. Trust me Elena, that man, no one misses him. We are nothing-- nothing-- like our father."

I silently nod. This is the first time I'm seeing Nate with such a dark expression on his face. For a while, he stays lost in his thoughts, in memories probably too dark to imagine. I spent my childhood looking for who I am, while Nate spent his trying to escape who he was.

"I always dreamt of that day we would be rich, free of any worry. Truth is, as you grow up, you realize how far you've come but also how it never ends. Like, you can have money, a bed, a job, stability, and there is always something… something missing."

He says that while looking at me, as if he was reading my soul. It's a bit hard to breathe. Is it because I feel the same? This little piece of emptiness inside, that missing piece I'm so desperately looking for.

We stare at each other for a few seconds, before I can't hold it anymore. I climb on his lap, straddling him, my hands around his neck, and I kiss him. Nate is a bit surprised at first, but as usual, he answers my kiss. Deeply, passionately. Like a dance we both know too well, so synchronized and entrancing. The taste of his lips is my personal drug, and more addicting every time I get a taste.

"*Elena!*"

The familiar headache takes me by surprise. My wolf growls, annoyed by the interruption. I'm annoyed too and can't help but answer a bit angrily.

"*What, Levi?*"

"*You're not going to like this. Get to the Alpha's house. Right now.*"

"*What? Why?*"

"*He's fighting with Reagan, it's nasty.*"

Holy crap. I get off of Nate's lap, trying to focus.

"*What the hell? Why?*"

"*Your ex. He's been spotted in the west. Diego is coming back, Elena.*"

"*Oh shit.*"

You've got to be fucking kidding me! I jump off the couch under Nate's confused expression.

"You have to go. Now."

I storm to my bedroom and grab a pair of sneakers.

"Elena, what is it? Are you okay?"

"No, Nate, I'm not okay and I really, really have to go."

I know he's probably confused as heck, but I really don't have the time. What do I need? My keys, my phone...

"What's going on?" he insists.

"I'm sorry Nate, I can't tell you. It's complicated, it's a pack issue and... Shit, where the hell are my keys?"

"On the kitchen counter. But seriously, Elena, explain this to me!" He stands up and follows me around. What the hell can I tell him? 'Hey, my abusive ex is coming back in town and my mentor lost her shit on our Alpha'? No way. Pack matters are pack matters, and I especially don't want Nate to know about this.

I finally have my keys in hand, grab my backpack, and put on my shoes and a raincoat. I grab my phone and finally force myself to walk up to him.

"Nate, I'm very happy you came to comfort me, and I spent a great day with you. I really did. Oh, and I loved the pizza too. But now, I really have to go and you do as well, please."

"You'll explain later?" He frowns, although he does go to gather his stuff.

"What? Yes, I mean, no. Well, maybe. I don't know for now. Anyway, Nate, please!"

"Okay, okay. Just go, Elena, I'll lock up after myself."

"All right. Thanks."

I give him a quick kiss and run out. I feel like crap for leaving him like this, but right now, I need to hurry over there...

Chapter 10

When I finally reach the Main house, I'm soaked but I couldn't care less! All I keep thinking about are Levi's words. Anyway, he said he would meet me here, and indeed, he's the one to open the door. To think I have to wait for someone to invite me into my uncle's house…

I can already hear people yelling. Damn, Reagan is furious. I follow Levi to the main room, only to see her at Xavier's throat, with three poor wolves trying to separate them.

"You little son of a dog! Do you think you can mess with me? Brat! I was already a fighter while you were still crying on your mother's lap! You shameless dog! You don't even deserve to be called an Alpha!"

"Reagan!" I call to her, trying to get her away from my uncle, but she won't release her grip. Iris and Chris run to me immediately.

"Elena! Where were you? They started fighting a while ago…" says Iris, a bit alarmed.

"They said Diego was spotted in the west! Did you know about this?" asks Chris.

"How would I have known?" I reply to the two of them, annoyed.

How did they expect me to be aware of all this? I didn't ask for it! I walk past my cousins to try and get in between Reagan and my uncle. This time, with Levi's help, we finally pull them apart, and I have to use all my strength to restrain my mentor, who is yelling her lungs out.

"You watch it, Xavier! Someone's gonna have your head someday and that might be me, you son of a dog!"

"Watch it, Reagan! You might be tolerated on our grounds but that won't be the case for much longer if you–!"

"If I what, huh? What will you do? You little mutt! You think you're bigger than Clark? Than Sam?"

Damn, she said it. My dad's name, to my uncle's face. Xavier's face turns from an angry red to dark purple, which is not any better. He starts vociferating a long list of insults, under everyone's horrified eyes. But Reagan is just laughing at him.

"Go ahead, insult me all you want! Little mutt!"

"ENOUGH!"

This time, everyone shuts up. My order resonated loudly in the room, and everyone's eyes are on me, with shocked expressions. Only Chris whistles a little in admiration, but I don't have time for my cousin's childishness right now. I glare at Reagan.

"Shut it now, old hag."

She doesn't reply, just snorting. I turn to my uncle, who is pissed, not only because I gave him an order, but because he obeyed. But unfortunately for him, I am the stronger alpha in the room, and we both know that.

"Is it true? He's back?"

"That is not for you to–"

"ANSWER ME!"

He steps back, with a sullen look. I'm serious, and I'll keep insisting for as long as it takes, whether he likes it or not. Xavier growls as a warning, but I growl too. My wolf is just as pissed as I am, and we want answers. After a while, my uncle's wolf finally backs down a little, surrendering.

"Yes… He was spotted. In the west."

"Why the hell is he back?" I ask, still growling.

"Isn't it obvious? It's almost time. He's making it clear he will come back as soon as his banishment order is lifted."

I clench my fist, hard.

"You said he wouldn't come back."

"I know what I said. But the ban was five years, Elena. Those five years are coming to an end, and if Diego comes back, I can't stop him."

"That guy is a fucking murderer!" I yell.

Xavier glares at me.

"Who is the murderer, Elena? You think we forgot just because you missed?"

I stand there, in shock. Is that really what my uncle thinks? I turn to my cousins, but Chris is looking down, embarrassed, and Iris isn't saying anything. I can't believe it. But someone puts a hand on my shoulder.

"Elena was pardoned long ago, and you all know that. She completed her sentence and earned forgiveness. You know it wasn't easy for anyone, Xavier."

I mouth a little thank you to Levi; he smiles at me.

"*You know I got your back, princess.*"

"Levi, this is none of your business," growls Xavier.

But Levi isn't afraid to growl back. Their wolves show their fangs for a while, and I wonder how Levi is not afraid to stand up to my uncle. He's only a Beta, while my uncle is an Alpha. It's only his protective instincts kicking in.

"Enough, both of you!"

I turn around. Clark just entered the room, visibly angry too. Following right behind him, Isabella growls at Levi.

"Don't growl at an Alpha! Who allowed you to do that, Levi?"

But he only stops growling, not glaring, at Xavier and stays beside me. Now, Clark is the one furious at my uncle.

"And you! Can't you control your own pack? Why do I have to come all the way here? In this shitty weather and at this late hour, too! What the hell, Xavier?"

"Say that to the old wench! She's the one who came here to defy me in the first place!" growls my uncle, glaring at my mentor.

Reagan doesn't even bother answering him, choosing to turn to my godfather instead. I've never seen anyone able to glare so long at Clark without flinching. But as expected, Reagan is an omega, she is not as sensitive to his Alpha Aura as regular wolves.

"Seriously, Clark? A five-year ban? That is all you could do?"

For the first time, the Alpha seems a bit embarrassed. He sighs, conflicted.

"It's not like I had much choice, Reagan. No matter what, Elena was–"

"She was right to do whatever the hell she had to! Are you fucking kidding me, Clark? What is wrong with you alphas these days? If this mess had happened in my time, that guy would have been fucking killed right there and then!"

"Reagan, enough! You think that it was an easy decision for me?" pleads Clark, annoyed.

But my mentor only gets angrier.

"Hell yeah, I think it was! You took the easiest path possible and did whatever the hell those idiots asked you to! A five-year ban, Clark? That is nothing! What happened to you to allow such things?"

"I protected Elena!"

"Don't fucking tell me you protected her!" yells Reagan. "You weren't there, no one was! She was fucking sixteen, Clark! And where were you? Where was Sam?"

"Reagan, enough. Please," I ask.

I'm not asking for Clark, but for myself. I don't want to hear this. Not again. Reagan's anger is only making things worse. I sigh, push my wet hair back, and turn to Clark to ask him very seriously.

"Can't you do something about it?"

My godfather looks at me with a very sorry expression. I can see the guilt on his face, and I feel my heart sink. He shakes his head slowly.

"I'm sorry, Elena."

Fuck.

I turn around and leave the house despite Levi and Chris calling my name. I don't want any of them to hold me back. As soon as I step out, Reagan and Xavier start yelling at each other again, but I just don't care anymore. I keep running, faster and faster, until I shape-shift mid-jump.

Running in my wolf form doesn't make anything less painful, I'm just faster. I keep running, across the familiar streets, looking for somewhere to go. I don't even know where to go. Not west, definitely not west.

I head north without thinking. I just want to be alone and cry my sorrow away. My steps naturally take me to our northern border, to the wild forest, where no one goes at this hour during such a downpour. I hear people calling me, trying to mind-link me, but I shut the voices out. I don't want to hear or listen to anyone now.

I find a large tree to crawl under and curl up around some roots.

I finally let myself cry. It's not just a few tears, I'm fucking bawling like a kid. I can't remember the last time I cried so much. My tears melt with the rain, but I can only hear my wolf's sorrow. I'm mad at the whole world right now.

It's not fair. This is all so fucking unfair. Why do I have to go through all this shit? After everything I've already gone through? Haven't I paid enough for my mistakes? I can't go through it all again. I just can't. I don't want to let that nightmare happen again.

I freeze when I sense a wolf close by. Fuck.

"*Hey, babe.*"

The tawny wolf has to dig a little to take the small spot next to me. Thankfully, Danny is a little smaller than me. He crawls to get beside me, ruining his fur with the mud. My best friend's green eyes finally meet mine, and I feel even more tears coming.

"*It's okay, babe. Just go for it.*"

I let my tears flow, and Danny rubs his head against mine, trying to comfort me. Damn, thank Moon Goddess it's him. Danny is probably the only person I'm willing to see right now.

I spend a long time crying, letting my feelings out without restraint. It's like I've been holding it in way too long.

"*Danny...*"

"*I know. Levi called me.*"

"*What are you doing here? What about your seminar?*"

"*Are you kidding me? Who gives a shit about some stupid seminar? My babe needs me, so I ran here!*"

"*Gosh, Danny. I love you.*"

"*I know. But I'm taken, you know. And a bit too gay.*"

"*Idiot.*"

"*Yeah, yeah, love you too.*"

We stay like this for a while, two wolves curled up against one another. I don't want to talk, and I don't care about the rain drenching us. I just keep crying silently with Danny's head resting on mine.

"*Elena...*"

I growl a bit. I don't want to talk. But of course, Danny ignores me.

"*We need to think of a plan, babe.*"

I growl again. What plan? Aside from killing Diego, I can't think of anything as satisfying.

"*What if you stayed with him? With Black, on his territory?*"

"*Are you nuts, Danny? On the Velvet Moon's territory? You can't be serious.*"

"*I am dead serious, babe. I know it's not our turf, but anything is better than having you anywhere near Diego.*"

"*Nate has no idea, Danny.*"

"*Tell me he wouldn't agree.*"

I think for a second. A few days back, I probably would have said there is no way he would. But after today, I mean, yesterday since it's probably way past midnight... would Nate agree to it? I can't believe I'm even considering the idea!

"*Elena, think about it, babe. Even that crazy-ass Diego wouldn't dare to chase you all the way to the Velvet Moon's territory. If you go anywhere else, he wouldn't think about it twice, but that is the King's turf.*"

"*The King doesn't even know that I exist, Daniel!*"

"*He doesn't need to know. Seriously, Elena. If Black hides you, you can stay away from Diego and his shit.*"

"*Then what, Danny? I stay trapped there forever? It's not my turf, plus why should I be the one to hide?*"

"Babe, I know it's not easy. I know Diego should have paid much more for what he did, but-"

"I was the one who lost and paid the most, Danny! That son of a bitch got away with just a fucking ban after what he did! After killing my baby!"

Daniel stays silent for a while but sighs eventually.

"I know, babe. I know all that. But right now, I want to protect you and the only one who can do that is Nathaniel Black."

Chapter 11

Sipping my coffee, I still think that this is the shittiest idea ever. Daniel spent half of last night trying to convince me before we both fell asleep, exhausted. And he's at it again this morning. The only difference is that while I was away and busy with the training, he brought reinforcements.

Caught in between us and standing in the kitchen, Bobo is looking at me, a bit surprised and confused after we explained a lot of things. Things he probably didn't want to know in the first place.

"So, the man you were seeing…"

"... was Nathaniel Black," I sigh, repeating myself again.

That's right. Boyan didn't know anything about my relationship until now. For starters, Daniel and I had agreed it would be best to keep his boyfriend out of it, especially since their own relationship was already complicated enough. Moreover, we thought it would probably be better for him not to know his boyfriend's roommate was having sex regularly with his Alpha's little brother, who also somehow happened to be his boss.

But now, the poor guy is totally at a loss, trying to put the pieces together.

"And you want to stay on the Velvet Moon territory because your ex-boyfriend is returning here?"

"Well, that's Daniel's idea, but yes."

"Daniel, who has great life-saving ideas," adds my best friend, humble as usual.

I ignore him. Boyan is frowning, his eyes on his huge cup of coffee. I thought he would side with Daniel right away, but I might have been wrong on this one. After a while, he raises his head to look at me.

"What's the deal with your ex-boyfriend? Why do you want to elude him?" he asks.

I don't know how to answer that. I leave the barstool to go sit on the couch, a bit annoyed. That's why I didn't want to involve Bobo. From behind the kitchen counter, Daniel explains first.

"He is a bastard, a good-for-nothing asshole. Everything's wrong with him, baby bear, that's all you have to know."

Baby bear? Damn, Danny has used almost every existing cheesy pet name by now. At least he's moved on from pumpkin or sugar.

Boyan glances at me, a bit confused.

"I don't wanna talk about him, Bobo. The guy's a mythic jerk, that's all you have to know, okay? I don't want to see him ever again."

"Okay, but can't you just ignore him?" asks Bobo.

I shake my head at the same time as Danny.

"No, baby bear. That dirtbag will definitely come after Elena. It's already a miracle that he respected his five-year ban, trust me."

"*You don't want to tell Boyan about the baby?*"

"*Hell no, Danny.*"

"*Got it.*"

I don't want to talk about it to anyone, at all. Even within our pack, very few people know exactly what happened back then. Aside from my parents, Daniel's family, Reagan, Clark, and my uncle, we didn't let anyone know. I am not even sure if Isabella or my cousins know about it. It's such a sensitive topic, everyone was relieved when it was settled.

Moreover, I didn't want people to pity me. I just wanted to get better and move on. I could hate Diego all I wanted and regain my freedom.

"I still think it might not be a good idea."sighs Bobo.

"Why?"

"I think Damian knows about you."

Daniel and I freeze. Damian? Does he mean the King, for real? How would he know? Nate told me he didn't talk to his siblings about me! He only told his Beta, and only because the guy was the nosy type! So how the hell would his older brother know I even exist? I exchange a glance with Daniel.

"Is that bad?" asks Danny.

"Not really. But my older brother is the King's Beta. He's the one who told me that Nate was seeing someone and he had to look into it. I never thought it would turn out to be you," he says with an apologetic face.

"He didn't say anything," I sigh.

Nate was long gone when we got home last night. It feels a bit odd to think about everything that happened yesterday, all in one day. There's still the cold pizza in the fridge, and some leftover ingredients.

Daniel clicks his tongue. I guess going to the Velvet Moon territory is out of the question now. I don't feel too good about it, either. Being on the King's radar is never a good thing; I'm starting to get a bit worried. I peek at my phone. Should I call him later? I was a bit mean when I threw him out last night.

"Don't you have anyone else who could help out? I thought you were close with the Alpha?" asks Bobo.

I shake my head.

"Clark is my godfather, but the Opal Moon is part of the White Moon. He can't hide me, and he can't really interfere either. If he wanted to, he should have done it earlier. That's why Reagan was so mad."

"Maybe you should leave with Reagan."

I glare at Danny.

"Seriously, Danny? I should run away from my territory because that asshole is coming back? No fucking way."

"There isn't a big difference."

"He should be the one to leave in the first place!" I growl, annoyed.

"I know that, babe, but I'm not taking any chances of having you near him. We're running out of ideas here. We can't keep him out and we can't find a place for you to stay! Once his ban is lifted, there will be no place that you can go where Diego can't go either!"

Damn it. I know Danny's right, but it's painful to hear.

"Is it that bad?" asks Bobo.

"Yes, it is that bad, Boyan. If my ex comes back, I'm going to be in big trouble, trust me. He won't leave me alone. So, I have two weeks to find a solution, or else I'm going to do something I'll regret."

With that, I get up and head to the shower. I'm so mad I don't even know what to do. I tried to exhaust myself with training this morning, but I only managed to scare the younger ones, while I didn't even calm down one bit.

I pick a new outfit from my wardrobe, something boyish and practical, and go back to the kitchen. Danny just finished preparing breakfast, and I grab a burrito for myself. He clicks his tongue at my lack of manners as I walk past the counter with my mouth full to grab my shoes.

"Where are you going?" he asks.

"To grab some fresh air."

"Where, Elena?"

"I'll text you. Can I take the car?"

"Not when you're mad like this, babe. Text me later."

I roll my eyes and exit the apartment promptly. I know Danny's just worried about me, I don't hold it against him. We've been friends for so long, he knows I'm mad at pretty much everything and everyone right now.

Walking down the familiar streets, I'm in no mood for chit-chat. I decide to avoid the main street and walk through more deserted alleys. The weather is still cloudy, with a light drizzle. I put my hood over my head and grab my phone and earbuds. A few seconds later, some adequate music is echoing in my head.

The singer's voice calms me down for a while, and I decide to head for the hospital. I didn't visit my dad yesterday. I miss him. I visit the hospital for only a couple of hours, but my gloom is back again once I leave my dad. I stand at the entrance, a bit lost.

Where to go now?

I don't want to go home yet. For a while, I stare at my phone. Should I call Nate? The fact his brother knows about us is seriously worrying me. I should probably leave him alone for a while, right? Seeing an Opal Moon girl probably isn't any good for him, I guess. Nate always acts as if he controls everything, but I feel like it might not be the case when the King is involved.

When I'm about to press the call button, I stop. I know I said I'd call, but to say what? "Hey, my ex is back, the situation is crappy, how have you been doing?" What a mess… I can't clear up my own mind, yet I can't involve Nate in all this. I sigh and put my phone back in my pocket. I stay here for a while, leaning back against the clinic's wall, watching the downpour amplify on our little turf of Silver City.

"Elena?"

I turn my head. Bianca is here, just exiting the hospital holding an umbrella over her head. She walks up to me with her little smile.

"So, it is you! What are you doing here? Got caught in the rain?" she asks, innocently.

"Hi, Bianca. Yeah, you could say that. I'm just waiting for it to pass."

She frowns in a cute pout.

"It will last for a while, you know. How about you come with me to Henry's bar? My friend's band is about to rehearse!"

Damn, that girl is so cute and nice. I give in and nod. A cold beer and hanging with the kids might do me good and help chase away all the gloom. Bianca, all too happily, shares her umbrella with me until we get there, about ten minutes later. The bar is not very lively, as usual, but a few teenagers are setting up their instruments, very enthusiastic about their rehearsal.

At the bar, there's only old Henry, grumpy as always.

Bianca greets her friends, forgetting me for a few minutes. I just ask for a drink meanwhile, wondering if my mentor is around.

"That's right, Elena! Don't you want to play for us?" says Bianca, turning to me.

"What? She can play something?" asks one of the guys, another of my cheeky trainees.

Bianca glares at him.

"Of course, she can, she has the best ears in the pack! Come on, Elena!"

The guy, a bit surprised that Bianca rebuffed him, looks down. Seems like he was just trying to act cool, but her answer wasn't what he expected. So cute, these teenage crushes. I smile at her and walk over to borrow one of their guitars.

"What should I play?" I ask.

"Anything! Whatever comes to mind," says Bianca. "I just want to hear you, it's been a while!"

Her smile is contagious, but I'm still feeling a bit down. What should I play? Something that matches my emotions. It might be a bit sad though. I strum a few chords on the guitar and decide to play the acoustic version of "Let You Love Me" by Rita Ora. It's so similar to my current thoughts.

"I should've stayed with you last night instead of going out to find trouble. That's just trouble... I think I run away sometimes, whenever I get too vulnerable. That's not your fault... See, I wanna stay the whole night, I wanna lay with you till the sun's up, I wanna let you inside. Oh, heaven knows I've tried. I wish that I could I let you love, wish that I could let you love me..."

I keep singing, that song I know by heart, my eyes closed. It reflects my thoughts about Nate so well. In another life, with different pasts, maybe we would have been great for each other. If we both weren't so afraid to love, perhaps we could have healed each other.

I immerse myself in the song, pouring my heart and feelings into it, in the strings under my fingers. I sing loud until the end, not caring about anything else but the song. It's been a while since I last sang my heart out like this, it feels great.

"Say what's the matter, what's the matter with me? What's the matter with me? Oh, I wish that I could I let you love, wish that I could let you love me now…"

I pour out the last words and stop, satisfied. When I open my eyes again, Bianca and her friends, their eyes shining, suddenly start clapping, excited.

"Moon Goddess, Elena, that was so good!"

"You have such a good voice!"

"Can you sing again?"

I shake my head.

"Thank you but it's your turn now. I have my beer waiting for me."

Because of their insistence and disappointed expressions, I have to promise I will sing again later before I can breach the wall of excited teenagers to reach the bar again. Once I finally get there, I notice someone had taken the spot next to mine.

"Hi, kiddo. It's been a while since I heard that singing voice," says Reagan.

I look at my mentor, suspicious. What is she doing here? Her leather jacket is still dripping. Did she come all the way here despite the rain? The way she took the seat next to mine too. Usually, Reagan avoids me, so what now?

I grab my beer and take a sip, waiting to see what the old woman has to say. She sighs.

"What's your idea?"

"For what?"

"Your ex, Elena. You know it's going to be a problem," she says, tapping her finger on the counter.

"Of course, I know."

But I haven't figured anything out yet. All I've done today is be angry about it and wonder what to do next. The idea of Diego coming back is just driving me nuts. It brings back way too many dark memories that I can't handle. Reagan growls.

"That dog. I should have killed him while he was still out."

"What for, Reagan? And Diego is not weak either. You probably would have been killed instead."

"Doesn't matter. As long as I keep that mutt away."

I frown. What is that supposed to mean? I'm not overestimating him. Five years ago, Diego was undoubtedly one of the strongest alphas in our pack, aside from myself. Now I wonder if he's gotten any stronger... well, probably. Many years spent as a rogue should do that, right? I drink some of my beer again.

"Let him come," suddenly says Reagan.

I almost spit out my beer before turning to her. Is this old hag going nuts?

"You've got to be kidding me, Reagan."

"No."

She puts her beer down and looks me right in the eye, resolute.

"Look at me, Elena. I did not train you to be a she-wolf that runs away. You were born and raised as an alpha, and you're going to act like one."

How did she know that was my first idea? And why is she going on about my alpha condition all of a sudden? It is true she raised me, trained me to be a strong woman, but I don't think this is going to help at all!

"But Xavier–"

"I don't care what your uncle says, kid. Stop using him or Clark as excuses. You know what you are, and you should not submit to them, your ex, or anyone."

"I am not using them as excuses!"

"Oh yes, you are," says Reagan, angry. "Look at you. Why are you even here? You don't meddle with the pack's affairs. You never fight. You stay the farthest you can from the rest of the pack. You only train those kids half-heartedly."

I glare at her, angry. How dare she judge me? I've only been trying to do what I'm supposed to do ever since I was raised here. What does she know about my childhood? What it was like to be the outcast of the pack while she was gone Moon-Goddess-knows where!

"You're the one who never gave me any answers!" I growl back.

"You don't need that to know who you are! You have an inner wolf! You have your Alpha Aura, even if you never use it! Stop acting like a coward, Elena! If your ex comes back, do what you must, but don't you dare lower your head to anyone."

I'm speechless. Since when does Reagan push me like this? She is the one who's never around and when she is, she eludes me! I remember her conversation with Clark, the one Levi recorded. Reagan always denied it, but she knows who my mother is and where I came from. But if I ask her about that, she might run away from the White Moon again.

I grab my sun necklace between my fingers, trying to calm down with the cold metal under my fingers, and take a deep breath.

"I've always wondered why I had this, why I was different. I tried so hard to be like the other pups in this pack, Reagan. But I couldn't. I was too strong, too fast. The only ones whom I could fit in with were the other misfits. Daniel and Diego. They became my whole world… my only friends in this pack."

"Elena..."

I shake my head. I need to finish speaking, to let her know what I've been carrying around all these years.

"When I stopped trying to fit in, I thought I had finally found my place. But that's when everything changed, again. You left, and Clark made me his goddaughter. I was placed a step higher than the others, and I didn't understand the reason why. I thought Clark had chosen me because I was the strongest, but neither Eric nor Orpheus are anywhere near as strong as Diego was. I wasn't leader material either. I was just a wild, rebellious, teenage she-wolf. I knew it had to be something else."

Reagan ignores me, her eyes wandering to the foam of her pint.

"There is something about me, something that you and Clark know and are desperate to hide. Something that is connected to me being so strong."

The old woman sighs. She turns to me, whispering in a very low voice so that no one but me can hear her, even with werewolf ears.

"All right, I will tell you more."

I stare, shocked. Is she for real? She never agreed to say anything no matter how long I begged for it before!

"What, really? Are you serious?"

"Yes, yes. But you have to promise me two things, Elena."

I frown. Why are we bargaining now? It's never easy with this woman! After a while, she looks around us and murmurs again.

"First, I want you to promise me you will not leave Silver City once I tell you this. I don't even want you to leave the White Moon or Opal Moon territories, you hear me?"

What the heck? I thought she would ask me to keep it all a secret.

"Why?"

"Because once I start talking, you will want more, and I don't need you to be in danger recklessly."

"All right. What is the second condition?"

"Everything has to stay between us. Only Clark and Xavier know what I'm about to tell you... well, your uncle Xavier knows the big lines. But aside from them, you have to promise me you won't tell anyone else."

"I'll tell Danny," I answer honestly.

Whether she likes it or not, Reagan knows how close I am to him. There isn't anything about myself I haven't told Daniel, and I'm pretty sure the same goes for him. So, I know my mentor has to be aware anything she says will get to Danny's ears as well.

Indeed, she sighs.

"All right, I guess that kid is part of the deal. Are you sure you can trust him? He's not going to talk?"

"With my life, Reagan. And you already know how important Daniel is to me."

She can't ignore he was my only friend after everything that happened. There really isn't anyone else I would think of sharing my secrets with. Even Nathaniel only knows very little about me, despite the fact that we have been seeing each other for two months now.

"Just make sure he doesn't talk about this to anyone, Elena. This is very serious."

"I get it."

"No, you don't get it. It's your life that's hanging in the balance, kid."

Reagan's serious tone is giving me chills. What could be so big that it impacts my whole life?

Behind us, the group of teenagers is paying no attention to us, rehearsing their songs and joking around. They wouldn't think of getting involved with someone as odd as Reagan anyway. And the barman is busy wiping glasses while eyeing them too, not paying any attention to us.

"I get it, Reagan. This is serious, I can't tell anyone but Danny, and I can't leave the territory recklessly. Will you talk now?"

I'm seriously on edge. I want to know, I'm dying to know. Reagan brushes her gray hair back, taking a big breath before she starts talking.

"First, I lied to you. I never belonged to the White Moon clan in the first place."

What? She and Clark had always told me that she was just an omega that had left the pack many years ago and came back when she found me! I did find it weird that she was allowed to come and go as she pleased, though.

"I was born in a much, much older pack than this one. Far in the north, a clan so big it had over a thousand members."

A thousand! That is at least twice the size of any of the big packs.

"We had a Luna Queen, a very powerful woman. She was as strong as she was gentle. We all loved her and worshiped her. She was special."

It is unusual for a Luna to rule a pack by herself indeed. What about her mate? Didn't she have one?

"Once, I had a big fight with her. We couldn't agree on something and argued a lot."

"About what?" I ask, curious.

Reagan growls.

"You don't need to know that! Anyway, since I was being stubborn, she decided to send me to the south. She asked me to go find a smaller group that belonged to our pack. Her younger sister was leading it, but they had been gone for a long time, and we didn't have any news. She asked me to return once I had found her younger sister."

"Did you find the group?"

Reagan shook her head, looking very sad.

"No. Many years had passed since that sister of hers had left, and we had no idea how far south she had gone. I kept going, but after a few months, I decided to turn back."

"Wait, you were gone not for days, but for months?"

Reagan nodded.

"I've always been very stubborn, okay? I just didn't want to go back until I had found them, and I was still mad about the reason I left in the first place. But... when I got back..."

"What?"

She suddenly looks very sullen, frowning, and staring at her beer with a mix of anger and sadness in her eyes. I wait for a while and see her fist clenching.

"Reagan, what happened to your pack?"

"They were killed. All of them."

... What? It can't be... Such a huge pack? How could that happen? I've heard of big fights between packs, but never a full clan being killed! And from what she had said, their Luna wasn't weak either.

"B... But how?" I ask, restless.

"I don't know. Whatever it was, it slaughtered all of them, Elena. This is why I'm telling you this is very, very serious. Something was strong enough to annihilate a full pack of werewolves."

"... Then, what about me?"

I remember a bit of her conversation with Clark that Levi recorded and try to piece it all together with what she said so far. That would mean... Reagan looks at me and seems to hesitate a bit. What is it that she can't tell me? She turns her eyes away, staring straight ahead as if she couldn't face me.

"I found you in the middle of the massacre. Alone."

So, what I heard was true...

"What about my parents?"

Reagan suddenly frowns and shakes her head, upset.

"Dead. Both of them."
Why is that old hag lying to me again?

Chapter 12

That can't be true. On Levi's recording, Reagan clearly mentioned my mother, and how she was alive when she took me! So why is she lying, saying my parents had already died? I stare at her for a while, wondering how to go about this. I can't let her know that we heard her conversation with Clark.

"Both my parents were dead? Are you sure?" I ask again.

"I just told you so," groans Reagan, impatient. "You were the only living being I could find, so I took you with me and fled the place."

"Wait… Didn't you try to figure out what had happened? Who had done this to our clan?"

But Reagan shakes her head.

"I couldn't, Elena. I had a two-year-old brat in my paws, and something bad was there."

"What do you mean, something bad?"

She sniffles, a disgusted expression on her face like she saw something repulsive.

"I don't know. My inner wolf couldn't calm down, my spine was constantly tingling. I could tell something filthy was there, something dangerous. Whatever had attacked was still there, and lurking, waiting around for more. I ran away with you and headed south."

"All the way to the White Moon territory," I say, putting the pieces together.

"That's right. That was as far as I could go with a two-year-old. Since I was a renegade from another pack, they had no obligation to accept me. But you were there. No werewolf can ignore a defenseless pup, let alone a little orphan alpha, like you."

She's right. Our wolf instincts are always pushing us to protect the younger ones of our kind, even if they don't belong to our pack. Any cub is a werewolf's responsibility, that's something we cannot ignore. No wonder the White Moon didn't reject her when she brought me with her.

"You still haven't told me why I'm different."

She sighs.

"Our whole pack was different, Elena. Our Luna made it so. I told you, she was very powerful and blessed by the Moon Goddess. Everyone in our pack was stronger than common werewolves."

I'm not sure I believe that. Once again, Reagan is not looking at me while speaking, and I feel like there is still a lot she isn't telling me. I'm a bit disappointed. I was hoping she would tell me more about my parents.

"I tried to go back several times after that," sighs Reagan.

"That's why you left for so long each time?"

She nods.

"It takes a while to go so far to the north, but I could never reach our homeland anyway."

"What do you mean?" I ask, perplexed.

"I don't know. Something is blocking me. Every time I should reach the destination, I get lost, as if I couldn't find my way, like a maze. I should know the place by heart, but something very, very odd happens. I'm not that old that I would forget the way back! Moreover, it's coming closer. Whatever it is, it's headed south, our way."

"… So this is why you don't want me going north?"

She turns to me, looking very serious. She puts a hand on my knee, whispering.

"Elena, whatever attacked our pack is coming to us. It's slow, but it is."

I sigh. Listening to Reagan, even despite her serious tone, I can't tell how serious she is. An invisible threat, coming after us? And after killing our entire pack too? Is she just trying to keep me distracted with more lies?

"Reagan, are you lying to me again?"

"Elena, I'm serious!"

"But none of this makes sense! Seriously, all I hear are excuses for me not to leave the White Moon! Why do you always lie to me? How old do you think I am to believe in an invisible threat who decimated a full, super-strong pack?"

She growls, seriously angry.

"You think I'm joking?"

"I think you're lying to me, again!" I yell back. "You never, ever tell me the truth!"

"That was the truth, you brat!"

"How am I supposed to believe this? None of it makes any sense, and it doesn't answer my questions either! You never tell me what I really want to know, about my parents, where I come from!"

Reagan stands up, grabbing her backpack and leaving money on the counter.

"Enough with your whims, Elena. If you don't want to listen--"

"I am listening, but you're just spitting nonsense, Reagan! I don't know if that pack really existed! If it did, and we were both born there, how could you not even know about my parents?"

She's glaring at me, but I won't back down. We are both angry and frustrated. Around us, all our yelling has silenced the rest of the people present, who are watching the scene with curiosity. I couldn't care less.

Reagan pushes her gray hair away from her face and turns around.

"I am not talking about your parents. This is about our pack, Elena, that's all you need to know!"

Of course. Once again, she gets to decide what I get to know or not! I can't believe that old hag! She leaves while we're still angrily growling at each other. I'm left watching her back as my mentor exits the place, leaving me speechless.

"Elena…?"

Bianca approaches me with a sorry look, but I can't handle the pity on her face right now. I shake my head, meaning I don't want to talk, and leave the bar.

Damn, I forgot about the rain. It's pouring. Reagan is already nowhere to be found, of course. She disappears so easily. She came, said what she had to, and left. That old hag… Was the story made up just because she doesn't want me to leave the territory? I don't even know what to believe in that incredible story she told.

Some parts do match with what I thought, but she also lied about my parents, and that so-called attacker or whatever. I don't know what to believe.

I'm feeling so lonely right now.

Maybe it's this rain, or because I'm tired, but I feel like crying again.

"*Danny.*"

"*Babe, what's wrong?*"

I reached out to him by reflex, but my thoughts aren't even clear enough to explain them to him. I can't think of words to express this feeling of uneasiness I feel piling up inside.

"*Bad day?*"

"*Yeah.*"

"*Wanna come home?*"

"*No.*"

I don't want to go home right now. If I go home, I'm just going to get even gloomier, and I don't want to hinder Danny's time with Bobo like that. He probably needs to catch up on the work he missed for me too. I hear his wolf sigh.

"*Okay, babe, what do you want to do then?*"

What do I want?

A face pops up in my mind immediately. I know exactly what I really want right now.

"*Babe, go see him. I know you want to.*"

I sigh. I love Danny, but sometimes he reads my mind way too easily and it's scary. And I know I shouldn't listen. I still can't come to a proper decision, about Nate or Diego.

"*Elena, you need this. So go for it. Plus, you owe him an explanation, remember?*"

Damn, he's so right.

He makes me promise to call him later, and I start walking again, heading south.

I don't know why, but I can't summon the courage to call Nate first. Playing with my phone in my pocket, I try to think of something to say while walking, but nothing sounds right, not after what happened last time. Nathaniel was adorable with me when I was unwell, but I had to leave so abruptly, and I didn't explain anything. How could I? I don't want him to know anything about my past or Diego.

While walking, I suddenly get a chill. I stop, warned by my inner wolf's instincts. Something's wrong. No, more like a threat, something's behind me. Someone is watching me.

I turn around, trying to use my wolf's vision despite the downpour. But no one seems to be there. I wish I could smell something, but it's impossible with this rain. Why would someone follow me? Diego can't possibly be here already. So, who?

I start running. Will they follow me to the border? I can feel someone following me again, but they're staying far enough away to not be spotted. It's all about instinct, and I can tell my wolf's annoyed by this little game. Whoever it is, they won't show themselves.

I finally reach the Blood Moon territory's border. Seems like whoever it is didn't dare to follow me. I adjust my hoodie on my head and keep walking. I decide to head straight for Nate's hotel where we meet the most, but I really hope there won't be any trouble. I usually let him know before coming, but right now I'm behaving like an intruder.

I decide to go the long way around so as to not attract too much attention. Some streets in the east are not the most welcoming, but there aren't many people who go there. We call it the slums for a reason. It's the riskiest place for humans and werewolves alike, full of deserted, filthy streets and blind alleys. I'm confident in my strength, though. Even if I meet a few rogues, I should be strong enough to get out of there unscratched.

I suddenly stop. My wolf is on all fours, growling, ready to defend herself.

I can feel that alpha aura all the way from here. Shit, I didn't expect to meet such a strong wolf here. A shadow dressed all in black is slowly walking my way. I can't see his face; he's wearing a hoodie too.

Involuntarily, I take a step back. Damn, am I really that scared? I can feel his aura, like an icy wind crawling all around him. It's almost as if I could see the beast before the man. My legs want to run away. I'm shivering, not because of the cold. Whoever it is, he's very, very angry and restless. Someone looking for a fight. For blood.

His pace is strangely slow for someone whose aura is going so wild, like a hurricane behind the surface. My breathing quickens as he comes closer. I should run. Whoever it is, I might not be able to fight him. Who the hell would be that strong?

I'm frozen right where I am, but before I can make a decision, he's already too close. Dangerously close, maybe a few steps away. I look up, and suddenly I think I recognize the lower part of his face.

"Nate…?"

Something feels wrong, though.

When he raises his head to look at me, I gasp. He does look a lot like Nate.

But his eyes are silver, and his hair is pitch black.

Moon Goddess. It's not Nate. It's his brother, the King. Why in the world would he be here, in the slums, alone? This is my first time meeting him, but there is no doubt. That man is way too scary and looks too much like Nate to be mistaken for anyone else. I try to remember his name. Damian, Damian Black. The eldest brother, Alpha of the Blood Moon, and alleged werewolf King of Silver City. No wonder everyone fears him, I can barely breathe in his presence!

In my pack, I am among the strongest, but I feel like a defenseless pup in front of this guy! How come I never felt that in front of Nate? Is it because this guy is currently furious and displaying his Alpha Aura carelessly? Is Nathaniel usually holding back? I have a hundred questions, but I have no idea what to do or how to react.

His silver eyes are piercing me like daggers, cutting me open, gauging me. I feel vulnerable. My inner wolf is torn between running away and fighting. Her instincts are messed up in front of a stronger alpha. This is not our territory, and we have no advantage here.

He comes closer, his eyes not leaving me at all. For a second there, I have one thought.

This guy is going to kill me.

But right when he's almost at my position, a shadow jumps in between us. Someone grabs my arms, and I'm pushed back.

"Damian, she's with me."

Nate. Nate just arrived, standing between me and his brother. He's holding me close, but his eyes are fixed on Damian. He doesn't seem scared though. More like wary, and he's making sure to hide me as much as he can from his brother's sight.

"Is this her?" whispers his brother.

His older brother has a gentler voice than I thought. I sense his murderous aura somewhat calm down, and it gets a bit easier to breathe. But why is he asking this? What does that mean? They both stay silent for a few seconds, but I guess they are mind-linking. I wish I knew what the brothers were saying. A few seconds later, Nathaniel turns to me, and immediately puts his hands on my cheeks, looking worried.

"Elena, what the hell are you doing here? Are you alright?"

Behind him, the King is already gone. I didn't hear him move at all, but we are definitely alone in this alley. Nate pushes back my wet hair on my shoulder, and his touch makes me shiver. Damn, it's only been a day, but I missed him.

"Sorry, I wanted to come to see you, but someone was following me, and..."

"What? Who was?" he asks, looking behind my shoulder like he was looking for someone.

I shake my head. I have no idea, but right now, I don't care. Unable to hold myself back, I step forward into his embrace, grabbing his shirt in my trembling fingers. I bury my face in his shoulder, and my tears start flowing as if something had just broken inside to let them out.

"Elena…"

Nathaniel immediately hugs me back, and I feel his hand on my drenched hair. I just keep crying like a child, unable to hold back. I just needed this. Nate's arms, around me, shielding me from anything that's been making me crazy these days.

We stay like this for a long time, in the rain, and he doesn't even ask. He just holds me, for as long as I need.

When my tears finally seem to stop a little, Nate takes my hand and guides me out of the slums. We walk in silence for a bit, still in the downpour. We are literally soaked when we finally reach a building that I don't recognize; I assume it's another one of his hotels. We stay against each other until we finally reach the entrance. When Nate opens the door with regular keys, I suddenly realize.

"This place…"

"It's my apartment. Come."

Surprised, I follow him inside. Actually, except for a few details, it feels like we could be in a hotel suite. The place is very clean, everything is in perfect order, and decorated with a modern taste. But there are shoes at the entrance, a few financial magazines on the table, and some personal items here and there.

"Elena, here."

He guides me to the bathroom, where he fills the bathtub with hot water before undressing himself. I won't refuse a good bath, I'm chilled to the bones. And that bathtub is big enough for two or even three people.

Nate gets naked in no time and gets in with a deep sigh of satisfaction. I abandon my clothes on the floor, perfectly aware that he is watching. Once I'm naked, I step in, and Nate guides me to sit in front of him, between his legs. I can finally relax, sitting with my back against his chest, his arms around me.

This is what I've needed all along… His warmth. I close my eyes, indulging myself in this bliss. I feel Nate pouring some hot water on my shoulders, helping me warm up. His lips, too, fleeting on my neck. But his hands are the best. Caressing me gently, spreading his warmth on my skin. He kisses my temple gently, and I feel his breath next to my ear.

"Better?" he asks softly.

"Much better."

He kisses my shoulder again and locks his arms around my waist, while we stay like this in a long silence. I can finally let go of all those dark thoughts that have been clouding my mind these last couple of days. I don't want to think of anything, just savor this little taste of happiness for a while.

His fingers gently brush my stomach, and I hear him breathing deeply like he's lost in his thoughts. I reach out for his hand, intertwining his fingers with mine. He hugs me a bit tighter.

"What were you doing there? You could have gotten killed."

"I told you, I just came to see you. I didn't expect to have to make such a detour. What about you? I didn't expect to meet your… the King, this way."

"I was just accompanying him. Someone had spotted a strange she-wolf in the slums. He checks every time."

"In case it's his mate," I guess in a whisper.

Nathaniel nods. I can barely imagine such devotion. It seems that no matter how scary the King is, nothing really matters to him but the mate he lost. I wonder what his mate must be like, to be a match for him, who's so strong and scary... Would she be scary as well? What kind of she-wolf is a good mate, a good Luna?

If only I had been Nate's fated mate... I've had this thought so often these days, it even scares me sometimes.

"Nate, I wanted to talk to you."

"About what?"

His voice indicates he suspected something. After all, I came all this way, in this shitty weather, totally unannounced, and bawled to him without warning. He took care of the emotional mess I am without question, but I should explain.

"My ex is coming back."

I feel him freeze. His whole body is tensed up, and I give him a few seconds.

"Okay… and?" he asks.

"And… I'm a fucking mess because of that."

"How so?"

I search for words, trying to think of a way to explain things to him without getting too deep into it. Nathaniel really doesn't need to know about all my shit, and Moon Goddess, I hope he never does.

"Is it the one you mentioned?"

I know he remembers our conversation, the one where I explained why I would never fall in love again. I slowly nod. I don't want to move, but I would be curious to see Nate's expression right now if he wasn't holding me tightly.

"Why is he coming back?"

"My Alpha had banned him for 5 years. I didn't think he would really come back. No one did. But he was spotted in the west, so there is no mistake."

I shiver just thinking about it. The idea of confronting Diego again, whatever he's become, is making me crazy.

"Elena, what did he do to you?"

I shake my head. I don't want to talk about it, and he knows that. I can feel his frustration, but there is no way I'm telling Nate. Moreover, I don't know what he would do if he did know, and that isn't good either. I don't want to implicate him any more than that in our pack's problems, and mine.

But to my surprise, he doesn't ask again. Instead, he suddenly holds me tighter and kisses my nape. It's not just sweet this time, it's more… sensual. I breathe in, Nate sucks and bites my skin gently, playing with it.

"I won't let him touch you," he suddenly whispers.

"W…What?"

"I'm serious, Elena."

If only he wasn't holding me so tight against him, I could see his expression, and have an idea of what he was thinking! But I can only feel his mouth, attacking my skin restlessly, his hands caressing me and holding me close against him.

"I could have him banished forever. Or kill him."

"No!"

I suddenly free myself from his grip and struggle to turn around and face him. I grab his face, as worried as I am serious. I look straight into his blue eyes.

"Nathaniel, no. Please. Don't you ever, ever get close to Diego."

"So, he's named Diego."

I growl, annoyed. That is so not the point! I can see the anger in his eyes, burning like fire under the ice. Thank Moon Goddess I haven't told him anything.

"Nate, I'm very serious. I don't want you to get involved with him, okay? Please. Let me handle him."

But Nate growls, not annoyed at me but the situation.

"To handle him? How? Elena, he's not even here and you're already freaking out. Whatever he did to you, it had to be big for him to get banned from his pack for five years!"

In my opinion, that sentence was too light. But that's not the point. I caress Nate's cheeks with my thumbs, hoping to keep him focused on me instead of Diego.

"Nate, no. This is my pack's issue, not yours. Don't worry about me, I'm strong enough, okay? Please, promise me you won't get involved."

Nathaniel is still obviously angry, and very unwilling to answer. I can almost see his inner turmoil, but I wait, hoping he will listen. He cannot act rashly. He's the King's brother, for Moon Goddess' sake!

"Nate…"

"Promise me you won't get involved with him either."

"What?"

"Elena, I'm not stupid. He did something big to you and traumatized you somehow."

"I'm not--!" I want to protest, but Nate interrupts me.

"Yes, he did. Don't lie, not to me. I know enough already, Elena. And I swear to Moon Goddess, if that guy takes one step into the Velvet Moon territory, I'll kill him."

There are a lot of words stuck in my throat right now, but none can come out when Nate is angry and determined like this. So, instead, I lean forward and kiss him.

He doesn't answer at first, but he doesn't push me away either. I knew he wouldn't. I insist a bit, playing with my lips on his, biting a bit, and insisting until he finally responds. Of course, our kisses are way too familiar now. We fight a bit, his mouth eager for more and mine trying to tame his. Our tongues collide for something deeper. Moon Goddess, I know I'm cheating, but I want him and not a fight about my ex. I can handle Diego. But not without Nate. I need him to be there, somewhere I know I can run to like I did tonight. My refuge, my warm place to be on rainy days like this.

Our kiss gets more intense, and so does my excitement. I want more, and I can feel his arousal as well. I straddle him, his hands running on my back, while my fingers play in his hair. The heat goes up, my body goes down. My heart is beating in my ears like the rain against the window. I want more, always more.

Chapter 13

"We need to talk."

He looks at me with a confused expression. I was waiting for him to come home, and he probably didn't expect that kind of greeting.

"Talk about what?"

"Nate, I… I won't be coming back here."

He frowns and I feel my heart waver a bit, but I can't change my mind now. I have been gathering my courage all afternoon leading up to this point. I cross my arms around me, but I can't bring myself to look him in the eye.

"What do you mean exactly?"

"I can't come back to the Velvet Moon territory, Nate, I think we should stop seeing each other."

"Why?"

He's starting to sound upset now. Hang on, you expected this much. I shake my head, trying to keep in mind all the excuses I gathered these past few days.

"Nate, I shouldn't be here in the first place and we both know it. Things have been going a bit too far these days. It's not what we had agreed on."

"Is that what it is? You're afraid of what we have nowadays? Are you scared of my brother, or your pack? I can—"

"It's not about any of that, Nate! It's about us, about me. I… You remember, when we first talked? You said you wanted one night. After that, we said it would be a simple relationship, no feelings involved."

"I also said we would play by your rules, Elena. That you get to decide."

"That's right. And right now, I decide that we should end this now before it gets too far. For the both of us."

I know he won't give up so easily. Not after all the amazing times we had together… So I have no choice but to do this. I take out that folder I found in his office. I'm genuinely annoyed about that one though, so it definitely helps. I see his blue eyes panic a bit as he recognizes it.

"Elena, that's not—"

"I don't give a damn, Nate. You had me investigated. I'm pretty sure you are using Boyan and Daniel too. I don't care about your reasons; this is not what I wanted."

He suddenly grabs it, throwing it in the trash bin before turning back to me, but I won't give in.

"Elena, I didn't want this. Damian and Isaac—"

"Nate, that's exactly the problem! Even if you don't want to, your whole pack is going to say no to me! And I don't want to fight with my pack for that reason either! I don't want a relationship where we have to investigate each other, sneak into each other's places in private, or hide to call each other!"

"That's how our relationship is, Elena! I decided I don't care what everyone else thinks about me being with you, I—"

"I don't want a relationship, Nate! I am not ready for that! My ex is coming back and this is going to be a hell of a mess already. I don't want to have to deal with you and your surveillance too! I don't want to deal with your brothers, your Beta, your exes!"

"What exes?" he frowns.

Shit, I shouldn't have mentioned that… Whatever.

"Listen, I didn't want to do it like this, okay? I just… I need to work on one problem at a time."

"So, I'm a problem now? And I only come after your ex?" he groans.

"Don't start, Nate. Maybe we'll see each other again when I'm done dealing with Diego."

"Oh, and I'm supposed to wait like a good boy for you to decide? What am I, a backup plan? I thought we had something serious going on. You know it."

I glare at him. He's making this harder than it needs to be!

"I thought we were supposed to be honest with each other, Nate."

"Honest? You never talk to me!"

"I have a past, and you knew that! I was honest when I at least told you that, and why I wouldn't want to get serious! Aren't you the one who was being dishonest? How long has it been since you had me investigated? How long ago did you break our promise?"

His expression suddenly gets a lot colder, and I feel a wall building between us.

"I didn't."

This hits me in the gut. I hesitate for just a second before I drop the question.

"You don't love me?"

"No."

... Fucking liar. We both are, but this still hurts.

"Fine," I mutter. "I guess we're good then."

I grab my stuff and leave before I change my mind and tell him the truth.

As agreed, Daniel is already waiting for me at the border. I get in the car and let out a big sigh. My best friend turns to me, worried.

"Are you sure?"

"I did what I had to, Danny. This is more important for now."

I take out the letter I received this morning. Just a simple card, with a question. But this is Diego's handwriting, no doubt. I crumple up the fucking "Missed me?" note that the bastard sent me. I don't even have the words for how much I hate him.

"Why didn't you just tell him?" asks Danny while starting the car.

But I shake my head. I already made my decision this morning. This past week with Nate was heaven. I lived without worries, with the best lover one could hope to wake up next to, every morning. I could have gotten seriously used to that, and easily too. But the longer I stayed, the more I felt like I was running away.

From my pack, and my problems. I avoided Xavier, Reagan, even Clark and Isabella. I avoided the days passing and Diego's return coming closer. Being with Nate was like a dream I didn't want to wake up from. Diego's message was a brutal fucking reminder. I have no idea how he knew where to send it to, or what his aim was, but it was a shock to me. No matter what, Diego was coming after me.

And I didn't want to involve Nate in that.

"I still think this isn't good, babe. To leave like that."

"Nathaniel would never have stopped at that. He already asked me twice if I wanted him to ban or kill Diego, Danny. I know he would break the rules of both his pack and mine and I can't let him do that for me. He's the King's brother, his position is too important to do that."

"But still, starting a fight?"

"That was all I could think of for him to let me go. Thank Moon Goddess I found this stupid folder this morning, it helped me come up with an excuse."

To be honest, I didn't find it by accident. I was looking for something that would make our fight a bit more genuine, but I didn't expect Nathaniel to keep a whole file on me and Diego. I still can't believe he knew I went to jail and didn't say anything about it. How long had he known for? He obviously read it, so does that mean he doesn't care about living with a criminal? About the ghosts of my past?

The more time I spent with Nate, the more it became obvious to me that we were moving on to a new relationship, something that couldn't be seen as simply friends with benefits. We kissed a lot for no reason, cuddled whenever we felt like it, and did pretty much everything together every night this week. Even the sex was much sweeter and more romantic, despite our carnal desire for each other.

If it wasn't for Diego, maybe I would have given us a chance, listened to our whims, and stayed longer at Nate's place. Maybe a few more days, and we would have become lovers without saying it.

"He said he doesn't love me."

"Well, that guy is either completely blind or very stubborn," replies Danny while turning left.

I chuckle. I know Nate was lying. He said what he thought would hold me back. Because that was the rule we had agreed on from the start.

But Moon Goddess, it's too late, way too late. I fell for that man, hard. For his kindness, his disarming honesty and smiles, and his gentle, electric blue eyes. The way he doesn't hesitate to caress or hug me, or how he kisses me softly. Damn, I already miss him.

I think about our argument again. What will he think? I purposely didn't give him the chance to speak as it was hard enough for me already. But even so, Nate still tried to make me stay, and that broke my heart. Because the truth is, I didn't want to leave him or make him think I wanted to. If things had been different, I would have trusted him a lot more than that, enough to confide in him about my past and let him back me up against my ex. I couldn't. Our relationship was too fresh for that, and I was scared that Diego would shatter it all before I had a chance to do anything. I was too afraid. I could stand to lose Nate because of our feelings, but if something happened to him because of my ex...

Daniel finally parks the car at our home an hour later. We stopped by the hospital to give flowers to my dad, but it's pretty late now, and I'm exhausted.

"What about Bobo?" I ask as Daniel opens the door.

"Too busy. I think his brother is giving him more work to keep him away from our territory."

For some reason, our apartment feels pretty lonely now. Damn, I didn't realize I would miss Nate so much. I change into my nightgown and curl up in my bed. I haven't slept here in a while. Has my room always been this cold and silent? I close my eyes, hoping everything will be fine. Between Nate and me, and tomorrow, too.

Tomorrow, the cursed day Diego is allowed back on our turf. I spend all night thinking about how to behave, what to say, and how I can ignore that bastard. The next morning, when I get up very early, I have a simple strategy in mind. It's Sunday, and for once, I'm up before Danny. Hence, he is shocked to find me making coffee when he comes out of his room about half an hour later.

"Damn, someone fell out of her bed."he whistles.

"More like I didn't sleep a wink," I sigh, going to the couch with my cup.

"Mmhmm. Bad thoughts?"

I nod with a frown before taking a sip. Daniel sighs before taking a cup for himself.

"What's the battle plan?"

"There isn't one, Danny. I've decided, I don't care about this jerk. I don't want anything to do with him, I'm done. He can do whatever the hell he wants as long as he stays the hell away from me."

Daniel stays silent for a few seconds and eventually comes to sit next to me on the couch.

"You know it's not going to be that easy, right, babe?"

"I know, but I'm not going to give in. I'm over whatever happened, Daniel, and that's what I will stick to until he understands. I don't want him back in my life. He had better stay the hell away, because I'm not going back to jail."

My best friend sighs and gently brushes my hair with his fingers.

"All right, you're the boss. Ignore the jackass until he gets bored. I bet Clark will give orders for the others to try and keep you two apart anyway. Okay, do you want some jam? Bonnie made a mean apricot jam."

I laugh and nod. Like any Sunday, Danny and I have breakfast together, chatting about our week with our respective lovers. To be honest, I feel like we haven't seen each other in forever, and it's good to spend time with just the two of us. I'm happy to hear his relationship with Bobo is going smoothly, despite the hardships that come from being from different packs. Seems like neither of them has talked to anyone else about this, not even their siblings. I remember Bobo's sister from the dinner, Tonia, and his older brother who is the King's Beta, such an important member of their pack.

"You think Levi knows?" I ask, taking a bite out of my bread.

"I bet he's too smart not to have caught on to something. He is always watching your back; it would be funny if he let me be. He argued a lot with Clark about Diego, you know. Those two better not meet either."

"Shit. I don't want to have Levi involved too."

His overprotective brother would definitely take my side and still hates Diego for what happened back then. Daniel licks the jam off his fingers, frowning a bit.

"He will get involved. You know Levi. Aside from being a beta to the bone, he has some feelings for you."

"Oh, shut up Danny, I am not talking about that."

"As you wish."

I am not blind to Levi's feelings for me, but I've become good at pretending. I already have enough to deal with in the love department nowadays. I finish my breakfast and head to the bathroom first, changing into a comfortable workout outfit: leggings and an oversized crop top.

"Whoa, that's one hot babe ready to do some punching."

"Come with me, Danny, you need to exercise sometimes."

He growls a bit.

"Are you hinting at something?"

"Yes, you're getting skinnier and losing muscle. Now get up and come train with me. I need someone who can keep up."

Daniel rolls his eyes but takes the rest of the breakfast dishes to the kitchen.

"Oh well, I guess it can't hurt from time to time."

Indeed, two hours later, we are just finishing the first round. Daniel is now growling at me, annoyed. Maybe because I won another match, the sixth in a row. I try to play innocent while grabbing some water.

"You agreed to train with me, babe," I remind him.

"I agreed to do training, not a beating you brute! Look at that! I'm going to have bruises all over! Bruises are not sexy, Whitewood."

I laugh a bit while he's still examining himself. Even if he complains, Daniel is a decent fighter. He may not be a match for me but having Levi or me as his training partner has shaped him into a good fighter. I'm kind of proud.

"Come on, babe, one more round?"

"You can have more rounds with the boxing sack, I'm done with you kicking my ass for today."

"Your scrawny ass."

"My perfect ass, if you want to ask my handsome and adorable boyfriend."

There he goes again, bragging about Boyan. At least he's not complaining anymore. I let him keep talking while I drink more water and go grab a towel, wiping off my sweat. A good sparring does make me feel a lot better. I have been lazy about training these days, but if I'm not seeing Nate anymore, I should probably focus on something else.

I check my phone, but nothing from him. Of course. He's probably still mad or at least perplexed by our fight from last night. No matter what, I hope this will be over soon, and I can go back to him. It may be a bit shameless to hope Nate will be that patient with me, but I somewhat believe he will be. I know what we had together was fucking good and real.

"Elena."

I turn to Daniel, wondering why he called me by my name all of sudden, but his eyes are set on the dojo's entrance. My wolf instantly starts growling. Damn.

Standing nonchalantly at the door, a tall silhouette with their arms crossed is staring right at us with a smile. I would recognize it anywhere. It's been five years and that asshole has barely changed. His black hair and dark skin. How he moves like a predator. He has a new scar on his face, across his left cheek, and a large tribal tattoo I had never seen before on his torso. He's only wearing ragged jeans, walking barefooted on the tatami.

Daniel moves to stand between me and him, but I gently stop my best friend. I don't care if he comes close. Diego walks up to us with an annoying smirk stuck on his face. Moon Goddess, how in the world did I ever fall for such a jerk like him. When he's a few steps away, he smiles at me, acting like a good guy.

"*Te extrañé, mi amor.*"

"Fuck off, Diego."

No matter how much you prepare yourself, I guess you can't do much against your worst nightmare. Strangely, reality is very different from the mess I had imagined. I didn't think I could stay so composed, or even stand being in the same room as him. I thought maybe I would go insane, scream, or jump at him to kill him.

But I don't feel any of that right now. Seeing my ex standing there in front of me, smiling at me as if nothing had happened, fucking disgusts me, and my wolf is growling loudly too, but there isn't much more. I realize it now.

I'm furious at him, and Moon Goddess, I still hate him to the core. But some of that hate has been subdued and forgotten by now. I am not the same helpless, idiotic teenage girl I was back then. I'm older. I have moved on. I found a new love.

Diego hasn't.

I turn around to ignore him and signal to Daniel that I want us to spar again. My best friend understands, and we exchange a few hits.

Honestly, I knew it wouldn't be enough to drive Diego away. Instead, he stays on the side of the ring.

"What? I don't even get a welcome kiss?"

I ignore him. Daniel throws a punch at me, and I manage to avoid it, sending back an uppercut. He growls a bit and kicks back. Maybe because of Diego's presence, Danny is angry, and his punches are fiercer.

"Elena, I'm talking to you."

Well, I don't give a damn. I keep ignoring him, even after he calls me one more time. I focus on my fight with Danny instead, and my best friend manages to keep me busy for a while. That is until Diego jumps on the ring to get in between us, dangerously close to me. I step back as a reflex. My wolf is furious. She doesn't want him near us, not after what he did to our baby.

"I said, I am talking to you," he growls.

"And I said fuck. Off."

I repeated that slowly, glaring right at him, showing him that he doesn't have any fucking right to order me around. He frowns, visibly a bit surprised. Seriously, what in the world did he expect? For me to be happy about his return? Really? After all that shit I went through five years ago?

"Five years without seeing me, and that's what I get? Fuck off, really? *Estás enojado conmigo, amor*?"

"Last time, Diego. You get the fuck out of my ring and out of my dojo," I warn him.

He seems shocked to see me standing my ground. I'm proud of myself. I don't even let him see how angry I really am and stand my ground without fail. Even I didn't think I could control my emotions so well.

Diego seems to hesitate a bit and slowly takes a few steps back. I can tell he is re-evaluating me, changing his attitude upon seeing my reaction.

"We are not done talking," he growls.

I watch him leave without answering, but I make sure to glare his way and let my wolf growl with all her might until he's out of sight. As soon as he's exited the dojo, I take a deep breath again.

"What a son of a dog, are you okay, babe? Damn, I don't think your Alpha Aura has ever felt that scary! If you were growling at me, I swear my pants wouldn't be dry right now!"

I chuckle. Only Danny can crack jokes at times like these. I sigh and rest my arms on the ropes of the ring, gazing in the direction Diego went. Around us, the few people who listened are sending glances my way, but I ignore them to talk to Daniel.

"He's going to be pissed now."

"You think?"

"I'm sure. He will be mad that I ignored him; that's the worst for him. I made him understand he won't be able to control me like before and he will not like it."

"Whatever. If he's unhappy, it's his problem. Come on, I'm done getting my butt kicked. Lunch is on me today."

I wish it was that easy. I know Diego won't let it slide. Nevertheless, I grab my bag and follow Daniel. Just as we exit the gym, my cousin Iris suddenly walks up to us.

"Elena! I'm so sorry I couldn't let you know earlier, Diego is back," she says, out of breath.

"I know. He was here just a minute ago. Don't worry, I'm fine."

"Really? I asked Dad to not let him back into the pack, but–"

"I'm fine, Iris. Xavier can decide whatever he wants," I reply.

"Come on, sweetheart, we were about to go get lunch. Are you joining us?" asks Daniel with a smile.

"Sure! Should I call Chris too?"

It's been a while since I ate with my cousins. For some reason, I have never gotten very close to them. Maybe because their dad never really liked me. However, Iris is only a few months younger than me, and Chris loves training with me.

They join me and Daniel for lunch, and we decide to go to George's. Because of their Sunday brunch, the place is crowded, and we have to wait at the entrance for a table to become available.

"Danny! Elena!"

We turn our heads. Across the restaurant, Levi is waving at us. He is at a large table with three other guys from the pack, including Orpheus. Danny gives me a little poke.

"Here's our entrance ticket! Come on, Iris, Chris!"

We skip the line to join their table, and Daniel's older brother and his friends welcome us with a big smile.

"I guess we had the same idea!"

"This is the only place that is almost as good as Mom's brunch," says Daniel.

"Hi, Elena, princess!"

Orpheus gives me a hug, and the two other guys, Jace and Kentin, greet me too before welcoming my cousins. They scoot over a bit on the leather bench and find a couple more chairs so we can all sit together.

"We just ordered, too!" says Jace. "You can just add whatever you want, Orpheus is buying lunch today."

"Seriously? What bet did you lose?" asks Chris with a smirk.

But Orpheus blushes a bit and refuses to answer, so Jace does in his stead.

"That idiot bet he could beat Eric!"

"You should have bet on hunting instead," sighs Daniel. "Eric is good at fighting but he's too clumsy to hunt anything."

"I thought this time I could do it!" insists Orpheus.

"No one can beat Eric, aside from Elena, you dummy."

"I'll beat him soon!" exclaims Chris, full of confidence.

I chuckle and ruffle his hair a bit.

"You need a bit more muscle and training before that happens, kid."

"At this rate, Xavier will pick Elena as his heir before that happens!" says Jace with a smirk.

"*Uh oh. Hey, babe.*"

"*What?*"

"*Look at Iris.*"

I follow Daniel's little chin movement to look at my cousin Iris, sitting next to Levi. She is glaring at Jace, looking pissed. Is it because he's making fun of her little brother? I didn't think she would get mad at such a lousy joke. Jace notices too and stops laughing.

"Sorry, sorry, I was just kidding, heh? Come on, I'll pay for the drinks."

Since Iris is an alpha too, he probably couldn't stand being glared at. But she soon calms down and sighs.

"That's fine."

I smile a bit. I forgot Iris is always a bit uptight about the pack's rules. The guys move on to discuss the last fights that happened within the pack, joking about who is making progress or not. Meanwhile, George spots us and comes to take our orders, adding a freebie for Daniel. Those two are super close after all. When he leaves, Jace turns to me.

"By the way, Elena, I heard Diego's back?"

He immediately gets a lot of glares and goes white. I sigh.

"Yes, he is."

"I can't believe Xavier let that fucker back in," growls Orpheus.

"It's a difficult situation. He belongs to our pack and is a good fighter too," says Iris, trying to defend her father's decision.

"Come on, Iris, don't defend that asshole. Everyone knows what an asshole he was to Elena," growls her brother.

"But--"

"Elena, if you're looking for a new boyfriend just to piss him off, I'm available!" says Jace with a little wink.

Daniel rolls his eyes.

"Moon Goddess, Jace, that is so uncalled for, dude. Get off your high horse a little, will ya? There's a whole line waiting to date my babe, and you're at the bottom. The very bottom, Jace."

"I don't wanna get anywhere near your bottom, Danny," mumbles Jace.

Levi and Orpheus, who are sitting on each side of that idiot, immediately smack him behind the head at the same time.

"Ouch! What the hell?"

"Thank you," says Daniel with a satisfied smile.

Iris and I laugh, almost spitting out our coffees. Damn, Jace is an idiot but a funny one. Levi growls at him when he protests again, putting an end to his childishness.

"But seriously, Elena, we got your back," says Orpheus to me.

I smile at him.

"Thanks."

They all give me some word or gesture to say they are on my side no matter what. I wish things had been this way back then. But the truth is, no one knew exactly what was going on between me and Diego.

Like Danny and I, Diego was some sort of pariah among the pack. His father was on bad terms with the Alpha and was always training him to become stronger. He had a rough, violent upbringing. His father justified anything with the werewolf condition. As an alpha, he had to be strong, to be tough, and not show his weakness. But Diego did end up showing his one weakness: me. I was the only girl he got along with, the only one he really liked. We fell in love like any other teens would have had they hung out together every day for years. We had grown up together. There wasn't anything we hid from one another, same with Danny.

He was my teenage crush, as well as my rival. We fought a lot. Because we were alphas, we fought seriously every time. But as I learned later, being an alpha doesn't justify violence. Diego didn't learn that. He fought with anyone in the pack, weaker or stronger than him, and there weren't many people who could stand up to him aside from me. As the years went by, his tendency to violence got worse. He injured several people in the pack under the pretense of "serious training," including Danny. The Alpha got mad, but I would always find excuses for his behavior.

I was an idiot in love, and I didn't know any better.

"Elena, babe?"

I return to reality when Danny puts his hand on my knee.

"Sorry, Danny, you were saying?"

"Your phone. It's vibrating in your bag. You might want to check it."

I almost jump down to grab the bag at my feet and take out my phone. It's a text from Nate. I smile but then worry. Is he mad about yesterday? What is this about? Did he believe me? Or not? I'm not sure what I want… I mumble some excuse about going to the bathroom and take my phone with me. Danny gives me a little wink. I take a deep breath in the unisex restroom and open Nate's text.

Chapter 14

"Stop staring at it."

I blush. Daniel caught me reading Nate's text again. I try to put my phone away, but Ben grabs it before I do.

"Elena's got a boyfriend?" he suddenly asks.

"Give that back!" I yell, annoyed.

I try to climb over the couch to get my smartphone back, but Daniel decides to team up with his brother and holds me back, long enough for Ben to throw it to Bonnie.

"This is so cute. Text from Nate: 'I'm sorry we fought. Can we talk? I miss you,'" she reads.

"Bonnie!" I protest.

Come on, even she betrays me to gang up on me with her brothers? She smiles and gives it back to me only because everyone's already heard the content! The Lewis twins sit on either side of me, Bonnie grabbing the popcorn bowl and Ben annoying me to no end with his questions.

"Who is Nate? Your boyfriend? Ex-boyfriend? Crush? Potential boyfriend?"

Daniel is laughing behind his little brother's back. Can't he help me out of this, that idiot! When I went along with him for a movie night at their family house, I didn't think I would fall into a trap about who's going to gossip more about my private life! Their father laughs, sitting in his armchair next to us.

"Ben, enough. It's Elena's private life, don't put your nose into it."

The twins laugh a bit but eventually, the conversation changes to who will have the final word about which movie we will watch. I sigh and scoot over to get next to Daniel, pinching him as revenge until he squeals.

"That wasn't necessary!"

"You deserve it, you traitor!"

"All right, all right, sorry. But you've been glued to your phone, girl.

Just text him if you miss him that much already."

I sigh.

"You know I can't, Daniel."

He rolls his eyes.

"Yeah, whatever."

Half an hour later, Bonnie got the last word, and we are watching some catchy sci-fi movie, something pretty interesting with spies and con men. Suddenly, Joseph jumps up, surprising all of us. Ben even drops his soda on the couch.

"What the heck, Dad?"

But Joseph stays standing, frowning, as if something was bothering him. I understand right away he's mind-linking. His eyes turn to me, and I immediately get a hunch as to what this is about.

"Is it Diego?" I ask, worried.

"Yeah. He's fighting Eric and Jace."

"Shit!"

I grab my jacket and prepare to follow Joe, but Danny suddenly grabs my arm.

"Babe, you really shouldn't go."

I hesitate for a second. Damn, I know I shouldn't. I really shouldn't get involved in anything Diego is involved in. I spent the last three days avoiding him, brushing him off, and ignoring him, but it wasn't easy. He almost fought with Levi yesterday just because I refused to answer when he talked to me at the pack's reunion.

But…

"Daniel, if he injures them, I won't forgive myself for it."

Danny spurts out a profanity I really don't hear often from his mouth and comes after us. The twins are about to come too, but their father orders them not to. We run outside, all three of us shape-shifting right away into our wolf forms.

Damn that guy! He hasn't been back for a fucking week and he's already messing with others!

Joe guides us all the way to another street, actually pretty close to where we were. When we arrive, there's already a crowd around the fight. We have to growl to get through it, until I can see the scene.

A dark-gray and a brown wolf are fighting, all claws and fangs out. It's a mess, there's fur and blood flying. I immediately recognize Eric's dark gray wolf, covered in blood. He is fighting angrily, growling, and standing his ground. The other wolf, however, barely has any injuries, but its maw is covered in blood.

When he is about to attack again, I instantly jump in and growl furiously. He stops his attack, stumbling to the side. My wolf warns him in an outraged growl.

"*Don't you fucking touch him!*"

"*Elena.*"

He steps forward, but I growl even louder.

"*Fuck off! Get away!*"

He stays nearby, though, walking left and right as if there was a perimeter around me he couldn't approach. Joe, in a dark brown blur of fur, suddenly gets in between us, growling at Diego too. But Joseph is a beta, and Diego isn't afraid to growl back. I feel Daniel's father trying hard to stand his ground, but I know how strong Diego is. I step in front of him and growl again, keeping Diego from approaching.

"*Let me finish him. He asked for it!*"

"*Don't you fucking touch Eric! You stay away!*"

He tries to come toward us, and my wolf growls even louder as a warning.

"*Don't.*"

"*You can't attack me anyway. Let me finish him!*"

I keep growling, ignoring the mind-link to use my wolf's full aura.

Diego takes another step, but suddenly, a big silver wolf jumps over my head and hits him full force, growling.

"*What the hell is going on here?*"

Clark's furious voice resonates in our heads, and a lot of werewolves that were watching on the sides until now flee the scene quickly, unwilling to be exposed to the Alpha's wrath. Only a few of us remain, and that's when I finally notice Jace, his wolf knocked out on the side. I run to him, worried, while Joe stays by Eric's side.

Clark's growls are directed right at Diego, but he doesn't stop growling despite facing the Alpha.

"*Diego, are you fucking trying to piss me off? Attacking pack members!*"

"*They started it. You should discipline them better, Clark. Those bastards don't even know how to show respect to an alpha.*"

I growl even more furiously. He is obviously doing this to piss me off! Of course he's doing it on purpose, this dirtbag! My wolf wants to attack him, make him pay for what he did! I keep growling, and Clark does too.

"*Shut up! Don't you dare start fights on my turf, with anyone! I don't care who instigated it, Diego, everything was fine until you came back and I'm not an idiot! This is a warning!*"

Diego turns his head away, not submitting but not admitting to his wrongs either. I'm so mad at this bastard! Jace is unconscious, and Eric needs to go to the hospital! How could they be stupid enough to even agree to fight him?

Joseph pushes Eric with his head. With the light rain falling, the blood is slowly washing off from his injuries, but he obviously needs stitches. The beta keeps pushing him to move in the hospital's direction. They both leave, and two other people from our pack run over to carry Jace.

Clark growls to chase away the few people left, and now it's only Diego and us.

"*I don't know what game you're playing, Diego, but it won't last long. Next time you pull some shit like this, I'm banning you again, and for good this time!*"

I can't tell if Diego is listening to him or not, his eyes are riveted on me. I'm still growling, and Daniel has come over to my side to growl at him with me.

Clark has to run off to the hospital, but he keeps growling at Diego until he's gone. As soon as our Alpha is out of sight, my ex walks over. I growl in warning.

"*I told you to stay the fuck away from me.*"

"*Now at least I got your attention. Do I have to injure your friends every time? Or should I kill one?*"

"*You sicko.*"

But he ignores Daniel as if it was just the two of us.

"*So, what's it gonna be, Elena? Shall we do this the easy way or the hard way?*"

"*What do you want? We are done, Diego. I don't want to see you, hear you, or even breathe the same air as you!*"

"*Really? Do you have to act so pissed off? Just because we had a fight before we parted?*"

I'm beyond furious right now. A fight? He calls what happened a mere fight? I want to kill him! But Daniel holds me back by biting my paw and then pulling my tail. I know I can't fight Diego, but damn, I can't even stand the sight of that bastard!

"*We didn't have a fight, Diego, you tried to fucking kill me!*"

"*No, you were the one who stabbed me, Elena! Who was trying to kill who, exactly?*"

Moon Goddess, I still remember it all, way too vividly. Like it was yesterday. Every word, every hit, every wound. Like a fucking nightmare I have to live over and over again. I growl, barely containing my rage.

"*You fucking raped me, Diego. You started it the second I said no and you kept insisting. You did it, you did that to me, and I fucking fought back exactly as I should have!*"

"*What the hell is wrong with you? That wasn't rape, you were my girlfriend! I'm a wolf, and your mate, I could fuck you anytime I wanted! That wasn't rape, that was merely us playing around! We are alphas, Elena, that was just a game like we always played! Because that's what we've always done, right? Fighting, testing our limits!*"

I can feel Daniel's wolf, so disgusted at Diego's words that he wants to jump in and kill him too. But I'm so furious it actually helps me focus and answer him coldly, like the current beneath the ice.

"*No. There was a fucking limit, and you didn't care about it. You never knew when to stop. You didn't care about hurting me or anyone else. You thought I said no to 'playing' because that's what you wanted to think, Diego. Being your girlfriend never meant it would be fine to fucking have sex with me when I didn't want it.*"

"*Is that what you told the pack? That I raped you, really? Was it fun to play the victim to Clark and the others? You liked it, Elena, you--*"

"*I LOST MY CHILD TRYING TO FIGHT YOU OFF! TELL ME HOW I COULD HAVE EVER WANTED THAT!*"

He growls back at me, acting angry for the first time.

"*I didn't know you were pregnant! You didn't tell me, how could I have known, huh? You fucking brought it upon yourself! The child died all because of you!*"

Before I can even react, I suddenly see Daniel jump at Diego. I scream.

"*DANNY, NO!*"

For a second, I'm the most terrified I've ever been in my entire life. I think that's it; my best friend is going to get killed in front of my eyes.

But right before they make contact, two other wolves jump in, pushing Danny to the side and out of Diego's way. I immediately run in to bite my best friend's ear, standing between him and Diego, and keeping him from getting killed.

"*You idiot! You could have gotten yourself killed!*"

Daniel doesn't listen to me; he's still growling furiously at Diego. However, with Levi right next to me holding him back too, he can't get through. His older brother is growling at him as well, trying to get him to calm down.

"*Let me through, Levi, this sucker needs a lesson!*"

"*Enough, Danny! You're only going to get hurt and punished! Back off!*"

While the two brothers are arguing loudly with growls and through mind-linking, I glance back. An old, white, and silver wolf is furiously growling at Diego and keeping him away from us.

"*You take one step forward and I swear you'll lose a limb, you little mutt.*"

"*Fuck off, Reagan!*"

But my mentor is not having it and is standing her ground. Diego's definitely not scaring a veteran like her, especially when she's this angry. She's showing her fangs and I know she is more than able to fight Diego. He knows it too, as he goes back and forth, trying to find a way to get to me and Daniel, but he is not getting one step closer.

She growls again.

"*Walk away before I really lose it and kill you, damn dog! Now!*"

Diego growls in response, but Reagan is even scarier. His tail and ears betray him. He's acting tough but he is scared and wary of my mentor. He slowly steps back, growling but also showing his defeat. I can't believe she really got him to step back and leave us alone. Reagan stands guard for a while, making sure Diego's gone for good.

I can finally catch my breath a bit. This tension is too much for me. Moon Goddess, I haven't felt this panicked in a long while. Daniel finally seems to calm down, shaking his head.

"*Danny.*"

"*What the fuck happened?*"

I explain everything that happened before Levi and Reagan jumped in while keeping an eye on Daniel. My mentor growls, annoyed.

"*Damn your Alpha. He should never have allowed that scum back onto your territory. See what's happened already.*"

"*Let's just go home for now. Your family must be worried, Danny. Reagan, can you go check up on Eric and Jace for me?*"

"*Sure. I have a few words for your Alpha.*"

She walks away, taking the direction of the hospital. I'm so freaking tired. Levi mind-links us, not hiding his annoyed tone.

"*That was fucking reckless of you, Danny. You could have gotten hurt!*"

"*Did you even hear what that asshole told Elena, Levi? I was not going to let that slide!*"

"*Daniel, enough. I don't give a damn what Diego thinks or says, okay? I know where I stand on that matter and I don't want to discuss it. Now can we go home, please? I'm cold and my fur is freaking soaked.*"

The downpour is drenching us, and I really don't want to get sick again. I have a headache already. Daniel growls a bit, unhappy, but the tawny wolf eventually agrees to follow us back to the Lewis house.

By the time we get back, my headache is way worse. Bonnie makes me a hot cup of tea and hands me some medicine while Daniel and Levi, back in their human forms, explain to the rest of the family what happened. It's a pitiful scene, the three of us soaking wet in the Lewis' salon, towels on our heads. I had to borrow clothes from Rachel and one of Levi's old sweaters too.

"You shouldn't have gone," sighs their mom. "What if one of you had been injured, like Jace and Eric!"

"You think Diego is going to get punished?" asked Ben.

I exchange a look with Levi.

"Clark gave him some sort of warning. It's probably a bit complicated. If he banishes a wolf he had just let back in the pack, it will be bad for his position. People will think the Alpha isn't making good decisions."

"He obviously isn't!" says Daniel. "What kind of idiot would let a jerk like Diego back into the White Moon clan! That guy is like a pest! Wherever he goes you can be sure there is going to be some sort of trouble!"

"I wonder what he was doing for five years outside of the city," whispers Bonnie.

"Who cares! He should have never come back and that's it. If only he could have gotten himself killed or something," grumbles Daniel.

"Enough, enough!" his mom says to stop the conversation. "I don't want to hear any more about that disgusting person! You change the subject to whatever you kids want, but enough of this!"

Everyone obeys and a heavy, awkward silence follows. Eventually, Bonnie and Ben agree to continue with the movie night and pick another movie to watch. I exchange a look with Daniel and Levi, and we agree silently. I don't want to talk about Diego anymore, either. This headache is just getting worse and killing me.

After a few minutes, I stand up and excuse myself to go to the bathroom. Maybe a bit of fresh water on my face will help. Gosh, I haven't felt this bad in a while. It couldn't possibly be my period, I had it just last week.

"*Help me.*"

What the hell? I hear a voice echoing in my head, like someone I know. Who is mind-linking me? It's not even someone from the pack! Aside from me, I don't know anyone who would be able to-

"*Help me!*"

I feel weird. I'm cold, and out of breath. So fucking cold, as if I was outside, in the rain, under that downpour. What the… I look at my face in the mirror, clenching my fists on the sink as if I'm about to fall. I look behind my shoulder as if someone were there, someone is pursuing me. What the hell is wrong with me?

Who's voice is that? It's a woman, no, a girl's voice I've never heard before. Yet, it's resonating like an echo in my head, like someone talking underwater or behind a wall.

"*Run, run…*"

Who is running? To where? Is she in danger?

I stagger, trying to distinguish between what's real and what's in my head. Her voice is so strong, I have to fight to remember where I am.

"*He will kill me!*"

I start crying, irrepressibly. I'm scared, I'm so scared. I crouch down, unable to keep my balance. My tears pour out, without me being able to control them. I don't know what's going on!

"Elena? Elena, are you okay?"

Bonnie just appeared at the entrance of the bathroom to find me sitting down and crying. She runs to me, putting her hands on my shoulders.

"Elena, what's wrong? Elena? Danny! Levi! Mom! Elena, tell me what's wrong, please?"

But I have no idea what's wrong with me, or why I'm so cold and scared. A few seconds later, half the Lewis family is around me, trying to soothe me and get me to calm down. Their mom even puts a blanket around me, and Daniel checks me everywhere to look for an invisible injury.

"Babe, talk to me, what's wrong? Did something happen?"

I just shake my head and struggle to calm down. I should probably try to ignore that voice, break that link between her and me, but for some reason, I can't. I don't want to lose it, to lose that connection.

At some point, I realize Levi is carrying me out of the bathroom. I'm taken to the couch, where they surround me again, trying to decide on what to do.

"Should we get a doctor?" asks Bonnie, worried.

"She is not injured, it looks like a panic attack. Can you grab the tablets in my bag? Levi, go get another blanket, she's shivering. Get the thermometer, too! Mom, can you make us some hot chocolate?"

Everyone runs to do whatever Daniel said, while I'm still struggling. My crying has stopped, and I'm getting less and less scared too. It's like it's fading away.

"Babe? Elena, are you with me? Talk to me, babe."

"I'm fine."

Daniel rolls his eyes.

"How are you fine? I've been trying to get you to talk or mind-link for at least ten minutes! What happened? Do you need anything?"

I try to catch my breath and think.

"Can I get something to drink? My throat feels awful."

"Mom's making it. Elena, what was that? Your skin is freaking cold, too. That wasn't a panic attack, right?"

"No… I think someone mind-linked me?"

Danny and Bonnie exchange a look, surprised. Behind them, I notice Ben's on the phone, talking about my condition to someone.

"Mind-linked you? Someone in the pack?"

"No, that's the weird part. I think she was someone outside of the pack."

"Wow, wait. I thought you were the only one who could do that?"

Abigail comes back before I can answer and puts a huge mug of hot chocolate in my hands, and I drink it right away. Levi comes back at the same time, carrying a blanket, and covers me up with it. He sits beside me and rubs my back to help me warm up while all the others sit on the table, the couch, or the floor in front of me. Daniel quickly tells them all what I just said.

"Sweetie, are you sure?" asks Abigail. "Aside from you, no one can mind-link someone who isn't part of the pack."

"Could it be someone you just didn't recognize?" says Ben.

"No, it felt totally different. It sounded like she was very far away, but I feel like I've heard her voice before, a very long time ago. Her wolf felt like... like mine."

They all exchange looks, while I take a sip of that hot chocolate. Moon Goddess, it's hot but it feels good.

"What if… it's someone from your family?"

I almost drop my cup and look at Bonnie, totally surprised. What… What did she just say? Her mother frowns, looking lost in her thoughts for a while.

"Bonnie's theory could explain it… The only other way you can mind-link someone who isn't from the same pack as yours is if they are your family member."

"Either that or this person has the same power as Elena," says Ben.

"If that were the case, I doubt this person would have reached out to her specifically."

Levi's right. If I was in utter panic like the girl I heard, I would have reached out to anyone, not to one specific person, but I felt like I was the only one with her at that time, if she even felt me at all.

"I'm not even sure she realized she was mind-linking me. She was in total panic, like she was in great danger. She kept saying someone was about to kill her. And I could feel she was outside, in that rain, as if I were too…"

"How did it stop, then?" asks Ben.

I shake my head.

"I'm not sure. It was very weak, to begin with, and it just faded away, like she was falling asleep or losing consciousness."

They all keep quiet for a few seconds, while I try to find that link again. This is so weird. It was as if the connection had reached out from the surface for a few seconds, and suddenly went away again… so confusing.

I try to warm myself up for a few minutes. Abigail, Ben, and Daniel are discussing what else could have caused it. Abigail even wants me to see a doctor, but my temperature is back to normal, and whatever happened, it's gone. Meanwhile, Bonnie is curled up next to me, sipping her own hot chocolate too. Levi has his arm around my shoulders, listening to them without taking part.

"Your headache?" he asks in a whisper.

"Gone," I sigh. "Probably something to do with the mind-linking as well."

I keep thinking about what Bonnie suggested. What if that girl, whoever it was, was really part of my family? Could we really be related? Our connection felt real, like something I had forgotten from long ago. I try to seek for remnants of that link, but my wolf is as clueless as I am. This is so strange.

Joseph and Micah come home, and everyone turns to them. Micah is in his wolf form, and completely soaked. Bonnie immediately brings him one of the towels to help her blind brother dry his fur. Joseph, too, gets a towel for his hair.

"Something happened."

"Elena's fine, dad," says Ben.

"It's not about Elena. Or Diego. Something's up with the Blood Moon pack, they've gone crazy."

I immediately get worried, thinking about Nate.

"Crazy?"

"Yeah. Clark and Xavier are freaking out. Their whole clan is running through the streets of Silver City. They are growling at all the borders like they are going to trespass. Rumor has it they already went to the Gold Moon and Jade Moon territories, totally unannounced."

"Moon Goddess. Could those be clans who refused to meet them? Is it a punitive expedition?"

"No, they met with the Jade Moon last Saturday."

A few of the siblings realize I shouldn't know that information and send me a glance, but Abigail is totally focused on the matter.

"Do you think they will attack?" asks Ben.

"I don't know, son. This is a first, no one knows what to do. The King hasn't said a thing, and their people haven't told us anything either. With so many people running around, it's chaotic outside, so Clark sent everyone home for now."

They continue to discuss what could be going on for a few seconds, but I slowly walk away, followed by Danny. I take out my phone.

"What are you- Moon Goddess, you're calling him?" whispers Danny.

I just nod and press the call button. Moon Goddess, I'm calling him when I haven't replied to his text in days... It rings for a while. Could it be that he's really not available? Or injured? I'm making up all kinds of stupid scenarios for a while, but Nate doesn't answer.

"What the hell!" I growl, frustrated.

"He's not picking up?"

"No..."

I try to call him again, with no luck. I give up and just send him a text, asking him to call me as soon as he can. Is he ignoring me, maybe? Daniel takes me back to the salon where Joseph and Levi are arguing about what to do.

"What if they attack?!"

"Levi, Xavier said to stay home. Nothing's happened for now, so we should stay home and wait. Maybe it's just an issue with their pack."

"But our borders-!"

"They're staying on their land, and they are not threatening us. Now calm down, you're going to make everyone worry twice as much. Ben,

Bonnie, Micah, go upstairs. It's late already."

The three younger siblings obey right away, leaving the room even if it's not actually that late. Abigail gets up to call Rachel. I sigh and sit back on the couch, curling up on my corner. What the heck is going on? Unhappy, Levi leaves, followed by his Dad, leaving me and Daniel alone.

"Moon Goddess, that's way too many emotions for one day," sighs Daniel.

I couldn't have said it any better. I keep looking at my phone, hoping to hear from Nate. I'm dozing off when it finally vibrates a few minutes later.

"Elena?"

"Moon Goddess, Nate, what's going on? Are you okay?"

"What? Yes, I'm fine. It's a bit chaotic here."

"They said your pack is at our border!" I whisper, hoping no one but Daniel can hear my conversation.

"It's okay, Elena, we are going back now. Something happened, I… I might not be available for a few days. I'll be in the hospital; I can't really call you whenever I want."

"Moon Goddess, the hospital? Are you injured?"

"No, no, not me, don't worry. Someone, uh… close. I have to watch over them for a while. Just… don't worry, okay? I promise I'll call you later."

I finally calm down a bit, letting out a sigh of relief.

"Okay. Anytime you want."

I hear him chuckle.

"It's nice."

"What?"

"Having you worry about me. I thought we were fighting."

"We're not fighting. I just said I needed a break to cool off."

I'm dying of embarrassment, and Daniel is looking at me like I'm crazy too. He kicks my leg, mouthing "you idiot" with his lips.

"A break, okay, well, I guess I need my share of a break for now too. But I'll contact you later. If that's okay?"

Facing me, Daniel is repeatedly making a big X with his arms and whispering "no, no!" but I ignore him.

"Okay. Later then."

Chapter 15

"You think this is too much?"

Daniel rolls his eyes at me. He's lying on our couch, surrounded by his notes for his presentation tomorrow about his samples or whatever. Meanwhile, I'm busy trying on a dress, something short and sexy.

"Girl, you are too much. There's going to be a fucking riot if you walk around wearing that napkin on your booty."

"Danny, you're not helping. I just can't find the right thing."

"Moon Goddess, the guy has seen you naked a hundred times! Why would he care if you're wearing last season's Chanel or a trash bag? We both know it's going to end up on the floor anyway."

I throw my dress at him, annoyed.

"I haven't seen him in a week, babe, and the last time I did, I yelled at him."

"With valid reasons."

"With a schedule, Daniel."

"You should have kept with it! One week?! Every time you take one step forward, it's two steps back with Black. You two are like magnets that just can't stay away from each other. It's painful to watch, I swear."

I sigh and look down at the pile of clothes at my feet. I turn to Daniel again, worried.

"You think I'm making a mistake, right? Seeing him again?"

Daniel seems to hesitate for a bit, then shakes his head.

"Honestly, Black is still a hundred times better than Diego, so… I don't know. This is all super complicated, especially with the pack's stuff and all. I feel like I'm watching Romeo and Juliet, the modern and adult version."

He's not wrong, sadly. Whatever we will be doing tonight, we are not supposed to. I have to sneak out of our territory, and Nate has to avoid his brothers. The worst thing is, I don't actually care about all that. I just want to see him, badly.

It's strange, but seeing Diego again has made me realize how much I love Nathaniel. As if the contrast between the two of them had made it more obvious. I growl and pick a sparkly white skirt.

"This one?"

"Yeah, with your blue top and dangly earrings. Seriously, Elena, you have to be careful. Do you want me to accompany you to the border? I really don't like you going out like this when Diego is in the neighborhood. There's no telling if that guy will listen to the boss' order to leave you alone."

"Don't worry, I'll be careful. Can I borrow your jacket?"

I finish getting ready, sending glances at the clock from time to time. Damn, I can't keep still, and I'm an hour early! Nate proposed we meet at The Rain, the nightclub where we first met. It's deep in his territory, surprisingly. Is it because he can't go too far from the hospital?

Boyan's recent texts explained the situation to both me and Daniel. The King finally found his lost mate. She's in critical condition, hence he and Nathaniel were appointed to watch her these last few days. Poor girl… At least she was finally found and reunited with her fated mate. I wonder what it's like to be chosen as the King's partner.

Gloomy thoughts of Nate's former fated mate come to haunt me again. Moon Goddess, I hate thinking about it.

I sigh and grab my keys, putting on my shoes.

"Babe, you're an hour early!" exclaims Danny, shocked.

"I can have a drink while I wait, okay? And you need some peace and quiet to study, no?"

"Don't use me as your excuse, you impatient babe!"

I stick my tongue out at him and leave the apartment. Daniel's not wrong, I'm just so excited and restless that I'm embarrassed at myself. I check my phone and Nate's text again, but nothing has changed. I walk out to the parking lot, looking for Daniel's car when I suddenly hear a noise behind me. I turn around by reflex to check, and almost immediately growl.

Diego's there on a huge bike.

"Going somewhere, love?"

Oh, Moon Goddess, I don't want to deal with that asshole right now. I ignore him and keep walking to the car, a bit faster. I hear him loudly start his bike, and he suddenly rides right in front of me, so close he almost runs over my feet!

"What the hell, Diego! Fuck off!" I yell.

"You're well dressed, mi amor. Where are you going at this time?"

"It's none of your fucking business."

When is he going to understand that I want him to leave me alone, for fuck's sake? I just can't stand the sight of him, why does he have to follow me everywhere!

"Tell me, could I accompany you there? We could talk."

I glare at him, using all the hatred I have. My wolf is furious and growling too.

"I don't want to see you; I don't want to talk to you. Fuck off, Diego, I can even say it in Spanish if you want! *Vete a la mierda! Joderte!*"

"Wow, calm down, amor."

"Don't ask me to calm down! I can't stand you, why the hell can't you leave me alone?"

"Really? That's all you got? What, you're going to ignore me? Until when? Are you going to stay pissed at me forever? Can't we talk?"

"Moon Goddess, I made it clear, Diego, I have nothing to talk to you about! I'm so done with you and your shit! I've moved on! From you, and everything!"

He growls, and I have to take a step back cautiously.

"You're my girlfriend, Elena. Just because we fought, doesn't mean we–"

I laugh. It's nervous and irrepressible. Does he have any idea how ridiculous he is right now? I need a minute to calm down, while Diego is staring at me with shocked eyes.

"I *was* your girlfriend, Diego. We are done. Do you get that? You and I, it ended five years ago. I am not that girl who needed you all the time and was crazy about you. I've moved on, I don't need or want you in my life anymore. Actually, I want you to stay as far away from me as possible, got it?"

He growls, seriously pissed this time.

"Is that what you have to say? Do you expect me to believe this? This ridiculous grown woman act? Who are you kidding, Elena? You love me. You're obsessed with me, that's why you're still so mad at me."

"I'm mad at the man who killed my child!" I scream. "I went to jail for what I did! Yes, I am fucking mad for ever having loved a jerk like you! But guess what? It's. Fucking. Over. Get that through your thick skull, Diego. You're nothing but a bastard from my past to me, you get it? Do you really think I still love you? Then I have some breaking news: I'm over you!"

Before I can even react, Diego suddenly grabs my wrist and tightens his grip so hard I cry out. I react with a pure shot of adrenaline and use my free elbow to hit him in the solar plexus. He lets go by surprise, and I take a few steps back, raising my hands, ready to fight if he wants to. He gets off his bike, and I think he's about to hit me, but someone suddenly grabs my shoulder to pull me back.

"Levi!"

Daniel and Levi ran over, one holding me and the other in between me and Diego. Levi is growling furiously at my ex.

"Last fucking warning, Diego. You get away from her right now."

"What… you're acting like Prince Charming again, Levi? Ready to be the good puppy, as always?" Diego snickers.

But Daniel's brother is too smart to fall for Diego's petty provocations. Instead, he takes a step back and suddenly puts his arm around my shoulders.

"I told you to stay the fuck away from Elena. Get close to my princess again and I'll rip your head off, Diego, alpha or not."

I finally see a hint of doubt in Diego's eyes. He glances back and forth between me and Levi, and I finally get it. He's wondering if Levi's my boyfriend now.

"Yeah, she's moved on, dickhead," adds Daniel, with a smirk.

What are these two playing at!

"*What the heck are you idiot brothers doing?*"

"*This guy won't leave you alone. And we can't exactly tell him whom you've really been seeing, right?*"

"*It's fine, Elena. Just play the part until that idiot goes away.*"

"Are you going to ruin date night, or do I have to chase you away?" growls Levi.

I can't believe they are pulling this kind of cheap play. This is so freaking ridiculous. Why do I have to play pretend with Levi just so Diego will leave me alone? Damn, that jerk really hurt my wrist.

"You're lying," mutters Diego, suspicious.

"It is what it is. I told you, I moved on. Now fuck off before I call Clark for real."

I don't like the idea, but if that can help get him off my back… Levi growls at Diego, as a warning. My ex keeps looking at us, skeptical, before starting his bike and finally riding away. I let out a big sigh and turn to Levi.

"Thanks. What are you doing here?"

"I came to drop Danny's books by your place. I heard you arguing with that jackass. Are you okay?"

I check my wrist. Damn, it's red and swollen. That jerk almost broke it.

"I'm okay, it should be healed in a few days."

"No, no, babe, let me at least get you a bandage from upstairs!"

Daniel runs off to our place to get the first aid kit, and I lean against the car with Levi. I sigh.

"That was a stupid lie, Lev."

"Oh, whatever. As long as it can get him off your back."

If only it would be that simple; I'm fully aware of Levi's feelings for me. We've never talked about it, but we both know that I know. He's just way too nice and understanding to voice it out loud, and I'm too much of a coward to face it.

"Were you going out?"

I nod. Levi is turning a blind eye to my little outings to the Velvet Moon territory. I don't know how we convinced him to ignore it, but he never mentions Nate and just helps cover for me.

"I'll accompany you to the border?"

"What?"

But before he can answer, Daniel comes back and helps me bandage my painful wrist. I hope I hurt him with my elbow, that dickhead! Once I'm bandaged, Levi insists on driving me there. We take Danny's car and chat about trivial stuff until we get to the club. I don't feel too good about Levi being here. He shouldn't have come, even less than me. Hopefully, no one will say a thing.

"Thank you for driving me."

"Do you want me to come pick you up later?"

"Don't worry Lev, I'll text Danny. Good night?"

"Good night, princess."

I give him a smile before getting out of the car and watch him drive away. Gosh, what are you thinking, Levi? That was a bit awkward. I wish I could just see him as an older brother.

I walk off to the club. Despite that stupid encounter with Diego, I'm still about twenty minutes early. I keep looking at my phone, but I don't get any news from Nate. I order a drink and head upstairs. I don't even have to ask or hesitate anymore; the staff knows who I am. What a change compared to my first time here…

To my surprise, the VIP floor is crowded. There might be a special event or something, a lot of people are here and well dressed. Thank Moon Goddess I picked one of my fancier skirts. I'm bored and sipping my cocktail when I suddenly feel two arms around me.

"Moon Goddess, I missed you."

Nate's lips are already on my shoulder, kissing me restlessly from behind, all the way to my neck. He doesn't even seem to care about the crowd around us, he is covering my skin in kisses, caressing my arms, and holding me close. Moon Goddess, I missed him too.

I turn around and shamelessly kiss him, feeling the taste of his lips for the first time in what seems like forever. He suddenly stops and growls.

"What's that smell?"

"What?"

"You have another man's smell on you," he growls, frowning.

Shit, probably Levi's. With his arm around me earlier it can only be him. Wait, does that really matter now? I put my glass down on a table and grab Nate's shirt.

"Just a friend, Nate."

"Your friends hug you often?"

I roll my eyes at him. Really? Now?

"Seriously, Nate, let it go, I've had enough jealous disputes for today!"

"What, what jealous disputes? With whom? Your ex? Is that his scent?"

I grab his collar and pull him behind me, all the way to the bathroom. It's so not classy, but I growl at two girls who were fixing their makeup for them to leave us alone. At least now I don't have to yell over the crowd and the music.

"No, my ex hasn't touched me except for this!" I growl, showing him my injured wrist.

Nathaniel immediately frowns, and I hear his wolf growling in anger. He takes my hand to look at my injury, but I keep it away.

"He did this? Your ex?"

Shit, I should have kept quiet about it. I sigh and decide to tell him the truth.

"Yes, he did. I told him to leave me alone, he didn't like it, and Levi intervened to help me so Diego would back off. That's it. Happy?"

"No."

Of course, he's even angrier now. I can't believe we are having an argument about this. I wanted to see him again and have a good time, not talk about Diego or Levi!

"I told you I had issues with my pack, Nate. I'll deal with it, okay?"

"He fucking hurt you, Elena. Don't tell me you can 'handle' that kind of asshole who does this to you!"

Shit, why does he have to get so protective now… I put my arms around his neck and kiss him. I know I'm cheating but he just can't refuse me. And I'm right. After insisting a bit, Nate puts his arm around my waist, a hand on my ass, and kisses me back. I missed him so much… I kiss him back hungrily, caressing his neck and grabbing his hair, feeling the heat rising. I want him. I feel him sliding a hand under my top, caressing my back, looking for my skin to touch. I catch my breath for a second, but Moon Goddess, that's not going to last.

"Tell me there's a lock on that door," I whisper.

I feel him snicker against my lips, and his hands lift my skirt up.

"No one will intrude," he promises while touching me.

I gasp.

It's been too good of a night… We had some quick but incredibly good sex in the bathroom, and I came fast like a beginner. Then, we went back to dancing, stuck to each other like a young couple intoxicated with each other. And on the way back, Nate just won't let go of my hand for more than a couple seconds while driving to his place. It's a quiet ride… and I'm getting tense as we enter his apartment. Everything is going far too well.

"So, I guess we're back together."

Oh, Moon Goddess, I knew it…

"We're not, Nate," I answer, calmly but firmly. "What I said last time still stands."

He drops his keys, but I ignore him, walking all the way to his bed and sitting there. This bed is all it should be about. At least for now, I can't afford for us to be more than that. Nate sighs and comes to sit next to me.

"I don't want to bind you to a serious relationship," I say.

"Tell me why again."

"I already told you, Nate. Neither of us is ready for that. We each have our own responsibilities, and honestly, I'm already dealing with a lot now that my ex is back."

He glances at my wrist; we both know what the real issue is.

"Can we keep things how they are?" I insist.

"Don't you trust me?" he suddenly asks.

Trust? He's really the one bringing up trust now?

"Who doesn't trust whom, exactly? What about that file, Nate?"

"I told you, that wasn't my intention," he . "I didn't ask for it."

"See? That's exactly what I'm talking about. I don't want your pack watching me, Nate. And even if you manage to make them stop, we are not supposed to be together. We have different packs, different interests."

He rolls his eyes, but I won't be the one to give up.

"Nate, let's just go back to the start," I ask him, taking his hand. "To our promise."

"That will not change my feelings for you."

… What? His feelings for me? I thought we were supposed to keep our feelings out of it. He literally looked me in the eye and said he didn't love me just days ago! I take a deep breath to calm myself down. Don't give in, Elena, don't.

"I know. It won't change mine either, Nate. Let's just… take the easy way until we can sort things out, okay?"

"When is that, then?"

I hesitate. He won't give up until I give him a real deadline…

"Not until my ex is out of the picture, and your brother sorts things out with his mate. I know it's complicated for your pack right now. Let's just wait and see how it turns out, okay?"

"Promise me something," he says.

"What?"

"If you ever need me, call me. I don't want you to hesitate, Elena. I'm serious. Use your wolf. Call me if you need me."

I can't help but smile. He can be so unbelievably sweet at times… and it makes it even harder.

"You too, then."

"All right," he chuckles. "I promise."

I lean in to kiss him, softly.

"And when is all of this going to be sorted out?" he insists.

I roll my eyes.

"Moon Goddess, Nate, shut up and get naked."

Chapter 16

"Why don't you just call him?"

I glare at Daniel.

"When I do call him, all he says is that he's busy with his brother's mate or work, Danny. If this goes on, I'm going to be jealous of a girl I don't even know!"

He sighs and takes a bite of his sandwich. It's lunchtime, and we managed to find a break between my classes and Danny's experiments to talk to each other. I haven't seen Nate for a few days, and it's driving me crazy because I have a feeling he is mad at me. I have no idea why. The last time I was over at his place, he suddenly went out in a hurry that night because of some issue with his brother's fated mate and didn't come back. Instead, all I got was a stupid text saying he would be busy for a few days.

"Maybe he's really busy?"

"Trust me, he had busy weeks before, but when he wanted to see me, he could. No, I feel like something's wrong. I don't like it."

His texts are too short, and his voice was so cold over the phone. I just don't get it. I feel like I'm missing something. Is it something I said? But everything was fine until then! He wouldn't have changed his mind so quickly, right?

"Babe, it's only been a few days, maybe you're thinking too much!"

I know Danny's just trying to cheer me up, but I don't believe it.

"How do you cope without Bobo?" I sigh.

He frowns, furiously biting into his vegetarian sandwich again.

"I do without! That idiot can go and do whatever he wants, I don't care," he says with a pout.

"Seriously, Danny? It's his work! The King appointed him as that girl's bodyguard, you can't ask him to drop everything like that."

"He could at least answer his texts! Can you believe he stays in wolf form? I mean, he did spend a lot of time in his wolf form, but all I've gotten so far are texts from his sister! His sister, Elena!"

I try hard not to laugh. My goodness, poor Bobo. I know he doesn't have much of a choice, but I hope he's ready for a big fight with his possessive boyfriend when they meet again… I can't blame Danny, though, he's barely gotten any news in three weeks.

"Anyway, I say you give him a few more days, girl. I mean, so far, Black's been very understanding with you, right? Plus, Xavier is all over your back these days, if you want to go to the Velvet Moon territory again it's going to be a serious hassle."

Daniel's right.

When I got back from the Velvet Moon that same night, my uncle caught me right at the border. It was a nightmare, and he asked a thousand questions. He was furious about me sneaking out, even more so when I refused to tell him where and why.

"That was super odd too."

"What?"

"My uncle was right there when I got back, waiting for me. As if he knew when and where I was going to come back. Isn't that weird?"

Daniel frowns for a while, then shrugs.

"I don't know, babe. You know, with all that sneaking in and out, I figured someone would catch you someday. You've been doing that since June, Elena. Almost four months, now! You're lucky no one caught you earlier, in my opinion."

Maybe Danny's right about that too. But I can't help but think my uncle Xavier's timing was way too perfect. Did someone tell him about it beforehand? Anyway, it's been a nightmare since. My uncle is keeping me as busy as he can, and watching me like a hawk. Even Isabella and Clark heard about it and scolded me like a pup too. I had the full speech about border security, me being irresponsible, the threats coming from the different packs, and so on. As a bonus, they doubled my training shifts.

"I'm tired," I say, massaging my stiff neck.

"According to my observations, waking up at 6:00 a.m. to train the kids, going to the hospital every day, then to your classes until 6:00 p.m., to the library until 10:00 p.m. and only going to bed around 11:00 p.m. will do that to anyone, babe."

I rest my head on Danny's shoulder, closing my eyes for a while. Damn, I could really use a nap right now.

"How about this?"

I jump, surprised to hear a feminine voice. I calm down when I recognize Daniel's colleague, though: Sylviana, an odd woman with crimson hair and a gentle smile. She's handing me a little wooden box that smells good. I grab it.

"Hi, Sylviana. What is this?"

"Just some tea to relieve fatigue, a little."

"Thanks…"

She smiles at me, and turns to Daniel, talking about one of their experiments. I've only seen Sylviana a few times before, but I always get a strange feeling about her. Maybe it's her green eyes. For some reason, I sometimes get the impression that their color changes with the light. But they look normal when she's chatting with Daniel.

"Yeah, I'll transfer it to you later. Thanks, Syl."

"You're welcome. See you later!"

She walks away, her long skirt floating a little with the wind. I watch her go until she enters one of the science faculty's greenhouses.

"Don't you think she's a bit weird?" I ask Danny.

"That sounds mean, babe."

"No, like… I don't know, she feels a bit strange, don't you think? I mean, she sometimes has a wolf's smell on her."

"Sylviana smells super good, and she's obviously not a werewolf! Maybe she knows other werewolves, but she's human, I don't know what you're thinking about."

Still, I can't shake that odd feeling about her. It's nothing wrong, but my wolf is always alert when Sylviana is nearby. Daniel finishes his sandwich and licks his fingers, then turns to me.

"Anyway, no studying tonight, babe, you need to rest a bit, okay? If you're dozing off in class it's not going to help, all right?"

"Yeah, yeah… But I'll drop by the cemetery after class. It's been a while since I went to change the flowers."

"Go with Levi."

I roll my eyes.

"Seriously? Since when is your brother my bodyguard?"

"He's your alibi!"

"I don't need Levi to be glued to me all day! Diego has been backing off these days, all right?"

"Only because of my genius plan!" insists Daniel.

Seriously, what genius plan? It's a stupid plan. Ever since Levi posed as my boyfriend in front of Diego, Daniel has insisted that we keep up the act. It's not that hard anyway, Levi and I have always been close. What I don't like is the feeling that I'm giving Levi false hope and using him to keep Diego at bay. He's assured me that he doesn't mind and understands a thousand times, but still.

"I'll go alone, Danny. Levi's probably busy with the patrol anyway, and Diego is not going to follow me all the way to the cemetery; even he is not that nuts."

Probably.

"What about Reagan?" asks Danny.

"Avoiding me again."

I'm so used to it that I don't even care anymore. Since she scolded me along with Clark for leaving the territory, my mentor has been set on watching me from afar. Probably because of Diego, too. But my ex strangely hasn't approached me for a while. Not that I'm going to complain about not seeing him, though. I just don't like not knowing what he's been up to.

"Okay, you go to the cemetery and then straight home. Mind-link me if anything happens. All right?"

"Yes, mom," I answer with a smile.

Daniel rolls his eyes.

"I'll really have Mom scold you if you keep going, babe."

"Your mom loves me too much. Anyway, time to go back to class, and you probably have some stuff to check with your microscope or whatever too."

Indeed, Daniel has too much to do on his own to complain any further. We part ways for the afternoon, each heading back to our respective departments. I wish I could finish my studies soon, but I still have two years to go.

I'm lucky, though, my last class is canceled at the last minute. I text Danny to let him know and head back to the Opal Moon territory. It's such a good day, I don't even need the car and walk all the way back, heading to the cemetery.

I buy flowers before going, since my mom loved them.

To be honest, I hate going to the cemetery. It's a cold, sad place. When I get there, there's a heavy silence reigning over the tombstones. I walk a bit between the rows. I forgot how big the cemetery was. When I'm about to reach my mom's tomb, I stop.

Reagan's there.

She's sitting in front of it, in her wolf form. I'm shocked. I had no idea she ever visited my mom. I step closer, and she notices me right away.

"Hi..." I say.

"*Hi, brat.*"

"You could be nice at least in front of mom."

She growls a bit. Yeah, she probably doesn't give a damn. I turn around to look down at the white stone. "Ivy Whitewood, dedicated wife and mother."My adoptive mom, and the only mom I remember. Moon Goddess, I miss her.

I tear up anytime I come here. As if the memories submerged me like a wave, a whirlwind of emotions twists my stomach into knots, and I have to repress those feelings. I don't want to cry in front of Reagan.

"*I went to see your dad, too.*"

"He's the same since the accident."

"*Who's paying the hospital fees?*"

I roll my eyes. Seriously, why does she care about that now?

"I sold the house," I confess.

I didn't have much of a choice. My parents' savings and mine were not enough to pay for Dad's hospital bills and my mom's funeral. It broke my heart, but I didn't want to accept Clark or Joseph's money. Reagan doesn't say anything.

We both stay here in silence. I never talk to my mom, not even in my mind. I just pray she's at peace, with the Moon Goddess watching over her. I'm not much of a believer, though.

After a while, Reagan walks away without a word. So much for comfort.

I don't feel like staying too long, either. It's a depressing place to be, and my mom's not here. I change the flowers and clean the stone a bit until it looks good enough. With a silent goodbye, I walk away, hands in my pockets. It's still early, but I promised Danny to go straight home. When I reach the cemetery's entrance, I'm suddenly faced with Sylviana, who had just walked in.

"What a coincidence," she says with a gentle smile.

She's carrying a small bouquet of white lilies. Is she visiting someone's grave too? She notices my eyes on her bouquet.

"Family," she just says with a sad look in her eyes.

I suddenly feel very impolite, as if I had asked out loud. I look away from the flowers, trying to think of something to say.

"Don't you miss them?" she suddenly whispers.

"What?"

Her tone is a bit strange, lower than usual. When she looks at me with those green eyes of hers, I can feel that odd sensation coming again. Is she talking about my mother? But I have a very strange impression that isn't the case…

"Who are you talking about? Who should I be missing?" I ask, completely lost.

She caresses her flowers, and I notice the little blue butterfly resting still on one of them. It only distracts me a second, though, and I look at Sylviana, but she just smiles and suddenly resumes her walking. I hesitate for a second and turn to follow her.

"Who are you talking about?" I ask, feeling strange.

"Have you ever been to the Jade Moon's territory, Elena?"

The Jade Moon territory? Why would I be interested? It's a minor clan and located almost on the opposite side of Silver City too. How does she even know about that name? It's a clan of werewolves… Does she really have werewolf friends? That's not completely unusual for a human, especially in Silver City, but… Sylviana doesn't answer me again but just keeps smiling and walking away.

That girl is just blurting things out, but why do I feel so weird listening to her?

My wolf is a bit restless, too. Her voice awoke something in us, and I really want to visit that territory suddenly. Why the Jade Moon? I shouldn't go, it's far and I have no reason to be there! Especially after I was caught and scolded for going out a few days ago.

I decide to leave her and quickly run out of the cemetery. I'm not thinking straight. I walk east and drop my backpack at Henry's bar on the way. I don't know why; I just keep walking east. I'm about to cross the border when I shape-shift and run away.

I'm headed east, to the Jade Moon territory. I have no idea why, but my werewolf just wants to go.

I run, in my wolf form, across the Pearl Moon territory, rushing and praying that no one will say anything about my presence here. Hypothetically, we are on good terms with their pack, but I wouldn't push it. Damn, if Clark or my uncle hear about this, I'm dead.

However, my wolf is pushing me even faster. We have to go. I'm still unsure about that weird thing that happened with Sylviana. It was a strange sensation. That girl is weird, creepy weird, but I still did what she suggested. Why? Why are my guts pushing me towards the Jade Moon right now?

I finally reach the border.

I'm prepared for tighter security, but to my surprise, there is absolutely no one guarding their border. What's going on? I walk a bit further, my wolf guiding me. What the hell? I pick up Nathaniel's smell out of the blue. What is he doing here?

I carefully approach. After walking a bit, I reach a clearing, where a crowd has gathered, split into two groups.

First, I spot Nate, standing in his human form next to a young, black-haired woman. All I can see are their backs; they are turned towards the other group, and I hear some argument going on. I walk closer, curious. Some wolves turn their heads towards me and growl, but they stop quickly.

I spot a big, brown wolf in the group, standing next to the young woman. Boyan! He briefly looks at me, and I get he's the one who told the others to leave me alone. Everyone is more focused on what's going on, though. Standing a bit to the side, I try to listen too.

"Food and shelter?" says the girl. "You put me in the basement. You made me work from dawn until dusk, and never let me eat with you. You never even considered me a part of our pack."

Is that her? Nora? She seems so young and frail! Is she really his brother's mate? I wish I could see her face. Why does she feel so familiar? My wolf is restless, too. It's funny, though, I can barely feel her inner wolf no matter how hard I try, like she is hiding.

"Everyone has to work to earn their living! You... You would have died in the streets if it wasn't for me, Nora. Nobody else would have helped you, but we did! Doesn't that count?"

Is that her Alpha? She was in the Jade Moon clan all this time? Damn, the guy doesn't have much of an Alpha Aura.

Compared to him, Nate is much more imposing. I notice another wolf standing in the front, a black one. Is that the younger Black brother? I've not seen him yet. The young wolf is growling furiously. I can feel Nate's anger from here, too, even if he's acting calm.

"You never really meant to help me, did you? All you saw was a helpless child, a free slave you could make use of. I was young, and you knew no one would protect me. Nobody would care no matter what happened to me. You never did. You are not my Alpha! You never acted like one to me. You never protected me or considered me your family, not in the slightest. All you did was use me, like some tool you could throw away anytime. I was broken, and all you did was break me even more."

Damn, I have to give it to her, that girl has some backbone. Is she an Alpha? She sort of feels like one, despite her very quiet wolf. More than that, listening to her, I feel something strange inside… I can't name it. My wolf wants to go to her, too.

I know that familiar feeling, I've felt it before, but where? Damn, if only her wolf wasn't so concealed!

"No, Nora. I didn't do it. I never laid a hand on you, did I? I even tried to keep Alec off your back, sometimes, I—"

"You didn't do anything! You let others do it for you, and that was it! You saw what they did to me, and you closed your eyes a million times! A million times you could have put an end to it with a single word, and you never ever did! You are worse than any of them! You are not even worthy of being called an Alpha!"

When she yells, her Alpha Aura shines a bit brighter, and I can feel it too. Around us, people are impressed or shocked. Yeah, that's what a young Alpha's Aura feels like. Only that she's not that young for a werewolf. A late awakening, possibly? I could use my wolf to yell like that when I was just six or seven, but for that girl, Nora, one can tell she's not used to it at all. It's almost as if she wasn't doing it on purpose, letting it flow naturally.

I look at Nate, and I can tell he's feeling it too. He looks surprised. Didn't they know about it?

"You wench! You should just shut up and be grateful the Alpha accepted a cursed, damn freak like you! No one wanted—"

But before she could finish, the black wolf jumps at her. I could tell before it started, that girl had no chance. In a couple of minutes, it's over. What an idiot… Smart werewolves don't fucking provoke one of the Black brothers! Despite my relationship with Nate, I can never forget how powerful he and his brothers are. That girl was probably blinded by her wrath, but attacking at that moment was clearly suicide.

It's my first time seeing one of them kill someone, though. It's the younger brother, but I'm very aware it could have been Nate. I can feel his cold anger from here. He could have killed her exactly as his sibling did.

Next to him, Nora seems shocked, looking at the body in horror. Welcome to the Black brother's world. I try to step to the side, but I still can't see her face. I want to get closer, but that's just when Nate's voice resonates.

"This was the last time I hear one of you talk like that about Nora ever again. We will leave behind as many corpses as necessary for that."

I felt that. It's the same voice he used whenever he was angry. So cold and frightening. I don't get to hear it often. A typical dominant Alpha warning. That Jade Moon Alpha is such a weakling compared to them. I don't even understand how he could have mistreated that girl all these years?

Suddenly, another of his wolves attacks. Did I miss something? His attempt is cut short. Another wolf dies right in front of us. Another wolf jumps, right after his death. A female, this time. Moon Goddess, are all the Jade Moon wolves idiots? They are all going to get killed at this rate! I don't know what they did to that girl, but this is suicide!

This time, Nate is the one to stop her. I barely saw him move. He was so fast! When I look, he is holding that she-wolf by the throat. I know what's about to happen, and I can't help it, I close my eyes. I wish I didn't hear it, either. The horrid sound of bones breaking and death.

"I warned you. Anyone else wants to try me?"

The body falls at his feet. Moon Goddess, I've never seen him like this before. I can't control myself and take a step back.

This isn't the Nate I know. The sweet, gentle, and patient Nate. This man is Nathaniel Black, the Alpha, angry and impatient.

"Enough, enough, please!" begs the Jade Moon Alpha.

"I have yet to hear any names," hisses Nate.

"Nathaniel, stop it."

I'm surprised to hear her speak so familiarly to Nate. And somewhat bitter to hear that, too. How did they become so close? He's only known her for a few weeks, right?

No, Elena, you idiot, it's his brother's mate. What am I thinking...? But I hate to see them look at each other. Moon Goddess, is it because he's been ignoring me? I can't believe I became jealous so easily. I have never seen Nate interact with another she-wolf, I think. Not so close, not so familiarly. I try to bury those idiotic feelings, as Nora steps closer to her Alpha. Moon Goddess, why can't I see her face, I'm too far back!

All the wolves accompanying Nate and her suddenly start growling even louder, intimidating the pitiful Jade Moon clan while she speaks.

"I'm not stopping them because of you. I still hold you responsible for what happened. But this clan needs its Alpha, and I'm done with seeing blood spilled today."

"From today on, the Blood Moon clan is hostile to the Jade Moon clan," declares Nathaniel. "Any of you takes one step into our turf, and you will face the consequences."

Wow, this means huge trouble for them. This is why no one ever gets on the Blood Moon's bad side. If you're any kind of werewolf with a brain, you don't want the strongest and wealthiest clan, which basically controls half the city, for an enemy. Those people are even lucky to still be alive, in my opinion. I bet if it wasn't for Nora's words earlier, this place would already be a bloodbath.

"In ten days at dusk, I want this whole pack to come to the East Point Ground. If a single person is missing, no matter the reason, we will hunt them down," suddenly says Nate. "This is a challenge for the Alpha position."

What? They want to take full control over the Jade Moon clan? Why would they even bother with a duel? They could wipe them all out here and now, right? I look at their Alpha. He looks like he's about to vomit…

Nathaniel doesn't add anything and turns around to leave with Nora.

I finally see them both. Nate sees me too, and the surprise on his face is something else. I know, I shouldn't be here.

I'm more intrigued by the young woman, though. Damn, she is pretty, but she looks so frail… Her skin is milk-white, and she's too skinny. But Moon Goddess, her eyes are beautiful. Striking, sapphire-blue eyes, like the night.

As I'm looking at them, a thought comes to my mind. *I've seen those eyes before.*

Why? Why the hell do they seem so familiar… I don't remember ever seeing Nora before, so how could I feel like this? I wish her wolf had a stronger aura, so I could feel it properly. But it's like reaching out for a cloud of smoke, it fades before I can touch it. So frustrating!

Nathaniel's eyes are riveted on me, trying to make sense of me being here. He stays close to Nora, though, accompanying her to a car close by. All the wolves around them quickly disperse, only Boyan and a few others staying like some security group around Nora. I recognize Tonia, his elder sister, when she shape-shifts back into her human form. She recognized me as well, it seems.

I don't really care about catching up with Boyan's sister, though. I'm still confused about that girl, Nora, and I need to talk to Nate. He seems angry at his own brother, though, glaring at the young black wolf the whole time. That's when I notice Nora is looking at me. For a second, she seems a bit surprised too, but Nate asks her to follow Tonia and soon, she disappears into a car. Did she feel something too?

"Elena."

I've caught up with reality. Nate has opened another car door for me. Now that the other car left with Nora, Boyan, and Tonia, it's just Nate, his brother, and I left. And it's awkward.

I jump in, trying to sit as best as I can. Yes, a car isn't the best place for a wolf. I can't even shape-shift, I don't have any clothes! So annoying.

"Who is that?"

I realize his brother shape-shifted into his human form on the back seat and pulled out clothes from his bag. I can hear him changing, so I look forward.

"Mind your own business, Liam. What the fuck were you thinking? Bringing Nora back here!"

"Hey, that was the only way to find out about her clan, okay? And I warned you right away, didn't I? Nothing happened to Damian's precious princess, so chill."

"This is not for you to decide!! We have half the clan trying to protect her and you fucking help her sneak out! When are you going to think before doing things like this! What if she had been injured? What if things had gone wrong with her pack, if I didn't get there in time? Did you even stop to think about that? About Damian, too?"

I hear that boy, Liam, sigh loudly.

"You are all so overprotective over Nora. You just saw her, didn't you? She's an Alpha! A freaking Alpha, you can't keep her locked up in an apartment! She spent half her life locked in a basement, see what it did to her wolf, she can't even growl properly!"

Suddenly, I feel some movement, and the younger brother puts his head between the front seats to smile at me, ignoring his older brother.

"Hello, pretty lady! Nice to see you again!"

I see Nate roll his eyes at his younger brother, exasperated. Damn, Liam seems like an energy pill. He hands me a large, black sweater.

"You can take it to change if you want! I don't want to leave a pretty lady naked."

Okay, Black brother number three is rather cute. He smiles and goes back to his seat, looking away. All right, time to change, I guess. I do my best to quickly shape-shift and put on the large sweater. Damn, it's big and covers down to my thighs, but I'm still totally naked underneath.

"Thanks, Liam," I can finally say.

He gives me a big smile in the mirror.

"Wow, you're even prettier in your–"

"Liam, shut up," growls Nate.

The atmosphere in the car goes cold again with Nate's words. He avoids looking at me, but I can tell he's only pretending to be focused on the road.

"Why did you come, Elena?"

"To see you," I reply right back. "You've been so busy."

I made it clear the last word is sarcastic because I don't believe him.

"As you can see, I was busy watching Nora and this idiot."

"Hey, don't lie to the lady when I'm right here, Nate. You only check on Nora and I once a week."

Thanks, Liam. I glare at Nate, who's a bit uncomfortable now. Damn, caught lying to my face.

"We'll talk once we get back to my place," he finally growls.

Whatever. I'm not leaving until we are done talking anyway. He drives back to his apartment, after we dropped off Liam at another one of their properties; the atmosphere was ice cold in the car. We finally reach his building and walk silently to the elevator. I don't even care that I'm almost naked and with bare feet, his attitude is pissing me off. Ignoring me for days and now this? Seriously? What the heck is wrong with him! The elevator stops on his floor, and we walk out. Damn, that silence is getting on my nerves. My wolf is almost about to growl. Nate is about to enter his passcode when someone suddenly opens the door.

It's a woman. Tall, pretty, and looking damn sexy in a tight black dress. She looks at him with a big sigh, but then her eyes fall on me. Who the hell is this? And what the hell is she doing at his place? She eventually ignores me to look at him.

"I was waiting for you."

I see Nate's eyes, going from her to me very quickly. I'm really, really tempted to fucking slap him right now.

"Narcissa. You shouldn't be here."

Damn, that embarrassed look on his face.

I'm so fucking stupid. I don't want to go through this. This is so fucking stupid.

"Looks like you two need to talk," I say with a bitter taste on my tongue.

I turn around. I suddenly feel Nate grabbing my wrist, but I push him away.

"Elena, wait!"

"No, I'm done waiting!" I yell back. "If you didn't want to talk to me, you could have said so, Nate. I'm not that stupid."

I walk away, so pissed I feel like I could murder someone. That jerk! I need to go back but fuck, I'm only wearing this stupid sweater! Never mind, I can always shape-shift.

"Elena, stop, let me speak!"

"You had days to speak, Nate! But every time I called, you were busy! Now I know what you were busy doing!"

"It's not what you think, okay?"

He follows me into the elevator. I'm thinking about throwing him out, but it's his place, I can't just push him out. Never mind, it's only a matter of seconds before I'm out of here anyway.

I just cross my arms and keep my eyes fixated on the wall, ignoring him. Nathaniel takes his chance to speak anyway.

"I have no idea what Narcissa is doing here, okay?"

"How she mysteriously got into your place, where you supposedly never invite anyone but me and your brothers? Are you going to tell me she teleported here, or got your keys by mistake? How stupid do you think I am!"

"I don't know! Someone must have let her in, but–"

"Oh, shut up, Nate, can't you just admit you're seeing someone else?"

He becomes red with anger, slamming the elevator's wall next to me. Damn Alpha, I'm seeing red too, and my wolf is angry at him, growling furiously. She feels betrayed, and so do I.

"I am not! You're the only one I–"

"Tell me you never had sex with her," I suddenly ask, looking him right in the eyes.

For a second, he's taken by surprise and stays silent, visibly shaken. Moon Goddess, I knew it. I'm so fucking stupid.

"That was before I met you, Elena," he answers very seriously.

"Before and after, I suppose. You could have just told me if you were bored with me, Nate."

"I am not bored with you!"

"You ignore me for days with stupid excuses about being busy and when I finally cross two territories to talk to you, you happen to have an ex-girlfriend in your apartment! Seriously, how do you expect me to believe you?"

"She was never my girlfriend, only a fuck buddy!"

"For Moon Goddess' sake, Nate, just shut up!"

I push him out of the way and exit the elevator, angry like never before. Moon Goddess, how could I be so stupid to not see what a player he was! It's only been a few days, and he sleeps with someone else? I'm such an idiot!

"Elena, if you would just listen–"

I turn around and growl at him once more. I'm pissed and angry, and I don't want to listen to him and his stupid excuses!

"I don't want to listen, Nate. If you wanted to fuck someone else, you could have told me we were over, not just ignore me like some high school brat!"

"What about you then? You're the only one who gets to play around with other guys, and I have to just wait?"

I stop, completely lost. What the hell is he talking about? I made it clear that I wasn't sleeping with anybody else!

"Excuse me?"

He suddenly rolls his eyes and takes out his phone, showing me a picture. What the–? Why the hell does he have a picture of me and Levi kissing?

"What is this then?" he asks, furious. "I thought things were over with your ex? It doesn't seem like it!"

"That's not Diego, you big idiot, that's Levi, Daniel's brother!"

Nathaniel shakes his head in disbelief. I let out a big sigh. Why am I the one justifying myself right now? I'm not the one with another woman waiting upstairs in a fucking sexy black dress!

"So, even your best friend's brother, now?""

Moon Goddess, if I wasn't repressing myself and my wolf right now I would slap him! What's that look he's giving me?

"I never slept with Levi, what the hell are you thinking, he's like a brother to me!"

"That didn't prevent you from kissing him!"

"That wasn't real, Nate! Levi is passing as my boyfriend so that Diego would leave me alone!"

I can see the shock on his face. Yeah, I guess he didn't expect that. That was a shitty plan, but the only one that worked. Whether Diego believed it or not, he backed off a little when Levi was around.

"Why would you do that?"

"Because Diego is a fucking psycho, and that was the only idea I had for him to back off, Nate!"

"So you picked your best friend's brother? And he believed it?"

"Yes, we have been pretending for a week and that's working, for now," I sigh, exhausted by this fight.

"So, there's nothing between you and that guy, Levi?"

"Of course not…"

"He doesn't like you?"

I freeze. Oh, damn it. If only I had ignored that question. Nathaniel looks like he is about to vomit, and takes one more look at the picture.

"So, you're pretending to go out with a guy who is in love with you?"

"Stop that, Nathaniel. Levi knows perfectly well that I don't love him back."

"Certainly. Your best friend's brother, you're definitely not leading him on by kissing him and pretending to–"

"Levi knows I don't have any feelings for him, Nate! Enough! Moreover, he knows I'm sleeping with you, okay?"

"You said only Daniel and Boyan knew!"

"Well, now Levi knows too, okay? He overheard Daniel and I, earlier this summer! So yes, Levi knows I'm sleeping with you and he's covering up for me because guess what? He's my only believable boyfriend!"

"You're happily kissing him and going out with him when I'm not available, I guess," growls Nate.

Moon Goddess, why is he the one having a jealousy tantrum now? I didn't come here to explain myself!

"Well, we could have held hands, but we are not five years old and Diego isn't a fucking moron, Nate."

"So you choose a guy who loves you to pass for your boyfriend instead."

"Yes, I fucking did because I can't have you do it for me! So guess what? I had to sort things out by myself with who I could, and Levi knew that! You knew us being from different packs wasn't going to make things easy, well here you go! Now, if you're done questioning me, you can go back to that whore waiting for you upstairs! And tell your brothers, your beta, or whoever took that to fucking stop watching me!"

I can't believe he is still monitoring me! How the hell did he even get that damn picture? It had to be taken within my territory!

He doesn't reply back, and I run away as fast as I can, shape-shifting as I leave the building. I hear him call my name, but I'm too fast and far already. I just can't believe him! That jerk! I'm so disappointed. Who was that woman anyway? Could it be she's not the only one he's been seeing? Who can tell what he's been doing behind my back?

I finally reach our border without trouble. I can't believe how easily I got in and out! No one bothered me, I only watched out when entering back into the White Moon territory. I grab my backpack and finally head home. I really hope Daniel hasn't noticed my absence.

Of course, he's home when I enter. Crap. I feel like a kid that was caught stealing when he's glaring at me like that. I sigh.

"Sorry."

"Seriously, Elena? What happened to coming straight home?"

He gets up from the couch, arms crossed, waiting for my explanation. Shit. I head to the kitchen to get some coffee when I spot his teapot. I suddenly remember Sylviana's words, and how it all started.

"Daniel, I really need to talk to you and for you to listen only for like ten minutes, please."

He looks at me, surprised by my guts.

"Seriously, Whitewood?"

"Daniel, I'm serious. Ten minutes."

He rolls his eyes and goes back to the couch to listen, still frowning behind his glasses.

"All right. But after that, I'm giving you a hell of a scolding, Elena."

I sigh, drink a bit of coffee, and tell him everything. My encounter with Reagan at the cemetery, Sylviana's weird attitude, how I suddenly went to the Jade Moon clan, and my encounter with that girl Nora and the strange feeling I got from it.

Daniel is about to talk or has weird expressions several times while listening to me, but he manages to hold back and stay quiet. Then, I tell him about how I briefly met Liam Black and the whole episode with Nathaniel. I see him go white when I tell him about the woman and our fight.

I don't know when I started to cry. I only realize I'm crying because he hands me a tissue in the middle of my monologue and the salty taste on my tongue. It's hard to breathe, sob, and still talk at the same time, but I don't want to stop until I'm done. I keep telling him everything until the point when I returned to our territory. By that time, I'm crying loudly and shaking.

Daniel's anger has died while watching me cry.

"Babe."

"I just… I feel like I had a nightmare, Danny. How could he do that?"

"I know… Men are jerks, okay? But how did he get that picture?"

I roll my eyes. Who cares about that stupid picture? That's not the point here! But Daniel shakes his head, putting his hand on my knee to comfort me.

"No, Elena, seriously, don't you think that's odd? He never knew about what happened here before. You told me he only accessed your police records, right? He didn't even know who Levi was until now, and aside from me, my brother is someone you hang out with a lot. Shouldn't he have learned about him sooner? And how would someone from his pack get–"

"Danny, I don't give a damn how he got that picture, okay? Did you miss the part where he was with that–"

"No, I get you, babe. I really do. But doesn't this seem a bit too big for you? A pretty chick waiting at his place right when you come? It's like a movie to me."

"What movie? She wasn't there at the right time, Danny, maybe it's even a regular thing since he got tired of me! He even admitted he's been with her before!"

"True," sighs Danny.

I try hard to stop crying. Gosh, when was the last time I bawled like this? I'm feeling so childish and stupid right now. I try to dry my tears until I'm out of tissues and Daniel makes me some tea.

"Okay, putting that jerk aside, Elena, what was that thing with that girl, Nora?"

"I don't know, I had a really weird feeling when I saw her, like déjà vu, you know? As if I knew her from somewhere."

"That would be weird if she's from the Jade Moon clan. And they kept her locked in a freaking basement, too? The King is going to wipe the floor with their limbs!"

"Well, I really couldn't care less about the Jade Moon, but it was already a bloodbath when I got there. Even your boyfriend had a bite, you know. Quite literally."

"That's my man," says Danny with a little smile.

Look at him. He was so unhappy at Boyan not too long ago…

"Danny, I need to see her again."

"What? That chick, Nora? Elena, she's the King's mate, you can't visit her like you visited Nathaniel, you know? She's probably going to be watched like the Pope! And after that fight you had, I'm pretty sure your man is not going to watch your ass if you get caught! Moreover, Xavier and Clark are watching you, remember that? Reagan, too! No, no, bad idea babe."

"But Bobo–"

"Bobo is too busy watching her to even answer my texts! He's probably guarding that kid all day and night. Not that I'm jealous, but even I wouldn't be able to get close!"

I frown.

No, I'm pretty sure that's not impossible. My instincts and my wolf are telling me to see that girl again, and I really need to. I have to figure out the odd feeling that I had with her.

"Babe, your phone."

I notice my phone's been vibrating in my bag. I grab it, and frown. Fuck, it's Nathaniel. Really, what does he want now? I decline. I don't care what he has to say, I'm certainly not in the mood for it. Daniel, who saw the name too, sighs.

"Damn, you two have one hell of a complicated relationship. I don't even need to watch TV anymore."

"Great to know I'm entertaining you."

"Don't be angry, babe, you know what I mean. You've got a fiery personality, and Black is not making it easy either, okay?"

"I'm so tired of trying to work things out. He even got jealous of Levi, seriously!"

"Well, I can understand that. Levi loves you, you both know it. If he has any kind of feelings for you, he wouldn't appreciate that you're passing a guy who has a crush on you as your boyfriend."

"That was your idea!" I reply, annoyed.

"I know, but I was putting your safety first, okay? Diego is still crazy as fuck. But I also understand Black's concerns. But guess what? I don't think you have a choice, and he just doesn't get that. He doesn't know how crazy and dangerous Diego is, even if he's been quiet these days."

Daniel's right. I feel like Diego has been too quiet these days, and it's worrying. I sigh and grab his cup of coffee, tired of the tea, but I frown as soon as I taste it.

"Daniel, you have to stop changing our coffee brands, this one tastes disgusting."

"No one likes salty coffee, babe. Just leave it, I'll make you some more tea."

I sigh and put the cup down. I'm tired and sad. It's like I'll never see the end of that black hole of a relationship with Nate. I close my eyes, letting out a big sigh.

"You know Danny, maybe you were right. Maybe I should have never accepted his deal in the first place."

"Okay, do I have to answer that, or will an 'I told you so' suffice?" he says with a smirk.

I growl at him, a bit pissed. He comes back with my lemon-flavored tea. Damn, that smells a whole lot better.

"All right, babe. You know what, let's do this. You cool down for a few days and focus on school and training. Ignore Black, give him a taste of his own medicine, and see how he reacts. Meanwhile, I'll try to get a hold of my man, and find out more about that Nora girl, okay?"

"Fine. But I want to ask Reagan."

Daniel scratches his head.

"Why Reagan? I thought she was avoiding you?"

"I don't know. I just have a feeling, you know? That she might know something about that girl."

"Well, you can always try. How about asking Eric if he can dig up more about her, too? Being friends with a cop should be beneficial at times like this."

"Yeah, fine, I'll text Eric and–"

My phone vibrates again. I sigh. Daniel walks over and grabs it. I thought he was going to block Nathaniel or something, but to my surprise, he answers!

"Hello, this is Daniel Lewis, her best and oldest friend. First, Elena is not available at the moment, and she won't be for a while. Second, Levi is my older brother and no, there is nothing Elena has done with my brother that she should apologize for. Third, if you're cheating on my babe with another bitch, you're an ass and you don't deserve her. Fourth, she's dealing with enough as it is with her jackass ex, so don't be a pushy jerk and deal with your own shit before coming back to her. I'm done, so don't call back. Bye and have a nice day."

He hangs up and hands me the phone with a satisfied look.

"Here you go, babe. Done."

I'm speechless.

Chapter 17

"Miss Whitewood? Any thoughts on this?"

I raise my head. Crap, what was he saying? I completely dozed off… I check the screen behind the Economics professor, but I'm clueless.

"Sorry sir, I–"

"You may want to nap outside of my class, Miss Whitewood. Thanks."

Damn. Everyone is staring at me while I gather my things. In this class of all classes, I had to feel sleepy! My marks are not going to be good for this semester if I can't stay focused. What's wrong with me? I can't sleep at night so I end up dozing in class. Great. I text Danny to let him know I'm going back to our place, but he's buried in his work this week. I'll let him have the car, I guess I can walk home.

I take out my earbuds and head back to our territory, a bit unsure. I feel bad about missing my class, but I don't feel good about anything these days, not since my argument with Nate. Danny did end up blocking him. I still don't know if I'm thankful or resentful for that, but he's got at least one thing right: I need a break from all the drama.

Suddenly, a car honks at me. I'm about to give him a finger when I realize it's my cousin.

"Moon Goddess, Iris, you scared me!"

"Sorry, but you really shouldn't keep both your earbuds in! Are you going home?"

"Yeah, after getting ejected from my class."

She frowns, looking sorry.

"Oh, well, get in, I'll give you a ride, I'm going back too."

I nod and get into her little car. Unlike Danny's, hers is brand new, and perfectly clean, even with a white interior. I put my bag down and Iris drives off as soon as my belt is on.

"What about you?" I ask.

"Cancelled, my biology teacher got sick. Not that I'm going to complain though, she's terrible."

"If you say she's terrible, she must be really bad."

Iris chuckles. My cousin is a straight-A student, the perfect little girl since she was born. Nothing out of place and never took one step out of line. Except…

"Iris?"

"Hm?"

"Why does it smell like Eric in here?"

Iris gasps, totally surprised by my question. She looks away, obviously awkward.

"Well, he… I mean, we sort of…"

"Oh Moon Goddess, you're going out with Eric? For real?" I ask, completely shocked.

"Elena, hush, please! I mean, my father doesn't know and it's not really official either. So… Can you keep it a secret, please?"

"Sure, sure. I can do that."

I can't believe it! Iris and Eric! I mean, he spent so much time chasing after me, I wouldn't have believed he moved on out of the blue! Now that I think about it, he did stop pursuing me these last few weeks. I guess that's when he and Iris got together. Who knew?

She sighs.

"He's a great guy," I say, watching her reaction.

"Oh, I know! He's a gentleman, though he doesn't show it in public. We sort of… got together on my birthday. I mean, that's when it started."

Iris had such a big party for her birthday, I didn't exactly keep track of everything that was going on that evening. I was busier trying to avoid my uncle, and I'm pretty sure I left as soon as I could to meet up with Nate. Seems like I missed the juicy part, though!

"Anyway, what about you? Any prospective lovers?"

I appreciate she's not mentioning that stupid Diego. However, I can't tell her about Nate. I like my cousin and she's super sweet, but things are complicated enough and she's still my uncle's daughter, with a tendency to let some things slip out.

"No, not really. I'm focused on other things these days."

"Like what?"

I hesitate a bit. I can't tell her it's my studies after getting kicked out of my class, I guess. I decide to tell her the truth, or like, a portion of it.

"You know how I've always tried to look for my biological parents? Well, Reagan still won't talk, but the other day, I got a weird, I don't know, a weird feeling, about some girl I met."

"A girl? One of ours?"

"No, not from the White Moon clan, another pack."

"Moon Goddess, Elena, you know you're not supposed to–"

"I know, but I really think there's something about her, and I swear, everything's fine, Iris. I just need to find out more about her."

"Okay… Well, do you know her name?"

"Just Nora."

"Nora? Nora, like the King's mate? Nora Bluemoon?"

I freeze. Wait, what?

"Yeah! That's her, but how do you-?"

"Elena, Eric was looking into her! I mean, remember how the King's brothers came, looking for her and so on? Well, they actually found her the other night, and Eric was working at the police station that night. So, he's been the one in charge of her case since then. The Blood Moon asked for a full investigation on her! She was attacked when they found her, and they're looking for who did it. Also, her whole background is a mystery…"

I bet they eventually learned she was from the Jade Moon, that would explain that whole scene the other day. But I didn't think Iris would know so much! I already got most of that information from Eric, though.

"Wait isn't it tonight?" suddenly said Iris.

"What?"

"The duel!"

"Oh, yeah, they are challenging the Jade Moon Alpha, but–"

"Elena, that girl is the one fighting. Nora! She's the one who is supposed to fight her former Alpha."

Wait, what? I had no idea! I thought Nate or one of his brothers would do it! They are making that girl fight? By herself?

"How do you know?"

"Someone from the Blood Moon pack called the police station so they wouldn't, you know, get involved and all that. Eric just got a few more details because everyone was talking about it, and Dad asked about it too. I mean, the Blood Moon dueling another pack isn't something small, you know! But turns out it's just that girl. I think many people are going to watch, though."

Oh Moon Goddess! I didn't think I would get an opportunity so soon! It's been what, ten days? I can't believe my luck!

"Elena? You look like a kid on Christmas morning."

"I have to go!"

"What? Elena, we already caught you twice at the border. My dad and Clark won't like it."

"If I'm just going as a White Moon clan representative, Iris, it should be fine, right?"

She hesitates, opening and closing her mouth several times. After a while, she sighs and grabs her phone.

"Hi, Dad. Hey, you remember talking about that duel the Blood Moon is supervising? Yes. I know Uncle Clark is already sending people, but I was wondering if I could go? You know, it would be a good opportunity for… Yes, yes… Elena is coming with me, too, it's fine, right? No, it's fine. Mmh, I don't know… Is it okay if we go then? Okay. Yes, sure. Okay, thanks Dad!"

She hangs up with a big smile. I can't believe her!

"Really? He said yes?"

"Yup! I told him we were just going to watch for training purposes, and he agreed. All right, I think we should be on time if we go now. Crap, we have to take the long way around, too."

Iris keeps driving to the highway, heading to East Point Ground. Easy to figure out why they picked that spot. It's a wide area, not specifically owned by any territory, and a bit outside of the city too.

It takes us a while to get there, but I'm more impatient than ever for some reason. It's that feeling in my stomach, the expectation makes me hold my breath. I'm going to see that girl again! Whatever it was that I felt when I met her, I need to confirm it. Our bond, what it really is. I still can't forget that feeling from last time, like an intense déjà vu, and some unexplainable wave of nostalgia.

My cousin finally parks her car in an empty parking lot. Honestly, it's not the best part of the suburbs. We are close to the slums, and there's a feeling of danger hanging around, keeping us on our toes. We keep our bags with us just in case and walk the rest of the way. I really hope her car doesn't get hijacked or something.

When we finally arrive, a lot of people have gathered already. It's been a long time since I've seen people from so many packs. I try to guess who's from which clan. Some dark-skinned people wearing leather are probably from the Purple Moon clan. A bit farther, I spot a couple of people that look wealthier and more dignified, the Pearl Moon, most likely. There are a few people already in their wolf form, so it's hard to say. Of course, the Jade

Moon clan has to be here too. Even if I hadn't seen him before, I can tell who their Alpha is: he's fidgeting and letting his aura out clumsily.

Iris is also looking around.

"At least six different clans," she whispers to me.

I nod. I wouldn't even be surprised if there's a dozen different packs represented here. It's quite an event, seeing the Blood Moon going all out. I wonder if Nate's brother will be here. He's never appeared in public, and I've only ever met him once, but for his mate, maybe?

After a while, several black cars arrive. I step back a bit. I was so excited to see Nora again, I almost completely forgot Nathaniel would probably be here as well. Crap. I just hope he doesn't spot me. It should be fine. There are hundreds of people here; we are not really in the front row, and I'm concealing my aura.

Nora finally appears, and she's flanked by two wolves. Damn, I forgot how big Boyan is in his wolf form! The guy is so huge, he's closer to a bear than a wolf! Next to me, I see Iris' eyes widen in surprise, and she's not the only one. Yeah, the Black brothers aren't the only scary individuals around. The other wolf is the younger one, Liam. Mostly black, only a few reddish spots. I wonder if he's in his wolf form to intimidate the other side or protect Nora?

Nathaniel comes out too. Moon Goddess, I try to stay calm, but my heart's not ready for this. I'm still so shaken by our fight from last time. We haven't spoken since, and I'm probably not ready for that.

They start talking, Nathaniel, Nora, and the Alpha. We are too far to hear everything, but it's not that hard to get what's going on. People are growling at one another, and I'll bet they are not exchanging niceties either. I'm surprised how Nora can endure all that, with such a weak Alpha Aura. But once again, it's not like her aura itself is small, more like it's concealed. It did grow bigger since last time though, much bigger. The difference is stunning, but she's still below an average alpha. Moon Goddess, they wouldn't let her get killed, right?

"I didn't know she was so pretty," Iris whispers to me.

That's right. Nora is a very pretty girl, now that she looks healthier. She has fair white skin, and her luscious black locks float around her face. Aside from the scar on her left eye, her face is quite pretty too, and she has those gorgeous blue eyes.

Those blue eyes that seem so familiar to me. Why is that? I just can't…

While I'm lost in my thoughts, things suddenly get a lot tenser. Nora and her opponent, the Jade Moon Alpha, start circling each other, in an obvious duel stance. My inner wolf immediately tenses up, as if I was about to fight myself.

The Jade Moon Alpha strikes first. I was worried for a second, but to my surprise, Nora dodges exactly when she has to. Not only does she dodge it, but she even throws a kick back! Iris gasps next to me, admirative too. We both keep watching, but it's obvious: Nora is doing a good job defending herself. The Jade Moon Alpha is a decent fighter, but the King's mate is not letting him dominate her. I'm on edge. Every hit she takes, I feel like jumping in to help her. I can't believe everyone else is remaining calm, I'm boiling inside!

She doesn't seem to need it, though. Her opponent is showing his weaknesses, and more importantly, his fear of the Black brothers present. It's obvious. He keeps glancing at them when he should be focusing on Nora, and she makes good use of that. I see them talking again, but the growling of the wolves around makes it impossible for me to hear.

Then, they attack again, until the guy suddenly shape-shifts. He's about to jump at her when Nora shape-shifts too, and incredibly fast!

"Oh, Moon Goddess!"

But it's not her speed Iris is shocked about.

Nora's wolf is white. Completely white, snow-white, with blue eyes. I've never heard of a wolf looking even remotely like that before!

We have no time to contemplate though, the fight is still ongoing. But despite their attacks getting more brutal than before, I can tell many around us are still shocked by her appearance.

"I didn't think they really existed. The white and blue-eyed wolves..." mutters Iris.

I'm just as shocked as she is, but my wolf doesn't care about Nora's appearance, she's too worried about her to focus on such details.

However, the fight is over almost instantly after her shape-shifting. It was a perfect move, and in a split second, Nora is holding her Alpha, her fangs biting tight on his throat. He knows she can kill him any second, the guy has lost, or so it seems.

I just saw his arm rise at the last minute, and Nora backs off all of a sudden. She's really wounded, her fur is turning red! My wolf is all fidgety, urging me to go help her. I just can't, I...

"*Stay with your wolf.*"

I don't know why I'm mind-linking her, but I do, and it's incredibly easy. I can feel her wolf as if she was standing right in front of me. It's indescribable, the strongest bond I've ever felt before!

"*Don't let him dominate you!*"

I know she can do it. I feel her wolf sensing mine, she definitely heard me. Get him, girl, I'm right there with you. Her wolf's mind grows stronger from mine communicating with her, and she's ready to attack again. I'm with her.

Nora's doing great despite her fighting. I wait for the perfect opportunity, as if I was seeing through her eyes. My years of experience are all for this moment, to help her out. She sees it too. For a split-second, he makes a mistake, exposing his shoulder; she jumps and bites.

"*Take him down… Go for his neck.*"

She's listening to every each of my word and doing great job executing them. When she attacks again, I know this time's the right one. Nora bites furiously, and she's holding on, ready to bite until he submits.

"*You got him.*"

She keeps him down, and people around start cheering. They know it's over, and they are right. The Jade Moon Alpha gives up eventually. She won! She freaking won!

I'm happy like it was my own victory, it's unexplainable.

Nora lets go as soon as her Alpha, or former Alpha now I guess, gives up. I'm so happy for her, my heart is about to burst. Even my wolf is excited! Tonia gives her some clothes to put on, and she shifts back quickly.

The other's demeanors around her are speaking for themselves. Boyan and Tonia are flanking her like bodyguards, and Nate seems protective of her as well. However, Nora doesn't need anyone to speak for her. We hear the Jade Moon reluctantly concede his defeat once more, but she still acts very politely and reserved. Their whole pack is ready to submit to her, and everyone waits for her words. Actually, a few are ready to leave now that the fight is over. I get a bit closer, trying to hear her decision.

"I don't want to be your Alpha. That will only be an excuse for you guys to hate me more than you already do, and you will turn against me on the first occasion. I don't want to have to fight every day until one of you kills me. However, I do have conditions."

The determination on Nora's face is sort of impressive. She is standing like a real Alpha, despite her petite stature. The Jade Moon pack may be growling, unhappy, but they are at her mercy.

"The Jade Moon clan will pledge full and complete allegiance to the Blood Moon clan from today on. Your turf will become part of their territory, and your clan members will follow the same rules as theirs."

Wow, that's big. A lot of them protest, but Nora ignores them, or makes them shut up with a glare.

"I just dominated your Alpha, I'm free to do whatever I please with this pack. You guys never cared about training properly, so it's high time for things to change. Your turf is one of the first grounds at the border of Silver City. If anyone launches an attack on the area, you will be the first wall of defense. Do you want to stand on the frontlines being unprepared like you are now?" she says, before turning to her Alpha. "And you, you'll have to finally act like a real Alpha. You will train the young ones properly, watch the border, and make sure everyone in your clan is treated fairly. Am I clear?"

"Who are you to decide what kind of Alpha I should be? Aren't you washing your hands of my pack? You are giving us to him, and now you get to decide what we—" protests the defeated guy.

But Nora's eyes suddenly burst in anger, and I can feel her aura, like a cold flame, burning all the way to us. Many people take a step back, their wolves wary or intimidated by hers.

"Protecting their pack is the duty of any Alpha here!" she starts yelling. "Stop being so lazy and do what you were named Alpha for! You may have their respect, but you are worse than a dog if you think you can sit comfortably and relax just because of that! Any clan could overpower yours, and yet I'm giving you a chance to keep your turf and pack and turn them into a proper one! If you don't like it, then all of you can leave!"

Holy shit. She's the real thing. The guy is so speechless, he looks like he got whipped. Damn, Nora's aura is on a whole other level once she unleashes it! Is this the same weak girl they were talking about? That girl is one hundred percent Alpha material!

"Moon Goddess," whispers Iris, just as impressed as I am.

"I know."

"This is for real," says my cousin. "She's going to become the Luna someday."

That, I have absolutely no doubt about. All around us, people are whispering about her already, some still stunned by her incredible inner wolf. That, plus her appearance that is one we've only heard about from legends. No doubt, everyone will keep a close eye on her from now on.

"Elena, look!"

Iris gives a little nod in the direction, and I suddenly feel it. Like an icy wind, a cold chill hits me. I recognize that sensation.

The King is here.

That guy is about twice as frightening as Nora. Not only is his aura terrifying, but he's expanding his aura like some death warning. It's like being stared at by a cold-blooded killer, except that he doesn't even have to look our way.

He slowly walks to Nora, but everyone else is so tense they have backed off. I'm pretty sure a few wolves even ran away, too intimidated to stay. Honestly, I can't blame them. My own wolf is not feeling too good either. It's werewolf instinct, we just know who the bigger monster is. He whispers something to Nora, and I realize how calm she is. I'm about fifty feet away, my wolf is freaking out and I'm scared, while she's perfectly fine standing right next to him! Iris is frowning too, and I can tell she's terrorized by the King's murderous aura.

As soon as he starts talking, though I can't hear what he says, more people run away. With all of the Black brothers present, there is no way the Jade Moon has anything to say anymore. Eventually, from their behaviors, I understand the guy submitted to Nora. It's over.

"Elena, let's go back. We shouldn't–"

But I stepped forward, ignoring Iris. I want to talk to Nora and understand why we are able to mind-link. This isn't my first time connecting with another alpha, but there's something completely different about our link. Like it's engraved in us, something that was there and wide open from the start. I can feel her wolf so easily, this can't be a coincidence!

"Elena!"

Iris insists, but I'm already heading towards the little crowd. Crap, how do I get to her with all those Blood Moon people and wolves surrounding their group? Nora is more heavily guarded than the mayor.

But suddenly, she turns her head to my left and starts running. What the hell? She's really fast, too!

By reflex, I start running too, trying to follow her from afar. Nora left so fast, only Boyan followed her right away. Everyone departed late, and she's now way ahead. Her wolf is so fast, too, I didn't even see the moment she shape-shifted. I keep running, too, but on my human legs.

Damn, that girl is fast. Thank Moon Goddess, I was in the right direction to follow her, even if it's from afar. Nora's headed right into the Sea Moon's territory, too, this can't be good. Where is she going anyway?

She suddenly ran off. I keep tracking her, all the way to the docks. This is no good, none of us should be here.

Bobo and I make eye-contact, though I can't tell if he had noticed me before. He doesn't slow down, though, and we keep running. Crap, I need to shape-shift again or I might lose them.

I look for my wolf, but just when I want to shape-shift, she refuses and ignores me. What the hell? Why is she acting stubborn now!

Suddenly, I hear a splash. Something fell into the sea? Bobo runs by me to keep going in that direction, as if he didn't hear it. I hesitate and go for the seafront. I can feel Nora's wolf that way! Oh Moon Goddess, don't tell me she…?

"*Boyan!*"

"*Grab Nora, I need to get him!*"

Get who, exactly? I growl and jump into the water. Fuck, it's the end of November, that damn water is freezing! I can almost feel my clothes getting iced around me!

"*Hang on!*"

Thank Moon Goddess, she didn't sink too deep yet. I grab the white wolf by its neck and pull her, swimming to the surface. I'm so freaking cold. I finally get us both out of the water. Damn, that wind makes it way worse.

Nora is coughing, shape-shifting back and trying to catch her breath. She swallowed a lot of water. I pat her back, hoping she'd warm up soon.

"*Are you okay?*" I ask, shivering myself.

She nods weakly, while I try to push her hair out of her face, helping her sit up.

"*It's okay, breathe. Use the mind-link to talk to me, don't waste your strength.*"

I feel her inner wolf hesitate, and she finally finds our mind-link.

"*Thanks.*"

I nod. Damn, she looks exhausted. And I'm strangely happy to be so close to her. I can't describe that feeling, like… we should be together. What the hell is that? I look for my wolf again. Come one, we have to! This time, she shape-shifts, a bit reluctantly. Nora is finally looking up, looking at me, her eyes a bit red and watery from coughing so much.

"*Elena, you need to get out of here. They're coming.*"

Bobo's voice suddenly reminds me I'm totally not supposed to be here. Crap.

"*How far, Bobo?*"

"You got a minute or two. I got the guy, they'll catch up to you in no time to check on Nora. Nathaniel and Liam too. Just go, I'll cover for you."

I thank him silently and turn to Nora again to address her.

"Don't worry, they'll be here soon. Bobo got him. Just catch your breath, your mate is coming. I got to go."

"Wait! Who are you?"

Moon Goddess, I wish I could stay and tell her everything I know now. Even discuss with her this bond between us, figure out what it means! I have so many theories, it's driving me crazy. But I already hear the other wolves coming. Boyan's right, I have to go.

"I can't stay, I am not supposed to be here. Don't worry, I'll find you again. Don't tell anyone about me. Especially not Nate."

I run away, after one last look at her. I swear, those eyes. I've seen it all before. I run between the docks, trying to evade both the Sea Moon wolves and Nate's pack. It's not easy, but I finally manage to find the road Iris took to get here. I'm still in my wolf form, my fur is soaked with ice-cold water and I'm in the middle of nowhere, without any clothes to change into.

"Iris? Iris, please tell me you're still around."

"Elena! Moon Goddess I was freaking out! Where are you?"

She finds me a few minutes later and picks me up in her car. She sighs when I get on the backseat, still in my wolf form. Seeing how I'm soaked and soaking her car too, she puts on the heater full blast.

"Seriously, Elena, you just ran off and I had no idea what to do! Half the Blood Moon started running after you and that girl, I was shocked."

"Sorry, sorry."

"What's the deal with that girl? Why are you interested in her?"

"I'm not sure. I think we're somewhat... connected."

Iris frowns.

"Connected? Elena, you're always so complicated... Anyway, I'll take you home, okay? You'll die if you stay like that. How did you even get drenched?"

After that, we don't really talk for the rest of the trip. I'm exhausted anyway, and probably in the middle of getting sick too. Iris drives me home, where Danny is waiting for me after I mind-linked him.

Back in my human form, I get into the warm bath he got ready for me first, while he sits down next to the bathtub. Danny poured us some cold beers, and listens while I tell him everything that happened today. When I finally catch up to the present, he is frowning.

"The way I mind-linked with her… Danny, I swear, I think I'm related to her somehow. It felt like… well, like I guess it'd feel to connect with a sibling."

"Yeah, to be honest, the first time you mentioned it, I thought it might be that, but you really don't look like each other?"

"Not really. She's got dark hair, white skin, and sapphire-blue eyes. And she's rather petite, too, while I'm tall like a giraffe. And to be honest, I didn't have time to really take a good look at her, there wasn't much time."

"Thank Moon Goddess the Blood Moon didn't see you."

I nod while drinking a bit more beer. That's for sure. Danny sighs and puts his chin on the edge of the bathtub, lost in his thoughts again.

"All right, let's assume you're from the same family. She might be a distant relative then. But you know, that means we could have another clue about your birth parents, starting from there. Do we know anything about her?"

"Well, that's another problem. We don't. According to Iris, the Blood Moon is already trying to find out more about her, but they don't have much. We know she lived in the Jade Moon pack all this time, but it's clear she wasn't born there. Damn, I'll have to ask Eric if he found anything else, because with just a name we won't get there."

"Her name?"

"Nora Bluemoon, I actually found out today, from Iris."

I wonder if I can ask Eric to call me if he finds anything else again. Maybe he can give me the info without the Blood Moon knowing. It would be a bit risky for sure, but that's why we have cops among us too.

"Nora Bluemoon?" suddenly repeats Danny.

I'm surprised, since he was silent for a while. I nod.

"Yes, Nora Bluemoon."

"Bluemoon?"

"Daniel, are you playing deaf or what?"

"Elena, what's your last name?"

I frown. Where is he going with this?

"Whitewood?"

"Why?"

"Because our clan is named the White Moon, and my dad's family were the first to be established in this for–"

Oh Moon Goddess. I suddenly understand what he was getting at. I stay speechless for a second, my mind going crazy with ideas and theories. I look at Danny, my heart beating crazy.

"Bluemoon," I repeat.

"Yup. A Blue Moon," says Daniel.

"Like a Blue Moon clan! Oh Moon Goddess, Daniel Lewis, you're a fucking genius!" I yell, running out of the bath.

"Thanks, but I already knew that. And, Elena, you're naked in the middle of the living room!"

I don't care. I have to make a call right now!

Daniel brings me a bathrobe while I'm still on the phone, waiting for someone to pick up.

"What are you doing? Who are you calling?" he asks, confused.

"The one person who might know if that Blue Moon clan was a real thing," I reply.

I can't calm down, I want to smash that smartphone. Someone please pick up! After a while, he finally picks up.

"Henry! It's Elena. Is Reagan there?"

"No. She came yesterday. Haven't seen her since."

Damn! I thought she might have been at her favorite pub. I thank Henry briefly and hang up. Where might my mentor be right now? It's almost 8:00 p.m., she's usually drinking at this time. If not, I don't know where she could be. Daniel crosses his arms.

"You want to try asking Reagan?"

"If it's my birth clan, she might know something."

"Sure."

"Who should I call? She wasn't at the bar."

Daniel sighs, nods, and goes to grab his own phone.

We spend the next hour calling almost everyone we know to try and figure out where Reagan is, but as usual, my mentor is a real mystery. No one knows her whereabouts since she was spotted earlier this morning in the forest by one of Levi's patrol friends.

I'm exhausted and angry when we finally give up. At least we know they'll call us back as soon as they see Reagan somewhere again. I growl and sit down on the couch. Daniel tries to soothe me, but I'm stuck in that whirlwind of emotions.

"It's a nightmare, Danny. Every time I think I've found something new, it just turns into a dead end again! And Reagan is just…"

I can't even express my frustration. If only she would talk! She knows, I know she freaking knows something, but won't say it. I sit down on the couch, desperate. Daniel heads to the kitchen.

"Don't worry babe, we're making progress. I'm telling you, that Blue Moon clan theory might be a real thing!"

"And how would we know? Reagan's playing dead and I have no one else to ask."

I pause. Actually, I do. I kind of put this at the back of my mind since it was complicated enough just to see her once, but… Danny spots my expression while bringing two cups of coffee.

"Babe, you got that face you make when you're about to say something crazy, reckless, dangerous, or all of the above."

"I have to meet Nora again," I say.

"I knew it," he sighs. "Okay, let's skip the 'this is a dumb idea' part and get right to when you explain your idea to me."

"I don't have an idea, I just need to meet her again. I'll ask Boyan to help."

"Boyan has been unreachable since he's been guarding her!" says Danny.

"I can mind-link him. It's hard, but, if I force it a little, I can reach him."

Daniel looks at me, totally shocked. Yeah. I kind of forgot to tell him about that. He takes a step back, frowning at me with a confused expression.

"Boyan is a beta," he says.

"I know."

"You mind-linked a beta. From another clan."

"Yep."

"Elena!"

"I know! I know it's kind of crazy, but it just happened and back then, I didn't really, you know, realize."

"Elena, it's already crazy enough that you can freely mind-link any alpha, but now you can mind-link betas too? Babe, this isn't a trivial matter!"

I understand Daniel's concerns, but really, I don't think it's that big of a deal. I sigh and grab my cup, trying to act calm.

"Listen, it was already kind of weird that I could mind-link alphas. So honestly, being able to mind-link Bobo is kind of a drop in the ocean… and maybe it's because we're close?"

"I am close to Boyan. You're close to Boyan because he's my boy–well, soon-to-be-ex-boyfriend, okay?"

"Stop the drama, Danny. Anyway, back to the main topic, Boyan can help me talk to Nora."

"So your idea is to harass Boyan through mind-link until he calls you back to let you meet with that Nora girl?"

I nod. I gulp down some coffee while Daniel shakes his head, not convinced. Damn, this coffee is disgusting! I put it down with a frown while I still taste the bitterness on my tongue.

"Seriously, Danny, I told you to stop buying that stupid coffee brand, it's disgusting!"

"Yeah, yeah, next I'll buy your Cuban coffee. That is so not relevant right now."

I roll my eyes and get up to make myself some tea, I'm craving something sour. He keeps telling me this isn't going to work, but I'm now dead set on the idea.

"Listen, Danny, I'll try to wait, okay? At least until we hear from Reagan or something. Your idea is the best we've got so far about my origins! I mean, it is a bit of a jump to assume that last name really is a clan's name and mine for that matter, but…"

Daniel sighs and drinks my cup of coffee, frowning.

"I get it, babe. You're desperate for answers anyway. Let's just ask Eric for help and wait. I mean, I wouldn't be against Boyan resurfacing from whatever ivory tower the Luna's locked in… speaking of towers, did you see you-know-who?"

I glare at him.

"Yes. Not gonna talk about it."

"Got it."

Damn, I didn't want to think about that jerk now. I just want to think about Nora, and how to get in touch with her. Damn, if only Boyan would answer. Daniel sighs.

"How about we do this; I can ask if anyone's heard anything about a Blue Moon clan, while you try to reach Boyan or Reagan, okay?"

I watch him grab his jacket, confused. Can't he just phone them?

"Where are you going?"

Daniel hesitates for a second, then grabs his phone and keys, a bit distracted.

"I'm gonna ask a friend. Someone who might know."

"Your friend doesn't have a phone?" I ask, raising an eyebrow.

"No, well… I mean I need to go to them directly, okay?"

"Are you going to see an ex-boyfriend, Daniel? Because I'm still rooting for Boyan, you know."

"I'm not!" he sighs. "I'm just going out, and I promise I'll be back soon, okay?"

"Okay."

I watch him leave in a hurry, still confused. What was that? And why is he acting so secretive suddenly? Except for a few of his shameful relationships, Daniel never hides anything from me! Why would he need to meet someone I don't know about?

I sigh and go grab a change of clothes. Damn, I'm tired and hungry now. I head to the kitchen and grab some toast and cheese. I'm really starving! I eat three pieces of toasts, but I'd rather have Danny's cooking, or Nate's.

Damn, that idiot. I check my phone, but still nothing since last time. It's tiring, how we keep fighting, getting back together, fighting again. I know it's not good. Too reckless. I can't afford that anymore. Especially when I think about whoever that bitch was at his place.

I decide to give Eric a call to ask him if he knows anything more, just because I need to keep myself busy. He only tells me that Nora was checked at the hospital, but now she's back in the Blood Moon's territory again. Crap, if she's so heavily guarded, it's going to be really, really hard…

Damn, I don't even remember falling asleep. I called Eric, and then... nothing. It's so dark in the apartment. Is Danny not back yet? I check my phone, but the battery died. Crap. I struggle to find my charger when someone bangs on our apartment door. What the heck?

"Elena! Open up, right now!"

Shit, what does my uncle want now? He never comes here!

I go to open the door, but Xavier barges in, literally furious. I don't think I've seen my uncle mad like this in a while. He almost runs into me while heading to the middle of the living room, red with anger.

"What the hell, Xavier?"

"I should be the one saying that! What the fuck were you doing outside our border again?"

What the... I stare at my uncle, completely lost. Has he gone nuts? The only time I went outside was for Nora's fight today!

"Are you kidding me? I had your fucking permission!"

"My permission, Elena? Seriously? To go out? When did I ever give you that?"

Oh Moon Goddess, is he fucking playing dumb on purpose?

"Iris called you! I was right there, Xavier, I heard you tell her it was fine for us to go!"

"I never said you could go anywhere! You disobeyed me on purpose! Are you trying to test my limits, Elena? I had told you if you left our territory again, there would be consequences!"

I can't believe this man! Is he pretending it never happened just to rant at me? As if I didn't have enough shit to deal with right now! How dare he pretend he never agreed to it? Is he just trying to screw me over for the pleasure of it? I can't believe him!

"So that's it? You found a way to fuck me over, Xavier? Really? I didn't think you would stoop so low!"

"I agreed for Iris to go there, I never said you could go! Now if you blame this on my daughter this will really go bad for you, Elena!"

"Don't you fucking threaten me on top of it!" I yell, my wolf growling.

He steps back, surprised at how I'm mad at him too. I can bear it when he's angry at me for disobeying him, but this is fucking unfair! My wolf is furious, growling at my uncle and telling him to keep away. She's mad and warning him to stay away from her for real. My aura is fuming, I'm so fucking mad at him!

But he suddenly comes back at me, growling even more furiously, gathering his Alpha Aura to growl back at me.

"You little bitch, how dare you rebel right in front of me! And disobey my order on purpose too! You really asked for it this time, Elena!"

He suddenly raises his hand.

"This time you're going to–!"

But before he finishes his sentence, I see my uncle fall on the floor. I was prepared for the worst, for him to punch and fight me, but he just collapsed at my feet. What the heck?

"Hi, Elena."

To my surprise, Sylviana is standing right there, perfectly calm. I was not ready for that. What is she doing at our place anyway? Daniel is right behind her, too, looking down at Xavier in horror.

"Oh Moon Goddess, Sylviana, please tell me you didn't kill him!" he shrieks.

"What? Oh, of course not, I just made him sleep a little."

Sleep? He looks like he's in a freaking coma! My uncle is lying on the ground in a weird position, like an inanimate puppet. It's disturbing. My eyes go from Danny to Sylviana, then to Danny again, who's closing our door.

"Okay, is anyone going to explain to me what just happened?" I say, exhausted.

"Sorry, I'm not fond of violence," Sylviana replies, going to our kitchen.

I look at her, completely stunned. This situation is surreal! She just had my uncle collapse out of the blue, and in front of my eyes too!

"You did something weird to me last time too!" I insist. "You were the one to give me that weird feeling the first time I met Nora!"

"Yes, I know."

Is she going to keep talking in enigmas? Because this is frustrating! Danny walks to me with an apologetic look. He puts his hands on my shoulders and gently pushes me back to our couch. I notice his hair is still wet from the rain outside. Did he just go to get Sylviana and came back here?

"Sit down, babe. I have a couple of things I have to tell you, okay?"

"About your weird friend?"

I keep sending glances in Sylviana's direction, unable to decide if she is supposed to be here or not. Daniel's worried face is not making me feel better at all.

"She's not weird," he replies.

"She just made my uncle sleep like a baby!" I say, pointing at the evidence lying on the floor a few steps away.

My uncle is in a weird position, and lying in our living room! Tell me again that his friend is not weird! I look in her direction again, but the more I see of that red-haired girl, the more confused I feel.

Now that I'm looking at her more clearly, I can tell there's something abnormal about her. My instincts tell me to stay away, there's something wrong. Something not human. Sylviana pours herself a cup of lemon tea as if it was her house and comes to sit next to me on the couch. I can't help but move farther away from her a little.

"Okay, if one of you doesn't start talking now, I'm really going to be mad," I warn them.

"Babe, Sylviana and I are university friends, you know that, right?"

I want to ask Danny why he is talking to me like I'm a child, but I don't and just give him a pissed off look. He sighs.

"When I started working with Sylviana in Biology, I noticed she... was very good, extremely good, to be honest. Her experiments were going too well, our entire greenhouse was doing awesome compared to others. Eventually, Sylviana and I became closer, and we started talking. And she told me a secret I couldn't tell anyone, not even you."

"A secret?" I repeat, a bit lost.

Sylviana gives me a big smile.

"That's right. Your instincts were right about me. I'm a witch, Elena."

I look at them, annoyed.

"That's a lame joke, Danny."

"It's not a joke, Elena."

I hesitate for a second, looking at both of them, doubtful. But no... Moon Goddess, they are fucking serious!

"Babe, you need to breathe, you're scaring me."

"Breathe? Danny, we have a witch in our living room!" I yell.

Daniel and Sylviana exchange a look, but I'm just feeling completely astonished right now. A witch. My best friend, my childhood friend whom I thought I knew by heart, has a witch friend that I had no idea about and has been working with her for three years too!

"It's normal to be shocked, Elena. Just don't be mad at Daniel, I asked him to keep this a secret when he found out. It's not easy to be a witch in a city full of humans and werewolves."

"So... you're not a bad witch?" I ask, a bit awkward.

Sylviana chuckles.

"No, Elena. I don't turn people into frogs, I don't eat children, and I'm not green, either. Just a good witch, minding her own business most of the time."

"So, what do you do?" I ask. "I mean, no offense, but we don't get a witch or vampire history class at school."

She got up and walked across the room. Because I now know that she isn't human, she feels even more eerie than usual. Her red, wavy hair, especially, and her green eyes are natural, right?

Sylviana checks one of our fanned plants. Danny grimaces, since it's one of his. I guess he's been lazy with gardening lately. But as soon as the witch's fingers touch it, it immediately changes to a bright green, and a few flowers even bloom within seconds! I'm witnessing real-life magic! I'm speechless.

Sylviana smiles at me and comes back to sit.

"I am an Earth Witch. My main domains are plants, living creatures, wood… Basically anything linked to earth."

"So, there are… other types of witches?" I ask, unsure.

She nods.

"For witches, the world is divided into three elements: Water, Earth, Fire, and all of that is in a cycle."

"What about wind?"

"Different element, not for witches," Sylviana simply answered. "Anyway, a witch gets her element from birth to death, we don't change. I was born under the Earth element, and I'm able to learn and grow my powers within that element."

"Okay, but… I mean, why Silver City? It's packed with werewolves! And are you alone?" I ask

"I am alone now. Though it wasn't always the case… You werewolves think you were here long before us, but it's the other way around. Witches lived among the humans in Silver City, and probably in any other city, long before the wolves came to settle in cities. We just didn't make ourselves known. I'm the only one left, though."

I take a deep breath in.

Moon Goddess, that's a lot to take in. It's like a whole new world just exploded in front of me. As a werewolf, I always knew about witches and that they existed somehow. As pups, we were always told stories about the bad witches who come and take the bad pups away, but I never thought I would meet one in real life!

I still think it's hard to believe a witch has been freely living in Silver City all this time. Half the population here is werewolf, and witches are our natural predators. It's all about the food chain, or its supernatural equivalent, the one we heard about from our parents. Werewolves chase vampires. Vampires feed on humans. Humans hunt witches. And witches attack werewolves. Sure, it has evolved a lot since then, but…

"So, you don't use werewolves for secret potions and stuff like that?"

Yeah, I know how stupid and childish that sounds. No need to give me that look, Danny. To my relief however, Sylviana takes my question very seriously.

"No, I'm not a witch who does that, to anyone. I tend to like werewolves and live in peace with them. It's true that some witches use werewolves for bad things, though."

Great, I'm not sure I was ready to hear that, but whatever. It's not like we have other witches waiting around in gingerbread houses anyway. I sigh and grab my cup of lemon tea to try and calm myself down. That's a lot of emotions for today.

I look at my uncle, lying on the floor, and point at him with my index finger.

"Should I be worried about that?"

"Oh, it's not like I can do that to anyone. It only works on weak minds, whether it's humans or werewolves. You do not have a weak mind," she says with a big smile, "but don't worry, he won't remember what happened when he wakes up."

"When will he wake up?"

"Hmm... In an hour or so?"

I sigh. Well, frankly I'm not too sorry for him, and at least I get an extra hour of peace. For now, I turn to Danny, who looks half worried and half sorry.

"Are you mad?"

"I'm not sure," I answer. "Sylviana asked you to not say anything, right?"

"Well, it took me a while to figure it out and a bit more to confirm, and you kind of already had a lot going on, babe."

"You're not wrong, but… Oh, well, fine, I get it. You had reasons. Now, why are you guys telling me all this now?"

Daniel turned to Sylviana.

"Can you tell her?"

Sylviana sighed, and after a while, spoke in a very calm voice.

"Daniel knows I have another power. Like most witches, I'm a seer."

"You can see the future?"

"The future, the past, the present. I get a glimpse of each if I focus on something. It's like looking into a very, very large and complex picture looking for a grain of sand. I need to know what I'm looking for exactly."

I exchange a look with Daniel and understand. Sylviana could know more about my past, about my family! I turn to her.

"How does it work?"

"The more I know, the better."

I nod and take out my sun necklace, to show it to her. I start explaining to her how I got to the White Moon clan, my adoption, and everything Reagan told me so far.

"Lately, she told me something else. She said her and I were born in an old pack, one far in the north. According to her, it was so big it had over a thousand members, and there was a Luna Queen. From what Reagan said, she must have been damn powerful because she didn't have a mate and still ruled. But Reagan told me our pack had been killed, and she had brought me here while trying to find the other half of the pack, a group that had parted with their clan decades before. She said she didn't know what had attacked our previous pack."

Sylviana listened to my story in silence, not acting surprised or anything. I hesitate a bit, and resume talking, Danny's hand on my knee to encourage me.

"Reagan said my parents were dead, and she is very unwilling to talk about that former pack, or why I'm stronger, different from other wolves. But…"

"You do not believe her," said Sylviana.

I nod.

"I just know when she lies or hides things. She's bad at lying but good at keeping secrets. And recently, there was this girl."

"You met Nora Bluemoon."

I look up at Sylviana, shocked. How the hell does she know Nora? Did she see something about her somehow? It's so intriguing to talk to her, I can't tell what she thinks or how much she knows!

She smiles gently.

"I've had my eyes on Nora for a while. She's the King's fated mate after all. And she's somewhat special."

"I've seen her wolf, too. She's white like snow, and her eyes are…"

Sylviana nods enigmatically, but she doesn't answer me, and grabs her cup of lemon tea to drink a bit. I sigh and understand there are some things I should focus on first, starting with my theories.

"Her last name is Bluemoon, and when I met her, I felt we were connected, like wolves of a same pack or family."

"You want to know if Nora is part of a Blue Moon clan you would have belonged to as well."

I slowly nod.

"Reagan said everyone but her and I had died. If Nora is really one of my kin, and alive, maybe…" I say, with hope.

But Sylviana shakes her head.

"I'm sorry, Elena. But your family, your parents really are dead, like Reagan said."

I feel my heart drop, like something very, very heavy just crushed it. It's hard to hear. I knew it was only a faint hope, but... I gulp down and try to repress a tear.

"How do you know?" I ask.

"I know."

I frown. So, she's just going to answer by enigmas, too? But to my surprise, Sylviana sighs and puts her cup down.

"Witches, werewolves, and vampires are children of the Moon Goddess. We are all different but connected. So, when a Luna as powerful as Queen Diane emerged and passed, there was no way I wasn't aware as well. Every witch around felt it."

I almost choke. Queen Diane? I've never heard of that name!

"Was that the Luna?"

"She was the Luna of that former pack, that's right. The Blue Moon pack had a Luna so powerful, she was filled with the Moon Goddess' power, and was a Royal werewolf so pure, like no one had seen for years."

"Wow, wait a second, Syl," said Daniel. "A Royal? We're talking about the real thing, a Royal werewolf? Like the legends?"

Daniel is right, this is insane! The Royal werewolves are no more! Long ago, the purest, strongest of our species were called the Royals, because they were like royalty to us: so strong, so wise, and pure-blooded they radiated with Alpha Auras.

But that was centuries ago! Now, we have mixed our blood with humans for so many generations, the Royals eventually became regular werewolves and just disappeared. But for one to come back, they would have to be a reincarnation of the Moon Goddess, like Queen Diane.

An image comes to my mind, something I couldn't forget even if I tried.

"Nora's wolf was white and sapphire-eyed, like the legends," I whisper, still in shock.

"She could be that woman's descendant," says Danny. "Right? Could she be that Queen Diane's child or…"

"Grand-child," said Sylviana. "Queen Diane died fifty years ago. If she had a child, it could be Nora's relative, yes. Possibly."

"You can't make sure?" I ask her, febrile.

Sylviana shakes her head.

"My power has its limits. There was no way for me to ignore Queen Diane's existence, since all witches knew such a woman existed. My mother told me about her, and even I felt the remnants of her power despite her death. But if Nora is linked to her, it is for her to uncover the truth."

I sigh. Moon Goddess, I thought we were making progress, but it turns out we have even more to uncover.

"So, that Royal family is…"

"Dead, yes. Reagan told the truth."

"But Nora!"

"Reagan couldn't have known of a child born after she had left the pack," suddenly said Danny. "Babe, think about it. The Black brothers said the girl was seventeen, right? If we believe Reagan, she had left the Blue Moon pack before that! If when she got back, someone else had taken Nora or whatever, it could explain why you had no idea about each other! I bet she has no idea another child survived, and you were too young to know. If that's what happened."

I stay silent for a while, trying to digest all of this.

The Blue Moon clan, and a Luna Queen, Diane.

Nora Bluemoon, who might be a Royal's grandchild, and a relative of mine.

My parents, dead for real.

Danny puts an arm around me, trying to soothe me.

"You okay, babe? That was a lot."

"I just... I really need to talk to Nora again, Danny. She needs to know, and I need to know more."

"About your pack?"

I turn to Sylviana again, frowning, remembering what Reagan had told me.

"When Reagan mentioned she had found me in the middle of the slaughter, she said something… She didn't really know what had attacked them. Something she couldn't understand. I know my mentor, and she's seen a lot of things. She would recognize a vampire's doing, or even another werewolf pack. So, what attacked them?"

Sylviana nodded, glancing down.

"That's another issue to solve, I fear. You should handle one problem at a time, Elena."

"Right. Thanks, Sylviana, that's still a lot more than what I had gathered in all these years!"

"Babe, I still think you should talk to Reagan," says Daniel.

"Why?"

"This is her story as much as yours. And since you know so much now, maybe she'll talk more. I still don't get why she was not willing to talk, but…"

"Reagan is trying to protect you, Elena. And she still feels guilty about what happened," explained Sylviana.

Guilty for what? I know she couldn't find her pack, but why would she feel responsible for what happened, and hide everything from me? Moon Goddess, I'm tired of all the lies, and secrets. I show my necklace to Sylviana.

"Do you know anything about this? About the sun?"

She barely looks at it.

"Danny is right, Elena. You should talk to Reagan."

I sigh and look at my necklace, that little, mysterious sunshine.

"Okay, I'll just ask Reagan. As soon as I find her, I guess."

"She's in the north-east forest, Elena, but she'll be back soon," says Sylviana.

I nod. Well, at least I finally got to know where my mentor is hiding! I get up and head to the kitchen, exhausted.

"Babe?"

"I need a drink, after all this. Sylviana, do you drink wine?"

"I do, but you really shouldn't drink, Elena."

I frown while taking the bottle of white wine.

"Why not?"

I mean, I could really use a drink. Sylviana sighs.

"Elena, you can't drink. You are pregnant."

The bottle of wine drops and breaks at my feet. I don't even care. I'm staring at Sylviana, still unable to process what she just said. I blink a couple of times. I try to breathe.

"Sorry, you… What?"

"You're pregnant, Elena."

Moon Goddess, no, no. I smile nervously, but there's nothing joyous about it. I shake my head, unable to hear it. She's wrong, she's got to be wrong. It can't be. How would she even know? I see Daniel, next to her, in the same state as me, his eyes going between Sylviana and me.

"I'm not pregnant. I'm not," I just mutter.

"I'm sure. You are pregnant."

"I'm not pregnant!" I yell.

I feel the tears before they even come out. My crying gets intense, erratic, loud. Daniel almost runs to me to try and help me calm down.

"Hey, babe, calm down, calm down."

"I'm not pregnant, Danny, it can't be, I'm…"

How could I be pregnant? I lost a baby before! I don't even know if I can have another baby! I don't feel pregnant at all, I don't even know what I'm supposed to feel!

Daniel hugs me, patting my back and holding me against him.

"Danny, I can't."

"It's okay, babe, I'm here, I'm here. Breathe. Calm down, Elena, it's okay, babe. It's okay…"

It takes a while for me to actually calm down. I cry, a lot. Because it's too sudden, because I don't, I can't, hear about a pregnancy now. I'm not ready at all. I just freaking broke up with Nathaniel! How can I be pregnant now?

I listen to Danny's voice for a while, trying to take deep breaths and slow down my weeping. I ruined his shirt with my tears and snot, but Moon Goddess, I don't care. Danny holds me for a long time, caressing my hair and soothing me until I can sit down and breathe without choking up.

I look at Sylviana, almost mad at her for telling me right now. I don't even know if she's right, and I'm not sure I want to confirm it.

"Syl, are you sure?" asks Danny.

She nods.

"If a witch says you're expecting, you are, Elena. You're about ten, no, almost eleven weeks."

"Eleven weeks!"

That's nearly 3 months! Moon Goddess, I can't have been pregnant and not noticed a thing, it's not possible! I can't possibly…

"Babe, when was your last period?" asks Daniel.

I glare at him. Really, now? But I still sigh and make the effort to try and remember.

"Probably… when Nate came over and made me pizza."

"Elena, that was in September, 3 months ago! Are you kidding me?"

"You know my period is irregular! And with everything that's been going on, I just didn't pay attention to that."

"That's the kind of thing you're supposed to pay attention to, babe, especially if you have sex with you-know-who!"

I sigh. I know, it was stupid of me to not check earlier about my period! I turn to Sylviana, trying to understand.

"I'm on the pill, how can it…"

"Pills are not completely effective, even more so with alpha werewolves, Elena. I wouldn't rely on it as contraception. In your case, well, you have proof now."

My gosh, I don't know if I want to scream or slam something. Worse thing is, I'm pretty sure I might have forgotten the pill a couple of times back when I was living with Nate. No way I'm letting Danny know about that, though.

I can't believe this is really happening. Moon Goddess, if I really am pregnant with Nate's baby…

"Daniel, I need to check. I'm sorry Sylviana, I'm not saying you're lying, but…"

"It's all right, I understand," she says with a soft smile.

"I can call the clinic," says Danny, grabbing his phone.

"Daniel, I'm pregnant with Nathaniel Black's baby! I can't just walk into the White Moon clan's clinic. Everyone will wonder what the hell I'm doing at OB-GYN!"

Moon Goddess, Xavier and Clark will kill me if they find out. Daniel nods.

"It's all right, we can ask Iris and Mom to help, they both work there, and we can trust them, okay?"

"Okay."

He sighs and turns to Sylviana.

"Girl, you can't drop bombs like that."

"Daniel, she's nearly three months. I thought she knew."

She does look a bit sorry, but honestly, I don't really care about being mad at her right now. I'm still in shock.

Nate's baby. I might be pregnant with Nathaniel's baby. I turn to Sylviana, a bit intrigued. Without thinking about it, I already have a hand on my tummy.

"How can you tell?"

"I told you, it's a witch thing. We are good midwives. I can tell you more if you want to hear it."

"More?"

"Your baby's health, the gender."

What the heck, she can already tell my baby's gender? He or she is only 11 weeks old! Does it even have a gender yet at that stage? I sigh and sit back down. I forgot about that stupid wine I spilled on the floor, but Danny is already taking care of it. Moon Goddess, I love my best friend.

"I want to know!" says Danny from the kitchen.

Sylviana smiles at him, but I know she's waiting for me. My gosh, I can barely believe I'm having a baby right now, do I really want the specifics? Moon Goddess, I can feel my wolf is anxious for her pup and urges me to ask the witch. Is that why she wasn't allowing me to shape-shift lately? Because she knew by instinct?

I nod.

"All right, well, first, you're expecting a girl. But Elena, you have to know, irregular periods are a sign of a weak uterus. Your chances of miscarriage are high."

Oh Moon Goddess, no. I turn to Daniel, but he already knows. I'm not losing another baby again, and certainly not Nate's baby. No fucking way.

"Don't worry Elena, I'll help you out. You want this baby, don't you?"

I slowly nod. I know I already love this baby of mine, even if I say I don't really believe Sylviana's words yet. Moon Goddess, there better be a child in there. I'll break that witch's neck if she gives me false hope like that.

"No more caffeine, alcohol, or shape-shifting for you. Only lots of rest and no stress, Elena."

That's going to be hard. And how will I hide my pregnancy? If the pack members don't see me shape-shifting for training and all, people will start asking questions. Moreover, how do I even hide a pregnancy? I mean, there's about 5 months of tummy growing left, and after that, I supposedly will have a whole baby! I turn to Danny, a bit panicked.

"Danny, if anyone knows who the dad is..."

"I know. It's okay, we'll come up with something. But you're going to tell him, right?"

Tell him. Oh, Moon Goddess, I didn't even think about that! Damn, how will I even tell Nate? The timing couldn't be worse! Hey, I know we fought about you having a mistress behind my back, but guess what? I'm pregnant with your baby! Oh, damn.

I have no idea how he will react. And there's the King, too! Holy crap, what did I get myself into now. I sigh, and Sylviana pushes my cup of tea towards me with a warm smile.

"I guess that means tea is fine?"

"It is."

I sigh and grab my cup, getting the hot drink down my throat. The lemon helps me calm down a bit, but it's a drop in the ocean. Danny just finished cleaning my mess and joins us, sitting next to me again.

"Babe, we have another problem."

"I know."

Diego.

If that butthole knows about me being pregnant, I have no idea what he'll do, but it's going to be bad. He is the last person I want to know about my child, my daughter. I get the chills just thinking about it. Remembering how I lost Angel… No way I'm losing another baby. I wouldn't survive this pain a second time.

Moon Goddess, that's a lot to think about.

"So, we need to hide the real father from the pack, and ideally, hide this pregnancy as long as possible so your ex doesn't go nuts. All that added to our secret meeting with Nora."

"I can help with that," said Sylviana.

I turn to her, intrigued.

"Nora? You know how to contact her?"

"Not yet," she says with a smile, "but I know someone on the inside."

"So do we," sighs Danny. "I mean, if we can persuade Bobo."

"Nora's birthday is coming up the day after tomorrow," says Sylviana. "They will most likely take her out at that time."

"Okay, so we know when to strike! You can mind-harass my boyfriend to know where, Elena."

I nod. Seems like we are getting somewhere, after all.

I look down at my uncle still lying there.

"What do we do about him?" I sigh. "I don't want to continue where we left off, to be honest."

"It's fine, I'll just have him forget what happened and go home. He'll be confused for a while but at least he will leave you alone."

"Great. Daniel Lewis, if you have other witch friends I need to know about, you better tell me now."

He chuckles.

"Sorry, babe."

We wait for another half-hour for my uncle to wake up. As Sylviana said, he was very confused, almost like he was drunk, and left without complaints or any memory of why he had come here.

Good grief, I can use one less thing to worry about. Sylviana leaves right after him, though I apparently can ask her for help anytime if I need to. Looks like I got a midwife out of the blue. It's late when I'm finally alone with Danny.

I'm exhausted. I just want to sleep and forget about how complicated my life has become for a while. Danny comes to sit beside me, putting my legs on his. He smiles at me.

"What?"

"You're having a baby."

I nod, still kind of in a weird state from hearing that.

"I still want to confirm, Danny."

"I know. But I believe Sylviana. She's weird but she's great."

"So, I can say she's weird now?"

"You know what I mean. She's the witchy kind of weird. It's cool."

We both laugh a bit, more to release all the nervousness than from anything funny. It's been a freaking weird day today.

"So many things happened today," I sigh, "and now it turns out I'm pregnant with that jerk's baby."

"You have to tell him, Elena. I know you still love him, too."

I glare at him. Why does Danny have to be so good at reading my emotions?

Yes, I won't ever say it, but I do love Nate, despite him being a two-timing jackass. I still have such vivid memories of that woman on his doorstep. Fuck him. I sigh and think about my child, our child. Damn, someone is going to get a rough wake-up call.

"I want to wait until I get medical confirmation, Danny."

"Okay. I'll talk to Mom tomorrow, okay? I'm sure she can help us check your condition in secret or something like that."

"She's going to ask who the father is. Iris, too."

Daniel nods and seems to think about it for a few seconds.

"My mom won't believe us if we tell her it's Levi, but I think she won't push it if you just tell her you don't want to talk about it. She's good with people's privacy. And Iris, well, we'll see if she asks, okay?"

"Iris will think Levi is the father, Danny. I've been pretending to date him for three months; everyone is going to think the baby's his. I can't push that onto your brother."

"You know what? Let's invite Levi for breakfast tomorrow morning and let him know first, okay? This way, he can voice his opinion, and we can discuss a plan together. But I doubt anyone's going to notice for a while, Elena. You're not showing, and you always wear baggy clothes. I'm your best friend and even I didn't have a clue. I mean, the coffee part was suspicious, but…"

"Your coffee really is disgusting, Danny!"

"Yeah, whatever, you're banned from drinking it for five months anyway so shut up about my coffee. Just concentrate on harassing my boyfriend so we can get some time with Nora in two days while I call my family."

He grabs his phone and calls the Lewis family house, while I resume trying to mind-link Boyan again. It's not easy, he's super far. And it's much harder to mind-link a Beta. It's like trying to find someone whispering in the middle of the crowd.

As usual, Daniel chats about trivial stuff with his mother, and I have plenty of time to think about random stuff while trying to contact his boyfriend. Seriously, I wish Bobo carried his own phone for once.

Meanwhile, my mind can't help but wander somewhere else. To my tummy, to be precise. A baby. I can't believe I'm pregnant with Nate's baby. This is so unreal. I didn't even dare to hope I could ever get pregnant again, after what had happened with Diego. The doctors had told me my miscarriage had reduced my chances drastically to ever conceive again. With the grief of losing my unborn child, I just never processed the thought of ever becoming a mother again.

My wolf is in protective mode. She doesn't want to lose her pup. She already knew, and I had no idea. This is so strange. No wonder she didn't want me to shape-shift. I take a second and a deep breath. I need to be careful. I can't lose this baby, my baby. No matter what, I'll protect him. I mean, her. Even if my clan disapproves, or Nate is against me having his child. I already know I don't care.

My child comes first.

Chapter 18

My heart is beating so fast.

It's a strange feeling, with my wolf being even more excited than I am, and it's not only because I'm back on the Blood Moon territory for the first time in a while... actually, the fact that they let me through is already surprising enough. I mean, am I still welcome after my parting with Nate? I shouldn't be, right? Yet, all the wolves guarding the border let me in, even though I know I'm being watched and followed closely.

I feel like every step closer to Nora is a step closer to the answers I've been looking for all this time. I'm so excited, maybe because I believe in Danny's theory and Sylviana's words too much. I'm on guard, but if I had wings, I would fly all the way there right away.

Today is going to be one hell of a day. First, meeting with Nora, and then, that appointment at the clinic. I'm not sure which one I'm more nervous about.

I finally find the salon, and I spot Boyan and Nora, along with an army of hairdressers. Moon Goddess, did they seriously book the whole salon for her?

I walk in, taking off my cap, hoping she will be able to recognize me from our short first encounter. Bobo raises his head, frowning.

"Hi, Bobo," I say with a little smile.

He frowns.

"Elena. You're not supposed to be here."

So I guess he did not completely agree with the plan. I knew it was weird he wouldn't respond to my mind-linking.

"I know. Are you going to stop me?"

"If Nathaniel or the King find you here, you'll be in serious trouble, Elena. I understand you want to speak to Nora, but..."

I know he switched to mind-linking not to include Nora, but I can't help but smile a little. That is so Boyan-like.

"*It's okay, Boyan. Is that why you didn't agree to it? You were worried for me?*"

"*Beta instinct. Protecting people is what I do.*"

"*Thanks, Big Boy. I'm okay.*"

He sighs.

"Okay. You're already here anyway."

With his approval, I can finally approach Nora. Moon Goddess, my heart is beating so fast now that she's right in front of me! And we can finally have a real chat, too. She's even prettier up close, and I can tell she's getting all dolled up for her birthday. They probably have a whole party ready for her as the Blood Moon's future Luna.

I take the seat next to her, a bit nervous but excited.

"Hi, Nora."

"Hello..."

She is a bit hesitant, with her cheeks blushing. She's observing me so intensely, I can tell she's as curious as I am.

"So, you recognize me, I guess. Sorry, I had to leave suddenly last time, but I don't really want Nate to know that you and I are acquainted."

"Why?"

Damn, why did I have to mention Nate. I shrug, trying to think of something.

"Personal reasons. Let's just say it would make things a bit more... complicated. It made it hard for me to get to you already. Your security is quite tight! Thankfully, your bodyguard is a friend."

I wink at Boyan, who's still a bit stiff and uneasy. I can tell he's sending glances at the door and mind-linking to see how much time I can have with Nora before people from the Blood Moon clan intervene.

"*Are you sad that Danny didn't accompany me?*"

He hesitates a bit before answering.

"You owe me one, Elena."

"I know, I know, Big Boy," I answer with a smile. "I'll talk to him, I promise."

I guess I owe him that much. And Danny isn't that mad at him anyway. He loves Boyan more than he's willing to admit.

"Anyway. I really wanted to meet with you, Nora," I say, finally addressing her.

"Me too. I have so many questions for you! What happened last time? How can we mind-link? I never did that with anyone!"

Oh my gosh, she's so excited! I'm happy someone is as enthusiastic and curious as I am, but I don't have all the answers! I take a breath and think about what I really need to tell her first.

"Easy, girl. I know you have a lot to ask, but I can't stay long," I say with a glance at the door, "and I may not have all the answers you are looking for. First, our mind-link suggests we are related somehow, though I'm not sure about the details. When we met on the Jade Moon clan's turf, I felt it. My wolf reacted strongly to your presence, so I came to your fight against the Alpha to confirm it. That's why I tried the mind-link, and it worked!"

She nods strongly, her eyes shining.

"Yes, I heard you during my fight. And after that."

"Exactly. You did great, by the way!" I say with a smile.

She immediately blushes. I didn't imagine she was this shy and modest, from her attitude last time! But she's obviously younger than me, and still a bit unsure of her actions. Seems like her inner wolf brings out her strong side, but on the inside, she's still a teenage girl. My gosh, I find her so adorable!

"Thanks," she says, "but I still have no clue as to how we are related... I just learned that my father was from the Gold Moon clan, but I have no idea who my mother is. All I know is that I didn't inherit my father's last name. When we searched for it, Nathaniel said the name Bluemoon doesn't appear anywhere."

Moon Goddess, it's thin, but it may confirm Danny's theory. I didn't know about her links to the Gold Moon clan, but if she has no idea where her last name and her mother are from, then…

"Because that is not a last name, Nora! Didn't you notice that it sounded a lot like a clan's name...?"

She stays speechless for a while, thinking about that information. I know, it's a lot to take in. I exchange a look with Boyan.

"Shit, Elena, that's big."

"I know. I just want to see if it might be real, both for me and Nora."

He sighs, and I focus on Nora again, who is still shocked.

"You mean, like a Blue Moon clan?" she mutters.

I nod, but Nora is still very confused. Behind her, Boyan frowns too.

"There is no Blue Moon clan in Silver City."

"To be exact, there is no Blue Moon clan at all," I explain. "Not anymore. But from what I've discovered, there used to be one, far up in the north. I don't know why or how, but they were all… killed. The entire pack, about eighteen years ago."

Nora stays silent again for a few seconds, making me even more nervous. She seems so surprised, yet I know a part of her sort of believes me…

"Killed? An entire pack? But... how?" she asks.

I shake my head. I wish I knew!

"I still don't know yet. But you and I are proof that some people from this clan survived."

She suddenly turns to me.

"Wait, you are… I mean, you think you are from this Blue Moon clan too? Did you grow up in this clan then?"

"No, no, someone saved me when I was an infant, and brought me to a childless couple of the Opal Moon clan here, in Silver City."

She looks at me a bit more intensely, like she's scanning me. Is she looking for something that would link us together? A resemblance or something? Or is she doubting me? I keep talking, telling her all I know.

Moon Goddess, I hope she believes me.

"The woman who saved me said that a Royal family had been killed and that she had found me alone in the middle of the... slaughter."

Nora is completely shocked when I mention the Royals. I know, it's big. Royals are more of a legend than a real thing, but…

"Royals? Are you sure?" asks Bobo.

"For now, I am not sure of anything! I have no memories of surviving a massacre either. I just got pieces of information from the woman who saved me... But I've seen Nora's wolf, and you did too."

Bobo nods slowly, and turns to Nora, thinking deeply. I know he's having doubts too, but Nora's wolf form is legendary! A white wolf with blue eyes, I didn't even think that was possible! Between us, Nora seems confused by my words.

"What do you mean?"

"You are a pure wolf, Nora. Dark blue eyes and perfectly white fur. Do you have any idea how rare that combination is amongst werewolves? It's almost legendary! And you even have a clan's name as your last name!"

She looks at me, speechless again, before shaking her head vigorously. I know it's hard to conceive, being a Royal, but I'm really starting to believe in that theory strongly as well. And if Nora really is such a werewolf, then…

"No, no, you said yourself, it is probably only the clan's name," she says, still shaking her head. "Even if I am from this Blue Moon clan, it could just be—"

"Royal families do take their clan's names as a symbol of power, Nora," says Boyan. "They carry it for generations until there are no more descendants, and usually a new Alpha from a dominant but non-Royal family takes over. Any clan's name can be old or newly made up, but only the Royals are entitled to carry it. And your father knew who your mother was. Why would he have told you this was your last name otherwise?"

Wow, since when did Boyan know so much about Royals? Is it because he's close to the King?

"One does not simply give a clan's name to their child!" I add.

Nora looks at us, completely stunned. Seems like she has a hard time believing any of this, and truthfully, I can't blame her. She just went from being an orphan to a potential Royal!

"Then why wouldn't that make you a Royal's child too? Aren't we related?" she suddenly asks me.

Wow, no way. I may be stronger than the usual wolf, but I'm far from being a potential Royal… though Nora's question is something I hadn't thought of. Could I be related to the Royals? I don't look like Nora, but if we were from the same pack originally, there's a chance that we are related. Remotely related, I'd say.

"We are related indeed, but I don't believe I am the child of a Royal. Not directly, at least. I have golden eyes, and my fur isn't completely white like yours. One of my parents probably wasn't a pure werewolf."

Nora frowns and shakes her head. I guess she wished I knew more than that, but I'm guessing here too.

"So, you think my birth mother was…"

"A Royal, yes," I tell her.

If she knows for certain that her father was from the Gold Moon, then that's the only logical explanation. Nora said it herself: her mother is a mystery, and she doesn't have her father's last name, so the Blue Moon wolf, and potentially Royal, has to be her mom!

Boyan seems worried seeing her so confused, and gently pats her shoulder, his beta instincts in action. I can tell she trusts him a lot from the way they interact. He's not like a bodyguard, more like… a big brother. A huge one.

"You're probably mixed, Nora. He might not have been an Alpha, but your father's blood was most likely pure enough for you to keep some of the characteristics."

"Not all of them. I can't heal properly, and my shape-shifting isn't ideal either."

Moon Goddess, what did she just say?

"Wait a minute… You can't heal fast?" I ask.

"No…" says Nora, shaking her head with a cute frown. "I still heal faster than a human, but my healing ability is not as good as regular werewolves."

Only then do I notice all the thin, white scars she has. Is it from before? A werewolf shouldn't have so many scars, unless she's just like me, unable to heal correctly!

"Nora, I have the same issue! As long as I can remember, I've never healed properly!"

"Really?"

"Yes! So far, I thought it was just me being weaker than other werewolves, but now…"

I keep looking at her scars, searching for an explanation. What kind of pack has werewolves that don't heal fast? Why would we be like that? We are stronger than other werewolves, is that a compensation of some sort?

"Have you experienced anything else that's different?" Nora asks.

The only thing I can think of is…

"Mind-linking. I'm much better at that than anyone I know, including my own Alpha. No matter the distance, I have no problem communicating with my pack members. I can even communicate with other packs' Alphas."

Nora tilts her head, a bit surprised.

"Wait, aren't you an Alpha?"

Ugh, I hate to say it.

"No, I'm not. And I don't want to be."

Nora seems confused, but my answer isn't going to change. I don't want to be considered an Alpha, even if it's in my DNA. I just… I want to be a normal wolf. I hate the struggles for the Alpha positions, be it in the White Moon or Opal Moon. I'm not interested in battling my cousins for Xavier's position, I have enough to deal with as it is.

"What about you?" I ask Nora, trying to change the subject.

"I can't, for now," she says. "I don't belong to any clan at the moment, so..."

I'm pretty sure it's not about belonging to a clan. Nora is definitely strong and very much like me, so I bet if she just tried, she could mind-link any alpha as well. She just needs to build up her self-confidence and break out of her shell.

"*You should try it. With your Alpha mate,*" I suggest, using my mind-link, forcing my power a bit.

"*I don't really get how it works yet...*"

"*Nora, you're mind-linking. Like, right now.*"

She's so surprised, I can't help but chuckle. She exchanges a look with Boyan, who probably understands what's going on already.

"*Don't use it too much on others though. If you're like me, people might... not really like it.*"

"*Why do you mean?*"

"*You'll see.*"

People don't like when you force the mind-linking on them. Especially if you're not from their packs, they perceive it as an intrusion. But then again, Nora will probably experience it for herself soon too.

"You should go, Elena. Our pack will have noticed your presence by now," says Boyan.

"*Nate is coming, Elena,*" he adds through our mind-link.

"What? Wait! We are not done talking!" says Nora.

Does she realize she's using her Alpha Aura anytime she's unhappy? Damn, her potential is a bit scary. I grab my cap to put back on and turn to her.

"Sorry, Nora, Bobo is right. I really wish I could, but I already stayed longer than I had planned to. But don't worry, I will keep searching for more information about the Blue Moon clan."

"When can we meet again?"

"I will find you, don't worry. For now, don't tell anyone about what we discussed today, okay? No one but Bobo must know, Nora, it is crucial."

She frowns, and I can tell right away who she's thinking about.

"*Not even your mate, Nora.*"

"*But...*"

"*If it makes you feel better, you are not the only one with secrets. I wouldn't trust Damian Black so easily if I were you.*"

"*What do you mean?*"

"*You'll see.*"

She's with the King, she can't really expect the guy to be completely clean, right? He's a known killer, and I can barely stand being in the same room as him. How does she do it? Damn, I really wish I could stay, but I gotta go. If Nate is on his way…

I walk to exit the salon, but right when I get to the entrance, Nathaniel walks in. Fuck.

"Elena... What are you doing here?"

Breathe, Elena. This is his territory, not yours. It's normal for him to ask.

"I came to see Bobo."

"Bobo?"

He turns to Boyan and Nora, looking for confirmation. Meanwhile, I'm still looking at him. My wolf is going crazy. It's only been a few weeks; did he change a lot? He looks perfectly normal, in his usual black suit, his hair a bit disheveled. Has he thought about me at all? Are we really over?

When he finally turns to me, he puts on an angry front.

"You're not supposed to be here."

"Are you going to kill me then?"

That doesn't work on me, Nate. I can tell when you're angry for real, and you're not. I don't even feel his aura, or his wolf growling. More importantly, I'm not scared of him at all. He's not Diego, Nate would never, ever touch me or hurt me.

"*What are you really doing here, Elena?*"

"*I told you, I just came to talk to Boyan.*"

"*I don't buy it.*"

I sigh internally. Damn, I forgot how stubborn he can be.

"*Elena, we need to talk.*"

"*Do you really want to talk in front of your brother's mate? And Boyan? … See you later, Nate.*"

He's still speechless, and I use that opportunity to leave. A bit too fast, but I just want to walk out of here before he realizes how nervous I am.

I don't even know how I can stand before him without exploding. I'm potentially pregnant with his child. Nate's baby. And he has no fucking idea, Moon Goddess. I feel like I could drop the bomb on him at any given moment, like it's struggling to get past my lips. When I saw him, I freaked out. I didn't plan to see him, and I had no idea what to do. He's still the same man, but Moon Goddess, so much has happened in the meantime.

I try to walk back fast, leaving the area as quickly as possible. I can still feel their people following me from a distance. If only I can get to the border before I get myself into serious trouble.

"*Daniel?*"

"*Waiting for ya, babe.*"

"*I ran into Nate.*"

"*What? No shit! You told him?*"

"*Of course not, you idiot! I'm not even sure I'm pregnant yet, and even if I do, I... I'm not sure I'm ready, Daniel.*"

"*Okay, okay, you're right, it's a bit too soon. Just come here and we'll go to the clinic, to clear up everything. Mom's waiting for us.*"

"*Yeah, I...*"

"Elena!"

Oh, fuck.

I didn't expect Nathaniel would come after me once I left the salon. I hesitate, but I can't just keep walking while he's running after me and calling my name. I sigh, and turn around to face him.

Looks like he really did run to catch up, his suit is a mess. I resist the urge to arrange it for him, crossing my arms against my chest.

Facing him is making me more nervous than I thought. I purposely wore baggy clothes to cover myself today, and I don't think anything is showing, but having Nathaniel right in front of me is making me feel pregnant as hell. My wolf, too, is taking a defensive stance. She's constantly worried for her pup, and an alpha male doesn't calm her down, even if he's the father.

"We need to talk," he says, out of breath. "I have not had sex with Narcissa since I met you. I swear."

My gosh, did he have to remind me of that bitch?

"Even if you didn't, Nate, and I'm not saying I believe you or not, it doesn't change things. We can't be together, and you know that."

"If it's only about our packs, I don't care, Elena. I can talk to my brother. Damian will–"

"What about my pack, Nate?" I shout back, exasperated. "I'm supposed to leave everything behind for you? Did you ever consider my position in your plans? I'm the Alpha's niece! And the White Moon Alpha's goddaughter, too! Imagine if they found out I'm going out with the King's brother!"

Let alone having his child. I would be banished from both the Opal Moon and White Moon clans, cut off from my family. I wouldn't even be able to see my dad in the hospital, or talk to any of my friends again, and it's not something I can afford right now!

"You could live with me, Elena, in the Blood Moon pack."

Oh, Moon Goddess, he can't be fucking serious right now.

He's tempting me, and I don't want that. I'm already too torn between him and my pack, and now I have his child to take into account, too. I have no idea how Nate would react to the news, and that terrifies me.

"*Elena, hurry up, girl.*"

"*Nate's here, Danny. Talking to me right now.*"

"*Oh, shit. Elena, you have to get out of there, seriously. Sylviana said no stress.*"

"*I know.*"

"Elena, I'm dead serious. I know we've had our ups and downs, but I want to sit down and discuss things seriously with you. I'm not over you, I'm nowhere near that. I want you back, I want the relationship we had back."

I shake my head.

"I'm not going back to being your fuck buddy, Nate. I believe you had plenty of candidates for that," I say, still bitter about last time.

"I meant as my lover, Elena, my girlfriend."

Fuck. Why did he have to say that now? He has never said that damn word, and I wasn't ready to hear it. I just can't! I have way too much going on right now! I'm close to uncovering the secret behind my birth, I just found Nora, my uncle is seriously after me, and Diego, too. And I'm fucking pregnant with his child!

"Elena?"

He comes close, worried about my sudden tears, but I step back. I feel like I'll explode if he touches me. I'm such a mess right now. I try to wipe them away clumsily. Damn, if only I could control my emotions a little!

"Elena, talk to me."

"Nate, I can't. Not here, not now, okay? I don't… I don't feel like talking. It's really not a good time right now."

He frowns, and his eyes go down on my oversized denim jacket.

"Is it because of him? Daniel's brother?"

Shit, he smelled it was Levi's. Damn, I only borrowed it to cover up my tummy! I didn't think that would lead to another jealousy crisis with Nathaniel! I shake my head, annoyed. This is not what I came for, and I don't want to fight him again!

"Leave Levi alone, Nate, seriously. He's got nothing to do with you."

"Are you going out with him now? For real?" he asks, his breathing becoming more intense.

"Moon Goddess, Nate, I told you a hundred times, no! I only borrowed his jacket, okay? Enough with this! I'm fed up with your jealousy!"

"Then why did you block me? It's been weeks, Elena! I couldn't call or text you. I couldn't reach you at all!"

"I needed time alone, Nate! Okay? Things have been hard lately, and I have had enough to deal with already! I'll unblock you if it makes you happy, but I don't have the luxury to stay right now, okay?"

I turn away and start walking, trying to stop my tears. Fuck, I really wish I hadn't cried in front of him…

"Elena!"

I keep walking, trying to ignore him, but he suddenly grabs my wrist and, before I can even react, kisses me.

Moon Goddess. I feel my whole body going numb under his lips. How long has it been? I just can't move. I don't push him away, I don't answer his kiss, I can't do anything. Nate's kiss is driving me crazy. I want to scream and cry again, I can't take it. Why is he doing this now?

He separates from me, putting his hands on my shoulders, while I'm still standing there like an idiot, confused as hell.

"Elena, I'm sorry. I'm sorry I lied to you. I'll say it now. I love you, Elena. I really love you."

Holy shit.

He really said it. I am shivering with something I can't identify right now. My heart's bursting with happiness, but my head is freaking out. Why now, of all times? This is so brutal; I have no idea how to respond to that. I stand there, speechless, lost.

Moon Goddess, is this even real? And why the hell does he have to confess when I'm already a hormonal mess!

I try to calm down. Think about the baby, think about the baby, Elena, Sylviana said no stress. My gosh, he's so not helping!

"Nate, I… I can't…"

"You can't what, Elena?"

I take a deep breath in. I can't handle the bomb he just dropped on me! I shake my head, trying to find the right words. I wish I could tell him how I feel, too, but I'm just so confused right now, I feel like crying, screaming, and literally exploding.

Deep breaths, think of something to say. Something that will not make me look totally nuts.

"I can't answer you right now. I have things to sort out, and–"

"Elena, why is it never the time with you?" he suddenly bursts, angry. "I'm opening my heart to you, putting my feelings out in the open, and it's not the right time? Are you kidding me? I just need a yes or no, Elena!"

"You can't just ask me that, Nate! You think it's easy! I have a million things to consider, and you just think I would let it all go for you! Put yourself in my shoes, for once! I'm not powerful like you, I'm not the King's brother! I can't just decide to throw my whole life away on a whim!"

"Seriously, what's holding you back? Can't you just admit that you're too scared of your feelings for me? I know you love me too, Elena!"

"It's not that easy! My father is in the hospital. My uncle and godfather are freaking Alphas, Nate! I can't just throw away the pack I grew up in, do you realize they adopted me? I wasn't even born there, and yet they gave me a home, a place, and responsibilities! I can't just leave them like that, Nate! You don't know what it's like!"

How can I still be angry with him? This whole damn conversation is exhausting, why are we yelling and screaming every time we see each other! He sighs, shaking his head, visibly annoyed. I know he's serious, but I'm not as free as he is!

"I have to go," I say, retreating a bit.

"So you're going to leave me without an answer? Again?"

"Not now, Nate, seriously."

Moon Goddess, I have to go to the clinic so I can confirm I'm pregnant with his baby, why do I have to deal with this first? He frowns, looking at me. I need to go back to the border, so I take my courage and turn around, wrapping my arms around me. I walk fast, and I know he's following me. I know it's his territory, his right, but…

"Elena!"

As promised, Daniel is waiting for me at the border, along with… shit, Levi. Nathaniel clicks his tongue.

"Of course."

"He's only here to accompany me, Nate."

"Yeah, I bet."

I turn to him, angry.

"Nathaniel, enough. Levi's helping me where you can't. If you don't like it, I don't care. We'll talk later."

He stays silent, but his glare towards Levi speaks volumes. Seriously. I turn around and finally get in the car, unable to hold it anymore. Levi's driving, and I purposely sat in the back with Danny. My best friend looks at me, worried.

"You okay, babe? Your eyes are red."

"Levi, just start the car, please."

"Yeah."

I try to ignore Nate's stare I can feel from the other side of the road. Moon Goddess, I'm so tired already.

"Elena?"

"I'm not feeling well," I admit.

"Hang on, babe, we're going to the clinic, getting you all checked up."

I doze off on Daniel's shoulder until we get there. I'm trying to forget my dispute with Nate. This all came at such a bad time. Why is the timing always so off? I have to say, I'm feeling weaker than usual. It's a relief when Levi finally parks in front of the clinic.

The Lewis brothers help me out, and Iris comes to meet me in the parking lot, looking worried.

"Are you okay, Elena? You look very pale. Come, Mrs. Lewis has the room ready for you."

My cousin guides us through the hospital and as promised, I'm taken into an isolated room. I don't know why, but the sight of the medical equipment makes it all a bit too real. Daniel holds my hand even when I sit on the weird seat for observation. Levi holds my jacket for me and leaves the room quietly. I'm a bit grateful. I'm nervous enough without an audience.

I don't know if they told their mom beforehand, but Abigail is very nice to me.

"Okay, sweetheart, we are going to take an ultrasound too to confirm. The gel will be a bit cold."

She puts some sort of gel on my tummy, and Daniel helps me keep my shirt up. I take a deep breath in, trying to relax. It feels good to be laying down, but I can't keep my eyes off the screen. Abigail's strange probe is going around my tummy, until she stops.

"There it is."

"What? Where?" I ask, squinting at the screen.

She smiles and points her finger at a little shape on the screen, and zooms in a bit.

"Moon Goddess," whispers Daniel.

Holy shit, he means! I can see my baby. I didn't expect it to be so obvious. Its shape, I can even see his– her head! And she's freaking moving, too! I start crying again, shocked. Moon Goddess, how can she already be this big! And I had no freaking idea!!

"There he is. About 1.5 inches, Elena. Danny's friend was right, you're in your eleventh week."

"It's a she, Mom," says Danny.

Moon Goddess, it's my baby right there! I keep crying, shocked beyond words. Danny gives me a hug.

"Congrats, babe, you're going to be a mom!" he whispers.

"Danny, I can't believe it, it's… it's really…"

"Yup. Your little baby daughter, live broadcasting from your belly!"

I chuckle. My gosh, only Daniel can make me laugh in such a situation… I'm both crying and laughing. I can't believe it. There's really a baby in there, my baby. Nate's baby. Our daughter!

Chapter 19

"Will it take long?"

"Just a couple of tests, sweetie," says Abigail. "I just want to confirm since your blood pressure is a bit too low."

"Sylviana said something as well, that Elena needed to be careful."

His mom sighs and sits in front of me.

"Elena, she's right. Once you've had a miscarriage, you're more likely to have another one. If you strain too much, it will be hard on the baby as well. You have to take things easy from now on and get lots of rest, sweetie, okay? It's for your child's sake, sweetie."

I nod. I get it, keeping the baby safe. I'm not losing another child. Danny puts a hand on my knee, with a big smile.

"Don't worry, I'll keep you in check. I know how you tend to get yourself in trouble sometimes."

I chuckle. I'm glad he's here to support me, as always. Abigail smiles.

"You better watch the future mom. Elena, no more fighting or shape-shifting from now on. You have to be twice as cautious, for your daughter's sake. She will do her best to grow, but Mommy has to do most of the work, all right? I will monitor you often, too. You need to come every two weeks."

"Every two weeks?" I ask, surprised.

"Yes, sweetie," she nods. "This is a high-risk pregnancy, Elena. So, every two weeks, and if you feel anything wrong, you call me right away, okay?"

Her question is directed at both me and Daniel, but now, I'm even more worried. Is it that bad? I feel fine, honestly, so fine I had no idea I was pregnant until yesterday. But Abigail is a trusted doctor of the pack, and one of the few people aware of my previous miscarriage. I have to trust her.

"Who is the father?"

I turn to my cousin Iris, shocked by her question. Since when is she so blunt? Daniel clicks his tongue.

"Seriously, Iris? Why do you ask?"

"I don't know. I find it strange that Daniel accompanied you here instead of Levi."

"I wanted Daniel here, he's my best friend."

"You should start paying attention, Elena. That kind of lie won't get you anywhere."

What is wrong with her? She sounds almost jealous! I've never seen my cousin act like this. Daniel growls at her, annoyed by her sudden attitude, and she leaves the room, still visibly upset. I can't believe Iris just talked to me like that!

Even Abigail looks a bit taken aback. I turn to Danny.

"*You think she knows something?*"

"*How could she?*"

"*I don't know, but her reaction...*"

"*Ignore her, babe. She was probably just in a bad mood for some reason.*"

Why do I feel like there's more to it? Abigail makes me go through some more tests, but I can't shake off that weird feeling I've had since hearing Iris' words. She's right, in a way; the list of my lies keeps getting longer, and harder to hide.

A while later, I'm done with all of Abigail's tests. Her recommendation is still the same, and she gave me some diet restrictions and tips, along with a bunch of vitamins I'm apparently supposed to take daily. Back in the car, I look at everything we got from the pharmacy, completely lost.

"Wait, so iron once a day, the pink ones twice a day and..."

"These two in the morning, two of these daily too, babe," says Daniel. "Don't worry, I'll make you sticky notes before you overdose yourself."

"Elena is probably the only woman who could give herself a vitamin overdose," laughs Levi.

"Hey, how about you concentrate on driving?" I reply, a bit offended.

The brothers laugh while I sigh and just throw everything back in the bag for Danny to handle. This is too much organization for me. I take out the envelope and look at my baby's picture once more. I can't believe she's so big already.

I try to remember when I could have gotten pregnant, following Abigail's calculations. Probably that night at The Rain. Or at his apartment later the same night. Damn, I kind of hope my daughter wasn't conceived in a nightclub bathroom!

"So? When are you going to tell him?"

I sigh at Daniel's question. I know who he is talking about, of course, but still.

"I have no idea."

"Elena, you should hide your pregnancy as long as possible," says Levi. "If Xavier finds out, he will give you hell. And don't even get me started on your ex."

"I know."

I'm freaking out about Diego knowing. I can avoid my uncle and my pack's suspicions for a while, but if I can't shape-shift into my wolf form for weeks, or if my belly starts showing, it's going to be harder. It's a very small bump for now, but according to Abigail, I'm almost in my second trimester already. I hope the oversized sweaters will cover it for a while.

"Okay, so, for now, only four people know: Levi, Mom, Iris, and me. Do you have anyone else you want to tell?"

"No, Danny. The fewer the better," I sigh. "For now, I want to make sure I— Wow! Levi, what the hell??"

"Sorry, some wolf just–"

But we all shut up as three other wolves suddenly run in front of the car, headed north, and I recognized at least two of them. What the heck is going on?

Levi quickly parks and we exit the car, kind of lost about what is going on. We are almost back in the Opal Moon territory, but so many wolves are running past us and heading north. I immediately mind-link my uncle.

"*Xavier, what the hell? I just saw–*"

"*VAMPIRES! VAMPIRE ATTACK ON THE NORTH!*"

I exchange a horrified look with Danny and Levi. They probably know, too. Shit, a vampire attack! Why now, of all times? We start following everyone's direction, Levi shape-shifting immediately and running in front.

"*Elena!*"

I stop walking, surprised to hear Nora's voice. Looks like someone has improved her mind-linking skills already. How did she get so good so fast? She's probably miles away!

"*Nora? Where are you?*"

"*On the sea with Damian. What's going on? There's too much agitation at—*"

"The north end, I know! I'm headed there now, we're under attack!"

"Rogues?"

"No, damn vampires!"

She cuts the mind-link, and I want to resume walking, even running to follow my pack, but before I can take another step, Daniel holds me back.

"Elena, hell no!"

"But, Danny, the–"

"Are you kidding me? Mom told you not even two hours ago! No fucking way, girl, back off!"

I bite my lip, but shit, Daniel is right, I can't go.

"Elena, where the fuck are you? There are dozens of them! Get over here, now!"

My uncle's voice keeps yelling in my head, along with many others. I can sense the attack going on a few paces away, all of my peers fighting hard to protect our territory.

"Come on, Elena, let's go!"

Daniel pushes me east, and we abandon the car to start running in the streets, not very fast but still at a good pace. Shit, shit. Moon Goddess, why now? We cross paths with dozens of people from our pack, headed north, and humans trying to flee the area. It's like a movie scene, with people crowding the streets in panic. I have to stay close to Danny to not lose him, and I focus extra hard to keep track of what's going on.

"Chris, get the right side!"

"Here, three more!"

"Watch out for the daggers! Silver!"

"Orpheus, here!"

"Got this one!"

"Anyone seen Isa?"

"Look out! You okay, man?"

"Help, Jace is hurt!"

"Someone catch this one!"

I'm hearing so many wolves' voices, I almost can't keep up with what's going on in front of me. I didn't realize Daniel's grabbed my hand until he suddenly pulls me to the side to avoid a gigantic brown wolf.

"Wait, was that…?"

"Boyan's sister, yeah. The Blood Moon is here!"

"Yeah, the Sea Moon too!"

"Elena! Come here, you traitor!"

My uncle's voice is like a knife piercing my head. I try to shut it off as he keeps calling me, yelling my name. My eyes tear up. It's so frustrating! I can't reply, I can't do anything but follow Daniel through the chaos.

But the fight is catching up to us. I can feel my pack's voices getting closer, people yelling to watch the east.

"The Sea Moon wolves are here!"

I see them, running from the waterfront towards us, ready to attack. Not only because of those wolves, but I realize we are going to get caught in the battle whether we want to or not. Daniel's probably realized this too as he keeps looking in all directions with panicked eyes.

"Babe, we really gotta go."

"Nora's at the waterfront too."

"Nora? Okay, better go this way then," he says, pulling me to the east.

We try to head in that direction, where I can hear Nora's wolf, but as we feared, it only takes a couple of minutes until a vampire suddenly runs our way. I jump in front of Danny and send that damn blood-sucker away with a high kick to its face.

"Elena!" screeches Daniel.

I know, I know. But I can't just do nothing! What's the point of not fighting if I get killed so stupidly anyway?

Danny stops protesting soon enough, because there is no other choice. Right after the first one, more vampires rush our way, obviously ready to attack. My wolf is ready to fight, but she also knows our baby comes first. I grab an iron pole to defend myself, but even in my human form, I'm a good enough fighter to keep them at bay. Vampires are fast, but werewolves are vampire killers to begin with. And I'm a damn good warrior, too. Using my fists, feet, and pole, I send them to the ground or flying one after the other.

"*Elena!*"

This time, it's my cousin Chris. I feel relieved to hear his voice among the others.

"*You okay?*"

"*They just keep coming! Hundreds of them!*"

"I know, they are already at the harbor! I'm in the middle of the Sea Moon pack, I think."

I can't even recognize anyone but Danny. I was so focused on defending myself, I didn't realize so many wolves and vampires had gathered around us in a raging battle. I keep fighting and mind-linking my cousin, worried for everyone.

"*Okay! We got two... no, three other packs helping us here, I think. But seriously, Elena, their numbers...*"

"*I know.*"

It's the biggest vampire attack I've ever seen. No matter how many I fight, it just doesn't stop, they keep coming at us in hordes. Where the hell did they come from? Vampire clans are never this big in the first place!

Next to me, Daniel is at his wit's end too. My best friend tried not to shape-shift for the longest time, but Danny is not a fighter like me, or an alpha. He's getting tired and can barely keep up with his enemies.

"Danny, shape-shift before you get killed!" I insist.

"I'm not leaving you alone!" he yells, out of breath.

That idiot! I'm about to yell at him again, but a sudden new attack keeps the words stuck in my mouth. I don't know if they understood that I'm the strongest in that area, but several vampires suddenly aim at me, fangs ready to bite and daggers in the air.

"ELENA!"

But before I can get in position, a gigantic wolf suddenly flies over me, and takes out two of them in a flash.

"Boyan!"

The huge brown wolf keeps fighting close to Daniel, and I suddenly realize what a death machine his size is capable of. It's like sending a tiger into a battle. Boyan's may be the size of a bear, but he's much more agile and faster than he looks. I'm starting to get why he's Nora's bodyguard.

"Blondie?"

This time, it's Tonia, his sister, looking at me in surprise. She doesn't stop, though, and keeps running towards the harbor, probably headed to Nora's location. But to my surprise, when her younger brother is about to follow, Daniel suddenly grabs his fur and holds him back, whispering something in his ear.

What the...?

I want to ask why the hell he's exchanging secrets with him in the middle of the fight, when a new bunch of wolves suddenly appear in the distance. Opposite to the harbor we have been pushed to, they are running in the streets, among the buildings, heading south.

"Was that the Rising Moon pack?" asks Danny

"Yeah, and the Gold Moon too!"

If they are headed south, it means the attack is even bigger than we thought! I hear some distressed wolf yelps around us. The Sea Moon wolves are losing ground with us. I try to reach out to my peers from the White Moon and Opal Moon to check the situation in the north, but before I can decide on someone, Nora's voice resonates clearly in my head again.

"*Elena, are you there yet?*"

"*On my way. But my friends told me there's a lot of them. Really, a lot.*"

"*Is your pack okay?*"

Moon Goddess, if only. I wish I could be with them! Right when I'm about to answer, five or six new wolves join us. This time, I recognize them. They were at the Jade Moon territory the first time I met Nora.

"*For now. The White Moon is there too and some of the Sea Moon pack warriors joined, as well. But those damn vampires just keep coming.*"

"*The Blood Moon is on their way.*"

"*I figured so. Nate's guys just arrived too.*"

"*What about the other clans?*"

"*They have to watch out for the other sides of the city. This might be a massive attack. I just saw some guys from the Gold Moon and Rising Moon packs heading south.*"

I'm starting to think Nora might get seriously good at this mind-linking thing, I feel like she's right next to me, talking to me! I have to focus though, the battle is raging around me. Boyan and Daniel are both staying close to me, our trio fending off the vampires the best we can, trying to keep our position.

Damn, they just keep coming. I don't even understand why they keep trying to go east, as if they were aiming somewhere specific. We are just at the edge of the harbor, but more and more keep coming, in a rhythm.

Suddenly, I hear screams from the vampires. Many wolves turn their heads the same way too. I can feel it even before we see him.

"*Holy fuck, is that...*"

"*Yeah. The King.*"

The huge, ferocious black wolf appears suddenly, his Alpha Aura oppressing everyone like a dark hurricane. Many wolves completely forget about fighting for a second just to get out of his way. He storms through the battle, killing the vampires within his reach one after another in front of our eyes. He tears them apart like freaking puppets, their limbs flying in every direction. It's a horror scene. Thank Moon Goddess that monster is on our side.

The King goes past us without giving us a single look. Damn, he is even scarier when he's fighting, that killing machine.

Next to me, Daniel even shape-shifted out of fear. His wolf took over because he sensed a stronger alpha, I can't blame him. I really can't believe the King's hellish aura.

"*You okay, Danny?*"

"*Yeah, well, much better now that he is going away. Moon Goddess, I swear I was that close to wetting my fur.*"

"*I know.*"

Despite how scary he is, the King cleared a lot of the vampires for us. Even the Sea Moon wolves look like they're in better shape now that there's a lot less blood-suckers to deal with, and I can take a few steps back to catch my breath.

I pray silently that my baby can hold on. I've been moving around so much. But she was fine so far despite my training, right? I spot more vampires coming, and growl automatically, fucking annoyed and exhausted. Hold on, baby, Mom's got a few more vampires to fend off.

We keep fighting, and I start to understand why Boyan is still here instead of following his sister to Nora's location. That idiot is protecting me, just like Danny! Did he tell him? I can barely get my hands on any vampires now, Boyan is like a wall of fur in front of me, while I just have to wave my iron bar around to keep my surroundings clear.

I don't have time to complain, though, as the vampires keep trying to get past us. Where the hell do they want to go? Are they aiming for the city, to the humans? Why the east? The Sea Moon wolves are gathered with us at their border, but we are now pushed a couple steps into their territory.

Suddenly, several vampires manage to kill one of them, and run past us. Fuck!

"*Nora! Some passed through our defense! They are running through the city!*"

"*What? Where are they headed to? They're targeting the humans?*"

"*I don't know, but it doesn't look like it. They are staying west on the Sea Wolves' turf! Following them now!*"

I completely forget about Boyan and Daniel and start running after those vampires. Where the hell are they going?

It was obviously a planned attack. There are too many of them, and they are too well equipped. Something's wrong, even for a vampire attack. I meet up with a group of Sea Moon wolves, but they are too busy to complain about me intruding on their turf. I feel Nora coming closer too, did she shape-shift? Her Alpha Aura is completely different from her mate's. While the King's aura is like a dark hurricane, Nora's is more like a white, silent shadow spreading around. I can't tell which one is scarier.

I feel her approaching, and stop running to focus on my surroundings. I'm worried because I can't reach my pack anymore. Moon Goddess, I hope they are fine!

"*Chris! Update!*"

"*Update, my ass, where the fuck are you? It's a war zone here!*"

"*Chris!*"

"*I can't even tell you, Elena, there are so many people here! All the packs, almost! But the vamps- Shit!*"

I panic for a second as I suddenly lose our mind-link, like he was pushed away or something. I try to mind-link someone else to check on my cousin, but he is back before that.

"*I have no idea what's going on, Elena, the water is attacking us!*"

The water? What the hell? I probably misheard.

"*Chris, what? The water what?*"

"*It's attacking us! For real! Ouch! Anyway, get over here!*"

I feel like the battle is taking a turn for the worse in the north, and I'm dying to go there, but… I try to focus on our position first. We got some rest after the King's arrival, but now that he's gone further north, those damn vampires are just going at it again. It's a never-ending battle! I keep fighting back and trying to get closer to Nora, resisting the urge to shape-shift. So much for no stress!

Suddenly, I feel something like a tingling at the back of my head, a ghost sensation.

"*Elena?*"

"*It's Nora. I think she's hurt!*"

"*How would you know, she's…*"

But I ignore Daniel, turning to Boyan.

"Boyan, get your damn ass to Nora! Now! Leave me alone!"

I try to focus on her, and it's surprisingly easy for me to locate her aura, even in the middle of that frenzy. Seems like she's fine, and she's got back-up too. Did Tonia join her? Or people from the Blood Moon? She's on the Sea Moon clan's turf, quite close.

"*Elena! Are you okay?*"

"*Yeah, doing my best. I'm just a few blocks ahead of your position, but the situation's worse here.*"

I want to keep running in her direction, but Boyan suddenly gets in my way.

"Damn it! What is he still doing here? Stubborn wolf!"

"Elena?"

Crap, I mind-linked Nora without thinking, reaching out to her is even easier than I thought!

"It's Bobo! I keep telling him to go to you, but he won't leave me! His sister is running to you, though!"

Maybe Tonia's already there, but I don't have time to check. More vampires, always more vampires are coming. I even lose my iron bar at some point, and have to resort to using my fists again. Fuck, I can't take any hits!

"Elena!"

"I know, Danny, shut up!"

I finally grab what looks like a wooden pole and use it. Oh, right, vampires don't like wood, right? I manage to defend myself a bit longer, but this is getting really exhausting. Does it ever end?

"Elena!"

I turn my head, and just as I feel it, the white wolf is here. Right behind Nora is Tonia's big wolf. Damn, it was high time. Finally!

"Nora! Are you okay? Moon Goddess, you're bleeding!"

"It's okay. Why aren't you in your wolf form?"

"Don't worry, I can defend myself fine this way."

I forgot people would ask. Thank Moon Goddess we soon get busy enough that I don't have to explain myself any further. Damn, is it me or are we getting more and more vampires suddenly? Just like Tonia is dead set on defending Nora, Bobo and Daniel are fighting hard to not let anyone close to me.

"Nora, something's weird."

"What is it?"

"I feel like they're targeting you!"

It's obvious when you stop to watch. All the vampires are almost going completely past us to target Nora exclusively! Tonia is getting tired, even with her brother's help, and Nora's defense is close to perfect, but there are just too many vampires!

Nora jumps to the side to test my theory, and as it turns out, I'm right.

She's their target.

"Elena, it's going to be fine. The south is almost clear. They will go and help the White Moon clan."

Did she request the Jade Moon's help? That would explain some things. I nod and try to mind-link my uncle reticently to check on them.

"*You damn... Our river is still attacking us! Our warriors are poisoned, and you are not here, you useless wench!*"

"*Elena, Dad's right, the water is– Hey!– still slowing us down!*"

I report it to Nora, omitting my uncle's rage toward me. This is so weird. Water attacking werewolves? Seriously? I take a glance at the sea behind us, but everything looks normal! What the hell is going on in the north? Moon Goddess, I hope they'll be fine. The King should be there by now.

"*TONIA!*"

I turn my head, realizing our mistake. Nora and I got too caught up in the mind-linking! Tonia is struggling on one side, and Nora is cornered by vampires on another, too far away from us! I try to get to her, but she's surrounded. Fuck!

I feel the wave coming a second before it does.

"*HELP!*"

"*Nora, don't!*"

It's too late. Nora's mind-link literally hits us, and probably a lot of wolves around too. Holy shit, how did she even…? But before I can take a second to think and run to her, dark shadows suddenly jump into the fight from everywhere. I recognize the familiar piercings and markings.

"*It's Lysandra Jones! The Purple Moon clan!*"

Moon Goddess, they are the best fighters in Silver City, and right on time to save the day, too! The Purple Moon wolves attack without mercy, shifting the balance, clearing the attackers around Nora and Tonia in no time.

The fighting resumes, even fiercer, but things are looking better for us this time. Suddenly, I realize another wolf joined the fight, the younger Black! He's side by side with Nora, but before I can wonder what he is doing here, I suddenly hear Daniel's whimper.

"*Danny!!*"

"*Fuck!*"

I jump in, kicking away the vampire who managed to pin him down. My best friend, in his wolf form, is hurt, struggling to get back up.

"*You idiot, stop trying to protect me!*"

"*Hey, I'm not protecting you, I'm protecting my goddaughter!*"

"*You've got to be kidding me!*"

We don't have time to argue; Boyan jumps in to kill the other vampire who was targeting him. I help Danny up, but thank Moon Goddess, it seems the fight is almost over. The vampires are pretty much all dead or unable to fight in some way, the Purple Moon and Boyan are tearing the rest of them to shreds.

It's a bloodbath around us, quite literally. Everyone is a mess. I check in with the north but thank Moon Goddess, the nightmare is almost over there too. Nora lets me know the south and east are safe too, the packs are clearing up their territories. Thank Moon Goddess. I turn to Danny and check his leg, but damn, it doesn't look good.

"You're hurt... I told you to not shield me!"

"*Danny, you okay, baby? Does it hurt?*"

But Daniel has decided to ignore both me and Boyan. It's cute to see a two-hundred-pound wolf worry about Danny, but I won't say that out loud. I start tending to Danny since I'm the only one with my hands available, and get to burning those damn vampire corpses. Damn, it reeks, and there's a lot to do.

While I'm busy getting rid of them, it seems the Alphas silently agreed to a short meeting there. Lysandra Jones, the Purple Moon Alpha, Patrick Seaver, the Sea Moon Alpha, and Nora start talking, in their human or wolf forms.

"*Elena!*"

I turn around. Damn, The King and… Nate.

"*Elena, are you okay?*"

Damn, does he have to mind-link me when there are about fifty people around? Doesn't he have a lot of other people to care about first? I nod, trying to avoid his gaze. Damn, I must look like a mess, too.

"The Black youngsters. I don't like seeing the likes of you in my harbor, but I guess this is what they call an emergency."

"Indeed. How is the north?"

"We are fine. The remains are being burnt as we speak, and we chased them far enough. The White Moon clan is taking care of whatever is left," answers Nate to the other Alphas.

Does he really have to keep glancing at me like that? I try to stay close to Danny, acting busy or whatever just to avoid looking at him.

"What was that? They attacked at the south-east too," the Purple Moon Alpha ponders.

"They struck the north first," says Nate. "We received the northern packs' distress call early enough and went to help them, but there were about a hundred vampires."

"You mean only a hundred? How come the White Moon couldn't get rid of that? Did they get soft or something?"

I can't help but growl, Danny too. Is she fucking kidding me? When they only arrived last minute to help? Nathaniel speaks before it gets nasty between us and the Purple Moon wolves.

"It wasn't only vampires. Something was helping them. I saw the water from the river catching and trapping wolves. Some were poisoned too; there were many victims because of that. Something was definitely off."

Xavier and Chris were telling the truth. How is that possible though? I exchange a glance with Daniel, just as clueless as I am.

"Sounds like a witch to me," suddenly says the Sea Moon Alpha.

"A witch?"

It's the first time the King has spoken, but everyone immediately turns to him. Only the Alphas present don't seem intimidated.

"Witches are elemental creatures. If a Water Witch was helping them…"

"It would explain how they got past the first defenses so easily," whispers Nate.

"Then what drove her off? Did anyone get her?" asks Jones.

"We didn't even see one. Only vampires. But she could have attacked from farther away. I don't know how their magic works."

"Send some people to look at the bodies," suddenly orders the King. "See if they find a witch among them."

Some wolves depart immediately, and I realize there are a lot more Blood Moon wolves than I thought, too. Moreover, a lot of them look perfectly fine. What are these monsters?

"What about what happened in the south, then? That time, the trees helped the packs. I don't think a witch would have changed her mind."

Wait a minute, trees helped the packs? I exchange a glance with Danny. As far as we know, there's only one Earth Witch in the area! Don't tell me…

And they can't change their elements, either. What if there is another Witch left in the South?' asks the Sea Wolf Alpha.

"If there is, she helped us. She was on our side," I suddenly blurt out.

Fuck, everyone's eyes are on me now. Why did I even open my damn mouth? I was suddenly worried they would turn on Sylviana, and it just happened. Even Danny is giving me the are-you-crazy look. Are they going to overlook this?

This time, I can't help but glance Nate's way, and of course, he's looking at me too, as surprised as the others. Damn it.

"I don't like the idea of a remnant witch here," finally says the Sea Moon Alpha.

"Me neither."

Great, they decided to ignore me, but they are still after Sylviana. What do we do now? I exchange a glance with Daniel again, wondering what to do.

"*I will take care of it! Let me look for the witch!*"

All the Alphas suddenly look at the youngest Black brother, Liam, who's still in his wolf form next to Nora. Him? Don't tell me…

"*Elena. Do you think Sylviana might have a thing for younger guys?*"

"*That kid? He's just a teenager! How old is Sylviana anyway?*"

"*No idea.*"

I'm still dumbfounded while Liam Black is convincing his brothers and the others to let him take care of the witch. Now that I think about it, Sylviana did say she had some sort of spy close to Nora. Could it be that kid? Seriously?

A long silence follows Liam Black's words, but it's obvious Nate and his brothers are mind-linking between themselves. Damn, if our theory is right, I hope that Liam kid can get the last word.

"If you want, Liam, you take care of it," suddenly says Nate. "We have our hands full as it is with this mess anyway... Just ask if you need help. Don't take on a witch by yourself."

I guess the kid won, then. The Alphas start talking about what to do with the corpses, and I understand there has been a lot of damage throughout the whole city. Fuck, I didn't even think of checking in with them! With all that mind-linking, I kind of shut them out.

Once again, I ignore my uncle's voice, trying to find a friendlier tone. I guess Daniel is doing the same because I can feel his wolf too.

"*Elena?*"

"*Levi. How are things there?*"

"*It's bad. You should come back, quickly.*"

"*What? What happened? Is everyone okay?*"

"*No, Elena. It's better if you come, honestly. We are not even done checking on everyone.*"

I feel my throat tightening. Moon Goddess, our friends. Daniel's ears droop, too, his brother probably told him too. Fuck, fuck!

"*Is your friend okay?*"

I almost jump at Nora's voice in my head. I nod mindlessly.

"*Yeah, he injured his leg, but it's going to heal quickly. I'm more worried about the rest of my pack... We lost some people, so I want to go there soon.*"

"*Why don't you go now?*"

Good question. But I need to justify my presence here before I go back and Xavier kills me. I can't tell Nora that though.

"*My Alpha wants me to represent him here, see what the other packs will do. It's only the White Moon and Opal Moon wolves cleaning the mess up there now, so we need to make sure we will get some help.*"

It's a half-truth, honestly. I take a look at Nate, but once again, he was looking at me already. He asks if I'm okay again, but honestly, I'm not.

"*Nathaniel will help you.*"

Crap, did Nora catch that? I can tell she has many questions, but I'm not in the mood, I'm done for today. Thank Moon Goddess there isn't much left to say.

The Alphas get back to their usual bickering, before parting ways. I signal to Daniel that it's time for us to go too, before Nathaniel really insists on talking with me.

It's a slow walk back because of Daniel's injury and we are both exhausted. We don't even try to run while we leave the Sea Moon territory, we're done running for today. Danny shape-shifted back and he's a bit pale, though I can't tell if he's sick or worried. Levi hasn't told us what happened on his side yet, and I'm worried about finding out the truth.

"Elena!"

I turn around, but before I can see anything, Nate's arms are suddenly around me, hugging me tightly. Oh, Moon Goddess. I give in and hug him back too. Why is it that just one embrace from that man makes me feel so much better? He's half-naked, and I can smell the sweat on his skin… his smell.

His hands on my neck, he steps back to look at me.

"Nate, what about your pack? And Nora…"

"My brothers are with them. I wanted to check on you, make sure you were fine."

"I'm fine," I sigh with a nod, "but there have been losses in my pack."

"I know. I was up there earlier."

What? Nate helped the White Moon clan too? I only saw the King running there. I check up on him, but despite all the blood on his jeans, he looks completely unharmed.

"Are you okay?" I ask, still checking.

He chuckles.

"Of course I'm fine. Tired but fine. Elena…"

He suddenly looks at me again, very serious. His eyes are so close… I can see the fire behind them shining.

"Elena, I get you need time. But I'm not giving up on you, okay?"

Oh, Moon Goddess. He has no idea how badly I want to lay in his arms and cry at the moment. My heart feels heavier than ever, and the man I love is just in front of me, waiting for me. Ready for me. I put my hands on his face and kiss him, a short but heartfelt one.

"I know. I promise, we'll talk. I'm not leaving you, Nate."

He smiles, looking relieved by my words. We hug once more, with his lips close to my neck. I think about my baby, trying to tell her it's her dad, her father holding us both.

"Babe."

"I know, Danny."

Reluctantly, Nate and I part, with one last short kiss. He smiles softly.

"Talk later, Sunshine."

I chuckle and nod. I haven't heard my nickname in a while.

He watches us go, staying there with that lonely expression on his face while Danny and I get away. I keep thinking until we are almost back on our territory and exchange a look with Daniel as we cross the border. He sighs.

"I know what you're thinking."

"No, Danny, I want to tell him."

"That's what I was gonna say, babe, but today, every wolf in Silver City was possibly around. Don't worry, there'll be a better time. Let's deal with this shit at home first, okay?"

"Yeah."

We get to see the shit at home a few minutes later.

I feel like crying.

It's the streets I've known all my life, the same houses, but they are stained with blood. Lots and lots of blood. Thank Moon Goddess the few bodies are vampires, already burning with that hideous smell of rotten flesh. How many are there?

"Elena? Daniel?"

It's Ben, who walks up to us. He doesn't look too good. His left ear is covered in blood, and he's limping a bit. Plus, he's got a lot of cuts and scratches.

"Moon Goddess, Ben, you–"

"I'm fine, I'm fine. Trust me, there is much worse. Bonnie is helping Mom tend to the wounded, I was checking if we haven't forgotten anyone. Come."

He guides us back to the scene of the fight. People from both the Opal Moon clan and White Moon clan are gathered. I feel my heart drop when I hear it. People crying, screaming. What?

We suddenly see the first wolf's body. Moon Goddess, it's a guy from the White Moon… someone covered his head with a white sheet, but I can recognize his fur's white and gray pattern. Oh, no…

We keep walking, and I recognize two others. Moon Goddess, this one had just begun training, she was so young. This guy was at the club the other day. Daniel's face drops, I bet he knew him.

"Elena, Danny, I better tell you now… Eric is dead."

Oh, Moon Goddess, no. No, no, no… I start crying and walk faster to the pack. The atmosphere around us is so horrible. Dust and smoke are flying around, and the streets I once knew are no longer the same. A house has collapsed on one side. There are pieces of wood, metal, and bricks all around. Mud and blood mixed, as the ground was completely turned over by the wrestling tracks. It smells like rust, ashes, and rotten flesh.

We finally reach a crowd, and that's when I see it.

Several bodies, aligned on the ground. Someone closed their eyes.

I recognize each one of them. Maria, the girl who helped her mother with the shop on Second Street. Krystal, the pretty waitress from the Latin bar. Camden, Adrian, Javier, all kids who trained or used to train with me. Hugo and David, those two were a couple, they used to go dancing at Pepe's… The young Ava, a friend of Bonnie… and Eric.

Daniel is already crying loudly next to me, and I hear my own sobs among everyone's. I can't believe what I'm seeing. It's like I'm a step away from the scene. There's no screen, but I'm just not able to look properly. All those lives I knew, and they are gone… just like that…

Someone hugs my shoulders, but I have no idea who, I don't care. I feel my breath, my heart, choking desperately. My wolf is crying loudly. I can't look away, I can't accept it. I can't believe Eric got killed. Not like that, not so easily, Moon Goddess!

"Elena!"

I turn to face my furious uncle. I can't deal with him right now. I just want to be able to cry and mourn my friends' deaths.

But he walks up to me, in a storm.

Before I can say a thing, he suddenly slaps me.

"What the fuck, Xavier!"

I hear people screaming my name and his, and several people rush to us. But he pushes them away.

"Where were you, you little wench! Your brothers and sisters died in battle because you weren't here! How dare you betray your pack and run away from the fight! Look at what you've–"

"You shut the hell up or I swear I'll kill you, Xavier!"

To everyone's surprise, that voice was Isabella's. Eric's mother looks furious, but no one can ignore the tears on her cheeks, far from dry. She gets between me and my uncle, and pushes him away in a rage, completely out of control.

"Don't you dare accuse anyone of my son's death, you bastard! Elena was better wherever she was instead of under your shitty command! You're the worst Alpha! Any of those children would be alive if you had been able to lead them properly! But the only thing you led them to is their death!"

"Elena was gone! She should have been where she–"

"You can't rely on a single wolf just because they are stronger, you useless, damn idiot!" Isabella yells. "You would have gotten her killed just like you did with my son! Now shut your goddamn mouth before I kill you! You should be silent and ashamed of yourself!"

"Isa, calm down."

Orpheus takes her away from Xavier, glaring at my uncle in the meantime. What the hell did he do during the fight? I knew Xavier was a poor leader, but now that I look at him, he's barely dirty and looks almost unharmed too. How the hell can he be so fine when people died? He should have been on the frontlines!

"What the hell did you do?" I whisper, in shock.

"I want to ask that too, Xavier."

Clark. My godfather's furious voice clears a path between him and Xavier, who just literally turned white.

"Clark, I–"

But before he can say a word, Clark slaps him. Not a sharp slap like the one I got, but a violent, powerful one that sends Xavier to the ground with a nasty sound of bone breaking. Everyone holds their breath.

"That one was for laying your hand on Elena, you bastard."

Before Xavier even realizes, Clark kicks him violently in his stomach, causing him to lose his breath in a ridiculous grimace.

"And that one was for fucking abandoning your pack to hide Moon-Goddess-knows-where during the fight, you scum!"

Now that I look around, people from our Opal Moon clan are glaring at Xavier. I can tell they're satisfied by Clark's words. Did he really run away? I can't believe him!

"Enough! What about Elena?"

I turn around, and see Iris, still half-crying, standing among the pack, glaring at Clark. My cousin looks like a mess, her dress torn apart and covered in blood and dirt. Clark frowns and turns to her.

"Didn't she abandon the fight, too? We all saw it. Why are you only going after my father! This is so unfair!"

I can't believe her. She knows! She fucking knows why I couldn't come! Why I couldn't shape-shift and fight, Iris knows I'm pregnant! Why the hell is she going after me now? Is she just trying to protect her father, using me to distract Clark from him?

"You little..." growls Daniel, looking at her like he's about to vomit.

"Elena was fighting further in the east. Can't you see my brother's state?" suddenly says Levi, emerging from the crowd. "She's covered in blood and ashes as well. She was fighting on the Sea Moon wolves' territory!"

But Iris just growls at him and goes to her father. I can't recognize my cousin. Is she just angry because she lost her boyfriend? For a second, I had forgotten about the two of them. She helps Xavier up, and they leave the scene without adding a word. I shake my head. Moon Goddess, all of this is too much.

"What about Chris?" I quietly ask Levi.

"He was taken to the hospital earlier. They say he might lose his arm."

"What? He was fine when he mind-linked me earlier!"

"He probably acted like he was fine, Elena, you know how Chris is," he sighs. "How are you two?"

"I'm fine, but Danny needs–"

Before I finish my sentence, Clark walks up to me, looking very annoyed too. He sighs.

"Elena, we need to talk. What were you doing on the Sea Moon territory?"

"We were pushed that way during the fight," explains Danny. "We just… Holy shit, Elena!"

His face suddenly goes white in horror, but I don't know what's… That's when I feel it. A sudden, sharp pain in my lower abdomen. I look down. My pants are covered in blood, my blood.

Oh, Moon Goddess, no, no…

Chapter 20

When I wake up, my first thought is that I'm feeling super nauseous, and very heavy, like I've been sleeping too long. I'm familiar with the smells around me… is it the hospital?

"Hey, morning, babe."

Daniel is sitting next to the bed I'm in, smiling softly, leaning against the mattress. What's going on? I am so confused.

Then, it all comes back when I see the little bandage on his cheek. The vampire attack. Nora's white wolf injured, Eric's death. Oh, Moon Goddess! I turn to him, panicked.

"Danny, my baby. I beg you, tell me my baby is–"

"She's fine. She's fine, Elena, I promise," he says, grabbing my shaking hand to hold it. "Your little girl is a fighter just like her mom. She held on, don't worry. She's still there."

I let out a big sigh of relief and put a hand on my belly, where I feel like she should be. Oh Moon Goddess, if I had lost her… I was terrified for a second. Gosh, I already love you so much, little thing.

"There's bad news, though…" says Daniel, frowning a bit.

"What?"

"Well, since you were transported to the hospital and all, the wolf's out of the bag."

Oh, shit.

"You mean they know I'm pregnant?"

"Well, everyone suspects so, but only Clark, Isa, and a few other people are aware."

Fuck! Damn, we were supposed to keep this pregnancy a secret as long as possible, and now all of the White Moon and Opal Moon clans know. Great. It couldn't have been worse. And I haven't been able to talk to Nathaniel yet!

I'm about to ask more when Abigail walks into the room.

"Honey, could you help me put the… Oh, Moon Goddess, Elena! You're awake, sweetie! Daniel, I told you to tell me as soon as she woke up!"

"Mom, she literally opened her eyes half a minute ago."

"Oh, I see. All right, take this, let me check her up. Hi, sweetie, how are you feeling?"

His mom asks me a few usual questions, like if I'm in pain or dizzy, and does her check-up. I'm feeling so numb and my limbs are sore, I wish I could stretch.

"How long was I unconscious?" I ask.

"You weren't completely unconscious, you had short wake-up moments, but only for a few seconds. Anyway, it's been two days."

Two days. Did they hold the funeral yet? What did Clark say about my pregnancy? Has Nora healed already?

I look down at Danny's bandaged leg. He notices my glance and chuckles.

"I'm fine, I get to rest by watching you. It doesn't hurt and it's healing fast, as usual."

"My babies have good health and self-healing," says his mom. "But you, sweetie, you know you have to take it easy, right? Especially with your little one in there."

"What happened to me? Was it because of the fight?"

"Well, we took you to the ER and did an ultrasound–" starts Daniel, but I interrupt him.

"Daniel, English, please. Cut it out with the scientific stuff."

His mom laughs and is the one who turns to me to explain.

"It's called threatened miscarriage."

"I don't like how that sounds."

"It means you almost had a miscarriage, and right now your body and baby are fighting to prevent it. Your blood pressure was too high, Elena, and that leads to complications for pregnant women."

"You mean it can still happen?"

"Yes. Unfortunately, the only thing you can do is rest. Rest a lot and wait a bit to see what happens next. We will keep you here for a few days, do HCG tests and ultrasounds often to verify until we think it is safe for you to go home."

I want to cry. Damn, I knew it was going to be hard. I take a deep breath to calm down. Low blood pressure, Elena, low, low, low. I exchange a look with Daniel. I know my best friend is trying to be as comforting and optimistic as he can. He keeps holding my hand, rubbing it with his thumb.

"What do I do now?"

"Rest, Elena. Lots and lots of rest. Not just staying calm, but you need to lie down and rest. No caffeine, no effort whatsoever, and when you're released from the hospital, you go straight home and rest."

"You know Clark is not just going to let it slide. Did he say anything?"

"Well, he was mostly worried for you, but he wants to know who the father is. He kind of already suspects it's not Levi. But, trust me, he has no idea about you-know-who."

He's in for a big surprise, then. Daniel seems uneasy for a second.

"Clark's here."

"What?"

"Well, he was here a few minutes ago, and he just went to visit your dad, so he's probably still around."

I'm not sure I'm ready to confront my godfather and Alpha now, but after what happened with Xavier, and the fact that I'll be completely unable to move around or do any pack activities for a while, I guess I'm going to have to do this sooner or later.

"*...Clark?*"

"*Elena? You're awake! Wait a minute, I'm coming to see you!*"

I exchange a look with Daniel, letting him know. He nods. Abigail, who caught on to what was going on, crosses her arms, unhappy.

"Elena! Your blood pressure!"

"It's going to be fine, I promise to stay calm."

"You'd better! I'm staying here anyway!"

We hear someone outside the door, but to my surprise, Levi shows up instead of Clark, smiling from ear to ear as soon as he sees me.

"There she is! Hey, glad you're back with us, princess."

He comes and gives me a soft hug.

"Levi! How did you–"

"I was on my way here when Danny and Mom mind-linked me to let me know. You okay?"

"For now," I admit. "Clark is coming."

"Oh."

Levi exchanges a glance with his mom and brother and nods, taking a seat next to my bed. He's clearly not leaving my side even as Clark is on his way.

"I didn't confirm or deny anything, Elena. I…"

"I know. But I won't lie to Clark."

"Lie to me about what?"

We all turn our heads as the Alpha just walks in, looking concerned. He sighs and walks up to my bed, frowning behind his beard.

"You scared the hell out of me, kiddo. What if something happened to you?"

I smile. He's still my godfather after all. I know he feels he has to look after me since my mom's passing and my dad's coma. Clark is like family to me, my second father. I don't want to lie to him. I've grown tired of all the lies. If my pack has to know, it's better they know everything.

"Clark, I need to talk to you."

"Yeah," he says, suddenly serious again. "Elena, you're pregnant? How come you didn't tell me?"

"I only learned about it two– I mean, this week, and it is not an easy topic for me either."

He glances in Levi's direction. The two of us have pretended to be a couple for a few weeks, but truthfully, I doubt Clark ever believed it. He knows how close I am to Daniel's brother, but he also knows my real feelings for Levi.

Clark is the kind of Alpha who is good at reading people's feelings. He's good at catching lies too.

"I'll take it Levi is not the father, since you say it like that?" he sighs.

"He's not."

"Then who? Don't tell me it's…"

What? How could he already know about Nate? But after a while, I realize we are not thinking about the same person at all. How dare he? He's one of the few people who know I lost a child because of Diego!

"Holy shit, Clark, how can you even think I'd ever sleep with Diego again?!"

He lets out a big sigh of relief.

"Thank Moon Goddess. I don't know, with the timing, I… Then who is it?"

There's a long silence in the room. I exchange a look with Daniel, but he nods. I have no idea how he will react. Come on Elena, it's only one name.

"Nathaniel Black."

Clark freezes completely for a second, stunned. He turns to the Lewises, but none of them are saying a word or moving. Then, he turns back to me, blinking several times.

"Black? Like… the Black brother? The King's–"

"The King's brother, yes."

"Elena, are you kidding me? You slept with Black?"

More than once, actually, but he doesn't need to know that.

"Was it when they came? But you…"

Oh, Moon Goddess, no, he's thinking about that damn time when we went to fetch the wine! I sigh, a bit annoyed.

"No, Clark, I had an affair with Nathaniel before that."

"And after, too," suddenly says Daniel.

I glare at him. Can't he just shut up for once? Clark looks like he's about to pass out, so I just tell him everything, well, not the details, but how Nate and I met and agree to see each other up until now. I leave out our repeated fighting, though. It's annoying and embarrassing enough as it is.

My godfather takes it all like a slap in the face, speechless for a while. After a long moment, he looks at me like he doesn't recognize me.

"Elena, do you realize what you have done?"

"I know I shouldn't be seeing someone outside of the pack, but-"

"BLACK! A Black, of all people! The King's brother! Are you kidding me, Elena? And you're pregnant, on top of that?"

"Okay, stop, enough," suddenly says Abigail. "Yes, Elena is pregnant, and I understand if it upsets you, but she and her baby are not fine. So if you don't stop yelling at her right now, you're leaving this room, Clark."

My godfather glares at her, but Abigail is a nurse, and she has beta blood, too. She can take it and doesn't budge.

"Who knows?" he suddenly asks.

"About my pregnancy, people who saw me bleed, I guess. As for the father, only the people in this room."

"Fine. Elena, I want no one to know."

"Excuse me?"

Just when I was about to come clean about my relationship with Nate, and my child? Is this a joke? But Clark shakes his head.

"Things are complicated at the moment. The Blood Moon and the Gold Moon are negotiating and things are heating up with the other clans. Everyone's going to have to pick a side."

"We have always been neutral, Clark," says Levi, suddenly looking as worried as I am.

"Until now, but there is no way we are siding with the Gold Moon. And if the Sapphire Moon clan picks a side, we cannot abandon them. We were nothing before they helped us finance the hospital, the clinic, and the labs. It's old history but it's still relevant."

"You're talking as if some war was about to take place…"

Clark sighs, and puts his hands on his hips.

"I don't know. But having two clans negotiate an alliance is never good. Everyone's watching and getting ready, just in case. So, Elena, this child. I don't want anybody to know."

"I am not lying to Nate, Clark," I talk back, annoyed.

My godfather growls, pissed.

"Why? You were concealing this relationship just fine until now, weren't you? This is for the safety of our pack! Elena, if the Sapphire Moon knows my goddaughter and potential heir is having a child with one of the Black brothers, what will they think? You'll put us all in danger! You're smarter than that!"

"I spent more than six months hiding my relationship with him, do you think I don't know the risks?" I reply, angry as well. "I know it was wrong, I know he's not someone I should get involved with, but it happened, Clark, and I'm done lying to everyone about it."

"Elena, this isn't just about you! I was thinking of making you the Alpha of the White Moon clan, and now, this? I know how important having a child must be for you, but I don't want Black involved in any way with my pack! Levi, you could–"

"I am not lying about my baby's father!" I yell. "It's not just about my child, Clark! I love Nathaniel Black, whether you like it or not! You can forget making me your heir, you can banish me, I don't care anymore! I never asked to be made Alpha anyway, you can give it to Orpheus!

"Elena, I beg you, calm down!"

Abigail walks over to me, worried, checking my vitals. I take a deep breath in, trying to calm down, looking at my blood pressure on the machine. Think calm, think about baby girl. I wait a few seconds until I think I'm calm enough. Clark looks torn between worry and anger, saying nothing and fidgeting.

"Clark, I get things are heating up. But I won't lie anymore. I lied for too long already, and this baby is my baby and Nathaniel Black's baby. I grew up without knowing my biological parents. I swear to Moon Goddess, I won't let my child grow up without knowing who her real father is."

I see my godfather is just furious, but I am not changing my mind, he has to understand that. I see him take a deep breath. He doesn't want to yell and put me at risk, but we are not done.

"What about your father, Elena? If I banish you, what about him? You'll leave him alone?"

"My dad would understand, Clark."

My godfather closes his eyes, letting out a long sigh. I exchange a glance with Daniel and Levi, both looking worried. I know they're afraid Clark would really banish me.

Honestly, I'm afraid too. I don't want to be banished from the White Moon clan for the rest of my life. But I also understand the position he's in. If a conflict really arises and we are not clear on whose side we are on, we might get crushed by clans bigger than ours.

"Abigail. How long does Elena need to rest?"

"About two weeks, at least. She can leave the hospital in a few days."

"Fine. Elena, I don't want you to talk to anyone for now. I'll get back to you when my decision is made. And that includes Black. You'll do whatever you want after that, but for now, just focus on your health."

He leaves the room, and all four of us let out a collective sigh.

"Damn, that's my babe," says Daniel. "Always in trouble."

"Levi, what was that about a war? The Gold Moon and the Blood Moon clan?" I ask.

I didn't hear anything about an alliance back at the fight. The Gold Moon was far from us, but the Blood Moon stayed in the north to help. Does Nora know anything about this? Or Nate?

Levi exchanges a glance with his mother, but they both shake their heads.

"Elena, you should just rest and not worry for now. You just woke up, sweetie. Levi will ask, but please, stay still and rest for now, all right? Danny and I will stay with you. Don't worry about Clark, I'm sure we will find a solution."

I nod, and Levi bids me goodbye, promising to find out more about that conflict Clark mentioned. I comply with Abigail's new check-up until she leaves, and I'm left with Daniel.

"Babe, there is something else."

I roll my eyes. What now?

"Don't worry, it's good news this time. I mean, a good idea."

"What then?"

"Bobo called me. Nora had an idea. She wants to test your blood and hers."

"Test our blood?"

"Yeah. Apparently, the King and her entourage want to check if she is really a Royal or not, and we thought…"

"We could use the tests to check if she and I are really related?"

Daniel nods with a big smile.

"I mean, we had suspicions, but wouldn't it be nice to confirm if she is your family ?"

I can't help but smile a bit. Family? That sounds really nice.

"You can do that?" I ask.

"Of course I can! I'm already in touch with Tonia, we'll compare it. But babe, if you are related to Nora, you know it might complicate things further, right?"

"I know. Let's just keep my relationship with her a secret for now, right? Nate doesn't know, and I hope she hasn't told the King either."

"She hasn't, Boyan told me. But babe, if Clark banishes you… You think Nathaniel or Nora could…"

"Take care of me? Honestly, I don't want to think about that now, Danny. I can't even tell Nate about the baby for now, so… I'll see how he reacts when it happens."

Daniel chuckles.

"He's crazy in love with ya, babe. Of course he will be happy about it."

I hope so too.

One thing is for sure, I hate doing nothing. The long hours in the hospital were torture. I don't know if Clark forbade visits or something, but aside from Danny's family, I don't get any visitors my entire stay.

It's about the same once I can finally get home, except that now, Sylviana visits me too. I wonder if there was something keeping her from coming to the hospital, but it's probably just too deep into the White Moon territory, unlike our apartment. She comes about once a week to check on me and my baby.

I get calls from Nora, too. I guess we don't need any blood tests or proof to grow closer. I like when she tells me about her relationship issues, even if it's hard to remember it's about the King.

Somehow, I end up telling her to trust Liam instead of her own mate. No matter what, I can't trust the King. I still remember the chill running down my spine when I crossed paths with him… and there's the Gold Moon clan issue too. They are known to be a selfish and conceited pack, no one can trust them. They only have one redeeming factor: their wealth. But if they really make some kind of alliance with the Blood Moon…

I hear Nora sigh at the other end of the phone. She probably has a lot to think about on her own, too. I glance down at the papers on my knees, the ones I've been looking at for three hours now. Daniel is next to me, sipping his coffee and looking at the more detailed version of those tests.

I take a deep breath.

"Nora, anything yet on the blood results?"

I wish I knew if she really is a Royal. It could change so many things for everyone in Silver City, her mate, and even my relationship with Nate.

"Not yet," she answers. "Tonia said it would take time. Apparently, gene-testing is longer."

"I figured so," I sigh, looking at Daniel. "Danny said the same thing. But I have something else. Apparently, matching our blood is much quicker."

I hear her breathing stopping. Is she okay?

"Nora?"

"Sorry, I'm just so stressed suddenly! Do you really have it? You know?"

My gosh, she already sounds so excited, I can't help but smile.

"Yes. Daniel just got the results this afternoon. I wanted to see you in person to tell you, but now that you called me first, I really don't think I can keep quiet until then. But can you breathe first? You're scaring me a bit and if you collapse, I'm too far away to help."

"No, I'm okay! Just tell me, is it a match? Is it?"

Moon Goddess, she's almost screaming! I laugh and grab the paper to check again before telling the poor girl.

"Elena!"

"Nora, it is! We are related!"

I feel the tears coming as I say that, and she is crying too. Great, we are both crying like pups now!

"Are you okay?" she asks.

"Why do you ask? You're crying like a baby too!"

We laugh for a bit, and Daniel smiles and shakes his head too. This is so insane. I try to remember what Daniel said precisely.

"Nora, there's more."

"What do you mean?"

"According to Daniel, the percentage of matching DNA can indicate how closely related we are, so he brought the full results. 13.3% of our DNA matches."

I wait a bit for her to take in the info, exchanging a complicit smile with Danny.

"You're torturing her, aren't you?" he whispers.

I stick my tongue out. I've been locked up for days, I'm just having a bit of fun while I can!

"Elena, speak!"

"We are cousins, Nora," I finally say. "First cousins! One of my birth parents was your mom's sibling!"

I just wish I knew which! Like anything about my birth family. I envy Nora who at least knew her dad.

"Are you kidding?"

I shake my head. I asked Daniel the same thing twice, too. But he was very specific, I remember each of his words by heart.

"No, I'm not. Daniel just told me this much matching DNA can only be a first cousin! Can you imagine? Your mother is my aunt! We are cousins!"

Nora cries a lot at the other end of the phone, and it's hard to stop my own tears. For the first time, I know someone with whom I am blood-related! My first family tie found, Nora is linked to my lost past!

Daniel shifts position to come closer to me, smiling and holding my free hand. It takes a while for Nora to calm down, so I take deep breaths too and lie down, my head on Danny's lap.

"Elena, do you know what this means?"

I sigh.

"Yeah, I thought about it right away. That means if you turn out to be one, I would be a Royal's child, too."

"Could it be?"

I really doubted it, but...

"Daniel said so. I may not have as much as you, but I do have some Royal characteristics, after all... My non-Royal parent was probably less pure or something? I don't know... But I will need to find this out now."

Nora being a Royal means I am one of sorts too, but it complicates things. A lot. Reagan never mentioned I was related to the Royals. Did she try to hide it? Why? If the woman she talked about was Nora's grandmother, and mine too, she and I shouldn't have such a difference in our Royal blood. But Nora is the pure one, not me. She's got perfectly white fur, sapphire-blue eyes, and a monstrous Alpha Aura. I don't have any of that, and my aura isn't as powerful as hers. I'm pretty sure her mind-linking is stronger too, from what she's demonstrated so far. So what is that big difference? Was it what Reagan wanted to conceal at any cost?

"Elena? What do you mean you need to find out?"

"I know I said before it didn't really matter for me, but…"

I sigh. Daniel caresses my hair.

"Babe, you gotta talk with Reagan again," he whispers. "Now you've got all this information, plus what Sylviana told you. She can't pretend anymore. You even know the name of your former pack, and it's about Nora too. And there's…"

He's right, there's my baby. If she has Royal blood, it changes a lot of things. The vampires from last time were targeting Nora, it might have to do with this. I mean, it's the only reason they would target her, from what we've heard. But turns out, I might have Royal blood too, even though it's weaker. Nathaniel is an alpha too, this probably makes my baby ever stronger.

Daniel points at the phone.

"You can tell Nora, Elena. She won't tell anyone."

"Tell me what?" she asks.

I take a deep breath.

"Nora, I need you to promise me you won't tell anyone what I'm about to say. Especially not the brothers. Not even Tonia, or anyone else."

"I promise. What is it?"

"I learned yesterday before the battle. I'm pregnant. It's Nate's."

She stays silent for a long while, and for some reason, I start crying.

I've been moody these days, but saying it out loud to Nora, just after the good news of us being family, unlocks something in me that I haven't been able to release before. I can put up a good front for Clark, pretend I'm strong, act calm for my baby, but I'm completely lost inside.

I am fucking pregnant. I love this baby, but she wasn't expected. It changes a lot of things. My relationship with Nathaniel, which was already a mess to begin with. My position in the pack that I might have to give up for her. Even school. I haven't been able to go to school since I was discharged from the hospital, but even so, what comes next?

I'll have to give up on university to take care of my baby girl. I'll have to take on a full-time job to support her, maybe juggle with Daniel to take care of her properly. But before all that, I still haven't told Nathaniel.

Nora and Daniel both try to comfort me, but it takes a while for my tears to dry. He takes the phone from me at some point and hangs up for me.

"Danny?"

"Yes, babe?"

"I don't know how I'm gonna pull it off. The clan isn't going to help me raise a child from another pack, and you know all my paychecks are going to my dad's bills and our rent, and the school…"

I start crying even more, not making any sense between my sobbing and irregular breathing. Daniel caresses my hair to have me calm down.

"Babe, calm down, calm down. No stress, okay? First, you're not going to be alone, ever. You have the best friend in the world, me, who would go to hell and back for you, okay? If you're banned, they can ban me too. Plus, you know my family won't ever abandon you, you're like our secret third sister. So even if Clark decides on something really stupid, you know our family will be there to support you. Also, don't worry about school, okay? You can always take a year off and resume later, no? As for money, your baby's father is a freaking millionaire, Elena. He will help you with his magical bank account."

"Danny. Nate doesn't even know about this baby yet."

"But once he does, he's going to go crazy for his daughter, like any good daddy. Plus, do you realize? That kid will be the King's niece! And Nora's, too!"

Oh Moon Goddess, I didn't realize!

If Nora marries the King, she will become my child's aunt, right? That plus being my cousin. This is crazy. Out of all people, my long-lost cousin and I fell in love with two brothers.

As I think about our weird family tree, it reminds me…

"Danny, my dad."

"Yeah, I know. Don't worry, I'll go see him for you, all right? I can ask Mom and Bonnie to check on him too."

My poor dad. I keep imagining him, alone in that hospital room, still in his coma. If only he could wake up now. I know he would support me, tell Clark he's an idiot, and be happy for me and my baby. He would probably give Nate one hell of a pep talk too. I chuckle imagining that, and Daniel notices it.

"Babe, I prefer seeing you smile. No negativity in this house, just warmth and a nice environment for our baby girl. You know what? Next time I go to the university, I'll get you some books about babies and all the kinds of stuff you will suffer from with parenthood!"

We laugh together about what a struggle it will be to raise this baby until I get hungry for pizza and beg Danny to order some.

Actually, I crave pizza every day that follows. Sitting at home isn't much better than lying down on the hospital bed. I give up studying by myself as it becomes boring and makes me angry anytime it reminds me how I won't be able to attend university until next summer at least.

Daniel keeps his word and brings me dozens of books about pregnancy, kids, and parenthood. I become much more aware of everything that comes with pregnancy, and discuss it often with his mother at each of my check-ups. The next two hospital visits are a relief: my baby girl is still there and growing.

Daniel even starts buying baby stuff, and his mom brings me what she kept from her five pregnancies. Abigail and Bonnie are a huge support, but Sylviana is probably the person I come to trust the most. The witch comes often and gives me some tea to drink, soups, and other things she prepares herself. She teaches me some breathing exercises, how to stretch, and even how to make my own nutritious soups.

However, a few days have passed, and I'm still confined to the sofa. Even worse, I'm running out of things to read, and Daniel is especially grumpy.

"Consider it like he's working, babe," I sigh.

He's glaring at his phone as if it was some vicious creature. If it wasn't the expensive smartphone kind, I bet he would have already smashed it.

"I'm just saying. A call once in a while would be nice."

"He is working. In his wolf form, Danny. Have you ever tried texting with your paws?"

"Why are you defending him?" he pouts.

"I'm the one ignoring Nate so I don't have to tell him I'm pregnant before Clark decides to throw my ass in the street or not! So I kind of understand what Boyan is going through!"

"Who knows if he really is working? Hm? Have you heard from him? Or Nora?"

I roll my eyes. Daniel is a fucking drama queen when he is in one of his jealous episodes. At least it's better than watching TV.

"Daniel, stop the insecurity episode right now. Boyan is gay for you, like literally. He makes you breakfast every time he's here!"

"Carlo made breakfast too, and he still cheated on me!"

"Yeah, I remember, his coffee was disgusting. But Boyan is cute, nice, and caring. So now, can you grab that stupid smartphone of yours to order my pizza or do I have to get up?"

"That's a different matter. With Juan, anyway, I..."

"*Elena...?*"

I frown. Was that Nora? I can barely recognize her voice. What's wrong with her?

"*Nora? Nora, why are you crying, are you okay? What's wrong?*"

"*Elena, can I come to your place? I have nowhere to go.*"

Nowhere to go? Isn't she staying at that place the King bought her? Boyan told us it was a huge penthouse and all.

"*What? But what about your...*"

"*... I'm not going back there.*"

Something happened. I can tell in her voice. Her wolf's crying, whimpering loudly. It almost makes me want to cry too, our bond is so strong.

"*Okay, okay. Do you know where you are? We will come and get you, okay?*"

She gives me the name of some restaurant, and I recognize it immediately, I ate there with Nate before. I get up to grab my coat under Daniel's surprised eyes.

"What are you doing?"

"Grab the car keys, we are going to the Blood Moon territory."

"No, we are not! Why would we–?"

"Nora needs me. Danny, we are going or I'm going alone."

He opens his mouth to protest but realizes I'm serious as hell.

"Oh, damn you, woman!"

We get ready in a hurry, and that walk to the car is probably the longest I've taken in days, but Moon Goddess, it feels great! Daniel insists I get in the back, and I don't protest. It's pouring outside, but I can feel Nora so intensely. Her sadness seeps into me. What happened to her? What about Boyan? And her mate, the King?

Chapter 21

While we drive to the address, Daniel doesn't stop saying how we will get in trouble for entering the Blood Moon clan's territory, but I couldn't care less. I'm still mind-linking Nora, silently feeling her anger, her sadness, and her distress.

We finally spot Nora, standing under the restaurant's sign, and Moon Goddess, she looks like a mess. She gets in the car, soaked and crying loudly. Her black hair is stuck to her cheeks, and her makeup is running down her face. And why is she wearing an expensive-looking dress?

"Nora... What happened?" I ask, trying to calm her down.

"Wait, it smells like blood, babe," says Danny.

I check Nora. Is she injured? She doesn't look like she was fighting… I finally see her feet.

"Oh, my Goddess, Nora!"

Moon Goddess, how could she even stand like this! Her feet are covered in blood! Is that glass? Her white skin is cut in multiple places, it looks damn painful just by looking at it! But she acts as if she had only just realized it too, and keeps sniffling and sobbing the same, shaking her head.

"Danny, you think you can handle that?" I ask, looking at the injury. "Or do we take her to the hospital?"

Danny glances back a couple of times. I know this isn't exactly his expertise, but his mom and sister are nurses, so…

"It should be okay," he finally says, "but we need to disinfect it quickly."

"My Goddess, Nora... What happened to you?"

She looks at me, and starts talking, but also crying a lot more.

"I… I thought there was something wrong with Damian, and… and Liam said there was this party… for the Black Corp, their… company… so I… I hid that I was going, and Liam took me there, and Bobo too, and…"

She starts crying a lot louder, breathing with difficulty. I pat her back, feeling as sad as her, trying to comfort her. She keeps trying to push her messy hair out of her face, with trembling hands and erratic moves.

"Damian was… there, with that woman, and they said she's… his fiancée!"

What the actual fuck? Nora is his fated mate, isn't she? He even made a whole ruckus about finding her for years, and now the King is getting engaged to someone else? What the hell is going on!

"That… that woman, King, she… she was acting like they were really close, and she was by his side, and Damian was okay with it, and… and he said it's true… He's… He's engaged to her… Elena, I don't get it! He said he loves me, but he doesn't want me as his Luna… I don't get it! She's just… She was…"

But her words are lost in her crying, and it goes on for a while.

My gosh, poor Nora. How could he do that? The King is…

"Men are jerks."

"Not helpful, Danny!" I growl at him.

Seriously, can he not make it about him for once? I take a deep breath, even though I'm probably as mad as he is at the King for doing such a thing. Engaged to Alexandra King, of all people? The Gold Moon clan Alpha's daughter? That woman is known to be a mythic bitch! She's crazy rich and so full of herself, too, from what I've seen or heard of her. So that's the shitty alliance Clark mentioned.

I take a deep breath. I need to calm down, Nora is already enough of a wreck as it is.

"Nora, I'm so sorry about what you went through tonight, really. But don't worry, okay? Tonight you can stay at our place, have a good sleep, and calm down. And we can talk about it tomorrow when you feel better, okay?"

She nods weakly, her cheeks still soaked with tears.

"What is there to talk about? She needs to ditch the guy and basta–"

"Danny, park the damn car and shut up!"

It feels like a short ride back to our place, but Nora manages to calm down a little. Her feet worry me, though, her shoes literally turned red from all the blood. I wrapped her in the blanket meant for me, but she doesn't look good. She's whiter than usual, if possible, and the rain keeps her all cold and wet no matter how much Danny turns up the heat in the car.

By the time we get back to our apartment, she has somewhat calmed down, and I suspect all this crying has exhausted her. We get her to the couch, and Danny runs to get the first aid kit his mom gave us. I can't even look at her feet, all this blood makes me so nauseous.

"How is it, Danny?" I ask without looking.

"Well, bleeding. I'm going to have to make sure she doesn't have any glass left in her foot, but it should be okay. Not a good idea to run around with your feet in that state, sweetheart."

"Sorry... I didn't realize."

While Daniel starts to look at her feet and do whatever he can with a frown on, I get up and head to the kitchen to get her something hot to drink.

"I would love a cappuccino too," says Danny.

"I wasn't asking you!"

"Thank you, babe."

I roll my eyes but of course, I make one for him too. I grab the coffee out of habit, but Daniel's head turns like a hawk.

"No coffee for you, mama!"

"Crap, I forgot."

I'll just make myself some lemon tea then. We need to buy more soon; I've been drinking nothing but citrus tea lately. Suddenly, my phone vibrates.

"It's Nate..."I sigh.

Why is he calling now of all times? Danny frowns, turning to me with his gloves covered in blood.

"They are probably looking for her," he says. "You should answer before the whole Blood Moon clan rushes to our territory."

Damn, he's probably right. If they are intensely worried and searching, Boyan probably told them before it escalated. Of all places, this is the first one Nora could think of that is not within the Blood Moon's domination. Nora is looking at me with her eyes full of worry and something that looks like… wariness. I take a big breath. Damn, I haven't talked to Nate in ages, and we barely texted each other too. I was too busy hiding my pregnancy from him.

"Yes, Nate?"

"Hi, Elena. Are you okay?"

"I'm okay, thanks."

"I haven't heard from you in a while, I was… a bit worried."

I bet. He probably thought we would be able to talk soon. Honestly, I hoped so too. I didn't expect to be under Clark's surveillance so soon, but since he discovered the truth about the baby… I take a look down at my little bump, hidden under my sweater.

"I know, sorry, I've been busy."

Busy watching TV and eating pizza. I feel so damn useless now that I think about it. If only I wasn't sick on top of being pregnant. Deep breath, Elena, it's for your daughter's health too. Moon Goddess, it's so hard to hear his voice and not spill anything. But I still haven't heard from Clark, and one wrong word could get me banished and penniless in a minute.

"Sorry if this question seems really out of the blue for you, but have you heard anything from Nora Bluemoon, by any chance?"

I frown. So Boyan did let him know about my relationship with Nora? How much did he say? Damn, I don't know how much he knows.

"Yes, she's here with me, at my place."

"Really? How is she? Is she hurt?"

"Yeah, she's okay," I answer, a bit annoyed. "Well, a bit shaken up, but she is safe, and Daniel is taking care of her feet."

Who got her in this state in the first place? I seriously hope the King is regretting being a damn idiot and doing this to my cousin. At least they do sound worried about her.

"All right. Good to know. I'll dispatch someone to come and get her, and–"

I stop him right there.

"Not tonight, Nate. It's not a good idea. Nora is still upset, she needs some time."

A brief silence, and I wonder if he's talking to or mind-linking someone else. Is he with his brothers? Does the King know? He's probably with him, considering how Nate is not mentioning anything about our relationship. By the way, how much do his brothers actually know about us?

"Elena, do you mind looking after Nora for us? I understand if she feels better staying with you, at least for tonight."

"Yes, of course. As long as she needs."

She could stay a full month, I wouldn't mind. I'm happy she's here. I'm mad at her mate, King or not, for being such a jerk to her. To be honest, there are a few very impolite and disrespectful things I wish I could say to him but now is probably not the right time.

Finally, I hear Nate talking to someone, but then, his tone changes a little.

"Who is with you?"

"That's none of your business, Nate."

What, is he making this about Levi again, seriously, right now? I hear him sigh.

"It's… Boyan wants to come over."

Oh. Not what I thought then, well, I think Boyan is not to blame, but Nora needs some time away from the Blood Moon to think. Maybe not now, but at least tomorrow morning, when she feels better.

"Nora?" I call to her.

She was watching me all this time, but Daniel turns his head to me too.

"Yes?"

"Bobo wants to come and see you tomorrow morning... Is that okay?"

She hesitates for a while, but in the meantime, Daniel's eyes are literally shining. To think he was mad at him an hour ago. I can't believe him. He's so childish at times! Finally, Nora nods.

"She said yes."

"Alright, let's do that then," says Nate, with a bit of relief in his voice.

"Okay."

He hesitates a while, and I wonder if I should hang up.

"Elena, you… Are you sure you're fine?"

I immediately turn red. Why is he saying that? Did he sense something? He couldn't tell just from my voice over the phone, right? I get really nervous. Is he just asking to be polite? Or does he suspect something? Boyan wouldn't have told him, right? And he didn't seem to notice anything at the fight either!

"Yes, I'm fine, I told you. Good night, Nathaniel."

I hang up a bit quickly and let out a big sigh. Damn. Just five minutes on the phone and I'm such a mess already.

"Are you okay, babe?"

"I am," I reply to Danny, "Anyway, Nora is the one to be worried about."

I can't have too much attention on me right now, and I want to focus on Nora anyway. At least Nate didn't have the guts to get engaged to some other bitch.

"Well, she should be happy, Boyan is coming for *her*."

"Oh, stop being a baby, Danny! Bobo is worried about Nora, as a friend! Now drop the jealousy act or, baby or not, I'm really kicking your scrawny ass!"

Nora suddenly looks at us with her eyes wide open.

"So, you're Bobo's mysterious boyfriend!"

Oh, right, she probably had no idea about those two until now. Daniel immediately turns red as a beet while I chuckle.

"Bobo's mysterious boyfriend, what do you have to say for yourself?"

"I knew it! I always saw him texting someone, so I knew he had a partner…"

Danny's embarrassed face is priceless. He pretends to be twice as focused on Nora's feet, but his ears are red, very, very red right now.

"W-we need to disinfect t-this quickly, and–"

"You already disinfected it, Danny, stop pretending. Well, don't you have some things to ask Nora?" I ask, taking the spot next to her on the couch. immediately

Nora frowns and grabs the hot tea.

"I'm sorry, Daniel, Boyan is always with me, you must miss him…"

"It's fine, I understand."

"Really? I thought someone was on the verge of breaking up with him…" I whisper behind my cup.

"Elena, shut it!"

I laugh. My gosh, now that he's facing Nora, he is so embarrassed it's kind of cute.

They talk about Boyan for a bit, and now that she is thinking of something else, Nora looks a lot better. It's the first time we've seen each other since we found out about our family ties. I see her more like a little sister, though. It's hard, I can't remember much, yet I have this feeling of closeness with her like we know each other from before. I wonder how Reagan would react to Nora, actually. She probably has no idea there's another survivor from the Blue Moon clan.

Nora, Daniel, and I talk for a bit, mostly to distract Nora from her bad evening. She falls asleep quickly, though, and Daniel and I watch her for a while. She's even prettier than before, somehow, despite her red eyes and nose.

"It's funny," says Daniel. "She doesn't look much like you physically, but I still see how you two are alike."

"Really?"

"Yeah. I don't know, like an impression or something. In the way she talks and moves. Is it a Royal thing?"

I sigh and shake my head.

"I'm not a Royal, Danny."

"A part of you is. At a lesser degree than Nora, for sure, but… I want to see her results. If she is as pure-blooded as we think, it may explain why you are so different too. Your mind-linking ability, your slow healing…"

I put a hand on my belly, a bit worried. If I am any part Royal, my baby will inherit it. And her father is a pure Alpha, too. Will that reinforce her Royal blood? I have no idea how it works. I just wish she could live a normal, happy life. Her parents being from different packs is enough of a nightmare as it is.

"I will tell Nate. Next time I see him. Even if Clark banishes me."

Daniel frowns, unable to hide his worry.

"I understand, babe. I hope he doesn't, but… the King's engagement confirms there is something bad going on. Damn, Moon Goddess, please prevent a war. I thought things had been calmer after the Black father's death, but…"

We both look at Nora, whose eyes still get teary in her sleep.

"She will probably be the first to be thrown in the middle of all this, you know. I don't know why the King got engaged, but Nora won't put up with it. She's a Luna, deep down, she knows that."

"Oh, I would pay to see her get rid of that bitch of Alexandra King," sighs Daniel. "Damn the Gold Moon clan."

"Come on, let's get her to bed. Let's think about this mess another day, I'm tired."

"Alright."

Danny carries Nora all the way to his bed and agrees to sleep on the sofa. Thank Moon Goddess she's petite, Daniel's muscles aren't the most impressive of the pack. We finally get to bed, but I can't find sleep for a while.

Hearing Nathaniel's voice for the first time in a while made me feel a bit better. My wolf is yearning for him. I try to imagine how he'll react to my pregnancy. Nate can be really sweet sometimes. I just hope he'll take it well. If I'm rejected by both him and the White Moon clan, I really will have nowhere to go.

"*Babe.*"

"*Mmhmm?*"

Why is Danny mind-linking at such a late hour? I sit up in my bed, confused.

"*Look out your window.*"

I push my curtain aside, and it takes me a while to see it in the darkness. A wolf, sitting at the corner of the street, completely still. Damn it, it's Diego.

"*How long has he been here?*"

"*No idea, I just spotted him. What the hell is he doing...*"

"*I don't know, but it's odd he won't approach.*"

"*Clark may have put someone to watch you, don't you think?*"

"*Or he knows I'm not alone. Damn it!*"

"*Babe, you really need to talk to Black. I don't care about Clark's decision, but I don't want this guy to keep loitering around you. If he knows about your baby...*"

"*I know, Danny.*"

I growl unconsciously and keep watching. After a while, it starts raining outside, and Diego walks away, but I can't settle down.

As I hoped, after a good night's sleep, Nora already looks a lot better. Her eyes are still red, but she's feisty enough to argue with Boyan about keeping silent on the King's engagement when he arrives. Daniel is happy to see his lover again, obviously, but for me, Boyan's presence is a strong reminder of Nate. He even passed along some fresh-baked croissants for us. He knows how I love croissants with my coffee in the morning…

The four of us decide to stay home and have a lazy day, as it's a downpour all day long outside and Nora and I are tired. Nora talks a lot with us, sometimes crying, sometimes laughing when we share our childhood stories. We talk a lot, bonding over our werewolf selves, and I tell her about how I control my werewolf, as she still apparently struggles with hers. I don't think I've ever felt so close with another woman around my age before, not even Bonnie or Iris. It's like I found myself a little sister.

In the evening, Liam Black comes to see her, just so they can take some time to talk. He's probably going to defend his brother's actions. We let her go with him, as I'm in no condition to go anyway. I keep falling asleep, my pregnancy and the rain keeping me sluggish. I don't even hear Nora get home.

I wake up to someone's crying. Is it Nora? I get up from the couch to approach her. She's curled up in a corner, breathing and crying loudly, a smartphone at her feet.

"Nora? What happened?"

But she keeps shaking her head, like in a trance. Gosh, what is wrong with her? Is she sick? Do I have to take her to the hospital? Moon Goddess, if anything happens to her here… I call Danny, unsure of what to do. Once he and Bobo arrive, they are the first ones to understand.

"Is she…"

"Yeah, Nora's in… heat," says Boyan with a frown.

"I gotta call Sylviana," adds Daniel, grabbing his phone in a rush.

"Why?"

"There is no medical way to stop a heat, Elena, and I really don't think it would be good to have the King's fated mate in heat here!"

Okay, he's got a point.

While he's on the phone I try to take Nora to the couch, and Boyan walks away a bit. Oh right, he's probably not doing great if he's bisexual. I try to calm down Nora a bit, but as Danny said, there's not much I can do. Her temperature keeps rising, and so do her pheromones, making Boyan leave our place soon after.

"Thank Moon Goddess for the rain," says Danny. "It should cover the smell a bit. Damn, I don't feel anything, I'm definitely gay."

I chuckle. Who was doubting that?

Thankfully, Sylviana arrives incredibly fast. She doesn't seem bothered by the downpour outside at all and rushes to Nora's side very calmly.

"Her first heat. It's surprising she hasn't mated yet."

"Well, the King might not be as much of a jerk as we thought he was… At least he's got some self-restraint."

I give him that too. If Nora is his fated mate, the man must be really patient for not touching her, and from what I've seen of him, he didn't seem like a very patient man at all.

Sylviana puts her hands on Nora's forehead and chest, closing her eyes, and starts whispering something. I can't hear, but from the way her lips are moving, I don't even think I could understand anything anyway. Is it a secret witch language of some sort? At least it seems effective. Nora progressively calms down, and from her previous agitated state, she falls into a deep slumber, peacefully sleeping as if nothing happened. It takes a few minutes until Sylviana stops, everyone in the room totally speechless.

"She does smell weird now," says Daniel.

"That is because I covered up her heat with my power. You feel my magic on her, and her wolf is smelling it too, that's why she is calm. Her heat is still there, only toned down. It will stay that way until it ends, so don't worry about that."

I can't help but let out a long sigh of relief. I really didn't expect that... I've seen female wolves having their heat a couple of times before, but I didn't think Nora would still be a virgin. Sylviana nods, visibly satisfied, and turns to us.

"Thank you for that. It's my first time seeing her from up close!"

"You sound like a kid going to Disneyland," says Daniel with a frown.

Sylviana chuckles.

"Nora is somewhat special. Her aura is like... a warm fire, radiating with Moon Power. I can feel it so clearly."

"They haven't confirmed she's a Royal yet," I say.

"I strongly believe so. Her power is so pure. Your baby's aura is the same, Elena."

I frown. What? She never mentioned anything like that before, but Sylviana keeps staring at my belly and nods.

"It's different from yours. I think her father's strong alpha blood might have awakened a power that was dormant within you. Have you talked with Reagan yet?"

"No. I was confined here, remember? But I plan to. And Nate, too."

"If Elena's baby is a Royal, just like Nora..."

I know we are thinking the same thing. If the vampire attack was targeting Nora because of her special blood... Sylviana nods sadly.

"She will become a target too."

"Sylviana, that vampire attack. It wasn't just a vampire attack, right? A dark witch was behind it, and she wanted Nora. You said bad witches will target werewolves."

She looks at me with a sad expression, and slowly nods.

"Yes. Nora's power is very attractive."

I start to lose patience and growl, annoyed.

"Sylviana, if you know things, spill it. I have enough things threatening my baby, I would rather have the full list now."

Of course, she is not impressed in the slightest, and shrugs.

"It is as I said, Elena. The dark witch who attacked the city is most likely after Nora's tremendous Moon Power... and once she knows of its existence, she might go after your daughter too. For now, it's like having a candle next to a firepit. Nora's aura is much stronger; she won't even be able to notice your baby while you carry her."

"You mean until she's born," says Danny.

"Yes. I can't quite understand it, but somehow, Elena's aura is acting as a shield and hiding her baby's. That's why even I couldn't see her aura until I got close."

I don't know if I should feel good about that or not.

In other words, something we can't figure out about me is shielding my baby from Sylviana and that dark witch's powers, though we still don't know why until I talk with Reagan.

But once my daughter is born, she will become a target. Like Nora's firepit aura.

I take a deep breath. I'm going to need a lot of help to get through this. I need Reagan to spill the beans about whatever's unusual about me, and finally know the truth about my parents.

But first, I need to talk to Nate.

"What's next?" I ask Sylviana. "How much of a threat are we talking about here?"

"It will depend on how many packs Nora and the King can rally."

I exchange a look with Danny. Rally the packs? Like, an actual alliance? Is she nuts? We barely see eye-to-eye let alone talk to some of the other packs!

"Sylviana, I don't mean to rain on your parade, but… that sounds very crazy."

But the witch chuckles.

"I think Nora might surprise us. Anyway, I have things to do on my side too. I'll get going."

"Don't you want Nora to meet you? Like, officially?" I ask, surprised.

Sylviana shakes her head.

"It is not a good time. If I reveal myself now, it will be harder for people to trust Nora and follow her. Each thing should happen at the right moment."

Oh, right, I forgot she's some sort of seer. Before we can add anything, Sylviana exits our apartment, leaving us there like idiots. I growl.

"Damn, can we get some good news once in a while?"

"Speaking of good news, Reagan is back in town, and you'll get to talk to Black soon, babe."

"I'd better."

A few hours later, Nora wakes up, feeling fine as if nothing happened. She has no recollection of her heat, it seems, and of course, no clue about Sylviana.

Can my cousin really find a way to rally the packs against that Dark Witch? Before my baby is born? It's not that I don't want to believe in her, but right now, Nora's only an eighteen-year-old, heartbroken girl on my couch!

Though, my cousin seems to get stronger every time I see her.

On Monday, she goes to work, looking perfectly fine, and I know she won't come back here. She looks like someone who's ready for a fight rather than a work shift. I hope she can work things out with the King and have him cancel that alliance with the Gold Moon.

As for me, I'm back to my routine of resting, attending check-ups at the hospital, and waiting for Clark's decision… Though I know it's taking too long. It doesn't seem good.

One evening, he finally shows up, visibly annoyed. Daniel is by my side on the couch and Levi is standing behind us with his arms crossed. My godfather is in a bad mood.

"I'll take it you didn't find a satisfying solution," I sigh.

"Oh, I did, Elena. But I know you're stubborn and won't listen to what I tell you no matter what, and that's what's bothering me."

"What is it?"

Clark takes a deep breath in.

"I spoke to the elders. They agreed to offer you a choice. I already told them you wouldn't give up your child, and they understood that much."

"Right."

"I don't... fully understand how things are between you and… the Blood Moon clan at the moment, but this is the White Moon we are talking about. So, you have a choice."

I'm getting nervous. What could get Clark so annoyed? He knows what decision I would make, so why did he still manage to get me a choice?

"You have to give up any of your rights as the Alpha heir, but the elders agreed to let you have your child as long as its existence is concealed from its biological father. They don't care what story you want to tell, but no one else should know that it is Black's child."

I clench my fist. Those damn assholes.

"Elena, think about it. You haven't told him yet, so…"

"What's the other option, Clark?"

He sighs.

"Banishment. From both the Opal and White Moon clans."

"So that's it? Either Elena keeps it a secret from her baby's father, or she is banished? Are they fucking serious?" says Daniel, furious.

"It's not like she had a child with just anyone!" says Clark. "Trust me, I hate it as much as you do, but that's the best they agreed to! No one wants the King involved in our business, and they certainly do not want his nephew or niece in our pack! Elena, we already forgave you after that episode with Diego, this time you–"

"Forgave me?"

I look at my godfather, so shocked I don't even know how to respond to that. I get up, looking at him, disappointed. I see in his face he's already regretting his words.

"Elena, that's not what I–"

"I went to jail, and you think you can call it forgiveness, Clark? After losing my baby? After you only banished Diego for 5 years?"

"Babe, calm down," says Danny, worried.

But I don't care. I'm too disappointed and shocked to stay quiet now. I've always believed in Clark, I can't actually believe what I just heard from him. I stand in front of him, trying to hold my tears in.

"When Diego tried to rape me and made me lose a baby, you banished him for five years. Now, I'm having a child with a man who loves me, and you're asking me to choose between him, my baby, and banishment? Look me in the eye and tell me why I should accept that, Clark!"

"This is bullshit, Clark," adds Levi's furious voice behind me.

Our Alpha is clearly uneasy and angry about this, trying to find his words, shaking his head.

"Elena, we are talking about one of the most dangerous men in this city. Nathaniel Black is this city's number two, and you are someone important to our pack, too. You getting pregnant by that man is not something we can celebrate like some happy news."

"I never cared about being Alpha of the White Moon or Opal Moon, Clark, I don't care even if I'm the last omega! I'm grateful my parents adopted me, I'm grateful to you for being my godfather, but I never asked for any of these responsibilities you're pushing on me! You all made those choices for me!"

Clark suddenly goes silent, visibly shocked. The words stay stuck in his throat for a while, before he addresses me, looking furious this time.

"You think we made this decision, Elena? Really? You think I chose to be an Alpha? If you're unhappy with your position, you can blame the Moon Goddess! But when Reagan brought us a Royal's child, you think we could have treated you any differently than we did?"

I'm speechless.

"What… did you say?" I ask, completely taken by surprise.

"Yes, Elena, you have Royal blood. We've known since the first day Reagan brought you here."

"You said you didn't know about my parents."

"She didn't give us details about your parents, Elena. We just knew. You had a crazy Alpha Aura for a child your age, and she said you were from a Royal family. We had no choice but to believe it, but as soon as we did, we hid it."

I exchange a look with Daniel and Levi, completely taken by surprise. How the hell did Clark keep this hidden from me all this time? He knew so much!

My godfather sighs.

"That's why Samuel and Ivy, of all people, took you in. We knew we would need a strong Alpha couple to take care of you. Until you were an adult, we hid you from the other packs, and even your lineage had to be kept a secret. We thought…"

He pauses.

"We thought having you take over the White Moon clan someday, as my goddaughter and Samuel's daughter, would seem natural. Werewolves naturally look up to the strongest individuals. As an Alpha of Royal blood, you would make a great leader for us. At least that's what we thought, until…"

"Until Diego?" asked Daniel, disgusted.

Clark nodded.

"Strong Alphas in the same pack always end up looking for strong partners or fighting each other. I just didn't think it would get so bad, or make you lose a child. I admit I may have treated you more as a female with Royal blood than a woman, Elena. But I never, ever thought you would do the same thing again!"

Moon Goddess, it's my godfather standing in front of me, but I feel like vomiting right now. And I swear my pregnancy has nothing to do with it.

"I'm sorry your… weapon is not living up to your expectations, Clark."

"Elena, that's not–"

"Shut up. Shut up, and listen to me, for once. I respected you, as an Alpha. I really did. But now I realize you've only been grooming me like the rest of your warriors. You never actually listened to my feelings, you just thought about the pack. I get it. You may think this was your duty as an Alpha, but honestly, I don't care anymore."

I see the sadness in his eyes. I know he must feel guilty after realizing what he has done, but this time, I'm not going to stay silent and take it anymore. I step up to him, trying to calm down and control myself.

"So from now on, I'm going to be my own individual and make my own decisions. Not for this pack, but for myself. I will find out the whole truth about my origin from Reagan, and I will tell Nathaniel Black I'm carrying his child. That is my decision, so now you can go and do whatever you want with it, Clark."

Chapter 22

Under the hot water, I can finally close my eyes and stop thinking.

The argument with Clark has left me exhausted. I'm sad, disappointed, and lost. And somewhat angry, too. How dare they decide on all these things for me? Isn't it my life? They never bothered to ask what I wanted!

I don't care about being a Royal, but I was glad to find out that I still have a blood relative that's alive!

"*Elena?*"

I almost jump at Nora's voice. Damn, I will never get used to that; our mind-link is so clear, it's as if she is standing next to me.

"*Nora! What is it, too lazy to use the phone now?*"

I grab my bathrobe and put my hair in a towel while she answers.

"*I'm showering. Plus, Nate is right next door. You still don't want the brothers to know we know each other, right?*"

How funny, we were doing the exact same thing. Did she know somehow? Is that why she thought of contacting me at the same time? Now that she said it and I'm focusing, I can almost feel the water running. I remember her question and shake my head.

"*No, no. Are you alright, Nora? Your wolf seems all shaken up.*"

"*A lot of things have happened! Someone broke into my place, I mean, the apartment Damian arranged for me.*"

"*What? Are you alright?*" I ask, worried.

I exit the bathroom to find Daniel and Levi chatting, but I ignore them and head to the kitchen to make myself some hot water with lemon while Nora keeps talking.

"*I'm fine, I was at work. But Damian is completely furious. Whoever did it left some sort of threat, he has the whole pack looking for the culprit. I'm with him right now, and Nate and Liam too.*"

I bet he is. The King seems totally overprotective of Nora, but now that something like this has happened… Who could have done it? Is it the same person who was watching me? Or the one who assaulted her when they found her? Anyone who wanted to piss off the King could go after Nora, but this seems personal.

"*Any suspects?*" I ask.

"*We have some. But anyway, I'm fine. I wanted to tell you something else. You know, about the Royal blood? The results came in, Elena. My blood is 80% Royal!*"

Damn, that's a whole lot!! I mean, not that much of a surprise, but still…

"*Nora, that's a lot of information. I'm not so surprised about the blood results, to be honest, I always knew you were more… well, more Royal than I am. But what happened at your place? That's really no good.*"

"*I know, I'm totally freaked out too, though I don't want to worry Damian.*"

"*I understand. But stay close to your mate until they found this psychopath, okay? And you can talk to me if you need help, anytime.*"

I can't help but worry about her. She is going to be a target now that they are together for real.

"*Thank you, cousin.*"

I chuckle.

"*Cousin? I don't really like it. Let's call each other sisters instead.*"

I've already been calling her that in my head for a while now, though I didn't want to admit it. It sounds a bit too cheesy.

"*Sister? … I like that.*"

"*All right. I'm still the older sister, though.*"

"*I'm fine with having an older sister! Anyway, Elena, how are you and…*"

I sigh. Nowhere! I'm still stuck at home and Nathaniel's stuck with the Blood Moon clan. I try to change the topic instead.

"*How about you and the King instead? You didn't even tell me how you made up.*"

"*Oh… Well, we… discussed it, and sorted out our differences?*"

I can feel she's blushing and acting all shy. My gosh, Nora is so freaking cute at times!

"*So, all good?*"

"*Um. I guess. He will cancel the engagement… and announce me as his mate…*"

"*Way to go, girl! Nora, I'm happy for you!*"

And jealous, too. Nora doesn't have a whole clan holding her back from announcing her relationship to the world. I wish I could say the same.

Suddenly, the mind-link is cut, and I can tell she's talking to someone else. I finish preparing my drink and go back to the salon where the boys are waiting for me, both visibly upset.

"Clark left," says Danny, stating the obvious.

"He said he's sorry, Elena. Also, he will talk to the elders, see if he can't do anything. I think he's really regretting what he said and did."

I nod at Levi's words, but I don't have anything to add. This stupid fight has exhausted me, for real. The brothers exchange a look, unsure, until Daniel asks.

"Okay, babe, so, what's next?"

"For now, I'll wait and see until Clark officially kicks me out. I am not changing my mind. As soon as I can leave this house and move without risking my baby's life, I'm talking to Nathaniel."

"And Reagan?" asks Levi.

I think for a second. Sylviana said Reagan was back on the territory, and it's high time we have a good talk.

I take a deep breath and use my wolf to focus on finding her. Reagan may be good at ignoring me, but she's from my pack too, from the Blue Moon. She can't hide forever or shut out my voice.

"*Reagan, we need to talk.*"

"*Leave me alone, kid. I got bigger fish to–*"

"*More important than the Blue Moon clan?*"

There's a long silence; she's stopped answering. I can feel that she's on the move. Is she finally coming? I can tell our mind-link is thin, she is probably still far up in the North Forest. After a long while, several hours later actually, we finally hear some loud knocking on the door. How far was she? I exchange a look with Daniel, who goes to open.

"Where the hell did you hear that name?" asks Reagan, visibly shocked and sweating.

"Why would I tell you? Do you ever tell me anything?" I reply back, pissed.

She growls.

"Don't play with me, kid. Even Clark doesn't know of that name, so how..."

Daniel hands her the tests he did on Nora's blood and mine, showing both her name and our results. Reagan is left speechless, staring at the document as if she's seen a ghost.

"She… she's really… alive?"

"You know about her?" asks Daniel, surprised.

Reagan shakes her head.

"I… I figured there might have been another, but… I thought…"

"You thought she must have died with everyone else," I finish for her.

Reagan slowly nods and lets herself fall on one of the stools, still visibly shaken. I don't think I've ever seen her like this. My old mentor's almost about to cry.

"Reagan. I need to know."

"No, no, Elena, you don't know what that means. If she's alive…"

"The Royal line survived, right?"

She turns to me, shocked again. Then, she frowns, split between anger and defiance.

"How much do you know?"

"A lot. About Queen Diane, and the Blue Moon clan. Nora and I are… her relatives, right? I mean, if you know Nora is a Royal, you know who her… no, who our parents were. I will find the answers, Reagan, I have to know. Clark said you told him of my Royal blood, but I am not a Royal, right? Why am I different from Nora?"

"How do you even know about Queen Diane!" shouts Reagan, furious.

"I had to dig around for the answers, Reagan, since you wouldn't talk! Why can't I know about her! She was my family, wasn't she? What was so secret about Queen Diane that you couldn't tell me? Because she was a pure Royal?"

Reagan keeps shaking her head, horrified.

"Elena, shut up! Don't you get it? This is how your parents got killed!"

What? I exchange a look with Daniel, taken by surprise. Reagan is acting like the world is about to end, and that's really not good coming from her. Danny insists I sit back on the couch, putting me a good distance away from my mentor, and turns to her.

"Reagan, whether you like it or not, Elena has found out most of the truth. So I really, really suggest you start speaking now and let her know if there's anything else that's endangering her."

The old she-wolf turns to me, her eyes suddenly looking very sad. She lets out a long sigh.

"Elena, I… All right, I'll tell you. Just… just don't judge me too harshly."

I frown. Why? Why would I judge her?

"It's true. The clan we were both born in was called the Blue Moon clan. And Diane was at its head. Queen Diane. She was an incredible woman. Since she was born, we knew she was different from us. Our Alphas had always been powerful, among the oldest, purest werewolf families. But Diane was different. Our people believed she was a reincarnation of the Moon Goddess herself, and honestly, I believed it too. She could do things that were like magic to us. I wonder if she didn't have witch blood or something. She could communicate with any animal, not just wolves. She knew when disasters would happen, she was a seer… I even saw her heal dying people, and her aura was incredible…"

I keep thinking about Sylviana while Reagan talks, but this is even different from what Danny's witch friend can do. I've never, ever heard about someone as powerful as that, even in our legends. I mean, the Royals were already strong and incredible, but this woman, as Reagan said, was more on the Goddess level!

And from what Sylviana said…

"She was… my grandmother?" I ask, a bit unsure.

Reagan nods.

"Our clan prospered for as long as she was there. When she was very young, Queen Diane gave birth to twins. I have no idea who the father was. Either she didn't want to say it, or there wasn't one, I honestly don't care. If she said there wasn't, we all believed her and didn't ask."

No father? This is crazy! More like she didn't want to reveal who it was… But now, I'm more interested in the twins than their father. I glance at the blood test. Nora and I are cousins, so those twins must be…

"The twins' birth was a big deal in the pack. A boy and a girl, born on the full moon. She named them Lilyan and Gabriel… Gabriel was your father."

I feel my heart beat a bit faster in my chest.

Gabriel. My father was Gabriel Bluemoon. I grab my necklace between my fingers. It was signed G. G for Gabriel… Daniel puts a hand on my knee while Reagan keeps talking, lost in her memories.

"He was the bravest fighter I've ever seen in my life. So strong, he could fight ten wolves by himself. His sister Lilyan was a gentle soul, so sweet. She used the healing power she had inherited from Queen Diane to help others, even injured people from other packs. Anyway, those two grew up happy and cherished, like blessed children. But Queen Diane knew their

Royal power would make them targets for dark forces, like witches or necromancers."

Sylviana said so, too, that Royals would be targets.

"So, Queen Diane sent her younger sister, Cynthia to find somewhere else to settle, somewhere safe. She wanted a place where werewolves could help each other against any threat, and our clan wouldn't be by itself like it was at the time. Cynthia wasn't filled with Royal power like Queen Diane was, but she was very smart, and a great leader too. So, she left, with a smaller portion of our pack. However, even after many years, she never returned. It broke Queen Diane's heart."

What happened to her younger sister? Did she get… killed? It doesn't sound like Cynthia had Royal blood like Diane, though. Did she end up a victim anyway? Why would someone attack her?

I can't even begin to imagine how heartbroken Queen Diane must have been. To lose her sister without knowing what happened to her… Or not even know if she was alive. How long did she wait for a sign, for anything?

"So, as it became clear Cynthia wasn't coming back, Queen Diane was left alone to protect her children… She decided to confine our territory behind some magic barrier she made, with the help of a good witch, and forbade everyone from talking about their Royal blood."

I exchange a look with Daniel. A good witch? Sylviana wasn't even born at that time, but could she know which witch it was?

"It was to be kept a secret, to protect her children. We lived like that for many, many years. I kept going in and out to find Cynthia, without luck. Life went on, and your father, Gabriel, was betrothed to another warrior she-wolf in the pack, while Lilyan still dedicated her life to others. Things could have probably gone on like that forever, until one day, a young group of humans walked onto our territory by mere chance."

"Wait, humans? How did they break the witch and Queen Diane's barrier?" asks Danny, surprised.

"Because Queen Diane wanted to prevent any danger from intruding. But Lilyan had convinced her to have this magic allow people who proved themselves harmless in. Those humans weren't a danger, they were totally harmless. Just a group of travelers, gypsies. The kind that didn't even know about werewolves' existence."

"What happened?" I ask, a bit lost.

How could a mere group of humans, apparently harmless, cause trouble? Reagan looks down, and I feel like she's holding back her tears. When she looks up again, she's looking at me.

"You happened... Your birth mother, Elena. She was one of them."

Moon Goddess...

"Wait. My mother was... a human?"

Reagan nods.

"A simple human woman... Her name was Althea."

She points at the necklace around my neck.

"That necklace was hers... Your father gave it to her."

"The Sunshine..." whispers Daniel. "Your mother was human, so she was..."

"A Daughter of the Sun," I finish.

I take a while to think about it. With my hands shaking, I undo my necklace, looking at the engraving again. "*To my Sunshine, G.*"

For some reason, I always thought this memento and that nickname were meant for me. Yet it never made sense. I am a daughter of the Moon Goddess, a werewolf. I never imagined my mother could be any different.

"Damn, a lot of things make sense now," says Daniel. "This is what Sylviana meant when she said you were shielding your baby and hiding her power. She-"

"What! Whose baby? What are you talking about?" asks Reagan.

Oh, right, she hadn't heard yet. She was probably away from the pack, and unsociable as she is, there was no way she had heard the rumors.

"I'm pregnant, Reagan," I simply admit.

She looks at me, completely stunned.

"What? But I thought..."

"Yeah, we thought it would be hard for Elena to conceive again, but it happened, and it's confirmed," explains Daniel.

Reagan looks at him, suspicious, then turns to me.

"Don't tell me you're having a kid with this shrimp."

"What? Ew!" says Daniel. "Are you crazy, old hag!"

"Of course, it's not Daniel's, Reagan," I sigh.

"Then who?"

I exchange a look with Daniel. Well, Clark knows, and it is very likely that the rest of the pack will know soon, so... As I said, no more hiding.

"Nathaniel Black."

Reagan frowns, but before she asks, I sigh and reply.

"Yes, the King's brother. I met him last summer, we hit it off, kept this relationship going, not seriously until recently, and now I'm pregnant."

"He doesn't know yet," adds Daniel. "Clark asked Elena to... consider her options."

"You are not aborting?" asked Reagan, suddenly unhappy.

"I have no intention to, and I'm pretty sure it's too late anyway. Moreover, I'm already having a hard time keeping her as it is…"

"What? What do you mean?"

Daniel takes over in explaining everything to her again, on how we found out and what followed, including my threatened miscarriage recently and how I have to rest. Somehow, he goes on to tell her how we found out about Nora and the Blue Moon clan too. To our surprise, Reagan doesn't seem very surprised to hear about Sylviana's existence.

"Queen Diane's friend was a good witch, too… Though she wasn't an Earth Witch. But I know what kind of women they are… The werewolves of Silver City aren't used to witches, but the Blue Moon clan was."

That's a bit surprising to hear, coming from Reagan.

"What about the Dark Witch, then? Do you think it could be…?"

Reagan nods.

"From the moment I heard about the vampire attack, I thought the same. Water attacking wolves… I don't know what else it could be. What does Sylviana think?"

Daniel frowns a bit as we exchange a look. Sylviana thought the same…

"She said that the Dark Witch is most likely after Nora's power… and my baby."

Reagan sighs, looking at me, shaking her head.

"It's the same thing all over again."

"You didn't tell us why Nora and Elena were separated from their parents," notes Daniel.

Reagan looks down, appearing a bit lost for a while. I try to help her resume her talking.

"You said my mother was among the humans that came to the clan."

"Her name was Althea. She was a very pretty and bright woman. You look a lot like her. She had honey blonde hair, dark skin, and brown eyes. But you have Gabriel's eyes. Your father's eyes were golden."

"Not blue?" I ask, a bit surprised.

For some reason, I figured both twins would have the Royals' blue eyes, but Reagan shakes her head.

"No. Only Lilyan inherited Queen Diane's blue eyes. For some reason, your father's were gold. But Queen Diane's father had gold eyes too, so maybe it's a female thing."

It feels good to finally hear about my parents. What they looked like, what kind of people they were… It's like my own story is being completed, filling in the gaps I've been trying to fill my whole life.

"Althea was a dancer. She was young when we met her. Your father knew she was his mate right away. She was human, so she had no idea what that meant, but they fell in love anyway."

"My parents were fated mates?"

"Yes," nods Reagan, "and very much in love. Your father broke his engagement to be with Althea. She was younger, so they decided to wait a couple of years before getting married. Her family was supposed to leave, too… It took her a while to make up her mind, but she couldn't leave your father, so she parted with her group and stayed among us. Not too long after, she got pregnant with you."

"What about Nora's mom?"

"I don't really know. She must have met her mate one of the times I was gone. After Althea's pregnancy was announced, I left our clan more and more often to find Cynthia's pack. I couldn't…"

"You were the fiancée, weren't you?"

Daniel's sudden words surprise both of us. I turn to Reagan. My father's fiancée? She mentioned a warrior she-wolf. Judging from Reagan's reaction, Daniel is right. My gosh… Reagan used to be engaged to my father?? I never paid attention, but generation-wise, Reagan could have been my mom. give or take a few years. And if Althea, I mean my mom, was younger than my dad, it makes sense.

"Yes. Gabriel was a wonderful man, and I admired his strength. We were childhood friends and started dating. I won't go into the details. But yes, I was engaged and loved your father. When your mother came, and I understood he was leaving me, I was heartbroken. I didn't understand what a fated mate bond was, even less with a human…"

Moon Goddess. I'm feeling so sorry for Reagan right now.

I still vividly remember the pain I was in when Nathaniel mentioned he had met his fated mate. I can't imagine what Reagan went through. Falling in love, your happiness being so close to perfect when you're engaged, and all of a sudden, a woman appears and everything collapses. I know the said-woman was my mom and wasn't to blame, but…

"I kept leaving the clan, under the pretense of looking for Cynthia. Truth is, I was running away from the pain. Seeing your parents happy together made it feel worse every time I came back. I left for longer and longer periods of time. I would go farther, trying to forget my pain and focus on something else. Even Queen Diane asked me to stop and relax, but I couldn't. I just… wanted the whole pack to forget me. I was the poor girl Gabriel had thrown away for a human. Lilyan was nice to me though; she kept trying to console me, even introduced me to other men. I never really listened to her. I probably should have…"

I can't help but feel so, so sad when listening to her.

No wonder Reagan became so lonely and bitter. I see my mentor in a different light now. She was always that strong, fighting woman to me. I never realized she carried her own emotional baggage and scars. This explains why she never wanted to talk about the past with me. I probably wouldn't feel like sharing my story with a child my ex conceived after leaving me for another, either.

"What happened, then? You made it sound like the attack was your fault," says Daniel.

"It was more complicated than that. We knew vampires clans were watching us, but the barrier always protected us. We thought they wouldn't attack our clan, big and powerful as it was. And we had a witch on our side, just that was enough to keep them at bay. Until one day, I couldn't cross the barrier anymore."

"What?"

Reagan nods, frowning.

"I don't know what changed. It just became impossible, it kept rejecting me. I thought… maybe I had come to hate your mother too much, and that was why."

Something just doesn't feel right about this. It was her own pack, they shouldn't have shut her out… What kind of barrier was it? Reagan said it kept people with bad intentions out, but it doesn't seem like she fit into that category.

"So you were shut out?"

"It lasted for days and then weeks. I didn't know what I had done wrong. I even left a few times, thinking it would be better if I calmed down. At some point, Lilyan talked to her mother, asking her to put the barrier down to let me in. Queen Diane and Denica, the witch, were reluctant though. That barrier had protected us for years."

"But they did, didn't they?"

"Yes. Anytime I came back, they would temporarily take down the barrier for me."

"Is that how they were attacked, then?" I ask.

Now it makes sense. If they took the barrier down, that explains how the clan was wiped out even despite the Queen's efforts. Reagan sighs and nods.

"I believe so. It happened right after I had left again. I had a big fight with Queen Diane, who was reluctant on letting me go. Once again, Lilyan helped me convince her. They lifted the barrier for me to leave, and that was the last time I saw the clan alive. When I got back, the barrier was gone. And they were…"

She doesn't need to finish her sentence. I sigh.

Reagan wasn't responsible, she just… triggered things, I guess. Whoever attacked them was probably lurking and waiting for a long time.

"So you don't know who did it?"

"At first I thought it was vampires. From the fighting, many vampire bodies were left. But there was something odd."

"My mother was alive," I suddenly realize.

Right. If it was a vampire attack, why would my mom have survived? Of all people, she was the only human! It doesn't make any sense.

"Exactly. As soon as I saw the first bodies, I headed for the castle, where your family and Queen Diane should have been. The only person left was your mother… and you. You were both alive, but your mom was badly injured. She managed to hide somehow, but she had been injured by some debris. She begged me to take you away. She made me swear to protect you and leave. She died right after I left."

"What about the others?" asks Danny

"I never found their bodies. My guess is… they might have been burned."

"Burned?"

"The Good Witch that was on our side was a Fire Witch. There were burnt corpses in the castle when I got there, some of them that could very well have been your father, aunt, and grandmother. I spent a long time thinking about it. If the attack wasn't really the doing of vampires…"

"A Dark Witch might have been behind it. Like the one we had here in Silver City."

"Exactly. And if she was after the Royals, Denica, our witch, might have burned their bodies to keep her from using them against others. Denica's body was the only one I found."

"And if she didn't find what she wanted back then, because Denica burnt the Royals' bodies…"

"She might try somewhere else. Like Silver City," I whisper.

That's why we were attacked.

Nora is slowly unveiling her wolf's power, and that Dark Witch was probably waiting for an event like this to happen. If she is still looking for Royals, Nora's power must be attracting her to Silver City like a firework in the night sky. This vampire attack was probably only the beginning.

Moon Goddess, and I am pregnant with another possible Royal baby…

Chapter 23

The next morning, after talking a lot with Reagan and Daniel, all three of us agree on the same thing.

The truth about my origin should remain a secret. It's all about protecting my child, now. According to Sylviana, my baby girl will be a Royal, like Nora, and I'm going to protect her from whoever wants to harm her. She is still safe while she's in my womb, but in five months, it will be a different story.

I'm happy I talked to Reagan, too. For the first time, I could finally thank her for taking me in and protecting me, like she promised my mom. I finally understood why she never told me the truth before; she had valid reasons. Thinking back, my mentor could have left me behind so many times, but she never did. She protected me, trained me until she made sure I would be safe on my own, and even so, she found me a good new pack and parents to be with.

She got mad for my sake and stayed around for me. When I tell her all that and how grateful I am, though, she's back to her old self, telling me to shut up.

"Let's go talk to your imbecile godfather," says Reagan. "I'll let him know what I think about his stupid elders and their rules! This city is impossible as it is nowadays. So many packs, living together yet not allowing their werewolves to mix? So crazy!"

"The peace is probably only because of the King and the alliances between the packs," sighs Daniel.

Yeah, he's probably got that right. I can still vividly remember that feeling when the King was next to us… Damn, no wonder no one can stand up to him. I wonder if Nathaniel and their younger brother Liam are the same? It's hard to tell. Those three are feared for good reason.

I sigh. And one of those three monsters is my baby's father. How will he react when I tell him? It's so hard to tell.

"Anyway, babe's got a doctor appointment all day today," says Daniel. "Let's have dinner with my family after that. My dad and Clark are close. Maybe he'll be able to convince him."

The doctor's appointment is as long as Daniel said. Abigail insists on making me go through a whole bunch of tests, but there's good reason for all that: my baby is now officially stable, I'll be able to move around again without spending all day on the couch. I get a second ultrasound and get to see my thirteen-week-old baby girl once again. I try hard not to cry. She's moving and all, alive and kicking, even. I ask for pictures, wondering if it's okay to show Nate this the next time I see him.

Gosh, now I'll be able to go and tell him! I can't stop thinking about it at dinner with the Lewis'. I love Danny's family. They are all so happy for me about this pregnancy, regardless of who the father is.

When we get back from dinner with Danny's family, walking as I insisted, it's a calm evening in the streets. Like always, the dinner at his parents' ended pretty late. Everyone around here must be busy preparing for Christmas. It's funny how we celebrate it as werewolves too, but a lot of the families in our neighborhood are Hispanic and very pious.

"I wonder if it's alright to be taking all this," I say, looking at the huge box Danny is carrying.

"Of course it is. Mom is overjoyed like she's going to be a grandma, you know. And my siblings and I don't use this stuff anymore, anyway."

I've always been a bit envious of Danny for having siblings. Levi, Rachel, the twins, Ben and Bonnie, and Micah. There was some bickering while they were growing up, but all six of them got along, overall. I wonder if I will give my baby girl a sibling someday. It might not be easy though. This pregnancy was already a miracle as it is.

"Babe, look."

Danny suddenly grabs my hand, taking me to one of the narrow alleys. What's going on? But he puts a finger on his lips, telling me to be silent, and that's when I realize: someone's whispering nearby. Why would someone be whispering? We are so close to the border too. Danny silently puts the box down, and we both lean in to look secretly.

What the… What the hell is my uncle doing with another man, at this time of the night, in secrecy? I try to focus, but I can't hear much. I turn to Danny. He's got a better ear than me. Who the heck is he talking to, anyway? I don't recognize the man. He's small, and probably around my uncle's age. He's got an Alpha Aura, though it's not much… probably on Xavier's level. This is so suspicious, especially since they are alone!

Suddenly, they both turn their heads in our direction. Danny and I hide, in time, I hope.

"Let's get out of here," mimics Danny with his lips, and I nod.

This can't be good. As quickly and silently as possible, we leave, both totally confused. What was that? We rush back to our apartment, where Danny leaves the box on our kitchen counter, still looking astonished.

"Danny, that man was…"

"King. The Gold Moon Alpha, Taaron King. I'm sure of it, I've seen his face in business magazines, and he tried to buy our Opal Moon's clinic several times. Iris hates him, she's convinced her dad not to do so, but…"

"You think that's what it was about?"

Daniel shakes his head and scratches it with a confused expression.

"Babe, I wish it was just about buying the clinic. But that's not what it looked like. I heard King mention an alliance to your uncle several times. I didn't get the conversation in full, but it looked like Xavier was interested. It's bad."

"Of course it's bad. Clark would never agree to an alliance with the Gold Moon clan! He said if we had to choose, it would be the Sapphire Moon clan, we still owe them so much. We don't interact with them, usually, but it's obvious they hate the Gold Moon! If we are caught in a war between those two clans…"

Damn, what is my uncle thinking! The Gold Moon clan, out of all people? Why would he agree to that! Is it for money? Moon Goddess, we cannot do that! He will never convince Clark to ally the White Moon clan with them. No fucking way.

Is it about the Opal Moon clan then? Does he intend to have the branch pack betray the White Moon? This is crazy! Daniel and I keep discussing and trying to think of how to deal with this, but there is no way to know what it was about exactly, or if my godfather is involved, which I highly doubt.

The next morning, I'm up early, though we talked until very late in the night. I'm making myself some lemon tea, Daniel eating next to me.

"I should ask Nora for help."

Daniel almost chokes on his croissant.

"Nora? Why would your cousin help? This is White Moon clan stuff!"

"Don't be an idiot, Danny, this is bigger than our pack. If the Gold Moon is trying to rally the White Moon, either they are doing this behind the Blood Moon clan's back, or with their back-up. But with Nora meddling with the King's engagement, I bet it is the first one. And this is no good to either her pack or ours. So, I shall ask Nora if she knows, to confirm. And if they don't, and Xavier is really out of his fucking mind, I'd rather have the Blood Moon know than have them gang up on Clark and us."

Daniel stays silent for a moment, thinking. Eventually, he nods and gets up to make himself more coffee.

"Okay, but we talk to Clark next. I bet Xavier is acting behind his back, and if we let the King know, we've got to let our Alpha know too."

I nod and channel my inner wolf to contact Nora. As expected, no matter the distance, it's as easy as talking to Daniel who's next to me.

"*Hey, Nora?*"

"*Elena? What is it?*"

"*We have to talk, fast. I think the Opal Moon clan is about to do something really, really stupid.*"

"*What do you mean?*"

"*You are not going to like it. Our Alpha had a secret meeting with Taaron King last night.*"

I explain to her what we witnessed, and the current situation for us. She agrees it's no good at all.

"*Damian doesn't know, Elena. This is bad... Well, there has been some good news too I need to tell you about. Do you remember the Blue Moon clan?*"

"*Yeah, I have a bit of news too.*"

I tell her most of what Reagan said, except that I decide to leave my mentor's own story out of it. She's been through a lot already.

"*... and our parents were killed, though I don't know exactly by whom. We only have... suppositions for now. But do you realize? Your mom's name was Lilyan, and my dad was...*"

"*Gabriel! Elena, I know all this! How did you find out?*"

I frown, surprised.

"*How did you find out? Nora, I learned all this only yesterday, how could you uncover so much?*"

"*The Blue Moon clan! They're still alive! I mean, not the main clan, but... Do you remember how Queen Cynthia left for the south and never came back?*"

"*Yeah, she disappeared about... fifty years ago?*"

"*She ended up here, Elena! The Sapphire Moon clan is Queen Cynthia's pack! They settled here, but never were never able to reach out to Queen Diane until it was too late! They went so far south that they lost contact, but they are here. William Blue, the Alpha of the Sapphire Moon, is our cousin too!*"

Holy Moon Goddess. I sit back on my chair, stunned.

They are alive. A part of our family is alive! Moon Goddess, I never imagined… I turn to Daniel, still so shaken up I can barely believe it.

"Babe? You alright?"

I explain to him in a few words before reaching out to Nora again.

"*Nora, are you sure? William Blue?*"

"*William Blue, Elena! I talked to him yesterday, he told me so much. I even saw a portrait of our grandmother, Queen Diane! She looks a lot like me, by the way. How about you?*"

"*Nora, I learned about my mom too. Why I don't look like you, and why I'm not fully Royal. My mom was human.*"

"*Human…? Oh Moon Goddess, it does explain a lot! That's why… Oh gosh, Elena! You have to meet with William, let him know about you!*"

"NO!"

Damn, I screamed out loud too. Danny jumped and spilled his coffee. I whisper a sorry to him before taking a deep breath in and talking to Nora again.

"*Nora, I can't. For now. It's better if very few people know about our link, okay? I'm in a bit of a situation. I want my real identity to stay as concealed as possible, please. I'm not saying I don't want to meet the Sapphire Moon, but…*"

"*I understand, Elena. It's about the baby, is it? Okay, how about you come here? I have an idea on how to protect everyone from this Dark Witch, but I'll need your help. And you need to talk to Nate too, right? He's… missing you. A lot.*"

I take a deep breath in. Going to the Blood Moon territory again? I have Nora and Nate's permission, and anyway, there's nothing more Clark can't blame me for now.

"*Elena, can I tell Damian about us, at least? He's my mate, I don't want to hide things from him.*"

"*Alright, Nora, but promise me you won't tell Nate. I need to talk to him myself.*"

"*I promise. Come to Damian's building. You know which one, right?*"

"*Yeah. I'll see you there.*"

I take a deep breath and turn to Daniel, who's been waiting for me. I explain my conversation with Nora in detail, and he nods.

"I guess it's time, babe, huh?"

I nod.

It's high time I tell Nate I'm pregnant with his daughter.

I decide to go there as soon as I can. It's a bit intimidating after being away for so long. To my surprise, it's not Nora who lets me in, but the King's Beta, Boyan's older brother.

"Welcome, Miss Elena. My name is Neal Mura."

I introduce myself, trying to remember where I've seen that guy before. The fight with the vampires! That guy was there, in his wolf form. His wolf is exactly like Boyan's and their sister Tonia's, only a tad smaller.

He guides me all the way to the highest floors of the Black Corporation building. Damn, I'm invited to the King's private quarters… Is Nora living there with him now? It's not very cozy, all glass and metal, in shades of gray and black. Definitely intimidating, though.

Once we get there, Nora welcomes me with a big hug.

"Elena! I missed you! So, I told Damian, as discussed, okay? Nathaniel should be here any minute too."

She calls him Nathaniel instead of Nate? I wonder what their relationship is. Isn't Nora working at one of his restaurants?

I completely forget my questions when Damian Black appears behind Nora. Moon Goddess, I had forgotten how imposing her mate's aura is. Especially staying in the same room as him is suffocating. Like a living storm, a dark cloud. How does Nora handle this? My cousin looks perfectly fine around him. She's even happier the closer she is to him. It's interesting to see how the pair interacts and reacts to each other.

The King constantly has an eye on her. She is never out of his line of sight, like a bodyguard. If she moves, he adjusts to her. Nora is never far from him, either, like he's her landmark or something. They sit together, they move together, they breathe together. Are they even aware of it?

"So, Nora, what was your idea?" I ask, a bit anxious.

We are in some large room, Nora and the King standing in front of me.

"Gathering everyone," she says. "All the packs, in one place, to discuss a large alliance. No more little alliances between several packs and bickering between the others. I want to gather every Alpha, every clan, and ask them to cooperate against this Dark Witch that's coming for us."

"Miss Nora argued that her Royal blood and power might help convince everyone," says Neal. "Her bond with the Sapphire Moon, Jade Moon, and also with you."

I frown. My bond with her? Does she want me to act as a spokesperson for the White Moon? Oh Moon Goddess, I am not really in the position for that, at the moment… I may convince Clark to show up, at best, but…

"Elena, trust me, I can do this! I want to–"

But just when she was about to finish her sentence, someone walks in. Nate.

At first, he doesn't notice me, greeting his brother, Nora, and the other people present. Boyan and Tonia walk in right after him, both greeting me. That's when his blue eyes fall on me, making my heart go crazy. Oh, Moon Goddess.

He frowns a bit, surprised to see me here. Oh, right, he doesn't know about my relationship with Nora… He turns his head to his brother, looking worried for a second. But Damian Black is focused on Nora, as usual, only nodding at his brother's arrival.

Nate finally walks up to me, looking uncertain.

"Elena, what are you–?"

"Nora called me here."

"Nora?"

"She's my friend!" says Nora, with a big smile.

That's the most simple-minded explanation one could think of, and I see Nate give a glance in Boyan's direction too, trying to make sense out of it, but the huge wolf is just laying at Nora's feet like a furry carpet. Nate seems to give up with a sigh, and while I'm totally unprepared for it, takes me in for a hug.

Damn, it feels good. I missed his smell like crazy. So good, actually, I'm almost crying. I answer his hug, unable to hold myself back. My wolf is breathing again, too, soothed. Why does it feel like we're closer now? Is it because I'm carrying his baby? Or because we missed each other so much? His whole body against mine is calming me down. Behind Nate, Nora is giving me a faint smile, and the other people in the room are either observing us with a hint of curiosity or total disinterest.

"All right… shall we get started, Miss Nora?" asks Neal.

Nathaniel and I part, though he holds my hand a bit longer. Nora walks up to me, looking a bit worried, biting her lip.

"Elena… I'm not sure how strong my inner voice will be… Can you help me out? A bit?"

I nod.

"Yeah, sure. Don't worry, Nora, you're already way better than I am. Just take a deep breath, relax, and you'll do great."

"Okay."

Nora takes several deep breaths, exchanging looks with me, channeling her inner wolf. Is it just me or are her eyes shining stronger than usual? I sit on the couch and wait for it. Nate hesitates before slowly walking to stand behind me.

I hear her message, bright and clear, in my head. To me, it's like a clear voice. But as I observe in the room, only the Black brothers are fine. Neal, Tonia, and Boyan are making faces, probably a bit overwhelmed by her aura.

As discussed, Nora lays out her plan. She explains who she is, and I actually learn for the first time she was born in the Gold Moon clan. Nora's in a unique position, though. Born in the Gold Moon clan, raised by the Jade Moon, mated to the Blood Moon Alpha and yet, her true roots belong to the Sapphire Moon clan. And there's me, her cousin, from the White Moon pack.

The biggest surprise is her heritage as a Royal, though. She only says a few words about this, but I know she doesn't want to make a big deal out of it. It would only have people freak out. Yet, her dominant voice in our heads leaves no doubt. Hence, they have no choice but to listen to her warning. Her warning about the Dark Witch that will target Silver City, and finally, how the packs need to work altogether.

It's a crazy idea.

I know Nora's a believer, but when she gives the time and place for a meeting in three days, I'm wondering who will dare to show up. It's not just about her being a Royal, or the pending attack. Most clans, though they won't admit it, are crazy scared of the Blood Moon. To Nora and I, the Black brothers are just lovers, but to everyone else, they are cold-blooded killers, crazy strong Alpha werewolves. At least, having a Luna of her background next to Damian Black might draw a few curious people in.

Nora exhales and opens her eyes. Good job, girl.

"You did great, Nora," says her mate with that gentle expression he only has for her.

"I have to admit, I didn't think you could really do it, but I guess this headache is my retribution for doubting you," growls Boyan's older brother.

Nora chuckles with a bit of an apologetic expression. Damn, she is so cute. No wonder everyone loves her. I wonder how we got to be so different when our parents were twins.

Though, she frowns soon enough and looks down, holding her head. I can almost feel it. Everyone who heard her voice is responding, using the mind-link back, submerging her.

"Nora, are you okay?" asks the King.

"Sorry… It's my head…"

He rubs her shoulder, while Nora is struggling to clear the voices out. It's funny, I can feel them as if I have a little window in her head. She finally lets a few in, exchanging with some Alphas unknown to me. I hope people are responding positively. Everyone in the room is holding their breaths, waiting for her.

After a while, she nods and turns to us.

"The Sapphire Moon and Sea Moon clans are coming. The Jade Moon, too. I don't know about the others yet, it was a bit confusing…"

It's already a good start, though. With the Blood Moon clan in as well, it means two of the biggest packs are already interested. That's huge…

"We expected this," says Neal Mura, "but this is how it always works between werewolves anyway, Miss Nora. No matter what happens, you did what you had to. We know how risky this is."

"Don't worry, baby girl. It's going to be okay. Even if only a few packs show up, it's plenty, okay? We just need to open up a dialogue," adds his sister.

Nora looks a bit uneasy, but I agree with the betas. Nora's done great, especially since she was reaching out to mind-link so many people for the first time.

"Anyway, we need to get ready. Three days is a very short time to sort out everything. Securing the stadium, informing the human police, and preparing the lieutenants won't be an easy job."

Looks like the Blood Moon's Beta is already in work mode. He starts making calls, giving orders, and everyone in the room moves. The King is talking to Tonia, and Boyan goes to Nora, who's sitting facing me. I'm not sure what I'm supposed to be doing. I wait a bit and get up, but the King leaves the room with Tonia and Neal, while Nora goes to the kitchen. I'm left alone with Boyan, still in his wolf form, and Nathaniel.

Nate walks up to me in a hurry.

"Elena! I missed you. How are you?" he asks, looking worried.

His hand is already on my neck, and the other grabs mine, we're so close. I need to catch my breath for a second and nod a bit awkwardly.

"I'm… fine."

Damn, why is it so hard to talk now that he's here facing me, so close, so real! What was I expecting? Nate's right in front of me, but the words are stuck in my throat while I'm just trying to breathe normally. It's been so long already. I don't even know where to start! I can't just drop the bomb like that! Where is our relationship at, anyway?

"Talk to me!"

He's getting impatient, but I just keep avoiding his eyes and trying to come up with something.

"Elena, I can't go on like this!"

"I told you I'm fine, Nate. Stop asking, please."

Can't you give me a second to think, to figure out what I want to say to you?

"I don't believe you! You've been avoiding me for days; I can't take it! Do you think I haven't noticed it? You're pale, you lost weight... Elena, are you sick?"

"What?"

Oh gosh, why does he have to be so observant about those kinds of things? I barely lost a couple of pounds! Guess what? Your daughter only likes freaking pizza and lemon tea.

"No, I'm not, I swear, Nate. I'm fine, okay? I really am."

"Then why…!"

"I'll tell you later, okay?" I just say, shaking my head.

"Later? What do you mean later! Elena… When?"

When your brother and half of your pack's leaders are not freaking next door, for a start! I'm not ready, for Moon Goddess' sake.

"After the pack meeting. Once it's over, we can talk," I stutter. "I promise, but not now. It's not the right time, with all that is going on. Nate, please."

He keeps staring, and Moon Goddess, he does look worried. Well, guess what, I'm freaking out too, and scared like I've never been before. I just… I'd rather fight a thousand vampires than tell Nate the truth right now. It's so fucking scary. I'm doubting his response, how he'll react, what he'll say, what he'll do. It's like a fucking void scaring the hell out of me.

"Okay, but… you have to stop avoiding me, please… I miss you."

I take a deep breath. Damn, there's so much weight in those three words.

"I missed you too," I confess in a whisper.

I see Bobo leave the room in silence, giving us some space, but right when my eyes are back on Nate, he pulls me in for a passionate kiss.

Oh, Moon Goddess, this feels so good… I don't even resist and respond right away, grabbing his shirt, his hair, any part of him I can claim. I want him. I've missed him, oh, so bad… We keep going, kissing each other, our lips and tongues going crazy, my skin burning under his touch, my blood rushing. I want more, it's like a drug. It tastes sweet and addicting.

His hands glide on my skin, under my shirt, on my neck… I shiver a bit. I had almost forgotten what his hands feel like. I feel my desire growing, like ash burning underneath the long-extinguished fire. A small, shy flame, as the kiss keeps going… It's Nate, my man. Mine. The only one I want to allow on me, the only one that can touch me. My wolf softly growls.

"Nate… Nate, wait…"

He keeps going. He doesn't want to stop. Frankly? Me neither. I just want more of his lips, more of his skin and smell on me. It's driving me crazy. My wolf growls again. We are in his brother's apartment, damn it.

"Nate, stop."

This time, I put my hands on his chest, pushing him away, taking a deep breath in.

"Elena?"

"Give me a second. I have something I really need to tell you."

He raises an eyebrow, a bit surprised.

"Well, that's a first. Everything okay?"

"No. I mean, yes, but… Moon Goddess…"

I take a step back, a deep breath, trying to think. How do you say it? How do you announce this kind of thing? What's the right word? Damn it. Breathe, Elena, low blood pressure. Nate is staring at me, confused, a bit worried. He puts his hands on his hips, waiting. Fuck it.

"Nathaniel, I'm… pregnant."

There's a long silence.

His expression is undecipherable, and he chuckles nervously.

"You're what?"

"Pregnant. I am pregnant, Nate."

It takes him a few more minutes for it to sink in, and his eyes wander mindlessly around the room. I have no fucking idea what to expect. Honestly, I'm terrified. He doesn't seem happy, or mad. He swallows his saliva, and turns to me, looking a bit off.

"Okay… I… How long?"

"I'm thirteen weeks now."

"I see."

He's frowning, looking anywhere but in my direction. Looking like he's confused. It's not what I was expecting. I don't know what to say, what to do, I stand there waiting, nervous as heck.

"For Moon Goddess' sake, Nate, says something. Please."

"… Who's the father?"

I stare at him, shocked. Is he fucking kidding me?

"Are you kidding me? Of course it's you!"

"Seriously, Elena."

What the hell, now? He doesn't believe me?

"Nate, you're the father! What now, you think I fuck anyone? I'm thirteen weeks pregnant, we were together back in September!"

I'm almost crying, I'm so fucking mad. I did think he would be surprised, not that he wouldn't believe me! He shakes his head.

"Elena, it can't be mine. Think again. I'm not accusing you, I just…"

"You think I don't know who I had sex with? There's been no one but you since last June, Nathaniel! You can ask Daniel, I haven't been close to another man!"

"Is it Levi's?"

"Wha– Fuck you! I didn't sleep with Levi. Are you mad? What the hell is wrong with you!"

"Elena, I'm telling you, if you are pregnant, this child cannot be mine!

"I am pregnant! I am pregnant, you dick, so pregnant I don't know what to do with myself!"

I grab the picture in my jacket and throw it at him, pissed.

"Look at that! This is your daughter and mine! There is no way she's anyone else's but yours!"

But he doesn't even look at the picture, or me crying. He takes a deep breath in, like he's trying to control himself, and I can feel his unsettled wolf too. What the hell…?

It's like a nightmare. He's there, but he's just distancing himself from me, building a wall between us. I don't get it. I feel anger replacing the disappointment, and my wolf growls.

"What's wrong with you? I've been avoiding you, now you don't want to believe I'm pregnant? Is that it? This is too much for you? Or you don't trust me? Is it because of your status, you can't have this happen?"

"Elena, stop it! I know this child isn't mine, so just tell me whose it is! I don't even care at this point!"

"Fuck you! I'm telling you, this child is yours! What the hell is wrong with you?"

"It can't be mine, Elena!"

He lets out a big sigh, before finally looking at me.

"... I'm sterile, Elena."

I stare at him, speechless for once. What the...

"I can't have children," he continues. "I swear if there was a one in a billion chance this child could be mine, trust me, I would gladly believe you. I would be thrilled if you were pregnant with my baby, Elena, I swear. But here's the thing, it cannot possibly be mine. I'm sterile."

... This is a nightmare. I feel the tears coming, and I don't repress them. I can't deal with this right now; I don't have the strength for this. I start sobbing, unable to repress it. Sterile? What the actual fuck? How can he say he's sterile? I'm pregnant with his baby!

"What the fuck are you saying?" I ask, hoping I heard that wrong. "Sterile?"

"It's from many years ago," he nods. "I lost the ability to have children because of my father. One day, he hit me. He always hit us, though most days Damian protected me and Liam. That wasn't always the case, though. And, that one time, he... hit me so hard in my stomach, I started bleeding... I bled a lot. Damian took me to the hospital, but they couldn't... I learned I wouldn't be able to have children no matter how much surgery I underwent. There's nothing medicine can do for me, Elena, I'm sterile. I've been sterile since I was fifteen... That's the real reason my fated mate didn't want me. She had a choice between her rich fiancé and a damaged teenager who could never have children. I can't blame her."

No, no, no. There's no fucking way. I am pregnant, I am pregnant for sure, and there's no fucking way anybody else is that child's father. And he has the fucking guts to give me a story about him being sterile now?!

"... Fuck you, Nate."

That's all I could utter right now. I'm so furious. I'm crying tears of anger and frustration. I don't care what he thinks and I don't care about that stupid offended expression of his.

"You dare mention your ex now?" I go on. "Do you think I care? I don't give a damn what you think you can or can't do, I know what I'm saying. Those doctors were wrong, Nate. I am pregnant, I am pregnant and no one else but you can be the father!"

"I cannot be, Elena! Even if you are, I can't have children! At all! I have all of the files, my complete medical chart, back at my place, attesting why your child cannot be mine! If you want, I can show it to you, I–"

"I don't give a shit about your medical records, you idiot!" I shout. "I've been trying to think for weeks about how to tell you, and now, this? Nate, this child is my miracle! I didn't think I could have children either! I had a miscarriage, and–"

"But your chances after a miscarriage aren't zero, Elena. Mine are. I'm… I'll try to be happy for you that you got pregnant again, but… don't say I'm the dad. I cannot be."

He steps away from me. Moon Goddess… He really doesn't believe me, not even one bit. I keep crying, helpless. What the fuck do I do? I don't care about his sterility bullshit, I need him! I didn't think I would have to fucking convince him! But it's already over. Whatever I say, he won't believe me. It's all written in his eyes. Fuck… This is the worst. I knew it could go wrong, he could have not taken it well, but this is a whole fucking different level. I feel so stupid! I feel stupid for even crying, for being so disappointed! Worse, now he thinks I'm carrying somebody else's baby!

"Elena, I–"

"Nate, shut up."

This time, I'm the one to step back. I can't do this. I need to think of myself and my child… Nate doesn't matter.

"I don't… You know what? Never mind. I don't need you."

"Elena, I–"

"You don't want to hear the truth, fine," I retort. "I'll do it on my own."

"I'm not leaving you, Elena! You're the one who's not listening, this child–"

"Nathaniel, I never slept with anyone else but you for almost a year," I growl. "This baby was conceived thirteen weeks ago, and as far as I'm concerned, I'm pretty sure I'm not able to conceive on my own."

I don't give a fuck what he thinks. This is the truth, and if he won't hear it, I won't waste my time here. I don't care how sorry he looks. I'm so fucking disappointed in him, that he won't even try to hear me out, to trust me, but there's no use staying here. He thinks I slept with somebody else, he thinks I'm a liar and some hoe. I don't care about his excuses. He doesn't get to play the apology card now.

"Elena, I really wanted to–"

"To what? Believe me? Believe whatever you want, Nate. I'm tired of lies. I came here to tell you this, now I've done my share. You do whatever you want with it."

"What do you mean?"

"You heard me. I've told you, now whatever you want to believe is up to you. I'll have this child, with you as its dad or not. I don't give a damn about your story of being sterile. It's your problem now."

I grab my jacket before I really lose my shit. I've cried more than enough already, and even if this child's father won't fucking be there, I owe it to protect the both of us. I leave his place, slamming the door, feeling completely wrecked.

Chapter 24

"Where have you been?"

Daniel just got back from Moon-Goddess-knows-where, and shrugs.

"I went to talk to Levi. He was patrolling at the border."

I frown. Since when is Levi patrolling at the border? Oh, well, I don't really care. I finish putting on my jeans and a sweater in front of a confused Daniel.

"You're going somewhere?"

"To my uncle's. If he's about to do something stupid, it's my duty to stop him."

"Uh… Don't you think you should…"

"What? Stay at home, keep crying?"

That's right. I'm a mess, my eyes are all red and puffy, and I'm dead tired because I haven't slept a wink. I cried so much, my head hurts and I feel sick. What happened with Nathaniel was beyond anything I had imagined. It might have been easier if he had just rejected me, but no, he doesn't even think this is his baby.

What the hell. I know who I've fucked, and I couldn't care less about his sterility issue. Not only am I mad at him for hiding it, I'm fucking disappointed he doubted me too.

However, I'm done crying. I'm done with everyone keeping me on the sidelines, telling me to stay put and not say things. I need to set things straight. I am not the kind to not do anything, hell no. I grab my coat and Danny follows me, still worried.

"Babe, shouldn't you talk to Clark first?"

"I will, and convince him to show up to Nora's gathering too. As of now, I am still part of this clan, and I'll do what I can."

"To help the White Moon?"

"To protect my daughter, Danny. If Nora's plan to rally all the clans is a success, my baby will have a better chance. Silver City has never seen all of its packs united as one before, or a witch like Sylviana standing alongside them. I don't know about this Dark Witch, but I want to believe that Nora has the right solution. I don't really care if I'm banished from the White Moon or not, honestly. This issue is much bigger than me or a couple of packs, Danny."

He slowly nods and grabs his jacket.

"I hate when you're right about stuff like that. But you're still right. Let's go talk some sense into those stupid men."

We just take our jackets and walk out. Wandering in the streets of our turf has a different feel to me now. Something's changed. Not only inside my heart, but in the way our people look at me. I can feel it as I walk by.

Do they know already? Or do they still wonder if I'm really pregnant, who the father could be? They probably have suspicions. I don't really care, though. Strangely, a big weight was lifted off my shoulders once I told Clark and Nate the truth. Even if things didn't turn out well, I'm relieved that I don't have to lie anymore.

We arrive at the Main House as Clark, Isabella, and other important leaders of our pack are actually discussing Nora's invite.

"You saw her... like me, Clark," says Isa, "and if she really is a Royal, she may be right."

"Why should we agree to cooperate with the Blood Moon?" says Brant, a young fighter. "I don't care much about the new Luna, why do we have to listen to their whim?"

When I walk in, Clark, who was supposed to answer, shuts up. A couple of them growl softly, warning me I'm not welcome here. They don't worry me much, though. I ignore them to turn to my Alpha.

"Please go."

"What?"

"What if Nora is right?" I add. "She's a Royal, and some menace is coming. You were there, Clark, at the vampire attack, you–"

"Elena, get out! You don't have a right to speak here, you lost that right when–"

"Silence."

I'm growling for real, and Brant is taken aback by my sudden use of my Alpha Aura. That's right. If you want to get me out, you'll have to think twice. Let's see who should shut up.

I turn to my godfather again, the only person I'll submit to in this room. Not because I'm the lesser wolf, but out of respect for him. Clark is obviously unhappy to see me here, but he won't be as mean as to kick me out. He crosses his arms, conflicted.

"Elena, what is your point?"

"I'm close to Nora, Clark. I know she says what she thinks, and I believe her too. In any case, the White Moon should go. I'm sure the Sapphire Moon will be there too."

"The Sapphire Moon?" says Isabella. "Why would they go? They hate the Blood Moon the most!"

"They will because of Nora Bluemoon," I explain. "She's a Royal, and that's one thing the Sapphire Moon respects most. They may hate the Black brothers, but it's not the Blood Moon or Sapphire Moon this is about."

They all exchange glances. If they had doubts about attending, the Sapphire Moon clan going should be a strong reason for us to go. Clark will always observe what the Sapphire Moon will do, just because of our old alliance with them. If Nora is so sure they will answer her call, then…

"This is so strange. That girl came out of nowhere and now she's a Royal? And Black's mate?" says an elder, doubtful. "Until now, we thought Royals were extinct! What if this is all part of the Blood Moon's scheme?"

"What about our people who died, then?" I reply back, angry. "You think the Blood Moon was behind the vampire attack too? Even if there's a chance they are wrong, if we can have any clue as to why they died, we owe our deceased to go!"

Isabella looks at me with endless sorrow in her eyes. She was Eric's mom. She's probably the one who wants answers the most, and deserves them. She slowly nods and turns to Clark.

"Clark, I think Elena's right. To be honest, I don't care much about our feud with the Blood Moon clan. They showed up when we needed help. The Sapphire Moon didn't."

She's referring to the vampire attack, when the King and Nate came to our territory with their people to help us out. Isabella's right. No wolf from the Sapphire Moon was spotted that night, but if it wasn't for the Blood Moon clan showing up, we might have experienced much worse.

One of the elders gives me a glance before turning to Clark too.

"The King has changed recently. Maybe for the better. He's breaking all ties to the Gold Moon and looking back, we never had any bad encounters with them. We even welcomed them here recently for the first time."

Clark turns his eyes to me. I know he's thinking about Nathaniel and my relationship with him. He sighs.

"Leave me alone with my Elena for a minute."

Brant and a couple of others growl.

"Alpha, she is not–"

"As far as I'm concerned, she's still my goddaughter, and I'm still your Alpha! Now get out!"

They eventually obey, though they glare and growl at me on the way out. I ignore the petty pack fights, they are the least of my concerns at the moment. Only Clark, Isa, Daniel, and I are left in the room. I turn to my godfather, feeling a bit bad about this.

"Sorry you have to fight them about me."

"It's not just about you, Elena," sighs Isabella. "Those kids are getting cocky anyway."

"Reagan told me you two talked?" says Clark.

I nod, but honestly, I don't want to go over it again. My godfather already knows everything he needs to, and there is no reason to involve him any more than he already is in this mess.

"Yeah, but that's another topic. Clark, I'm concerned about the Opal Moon. Don't let Xavier attend the meeting."

Clark and Isabella exchange a glance, surprised.

"What about Xavier?"

"We witnessed him with the Gold Moon Alpha, two days ago, at the border."

"We couldn't hear everything," adds Daniel. "But it really didn't sound like they were disagreeing."

My godfather stays doubtful, crossing his arms.

"Are you sure it was Xavier and Taaron King? We have no business with the Gold Moon, and nobody reported such a meeting."

"Positive," we answer together.

"Fuck."

My godfather stays silent for a moment, frowning and thinking. What now? He cannot confront Xavier on our accusations alone, I guess, but it would be dangerous to have him come to the meeting as well. My godfather sighs and turns to me.

"Elena, you stop him. I know you cannot fight in your condition, but as an alpha, you have enough authority to stop your uncle without it. I know Iris and Chris will support you, too. Let him know I don't want him to come tomorrow, and you are there to say that."

"Won't he say I don't have authority anymore?" I ask, flustered.

"So far, nothing has been decided," explains Isabella. "To everyone, you're still part of the pack, pending Clark's decision. They don't know about your child's father either."

"Does that mean you'll go, Clark?" I ask my godfather.

He hesitates for a second, exchanging a glance with Isabella, but his Beta is already agreeing with me. He nods.

"Yeah. As you said, we owe them one, and I want to know if this witch theory is real. We haven't seen one in ages, but our pack is one of the oldest in Silver City, we know there used to be witches in the area."

I bet he would be in for a surprise if he met Sylviana.

"Moreover, if the Sapphire Moon clan goes too as you say, I do not want to miss that. I just don't hold the Black brothers in high esteem. Especially now."

Especially now that one got me pregnant, he means. Gosh, baby, you're really complicating a lot of things around here. At least I convinced Clark to go and I get to deal with Xavier myself.

"Elena?" he calls to me when I'm about to leave.

"What is it?"

"You still… haven't changed your mind, have you?"

I think for a second. Have I? I know Clark could turn a blind eye if I changed my mind and agreed to keep my baby's biological father a secret, but…

"No. Sorry."

"Don't be sorry."

I nod and leave behind Daniel.

I'm not going to lie. Whether Nathaniel believes me or not won't change anything, he is this baby's father. If I go back now, it will be like I lied this entire time, or I'm really confused about who I had this child with, and I'm not.

We rush to my uncle's house, following other people's directions as to where he is currently. I take deep breaths. This definitely won't be easy. I have to confront my uncle without getting into a fight with him and persuade him, or keep him from going to the gathering. Isn't Clark overestimating me?

I decide to mind-link my cousins to explain the situation on the way. Both Iris and Chris are shocked to hear what their father did. Iris is a bit more doubtful than her brother, but I expected so, she's always respected her father more. We agree to meet up at his house, as Iris is driving from the clinic to join us, and Chris is almost there.

When we both arrive, it's the evening already. Chris walks up to me, but despite his smile, my heart breaks upon the sight of his missing arm. I can't believe those damn vampires did that. He was such a strong fighter. Now everything from his shoulder down has disappeared; they cut it off after it became obvious the vampire's venom had filled his whole arm.

Yet, Chris is about the same as before. He runs up to me and gives me a hug.

"I missed ya, Elena! I'm so glad you're okay."

"Thanks, Chris, I'm… I'm sorry I couldn't see you earlier."

"Hey, no big deal. Seriously, they gave me so many drugs I couldn't remember my own name for two weeks, let alone remember who visited me! It takes forever to get vampire venom out of your system, did you know that? Moreover, you had a good reason, didn't you?"

He asks while pointing at my tummy, making me blush.

"Chris, you…"

"People talk, you know. I can't believe you're having a baby! Is it a boy? A girl? I'm sure my sister knows but Iris stayed quiet as a stone!"

"Because I cannot trust you to shut your mouth about it!"

His sister just arrived, and rolls her eyes before walking up to us, a bit awkward.

"Sorry I'm late, work at the clinic is a nightmare these days. Elena, are you sure about Father? I can't believe he would do that."

"Iris, I'm sorry. You'll see when we talk to him."

She sighs and nods, stepping into her house first.

"Dad?"

"Iris? What are you… Chris too? And…"

Her father, who stepped out to greet them, suddenly sees me and Daniel. His face immediately goes red.

"What are you doing here! How dare you–"

"Enough, Dad!" says Chris. "Elena is our cousin, she has every right to be here. Moreover, we have things to discuss. Seriously."

But his father won't stop glaring at me, pointing at me, furious.

"If you dare to ask for any support for you little bastard–"

"Shut the fuck up!" I yell, annoyed. "You leave my child out of this, Xavier, and to be perfectly clear, you're the last person I would ask for anything! I came here because I want to know what you're planning to do with the Gold Moon!"

His anger melts like snow in the sun when he hears those last words. He goes as white as a sheet, stepping back.

"What? How did you–"

"We caught you at the border," says Daniel, "discussing with them."

Xavier shakes his head.

"I wasn't discussing, I was chasing them out! Out of our territory! You don't know anything!"

"You're telling me you were chasing Taaron King out? You?" I ask, not believing one word of his. "Come on, Xavier, we know who we saw, and you certainly don't have what it takes to chase out another Alpha!"

"I don't owe you anything, Elena! You can't give me orders and you can't tell me what to do or not! You're about to get banished from the pack, and now you think you can give orders? Huh?"

"I am not banished yet, and you have some explaining to do before I do. Clark sent me here. If you are not willing to answer to me, you'll have to answer to him, Xavier, so spill it now."

"Dad, what were you doing? With the Gold Moon, no less!" insists Chris, annoyed.

Seeing his son question him too seems to take my uncle by surprise. His eyes go on Chris, then Iris, then back to me again.

"Answer me," I insist, using my Alpha Aura.

My wolf starts to growl, threatening. I may not be able to fight, but I can still make him obey. Even if there are only a few drops of Royal blood in my veins, it should be enough to have someone like Xavier comply.

"Elena, enough," says Iris, vexed. "You can't order my father like that, it's disrespectful to your Alpha."

"Maybe it's time for a new Alpha," I say, annoyed.

"Elena!"

My cousin looks at me, furious. But Chris is still glaring his father's way, disappointed.

"Dad, please, answer Elena's questions. You can't risk all of the Opal Moon clan because of your selfishness! What did Taaron King say to you?"

Xavier hesitates for a while, looking at me and his children. He avoids our eyes, looking down.

"He only wanted to discuss things! I never agreed to a… to a real alliance. I was… just intrigued. He said he could put more money into Iris' clinic, and make sure this would stay within the Opal Moon clan. He was saying the White Moon is underestimating me, but if I joined him, he could–"

"If you joined him! Father, how dare you even think of allying yourself with those sharks!" yells Iris, furious. "I can't believe you even thought of taking any actions for my clinic without even telling me!"

She's the one most disappointed in her father, and for good reason. I can't believe Xavier would be so greedy as to do such a thing or even consider it.

"Xavier, I want you to step down from your position as Alpha."

Everyone suddenly turns to me, shocked.

I'm using all of my Alpha Aura, and I've had enough.

"Elena, what are you…?" mutters Iris, shocked.

"I said, step down. You are not worthy to be anyone's Alpha. The Opal Moon deserves better, and you know it."

"You can't force me!" says Xavier, growling.

"I can."

I take deep breaths like Nora did, and use my inner strength to oppose him. We are a few steps away from each other, but he's already struggling to face my aura.

He always knew I was stronger. He only pretended not to. I guess now is the time, probably the last time, I use my Alpha Aura to do the right thing for this pack. Chris looks at me with uncertainty.

"Elena, you mean to–"

"I'm not competing to be the Opal Moon Alpha. I am only doing what's right for this pack. If no one can lead it properly, maybe the Opal Moon has lost its reason for existing. I am not worthy to be an Alpha for this pack, my priorities are elsewhere now. But I would rather give the ownership back to Clark than see my uncle put anyone in danger because of his greed."

Both siblings exchange glances at that moment, but I can tell they are mind-linking as well, thinking deeply about this situation.

"Chris, Iris! You can't allow her to do that!"

"Actually, Father, we can," says Chris, "and Elena is right. You've put us in danger one too many times. The Gold Moon clan? Really?"

"I…" says Iris, still unsure.

"How dare you! Both of you!"

"Enough, Xavier," I say, stepping forward. "Give up. Now."

"You can't!"

"STEP. DOWN."

I used my Alpha voice, at its strongest, for the first and last time. I am tired of this arguing. Xavier tries to think of something to say, but the words are stuck in his throat.

"Xavier, you know you were wrong. This is all wrong, for the Opal Moon clan to suffer because of you. If you step down properly, Chris can take over and make things right. Don't let things go overboard because of your greed."

"You have no right to–"

"I have every fucking right when it comes to protecting this pack!" I yell back. "I am a fighter of this pack, a guarantor of its safety!"

A long silence follows my words. Iris and Xavier are staring at me, and Chris and I are staring at his father. I don't even hold it personally against my uncle, I only want him to do what's right. After a long staring contest, I use my wolf again, making my eyes glow a little and growl again. Xavier looks down, helpless.

"Fine. I'm officially stepping down as the Opal Moon clan's Alpha from today onwards."

That's a huge relief. I'm not happy about it, however. I just feel sorry that things turned out this way. I turn to Chris.

"You can fill in for now, kid?"

He nods.

"You can count on me."

"Elena, you–" starts his sister, but I interrupt her.

"Iris, Chris will need your help too. You're smart, and you control most of the Opal Moon clan's facilities already."

Iris stays silent, obviously bitter. She faintly nods, but that's enough for me. I've done my share, but this Alpha position isn't mine to take. I'll leave it to my cousins. I have enough on my plate as it is.

I turn around to leave this place, Daniel following me, but I can tell that my best friend is irritated about something.

"What is it?"

"Don't you think that was… too easy?"

"Easy? How so?"

"Xavier is the proudest man we know, and he stepped down without a fight. Don't you think that's odd? He's got the guts to discuss business with the Gold Moon behind Clark's back, yet he barely argues when you force him to give up his Alpha position? I just think there's something strange about his actions."

I keep thinking about it. I know this is true in some way, but no matter what, Xavier did give up his position. He cannot go back on his word, and if he's not the Opal Moon Alpha anymore, whatever deal he made with the Gold Moon is void as well, isn't it?

"You think too much, Danny," I sigh. "I mean, Xavier's never been very brave."

"Yeah. Maybe you're right."

Suddenly, his phone vibrates. He takes it out, and answers it, sending me weird glances. Who is he on the phone with?

"Yes. Okay. Yeah, we'll meet you there."

He hangs up, leaving me confused.

"Babe, we're going to the university lab."

"Why?"

"You'll see when we get there."

After getting his car, we drive there, a long silence accompanying us all the way. I'm used to seeing Danny nervous, but now he seems more uneasy than usual. What is he up to this time? And at the university lab?

He parks, and I recognize the car next to ours immediately.

"Daniel! What the hell?"

He turns off the engine and brushes his blonde hair back before turning to me.

"Babe, calm down. I called him, there are a couple of things I want to discuss with you and him."

"How dare you call Nathaniel! And without telling me!"

"Elena, please. I'm trying to make things better for you and baby girl, okay? Just hear me out, and we can check what's going on with your pregnancy and his sterility thing. I promise I'll explain."

Damn, I feel like slapping him right now! How dare he fucking do something like this behind my back! How did he even reach out to Nate in the first place! Did Boyan help him? I'm so mad he did it without even talking to me first!

"Babe, please."

"Shut up, Danny! You traitor! You should have told me!"

"Elena, I know you by heart, you would have said no! I had no choice. So now, just suck it up and trust me! Come on!"

He gets out of the car, and honestly, I want to stay here and sulk. I can't believe him. After a while, though, I can't stand being so childish, especially with Nathaniel there. I get out of the car, not hiding how pissed I am.

Nathaniel is standing next to his car now, in his usual jeans and T-shirt outfit. Damn, I hate how handsome he is at a time like this. I probably look like shit, and angry too. I don't want to talk to him or Danny. I just cross my arms and look down, or anywhere but his direction.

"Hi…" says Daniel, a bit awkward.

"Hello, Daniel, Elena."

"Let's go, Danny," I just say.

My best friend hesitates before walking ahead, taking us to one of the labs he works in. I make sure to stay away from Nate despite the glances he sends me. Stay cool and calm, Elena. Deep breaths; don't get flustered.

Daniel takes out a large envelope, handing it back to Nathaniel.

"I checked your medical file. It is as you said: azoospermia."

I look at them, confused.

"You checked his…?"

"Yes, babe. When he mentioned his sterility, I wanted to check for myself. So we talked, and he gave me a copy of his file. Nathaniel has azoospermia; basically, when he comes, it's blank and, well, he cannot have children. It's due to trauma, and the surgery required to heal it, as it says on the file, is impossible by today's medical standards."

I just can't believe that. Daniel went as far as checking Nathaniel's medical file? To be sure? I stare at the envelope, and Nathaniel holding it with a long face, totally confused. I turn to Daniel again.

"He's really infertile?"

"Well, he was, back when he was diagnosed. To be honest, I'll say science is on his side."

"See? I didn't lie to you, Elena," says Nathaniel.

I glare at him. I am not crazy, or a liar. This baby is his, no matter how many medical files he brings. I turn to Daniel. At least I know my best friend trusts me.

Daniel takes a deep breath, crossing his arms.

"I want to check again," says Daniel.

"… Excuse me?"

"Those tests were done ten years ago. They reflect how things were back then, but maybe it has evolved. Science has yet to explain everything and, moreover, we are werewolves. Who knows if something has changed since then, healing you in the process? So, I want to retest you, do a new test. If the results are the same, then we can confirm you are not–"

"You think I wouldn't know if I could have children?" yells Nathaniel, suddenly furious. "Sorry to disappoint you, but I've had many, many women before Elena! I would have known if things had changed, and I would have checked!"

He takes a deep breath, trying to calm down, before turning to me.

"Elena, it's nothing against you. I swear I'd give anything to be this child's father, biologically. But your best friend just confirmed it: I cannot. Even if Daniel asks me to go through all the tests to check whether I'm cured or not, it won't be ready until–"

"Let's do a paternity test."

He looks at me, speechless. I try to look at him, keeping my cool as best as I can. Honestly, I want to slap him and make him go away.

"I don't care about you being infertile or not. Danny will do a paternity test and clear things up. It's quick and sure, alright?"

"We will do a real test, not that cheap stuff from a drugstore," adds Daniel. "I just need a sample of your blood, and we have everything at our clinic to test Elena's baby."

Nathaniel frowns.

"Isn't that illegal?"

I roll my eyes. Is he really testing my patience now?

"My cousin owns the clinic, she can have any doctor do it for me. Do you want to check the doctor's credentials too, perhaps?"

He seems a bit embarrassed for a moment. Yeah, it may not be their buildings but we do have our own facilities. Eventually, he sighs and turns to us, hesitant toward me and Daniel.

"Fine… Let's do that then. If it can put an end to this."

I hate the way he said that. Like a nightmare that should be over soon. Something he doesn't want anything to do with. I just wish he could understand I'm carrying his daughter, not anyone else's.

"Danny, just take whatever you need, and let's go."

"Wait, Elena, we need to talk."

I glare at him. Now he wants to talk? About what? I don't want to talk to him. I'm just mad and I haven't had time to sort out my feelings yet. Damn it. I exchange a glance with Daniel.

"*Five minutes?*"

"*I'll be right next door if you need me, babe.*"

"*Thanks, Danny.*"

Daniel walks out, but I know he's staying close by. I turn to Nathaniel, wondering what he wants with me now. I cross my arms like I'm protecting myself and my child.

"Elena, I'm sorry I–"

"I don't want an apology, Nate. Just tell me what you wanted to say and let's get on with it."

"... Fine. I don't want you to come to the gathering."

Wow, I didn't expect that one. I'm confused. Why would he suddenly say that?

"What? Why? What are you planning?"

"Nothing, Elena," he says. "The Blood Moon only wants to talk. But I'm afraid not everyone will be as nice and understanding as Nora and Damian. I don't want you there if something happens, Elena."

I'm speechless. He's worried about me? Is that why? This isn't what I expected at all. Seeing me hesitate, he resumes talking, thinking I'm doubtful.

"Elena, no matter what, I still love you. I'm still going to worry about you. If something happens to you, I won't be able to help; you'll be with your pack and I'll be with mine. I don't want that, but I need to be there fully to support my brother, too."

I'm choking up a bit. I did not expect those words or his concern for me. Why? Why does he always confuse me with his words? He steps closer, but my feet are stuck to the ground. He doesn't touch me though. Nathaniel stops a foot away, so close yet not touching me. It's even worse than I thought.

"Elena, please. Promise me you'll stay away, stay in your territory. If you don't do it for me, do it for your baby."

"...Okay."

He lets out a sigh of relief, nodding.

"Good. I–"

"Bye."

I leave the room, unable to bear it anymore. I don't want to be in there with him. I cross Danny's path on my way out, just letting him know I'll wait in the car.

It only takes a few minutes for Daniel to come outside, a sample from Nathaniel with him. My baby is his, I'll prove it to him. I insist on going directly to the clinic to do this stupid test, though it will take a couple of days for the results to come back.

"You think this gathering will go well?" I ask Daniel as we leave the clinic.

"I hope so. Nora can be convincing, and most packs will at least be respectful since she's a Royal and the King's mate."

I guess things will be over tomorrow night. I can't believe I promised him not to go. I should be there, by Clark's side, with my pack. So many things have changed because of this pregnancy… however, I'm not changing my mind. I will protect my baby no matter what.

Once we get home, I try to call Clark, to tell him I won't be going to the gathering. My godfather doesn't answer my call, so I just leave a message to let him know. He is probably busy, with the gathering coming up tomorrow.

I fell asleep without even realizing it again. I'm confused when I wake up, not to my alarm but from my phone's ringtone. Who calls me at… 6:00 a.m.? Half-asleep, I answer the call.

"Elena?"

"Clark? What is it?"

It's never good to receive a call from my Alpha at such an hour. I sit up. Is it about Xavier? Or the fact I saw Nate again?

"Do you know anything? About Diego?"

"Diego? Clark, why the fuck should I know anything about him?"

I feel anxious all of a sudden. Why is he bringing up that asshole now? He stopped stalking me two days ago, but I haven't seen him since and I didn't want to!

"I just needed to check."

"Clark, what happened?"

"Diego's dead, Elena. We found him an hour ago. His body was outside our border, in the neutral part of the forest."

"His body? What… How did he…?"

"He was killed, Elena. Someone shot him, one bullet, right in the head. No traces of any fight, and no one heard the gunshot either. It was an execution."

Holy Moon Goddess.

Diego's dead? And… killed? Who the hell did this? It wasn't even a fight, someone just killed him like a dog!

"Elena, stay at home for now. I'll alert the police, but… you might be a suspect, considering your past with him. I don't want you to go out for now. I got your message, too, I also think it's best you don't come. I need someone here to watch the Opal Moon clan, make sure no one tries to fight Chris or gets involved with the Gold Moon. I need you here."

He needs me here? More like he needs me to stay where he can watch me.

Who the hell killed Diego? I can't believe it! It doesn't feel real. For a werewolf as strong as him to simply be shot down like that? Who could have... and right before the gathering too! I doubt Clark will go public about it, but…

Suddenly, a thought crosses my mind. He wouldn't have done this, right? I hang up, and notice Daniel, in his pajamas, at my door.

"Is he dead?" he asks.

"Daniel, what the fuck do you know about this?"

Chapter 25

"You agreed to what! Moon Goddess, Daniel, have you gone crazy? Do you have any idea what you've done?"

I can't believe this is my best friend facing me right now. Daniel Lewis, who couldn't even look an Alpha in the eye three years ago, just sold someone out to the Black brothers? I am fucking dreaming right now!

Next to me, Reagan has her arms crossed, looking at me very calmly. She even has a bit of a smirk on, satisfied by Diego's death.

"The shrimp did something right for once."

"Nothing about this is right, Reagan! Daniel just–"

"Got rid of a rapist and a murderer who was threatening you."

"And you helped him. Of course," I growl at her.

She shrugs.

"It was just a matter of luring him out. I washed my hands of whatever happened next. If Black did things cleanly, I'm satisfied."

"Satisfied? Reagan! This is–"

"What needed to be done, Elena!" yells Daniel. "I am not kidding about my best friend's safety, Elena. That guy was stalking you, and he could have assaulted you anytime. He's a rapist, and he doesn't even feel sorry for causing the death of an unborn child!"

"That was not for you to decide, Daniel!"

He finally shuts up, and I just shake my head, exhausted. This all happened so fast.

"Daniel, even if Diego was an issue, it was mine to deal with. You can't dish out justice by yourself or let Nathaniel do it. He just killed someone from our pack because of you, and right before a gathering too! Do you realize how wrong that could have gone?"

"Elena, you don't get it," he replies. "This isn't about justice. I wasn't avenging you. We live in a world of wolves, alphas, and blood. You're having a miracle child, and this guy threatened you! I am not letting you take any chances; I won't let you lose that baby. It would kill you, I know it."

He sighs and shakes his head, resolute.

"Nathaniel did the first thing he should do as the baby's father and protected you. I don't care about the cost, and I don't care about an asshole like Diego. He should have been the one to go to prison, but everyone turned a blind eye and let him back in. Well, I am not making the same mistake of waiting for something bad to happen to you. I saw an opportunity and I took it. I don't care if you blame me for that, Elena. I am no alpha like you. I don't fight with my fists, but I do what I have to do."

Next to him, Reagan nods. I can't believe his nerve, or that he doesn't regret it one bit. We've killed before, fighting for our lives and pack, but this… this was simply murder, and I can't cope with that thought associated with my best friend.

"Daniel, I understand, but… I still think this was all wrong. I'm sorry."

"It's okay, babe. What's done is done. I'll live with it."

Just like that, we both agree to end that argument for now. I can only deal with so much. Moon Goddess, these last few days have been so crazy. I pray Nora's side can really come up with the solution to fight all of this madness.

As promised to Nathaniel, I am not going to the gathering, but it's hard. My heart's telling me something big will happen there, and I'm dying to go.

I decide to get out and go see my father to calm myself down. I haven't been to the hospital as often as I used to, and I feel like I haven't seen my dad in ages.

I manage to convince Reagan and Daniel to let me go alone as I need some time to cool off. With most of our pack gone to attend Nora's gathering, the streets are quieter than usual. I haven't been on my own in a while, either. I take my time getting there and enjoy the cold December breeze.

Right, it's almost Christmas. The Hispanic neighborhood had put up such pretty decorations a while ago, but I feel like I'm only seeing them now. The White Moon hospital is decorated nicely too.

A nurse put a little Christmas tree next to my father's bed. I take the stool next to him, observing my dad again. He ages so slowly, yet I start to see his little wrinkles, and his beard is growing a bit more sporadically. I miss the color of his eyes. My dad has deep brown eyes. I decide to add to the atmosphere, listening to some Christmas songs with him for a while. I don't feel like talking anyway. I'm just glad I can be next to him.

Suddenly, I realize I'm not alone. Sylviana is there, at the entrance of his room. She smiles softly.

"Good morning, Elena."

"Sylviana? How did you… Daniel called you?"

"No, he did."

She's pointing at… my dad? What the… She walks up to my father's bed and sits on the other side, looking at him.

"He's a very brave man."

"He's the best father in the world."

"Of course," she replies gently.

I don't really understand.

"Sylviana, what are you…? Why are you here?"

"It's time to let him go, Elena."

I stare at her, a bit shocked.

"What are you talking about?" I ask, in a hoarse voice.

"His fight is over, Elena. You're a stronger woman now. You're not alone anymore. It's time to let your father go."

I keep staring at her, trying to understand her words. No, I understand what she's saying; I just don't want to hear, I don't want to listen. Sylviana is speaking softly, so calmly I can't even get mad or cry. Is she doing this?

She turns to my dad, looking at him like he's an old friend of hers.

"Samuel needs to rest now, Elena."

"He won't wake up?"

"I think you have known the truth for a while now."

I look at my father, choking up a bit. He only seems asleep.

"Sylviana, I don't want to say goodbye…"

"I know."

"Can you not?"

"It's not me, Elena. It's your father. He's the one to decide. I'm not going to do anything. I only came for you."

I feel a few tears on my cheeks. It's so hard. I don't want to let go, to say goodbye. I take his hand, and try to think of words to say. What haven't I told him? In two years, I've said so much: I love you, goodbye, I'm proud to be your daughter… I never had any filter with him. Just my heart, poured out day after day to let him know how much I love the man who raised me.

After a while, I decide to take out my phone and select a song: Mom's favorite song. I let it play out loud, and Sylviana smiles.

"It's a pretty song."

The singer's voice is soothing, talking about love and his funny valentine. About his lover's flows and strength. About how she doesn't need to change a thing… I sing with him, softly. My voice is the worst it's ever been, I'm hoarse and trying hard not to cry. As the last note hits, a long beep follows.

I hold my father's hand a bit tighter.

"Elena, it's alright. You can let go now."

One of the nurses barges in, saying something I can't hear. I can only hear Sylviana's voice, trying to help me. I'm crying helplessly, unable to step away, unable to let go. She comes around and puts her hand on my shoulder, slowly whispering something to me. I don't understand what she's saying, but I feel something warm covering me, and my hands go numb. I can hear my own wailing, erratic and frantic. Sylviana pats my back.

They ask us to leave the room. I hear people giving orders, a doctor walks in as we walk out. Sylviana takes my hand and guides me outside. I'm not walking away from him; my father isn't in that room anymore

He's gone.

"Elena? Take this."

She puts a cup of hot tea in my hands. I don't know how much time has passed, how long I cried. I take a deep breath and drink a bit. It burns my throat, but I feel a bit better.

"I can't believe he went so fast…"

"He went peacefully. He was just glad you were there with him."

"Do you know… what happens after death?" I ask, feeling a bit stupid.

She chuckles.

"Witches don't have the same beliefs as humans or werewolves. We live different lives. I could give you an answer, yet like everyone else, I wouldn't be able to prove it. Witches are part of a cycle. We live, we die, and we are reborn."

"You believe in reincarnation?"

"Yes. Our souls live on in other witches to guide them. We carry the souls of our mothers and ancestors with us."

I keep listening to her, but my heart just feels numb right now. As Sylviana comforts me, I see my uncle and Chris running into the hospital, but I don't go in with them.

We sit outside in the little hospital garden. Despite the cold, I feel better here than within the hospital's white walls. Daniel is on his way, but I have no idea what I'll say. I just feel numb right now. My father just died, and my heart is as cold as ice. I can't think of anything else. I want to cry again, and I do every time I need. My eyes are red and puffy, my head hurts, and I'm a mess.

I lost my parents… twice. I really am an orphan now. When my dad was alive and hanging on, I was okay, but… damn, I've never felt so alone.

I put a hand on my tummy, thinking about the baby girl growing in there. Will I be a good mother? It seems so hard. I want this child so badly, yet my confidence is plummeting. Will I be able to do it on my own if Nate rejects her, rejects me?

I take a deep breath in. It will be fine. As long as I love my baby, it'll be okay. I'll do my best for her, be the mother I've always wanted to be.

I suddenly feel a hand on mine. It's not Sylviana or Danny, it's Reagan. She looks at me with a sorrowful expression, not saying a thing. I gather all my courage and nod.

"Dad's gone, Reagan."

"I know, kid. How are you holding up?"

"I…"

No words can explain what I'm going through. I just end up shaking my head and holding my tears back. She puts an arm around me, probably the nicest gesture she has ever done for me. I rest my head on my mentor's shoulder, closing my eyes and taking deep breaths so as not to fall apart again.

"You'll be fine, kid. Sam knew how strong you are. You're a woman now."

I listen to her words, and it's like a weight has been lifted off my shoulders. Why are Reagan's words so effective on me?

"… There's something else I never told you."

I sit back up and look at her, confused. Reagan looks around, making sure we are alone. Sylviana wandered off somewhere, so we are.

"When I took you from your mother's arms, she asked me to protect you," she whispers. "I had to hide who you were, any bond you had to the Royals. I also… changed your name."

"My name?"

"I'll say it only once, because it's a blessed name, and you should hide it for now. It would easily expose your link to the Royals, so only reveal it to people you trust, alright?"

I nod, despite my confusion. She gets close to me and whispers it in my ear, so low I barely hear it. However, when I do, something lights up inside of me.

"… That's my real name?"

"I didn't do much, but I thought it would be better to hide it for now. It makes your identity too obvious."

I agree. It's such a simple thing, yet…

"Elena!"

I see Daniel running toward me, out of breath. He pulls me in for a hug, holding me tight and close for a few seconds.

"Babe, I am so, so sorry about your dad. Are you okay? You weren't alone, right?"

"I'm okay, Danny. Thanks for coming."

"Actually…"

He seems uneasy for a while, hesitating. I frown.

"Danny, what is it?"

"I'm sorry, babe, but I saw a bunch of the Opal Moon clan heading south on my way here, I didn't know if I should tell you or not."

Holy shit. I jump back on my feet. Who would dare to…! I saw Xavier and Chris running to the hospital, who could be doing this behind their backs! And after Clark told the whole Opal Moon clan to stay put! I immediately start growling. This is not the day to fucking piss me off.

"Elena, wait!"

I ignore both Reagan and Danny and start running south. They're going to get it this time. I mind-link everyone I trust from the Opal Moon, including Daniel's siblings, our friends, and the youngsters I trained. None of them know anything about the group headed south, but agree to meet up with me.

I hear my best friend, already shape-shifted into his tawny wolf form, and my mentor running behind me. Sylviana's apparently gone Moon-Goddess-knows-where, but she doesn't need to be involved in this.

When I finally reach the group, they are about to cross the border. I growl immediately. Even in my human form, my Alpha Aura and angry wolf voice are enough to stop most of them. Some seem confused to see me here, and others are furious.

"Elena? What is it?"

"Where the fuck do you think you're going?" I growl back.

The sorrow from earlier adds to my anger, and the fuel in my voice impresses some of them enough to make them step back. I must look scary, with my red eyes, disheveled hair, and anger painted all over my face.

"I asked where do you think you're going?!"

They hesitate, looking at each other like no one wants to take the blame until someone finally steps forward to face me.

"Get out of the way, we have a gathering to attend, cousin."

"You?" I ask, confused.

Why the hell would my cousin Iris be leading this group? On her father's orders, perhaps? But Xavier just lost his brother, so why would he give orders now… Iris chuckles at my confusion.

"What is it, Elena? Surprised to see me taking the lead, perhaps? I bet you never thought one second your pretty, well-behaved cousin had the guts to overstep her own father's authority to make a deal with the Gold Moon."

Iris? Iris was behind all of this? Since when! I'm so shocked, I don't even know how to react. But my cousin steps forward, not impressed by my Alpha Aura.

"Elena, you're no match for me. Step aside and mind your own business, cousin."

I growl back. Hell no. I don't understand what's going on, but I am not letting her ruin Nora's hard work to organize this gathering. Iris may be my adoptive cousin, the one I grew up with, but Nora is my blood. She is the one I feel close to, and the one doing the right thing right now. She's trying to unite the packs and be a good Luna. And so will I.

I am Selena Bluemoon, and I am a fighter of the White and Opal Moon packs. And I'll fight for them.

"What is wrong with you, Iris? This isn't you!"

My cousin sighs, brushing her purple hair back.

"You don't know the first thing about me, Elena. Let me guess. You've always seen me as the quiet, shy, and good girl my daddy raised. Isn't that it? I was never on the stronger side, like you and Chris. I was barely average for an alpha. Do you have any idea what it's like to grow up in someone's shadow? In my own sibling's shadow? In yours?"

I don't even recognize her voice when she speaks. She sounds like someone else, yet she is still… Iris. An Iris I don't recognize. She steps forward again, defying me with her eyes.

"My father was always crazy with his jealousy. His younger brother was stronger, smarter, and more appreciated. He always felt like Samuel stripped him of his Alpha title. Even when my dad finally got it back, it wasn't enough. Your adoptive father's shadow was always there."

What does this have to do with her? Our fathers' rivalry is nothing new!

"Iris, that has nothing to do with us. Xavier got the Alpha position in the end!"

"Oh, but that was never enough. Actually, he trained us even harder because of that. Or more precisely, he tried to train Chris. Me? I was his smart little girl, cast aside because why would he consider me when he had a son?"

I'm confused. Didn't Xavier always treat Iris better? He cherished her like a little princess her whole life compared to Chris! Her brother always had to train harder, to prove himself to their father while Iris could do whatever she wanted.

"To be honest, I wouldn't have cared that my younger brother took the heir position if it wasn't for you, Elena. But you? You were always so annoyingly strong and perfect. Father grew obsessed about Chris being better than you. 'You can't be beaten by Samuel's daughter, by a girl!' Guess what? Your existence fueled our father's jealousy, Elena. And mine! You were supposedly only the Alpha's niece, but Clark had to make you his goddaughter and make you a possible heir for the White Moon clan! Do you know how humiliating that was?"

I'm completely in shock. I never thought Iris gave a shit about the Alpha position, in the Opal or White Moon clans!

"I didn't ask for anything, Iris! Clark and Xavier decided it all on their own!"

She sends me a glare back.

"Oh, shut the hell up, Elena. You've always known you were more cherished. The precious little orphan, so strong, so bright, so loved. After enduring my father's jealousy towards yours, now you were in the competition as well? But guess what, my father never, ever considered me as your rival or an heir for a single second!"

"I don't want to be anyone's rival, Iris! I even gave Chris the Opal Moon Alpha position!"

Iris laughed, rolling her eyes.

"You gave it to him? Do you even hear yourself? Even now you think you're so much better than us? Moreover, you're the same as my dad! You don't consider me at all!"

I'm getting tired of that attitude of hers. I've had enough emotions for today. I growl, warning her.

"You are who you are, Iris, and that is not a leader. You may be an alpha, but…"

"What? I don't have the muscles?"

I frown. She really thinks that's all there is? Is that why she's so delusional? And jealous?

"I have the brains, Elena! I may not be strong, but I was always the smarter one!"

"You're doing a great job with our facilities, Iris, I know that. You're an integral part of the clan, and so important, but…"

She scoffs.

"Oh, poor Elena," she sighs. "You really think that's it, right? Don't you get it? I'm so good at this game, I am the one who kicked you out of Clark's heir position as the White Moon Alpha in the first place."

What is she talking about? Clark took me out of his potential heirs because of my baby, and Iris has nothing to do with it. She shakes her head, with that annoying smirk of hers.

"I bet you never realized until now, cousin. Gosh, it wasn't easy, you know?"

She walks around me in a circle while talking, making my wolf wary of her. Out of the corner of my eye, I see Daniel, Reagan, Levi, Ben, and Bonnie arrive next to us, all the Lewis siblings in their wolf form. Reagan is still in her human form but growling.

"Let's go back to the start. When your father had his accident and you were sent to jail because you were stupid enough to get involved with Diego, I thought we would finally get rid of you. What I did not expect was that you'd be back and forgiven by Clark. Not only that, following Samuel's coma, he made your position official as his goddaughter and possible heir. You have no idea how furious I was! So I tried to find a way to kick you out discreetly."

What the hell? Behind her, the rest of the Opal Moon clan is listening as well, visibly as confused as I am.

"Luckily, you gave me an opportunity sooner than I thought; when you met Nathaniel Black."

A lot of faces cannot hide their shock and stare at me in awe. I guess the cat's out of the bag now, but I couldn't care less who knows or not. Iris continues her speech, ignoring everyone else, so full of confidence it's beyond irritating.

"I didn't think much of it at first, but when I heard about you two being together at the club, I thought this might be another opportunity."

"You saw us?"

"Oh no, Elena, I'm the good girl, remember? I don't go partying outside of the pack's territory. But some kids from our pack were there, remember? One of them saw you, how attracted you were to Black, and told me everything."

I can't believe it. This goes back to my first meeting with Nate! She chuckles.

"So I made sure you went back again. I know how attracted you are to bad boys, Elena, I knew you'd fall for him."

"You're the one who sent that text," I realize.

I had never understood how the club had gotten my number to send a private invite, but it turns out it was Iris?

"Bingo!" she says with a smile. "Clever, right? You ran back there, so I knew I had you in Black's arms. knowing you, I thought you'd sleep with him once or twice. But I didn't expect it to go on and on for weeks!"

"How the hell do you know!"

"I watched you, of course! To be honest, it wasn't easy. The Blood Moon watches their territory closely, and the Black brothers almost caught me more than once."

The female that intruded on their territory! Moon Goddess, so many things are coming to light now! I can't believe it. All those little details that had me intrigued earlier, even…

"You're the one who sent that picture of me and Levi kissing to Nate!"

"I did! Oh, it was fun, to be honest. Having you pretend you had a boyfriend here to keep Diego at bay while hiding your relationship with Black! Not going to lie, Elena, it was thrilling. In all honesty, I did it out of revenge too."

"I never did anything to you, Iris, all this jealousy was your own!"

She sighs and shakes her head.

"Oh no, Elena, you never did anything. That's right. But it didn't stop Eric from being crazy in love with you."

"Eric?"

I didn't expect him to be brought up. Right, her deceased boyfriend used to express his love for me, but I thought that was ancient history since he got with her! Iris loses her smile while talking about Eric.

"If I ever had one crush, it was Eric. For years, I got prettier and prettier, hoping he'd notice me. Yet, like an idiot, I had to watch him talk about how much he loved you day after day… It was so upsetting! So, when you pretended to go out with Levi, I knew it was my chance. I asked him out, arguing you'd never notice him anyway. Luckily, he agreed. Do you know how useful it is to be with a police officer, Elena? Much more than I thought."

I can't believe her. She even used Eric? Iris chuckled again.

"When Levi was thrown into your love affair, I didn't really expect it. But after that picture, I knew your relationship with Black would collapse at any time. I mean, any male would be jealous, right? Yet, it had already exceeded my expectations, so I threw his ex in the mix, just to be sure. With Eric's contacts, it was easy to get his passcode, send a little innocent text to his ex-girlfriend, and just as I saw you leave the pack again to see him, with the right timing… surprise!"

A wave of cold anger is rising in my bones. I can't believe her! She was evil enough to plot so much against me and Nathaniel? I've never wanted to slap someone so much!

"What was your plan, Iris? Bringing us together just to have us break up? Why?"

She shrugs.

"I told you, I expected you to sleep with him a few times, not have it go on for weeks and then months! Oh, I guess you fought a few times. You have quite a temper, cousin, after all, don't you? Yet, as time passed, you kept getting back together with him, and a thought hit me. I wanted you with Black to piss Clark off and have him take you off his list of potential heirs, but what if? What if things got serious between you and Black? What if you got the Blood Moon's backing eventually? I realized things were more complex than I thought when we went out together. I sensed something was going on between you and the King's mate, but I couldn't grasp what."

I remember. Iris picked me up at university, and we went to see Nora's fight.

"I had only meant to bring you to have you betray my father and Clark's order on leaving the pack territory, but…"

"You called your father, you said I had permission to–!"

"Oh, yeah, I lied. I pretended to call."

Holy Moon Goddess, that explains why Xavier was so fucking furious! He never gave me his permission to go out, yet I thought so and kept arguing with him! I can't believe Iris was behind all this from the start!

"Anyway, I had another problem on my hands. You got closer to the Blood Moon, and I couldn't understand why. Then, the attack. I lost Eric. I was so, so mad, and you… and meanwhile, you went and got fucking pregnant with Black's child!"

Everyone's eyes are on me, shocked or angry. If anyone wondered about my baby's father, I guess things are out in the open now. But I don't care. I'm angrier about Iris being behind all of this. I just can't believe her!

"I was furious. I had lost my lover, yet you of all people managed to conceive a child with Black? It was hard to swallow, but at least Clark knew soon enough, and I knew he would never allow that. I finally got you out of my way. But to be honest, I didn't feel relieved. It wasn't enough. Hence I decided it would be better if you didn't have this child at all. After all, I worked so hard for you to not become this pack's Alpha, I couldn't let you become another pack's Luna, right?"

What the hell? I try to think, but I don't understand what she could have done. However, Iris' unhappy face tells me things didn't turn out her way. She growls softly.

"So, I tipped off your dear ex, Diego, about your pregnancy. You should have seen it, it was funny how crazy and mad he went. You have a thing for psychos, cousin. Anyway, he started rampaging about how he was going to stab you, make sure your next child was his."

I get a chill down my back. Holy fuck, that sounds like the crazy Diego I once knew. But Diego is dead now. I swallow, trying to calm down.

"But it didn't go your way, Iris, did it? Diego is dead."

She glares my way, losing her smirk for good.

"Yeah, you're lucky your dear lover got a hold of him. Since Clark had you on lockdown, Diego had to wait for the right moment to get to you. It wasn't easy, since you were never alone. If it wasn't for Black protecting you..."

I frown. Black protecting me? Nathaniel never came to the White Moon territory, and I did leave the house a few times unaccompanied or with Daniel only… What is she talking about?

"Moreover, you weren't my only issue. I needed to do more for Father to consider me as an heir, and I did. To be fair, I'm sorry that my brother lost an arm, but it worked in my favor. I already had control of most of our medical facilities, our pack's main economy. All I needed was better control of the funds. And guess what? I could do so by an agreement with the Gold Moon clan."

I growl. She wants to shift the clan's money to the Gold Moon banks to gain more control! So far, the only place we have our money stored is under the financial establishments owned by the Sapphire Moon clan, the main reminder of our alliance with them! If we shift this money, we will clearly be losing the partnership with them!

"You're crazy, Iris! You can't manipulate our money in favor of the Gold Moon!"

"Oh, I will. My father was never good at handling these things or making big decisions, so I did. I let my dad think he could lead the negotiations, but I was the one behind it all. And you fell for it, cousin."

I growl. Damn it, she's right. I always thought Xavier was the one behind the scheming with the Gold Moon clan, not her!

"You can't do that, Iris," says one of the men behind her. "Chris is the new Alpha, you…"

"I control the clan's finances! I am the one in charge! My brother has lost an arm and has nothing, he is not fit to be an Alpha!"

"Chris is still better than you!" I yell back. "He is a brave, strong, and good kid! He cares about others, not only his little old self like you, Iris!

"That is not for you to decide, Elena," she growls back.

I glare at her, furious. Who the hell does she think she is? She's been deceiving not only me, but the whole pack for weeks, and now she wants to fucking claim ownership? Iris has a smirk on.

"They will never accept you, anyway. Not with the little bastard you're carrying."

I growl. How dare she insult my daughter! The people around her are confused. I bet they didn't expect Iris to have done so much. One of them steps forward.

"Iris, we can't move without the Alpha's permission."

"I am the Alpha! Didn't you listen? I control this pack's money, and I have the support of the Gold Moon. Chris and Elena have nothing, and my father even stepped down because of her. If you don't want to be exposed and penniless, you'll do as I say!"

Everyone hesitates, unwilling to say anymore. I cross my arms, staying right in front of her. She frowns, a bit surprised.

"What the heck are you doing?"

"You're not going anywhere, Iris. I'm still a fighter of this clan, while you are not its official Alpha. I say you're not going. Don't you dare take one step outside."

"Oh, and you're going to stop me, perhaps? I know of your medical condition, Elena, you can't fight or you'll lose your baby. And you would never risk that."

This time, it's my turn to smile.

"I don't need to shape-shift to fight, Iris. And I can assure you my human form is plenty enough to keep you here, cousin."

I hear Reagan step forward behind me, handing me a large pole. It shines immediately, and Iris goes pale.

"You… You can touch silver?"

I chuckle.

"Surprise, surprise, cousin. You're not the only one with secrets."

Even if I am not a full Royal like Nora, I guess being a daughter of the Sun also has its perks.

I glare back at my cousin.

"Now Iris, I would advise you to use your smartness and think twice before trying to cross me."

My cousin goes red with anger, probably the first time I have ever seen her lose control. Her eyes are glaring at me, yet staring at my silver pole with defiance.

Yes, I can touch silver. It injures me like any metal if I'm hit, of course, but unlike most werewolves, I am not that affected by it. I've known since Reagan started training me, but it had become something irrelevant in a city inhabited half by werewolves and half by humans, both living together in peace. I never thought it would come in handy at a time like this.

"You… Enough, Elena! Stand back and–!"

"I won't, Iris," I answer calmly. "Clark gave me one mission: making sure the Opal Moon stays out of the gathering."

"The Alpha said that?" whispers someone behind Iris.

My cousin immediately turns to him.

"Don't listen to her! Why would Clark trust her! Didn't you hear? She is bearing a Black brothers' child? He kicked her out for that! I forbid you to listen to her! I am the Alpha and–"

"Chris is the Alpha, Iris! You are nothing!"

She turns to me, turning so red I feel like she is going to explode.

"I have anything I want! I planned all of this, Elena. I worked so hard, and you are nothing! You're just an orphan, a little bastard picked up off the streets! I am the oldest child of my father, his heir! How dare you name Chris and tell me what I can and cannot do!"

"You are smart, but you are not fit for the Alpha position, Iris."

"Why? I have power, don't I?" she says with a confident smirk. "I have the entire packs' funds under my control. I'm in charge of most of our medical facilities. I rule our economy from one border to another. They can disobey me if they want to go penniless!"

Behind her, people exchange looks, somewhere between shock and fear. The White Moon clan's main income comes from the clinics, hospital, and labs we have, and indeed, Iris spearheads them all. There is one thing she can't control, however.

"Iris, we are werewolves, not humans. We don't just need money. We need hierarchy, relationships, trusted individuals. We need people strong enough to protect the pack, and some to rule it. We are a pack, a group. But you?"

I chuckle.

"You're just a selfish, self-centered little bitch."

"You swine! You–"

I slap her before she can finish her sentence.

I didn't hold back, and she stumbles a couple of steps back, astonished.

"How dare you–"

"You think you are an Alpha? Have it your way. Try to get past me or touch me. I'll show you how wrong you are!"

She growls furiously, and without thinking, runs at me. It's funny how conscious I am of our difference in strength now. Iris was never a fighter. I only need to take a step to the left to avoid getting hit. She is so mad and keeps coming at me, trying to throw punches.

Too bad she didn't pay better attention during training. I have no difficulties dodging anything she throws at me. For a few minutes, I keep dodging and she keeps attacking. She is using so much strength for nothing, it's pathetic. Having brains is of no use now. I am the stronger wolf. I keep going, but I make sure to fight back too: making her trip, hitting her back, and using my silver pole as a barrier. I am playing with her.

Iris is getting more and more exhausted while I flawlessly lead this fight where I want it. I don't even break a sweat, but Iris is out of breath in minutes. Behind her, people watch her with nothing left but pity and embarrassment. Such a weak wolf cannot be an Alpha. No way.

I can tell what they are thinking, but my mind is somewhere else. I wonder where the rest of the pack is, as well as Nora, the King, and Nate.

The gathering should have started by now. I don't even dare to mind-link them, closing my mind to focus on Iris. If anything happens, I don't want them to get distracted by my mind-link. I'll wait for the good news.

I hope.

"Iris!"

I stop fighting and turn to Chris. My cousin, completely lost, is watching me humiliate his sister until someone runs over to explain everything to him. His glare is already directed at his sister.

"What the fuck is wrong with you, Iris? Step away!"

"I won't! You are–"

"I am the Alpha of this pack!" roars her brother.

"*Elena.*"

I turn my head to Clark's mind-linking. Shouldn't he be at the gathering by now?

"*You were right. The Gold Moon expects the Opal Moon to follow them and betray us. Do whatever you need to, but make sure those traitors don't come here.*"

I glance in Chris' direction, but judging by his dark expression, my cousin got the info too. He growls even louder at his sister. Iris looks scared for the first time, stepping back. Did she not expect Chris to take my side and interfere? She looks around, but the Opal Moon people don't really look willing to follow her anymore.

I twirl the silver bar in my hand, reminding her about the additional threat.

"I can do this all day, Iris. Stay here or I'll really get mean and mad, cousin."

"Out of my way!"

Her anger isn't that hard to handle. She keeps struggling, trying to fight me off, but it's useless. I dodge every one of her attempts to kick or hit me back, except when I retaliate, I don't miss my target. I am a fucking fighter, no kidding. She may be smart and manipulative, but she is no match for me. I keep fighting her off, and Chris doesn't intervene. He knows his sister can use a good lesson.

"Elena, what about our money!" suddenly yells the guy from earlier. "We will never get it back from the Gold Moon clan!"

"Trust the new Luna. She won't agree to their terms, and the Blood Moon clan and the King will end all this."

I believe in Nora. Her idea will work.

Suddenly, we hear a huge explosion from afar. Everyone turns their heads toward… There's smoke where the gathering is happening! What the heck is going on? I turn to Chris, but he looks just as worried and clueless as me. Holy crap!

"*Clark! Clark, are you okay!*"

"*Elena, stay where you are! The Gold Moon is attacking the Blood Moon! Make sure to– Shit!*"

I lose him, and I'm freaking out. What the heck is going on over there? I don't dare to mind-link anyone else, what if they are distracted and take a hit because of me? I'm so powerless and furious! I turn to Iris, grabbing her collar.

"What do you know? Iris, what do you know about this!"

But she just laughs at me, despite her mouth covered in blood from my punches.

"How is it, Elena? Frustrating? Annoying? Well, you should get a taste too!"

I slap her, too pissed to control myself. Chris gets between us and grabs his sister by the throat.

"Iris, enough! Someone lock her away!"

Two of our men grab Iris and drag her away to Moon-Goddess-knows-where.

"Chris! Chris, you can't do this to me! I'm your older sister! I did this for us! I–"

"And have her shut the fuck up," he growls while turning his back on her to walk up to me.

I'm too worried to care about his sister anymore. I keep looking at the horizon in the direction of the Silver Stadium, scared. Chris puts a hand on my shoulder.

"He said to stay here."

"Yeah, but..."

Damn, fifty people from our pack are there, Nora is there, Nate is there! Reagan stands next to me, frowning.

"The Gold Moon had a trap prepared. Losing the Opal Moon will probably not help. Don't worry, kid, the clans are better than that."

That's the problem: What if they didn't manage to get everyone to ally? What if every pack is on its own? I take a deep breath and try to feel them. I can feel Clark's wolf, fighting. I check on our pack, but they are all fighting or fleeing the scene.

Then, Nora. She is panicked, but she is fine. For now. Moon Goddess, please protect her… I already lost my father today, I can't lose her too!

Suddenly, I realize. I don't feel Nathaniel's wolf. It's like a blank space. He can't be sleeping at such a time. Holy shit, why would he be unconscious? Now?

"*Elena, the fight's over! We are going to help evacuate people from here, a lot are injured! The Gold Moon clan's dead. Shit. There are bodies. The King is injured too.*"

"*What about his Luna? And his brother? Clark!*"

"*I'm busy! Meet me at the General Hospital!*"

I swear and turn to Chris, but he's already nodding. He was mind-linked and informed too.

"Go, Elena. I'll stay here and make sure everything's alright, okay? Don't worry about the Opal Moon anymore. But judging from the number of victims, they will probably send people to our hospital too, we'll be busy. Don't worry, just go."

I nod and start running without a second thought.

Moon Goddess, please let them be alright! Suddenly, as I'm close to the border, a bike's loud engine catches my attention. Reagan is waiting for me, handing me a helmet.

"Get on, kid, you'll get there faster."

Reagan rides as fast as possible to the General Hospital in the Blood Moon territory.

When we arrive, it's hell there. Dozens of people are running in and out, admitting more and more injured people. I jump off the bike and try to get a grasp of what's going on. Some people visibly fought other werewolves, while others were most likely injured in the explosion. Moon Goddess, how many people died? I run inside, trying to look for a clue, something, someone in this crowd who could tell me how Nora and Nate are doing. Even Boyan! He was there too, I just realize now.

I try to find Clark, but I don't know this place. I get so confused by all these corridors, and they are packed with medical staff and victims! Suddenly, I recognize a familiar silhouette across the crowd.

"Sylviana!"

The witch turns to me, surprised, while I do my best to get to her.

"Elena! What are you doing here! Are you okay?" she asks.

Who cares if I'm okay, I wasn't even at the scene! I want to ask her about Nathaniel when I recognize the guy right behind her. It's the King's youngest brother. He looks exhausted and a bit of a mess, but I unconsciously address him.

"Liam. Where is Nate?" I ask, my voice shaking.

"He's in surgery."

Oh, Moon Goddess. In surgery? Why? What happened to him! I can't hold back my tears, I start sobbing loudly, panicked. Why is he in surgery?! Sylviana tries to calm me down, rubbing my hand.

"He's fine, Elena, he will make it."

"Oh, Moon Goddess, Nate…" I sob. "What happened?"

The Good Witch holds my hand a bit tighter, while Liam Black steps away to make a call.

"The Gold Moon clan attacked despite Nora's attempts to calm them down. She had most of the clans agree to an alliance when they attacked."

"We heard an explosion."

"They planted a bomb ahead of the gathering; it took everyone by surprise. The clans fought the Gold Moon and Rising Moon clans, as well as a few others, and I intervened too. We won, but… there are a lot of casualties. The King is gravely injured as well, and Nora's gone."

What the hell, Nora is gone? Before I can even ask, Liam Black is back, with a furious expression that is scarily similar to his brother's.

"It's bad, really bad. The psycho who was after Nora, it's him. He took her and shot my brothers."

What?

"You've got to be kidding me?!" I yell.

Some sicko took Nora? And Nate and the King were shot? What the fuck happened there! And I couldn't even help!

"I'm not," he replies, annoyed. "We have to find Nora, fast!"

I focus on my wolf, trying to feel my cousin. Shit, it's usually so easy, but now…

"I can't! She must be unconscious, I can't reach her at all!"

"Maybe I can help."

Some shady guy just appeared behind Liam. He looks like a junkie that's about to collapse at any moment. Liam and he start talking in low voices, and Sylviana turns to me again.

"Elena, look at me. Liam and I will find Nora. Go and find Nathaniel. He's injured, and I believe he needs you by his side. His surgery is almost over, but you should stay with him while Liam and I are gone, alright? Don't worry, we'll find Nora, okay?"

I nod, unable to say anything to that. I can't believe it. I try to calm down, but I keep crying mindlessly. Sylviana and Liam get busy with finding Nora, while I rush to the nurses office I saw earlier.

"Excuse me! I'm looking for Nathaniel Black?" I ask the first nurse I see.

"Black? He's still in surgery."

But another woman behind her, a werewolf, shakes her head.

"Not that one. The King is still in surgery, honey, but Nathaniel Black just came out. He's in room 238, second floor, blondie. But you can't go in like that!"

The hell I can't! I'm already gone, running to the second floor. In front of his room, among a little group of people, I only recognize Isaac, his best friend, who's frowning.

"You… What are you doing here?"

"How is he?" I ask, ignoring his question.

He nods.

"He's doing fine, for someone who took two silver bullets. One in the arm and the other in the stomach, but his healing ability is doing what it should. He's still unconscious, though."

"Can I… go in?"

He seems to hesitate, then nods.

Of course, they gave him one of the best rooms. It's spacious, but not too big. Just enough for him to be alone and have room for visitors. Well, it's just me, actually. I choke up when I see him, lying on the bed. Moon Goddess… He has a lot of bandages, and a scar on the left side of his head where they had to shave his head to stitch him. I want to cry again when I see him like this. I stumble to the stool next to him and grab his hand, mine shaking.

"Moon Goddess, Nate."

What happened to him? Who did this? Fuck, I can't believe I wasn't there. I start crying without thinking, though I try not to make much noise. My father died, the man I love is lying in a hospital bed, and Nora is missing! What else could go wrong?! I keep silently crying those tears that I have been holding back since earlier while holding his hand. If something had happened to him…

I wake up a bit later, completely confused. Oh, right, the hospital. Where is Nate? The bed is empty, but as I look around, I realize Daniel is with me.

"Danny?"

"Hey, babe. Are you okay? Damn, your eyes are so–"

"Where is he? Nate? Where did he–"

"He's fine. He woke up an hour ago, but he asked me not to wake you. He went to check on his brother. The King is in bad shape, Elena. We don't know if he's going to make it."

Oh, Moon Goddess, no, no.

"What about Nora?" I ask him, suddenly stressed out. "She was missing! They said–"

"She's back. Liam Black and Sylviana brought her to the hospital and she had surgery. She was shot in the leg, but apparently, she's okay. She's… changed a bit, but…"

She changed? I get up and leave the room, Daniel behind me. We ask for the King's room, I know Nora will be there. On my way there, I almost run into some guy who is leaving the room.

"Ex…"

He looks at me strangely, before shaking his head and leaving. I turn to Daniel.

"Who was that?"

"Elena, I think that was William Blue, your… other cousin."

I didn't even realize. Now that I think about it, he did have dark hair and blue eyes like her! I can't stop to think about that, though. I almost run into the room, only to find Nora, alone with her mate. She's silently crying. She barely looks at me.

"Moon Goddess, Nora. How are you?" I ask while looking at the King.

He was so scary before, but now… he's obviously in bad shape. How bad were his injuries? He's got so much machinery linked to his body, it's unsettling. But the worst thing is Nora's expression.

"He… They say he won't wake up…" she sobs.

Chapter 26

It's been a rough six days. Nora just woke up yesterday, but her mate is still in a coma, and this morning, I buried my dad. We lost so many werewolves in this battle and the damages… The stadium and its surroundings are still ravaged, like a gaping wound within the city. Silver City is sad these days. The sky is dark, and we get rain from time to time. With the King in a coma and Nora in the hospital, all the Alphas are helping each other with the aftermath of the battle.

I know Nathaniel is stepping in for his brother Damian as the head of their pack, but I haven't seen him since. I've come to realize this is no coincidence, but I'm still unsure why he would be avoiding me at such a time. Is he afraid I'll distract him? Or…

When I show up at the office of the Black Corporation that evening, the secretary behind the welcome desk looks unsure and tired.

"Excuse me," she says, "Mr. Black is busy."

"Is he upstairs?" I ask.

"Yes, but he's–"

"Fine."

"Miss Whitewood! You can't!"

But I ignore her and walk to the elevators, hitting the button to go all the way up to his brother's office. Since the King is still in a coma, I bet Nate will have directly taken over. When I walk into their office, I notice he's busy, but Isaac and Tonia are also there. They both look surprised to see me.

"Hey, blondie," says Isaac. "It's been a while."

"Hello, Isaac, Tonia. Mind if I talk to Nathaniel for a few minutes?"

"We're busy, Elena."

I glare at him. Too busy to see the woman carrying your child? Tonia and I exchange a look, and within a few silent seconds, she understands and walks out. Isaac sighs and follows her out, too.

Nathaniel crosses his arms.

"Great. I never meant to replace my brother, but now I can really see I don't have his authority."

"So you still have some humor. Now I can see the resemblance between you and Liam a bit."

He shakes his head, annoyed.

"Why are you here, Elena? I don't mean to be rude, but with both Damian and Nora in the hospital, I have a lot to deal with, and no one is easy to deal with these days, including but not limited to your Alpha, who hates me."

I am not going to feel sorry for him. Clark is still my godfather and having to deal with the jerk who got me pregnant on a daily basis is probably testing his patience.

"You've been avoiding me."

He takes a deep breath in, not hiding his foul mood.

"No, I've been busy, and–"

"Don't give me that, Nate. Being busy never held you back before. So, what is it? I went to see you at the hospital, but when I woke up, you were gone."

"I was needed elsewhere."

"I get that, but it's been a few days now. Even Clark found time to come back to our pack. You're avoiding me."

He sighs. Does he think I haven't noticed? He's looking anywhere but in my direction!

"Nathaniel."

This time, I'm growling and using my Alpha Aura. He won't avoid me like that.

But to my surprise, he growls back. I think this is the first time Nate's ever growled at me.

"Enough with your insolence, Elena," he says. "If you have something to tell me, say it now, or be gone. Despite what you think, I really have more important priorities than you."

I'm speechless. What does he mean? Nathaniel has never talked to me like this before, or sent me away. He's always been the one to hold me back! What is this?

"Nate, what…?"

"Tell me again, Elena. The truth this time. Who is the baby's father?"

"It's you! Of course, it's you, for the hundredth time, I…"

He turns around and suddenly slams some files onto his desk, looking angry and… hurt.

"I don't understand how you can keep lying with a straight face like that, Elena. You knew you'd get caught sooner or later. I mean, maybe you didn't want to believe it wasn't mine at first, but when I told you the truth about my condition, you could have just apologized and said the truth!"

What the heck? I take a few steps to his desk, grabbing those papers. They are from the White Moon clinic, it's the paternity test from our samples that Daniel had sent. I check it out. Moon Goddess, the results…

How can it be negative? Nathaniel is the father! I check and recheck it, but it doesn't change a thing. According to the results, Nathaniel is not the biological father of my baby. I'm in such shock, it takes me a couple of seconds to understand… Iris.

It has to be my cousin. As of today, she's pending trial for her betrayal, and because we are so short-handed, she still runs all our facilities. Iris knew I was conducting a paternity test to prove Nate's the father, I bet she did this to punish me. Fuck.

I look at Nathaniel and his eyes that are full of anger and sadness. He thinks I betrayed him. That I slept with someone else, probably Levi or Diego, and lied to him. That I'm bearing someone else's child. This is so pathetic. I start crying silently, but it's only adding to his anger.

"Don't you cry, Elena! You're the one who lied! I gave you so many chances to say the truth, but now you're feeling sorry? Won't you even apologize?"

"Those papers are lying, Nate. You're the father. My cousin Iris did this, she–"

"No, no, enough with the excuses, Elena. I already gave you the benefit of the doubt when Daniel asked to retest my condition and give you samples for a paternity test. Now I'm done listening to your lies."

"Nate, I swear on Moon Goddess, this baby is–"

"ELENA, ENOUGH!"

I have no choice but to take a couple of steps back, shocked by his Alpha Aura thrown at me. I've never seen him so angry, and I've never been so scared of him. His wolf is so much like the King's: all dark, growling and glaring at me.

He really thinks I cheated on him, that I lied. I keep crying, tears rolling down my cheeks. I can't think of any words to say. He's too mad and too hurt to listen. I'm not going to convince him like this. I sob painfully, but that irritates him.

"Elena, we're done. I don't want to see you if you don't want to apologize and tell me the truth."

"I never said anything but the truth, Nathaniel."

He looks at me, shocked, but when he's about to yell at me again, I turn on my heels and leave this place.

I burst out in tears and cry loudly in the elevator, so loud it echoes in my ears. Why, why, why? It wasn't supposed to end like this! I thought the test would prove he's the dad, he'd be happy, and we could be happy together.

Moon Goddess, my baby. What am I going to do with her? Her father won't believe she's his, and my pack will reject her! I keep crying as I leave the building, and with no idea where to go. I don't want Nora to see me in this state. I don't even feel like seeing Daniel, he's helping at the hospital, there is so much work to do. I don't have the heart to call and tell him. He will be so devastated when I tell him Iris messed up the paternity test.

I slowly walk back to the White Moon clan, to our apartment. I feel like a ghost, walking in silence, by myself, a step away from the real world. I can barely breathe. All I can keep thinking is, what will I do from now on? I could ask Nora, but she's already overwhelmed by the King's state.

It's already late and dark when I go to my room, feeling like a stranger in my own place. It's like I can't recognize the smells, the pictures on the walls, anything that was so familiar. Everything that used to make me feel better is gone. I try to wipe the tears off my face, trying to think straight. I've reached the lowest levels of sadness, like my heart is getting swallowed by ice. I want to cry again, but I'm too tired for that.

"Elena?"

I turn around. To my surprise, Sylviana and Daniel are there, coming out of his room. My best friend's eyes are red. I frown, a bit lost. He runs up to me, however, and hugs me without a word. I don't understand.

"I already explained it to him," says Sylviana.

She knew that the results had come out negative? I can't hold back new tears as I keep looking at the witch.

"He's the father," I repeat uncontrollably. "Nathaniel is…"

"I know, Elena," she whispers, walking up to me to caress my hair, "but he won't accept it now. I'm really sorry, Elena."

"It's okay, babe. I'm here."

Daniel's words comfort me a little, but they can't fill that void in my heart. I'm too sad, too worried, too disappointed. When he lets go of me, I realize I won't be able to go on like this. Just when I'm about to talk, Sylviana takes my hand.

"Nora went into a coma again."

I frown.

"What? Why? I saw her yesterday, she was fine!"

"She couldn't take it anymore, Elena. I can't explain it to you, but… she went back into a coma, and the King woke up."

Damian Black woke up? I heard the medical staff had said he was not going to make it. What did Nora do? How did she do that? I have a feeling her fated mate's improved condition is because of Nora, but I don't understand.

"Elena. Nora is in a deep coma. Her power will go… dormant."

I frown. Dormant? Meaning the Dark Witch won't be able to feel it anymore. Then… I put a hand on my tummy.

"She will be able to feel my baby?"

"Her aura, yes. For now, she is still concealed in your belly, but…"

"When will Nora wake up?" I ask, realizing that's what all this is about.

If my cousin wakes up before my baby is born, it would be fine, but if she doesn't… To my surprise, Sylviana shakes her head.

"I can't tell, Elena. But no matter how many times I try to see, Nora won't be back before your baby's birth."

I take a few seconds to handle the shock. It means Nora will stay in the coma at least five or six more months.

Piece by piece, everything adds up, doing the math I've been too blind to realize. My cousin is in a coma, my baby will be more in danger than ever, and with no one but me to protect her. I chuckle nervously.

"It's just like when Reagan saved me."

Daniel shakes his head, confused.

"What are you talking about, babe?"

"I have to leave."

"What? But aside from the White Moon, the packs–"

"I'm not leaving the White Moon clan, Danny; I'm leaving Silver City."

My best friend stares at me, speechless. I take a deep breath. It's like I'm feeling better now that I've come to that conclusion.

"Danny, it's the only way. The White Moon pack won't accept my child, and Nathaniel isn't going to help me. With Nora in a coma, I can't do anything but leave. As soon as she's born, this baby will become a target. I don't want that."

"But..."

He stumbles on his words, unable to come up with something. I exchange a glance with Sylviana over his shoulder. I don't know how far ahead the witch had planned, but I know she saw it coming. She knew it would come to this.

I put my hair back, trying to get my ideas in order. I need to stop crying and think rationally. The truth hurts, but it's right there in front of me. I have to leave.

I turn to Sylviana, holding Daniel's hand.

"I just want to see Nora before I go."

"Wait! Elena, you want to leave now?" asks Danny, shocked.

"Daniel, every second I stay in the same city as Nathaniel, I feel worse. My father isn't here anymore either. With Nora in a coma, you're the only one I have left here..."

"... But! What about Clark, and Chris, and Boyan..."

I smile and hug him once more.

"It's okay, Danny. Clark is just making up excuses to not banish me yet, and I know Chris will understand. You can explain to Boyan and your family, too."

"What will you do! If you leave here alone, you..."

"She won't be alone," says Sylviana. "I will go with her, at least until I'm sure the baby is born safely. Elena will need my help and protection to settle somewhere the Dark Witch won't find her too."

I nod. I feel a bit better knowing our witch will help me. I need to ask Reagan too but I'm pretty sure my mentor will follow me anyway. I go to my room and grab a backpack. Daniel is crying, but he helps me gather some clothes and necessities.

"I can't believe it. This is so unfair."

He keeps mumbling and sobbing, but I don't have the heart to answer him. It only takes a few minutes for me to get all my things. I leave a lot here, but I have no idea when I'll be back, honestly. It may only be a few months, but it could be years. I take a deep breath.

I look around our apartment one last time before Daniel closes the door, and that's it.

This is so crazy, yet I'm feeling a lot better as we walk through the city, leaving the White Moon clan's borders to head to the Black General Hospital. It's the middle of the night, and I doubt Nate will be there.

Sylviana and Daniel wait for me outside. I silently walk up to Nora's room.

Just as I'm about to walk in, a shadow suddenly comes out. I hold my breath. Damian Black. The King looks at me, his eyes even darker than usual. Damn, he looks healthy but so sad. We exchange looks, and I'm very uneasy. Should I say something? I didn't think he'd be here at night too. But without a word, he steps aside and walks away. Is this okay?

Something strange happened here. Her bed is surrounded by roses, and I suspect Sylviana is no stranger to this eerie setting. My cousin looks like the modern version of Sleeping Beauty, lying in her hospital bed surrounded by roses as white as her new, strange hair. A huge brown wolf is sleeping at the foot of her bed, and Liam Black is snoring in the chair across the room.

I sit next to her on the bed and take her hand to caress it softly.

"I'm so sorry, Nora," I whisper. "I wish you were here. I wish I could tell you goodbye in person. I… I hope you'll be back soon. They all miss you. I'll miss you the most. Do you know how much you're loved, Nora? He is coming every day to see you… Liam and Bobo too. Everyone loves you. They are all waiting for you… I hope you will be back soon. I'm so sorry we have to part this way. I hope you'll understand, Nora. We will see each other again, I promise. … Forgive me."

I feel like crying again, but this is only a goodbye, not a farewell. I know I'll see her again. I know they will take good care of her. I stay a bit longer, holding her hand until I've calmed down. If only I could borrow a bit of your strength, Nora.

I place a long kiss on her forehead, taking one last good look at her. The next time I see her, she'll be awake, bright and happy. I really pray for it.

When I leave the room, still teary, I meet Damian Black outside again. But this time, he stands in front of me in the corridor.

"I'm sorry, I have to go…" I stutter.

"Take this."

To my surprise, he hands me a thick bundle of bills. Just by the number on the first one, I can tell it's a lot! What is this? I glance at him, surprised. Why would the King give me money? Did he hear me talking to Nora?

"I don't understand…"

"You'll need it. Nora thinks of you as a sister… and you're carrying my niece."

I frown. How did he..?

"Sylviana, Liam, and I talked a lot when I woke up," he explains.

He knows about my baby? Why would Sylviana tell him? I hesitate but take the money. If he knows, he probably already made up his mind about this.

"Thanks."

I wonder what to add, but before I can, he's already walking back into Nora's room. I guess that's it. I put the money in my jacket and leave the hospital.

Sylviana and Daniel are still waiting outside, and I mind-link Reagan so she can join me at the border. We walk there in silence, only Daniel sobbing softly.

When we finally reach it, I turn around and pull my best friend into a big hug.

"Be careful outside, okay? Don't drink, don't get sick. Sleep a lot, okay? And… if anything happens…"

"Don't worry, Danny. I'll keep my phone just in case. I'll text you where I am when I can, okay? Please explain everything to your family. I'm sorry I can't stay longer, but I won't have the courage to leave if I don't do it tonight."

He nods but cries again. Oh, poor Danny. I take his hand.

"Daniel, you're my best, best friend in the whole world. I love you, babe."

"I love you too, babe," he sobs.

"See you soon, okay?" I say with the bit of a smile I can gather.

"It'd better be soon. I want to see my goddaughter. She'll be so pretty."

"I'll do my best. Take care, babe. Don't fight too much with Bobo, and eat properly."

He's about to say something, but he's crying too much to make any sense.

I hug him long and tight.

"See you, babe."

"See ya."

I part with him and start walking away.

Away from Daniel, away from my pack, away from Silver City. I'm crying hard and ugly. It's so hard to go this way. Sylviana takes my hand, and Reagan is by my side too. It will be okay. I'll be okay…

Part II

Chapter 27

I double-check the recipe from the book, but it should be okay. A couple more minutes, and then I can add the veggies. I turn around, dancing to the soft jazz music coming from the old radio. It's sunny outside, just how I like it. I sit down to check my texts when I hear running steps. I told her a billion times not to run…

Suddenly, two small hands cover my eyes.

"Guess who!"

I smile immediately. I start patting the little hands as if I was wondering.

"Hmm… Who could it be? Two small paws… The smell of wild berries… Is it a baby bear?"

I hear the cutest baby giggling.

"No! Guess again!"

"Really? Let's see… Tiny fingers and small nails… Is it a baby monkey?"

"Hehe, you're wrong! Try again!"

"Oh! I know that little laugh. Is it my baby star?"

"Yes!

She laughs and I grab her, sitting her on my lap to tickle her. She tries to evade me, but she is way too tiny to escape me! My daughter is the most adorable thing in the world, of course. When I finally stop torturing her, she is still laughing, pushing her honey-blonde hair back. She looks up at me, with her father's sky-blue eyes.

"Mommy, I'm hungry. What are you making?"

"Your favorite Bolognese pasta, with Auntie Nora's secret ingredient," I answer while styling her hair into two little ponytails.

She turns her head toward the stove, but then, I see her frown.

"Carrots? But I hate carrots!"

"Baby, you need to eat your vegetables. And It's just going to be tiny bits."

She frowns, but she is eyeing the carrots with suspicion, thinking it over.

"You will make them super tiny?" she asks me.

"Super, super tiny, I promise. So tiny you won't see them."

"Okay, then."

She is still pouting a bit. Moon Goddess, she is so cute I want to eat her all up instead of the pasta! I kiss her chubby cheek, making her chuckle again, and she immediately wraps her tiny arms around my neck to kiss me back.

"What did you do this morning, my little star?"

"I draw bunnies! Wait here, Mommy, I will show you!"

And off she goes again, jumping off my knees to run and grab her drawing from wherever she left it. She probably played in the garden too, seeing how the bottom of her denim jumper is all dirty. When she comes back, she proudly shows me her drawing and starts explaining the names she gave to each of her colored bunnies.

"Stella, baby, you remember how to say bunny with your hands?"

"Yes!"

She brings two fingers from each hand up her head, mimicking a bunny's ears. I clap and do it too.

"That's right, baby!"

"Mommy, I'm better than you at talking with my hands!" she says, acting all proud. "Look, I can do a lot of animals too!"

We start having a little contest, but indeed, she is even better than I am at sign language now. When she gets tired of it, she runs off again to grab her coloring pencils. Dad told me that I was a little energy pill when I was young too, so I guess she gets that from me, but Estelle is a well-disciplined kid. She very rarely throws tantrums, and she doesn't really argue when I ask her to do something, even if she dislikes it.

The only thing I'm worried about is her insecurity issues. Sometimes, she asks for hugs all of a sudden and asks if I will leave her. I have no idea where she gets that from. Is it because she doesn't have a father? She asks about him sometimes. She has a photo of Nathaniel, one she loved from my phone, so I had it printed for her to keep. I didn't want to lie to her and tell her she doesn't have a dad.

"Mommy! Is it ready? I'm really, really hungry now!"

"Yes, yes. Go wash your hands and we can eat!"

"Okay!" she says, running off to the bathroom.

While I'm busy grabbing our plates, my phone rings. Before I can even move, Estelle is running over to grab it. She is too young to read, but she recognizes the picture.

"It's Dada! Hi, Dada!"

She starts happily chatting with her godfather, telling him all about her day. She has never met him physically yet, but they talk so often it doesn't really make any difference. Daniel is crazy about my little star. Every time he calls, he asks when I am coming back to Silver City with Estelle.

I don't know if I'm ready yet. I miss Daniel a lot, and all of my friends too. I miss Silver City, the Arts District, the Latin neighborhood. I know Nora woke up two years after I had gone, but I wasn't ready to go back. Going back would mean seeing Estelle's father again, and I don't know if I can handle that. She looks so much like him, I guess he'll finally believe me once they meet.

I watch my little star, on the phone. I wonder what my life would be like without her. Estelle is so well-behaved, sometimes I wonder if I really raised her alone. Well, Reagan comes often, too. My mentor never stays around, but she's never too far away either. She drops by whenever she feels like it and lives her life as a wolf most of the time.

We live in a large forest, miles away from Silver City. I can't remember how long we had walked until we got here. Sylviana knew about this old abandoned house, and in a few days of work between the three of us, it became perfectly fine for us to live in. It's even a bit too big for just a woman and child.

"Mommy, it smells bad again."

Holy shit! I turn around and jump on the casserole. Damn it, I let it burn again. How come I can never get even the simplest of dishes right? Estelle walks up to me and frowns, looking at my half-burned Bolognese.

"Sorry, baby. Don't worry, Mommy will eat the burnt parts."

"It's okay, Mommy, I like the crunchy parts!"

Moon Goddess, I love this child of mine. She even loves my burnt pasta. She sits down to eat, grabbing her fork and eagerly waiting. Like any werewolf kid, she's an energy pill and a big eater. I fill her plate, but everything's gone in a few minutes, and she smiles, satisfied, licking the leftover tomato sauce off her lips.

"Mommy, can I have a magic cake for dessert? The one with pink sprinkles!"

I smile. The only thing I never fail at: her favorite magic cake.

"Okay, baby, but…"

I stop talking, uneasy.

I have an odd feeling. My wolf is unsettled too, looking around for a threat.

"Mommy?"

After a few seconds of complete silence, the branches from the trees on the terrace all begin crackling at once. Holy crap!

"Estelle, come!"

I grab my daughter and run across the house, grabbing her little backpack from our room.

"Mommy, what is it? Mommy!"

I don't have time to explain. We need to leave this place and run.

It's Sylviana's signal. She said the trees would do this if the Dark Witch was near! I didn't think she would really find us! Estelle is scared and struggles to keep up with me, but I keep running until we're out of the house, a few feet away, and get on one knee in front of her to help her put her backpack on.

"Stella, listen to Mommy very carefully. We need to leave the house and run, baby. We are going to run very, very fast to the east, okay? We don't make noise, and we keep running until Mommy says stop."

"Mommy, why are we running? Why are we leaving home? Mommy, I'm scared."

Seeing the tears in my daughter's scared eyes breaks my heart, but I really don't have time to explain! Every second matters now. I shake my head.

"Estelle, don't cry, baby, okay? Just trust Mommy, you will be okay. You run very, very fast, like we did with Reagan, okay?"

She nods, a bit distraught, and I encourage her with a little smile.

"Alright, let's go, baby."

I start running and Estelle does her best to run after me. She's fast, for a four-year-old, but after a while, I have no choice but to carry her to keep up the pace. I hear her cry silently against my neck. My poor baby… I can't stop and comfort her, though. I know we don't have much time, and we absolutely can't stop if I want to outrun the Dark Witch, or at least reach Silver City in time.

I can feel her. It's like a dark shadow, some evil presence behind us. A cold wind chasing my every step. As I keep running through the trees, I also see her water streaming nearby. I need to avoid sources of water while heading east.

My wolf wants to shape-shift, but if I do, I won't be able to carry Estelle! I keep running, trying to think of what to do, how to get out of here. I still can't see Silver City, how far away are we? I feel like I've been running for hours!

I try to focus and reach out to Nora, my cousin. She would be the first one that I could reach out to as soon as I'm close enough… Back then, she could mind-link people from miles away. I really hope it works the other way too. I keep calling out to her with my wolf while holding on tightly to Estelle, running and watching out for nearby water sources.

"*Elena!*"

Finally! She heard me. We are close enough.

Right when I think things are getting better, I feel a sudden rumbling on my left. Crap, crap. The witch is catching up to us! If only Sylviana was here, or at least Reagan so I could give her my daughter! Where could she be at a time like this? I stop, looking around.

"Mommy?"

I finally find it.

A little opening in a large tree, just big enough for Estelle to hide. I take her there and have her sit inside the trunk. She is terrified, but I take her hand. We don't have much time.

"Estelle, listen to Mommy very carefully. You stay here, and you stay hidden, baby, okay?"

"Why?"

"Mommy has to go a different way, but don't worry, I won't leave you alone, okay? I will be back. Estelle, you remember how to talk with your wolf, right, baby?"

She nods, her eyes still teary. Thank Moon Goddess she's already been able to mind-link for a couple of months now. Maybe it's her Royal blood, but she's a precocious one. I see her frown a bit, and I finally feel her inner wolf, like it's waking up.

"*Yes, Mommy.*"

"*Good girl. Now I want you to not talk, Estelle, not at all. Just use your wolf's voice, like Mommy, and call Auntie Nora.*"

"*Auntie Nora?*"

"*That's right, baby. You call Auntie Nora with all your heart, okay?*"

"*Can I call Dada too?*"

I shake my head, desperate. Estelle doesn't belong to the White Moon clan; she doesn't belong to any clan! I don't think she can mind-link other alphas or wolves like Nora and I can, she can only call her kin… Oh Moon Goddess, I didn't even think of it earlier!

"Baby, you call Auntie Nora or Daddy with all your puppy heart, okay?"

"Daddy too?"

"Yes, baby," I tell her while putting my jacket around her. *"You call Nora and Daddy with your wolf until Mommy comes to get you, okay?"*

"Why can't I call you, Mommy?"

Oh, Moon Goddess, how do I explain to her? I need to get away, this might be the only chance to lure that witch away from her!

"Mommy knows where you are, baby. I have to go away, but… it will be okay, just promise me you will stay here, okay? You'll be a good girl and stay here, right?"

"I promise…" she whispers.

I take a deep breath and hold my daughter one last time, very tight against my heart. Moon Goddess, I love her so, so much. We are both crying silently. She's four years old and a bright girl, but I don't know how much of this she really understands.

With a heavy heart, I give her one last glance and run in the opposite direction, towards the north. I stop calling Nora for help, and pray to Moon Goddess that she can find my daughter instead.

I head west, shape-shifting as soon as I can. I'm faster, and letting my Alpha Aura out, hoping the Dark Witch will take the bait.

Finally, I hear it. A rumbling coming after me. That's right, bitch, follow me. Let's see how fast your damned water can be. I run faster, trying to mind-link Reagan at the same time.

"Kid! Where are you!"

"Headed north, Reagan!"

"Okay, I feel you! On my way!"

I keep running, praying for my baby to be okay. Nora will find you, baby, don't worry.

Suddenly, a sharp pain strikes me. I'm thrown several yards to my left, before violently hitting a tree. Holy shit, it hurts. I'm dizzy from the shock, but my shoulder is painful as fuck. I look, and my fur is covered in red. Damn it.

"Are you done running, dog?"

I turn my head, but my vision is all red and blurry. The woman walks up to me, I can hear her annoying laugh. Damn her.

"You... You're not the one I want. What are you, a halfling? Interesting. I've never seen a half-werewolf before..."

I feel her walk up to me and grab my neck. I try to bite her, and she takes her hand off.

"Feisty. But lucky for you, I need you alive so you can tell me where you left your offspring."

There's a sharp pain again in my shoulder, as she steps on it.

"Where is it? Where is the Royal?"

"*Fuck you!*" I growl back.

"*Elena!*"

Out of the corner of my eye, I see the old gray wolf jump in, and the witch screeches. I hear something like a fight, but I struggle to get back on my feet and retreat. I can't stay here. I'm too injured to fight. If only I could...

"Enough!"

I hear a yap, and a wolf's body falls in front of me, inert. No, no, no, not Reagan.

I'm suddenly dragged from behind while I struggle to stay with my mentor. I feel trapped, a weight on my body like a huge rock.

"I'll make you talk, wolf. You'll talk!"

A horrible pain pierces my legs, something sharp pinning them to the ground. I growl, furious and blinded by the pain. Moon Goddess, I swear she could kill me a hundred times, I'd never, ever give my daughter to that bitch!

"You damn stubborn...! Fine! I don't need you anyway, I only need the child..."

Chapter 28

"Man, you need a break."

Seven, eight… I keep ignoring Isaac and focus on my exercise, feeling the strain in my arms. He just keeps walking back and forth next to me. Damn, he's so annoying.

"No, you need a life, actually. Seriously, you're scaring me."

Thirteen, fourteen… I make sure to breathe in and out, despite the sweat on my forehead. I glance at the timer. Damn, it's been an hour already. I feel like I've only been here for five minutes. Maybe ten, since Isaac keeps ranting non-stop.

"Are you listening to me, Nate?"

"More like I am hearing you. I'm fine, Isaac. You can tell that to whoever sent you."

He growls,

"You're not fine, man. Honestly? I don't know if I liked it better when you were depressed or drunk every hour of the day. Now you're sober but you're a freaking machine."

"Thanks."

"No, no, no, man, that's not a compliment. For real, Nate. You wake up at 5:00 a.m. every morning, workout for two hours, get to work at 8:00 a.m., work until 8:00 p.m. with only a fifteen-minute lunch break, go clubbing, party like an animal, and start all over again. You know who sleeps as little as you? Insomniacs!"

I rarely wake up after 4:00 a.m. He doesn't need to know, though.

"I am fine. I'm over it, taking my life back, okay?"

"That's not a life, Nate, it's a freaking clock. Normal people, even workaholics, sleep late on weekends, watch crappy soap operas in their free time, eat burnt mac and cheese for dinner, and see their family for brunch, not kill themselves on a freaking elliptical!"

"So it was Nora," I growl.

My sister-in-law was probably worried since I ignored her invitation. Again. Damn it. I put the weights back and stand up to face him.

"Isaac, stop making a fuss. I just missed one brunch with my brother and Nora. It doesn't mean anything."

He shakes his head.

"One brunch? Nate, you haven't seen them in days! The boss is worried, and you've turned down all their invitations for two weeks. Do you even remember what your nephew looks like?"

Here he goes with the guilt trip. I didn't mean to worry Damian or Nora. But somehow, it hurts to see them. Since my sister-in-law awoke from her coma, they have been living the perfect family life. A big house, a son, and now a second kid on the way.

Meanwhile, I've been trying to drown myself. First, it was alcohol. When Damian told me about Elena, I couldn't believe it. It hurt so bad. I kept replaying my fight with her, how I never wanted to see her again. I didn't think she would really leave! Her words still haunt me, like some dark movie playing over and over in my head. I kept drinking, but it didn't change a thing. Sober or drunk, it hurt too much to think about her, yet I was unable to forget her. I even tried sleeping with other women, only to realize how useless it was. I couldn't go back in time to when I didn't love her.

Damian was angry with me, so was Liam. My brothers couldn't stand my dangerous behavior anymore. The more I drank, the more reckless I got. I almost died in a car accident last year. I had to promise I wouldn't drink another drop of alcohol anymore. Nora was worried for me too. She invited me over again and again to make sure I was fine, eating properly, getting decent sleep. After James was born, however, it became harder, because seeing my nephew reminded me of Elena's child.

We never say her name. They know how painful it is for me. It's no use, anyway. She's gone.

"I'll call Nora after I'm done with my workout, Isaac, okay?"

My Beta and best friend was frowning, doubtful, so I ignored him and moved onto the rower. He follows me, of course.

"It's not just Nora, Nate. How about you take a few days off work too, huh? I'm the HR Director and I know you haven't taken a day off in months!"

"Damian took days off to watch Nora and James. I can take over, I'm fine."

He rolls his eyes at me.

"You stubborn prick! The Black Corporation isn't going to collapse if you and Damian take a day off! We have Neal, Thaddeus, Victoria; they all work for you, you know!"

"Fine!" I growl, annoyed at him. "I'll take a day off tomorrow."

"Oh, so you will finally rest on a Sunday?"

Shit. Is it Saturday already? I lost count. I keep rowing, hoping he'll finally go away, but he stays there with his arms crossed. Don't tell me he is really going to wait and watch me call Nora?

"Seriously, Isaac, don't you have a wife and a kid to--"

"*Daddy...*"

I stop, the handle flying out of my hands. What was that? I swear I...

"Nate? What's wrong?"

I wait a few seconds, but it's gone. I look around, but there aren't any kids in the gym, of course, it's off-limits to minors. Did it come from outside? Or one of the TV screens?

"... Nothing. I thought I heard something."

I must be more tired than I thought. I get up, grabbing my towel and heading to the locker room, Isaac right behind me.

"Come have dinner at our place. Leah and Julian would be happy to see you."

"I'm good, Isaac. Anyway, your–"

Before I can end my sentence, my phone rings. It's Damian. I sigh and answer my older brother.

"Yes, Damian, I didn't mean to ignore Nora, I--"

"Nate, it's Elena. She just mind-linked Nora."

I stop breathing for a second... Elena? Elena mind-linked Nora? Why? Doesn't that mean she's close? Nora always said they couldn't reach each other because of the distance! I don't even know what to say.

"She said Elena's daughter mind-linked her too."

Elena's...? My heartbeat's thumping in my ears. Why would Elena mind-link Nora now? She's coming back? And why would she...

"*Daddy...*"

A chill goes down my spine. This time, I heard it, I really heard it. My wolf is on all fours, searching around, restless. Where is she? Isaac's about to say something, but I start running, leaving all of my things behind except for my phone, which is stuck to my ear.

"Nora's trying to focus on her, but she just lost the mind-link with Elena. Her daughter's–"

"Damian, I feel her too."

I almost choke up with those words, but I'm rushing outside, a confused Isaac following right behind me. My wolf's telling me to head west, and I'm running there. How could Elena's child mind-link me? She shouldn't be able to, right?

"Nathaniel?" calls my brother.

"I'm going… I… I'm headed to the west…" I say, trying to save my breath.

"Nate, what's going on?" asks Isaac, concerned.

"Just come!" I yell to him, annoyed.

I don't even know myself! Why is Elena's child able to mind-link me? And why can't I feel her mother?

"*Nathaniel?*"

"*Nora! Can you feel her? Elena? I can't feel her!*"

"*I know, I could feel her too until a few minutes ago, but... I don't know what's going on... I can still feel Estelle, but it's very faint...*"

Estelle. Her daughter's name is Estelle. I nod and keep running, following my instincts exactly where my wolf begs me to go.

"Nate, I don't want Nora out in her condition. I'm sending Liam with you."

I nod. Not only is she the Luna and needs to stay in Silver City for her protection, but she's six months pregnant, so she can't shape-shift. Damn, he has to send that idiot. Him and his witch girlfriend have been giving me hell since Elena left. Okay, I don't care for now. I just need to find Elena and her daughter. I don't want to be too occupied with mind-linking Nora, the connection to… to Estelle is already so faint, I'm worried I'll lose it.

"*Daddy... Auntie Nora...*"

I can sense her cries, and it drives my wolf crazy. I finally reach our border and run outside, right into the forest. She can't be that far.

A black wolf joins me, but I don't glance at my brother, we're both too focused on running as fast as we can for now. Something's definitely wrong. I feel a rumbling underground, and realize Sylviana's probably following us too. Why is the witch coming? Can she help find Elena?

"*Da...Daddy...*"

I turn left, my wolf guiding me by pure instinct. Why is it so easy? It's like an invisible thread guiding me to her. Within a few minutes, I reach the spot my wolf found, and look around. Where is she? I still can't feel Elena's wolf, and it's driving me crazy. Why can't I find her daughter either? She…

"Nate!"

Isaac is standing a few steps away, in front of a large tree with something like a large crack in the trunk. I walk up to him, my heart beating like crazy, my hands shaking.

My heart stops. Curled up there, looking at us with her eyes full of tears, a little girl is hidden. Moon Goddess. My wolf is going nuts, and I just lose the ability to think. She's… she's so like her mom. Golden blonde hair, slightly gold skin, and a little mouth and nose; her daughter is only a bit chubbier than Elena. But her eyes… She has my mother's eyes. This vivid shade of sky-blue. The exact same eyes as mine.

She's undoubtedly my daughter. The truth hits me harder than I ever expected. This little girl is the perfect mix between me and her mother. I recognize so much of myself in her, and my wolf is restless in front of his pup too. I… How…

"… Daddy?"

It's like an electric shock when she calls to me with her little voice. She knows I'm her father? How would she…? I exchange a glance with Isaac, but I'm the one she's staring at, with her eyes full of worry and hope.

"Moon Goddess, Nate, she's really your spitting image…" whispers Isaac.

She looks terrified, waiting for an answer.

I'm overwhelmed with emotions right now, but my instincts take over. I kneel and open my arms to her.

"It… It's okay. You can…"

Before I finish my sentence, she runs to me, burying her face in my torso and crying loudly.

"I want Mommy… Mommy left… and we left the house… and we ran fast… Daddy… Mommy… I'm really, really scared…"

Hearing her cry like this, I can't take it anymore. I hug her back and get up, carrying my daughter in my arms. My daughter. Moon Goddess, this is so crazy. I turn to Isaac, restless. I have Estelle now, but what about her mom? How do we find her if we can't mind-link her?

"Isaac, call…"

"*Nate! We found Elena!*"

I turn around, following my brother's wolf's voice. From the panic in his voice, I can tell something's wrong. I run, holding Estelle tight. What happened to Elena? Why would she leave her daughter alone in such a place? I keep running, she was so far away from Estelle!

When I get there, I spot Sylviana first, making a sour face. She's leaning over a dead wolf's body. Moon Goddess, no, no.

"That's…" starts Isaac, just when I'm too frightened to ask.

"Reagan," says Sylviana. "She was Elena's mentor."

Yeah, I remember that woman. She is the one I had met at the border. Now that I'm thinking it over, this wolf's fur is silver gray; Elena said hers was cream white. Then, where… I see Liam, back in his human form a few feet behind them, leaning over another wolf. Damn it, that's Elena!

I rush to his side, making sure Estelle's face stays against my shoulder so she doesn't look. There's so much blood. My heart goes cold. I can tell she's barely breathing, and her shoulder looks severely injured!

"We need to get her to a hospital, and quick," says Liam. "Sylviana, can you do something?"

His girlfriend is still by the dead wolf's side, her eyes red with sadness and anger. It takes her a couple more seconds before she leaves her side and rushes to Elena. She inspects her injury, frowning.

"I'll do what I can, but we need to hurry."

Immediately, she grabs some of the soil, pouring it over Elena's injury. What the heck? Will this do any good? I want to protest, but before I can, something happens. A lot of little red flowers suddenly bloom all over Elena's injury.

"Mommy? Grandma Reagan?"

"No, no, Estelle, don't look," says Isaac, worried.

She's struggling in my arms, trying to see her mother. Crap, she probably sensed she was close. How can her wolf be awake already? She is, what, four years old now? Isn't she too young for her wolf to be awake? I didn't even think about it, but she did mind-link me.

"Isaac, take her."

I hand my daughter to him, and rush to pick up and carry Elena. Damn it, I haven't seen her in over four years and now this… She is so light. Did she change much during all this time?

"Nate, let's go," says Liam.

He's carrying her deceased mentor. What happened to them? That was no weak woman, neither is Elena. How could they end up in such a state? Sylviana keeps looking around, visibly restless too.

"Sylviana, what happened to them?"

She shakes her head.

"Let's take them back. We will talk later."

I'm already hurrying to get Elena back as fast as possible. I can't stop glancing at our daughter in Isaac's arms. Truthfully, I wish I had enough arms to carry both of them. I still can't believe it.

"Nathaniel! Nathaniel, where is she? Elena is…"

I turn to see Nora, running up to me, with my brother and Boyan. They probably left in a hurry; her bun is messy, and my brother's shirt is wrinkled too. We're in the Emergency room waiting area, gathered around like idiots.

The wait is killing me. I'm only holding on because I have Estelle with me, who's been crying silently against my shoulder. She's terrified and I have no idea how to comfort her. The only thing I've done so far is carry her. She still has that jacket that smells like her mom around her, hopefully comforting her a bit too. Her little hands are holding on tight to my shirt, and she won't let go.

Isaac walks up to Nora and Damian to explain the situation to them, whispering.

"Elena's in surgery. Her injuries are bad, but the doctors said she will make it."

"Moon Goddess, Estelle…"

Nora walks up to me, seeing my daughter in my arms. Estelle looks at her with a little frown, confused.

"Estelle, honey, it's Auntie Nora. Do you remember me? We talked a lot on the phone."

"Auntie Nora…?"

"That's right, honey," says the Luna with a gentle smile. "You were a brave girl, weren't you?"

Estelle seems a bit hesitant. She probably hasn't met Nora in person before. She was already very scared when we reached Silver City, which is not surprising. She just went from the countryside she's known her whole life to a city full of skyscrapers and noise.

I am still too shocked from discovering I have a daughter, yet she's been holding on to me this whole time. How come she knows about me? She trusts me as her dad, like she has known me her whole life. I'm still baffled.

"Estelle! Elena!"

This time, it's Daniel Lewis and his brother who come running in. Shit, I didn't expect him… or his brother. He walks up to me, immediately going from worried to angry at me.

"How dare you pick her up! Let her go! Estelle, it's Dada! You know, your Dada?"

"Dada!"

This time, Estelle recognizes him immediately, and when he takes her from me, she doesn't resist. Shit. I have to control my wolf to not be angry at him. It's odd, that sensation. I didn't want to part with Estelle. Even now, she's only a few steps away, but my wolf wants his pup back.

"Dada… I want to see Mommy…"

Daniel turns to Liam and Sylviana, clearly ignoring me. Behind him, his brother is giving me weird glances too.

"Where is Elena? What happened?"

"Nora and Nate picked up their distress calls," explains Liam. "We found Estelle alone, but Elena probably acted as a decoy to save her."

"It was the Dark Witch," admits Sylviana. "I think she ran when she felt me coming, but…"

"How is she?" asks Daniel's brother, sending worried glances toward the surgery room.

"She's going to be fine. I won't make a full list, but she had a lot of injuries, though the medical staff said she will make it."

"Thank Moon Goddess," sighs Daniel.

"Daniel… We… found Reagan too."

Her sorry expression says it all, but Sylviana's probably careful with her words because of Estelle. Daniel's jaw drops.

"She…?"

A long silence follows. He looks terribly affected, shaking his head, holding back his tears. Boyan walks up to him, standing by his boyfriend to try and comfort him. Nora, too, walks up to him and rubs his shoulder.

"Daniel, I'm so sorry."

"Damn it… She's going to be so sad when she hears this."

He has a hard time trying not to cry, I can tell. I guess he was close to that woman too. I see his brother take out his phone from his pocket and leave. They probably need to tell their pack the news. What a mess…

Daniel puts a hand over Estelle's left ear, holding her with his free arm, and turns to us again.

"Elena, did she… say anything?"

"No, she only called out to me for help, and I lost the mind-link almost immediately," sighs Nora.

"Fuck! I can't believe this really happened. And Reagan's death… Moon Goddess."

I'm confused. Why the hell is he only blocking one of her ears, what's the point if she hears it? I understand his other arm is busy, but…

However, to my surprise, Estelle isn't reacting at all to his words. I stare at my daughter, who seems tired in his arms, but really, it's like she didn't hear.

"Estelle?"

She doesn't react, again. What the…? She really didn't hear. Daniel sighs and turns to me with an exasperated expression, like I did something wrong.

"What are you doing?"

"Why can't she hear me?"

He sighs again.

"Her right ear is deaf. She was born like that. She only hears from her left side."

What? Why? Why was she born with a deaf ear? Nora seems surprised, too, so I guess my sister-in-law wasn't aware either.

Understanding we're talking about her, Estelle pushes his hand away and turns to him.

"Dada, can I see Mommy now? I want to see Mommy."

"Not yet, baby star, Mommy is with the doctors. You will see her soon, I promise."

"The surgery will probably take a couple more hours, though," says Liam with a frown.

"Daniel, how about we take her for a little snack?" suggests Nora. "She must be tired from all that's happened. Estelle, do you want something to drink?"

"A hot chocolate."

Nora smiles softly, caressing her blonde hair.

"Alright, let's go get a hot chocolate, alright? Danny, come."

Like they had discussed this before, Nora gives a little nod to Damian, and she walks away with Daniel, Boyan following behind them.

"Liam, you're going with them," suddenly says Damian.

"But…"

Our brother's eyes won't take any refusal. Liam hesitates, sends me an annoyed glance, and then follows them.

I'm left with Damian and Sylviana, and my legs officially give up. I fall on my ass off one of the benches. That's too much emotion for one day.

"I have a child. Moon Goddess, Damian, I have a four-year-old daughter," I whisper, my head in my hands.

The truth hits me again, like a hammer hitting harder every freaking minute. Though Estelle walked away with her mother's best friend, my wolf can still feel his pup. I can tell exactly where she is in the building.

Damian sits next to me, putting a hand on my shoulder.

"Elena will be fine."

"She will kill me when she wakes up. She has every fucking right to. I can't believe it."

"Nathaniel, calm down."

"I can't calm down! I have a kid! Elena had my child, all by herself, and she raised her alone in the woods for four fucking years after I basically kicked her out!"

"You didn't kick her out."

Sylviana's voice surprises me. I didn't expect our friendly neighborhood witch to step into this conversation. She looks tired, with her sullied dress and disheveled red hair.

"Elena had many reasons to leave. You were one of them, but it wasn't only you. It was to protect her baby."

"Why couldn't she have protected her within Silver City?" I ask, angry.

"Nathaniel. Nora and Elena are related."

I turn to my brother, confused.

"What do you mean, related?"

"They are cousins."

I shake my head, doubtful. What is he saying? Where does this come from? His wife and Elena, related?

"It's a long story," adds Sylviana, "but Elena has Royal blood, just like Nora. She left because Estelle was your child. She knew that with your Alpha blood, her daughter would be a Royal too."

"It doesn't make any sense. Elena isn't a Royal! She doesn't even look like Nora!"

I'm exasperated now. Why are they telling me these crazy truths, after all this time? How does Damian know so much about Elena? He turns to me, using his big brother voice just when I'm getting too confused to think straight.

"Nate, you'll sort it out with Elena when she wakes up."

"How do you know these things, Damian? Why didn't you tell me before?"

"There are many things we concealed to protect Estelle," says Sylviana. "Other things Elena didn't want you to know, too."

"I've had my share of secrets," I growl. "Anything else I need to know?"

"She can't come back to our pack."

Surprised, I turn around and realize that Daniel's redhead brother is back. I had forgotten about that guy. What was his name again? Levi? I can't believe I suspected he was Estelle's father. He looks nothing like her. He has darker skin than Elena's, he's tall like a giraffe. and though his eyes are blue, it's a different shape and shade, nothing like mine.

"What? Why?" I ask, confused for the hundredth time today.

"She was banned five years ago."

"You mean before she left? Why would they ban Elena? Isn't her godfather your Alpha?"

He hesitates, looking a bit embarrassed. That's when I realize. I get up and grab his collar, furious.

"Because of Estelle? You bastards kicked her out because she was having my child?!"

"Nathaniel!" growls Damian.

My brother intervenes to get me off Levi, but I'm so angry, I just keep growling at him. He shakes his head.

"First of all, I am not our Alpha or our elders, we didn't have any say in this. And there were… circumstances, okay?"

"I don't care about your circumstances! You tell Clark that next time I see him, I'll–"

"Nathaniel, enough!"

This time, I can't disobey Damian. His Alpha Aura is suppressing mine. Fuck! I can't believe the White Moon banished a pregnant woman because of her relationship with me! I know it wasn't the best for us to be together back then, but still!

Damian insists on having me sit back down, where Levi is out of reach.

"Enough. First, let's focus on Elena and Estelle; we'll deal with Clark later. They will stay with our pack for now."

This time, Damian's glare is on that guy, meaning there is no arguing on this. Or maybe he's a bit pissed at the White Moon too. Even though the borders within Silver City are long forgotten and the packs' relationships have drastically improved, there are some things that won't be forgiven just like that.

Like a clan kicking his niece's mother out.

"Thanks. I know Daniel can freely go to your territory, so--"

"Anyone can come to our territory," says Damian. "If Elena's friends want to see her, they can."

Levi nods, looking a bit thankful. I don't feel sorry for them. If they hadn't banished her, I would have been able to see my daughter as soon as she was born. They--

"Daddy!"

I turn around. Estelle is already back, running to me with a Starbucks cup in her hand. She stands face-to-face with me as I'm still sitting, showing me her cup.

"Daddy, look. Auntie Nora bought me this, and the lady made it with the coffee machine, and she put whipped cream on it."

I can't help but smile while she tells me all this. She's so excited by a mere cup of hot chocolate, she looks better than when she was worried about her mom.

"She wanted to come back as soon as possible," says Nora. "She was afraid her dad would be gone."

I frown. Estelle was scared I'd leave? Why is she so insecure when she has only just met me? Behind her, Daniel is glaring at me with his arms crossed, but he doesn't dare say anything in front of Estelle.

"Daddy, do you want some? Auntie Nora, can I share?"

"Of course, honey."

"I'm fine, Estelle. You can drink it."

She nods and drinks a bit.

It's strange how curious I am about every one of her movements. I'm literally fascinated by my daughter. I turn to Nora, thinking about her own child.

"Where is James?"

"We left him with William," explains Nora.

Oh, her cousin. That makes sense. My two-year-old nephew is a bit too young to be in a hospital, and he has a bit of a temper, too. He probably can't sit still for a long time. Estelle, on the other hand, is very calm, though she sends regular glances to the surgery room, and seems a bit afraid by the crowd around her. Is that why she's staying right next to me?

"Estelle?" I gently call to her.

"Mhmm?"

"How did you know that I'm your dad?"

Daniel sends me another glare from behind her, but I don't care. Estelle smiles, all proud, and explains in her little voice.

"I have your picture! Mommy showed it to me, and I said I liked it, so Mommy printed it and now I have it! I put it in a pretty frame so I could see you all the time!"

My heart is torn apart from hearing this.

I'm such an ass. All these years… Damn it. I can't hold back; I pull my daughter in to hug her. I'm so thankful to Elena. She didn't tell her how much of an imbecile her father was, or pretend I didn't exist.

"But… Daddy… I left the picture at the house…"

I chuckle.

"It's okay, baby. I'm here now. And we can get it back later if you want."

"Can we?" asks Nora, turning to Sylviana. "You said she was…"

The witch seems to hesitate for a few seconds.

"She fled as soon as she sensed me, but from what I felt, she is stronger than before. I'm afraid we don't have much time left."

Damian and I exchange a glance. We were preparing for when this Dark Witch would attack, but… this is too soon. I only barely met Estelle, and Elena is in such a state!

"How long?" asks Damian.

"I'm not sure," sighs Sylviana. "It could be a few weeks, or a few months. But it will be before next year."

Next year? We are already in July… meaning we only have six months left, maximum. I look at my daughter, feeling like a vice is constricting my heart. At least now she's here with me.

"Tonia?"

Boyan's older sister just came out of the surgery room, wearing a nurse's gown. She takes off the paper hat and mask, walking up to us. I realize Damian probably gave orders right when we came back.

"Hi, everyone. Elena is fine. We managed to save her shoulder too. It will take a few weeks, but she'll heal. She's stable, but she will need to stay in the intensive care unit. She lost a lot of blood, and like Nora, she doesn't heal like a normal werewolf either."

"Thank you for taking care of her," says Levi.

"What are you talking about? She's family, of course we will take care of her, and Estelle too," replies Nora.

He looks down, a bit overwhelmed by the Luna's annoyed tone. Damian probably told her about the White Moon clan banishing Elena. Nora is usually gentle, but when she's pissed, you don't want to be in the same room as her. She learned how to be scary from my brother, but her Alpha Aura is no mere imitation.

"Nora, go home with Estelle," says Damian. "She won't be able to see her mother in the intensive care unit."

"But… I want to see Mommy…" Estelle starts crying.

She's standing next to me, opposite from my brother, but I can tell Damian scares her a bit. I caress my daughter's hair.

"Estelle, Mommy is sleeping now, and doctors are taking care of her."

She slowly cries, fidgeting. She grabs my hand, holding on to it.

"Daddy… Please… I promise I won't wake Mommy up… I'll be really quiet… please…"

Shit… I'm going to be one weak-willed father. I sigh a bit and turn to Damian. Maybe we can make an exception, just this once? I see Nora give him the look too. Thank Moon Goddess my sister-in-law is on my side. He nods and turns to Tonia.

"Make sure she sees her mom."

Tonia frowns.

"The hospital director won't be happy."

"The hospital director's salary comes from my wallet," growls Damian, "and the budget comes from our company. Let him know he had better think twice before being unhappy."

"Sure thing, Boss."

Tonia walks away to warn the nurses, and Daniel turns to us with a frown.

"Where will she stay? Elena doesn't have a place here; we left our apartment and she sold her parents' house."

"Both were on the White Moon territory, anyway," says Liam.

"I'm not homeless," I say to him.

"Why would she live with you?" says Daniel. "Technically, you were a stranger until two hours ago. You've never raised a kid, as far as I know, and you don't know anything about her."

I would argue against not raising anyone, considering what a pain in the ass Liam was growing up, but I'll leave that for now.

"I'm still her father," I growl.

"Her estranged father. I'm her godfather; I've talked to her and her mom every week since she was born!"

"Shut up, both of you!" suddenly yells Nora. "First of all, may I remind you this is a hospital, so be quiet. Second of all, Estelle is right here, so stop fighting in front of her. And third of all, she will stay with us."

Liam opens his mouth to argue, but she glares at him.

"Liam, I'm very tired, very pregnant, and your Luna. Don't you think about it."

"That's my wife."

Liam and I both glare at Damian and his smirk. Does he really have to brag right now?

"Anyway, we have plenty of room at home," she adds. "Everyone can sleep over for now."

"Guess I'll get to see my nephew, then," says Liam, avoiding my eyes.

I guess he is still mad at me too.

"Estelle, you'll be able to meet your cousin tonight!"

She looks at Nora with surprised eyes.

"My cousin?"

"That's right, honey. Your cousin James. He's younger than you, only two years old."

Estelle smiles, visibly happy, though she doesn't dare to add anything else. Her hand is still holding on to mine. Somehow, it's a huge relief to me. She doesn't consider me a stranger.

"Boss, you can go in now," announces Tonia. "Not too many people at once, though."

"I can see Mommy?" suddenly asks Estelle.

"Yes, honey, but you have to be very quiet, okay?" replies Nora.

"I will! I will be as quiet as a mouse," she says while covering her mouth with her little hands.

I get up, my heart beating like crazy in my ears. I get to see Elena in her human form. I try to calm down, but it's hard. Estelle is overjoyed, her hand still in mine.

"Where are you going?" asks Daniel with a frown.

"To see Elena," I reply, though I can already tell it won't be that simple.

"How dare you! She wouldn't want to see you!"

"It's not about her seeing me but me seeing her, Daniel," I say, trying not to growl to not scare my daughter.

"How easy, for someone who didn't want to see her for four and a half years," says Liam.

I growl at my brother, annoyed that he's on Daniel's side, but Damian steps in before I can say anything.

"Liam, enough."

"But–"

"I said enough!"

This time, our younger brother doesn't dare say a thing, and no one stops me when I follow Tonia to the intensive care unit.

I can feel Estelle's hand shaking. She's scared in this unfamiliar environment. A hospital is no place for a young kid. I decide to carry her again, since she seems a bit less frightened this way. I still can't get used to it. Carrying my daughter, having her little body against mine, her arms around my neck…

"Here she is…" whispers Tonia, taking us to the right bed.

Moon Goddess…

My heart is just about to explode. Fuck. She is even more beautiful than I remember, despite being stuck in a hospital bed with machines all around to help her breathe. I wish I could see her eyes though. Estelle doesn't have her mom's unique amber eyes. Elena's blonde hair is longer, and she's lost weight. I try to engrave her face into my memory, replacing all the images I had already.

"Mommy…"

Estelle is frowning, a bit impressed by the medical equipment.

"She is okay, honey, the doctors are taking care of her."

"She is sleeping?"

"Yes, sweetheart."

It's good that Nora is answering her questions because my throat is too tight to utter a single word right now. I want to cry, apologize to her. I'm such a--

"Nate, are you okay?"

"Take Estelle for a second."

I give my daughter to Tonia and leave the hospital, finding the closest exit I can. Fuck, fuck, FUCK! This all my fucking fault! I lost four and a half years with Elena and our daughter! And now she's in that state?! I'm the worst!

I fall on the asphalt and burst into tears, something I haven't done in a long, long time. But I can't hold it in. It just all comes back to me now: all the regret, the pain from these last few years. I can't believe it. All this time lost, and I'm never going to get it back.

"Nate, calm down."

I feel Damian's hand on the nape of my neck, trying to comfort me, but I can't. There's a torrent of tears that needs to flow out.

"I've been such an… an idiot…"

"It's okay. You'll earn their trust back."

"How? There's no fucking way Elena will forgive me!"

"Nate, you'll think of something later. For now, focus on your daughter."

Estelle… Damn it. It's a miracle she even knows I exist. I hang on to this tiny sliver of hope that maybe, just maybe, Elena told her about me because there's still something, a little something left between us…

"Nathaniel? Estelle's asking for you."

Nora's voice in my head makes me calm down. Damian helps me up, and we walk back inside. They're right. One thing at a time.

"Daddy!"

From the other end of the corridor, my daughter lets go of Nora's hand and runs to me. It's one of the best feelings ever. Opening my arms to her, seeing her shy smile before she hugs me.

"Auntie Nora said we can come back tomorrow to see Mommy."

"Yeah, let's do that," I whisper to her with a nod.

"The Lewis' are with her now," explains Nora, "but they will come over for dinner later. Let's go home."

We take the car back to their house, and for Estelle, it's a whole new experience. She keeps staring outside, asking us a thousand questions like what is that building, how does the car work, why do the streets have names, and so on.

We drive back to Nora and Damian's house. He bought it for them a few years ago, and they are properly settled in now. Even the room for the new baby is already prepared. They are careful with this pregnancy since James was a premature baby. Now that I think about it…

"Estelle, you're four years old? When is your birthday?"

"May 1st!"

So she was born a bit early too? If I remember correctly, Sylviana said Elena got pregnant mid-September, so she should have given birth late June. Maybe it's a Royal thing? The babies are more fragile?

We finally arrive at their house, and Estelle stays right next to me, a bit shy. I notice she doesn't go near Boyan. The huge brown wolf seems to scare her a bit.

"Mama!"

James is already running to us when we enter. My nephew is an energy pill, and very, very stubborn. I wonder who he got that from…

"My baby!"

Nora gets on her knees to hug him with a big smile. Behind him, her cousin William comes to greet us.

"Welcome back."

As usual, William and Damian are exchanging glares while he talks to Nora. He's just like a picky father-in-law. He leaves to go home to his wife and daughter after a while, and Nora takes care of James, who's being fussy as usual, while I give Estelle a tour of the house.

"This is Auntie Nora's house?" she asks, impressed as we visit the living room and playroom on the first floor.

"And your Uncle Damian's."

"Uncle Damian?"

I think my brother is still a bit too frightening for her. I can't blame her. Aside from his family, I haven't met anyone who isn't naturally scared of my brother. Nora comes back and decides we should order pizza for everyone to share, James following her every step as usual.

"Pizza?" repeats Estelle with a little frown.

Moon Goddess, she doesn't know what pizza is? Well, with her mother's cooking, I shouldn't be too surprised, but I smile and kneel to face her, a bit amused.

"You've never had pizza? It was your mom's favorite food."

"Really?"

"Yes. I made it for her when she was sick; she loved it."

"Can you make one for me too?"

"Nora ordered them already, but I promise I'll make you any dish you want later, okay?"

"Okay, Daddy."

I smile. This is a new sensation for me. Estelle smiles and goes to play with James, who's basically treating poor Boyan like a horse. Nora only introduced them quickly, but my nephew's apparently decided he loves his cousin already. They brought over some toys from the playroom to play with on the carpet, but Boyan is the main entertainment for now.

Meanwhile, I grab the backpack Estelle had with her this whole time. Was Elena ready to leave anytime? I check inside. There are children's basic toiletries, two changes of clothes, some money, and a letter. I hesitate a second. The envelope is blank, but whatever Elena wrote is inside. Before I can make up my mind, Damian takes it from me to open it.

"To whoever found her, please bring my daughter Estelle to her father in Silver City. If I can't be by her side, please make sure she meets him safely. His name is Nathaniel Black. He will take care of her, if you present her to him. He can even give you money in exchange if you want, but please, to whoever is reading this letter, take good care of my baby. I'm sorry I can't be there, but she is the most precious thing to me. Please."

I take a deep breath.

She trusted me. Elena knew I'd take care of Estelle if I met her. It's a huge relief. All the signs are there. She wanted me to know my daughter, and for her to know me.

Someone takes the letter from me. Isaac and Daniel are back, and read it together.

"Dada!"

"I can't believe it. She said to bring Estelle to you instead of me?" he sighs.

"You still belong to the White Moon clan," says Damian. "She doesn't. And Nathaniel is her father."

"He doesn't–!"

Damian suddenly gets up to face Daniel.

"Daniel, I'll say it one last time. Nathaniel made mistakes, but so did you. Who was in charge of that paternity test back then?"

He inevitably looks down, shaking his head.

"It wasn't my fault. Iris…"

Iris? Who is he talking about?

"I don't care what Whitewood did," growls Damian. "It was also your fault for not watching those tests. My brother has his wrongdoings but so do you, and so did Elena. Now if you still have a problem with Nathaniel taking care of his daughter, you'll settle this with him outside, not inside my house."

He used his Alpha Aura in that last sentence, and Daniel steps back instinctively, overpowered. I'm grateful to him. I'm feeling shitty enough without having to fight Daniel today.

"That goes for you too," Damian says to Liam, who had just walked in.

"Yeah, yeah, I get it."

Our younger brother just avoids us to go play with James, but Sylviana sits next to me. The witch is very comfortable around us now. Of course, given that I have been avoiding pretty much everyone recently, I didn't see her much either, but I know she hangs out a lot with Nora.

"How are you?" she asks me softly.

"A bit shaken up," I sigh. "It's… a lot for one day. I just can't believe they are here."

She smiles, and when James starts to whine about some toy, Sylviana agitates her fingers. A few flower petals appear out of nowhere around the kids, who immediately start playing with them, amused.

"You were there when she was born."

"Yes," she nods. "I helped Elena give birth to her. Estelle was unhealthy. I think Elena suffered too much stress during her pregnancy, plus the pre-eclampsia and her previous miscarriage."

I guess Estelle's birth was a miracle to begin with. How was she even conceived? Between both of our difficulties, it should have been impossible. So how?

"Nathaniel, don't think too much, for now," says Sylviana. "Even if she looks fine, Estelle is in a new environment, without her mother, and with people she didn't know until today. She probably trusts you more than any of us because of her wolf's instincts too."

I hadn't thought of that. But indeed, her wolf is already awake. She probably felt our bond before I did.

"*Estelle*?"

She turns her head and walks up to me, curious.

"You called me, Daddy?"

I can't help but smile. I caress her blonde hair, and she puts her little hands on my knees.

"Are you tired?"

"Mhmm. A little. But I'm really hungry."

"The pizza is on its way," says Nora from across the room.

"Pizza? You ordered pizza?" asks Liam, suddenly very interested.

"Pizza!" yells James, excited.

"Liam, take the kids to wash their hands first," says Nora.

Two hours later, we are done eating the pizza. It's the best evening I've had in a long time. Watching the kids play with Boyan, Daniel, and Liam, chatting with my brother and Isaac about company matters, and leaving Sylviana and Nora to talk about the garden.

When Nora decides it's time for everyone to go to bed, I realize she already prepared the rooms for us all. Estelle's is right next to mine, but I insist on tucking her into bed. I lay next to my daughter, while she's still glancing around the room, a bit uneasy.

"You don't like the room?" I ask.

"No, it's pretty."

She's probably just not used to the new environment. She's snuggling against me, unable to close her eyes despite the late hour.

"How was your bedroom? In Mom's house?"

"Hmm... smaller. And I draw bunnies on the wall too."

"You like bunnies?"

"Yes! I draw lots and lots. And Mom got me a bunny plushie. But I left it there."

"It's okay, we can go and buy you new plushies tomorrow, okay?"

"Really?" she asks with her big eyes opened wide.

"Yeah. We can buy whatever you want. And new clothes and pajamas, too."

For now, she's sleeping in one of Nora's shirts that falls to her knees.

"Daddy?"

"Yes?"

"We are not going back to our house?"

"I don't think so."

"Oh."

She seems a bit sad. She probably left all of her toys and stuff there. And she's lived there her whole life, too.

"Estelle, where did Mommy get your bunny?"

"At the village with the humans. But I don't like going there. They don't like us."

Probably because they were wary of werewolves. We are lucky in Silver City; decades of cohabitation have made it so that humans and werewolves get along. We don't get involved in each other's business, but we don't fight either. They hate vampires a lot more, but they don't mind us.

"I miss Grandma Reagan too."

"I'm sorry, baby."

"Baby star!"

"What?"

She suddenly smiles.

"Mommy called me baby star! She said my name comes from the stars, because I'm Mommy's little sun. So I'm a baby star!"

I chuckle. So that's how she decided on her name. Estelle. Did she pick a French name on purpose? I really like it. And I called her mom my sunshine, too. It's very fitting. I kiss her cheek.

"Alright, baby star needs to sleep now."

I'm about to get up and leave, but she holds on to me, suddenly losing her smile.

"Daddy… Can you stay? I'm… a little bit scared…"

I nod and take my position again next to her. Estelle smiles and grabs my shirt, satisfied. We stay silent for a while, and I think she's asleep, but then…

"Daddy? Can we see Mommy again? Tomorrow?"

"I promise. You'll see Mommy every day."

"And you'll stay with me?"

"Yes."

"You're not leaving?"

"Why do you think I'll leave?" I ask.

"I don't know. Mommy said you have a house in the sky."

A house in the… Does she mean my apartment? Elena really loved the view from up there. I smile.

"Would you like to come and see my house in the sky tomorrow?"

"Can I?" she asks, excited.

"If you're a good girl and sleep well."

"Okay! I will sleep now. Good night, Daddy."

"Good night, little star," I whisper.

I watch her sleep for a while, unable to find sleep myself. She's the cutest little girl I've ever seen, and she's mine. She's breathing slowly, her hand still holding on tight to my shirt. I just hope she's not remembering too much of her scare today. Sylviana gave us a dreamcatcher to hang at the end of the bed. I hope this witch stuff is effective…

Chapter 29

My first thought, the next morning, is about how well I've slept. For the first time in a while, the sun is already up outside, and I don't feel like jumping out of bed. I would rather not. Estelle is still sound asleep right next to me, in a curled-up position, so cute I can't bear it. I slowly recall everything that happened yesterday as if it was a dream. But it's not, and my daughter is right here.

I observe her for a while until someone slowly opens the door. I frown before realizing it's James, on his short legs, looking at us with his big blue eyes. Damn, this kid is an energy pill.

Having spotted his newly befriended cousin, he walks up to us with anticipation, but I frown.

"James, if you wake her up…" I whisper.

What time is it anyway? Probably not late, considering we are in July and the sky is still slightly pink. Of course, my nephew decides to play deaf, putting his hands on the bed.

"*Nora, Damian, your kid is here.*"

I sense my brother's frustration, while Nora is probably still asleep as well. A few seconds later, my brother walks in, but his sudden arrival makes his kid scream and run away. Damian grabs him before he can get out.

"James, you little…"

"… Daddy?"

Damn it, now she's awake too. I sigh.

"Sorry, Nate, I didn't realize he was up," says my brother.

"Good morning, Uncle Damian. Good morning, James," says Estelle in her little voice.

"Stella! Up, up!"

She smiles and slides off the bed to walk up to him. Damian gives up and lets his son down, who grabs Estelle and takes her somewhere else in the house. I sigh.

"Ever tried the leash on him?"

"Trust me, I've thought about it a couple of times," admits my brother. "Coffee?"

"Moon Goddess, yes."

We both head to the kitchen to prepare breakfast for everyone. From the snoring we can hear, Boyan slept on the couch. I check the cupboard to see what I can cook for everyone, and realize they are even fuller than usual. Who the heck eats this much pesto?

"Don't ask," sighs Damian, spotting my confused expression. "Nora eats like a dinosaur with this one."

I chuckle. It's probably better than being exhausted like she was with James. I finally find enough ingredients to make some pastries and hot chocolate while Damian is in charge of the coffees, which pretty much sums up his culinary skills.

"Daddy? What are you making?"

Estelle just walked in, curious. She climbs up onto one of the kitchen stools.

"Croissants. Do you like them?"

"I don't know. Can't you make a magic cake?"

A magic cake? What the heck is a magic cake? I exchange a glance with Damian, but he's about as clueless as me. I turn to my daughter, with her messy hair and oversized pajamas.

"What is a magic cake, baby star?"

She hesitates then points at one of the hot chocolate cups. Something with hot chocolate?

"A mug cake, honey?"

Nora just walked in, and quickly kisses her husband.

"Damian, I really hope it wasn't your son I just saw drawing on his bedroom wall."

"Crap."

My brother runs out, and Nora turns to us with a large smile.

"A mug cake?" I repeat, confused.

Stella nods, smiling from ear to ear, while Nora laughs at my confused expression. She grabs one of the cups and some of the ingredients I took out and puts it in the microwave.

"Well, you know how bad Elena's cooking is, so I gave her this recipe. Two minutes to make a chocolate mug cake, with a microwave and basic ingredients. James loves these too."

"You're telling me I just spent fifteen minutes preparing croissants for nothing?" I sigh.

"I love croissants, but for kids, this works better," she says with a confident smile.

As it turns out, Nora is right. Both James and Estelle eat their mug cakes in a few minutes, looking happy and satisfied. Okay, I may be the best at cooking, but my sister-in-law definitely beats me at handling kids.

Damian lets me know that after a call to the hospital, Elena hasn't woken up yet, but everything else looks alright.

"I'll go visit her this morning; I need to do my pregnancy check-up anyway. How about you take Estelle out?"

I nod. I did say I would take her shopping and to see my place too. I'm not sure how confident I am about watching a kid, though.

"How about you go with Boyan? He's good with kids, and it will give him a break from watching me and James all the time."

"Okay."

I'm still not confident about this. I've never spent the day alone with a child, let alone my four-year-old daughter who I didn't know until yesterday. However, I still want to spend as much time as I can to get to know her. I borrow one of my brother's cars and take us to the mall, which is not too busy on a Sunday. Plus, the huge brown wolf next to us keeps everyone at bay, meaning we can walk side by side and take our time.

Truthfully, it's even better than I thought. First, Estelle is impressed by everything. She's never been to a mall and seen so many things or so many people in one place. Though she doesn't let go of my hand one second, her eyes are everywhere. I'm also shocked by how well-behaved and shy she is.

Even if she sees something she really likes, she will just stare at it and not ask for anything. It takes me a while to realize every time, and I have to insist and ask several times if she wants it. If I make her try on clothes, she's happy to show it to me and blushes anytime I or any of the salespeople gives her a compliment. In the end, despite my best efforts, we only buy a few outfits, two pajamas, and a drawing set.

I sigh as we exit another shop empty-handed, but Estelle doesn't seem to mind at all.

"*Don't worry. You're doing well.*"

"*You think so, Boyan?*"

"*She's just not your average kid. She grew up in a forest; this is too new for her. Spending time with you is probably more important to Stella than all that stuff you want to buy her.*"

I realize he's probably right. Everywhere we went, Estelle made sure I was never out of reach or sight. She just won't leave my side, and looks to me for everything. I put a knee down to face her.

"Estelle, shall we have lunch now? Are you hungry?"

"Um… a little bit."

"What do you want to eat?"

She seems to hesitate, then looks around. This mall has a few restaurants open, and from across the hall, she spots the food court with people lining up. It will probably be easier if she can see the food. We walk over there, checking what's available. There are a couple of Asian food stalls, one for sushi, two famous fast-food chains, an Indian one, and a Mexican one.

"Daddy? What do you like best?"

"I'm not sure. Which one do you like, Estelle?"

"I don't know…"

A lady is giving samples a bit further along, and after trying it out, we settle for the Asian food one. It turns out my daughter loves the noodles and sweet and sour pork. It's nice to simply chat like this and eat together, trying each other's food. I realize it's also the first time I've really taken a day off in ages.

"… Daddy?"

"What is it?"

"Are we going to live at Auntie Nora's house now?"

I hesitate while Estelle is waiting for my answer with an anxious expression. What should I tell her? Until Elena wakes up, and even after, it will be a difficult question.

"I think so, until your mom wakes up."

"And when Mommy wakes up?"

"It will be up to your mom to decide?"

"We can't… live in your house in the sky?"

"Only if Mommy wants to, little star. But I'm not sure."

That will probably depend on how mad her mother is with me… and if there's a chance for all three of us to be a family again, I guess. Estelle nods.

"I understand. I hope Mommy will wake up soon."

"Me too, little star. Let's go see her after we are done shopping, okay?"

"Do we still need to buy more?"

"Didn't you want a new bunny?"

Her eyes suddenly light up, and I'm glad she looks happy again. We finish eating quickly, and do some more shopping, but without finding a new plushie to her liking. She seems happy about her drawing set though and keeps looking at it in the car as I drive to the hospital.

"*Nate?*"

"*Damian, we're going to the hospital with Estelle.*"

"*I was about to call you; Elena just woke up.*"

I stay speechless. Shit, really? Now? I can barely think. I park the car in the first spot I see, taking deep breaths.

"Daddy?"

"Give me a minute, baby."

I grab my phone, fidgety, calling Damian.

"What?"

"Is she… she okay?"

"Yeah. She's with a doctor, but she's fine. She asked about Estelle as soon as she woke up, and Nora's with her right now. Are you far from the hospital?"

"We were on our way. We'll be there in five minutes."

"See you then," he says before hanging up.

Crap. I'm not ready. Despite all this time with Estelle, I'm so not ready to face her mom. What should I tell her? Should I apologize straight out, ask for forgiveness? Or try the friendly approach first? Damn it, what friendly approach, you dumbass.

"Mommy is awake?"

"Yeah, baby."

"Can we go? Daddy, can we go see Mommy? Please?"

I take a deep breath.

No matter what, I want to see her. I don't want to push this back any longer. For Estelle's sake, too, we need to have this conversation, as painful as it may be.

"… Daddy?"

"Yeah, we're going. Let's go see Mom."

"Yay!"

She looks bright and happy again, unaware of my inner turmoil. I drive to the hospital, a hundred thoughts fighting inside my head. I'm a mess inside, and I'm so not ready when I finally park, helping Estelle out while Boyan takes the lead.

We walk inside, and honestly, I'm torn between running to her room and running outside. I'm just… so ashamed. Ashamed of the idiot I've been, ashamed of everything I've said to her. How mad will she be? How much can she really resent me, after all this time?

"Daddy!"

Estelle guides me back to her mom's room; she already remembers which one it was. We wait outside for a second, and Nora suddenly walks out.

"Auntie Nora! Mommy is awake!"

"Yes she is, sweetheart. You ready to see her?"

"Yes! Can I go in now?"

"Go, honey. No running and no screaming, okay?"

"Yes, I promise!"

After that, Estelle lets go of my hand to rush to her mom, yet not running as she promised. I stay outside the room, my heart thumping loud. Nora looks at me, a bit worried.

"Nathaniel? Are you okay?"

"I don't know… what to say."

"It's okay. You two need to talk, okay?"

"Yeah. Yeah, I know."

"Alright. I'll stay here with Bobo."

I nod, my mouth a bit dry. Yeah, I'll be fine. We will be fine.

I step inside, and the only separation between us is a simple curtain. I can already hear her voice, talking with Estelle.

"… he bought you new clothes?"

"Yes! Daddy got me a new drawing set too. It has fifty pencils, a lot of pretty colors, and even animal stamps."

"Whoa, you'll make pretty pictures with that?"

"Of course! I'll make new ones for you, Mommy. And for Auntie Nora too! And Daddy!"

I try to gather my courage and take another step, but Moon Goddess, I'm scared. I can't remember the last time I was so stressed.

"… Nathaniel, if you want to talk, you'll have to stand where I can see you."

Her voice takes me by surprise, causing me to jump. Damn it. Of course she felt me. I gather up all my courage and step forward, finally facing her hospital bed.

Damn it. It's so… awkward.

And Moon Goddess, she's so beautiful. Elena's sitting up, in a hospital gown, Estelle right next to her on the bed. Her hair is brushed compared to yesterday, and she looks a bit healthier too, despite the dressings on her head and her arm in a sling. Her face has better colors, and her eyes are open.

Open and looking right at me.

"… Hi," I finally manage to blurt out.

"Hi, Nate."

The simple fact that she uses my nickname means the world to me. I walk a bit closer, and Estelle, unaware of that atmosphere between us, smiles at me. Elena caresses her hair, and I can finally see how alike they are.

"Thank you for taking care of her," Elena says.

"I should be the one to say that."

I smile a bit, she knows what I mean by those words. I know, I know she's my daughter, and she had to raise her alone.

"… It's okay."

"It's not okay, Elena. I'm sorry."

"I don't need an apology."

"I'm really sorry."

She glares at me, a bit annoyed, but I need to say it. I need to lift that weight off my heart, even if it's just a little.

"Things shouldn't have turned out the way they did. I should have believed you, I should have helped you from the start."

"Nathaniel, I really don't want to hear this right now. Honestly, I'm just glad we are both fine, okay? I don't… I'm not in the mood to have that conversation now. Really."

Her last words sound a bit annoyed, and I realize. It's maybe a bit too… early for that. I nod, and Elena turns to Estelle again.

"You've been a good girl with Auntie Nora and Daddy, my baby star?"

"Yes! And Auntie Nora made us magic cakes this morning!"

"You slept at Auntie Nora's?"

While she tells her mom all about last night, I grab a chair and sit next to them, unable to take that stupid smile off my face now. I'm just an idiot, happy to be with these two. I feel a bit relieved, though I know we still need to have the talk later. I'm just glad she didn't refuse to see me, cursed at me, or kicked me out. It could have been way worse.

"Mommy, are you coming to sleep at Auntie Nora's home?" asks Estelle.

"No, baby star, I need to stay in the hospital. Mommy is still very tired, okay?"

"Okay. But Auntie Nora said I can't sleep with you."

"Yes, but you can sleep at Auntie Nora's house for now, okay?"

"Actually…"

I hesitate, but I really need to ask.

"I was thinking… I mean, Estelle was also asking if she could sleep at my place."

To my surprise, Elena nods.

"Sure."

"Really?"

I was prepared for her to say no, but she just smiles at Estelle.

"You can ask Daddy or Auntie Nora and pick where you want to sleep, okay? Auntie Nora says you and Daddy can sleep at her house too if you want, but I think your cousin is tiring her out a lot…"

Estelle chuckles.

"James runs around a lot!"

"Yeah, and you saw Auntie Nora's tummy? She is going to have another baby!"

"I know! I will have another cousin!"

"That's right, baby star, but until the baby is born, it's better to let Auntie Nora rest, okay?"

"Okay! I can go and sleep at Daddy's house then?"

"Yes, if Daddy is okay with it."

Estelle turns to me, excited.

"Daddy, can I sleep at your house tonight? The one in the sky?"

I smile.

"Of course, baby."

She smiles brightly at me. I'm so grateful she feels safe at my place… and it seems to show Elena I've been doing alright as a dad so far. The two of them exchange smiles, and Elena caresses her hair. Something in her smile seems forced, though. Is she in a lot of pain? Or trying to act tough for Estelle?

"Mommy, when will you get out of this hospital?"

"Um... When the doctors say I can, baby star."

Estelle frowns, a bit disappointed with her answer. She inevitably glances down at her mom's injuries, especially her arm.

"Does it hurt very bad?"

"It's okay, baby star."

It's probably not as okay as she wants to make it sound. For Elena to be faking smiles and allowing her daughter to see her wired to a hospital bed, her injuries must be greater than she's showing…

"Do you want me to blow on it? Like you did when I scratched my knee? It really worked, you know!"

"If you want, baby star. You'll give Mommy a kiss, so I'll be all better?"

"Of course!"

Damn, I could just melt from watching the two of them together. They hug, with a closeness I can only watch from the sidelines, making me a little bit jealous… until I catch Elena looking at me over Estelle's shoulder. We stare at each other, for just a few seconds, until loud steps come from the corridor.

"Elena! Elena! Babe, oh my babe…"

Her friend Daniel just barged in, looking panicked. He runs to her, but Elena grabs his collar right before he jumps on her.

"Daniel Lewis, if you hurt me with one of your herculean hugs, I'll kick your butt as soon as I can stand, you hear me?"

To my surprise, he just laughs.

"Moon Goddess, it's really you… Oh babe, I missed you."

The two of them hug, Estelle caught in between. I'm feeling a bit out of place now, but I just stay quiet, waiting.

"Are you okay? It doesn't hurt? I can ask them to increase the morphine dose, but…"

"I'm okay, Danny, chill."

"Babe. You could have…"

She frowns, and I know she's telling him to be mindful about Estelle, who's right next to them. To my surprise, she turns to me.

"Can you take her? I need to talk with Daniel."

I'm a bit disappointed that's all she asks of me, but I hurry over.

"Sure. Estelle, are you coming? Let's go grab the hot chocolate you liked last time."

"Oh, yes! Mommy, do you want a hot chocolate too? They are really good, and the nice lady puts sprinkles on it!"

"I'm fine, baby, eat a lot of sprinkles for me, okay?"

"Okay! See you later Mommy, see you later Dada!"

"Bye, baby star."

We walk out, Estelle still waving at her mom, while I feel like I left my heart back there…

I drive us back to my place, Estelle sipping her hot chocolate in the back seat, excitedly talking to me about how happy she was to see her mom.

I still can't believe it, either. I was prepared for anything, for Elena to scream or yell at me. I wouldn't even have blamed her if she punched me a few times. I'm still waiting for it. I take a glance at my baby star in the back seat. How did she raise such a precious, perfect little girl alone like that? I take a deep breath.

I need to make things right. Not just with Estelle; I want to resume my relationship with Elena too. Even if it takes years, I want to earn her forgiveness, have them both back in my life, and stop being that ghost I've been for the past four years. I'm the most selfish man there is, for sure, but honestly, I'd rather die than miss my chance again.

I finally park in front of the residence, escorting my baby star out of the car. She is amazed by the view of the sea behind us.

"Daddy! Is it the ocean? It's so big!"

"Yes, baby star. Come, you will see it even better from my apartment."

"Really?"

She takes my hand and follows me inside. The concierge, Harry, opens his eyes wide, seeing me walk in with a kid. Aside from Elena or my family, he's never seen me bring anyone else home.

"Good evening, Mr. Black. May I ask who the little Miss with you is?"

Estelle, a bit shy, exchanges a glance with me before smiling at him.

"I'm Estelle, mister."

"Nice to meet you, Miss Estelle, I am Harry. Please let me know if you need anything."

"Thank you, Harry!"

"Thanks, Harry," I say, a bit proud.

While we walk to the elevator, Estelle suddenly stops. You can see the pool from the other side of the glass wall, and she is stunned.

"Daddy! There is a huge pool too!"

"I know. Do you want to go for a swim later?"

She frowns, turning to me.

"I don't know how to swim… and I don't have a swimsuit…"

"Alright, then we can buy you a swimsuit, and Daddy can teach you to swim, okay?"

She nods with a big smile, her eyes turning to the pool again. It's cute how she can barely manage to hide her excitement. We take the elevator to my apartment, and when she walks in, she doesn't dare to walk away from me, even after we take our shoes off.

"This is… Daddy's house?"

"Yes. Go on. Don't you want to explore it?"

"But… you live alone, Daddy?"

"Yes. Your uncles come sometimes. But your mom is the only girl who came here before you."

"Really?"

With excitement, she finally walks in, looking at everything around her. Now that I think about it… maybe Estelle was even conceived here. Not a lot of things have changed since then. I like a somber, neat style. Liam always says my apartment looks like it's for sale, since it's so clean you wouldn't have guessed that someone lives here… Well, I usually only come here to shower and sleep.

"Daddy! There are so many rooms!"

I hear her running from one room to another, and I laugh. That place really is big. Way too damn big for just myself, actually. I remember I bought it because I had the means to get the best, but for one man alone, it's ridiculously big. What was I thinking? I understand Damian better now. He just lived in the place above his office, with just one bedroom, and waited until he had a wife and children to get a huge family house.

"Estelle, come see the view!"

She comes out of one of the rooms while I put our shopping bags in a corner. I take her to the balcony, which offers an incredible view of Silver City, its buildings, and the sea, on the left. She's silent, but I can tell she's stunned.

"Daddy… It's so big, like a forest of buildings…"

I nod and take a seat next to her. Elena loved this view too. I remember sitting here so many times with her, watching it while listening to her music. Even when it rained, she would lie on the couch and face the glass wall to watch it. Estelle goes to the edge of the balcony, looking at everything for a long time, sometimes commenting about some funny-shaped building, asking me what is this or that, and making me point out our company, the hospital where her mom is, and her auntie Nora's house.

"I miss Mommy already," she says, turning to me with a sad little face all of a sudden.

I open my arms, and she comes to sit on my lap. I gently tuck her blonde hair behind her ears, looking at my daughter up close.

"I miss her too, little star."

"Do you think Mommy can leave the hospital soon?"

I nod.

"Of course. Your mom is super strong."

"How soon? Tomorrow?"

"I don't know, baby. That's for the doctors to decide."

"Okay."

But I can tell she's unhappy, looking down. How do I cheer up a four-year-old, especially without her mom?

"You'll stay with me until Mommy gets out, okay? And we will go and see her every day, I promise."

"Really?" she asks, her eyes shining again.

"I promise. Meanwhile, we can do anything you want: go to the sea, to the movies, to your auntie's house…"

Estelle smiles wide again, making me feel I did something right.

"Can we eat more pizza?"

I laugh.

"You're already addicted to pizza? It really is in your genes. How about I make you some homemade pizza tonight?"

"Is that okay? We had pizza yesterday."

"Then… I can make something else if you want? Or we can even eat out?"

"I'll eat what Daddy makes!"

After a while, we agree to make some mac and cheese and rent a Disney movie. As expected, she had never seen one. We end up seeing two more Disney movies together before she falls asleep on the couch beside me, and I take her to the bedroom.

Damian gives me a call that night, making sure everything's fine. I don't think I've ever been so grateful to my older brother. He's always been on my side, but… It's a strange feeling, him helping me become a good father. He gives me a few tips about what I could do with Estelle, what kind of food I should try with her, and so on. He's been a dad for two years, but I have a four-year-old all of a sudden. I guess I'm doing something right if she's happy staying with me so far. I also realize my place isn't very child-friendly. I could use a few more toys and less impractical furniture.

The next day, I let Estelle pick one of the bedrooms to become her own. She's so happy about getting her own room at my place and picks one with a good view of the sea, but more importantly, the one closest to mine. I tell her we will decorate it to her liking, and we spend the day going to furniture and toy stores. After a while, she goes for a winter theme after her new favorite Disney movie. She is most excited that we will paint it together, as she picked some turquoise paint.

We visit her mother in the afternoon, but as expected, Elena only wants to see her daughter. We barely exchange a few words. I'm fine with just seeing her for a while though. I spend more time discreetly inquiring with her doctor. She's getting better, and should be discharged soon, much to my relief.

After two hours, Estelle agrees to leave, a bit sad to part with her mom again, and we spend the rest of the evening painting, as she was excited to start remodeling her new bedroom and finish the night by watching more Disney movies with my delicious homemade pizza.

While putting my daughter to bed, I realize I completely forgot about work, but Isaac didn't call me, and neither did my secretary, so I guess it's fine…

The next morning, Damian calls me.

"Elena can leave the hospital."

"What? Really?"

I'm busy preparing breakfast for my daughter who's still asleep, and I almost drop the pan. She… Elena can leave the hospital? Already?

"Yeah," says Damian. "Her shoulder is still injured, so her arm is not healed completely, but her legs are fine now. She can walk, and apparently, she insisted on leaving quite a lot."

"When?" I ask, fidgety.

"She'll be discharged after they give her a new cast and she gets the clearance, so… in an hour or so."

"Okay. Can you delay it? I want to bring Estelle there before she leaves."

"Fine, I'll talk to the hospital director. But hurry up."

"Yeah. Thanks."

I hang up, and notice Estelle woke up, walking to me half-asleep while carrying her new bunny plushie.

"Good morning, Daddy," she says in her sleepy voice.

I walk over to kiss her cheek, picking her up to carry her. Even her eyes are still fighting to stay open.

"Baby, I got good news from your uncle."

"Uncle Damian?"

"Yes. Your mom is leaving the hospital today."

Suddenly, she's completely awake and excited, her big eyes looking at me.

"Really? Really, Daddy? Mommy can leave? Today?"

"Yes, baby. So, you should eat your breakfast and we can go see her."

"Okay! Daddy, I'll eat fast so we can go right after, right? Daddy, what is this?"

"It's crepes, baby. My mom used to make them when we were young, with your uncles. I made ones with chocolate and sugar, so take what you want, okay?"

"Can we save some for Mommy?"

"Of course."

She smiles and starts eating happily, faster than usual. I may be more excited, though. I barely eat, just gulping down my coffee. I'm so anxious. I get dressed, a T-shirt and some jeans, and help Estelle get ready before we drive to the hospital.

I decide to make a stop on the way to buy some flowers for Elena's discharge. Is that too much? Estelle can give it to her, it will be less awkward that way. If only I could calm down. I hurry to the hospital, park, and walk inside with Estelle.

Damian is already there, discussing with Elena and some guy from the medical staff. Calm down, calm down. I try to calm myself, holding our daughter's hand a bit tighter. Elena notices me first, but turns back to the doctor.

"Is that all?"

"As long as you take the medicine and get lots of rest, you will be better in a few days, Miss Whitewood. Please don't stand for too long, and be careful with your arm. I will schedule a check-up for you in three days, just to make sure."

"About the hospital bill…"

"Elena, don't," says Damian with a frown. "Nora will scold us both. Don't you dare talk about money."

She sighs, turning to Damian.

"Can I at least say thank you?"

I see the slightest bit of a smirk on my brother's face. Since when were these two so close? I let go of her hand, and Estelle runs to her mother.

"Mommy!"

"Baby star!"

She kneels down painfully to hug her daughter. Is it alright for her to be crouching? Her arm is still in a sling, and she looks tired too. I quickly join them, grabbing Estelle to carry her. Elena barely looks at me…

"Mommy, can you really leave now?"

"Yes, baby, I'm leaving the hospital."

"Really? And you can come and live with Daddy and me? We painted my room! It will be dry in two days!"

Elena hesitates, looking at me. I take a deep breath.

"How about we discuss this a bit first? Maybe Mommy wants some breakfast too, baby?"

"We made some crepes!"

While she tells her mother all about her morning, Damian settles the last details with the hospital so that we can leave. Elena is obviously trying to avoid my eyes while talking to her daughter. Meanwhile, I take deep breaths, trying to calm down and act rationally. It had to happen sooner or later, right?

"Alright, it's settled," announces Damian. "I have to go home, Nora asked me to watch the kid this afternoon."

"She's not working?" I ask, worried.

"No, but Tonia is taking her shopping for the baby."

"Didn't you say you don't want to know the gender yet?" asks Elena, surprised.

Damian nods.

"We don't, but they still want to look for more baby toys and things to prepare for the birth. Nora is scared it will be premature like James. Anway…"

He sighs and says goodbye to us, giving a kiss to the girls before leaving.

Okay, now I'm left with the two girls. I take a deep breath and turn to Estelle.

"Do you want a hot chocolate, baby? So you can finish eating your crepes with Mommy?"

"Yes! Come, Mommy! Daddy, can we get another one for Mommy?"

"Of course, baby."

Elena stays silent and follows her to the hospital cafeteria. It's so awkward. I take a deep breath and follow them. I insist on paying for the drinks, getting myself an Americano and two hot chocolates for the girls, and we sit down, a bit uncomfortable.

"Do you like it, Mommy?"

"It's good, sweetheart," says Elena.

We stay silent a bit longer, and it's the most awkward we've ever been. I really need to say something, now. It's the time, if I ever want to make things right…

"Are you coming home with us now, Mommy?"

"I think I'll go and live with Auntie Nora for now, baby star."

Estelle immediately makes a sad face while looking at us, alternating between her and me, worried.

"But… Daddy has a lot of rooms… and the Disney movies… and he said you liked it at Daddy's place before…"

She's almost crying, and I immediately feel so guilty for it! I turn to Elena, talking very seriously.

"You could come to my place."

"Oh, heck no, Nate. We are done."

"I'm not asking you to get back together with me. I have a lot of spare rooms, and I can–"

"Your place is not a hotel, and I am not desperate. Nora can host me anytime, and we both know it."

"Yes, but I want to see my daughter, and we can't split her between my place and Damian's all the time. And Nora is pregnant and tired; she can't host all three of us."

"I'm pretty sure Damian can lend me a room anytime I ask for it, Nathaniel."

"Elena, I'm just asking you because of our daughter. You don't have to get back with me, just consider living in the same place as me."

"Nathaniel, do you even know what you're saying! It's not like we could just be roommates!"

"Why not?" I ask, very seriously. "Elena, you know I want you back. I'll be very clear right now about that. I owe you a hundred apologies, and we need a good, long talk. I'm asking you to have it now, for Estelle's sake. But my place would be better than a hospital cafeteria. You… You're free to go back to Nora's place with Estelle after that. All I'm asking is… you just give me time to talk to you before that. Please."

She takes a deep breath, visibly conflicted.

"Nate, we already had that talk about four years ago."

"You know I didn't have all the pieces of the puzzle, Elena," I try to argue. "It was unfair. I'm not saying it was your fault, but you can't… I mean, anyone would have had doubts. You had my medical records and the paternity test–"

"I told you," she immediately gets furious. "My cousin–!"

"Elena."

I give her a second to calm down, and she glances towards Estelle, who's staring at the two of us, anxious and a bit lost. She is holding on to her hot chocolate, trying to grasp what's going on between me and her mom. I sigh.

"Elena, I'm just asking we go to my place for now to talk. I don't want to just pick a random place, and Estelle's stuff is there too, she can just watch a movie while we discuss calmly, like adults."

"Mommy, Daddy and I watched Disney movies yesterday! It was very, very funny, and I even know the song a bit!"

Elena caresses her cheek, without answering me. She looks so conflicted, but I need her to agree. I'm desperate to patch things up between us, no matter how long it takes. And her coming back to that place where we have so many memories would be a huge step in that direction… She eventually sighs.

"Fine, but… just to talk, Nathaniel."

"Of course," I nod, relieved. "I promise, you're more than welcome to stay at my place, but I won't hold you back if you want to go to Nora's."

I grab her bag before she can change her mind, and we leave the hospital. Estelle happily walks between us, telling Elena all about her new room and the movies she watched at my place. I'm kind of glad she's helping me out a lot without knowing.

Elena sits next to me in the passenger seat, but we don't exchange one word; she silently stares at Silver City while I chat and entertain our daughter. Did she miss our city…?

We finally park in front of my residence and go upstairs. Does it bring back memories for her? Harry recognizes her and greets Estelle, professional as usual. The elevator ride is quick, and I let her step into my flat first… She glances around, but it probably hasn't changed that much since the last time she came here, except for our daughter's stuff… Should I have made some more family-friendly changes? No, that would be too much. Estelle runs to get her latest drawing.

"Look, Mommy! Daddy and I, we picked some really nice pencils! I did this yesterday!"

"It's very pretty, honey."

"Baby," I ask her. "Can you be a good girl and watch another Disney movie? Mommy and I need to talk a bit."

"Okay, Daddy! I remember how to pick a movie!"

She runs to grab the remote and climbs onto the couch, ready to watch. Meanwhile, Elena sighs, and I put her bag on the kitchen counter to leave her the choice of where she wants to settle, and I go to the fridge.

"Do you want something to drink?"

"I'm fine."

I pour a cup of water, nervous as hell. I got her to come here, now what? This is what I've been hoping for, but she's keeping her defenses up. Music from Estelle's movie fills the room, not exactly ideal. I head to the balcony, and thankfully, Elena follows. I take a seat, hoping she'll do the same.

"… You stopped smoking?" she asks, surprised.

"Yeah, about two years ago. I stopped a lot of things."

If she knew the wreck I was after she left… I hit rock bottom before I managed to climb back up. First, I started drinking a lot. Isaac and my brothers tried to help me as much as they could, but… I was a wreck. I put myself in danger so many times, Damian lost his shit. It's probably around that time I had my car accident… It took time, but I got better. A lot better. Damian thinks I went to the other end of the extreme, turning into a work and fitness junkie, but at least I don't put myself in danger anymore… And now that Elena and Estelle are here, I couldn't be more grateful. They both have no idea, but they're my best reason to live.

"Alright. I guess we need to discuss some things about our daughter."

"Elena…"

"Nathaniel, no."

She stops me with a determined expression, and I'm forced to shut up.

"We will only discuss Estelle. Because she's your daughter and if you have questions, I'm ready to answer them. Nothing else."

"Elena, it's not just Estelle I want to talk over with you. I know I really owe you an apology."

"Nathaniel, I–"

"No, listen."

I put my hand on hers. I'm the one who needs her to listen to me. I see she's mad, she's upset at me and rightfully so, but I need to speak up, at least once. I owe her that apology.

"Elena, I'm so, so sorry for not believing you back then. No matter the numbers, the tests, the hospital. I should have… I regretted it so many times, I swear. Even before I knew Estelle was really my baby, I wanted to bring you back and apologize. I didn't even care who her father was, I just wanted you back. You have no idea… how many times Damian and Liam kept me from doing some really, really stupid things. I was a fucking idiot, Elena. Because I was blinded by the idea you could have been with someone else. I died of jealousy. I just couldn't swallow it. When the results came back, I felt like you were betraying me a second time, and I lost it. I swear I never, ever meant for you to leave Silver City. I had no idea you would go somewhere I couldn't reach you."

"Nate, I didn't just leave because of you. So many things happened back then. I had no choice. Yes, you were part of the problem, but… it wasn't just about you."

It wasn't just because of me? Then what… I try to remember the situation back then, what else could have pushed her to leave not just me but the city…?

"Because of your pack? And your relationship to Nora?"

She growls, rolling her eyes.

"I'm not saying it wasn't partially your fault! But yeah. Because of all that. And Estelle… As soon as I announced I was pregnant with your child, things became complicated with my pack."

… What the fuck? Her pack pushed her to leave? For having my child?! I thought it was all my fault, but I never understood why she had to leave the city, and it turns out it was her pack's doing?!

"Elena, why did you leave?" I insist.

It has to be more complicated than that. Given Elena's personality, She wouldn't have just left if she had any other choice. Nora is a royal, and her cousin… I glance towards Estelle, and that's when it hits me.

"She's… a Royal?"

She nods. No way… Now that explains a couple of things…

"Why didn't you tell me? About your relationship with Nora?"

"It was so complicated, even for me, Nathaniel. I was barely sorting out who I was, no one wanted to talk to me about my origins. Even with Nora, we did nothing but guess until the truth came out."

"So it's true? You're cousins?"

She nods, and goes on to explain to me everything I was missing so far: how she felt her bond with Nora, how they both looked for answers regarding their biological family, what she learned from her mentor and Sylviana. That's a lot… I always knew she was special as a werewolf, but I had no idea how much.

"So that's why you're not fully Royal… but Estelle is?"

"Yes. Your Alpha blood was strong enough to awaken her Royal gene, or something like that. Daniel can explain it better than me."

Moon Goddess… I would have never imagined our daughter would be that special. Well, I had no idea her mother was either. I am glad a lot more things make sense now, though.

"Okay," I eventually mutter.

"That's it?" she frowns. "Okay?"

"What did you expect me to say? My daughter is a Royal, and you are Nora's cousin, though you're not completely Royal because your mother was human. I am not saying I wouldn't have wanted to know earlier, but it doesn't change much. I want you and Estelle back."

"She is your daughter, I never said otherwise," she immediately says.

"You know what I mean, Elena. I still love you."

Elena looks away from me; she probably wasn't expecting that, but I'd rather be honest and blunt. I'm not giving up on either of them.

"Nathaniel, no."

"I'm not going to do anything. I just needed you to know, Elena. I still love you, maybe even more than before."

"Can we just focus on Estelle for now?"

I nod. I know I won't convince her so easily… and I'm already happy with where we're at.

"Okay," she says. "I just want what's best for her right now."

"I still want both of you to stay here."

I insist before she changes her mind or thinks there's a better place for them to go, which I'm sure there isn't.

"I understand you want to spend time with Estelle, but don't include me in–"

"She is our daughter. And I don't want us to have to split our time with her, Elena. I'm not asking you to think of me like that. I mean, I do want us to get back together, but I know the most important right now is that we both stay with her. I have this huge apartment with enough rooms you can lock anytime. Estelle likes it here, and I know you do too."

I'm trying hard here, but I know I'll have to respect her decision, whatever it is. I'm just hoping that now that she's here, she'll agree to stay. I want her and Estelle here, I really do. Not only do I not know how I could spend one more night without her near, but I'm terrified at the idea that she'll put up more barriers and our relationship won't be rekindled. But I have hope. Lots of it; I can see in her eyes she's hesitating. Nora's pregnant, and her pack kicked her out. I know I shouldn't be happy about it, but I know that makes my place the most suitable home for the two of them. Moreover, we are a family. Estelle's our daughter, and she likes it here. She's waving at us from the couch, singing along to some Disney song.

Since she's taking a while to answer, I decide to give her the time to think; at least she won't make a rash decision and leave now.

"You can think about it until tonight, Elena. I know it's complicated for you to forgive me, but I'm not going to change my mind about anything I said. So, whether you leave or you stay, it's up to you. But I do want you here, and Estelle too, of course."

"Daddy!"

Our daughter comes running, getting tired of watching us through the window. She runs to me, all excited with her pink cheeks.

"Daddy, in the movie, they were eating spaghetti Bolognese! With big meatballs too! Can we eat that for lunch?"

Elena suddenly laughs, and I'm completely confused. She smiles at me between her tears.

"I was making Bolognese before we left the house."

"You made Bolognese?" I can't help but ask, a bit surprised.

"Mommy burnt it! With crunchy parts!"

I laugh, while her mother dies with embarrassment.

Chapter 30

"Daddy! Daddy, look!"

She runs to me, showing off her new drawing. This time, she used her new Disney stamps all over it, and a lot of blue glitter. I'm starting to regret buying her so much glitter. I feel like my black leather couch and white rug won't stay neutral for long.

"It's pretty, baby star. My daughter is an artist! Do you want to sell your drawings when you're a big girl? Or you can be an architect, and draw buildings and houses?"

"No, I want to bake cakes! I want to make cupcakes with lots of sparkles. I'll have one shop for pink cakes, one for blue cakes, and one with… um… orange cakes!"

"Woah, orange cupcakes? Alright, my daughter will be a pâtissière, then."

She nods, all proud of herself, and climbs on my lap, trying to peek at what I'm doing.

"Daddy, are you busy?" she asks, frowning at the numbers on my screen.

"Just catching up on some work. I'll finish later when you're in bed, okay? Are you hungry?"

"Um. No, I'm okay!"

I smile. We had crepes again for breakfast, and I think my daughter is slowly getting addicted to my cuisine. We discuss her drawing a bit longer, and I close my laptop. Isaac's emails can wait, I guess. To my surprise, someone knocks on the door, and Estelle runs toward it, curious.

It's her mom, who was waiting there for me to open the door.

"You can just come in next time, Elena. The passcode hasn't changed. Are you okay?"

She doesn't look okay. Her eyes are red, and I realize she was probably crying. I know she went to bury her mentor with Daniel and his brother this morning. She warned me last night, after she left to spend the evening with Nora, and I didn't see her since; I only know she came back here to sleep in one of my guest rooms, but she left early for the funeral this morning… I can't imagine how tough it must have been for her.

She nods, ignoring me to look for Estelle with her eyes. To my surprise, she gets on her knees, taking her hand gently and talking to her very seriously while I close the door behind them.

"Baby star, Mommy needs to tell you something."

"Are you okay, Mommy? You look sad," says Estelle, worried.

"Yes, baby, I'm very sad. Because Reagan left."

Estelle looks a bit confused for a second, glancing at me before looking at her mom again.

"She left? Why? Where did she go?"

"She went to be with the Moon Goddess, Estelle. Grandma Reagan won't be coming back, baby."

I don't know how much a four-year-old understands about death, but Estelle starts tearing up, biting her lip. She looks at me again, as if she was expecting me to say something, but when her mother and I both stay silent, she slowly starts crying.

"… She won't come back?"

"No, baby star. But she is with the Moon Goddess, and with your puppy heart, okay? If you want to cry, you can cry, baby."

"Okay..."

Estelle cries silently before her mom hugs her. Elena's grief is obvious too. I barely knew Reagan, but it breaks my heart to see the two of them like this. I step away, I don't know what to do. I know how tense things are right now, but the worst thing is, I'm just happy they are both here.

After a few minutes, Elena comes back, followed by Estelle.

"Can I have a coffee?" she asks, to my surprise.

"Of course. Baby, do you want a hot drink too?"

My daughter nods, wiping her tears clumsily.

"Can I get a hot chocolate, Daddy?"

"Sure, baby."

I start preparing it while Estelle proudly goes to show her latest drawings and new drawing tools to her mom. Thank Moon Goddess Estelle and I went to buy some groceries this morning, as it appears taking care of a child requires a bit more things than I thought, including but not limited to hot chocolate powder, chocolate sprinkles, and hazelnut paste. Once the coffee and hot chocolate are ready for the two women in my life, I proudly hand them their drinks.

"Here you go, young lady!"

"Thanks, Daddy!"

"Estelle, baby, why don't you make another drawing to show your auntie Nora later?"

"Okay! Wait here, Mommy, I'll do one with the princess stamp!"

She runs off to grab her pencils, and I prepare another coffee for myself. However, while I'm pouring, I realize Elena's eyes are on me.

"Nathaniel…"

"Yes?"

She puts her cup down, looking serious all of a sudden. Her amber eyes are a bit hesitant and shy, and she puts a strand of her hair behind her ear, her gesture when she's embarrassed.

"I… thought a bit about the situation. You're right on some things. I think Estelle should live with you, with her dad. She hasn't known you since the day she was born, and I want her to be able to."

I almost drop my cup, completely taken by surprise. Really? I did hope Elena would give it some consideration, but to think she would change her mind so fast. Did Nora or Damian tell her something? I haven't heard from them since Elena slept at their place last night.

She continues, looking down at her coffee, not showing too much of her emotions.

"I never wanted for her to live away from you, to begin with. It was just… too hard for me to come back."

"I know I'm partially to blame for that, and–"

"Shut up, Nate, let me talk first. I was in the wrong too. No matter how much grief I had against you and my pack, it was my own selfishness that kept Estelle from meeting you two years earlier. I should have come back when Nora woke up. I'm… sorry I didn't."

I'm speechless. I expected many things from Elena, but not an apology. I don't know how to react. I don't feel like I deserve it, to begin with. I was the one that acted like a jerk and didn't trust her. Why would she be the sorry one?

"I was given a lot to think about, after talking with Nora, and I realized it wouldn't be fair that you're the only one to apologize when we're both in the wrong. I'm not saying I'm forgiving you, remember that. I'm just saying I don't want us to lose any more time to fighting and bickering."

Wow. I'm speechless. I never thought she would come so far so fast. I know I'm still far from forgiveness, but I'm glad she's willing to give me a chance, even if it's for Estelle's sake. I can live with that.

"You can talk now," she says with a pout.

But I can't talk; I'm just smiling. Elena growls.

"Say something!"

"I love you."

She immediately blushes and looks away.

"Anything but that."

I chuckle. Moon Goddess, she's almost as cute as our baby. I lean closer, taking a sip from my cup of coffee. Elena sits back, crossing her arms and looking away, but I can tell she's still blushing a bit, embarrassed. I love this woman.

"Then, will you agree to live here?" I ask.

"Yes. Temporarily."

"That's fine by me. And the rooms next to Estelle's and across from mine are fully furnished and available. You can move your stuff in any time you want."

"Nathaniel, I don't have any stuff. I left in a hurry, remember? I only have this outfit, and a couple of T-shirts Nora lent me."

I doubt they are the right size. Nora and Elena may be related, but they don't have much in common. Elena's body is curvier than her cousin's, and she's taller.

"I can lend you a couple of shirts, but you should order something."

"It will take days before it gets here!"

I smile and take my phone out. Giving a quick call to my building's concierge, I make sure enough outfits for an adult woman will be delivered today for Elena's size and body build.

"Yes, Mr. Black, it will be delivered today before 6:00 p.m. Do you have any preference for brand or color?"

"I'll leave that to you, Harry."

I hang up before Elena's shocked eyes.

"Your concierge does your shopping?" she asks in disbelief.

"Rich people privilege. He gets some nice tips for such services."

"I don't know if I should be surprised or annoyed."

"It's okay. You can thank Harry later."

Elena rolls her eyes and gets up, going to check the bedrooms. I follow, a few steps behind. She stands speechless in front of Estelle's room, one of the walls half painted with blue and purple. It's a bit of a mess.

"What the heck happened here?" she asks, frowning.

"We started painting yesterday. It was more fun than I expected."

"Mommy!"

Estelle, who heard us, runs to her mom's leg and shows us her room, excited.

"Did you see, Mommy? It's the same color as Elsa's castle! And when it's dry, we can put some stickers, too!"

"Elsa's castle? Baby, are you going to redecorate all of daddy's apartment with a Disney theme?"

"I think we'll try to contain it to her bedroom for now," I whisper.

"Welcome to the world of a four-year-old," she whistles, amused.

I guess she had to go along with it long before me.

Elena turns around to check the other rooms, but as expected, she picks one of the ones I mentioned, leaving her backpack in it. Then, she turns to Estelle.

"What are you going to do with Daddy today, baby star?"

"We will finish painting my room! And then, we can build the princess castle Daddy brought!"

"Daddy opened his wallet, huh?" says Elena, sending me an annoyed look.

"*Stop buying her everything, I don't want my daughter to be too spoiled.*"

"*I'm just making up for missing the last four years. And she isn't spoiled. She is well-behaved and reasonable. Like her mom.*"

"*Mhmm...*"

"Come on, baby, let's go change before Mommy gets really mad at me," I say to Estelle, taking her to the bathroom.

We pick three of my T-shirts and spend most of the afternoon ruining them with paint. It was the most fun I had in years, thanks to them. We had to be careful because Elena's arm isn't fully healed, and though she won't admit it, I can tell it's painful for her.

She's relieved when we finish painting the wall, and heads to the living room to watch another Disney movie, at Estelle's demand. Elena actually picks her favorite, one with Greek gods and a lot of catchy songs for our daughter to learn. Thank Moon Goddess I subscribed to that new channel.

"Daddy…"

I hear a little whisper coming from the other side of the counter. I finish putting our plates in the dishwasher and turn to her.

"What is it, baby? You want more veggies?"

She frowns. I did notice she wasn't fond of the carrots in the casserole.

"No. Daddy, Mommy fell asleep."

"Oh, okay, I'm coming, baby. The movie is over?"

She nods, and walks back to the living room, with me following her. Indeed, Elena is profoundly sleeping on the couch, while the movie's closing credits are playing on the TV screen. I gesture for Estelle not to make any noise, and she smiles and covers her little mouth.

I pull a blanket on Elena and take Estelle to bed. Because of the fresh paint in her room, she'll have to sleep with her mom tonight, but I don't think it bothers either of them.

"... Daddy?"

"Yes, baby?"

"Mommy will live here too now?"

I chuckle. She sure is smart for her age, isn't she?

"Yes, baby, I think so. I hope so, baby star. But it's Mommy's choice, okay? So now, do you want me to read your book? Where did we stop last night?"

After reading a few pages of another Disney princess story, Estelle is deep asleep, and I silently leave the room. I clean the living room a bit, turning the TV off and putting Estelle's toys aside.

Suddenly, I hear a cry. On the couch next to me, Elena is frowning in her sleep, looking in pain. Shit, where are her meds? Can she take more? I kneel at her side, unsure what to do, panicked. It's surely her shoulder wound, she keeps moving in her sleep, looking for a better position. Is it too late to call Tonia for advice?

"You got some alcohol?"

Damn it, she's awake.

"It's been disinfected already."

"Not for that, idiot."

She sits up painfully, with my help, but she's sweating and frowning a lot.

"Elena, no, not with your meds. I don't have any anyway."

"Nate, it's only been 5 years," she says with a groan. "I remember your minibar."

I shake my head.

"It's long gone. It's been destroyed, emptied, and thrown out a while ago. You can ask Damian, he's the one who wreaked havoc on it."

For a few seconds, she stays silent, and sighs.

"Fuck, why did you have to go sober…"

"Come on, I'll help you to the bed. Or do you want me to call Tonia? We can ask her if you can take anything else."

"Help me to bed, then. Please," she sighs.

Gently, I take her to the bed, next to Estelle, who's still asleep. As soon as she's next to her, Elena smiles despite the pain.

"How did we make such a pretty baby…" she whispers.

"You tell me. You're the mom."

She smiles, caressing her blonde hair. I sit on the side of the bed, watching them, unwilling to part. Elena's face betrays the pain she feels, but she won't complain. At one point, I realize she's clenching her teeth, to endure the pain.

"*Elena...*"

"*Shut up.*"

I sigh, and move to sit behind her, putting my arm under her head.

"*... What are you doing?*"

"*Bite me.*"

"*Excuse me?*"

"*Bite me, Elena. You'll hurt your teeth if you keep going. And you're too stubborn for me to call you a nurse, so bite me.*"

"*I can bite myself!*"

"*I heal faster, Elena. Stop being so stubborn for once, okay? Even if it's for one hour, and then I promise I'll go.*"

"*...Stay.*"

"*What?*"

"*You heard me. Just... stay. Please.*"

I don't know how to answer. But, to my surprise, she takes my hand and holds on to it, tightly. We stay like this for a long time, until I slowly lay back behind her, with gentle movements. I can tell she's not sleeping, but she doesn't move, and rests her head on my arm, breathing slowly.

Chapter 31

I slowly wake up to that familiar feel of the sunshine on my skin. Where am I? I look around but nothing's familiar. Shit, it's painful. I look down at my arm, and remember. I am at Nate's place, with Estelle. What time is it? I'm alone in the bed, but I'm pretty sure I fell asleep with both of them by my side.

I struggle to sit up, putting my sling in the most comfortable position possible. Shit, I really wish I could heal fast like a normal werewolf. Wait, I'm in my panties? Who the hell took my pants off? I growl, annoyed.

Why can't I hear anything? It's quiet in here, isn't Estelle awake? She usually plays when she wakes up early.

I get up, and it takes me ages to put those damn jeans on. When I'm done, I'm exhausted, but still walk out of the room. Now that the door's open, I do hear a bit of music… Disney again? I walk to the living room and, as expected, Estelle is quietly playing with some toy castle, humming to the Disney music. Looks like Nate managed to trade a movie for a playlist this morning.

"Good morning, Mommy!"

"Good morning, baby star. Did you sleep well?"

"Yes! Daddy said to let you sleep, but that we should go out later, so I am playing now!"

"Good girl."

I give her a quick kiss and listen a bit to what she's playing with before leaving her to head to the kitchen. I dangerously need coffee at such a time, though it's probably later than usual. I freeze before I enter the kitchen, though.

Nathaniel is standing there, half-naked. How dare he be half-naked so early in the morning! He already had a nice body five years ago, but now, he looks like a damn model that just stepped out of a magazine. Who wears only jeans in a kitchen like some sexy movie! Gosh, I hate him. And his stupid abs. I close my eyes for a second. I need to adjust, or I'll literally jump on him.

"Good morning, Sunshine."

And his damn morning husky voice. I'm doomed.

"Hi," I grumble, trying to evade him while grabbing the coffee pot.

Coffee, I need to wake up and drink that damn coffee. Don't look, Elena. Don't look at those abs.

"You slept well?"

"Fine… By the way, did you take my pants off?"

"Um, you asked for it. Around 2:00 a.m. You were groaning a lot and basically kicked me a couple of times, saying you wanted to… undress."

Moon Goddess, if you're there, please let me die. Like, right now.

I take a deep breath. He's seen me naked hundreds of times anyway, right? No big deal that I was left in panties. Damn, what was I wearing again?

"I need to take a shower," I suddenly declare, gulping down my coffee.

"Do you need help–"

"Nathaniel Black, you stay out of the damn bathroom, or I swear I'll bite you."

I hear him chuckle as I exit the kitchen, but I don't care. He's playing with my nerves!

Taking a shower with one arm injured is even harder than I thought. I struggle to undress, struggle to take that damn sling off and struggle to shower without soaking my bandages. What a mess. My legs still have scars too, so I guess it isn't going to heal at all. I sigh. At least I'm alive and have all my limbs.

"Elena? Everything okay?" I hear him yell from behind the door.

"I'm fine!"

If he enters this room while I'm naked, I swear I'll lose it. I hurry up, making sure to clean myself the best I can, and grab a towel to wrap myself in, and… Damn it. I forgot to bring in new clothes. They were delivered last night, but I left them in my room. Crap. I need to cross the hallway in that stupid towel.

It's okay, he's seen it all already anyway. Just act calm, Elena, you've been in worse situations than walking around half-naked in your ex's apartment.

"Nice view."

"Why are you behind this damn door, Nate?"

He chuckles, glancing over without mercy.

"I was wondering if you needed help."

"Oh, shut up and let me through!"

I push him out of the way to get to the closet, torn between anger and embarrassment. I want to punch him, if only my arm was healed enough. I grab whatever clothes I can find in a hurry. Thank Moon Goddess, it's the right fit, and Harry has good tastes. I find a black undergarment ensemble, and a comfy sleeveless jumpsuit from an Italian brand I don't recognize. At least I don't spend half an hour putting it on or taking it off, I can slide into it right away.

"Still don't need help?"

"No!"

I hear him laugh and leave the room. He's doing this on purpose, isn't he?

"… Elena?"

"I'm almost done, Nate, can't you just…"

"No, I think you should come and… see."

His voice changed, and I realize something's wrong. He's in the living room? What is it? Did Estelle do something? I hurry over, and I can't see my daughter for a few seconds, making me panic. Until I realize Nate is behind the couch, looking down. Is she crouching?

I walk over, and stand there speechless. Oh, Moon Goddess. Nate looks at me, totally stunned too.

"I think we have a problem," he says.

I nod. Estelle is there. But not as a human.

My daughter turned into an adorable wolf pup, with perfectly white fur and big, blue eyes.

Oh, Moon Goddess. She looks like a mini-Nora. Like, a perfect Royal. White as snow, literally, and blue eyes like her dad. Holy Moon Goddess. Nathaniel is as helpless as I am, staring at her, not knowing what to do. I don't know either.

"Estelle, baby."

"*Mommy!*"

The puppy turns and throttles to me, all excited. How did she shape-shift? How can she even shape-shift when she's not even five years old yet! I kneel to her height. What am I supposed to say? I've never dealt with a werewolf cub, not one so young! Is it dangerous if she stays like that? I turn to Nathaniel, but he's already taken out his phone.

"Damian? It's Nate, um… We have a little bit of an issue here. Estelle shape-shifted. Yes, I know, but I swear, Damian, she's right in front of me, and she's a pup. No… Yes, yes, okay. I'll do that. Can you… Yes, please. Thanks. See you later."

He hangs up.

"What did he say?"

"He said to bring her over. He'll call Tonia so she can check."

"Check what? Tonia is…"

"A nurse now. And she knows a lot about shape-shifting and all that; Boyan was a super precocious one too."

He grabs his car keys, turns off the TV, and I see him run to the bedroom. What did he grab? Oh, a change of clothes. I feel totally useless, but my daughter looks fine, playing around in front of me and nibbling some toy. Is this okay?

"Elena?"

Nathaniel walks up to us, carrying a backpack. He crouches down, smiling confidently to our daughter.

"Let's go see Auntie Nora, baby. And your uncles?"

"*Now? Are we going now, Daddy?*"

"Yes. Come here."

He carries her in his arms, while I'm still completely at a loss. Nate notices my expression and takes my hand.

"Come on, let's go. It's okay, Elena."

I nod, but really, is it okay? We leave his apartment and get in the car, but while Nathaniel drives, I can't settle down. What does that mean? Won't the Dark Witch sense Estelle more easily now? Is she in danger? How can she already shape-shift, she's four years old! I have so many questions, I just can't calm down.

Next to me, Nathaniel is acting confident, talking to Estelle, who sat down behind us, looking out the window.

"Do you want some music, baby?"

"*Yes!*"

He puts on the same playlist from earlier on his phone, aiming the speakers toward the back seat. I let out a deep sigh. Before I can react, Nate puts a hand on my knee, whispering so she can't hear us above the music.

"It will be okay, Elena."

"She's just four! How can she…?"

"You know it happens. It's fine. Tonia will just make sure she's fine, but she doesn't seem to be in any pain, and nothing about her werewolf aura has changed. It's okay."

"When Nora shape-shifted, I felt it. "

"You weren't there when Nora shape-shifted for the first time. You probably only felt something because you were close, and her kin. Calm down, it's going to be okay. In any case, Sylviana can probably do something."

"Do what? We can't forbid our daughter from shape-shifting! She probably doesn't even know the difference!"

He sighs but doesn't answer. Meanwhile, I can't stop glancing at the puppy behind us, who's happily nodding to the tune. At least she doesn't seem too disturbed.

Nathaniel finally parks in front of Damian and Nora's house. They are both waiting for us on the porch. Nora opens her mouth wide, seeing Estelle confidently jump out of the car.

"Moon Goddess… She's so cute!"

Is that all she's thinking? Am I the only one literally freaking out? Damian seems to notice my expression and walks up to me.

"It's okay. Come on in."

We sit in their living room, and Boyan walks in carrying James. Of course, the two-year-old is overjoyed when seeing the puppy and runs to her. The two kids start playing a game of tag, while I sit next to my cousin, anxious.

"How come she shape-shifted? She's too young to shape-shift!"

"It's okay, Elena. Bobo shape-shifted for the first time when he was about her age too. And she is a Royal; she might be a precocious one because of that."

"I don't want her to be precocious, Nora! Look at her, anyone can tell she's a Royal like you!"

"I can barely feel the change in her aura, Elena, calm down. We called Tonia and Sylviana, they'll be here any minute, okay? Let's have some tea."

Nora gets up to pour some tea, kicking Damian out of the kitchen in the meantime. I can't calm down though. Boyan is watching over the two kids running around in the living room, laughing so much while chasing each other. Neither of them seems disturbed by the fact that my daughter is a white pup.

When Tonia finally arrives, I almost jump on her, but she frowns and gestures for me to shut up.

"No, don't start. First of all, yes, werewolves can shape-shift that young. No, she doesn't have any health-related issues because of that, and yes, she is fine. Okay, now you can ask."

"How can that happen?"

"Like any werewolf kid! Excitement, anger, any strong emotion can trigger our first shape-shift, Elena! The only problem with Estelle is that she is too young to even realize she shape-shifted! It's so natural to her, she doesn't care much about it. So chill, mama, she's fine, okay? Now, where are the brats…"

Tonia dismisses me and walks in, grabbing Estelle by her neck when she runs close to her. I don't like seeing my baby manipulated like that, even if she's in her puppy form. Right away, Tonia starts inspecting her, ignoring my daughter's annoyed growls.

"She's a normal size. With those paws, she'll grow to be your size, I'd say. Good fangs. Hey, don't bite or I'll bite you back. Her eyes are fine too. Her tail's a bit short but that's okay. Fine, you can go now."

She lets Estelle go and my daughter runs back to play with her cousin. At least she's okay. I let out a long sigh, and Nathaniel comes to sit next to me, putting his arm around me. I finally accept Nora's tea and, for a few minutes, we just watch the kids play.

"I wonder if James will be all white too, or jet-black like you," whispers Nora to Damian, who's caressing her big belly.

"Definitely white," replies Tonia. "His Royal aura is even stronger than Estelle's. There's no way he will have black fur."

"Too bad… Well, white is cute."

Damian chuckles.

"Nora, you should–"

"If you tell me to rest again, Damian Black, I'll kick you. I'm pregnant, not disabled."

It's my turn to chuckle. I can't pick sides on this one, Damian looks genuinely worried for his wife. Nora is almost seven months along now. Werewolf pregnancies are a bit shorter, so my cousin might give birth within the next two months.

"Good morning, everyone!"

Sylviana just walked in, followed by a tall black wolf. Did Liam Black get bigger? He's lost all his teenage attitude. Immediately, both James and Estelle run to them, excited by the presence of another wolf. Damn, it's going to be crazy in here if we have more pups that can shape-shift, starting with Nora's next baby. I notice Damian's frowning a bit too, probably thinking the same as me. How many werewolf pups can we handle at the same time? Those two have been running around for twenty minutes straight!

Sylviana smiles and sits on the floor to hug James, who's apparently very familiar with the witch, and Estelle is happily playing with her too.

"Elena freaked out," says Tonia right away.

"It's fine," whispers the witch.

"She will feel it, won't she?" asks Nathaniel before I do.

Sylviana nods.

"Yeah. Estelle's Royal Aura just increased; she won't miss something like that. She is probably waiting for the right moment, though."

"What is the right moment?" I ask. "Why would she delay her attack?"

The witch stays silent for a while, and Liam takes over playing with the kids, pushing Estelle around and letting James chase him. Sylviana stands up, crossing her arms.

"I've been thinking about what a good time would be. I think she's scared of Nora, mostly."

"Scared of me?" says my cousin. "I've never fought her."

"No, but she has experience with Royals. With your family. I was wondering why she hasn't attacked sooner. First, I thought the Black brothers had scared her after pushing all the vampires away four years ago, but… I think that now, you're the one she's scared of. Nora, you're probably as powerful as your grandmother was, and the Dark Witch was never able to attack until Diane made a mistake."

"You mean when she lifted the barrier for Reagan?"

"I think so. I think she is probably sensing that Nora is protecting Silver City in her own way. And Damian protects Nora, and all the packs protect them. She doesn't want to make any mistakes this time, so she'll wait until Nora is vulnerable to attack her."

"Define vulnerable?" says Nate, frowning and glancing at my cousin.

"The one moment Nora won't be able to fight her off…"

Nora is frowning, confused, but next to her, her husband's eyes are already murderous. He understood, too.

"… She's waiting for Nora to go into labor."

Nathaniel shakes his head, confused.

"Wait a second. If that's the case, why didn't she... Why didn't that witch attack when James was born?"

"I'm not sure. She might have missed her chance. Nora's power was even stronger while she was asleep, remember? Her aura could be felt all the time, and even stronger at night."

"When her hair turned white," whispers Tonia.

"That's right. And it was not that long after the vampire attack, which you decimated."

"She probably didn't have any army to attack with, even if it had been two years," I say.

Sylviana sighs.

"She's just like me. A woman, even if she's a witch, all on her own. I don't know how she can compel vampires to do her bidding, but if it were me, I would have taken my time to gather a new army, and focused on improving my magic too. Since she was beaten once and aware of the fact that I'm here, she wouldn't attack blindly a second time."

"You're still stronger than her, right?" asks Tonia, concerned.

After a few seconds, Sylviana sighs.

"I'm not sure these days. She's getting closer, and whatever I try to do, I'm barely slowing her down. I only win over her by a bit because of our elements."

"Because of what you explained to me?" asks Nora. "The cycle? Water beats fire, fire beats earth and..."

"Earth overpowers water. It's a very simplistic way to put it, but yes. But there's a lot more than that to take into consideration. Our race doesn't function like humans, even less like werewolves. We can change a lot in a few years' time. I've put all the defenses I can around Silver City, but without Nora..."

"Okay, time out," I exclaim, standing up. "Can someone explain to me what is Nora's superpower? Because I'm feeling like I really missed a chapter here. Her hair glows white, and she's got a big, mean, supersized Royal Aura. What else?"

Nora blushes a bit, and I frown. What now? My cousin turns to me, hesitating a bit.

"I have some sort of power that makes people listen to me."

"That's part of the aura thing."

"No, not just that," says my cousin, shaking her head. "I noticed it a few months after I woke up. It had happened before, but I can give orders, and people can't fight it."

I'm about to say something, but Damian puts his hand around her with a little smile.

"Even I can't say no when she gets mad."

Even the King? Okay, that's a bit weird. I turn to Sylviana. The witch is fidgeting, maybe for the first time since we've met her. She's brushing her long red hair, frowning, visibly thinking deep about all of this.

"You're going to tell us that's not… part of the aura thing?"

"Oh, it is. But just imagine it as Nora having an unfightable willpower. It's as if the Moon Goddess herself spoke. No werewolf can fight her, not even her own mate, or any alpha out there."

I shake my head. I'm getting very confused here. I had noticed that Nora's aura had gotten crazy strong, stronger than before, but it's not nearly as aggressive and scary as her husband's. She's like a calm force… It would be like comparing a small flurry of fresh white snow to a dark stormy hurricane. I can't even picture her making her husband submit to her.

"I know," says Sylviana, "but it's the truth. No living night creature in Silver City can refuse Nora. Even a human would feel something."

I chuckle nervously, as I start to understand.

"Wait, you're telling me Nora could potentially control that Dark Witch? For real?"

"I can't guarantee her aura is strong enough, but we are creatures under the Moon Goddess' power, just like you. If Nora ordered me to go and hang myself right now, I'd probably have a hard time ignoring her."

I stay speechless.

This is huge. My cousin's superpower is to give orders? Unrefusable orders? Like a… a Werewolf Queen, for Moon Goddess' sake. Even stronger than a Luna. I laugh nervously, but there's really nothing funny about it. I turn to Nathaniel, who's frowning, visibly confused too. I eventually turn to Nora.

"Why don't we just end it now? We could just find that witch, and if you–"

Next to her, Damian growls at me immediately.

"Nora is pregnant, she's not taking one step outside Silver City."

His murderous glare is convincing. I look down, reminding myself he's still the King.

"Even if she could potentially fight off that witch, there's still the vampires," says Tonia. "Her main problem is that, while she is pregnant, if she gets bitten just once…"

"She could die," whispers Nathaniel, bitter.

Why do I feel like this is a taboo subject here? I shake my head, annoyed. I can't believe we're stuck. On one hand, that witch is too scared of Nora's power to attack, and on the other, Nora can't risk a vampire bite.

I hate this. I hate not being able to do anything, waiting for something to happen in this stupid climate of fear. Nate walks up to me, putting his arms around me to try and comfort me, but I keep shaking my head. Why do I even feel like crying?

"Elena."

Here we go, I'm crying. I'm so fucking tired of crying these days! But I can't stop it, neither can I stop Nathaniel from hugging me, though he's careful not to hurt my arm. I hear Nora growl behind me, pissed too. She suddenly stands up.

"I'm not waiting and doing nothing. I want all the Alphas to gather tomorrow. Let's explain this to them. If hell must break loose when this baby decides to come out, I'd rather be ready. Sylviana, you too, please."

"Of course."

"I'm coming too," I declare, sniffling, but Nora shakes her head.

"No, Elena, you go home and focus on getting better, okay?"

"Don't leave me out of it!"

"Elena, I'm the one who's going to be left out!" she yells. "Don't you think I'm frustrated too? I'm already scared enough for my babies, now I'm going to be the trigger for when that damned Dark Witch will attack, and there's nothing I'll be able to do because I'll be too focused on giving birth!"

Only then do I realize my cousin's crying too, with red eyes and a raspy voice. She walks up to me, facing me, voicing her emotions out. She's twirling her messy curls, her thing when she's frustrated or stressed… or both, I guess.

"Elena, you're the fighter," she says. "I'm the healer, the protector. I was never a fighter, okay? It was always going to be this way, right? You'll be healed by then, but I won't be able to fight. Trust me, I hate it. I hate standing on the sidelines, but this time, I probably won't have a choice. You'll be the one this time. Okay?"

I shake my head. I hate this whole situation. Nora won't be in the battle, but she'll be the target. The first fucking target of that Dark Witch. She doesn't care about me, the half-breed. In a way, I was lucky to have a human mother. But Estelle…

I turn to my daughter, who's playing with James, trying to catch Boyan's tail and barking with excitement. Estelle will be a target too. I take a deep breath and turn to Nora, who's clumsily wiping her tears away.

"Promise me you'll protect her."

"What?"

"All three of the Black brothers and I will be fighting, so if anything happens to me and Nate, you'll be the only family Estelle has left. Promise me you'll protect her. I can fight, but I won't be able to focus if I don't know my daughter is safe."

"Elena!" yells Nate, but I turn to him.

"Don't act like you don't know, Nate. It's going to be an all-out war. They'll need both of us, and Estelle… I love Danny, but his family is mostly betas, and they'll probably be on the front lines too. Nora will be the only one to protect our baby."

"Stop it. Nothing will happen to you, to us."

"I'm just saying if…"

We stare at each other for a few seconds, a heated tension between us. I'm dead serious, and I don't care if he doesn't want to hear the truth. Nora gently takes my hand.

"Elena, it will be alright. We'll win, okay?"

I nod, but the truth is, I don't have the confidence.

Sylviana's expression is too dark to be confident. She's blankly staring at the children. How much does she really know? Our Good Witch realizes I'm watching her and leaves the room without warning. Liam follows right after her.

I let out a big sigh.

"Anyone else want to add something not depressing about this?"

"*... I'm hungry.*"

I can't help but chuckle at Boyan's out-of-the-blue sentence. Immediately, both kids jump on his back.

"*I'm hungry too!*"

"*Me too!*"

"Let's have brunch," says Tonia, heading to the kitchen as if this was her own house.

Meanwhile, I exchange a glance with Nora.

"Is it me or did James just…"

"Mind-link Boyan and Estelle? Yeah, he can do that. Estelle's not the only precocious one," sighs my cousin. "Royal babies are full of surprises."

Gosh, such a headache. Behind me, Nate chuckles and walks up to me, hugging me from behind. Damian and Nora silently walk to the kitchen, leaving us alone with Boyan and the kids.

"Aren't you taking advantage of the situation?" I ask.

"You think?"

He has no intention to let go, apparently. I sigh. I'm in no mood to fight now, so I just rest my head on his shoulder, enjoying this innocent hug for a while. It's too much emotion for one morning. Seeing this as a silent agreement, Nate goes ahead and kisses my shoulder.

"Hey."

But he ignores me, and keeps going, climbing up to my neck. Oh, gosh, he's so…

"*Ahem.*"

Boyan the bear-sized wolf is staring at us, with a blank expression, clearly reminding us we're not alone. Crap. I push Nate away and escape, hearing him chuckle behind me. He's so annoying!

After texting Daniel to come over, we enjoy a big family brunch in the garden. It's a nice day in July and frankly, when we're all gathered like this, it doesn't feel like it could end in a few weeks. Liam and Boyan, in their wolf forms, keep the kids entertained as long as we feed them too. I get why Nora needs Boyan as a nanny; James is an energy pill. Not in a bad way though, he does listen to his parents.

I realize my best friend is staring fondly at his fiancé. So cute. I can't help but wink at him, making him blush immediately.

"*Oh, stop it. Where are you at with Mr. Perfect Abs?*"

"*How do you know about his abs?*"

"*He was in an amazing sporty outfit when he got you. Very fitting. Tight. Well, I have an eye for that. So?*"

"*Nothing…*"

"*Oh, shut up, Boyan said you were shamelessly hugging just minutes ago.*"

"*Why did you ask if you already know!*"

We bicker a bit longer. Daniel and I got so used to mind-linking each other at his family dinners, we can keep going for a long time without anyone even noticing. It's a bit impolite, but with this topic, we are certainly not going to mention it out loud.

"*So, you're giving him the goods.*"

"*No.*"

"*You really want to give him the goods.*"

"No!"

"Oh, please, girl, you lived alone in a freaking forest for four and a half years. You're not a nun, and you live with your very, very sexy ex-sex-friend-almost-boyfriend who had the great idea to get an even sexier body in the meantime. You're hungry."

"Daniel, shut up."

"Hungry and starving..."

I decide to ignore him, but his smirk is not subtle. I hate how right he is sometimes! I need to focus hard on something else to elude both Daniel's eyes and Nathaniel's direction. I eat a bit more and try to participate in Nora and Damian's debate over the baby's name, which, surprisingly, they haven't agreed on yet.

An hour later, Daniel needs to get back to work, and James and Nora need their nap. I guess it's time for us to go back too. Thank Moon Goddess Estelle shape-shifted back, and we carefully explained to her why she should learn to control herself from now on. Though Silver City's humans are used to werewolves, we can't have people, especially young ones, running around and shape-shifting in front of their noses all day.

Nate drives us back to his apartment, and Estelle is sleeping soundly in his arms when we get to the elevator. I take note that playing with her cousin managed to make her that tired. I just hope she won't be sleeping too long and be hard to put to sleep tonight.

When Nathaniel closes her bedroom door, I let out a long sigh.

"What a morning, huh?" he says.

I nod, landing my ass on the living room couch. Nate comes to sit opposite me with a faint smile.

"What are you smiling for?" I ask.

"I think I'm a bit crazy. I know we're about to face a never-seen-before war, yet all I can think about is how happy I am that you and Estelle are living here."

"You idiot," I say, pushing him with my foot.

He grabs my ankle and, without warning, starts to caress my ankle. The feeling of his fingers on my skin makes me blush like crazy... I try to get away, but the sofa isn't that big. He pulls my legs onto his knee, and I don't have the strength to refuse him. Gosh...

I don't want to give in to him so easily, but when he keeps caressing my skin, I don't say anything. Why did I wear something so short? I mean, it's summer, but still. Nathaniel keeps going, silently moving to my leg, his electric blue eyes still on me. So annoying... I'm blushing.

"You're not too tired? You should take your meds."

I shake my head. I hate taking medicine, it makes me drowsy. I would rather stay here and snooze on the couch with him. Nathaniel doesn't add anything either, but he won't take his eyes off me. This is such a strange situation… A few days ago, we couldn't have been further apart. It took a witch's attack to bring us back together. So, what now?

"How are you feeling?"

"I'm fine. I may be a slow healer, but I can still heal. It doesn't hurt more than a sprain now."

To prove my words, I take off the useless sling that was holding my arm, and pull down my shirt to show the pink scar on my shoulder. I was wondering if he might feel disgusted by it, but he just nods with a satisfied look.

"Can you move?"

"Yeah. It just aches a bit if I use my muscles too much."

Wait, he's not thinking of doing anything too… straining, right? I frown a bit, recalling Danny's earlier words. I don't know how much I can trust my own self control right now. I've been sex-deprived for a few years, after all… I wonder if that's the case for him too.

"Nate."

"Hm?"

"Did you sleep with anyone else after I left?"

He doesn't answer, but goes as white as a sheet, which pretty much gives away his answer. Fuck. I had hoped for something different. I click my tongue, a bit annoyed. I guess I was the only one living like a nun.

"Nothing serious," he says. "It was only a few one-night stands."

"Fuck you, Nate."

"I swear, I never saw them twice."

"Fuck you and shut up."

He looks down, and from his expression, I can tell he is swearing internally, probably pissed at himself. Serves him right. I'm not in a forgiving mood anyway, so I'd rather not talk about this again. At least he's not giving me the alpha male excuse.

Following this, I see him take a deep breath. I wonder where his deep thinking brought him to. Back then, I thought I had learned to decipher his emotions but now, it's like we're back to square one all over again. It annoys me a bit. It's not like we both have a clean slate, anyway.

"Elena, would you marry me?"

… Has he gone crazy now? I look at him, speechless. What the heck was he thinking to utter those words now? Is he that desperate?

"No. Hell no."

No way I'm ready for this kind of thing, and certainly not with a man who just confessed he had sex with Moon-Goddess-knows how many women since I've been gone. Unlike my expectations, he slowly nods, not looking surprised.

"I thought you'd trust me more that way."

"You think marriage prevents cheating? Are you serious?"

"It works for Nora and Damian."

"Your brother and my cousin are fated mates, they'll stay faithful to each other basically for life. I don't know if you've noticed, but neither of us is anything close to that," I reply angrily.

I get up, annoyed at him for some reason. He can't compare me to Nora. I'm not my cousin. I love her, truly, but we're worlds apart. In the way we were raised, grew up, fought, and found love, Nora and I are absolutely nothing alike. If it wasn't for a blood test, I wouldn't even believe we're the same family and our parents were twins.

I see him get up too, and just as I'm about to walk away from him, this idiot follows me all the way to the kitchen. I try to ignore him and grab a glass of wine. Nathaniel chuckles, annoying me a bit because I'm torn between ignoring him and asking what is so funny.

"Stop laughing."

"I'm not laughing."

"You're having fun, anyway. Nothing is fun–"

"Elena, calm down."

Before I can protest, he corners me, putting his arms on either side of me, hands on the counter. I'm so surprised I miss the chance to say anything. Moreover, he's already dangerously close, and his scent becomes a bit of a problem. It's alluring. Too alluring.

"It's fine. Estelle will be fine, so will we."

"I saw my baby shape-shift for the first time today, Nate, it's not–"

"It's the natural order of things, she had to shape-shift one day. So what if she's early and a Royal? You already knew that, right? It's pointless to worry over that. She is who she is. I don't care how many witches come after her, I'll protect my daughter."

"Our daughter."

"Our daughter. Elena, I'm her dad, alright?"

"That's easy for you to say now!"

He smiles, annoying me to the core. Can he just drop that attitude of his? He takes one step closer. I didn't realize he could come closer and still not touch me. He's driving me crazy. I have to look away so as to not look at him now. It's unnatural. He knows. We both know.

"Estelle has two powerful uncles, the greatest Luna aunt, and her parents are warriors. Her mom is the strongest, toughest she-wolf I know. She'll grow old and beautiful like her mom."

"Stop the sweet-talking, idiot…"

Of course, he doesn't listen.

I freeze when his lips get dangerously close. I'm taking a deep breath in, but right before our lips touch, he suddenly changes direction, and softly kisses my cheek. I blush. That. That!!

"Elena?"

"You're kidding me, right?"

Before he can add anything else, I grab his hair, and pull him in, kissing him fiercely. "That's how you should be kissing me!" is what I want to say, but of course, my mouth is too busy for that. Moon Goddess, his lips, his taste… I missed this so much. His hands are already caressing my body, my neck, my hair, while I moan under our passionate kissing. How did I survive without his kisses for four years? How? Nate's tongue is on mine, driving me crazy, stirring up the heat from the depths of my body, making me burn all throughout. I'm trembling, grabbing him, kissing him hard and deep.

"Elena… Elena…"

His voice is consummated by desire, and driving me equally crazy… We're both going nuts. I don't know. I keep searching for air, but I want his kisses more. I'm cornered in his kitchen, his arms all around me, caressing my skin and undoing my clothes skillfully. I'm so hot… I want more, more.

My self-control flew out of the window as soon as he touched me. I hate him… I hate what he does to me, and this foolish body of mine for craving him when I should be resenting him for… I don't know, at least a few weeks more. Nate lifts me without warning, getting rid of my outfit and having it slide down to my ankles until it drops to the floor. He makes me sit on the kitchen counter, and I immediately entrap him between my legs. I'm in my underwear, in his kitchen, facing him. I'm hot. So fucking hot.

His fingers keep caressing my skin, my thighs, my waist, my back. I shiver and let the sparks crawl under my skin, a wave of pleasure slowly rocking back and forth. I struggle to get him out of his shirt, making him chuckle… I make him shut up with even more kissing, our tongues fighting to get a better taste of the other. When I suddenly feel his fingers on my panties, I grab his wrist, freezing.

It's… not…

"Elena?" he asks, out of breath too.

"I… I…"

My head is in such confusion right now, I don't even know how to formulate my thoughts into words. I'm red from head to toe, out of breath and excited. He stares at me, confused, half-naked and in about the same state as I am.

"I… I had a baby."

"I already know that," he replies, a bit confused.

"It means my body changed. I… My… I mean, sex is not going to be… to be like before."

He chuckles, caressing my nape with a tender look in his eyes. I don't think he's getting it, but a wave of anxiety overpowers me in a few seconds. What if he's disappointed? What if he doesn't like my body anymore? What if we have the lousiest sex ever and…

"Elena, look at me."

He manages to get my attention, but I shake my head.

"You know what? Let's forget it. This is a bad idea. I can just…"

But while I struggle to escape him, he keeps smiling and holds me back, until I stop fighting and sigh.

"Elena Whitewood, I love you."

Holy Moon Goddess, why does he have to be so cheesy right now? I'm blushing like crazy, trying to evade his eyes, but he caresses my neck, speaking softly.

"I don't care how much your body has changed. I want to embrace the woman I love. That's all I am thinking about. I'll love it because it's you. I don't care how much your body changes, my sunshine. Even if you get wrinkles or gain a hundred more pounds, I'll love this body of yours."

"Sh… Shut up…" I stutter, even more ashamed right now.

Is he saying that because he noticed I took on a bit more weight? Before I can say anything else, he slowly kisses the tips of my fingers. His mesmerizing blue gaze is on me, making me crazy. He kisses each of my fingers one by one, then goes to my palm. It's like this part of my body is suddenly connected to another, more intimate part, and sending electricity there. I shiver, burning inside. His kisses move to my wrist, and keep climbing higher and higher, until he reaches my bra. His lips go in between, and, skilled as he is, that bastard, he takes it off in a matter of seconds. It's best not to think about how he got so skilled. I breathe louder as he keeps kissing, fondling, and caressing me. I reach out for his warmth too, my arms go to his back, stroking it, going lower. I can't strain my shoulder, but I won't let him do it all by himself either…

The heat goes up in the kitchen, and before I know it, we're both naked against each other, hotter than ever. My heart is thumping in my ears, I'm… excited beyond words. It's Nate. Nathaniel. The man I left four years ago, the man I've been wanting for four years. I don't know if I should be glad or regretful, but it's way too late. I want him. I want him so bad. When we unite our bodies, I can't hold back a cry of pleasure. It takes the two of us a few seconds to recover just from that deep, forceful contact. We kiss again in that short lapse of time, unable to hold it. It's like it never happened. Like we're back to four years ago but… with something better. Something more fusional between us, something I don't want to miss ever again. His body is bulkier, manlier, and I can't handle it all. The muscles moving under his skin are driving me crazy.

Nate keeps moving, inside, and I can't hold it. He's gotten even better, if it was possible. My extremities are going crazy with lust, tickling, and I need to focus on breathing so as not to explode. He's not even going fast or wild, it's just… so, so good. He remembers my body, how to make me go insane with pleasure. My stomach is bursting, my insides overwhelmed by the friction of our bodies between my legs. Worst thing is, I have to be careful not to be too loud; I'm scared it will wake Estelle up, and I really don't want that.

"Nate… Nate… More… Please…"

As if he was waiting for my go-ahead, he suddenly accelerates, and I wasn't prepared. I breathe and moan, grabbing his broad shoulders to hold on, the blood rushing. After a while, I realize his erratic breathing mixes with his husky voice, calling my name. I hear it, again and again, as he keeps thrusting, creating sparks inside, making me cry out.

After a while, I finally feel it coming. I don't know how long we've been like this, but I can't take it anymore, and I can feel him tensing up, groaning louder. A few seconds later, we both explode, like a firework in my head and our joined bodies.

"You… Are you okay?" he asks, out of breath.

I slowly nod.

Moon Goddess. How did we spend hours having sex before? Just a few minutes and I'm so freaking tired. Nathaniel doesn't seem as exhausted as I am. He just kisses my shoulder while I rest on his, caressing my back.

"I missed you… I missed you so much…" he whispers while gently hugging me.

To my own surprise, his words bring me to tears. I hug him back, hiding my pathetic sobbing in his shoulder.

"Elena? Are you in pain? Did I…"

"Shut up…" I sob.

He sighs, and lifts me up again, holding me effortlessly. Damn it. Between his strength and his new muscles, I'll get really addicted to his new body.

"… I missed you too. You jerk."

"Elena, I…"

"You damn jerk. I hate you…"

I hear him chuckle and kiss my neck again.

"I know. I'm sorry. And I love you, too."

"Stop saying that. I still hate you."

"Mhmm."

I know he doesn't care, but I'm still annoyed at him.

A bit.

"Bath? Shower?" he asks softly.

"Hmm… A bath."

"Alright. And maybe we can go for a second–"

"Shut up!"

I hear him chuckle while he carries me to the bathroom. Damn it.

I wake up, completely bewildered, but the cries of my daughter are the best alarm clock. I frown, confused before I recognize Nate's place… and his voice. Sounds like he's already with her. I still need to go and check what happened, my wolf mom instincts won't have it. I find a shirt of Nate's and put it on before walking out of his bedroom.

When I walk into the kitchen, he's hugging her, while our baby girl is sobbing silently on his shoulder. He glances at my bare legs, but I ignore him and walk up to them.

"Oh, baby. What happened?"

"I woke up and… Daddy wasn't here, and you weren't here, Mommy… So, I was really scared and I cried a lot…"

"Don't be scared, little star, we're here. I always told you, didn't I? Mommy will always be here for you."

She had one of those panics again… I caress her hair and kiss her wet cheeks, but I leave her in her dad's arms since he's doing a nice job already. My heart becomes so warm every time I see him with her…

"Do you want a hot chocolate, baby star? I think you're hungry, my baby. You skipped dinner last night, remember?"

She nods and decides to come to me. Nathaniel hands her over to me without a word but keeps caressing her hair. She looks so much like him with those big blue eyes of hers still sparkling from all her tears earlier.

"Daddy… Can we have breakfast now… Please?"

He smiles and kisses her cheek, and we head together to the kitchen. I have her sit up on the counter and take a stool to sit on the other side with a little smile, brushing Estelle's hair. Looks like Daddy's in charge of breakfast.

"What does our baby star want to eat?"

"I think our empty stomachs call for brunch," I immediately state with a wink.

I know he gets what I mean. He smiles and turns to Estelle, kissing her forehead.

"You like a good potato omelet, baby?"

Estelle's all curious, watching him cook with wide eyes. Nate goes all out and makes three big potato omelets, with some bell peppers, smoked salmon on the side, and toast. Of course, our princess gets her hot chocolate while her dad and I gulp down our dose of caffeine. We cheerfully eat breakfast all together in the kitchen, and the tears from earlier are easily dried up. Estelle laughs with us about my useless attempt to help Nate and tells us all about her play date with her cousin last night.

When she's done eating, she runs to her bedroom to play, leaving us alone in the kitchen. I'm still chewing on that delicious toast when Nate walks over to my side, putting his hands on my ass. I'm so surprised I don't even have time to protest before he takes a bite of my food.

"Hey, let me eat, you wolf."

"I'm hungry."

"Well in that case you should have cooked more."

"I'm not talking about the food…"

Oh… I guess my bare legs did give him an idea, hm? He hugs me, taking a long sniff… Do I smell? Not that he seems to care. He puts gentle kisses on my shoulder.

"Nate, stop it…"

Estelle's literally next door, we can't go overboard here and now… although I feel his arousal tickle mine. He groans but finally gives up, leaning away.

"Someone's been working on their self-control."

"Don't tempt me," he sighs. "You're the one walking around with bare legs in my apartment."

"I didn't think the sight of my bare legs would get you excited."

"Any bare part of you is exciting."

"Even if I'm not shaved? And I got fatter?"

He rolls his eyes. I might as well get a check on my insecurities…

"Yes, and you didn't get fatter. I think you got even thinner, but no worries, I can take care of that for you."

"Are you planning on fattening me up?" I put the toast down.

"I like your curves. By the way, did you think about my question?"

What question is he talking about…? Oh, that.

"Oh, hell no, Nathaniel Black," I scoff. "I'm not marrying you. Or anyone."

"Are you sure? Estelle would look so cute in a little white dress."

"She can wear one when she gets married. I won't."

He frowns, either because of my refusal or the idea of our daughter getting married. Ugh, I feel like he'd be one very protective dad… let alone her uncles. Sorry, baby. Either way, I finish my toast while he's lost in his thoughts.

"Please marry me," he insists.

"No, Nate. I just agreed to live with you, now you want to wed me? Are you nuts? Do I get any room for thinking at all? You're rushing things."

"Well, considering we went rather quickly from being reunited, to living together, and then having sex, I figured…"

I slap his shoulder. He needs to learn to freaking slow down!

"It's a no, you idiot. And if you insist again, I'll even take a step back and sleep with my daughter instead of you."

"You'll miss me first," he mocks me.

"Oh, shut up!"

I push him away and walk to the bathroom, and I make sure to lock the door behind me. Since when was he so clingy?

I enjoy my time alone with my thoughts while in the shower. Since when was he so into marriage… Did Nora and Damian give him ideas? Or is it his way of making sure I don't run away again? Either way, I'm not ready. And there's so much going on… I go back to the bedroom to grab some jeans and a tank top when Nate walks in. I ignore him at first, and instead, try to desperately take care of the stupid mess that is my hair.

"I need a haircut, this is too annoying," I growl.

"I could recommend a salon down the street."

I nod.

"By the way, don't you have work?" I ask. "I don't think I've seen you on your computer since we came here."

"Don't worry, my HR director is happy to get rid of me for a while. And we have other matters at hand."

"What are you talking about?"

"Elena, if something big and bad will happen in a few days, we need a back-up plan to protect Estelle. I feel bad bringing it up, but I don't want to wait until it's too late. I know you've probably thought about it already, so tell me."

Oh… I do guess work is nothing compared to what's headed our way, and he does have a family to take care of now. We both do.

"Yes, I thought about it. I was thinking of asking Danny."

"What?"

He seems unhappy with my choice, so I explain.

"He's not a good fighter at all, but he's fast. If things don't end up the way we want it to, he can take Estelle away from Silver City, fast. We talked about it after Reagan's funeral, and Daniel agrees with me. He will hide during the fight with Estelle and leave if things turn bad."

"I hate that idea. And where would they go?"

"Well, from what Reagan said, my mom was a gypsy from the east, so I was thinking they'd run east until they find some human town to hide in."

"Elena, no. I'm not letting my daughter leave Silver City alone with a weak wolf. No offense to Daniel, but if anything happens to me, I want to be sure she'll be fine."

"If something happens to you, Nate, we will both be too dead to deal with what happens to her! Do you have a better idea? Everyone will be fighting, so–"

"Damian has a plan already."

"What?"

"We talked about it after you came back. Damian's been planning things for months, with William, Nora's… well, your cousin too. The Sapphire Moon has a safe house in the north, and they know how to get there secretly. When her labor starts, Nora will most likely be moved to the Sapphire Moon territory. The witch doesn't know of your connection to this clan, and will most likely focus on the Blood Moon clan's territory. She'll go with James, and the Sapphire Moon will protect her."

Nora didn't mention any of that when I saw her last night!

"You want Estelle to be with them?" I ask, surprised.

"Yeah. Sylviana knows about this plan and approves of it. She's already placed some more witch protection spells or whatever there. Elena, the children will be safe, and Daniel can go with them if it makes you feel better. Liam will be there too."

"What? Liam? Why would he be there instead of fighting with you?"

"He will be fighting, but from the rear, like a defensive position. That way, if things turn bad, Nora and Liam can leave together."

... My Goddess. They had this much planned already. I know this whole plan makes sense, but the mere idea of my daughter being forced to run away with her aunt and uncle, without me and Nate... I shudder. At least I'm glad Nate also thought a lot about it. I repress my tears.

"Alright," I nod. "I trust your brother anyway. If there's one thing he's good at, it's protecting his family, including his niece, I guess. I just... I hate that we're planning all this when we just promised we'd never leave her. I'll have to explain it to her before that time comes."

"I know," Nate sighs. "I feel the same as you."

"... Before that, I need to talk to the White Moon clan."

Nate's surprised, but there are a few things I need to settle before this all goes down.

"If we have to fight, I don't want it to be like last time's mess. We lost lives because our Alpha didn't make the right choices. I need to be sure things are as they should be over there. I need to talk to Clark and Chris."

"Okay."

I frown.

"I'm going alone, Nate."

"Yeah," he chuckles. "I'd expect so. I'll watch the baby meanwhile."

"And Nathaniel, I need to ask you something."

He frowns at my serious tone, especially as I rarely use his full name, but there's one thing I need to be sure of before I go back to face my pack once and for all.

"Who killed Diego, Nate?"

Chapter 32

I decided to walk to the White Moon clan's turf. I need some fresh air to clear my mind before I do this. Truth is, I'm not ecstatic about going back there, but some things need to be done and some things need to be said. I managed to avoid them when I buried Reagan, but it can't go on like this forever.

After all, that pack adopted me and raised me. There have been a lot of mistakes, and trust was lost along the way, but they are still my people. At least, in my mind. I know I was officially banned for birthing a child from a different clan, but that was four years ago. Nora and Damian got rid of any borders. Now, I can walk into my former territory without anyone stopping me. I knew it wouldn't be a nice return, but I did not expect to feel so… sad.

I spent my whole childhood in these streets, and until now, I hadn't realized how much I missed all of this. The familiar smells, the simple shops, the music streaming through the open windows. Especially in the summer, the Hispanic neighborhood is one of the liveliest ones in Silver City. Some people seem to recognize me, surprised, and greet me with a bit of hesitation. Not everyone is a werewolf around here; it's a rather mixed area, almost 50-50 split between humans and us. Hence, those who didn't know why I disappeared are surprised to see me back, and awkward.

After a while, the first wolves come to greet me. I was prepared to have to struggle a bit, maybe defend myself, but to my surprise they are happy to see me.

"*Elena! Welcome back girl!!*"

"*Missed ya, baby!*"

"*Guys, look, it's really Elena!*"

"Jace! Bianca! And…"

In a few minutes, not a few but a whole crowd of werewolves run to me! The ones that were probably on patrol right before are still in their wolf form, but they bicker to run to me, like a wave of fur around my knees. They all try to hug me, ruffle my hair, or grab my hand. I don't even know who to look at anymore!

"Elena!"

I can barely recognize them before the Lewis twins jump at me. Bonnie and Ben have grown up so much! They are freaking adults now! I hug them back, chuckling. I missed the Lewis family so damn much!

After a few seconds of hugging them, I recognize the young man behind them.

"Moon Goddess… Micah?"

He smiles and hugs me. How did he get so big too!

"It was high time you came home, Elena," he whispers with a smile.

I realize he's right. I was away for so long, and the White Moon clan is still a part of me, even if I tried hard to deny it and move on.

For a few minutes, I laugh and tear up a bit, catching up with my old friends, holding Micah's arm and walking with the little crowd to my godfather's house. Most people leave me before we reach it, making me promise to come by the pub or other places before I go back. I feel like this is going to take all day.

When I finally stop at the front door, I'm left with the twins and Micah. Their presence makes me feel a bit better, especially since Danny is busy at work and couldn't be here. I take a deep breath and knock.

To my surprise, someone opens the door almost immediately.

"Hey, beautiful."

"Levi? What are you doing here?"

He hugs me quickly, and shrugs.

"Patrol duty, and Ben mind-linked me to say you were on your way here. So, how have you been? Your shoulder?"

I nod and show him.

"I'll have a nasty scar, but it's doing well, for a slow healer."

"Good," he says with a smile, "but I'm still going to rip that damn witch apart for what she did to you."

"Alright," I laugh, "but you'll have to share."

"Elena?"

Behind him, Orpheus and Chris just appeared at the same time. Chris is already smiling from ear to ear. My cousin runs to me, hugging me tight with his arm.

"Hey, easy! Seriously, how much did you eat, Chris, you're as strong as a bear!"

He laughs while letting me go. Shit, he grew up too, and he's clearly been working out!

"I didn't stop training just because you were gone! Our training got even harsher since Isa took over. We almost missed you!"

"Haha, very funny."

"He's telling the truth though," chuckles Orpheus. "Isabella is one tough trainer. Welcome back, Elena."

I hug him too. Orpheus and I were never very close to begin with, but I don't think he's the type to be close to anyone. He's the typical workaholic introvert.

"Is Clark…?"

Orpheus nods, pointing at the back of the house. I follow him into the large living room.

To my surprise, I start tearing up as soon as I spot him, sitting on the couch with a frown, reading some document. Hearing us walk in, he turns his head to us.

"Orpheus, do you have the…"

He goes silent when he notices me in the middle of the little group. His mouth and eyes stay open for a few seconds while I'm trying hard not to cry. I didn't think I would be thrown into such disarray once I saw Clark, but I can't stop it. I even try to look away for a second, and one of the boys rubs my back gently.

Without either of us saying a word, Clark stands up and walks up to me. I have no fucking idea what to say now that I'm here, but before I can think of something, my godfather suddenly hugs me.

"Moon Goddess Mother. I'm so sorry, baby."

It's too much, I'm crying buckets already. Damn him. I missed my godfather more than I thought, and I can't help but hug him back. His huge arms are covering all of me, and I feel his hand gently caressing my hair, like a child.

"I'm so sorry Elena, I was wrong… This was all wrong…"

"Clark, it's over now, so…"

"No, Elena."

He grabs my shoulders, looking at me with a very serious expression and red eyes.

"It was my fault. Entirely. I'm your godfather. I should have protected you all the way, and I didn't. You did nothing wrong. I should have told them to fuck off, and never, ever agreed to your banishment. I know that now."

I wipe my tears and take deep breaths. I don't need a nervous breakdown now, it's not the time for that.

He takes me by the hand and pulls me to sit next to him on the couch. The rest of our little group spread around in the room, sitting or still standing, but no one's willing to leave. My cousin, Orpheus, and the Lewis siblings are all looking at us, waiting for what's next.

"It's good to see you back," whispers Clark.

"I know. I didn't think I'd be so happy to be back, to be honest. I guess I missed home more than I wanted to admit."

Everyone around us chuckles.

"Stubborn as ever," says Chris with a sneer.

"As long as you're back, I'm happy. Forget the banishment, we don't have any borders anyway, and–"

"Clark, you know it's not that simple."

My seriousness seems to pain him, but we have to set things straight. There are some things we won't be able to avoid.

"I'm no longer part of the White Moon, it's over."

"Elena…"

"No, listen. I'm saying this because I need you to know, and because now, it's okay. I'm fine with that."

"So you're with the… Blood Moon now?" asks Levi.

I shake my head.

"No. I'm my own wolf. I'm fine with not belonging to any pack. I've never liked answering to anyone, anyway. Alpha or not, I'm better off being a rogue. It's better this way."

Maybe because I'm voicing it out for the first time, I'm more convinced than ever.

I'm my own wolf. Not a White Moon daughter, not a Royal, not an Alpha. I'm just me, Elena Whitewood. Selena Bluemoon. I'm half-human, and half-werewolf, and a warrior. I'm different from my cousin, different from my peers.

And that's okay. I don't need a clan's backing, or a Royal's entitlement. I just need my family and my friends. I think I finally understand Reagan's feelings a bit better now, and that freedom she always cherished. She couldn't be tied down, she was a free wolf. I think I'm just like her.

For a while, I explain to Clark everything he may not have heard of already. From when I left the White Moon, to the attack, and the Dark Witch's threat. Levi and Daniel told him most of what he needed to know already, so I'm just filling in the blanks from my perspective. I stop at the point where I decided to get back with Nathaniel, so we could raise our daughter together.

"I know it's not what you would have wanted, Clark, but it's the decision I've made. It's better for her, too."

"No, it's fine, Elena. I've lost all rights to tell you what to do with your life, or your baby girl's. I would just like to meet her someday, if you'll allow it."

"Of course," I say with a smile.

I've been dying to show Estelle the streets I grew up in. I never had the chance to know much about my mother, so I want to do that with her, so she knows where I come from, and why our family is like it is now.

"Clark. I wanted to talk about the Dark Witch too. I want you to cooperate with the Blood Moon clan. Unconditionally."

He sighs.

"To be honest, we won't have much choice. We already lost too many people back then, four and a half years ago. If anything bigger than that is coming, I want to do anything I can to protect our clan, everyone. We've been watching the north for a while already. We will move first if anything happens. I just don't like to think we will be on the front lines, but–"

"We don't know that for sure," says Levi. "It might come from the east."

"Our clan will stand at the border no matter what," replies Clark with a dark expression. "We have always been. Everyone is preparing for what's coming. But even if I agree to it, Elena, it won't be easy to convince everyone. They haven't forgotten how the Blood Moon clan killed Diego. He was a criminal, but your mate had no right to kill him like a dog."

I take a deep breath.

"Nathaniel didn't kill Diego."

"What?"

"When I asked him, he said he couldn't answer. I know he wouldn't lie to me, so it wasn't him, but he probably couldn't tell me the truth either."

"Why would he–"

"Clark, I need to see Iris."

"What the heck? Elena, NO!" yells Chris.

I ignore him to address Clark.

"Clark, Iris knows what happened. She probably didn't say anything on purpose. My cousin might be a mythic bitch, but I must admit, she's a freaking mastermind when it comes down to manipulating people."

"Elena, if it's really the Blood Moon clan who did it, it could make things worse."

"I don't think they would have done this without a reason. I want to know exactly what happened. Moreover, I'm sure that Iris can help us convince everyone to rally with the Blood Moon."

"Elena, that's the shittiest idea ever," growls Chris. "My sister's been locked up for four years since we found out she falsified several documents of the clan for her benefit. You think she's going to be happy to see you? No way she'll agree to help you!"

I chuckle.

"You know Chris, one thing about being locked up is that by now, she might be craving some fresh air."

He shakes his head, unhappy. I can see they are all in disbelief, or seriously wondering if I've gone mad about letting my worst enemy out of prison.

Truth is, I'm not as sure as I want to sound, but at the moment, I'm more concerned about changing opinions in the White Moon clan. I know a lot of people missed me, and are happy to see me back, but a lot of them don't trust me either. Even if Nora and Damian did most of the job by erasing the borders, I know the White Moon clan still isn't ready to fully cooperate. Both times we did, we lost people, like Eric. We will probably lose a lot more this time, unless we unite as one with the Blood Moon clan. Not as a gathering of several packs, but as one, large pack. One pack of wolves, ready to defend one city. It's a crazy idea, but it's our only shot, I realize that now, especially since it will be the only defense between Estelle, James and the baby, and that Dark Witch with her army of vampires.

"You want to ask Iris for her help to convince the White Moon to unite with the Blood Moon?" repeats Levi, when I tell him my full idea on the way there.

"It's already starting, Levi. The Sapphire Moon and the Blood Moon are unified through Nora. Smaller clans will follow unconditionally. The only big clan that has always worked alone is the White Moon. It became worse after I left, didn't it?"

"Because our people thought you had been driven away by Black! And they killed one of our own, Elena. Even if it was Diego, it was–"

"I know. But I feel like there's something that still can be done about that."

"... The situation is already complicated, and you have to ask your psychopath cousin for help? Of all people?"

I sigh. Yeah, I have to.

I always imagined Iris to be locked away in some dark, creepy dungeon, but this is the twenty-first century. We don't have a prison on our turf, but we do have a hospital with a psychiatric ward. It's easy to throw someone in a tiny room, lock it, and forget the key for a few years.

So, my cousin is and has been confined in an all-white, rather spacious room with the simplest furniture and a few books. Her hair has grown a lot, so her lavender curls are now pushed down by her blonde roots. It kind of annoys me that, despite having been locked away all these years, she's still as pretty as before and looking fine. I take a few seconds to observe her from behind the tiny window; she's wearing some dark jeans and a sexy white top. Nothing like the quiet, shy Iris she pretended to be for years. I guess she has no more use in pretending. She's barefoot, but I bet she'd be wearing killer heels if she could.

I take a deep breath and walk in. She raises her eyes from her book and, as soon as she notices me, sneers.

"Look who's here. My dear cousin. How have you been, Elena? It's been a while! Did you bring me something, since you're visiting?"

Behind me, Levi clicks his tongue.

After a long argument, we decided it would be better for only him to accompany me. Chris strictly refuses to see his sister again, as it upsets him deeply, and the younger Lewis siblings are unrelated to her. Even Clark refused to come.

"I'm not here to play your petty games, Iris," I reply coldly.

She sighs.

"I know. Since you're showing up here, I guess you have something to ask me. I wonder what that is and, more importantly, how you're going to get me to comply."

She's not going to make it easy, I know. Behind me, Levi's already growling. She chuckles.

"You brought your little sweetheart? No, let me guess. You're a single mother now? I bet Clark changed his mind and let you stay... Well, that idiot would be happy to take a single mom as his girlfriend, but it doesn't seem like you two are together."

So she has no idea what happened after she was imprisoned. She doesn't know I was gone for four years or even about the witch's attack. I take a deep breath, and after hesitating a while, undo my shirt, showing her the large scar, still pink and wide. It runs from my back to my shoulder and down to my right breast. It's thick and ugly, and she probably can tell it's rather fresh.

Iris frowns. I managed to get her attention.

"Someone attacked you with a chainsaw?" she says in a mocking tone.

"Very funny, Iris, but no. The Dark Witch did this, and without a weapon."

She stays silent for a few seconds, staring at my injury with an indecipherable expression. After a few seconds, she tilts her head.

"Well, it looks painful. That bitch has some talent."

To my surprise, my injury doesn't seem to make her any happier. My cousin doesn't seem to care at all, in fact. She lets out a long sigh of boredom, sitting back on her bed.

"Oh, well. I guess you didn't come here just to strip, so let's get this over with. What's going on?"

"The Dark Witch will attack any time now," I explain. "I need the White Moon to trust the Blood Moon clan fully."

"Okay, and why should I care?" asks Iris, raising an eyebrow.

"You're the one who knows what really happened to Diego. If I want the White Moon to trust the Blood Moon, I need–"

Before I can finish, Iris bursts into an annoying laugh. She shakes her head, unable to stop, as if I had said something funny. What the heck is wrong with her?

"Seriously, Elena? That's why? You think resolving your ex's death will solve things? Are you dumb?"

I want to slap her so badly at this moment, but I'll restrain myself. She chuckles and gets up, walking toward me like a cat.

"You've always been so strong, but you haven't gotten smarter, Elena. You think that's all this is about? That if you can solve Diego's death, you can make things right between the White Moon and the Blood Moon? Does that mean you're still…? No way, you and Black?"

I growl, truly annoyed at her tone. Maybe it was a bad idea after all, I shouldn't have come here, she's so…!

Iris sighs, crossing her arms.

"Even if I tell you the truth, you think it will solve things? Get real, Elena. The real reason no one trusts the Blood Moon clan is simply because they are cold-blooded murderers."

I take a deep breath. Iris has no idea.

True, she played a role in getting me and Nathaniel together. But she doesn't know a thing about our relationship, about him. Sure, he's made mistakes. I know he's not as gentle as he is with me when he's being his Alpha self. I've seen it. I've seen him murder a man with his bare hands and not feel sorry about it. All the times I smelled blood on him, I didn't say a thing.

Because I know that man isn't my Nathaniel. Yes, we are werewolves, and we fight. We defend our territories, we get into battles. We growl when we feel threatened, and we bite when we have to. This is the world we live in, but it doesn't make us who we are. That same man can be the sweetest father, the gentlest lover. Those same hands that got dirtied can also hug and caress. It's just that too few people know about that side of them. That side of him.

The Black brothers aren't cold-blooded. They are Alphas, scary and mighty, but they are men too. Men who can be reasoned with, protect their packs, and love their families. They listen to their mates, they care for others. If they kill, they have a reason for it. It's never unjustified, or unnecessarily cruel.

The cruel one was that bitch witch that tortured me to find my baby and use her as a weapon.

"Iris, tell me," I growl. "Why do you care, anyway?"

"Why would I tell you? You had no issue with leaving me to rot here for months and months, and now I should be a good girl and obey? What about your little puppy here? You didn't even ask him, did you?"

I turn to Levi and sigh.

"I already know Danny and Reagan had an agreement with Nate and gave him Diego. They told me a while ago. What I don't know is what really happened after that. You're the one who was behind Diego's return, I bet you were watching him and know who killed him."

Iris clicks her tongue, meaning I'm right. She seems to hesitate for a bit.

"Why should I help you, Elena? I don't gain anything from opening my mouth, I might as well keep it shut. I do gain some satisfaction from it, so I'd rather stay silent. Unless you have something worth my while."

"I'm not playing, Iris," I growl. "We have a witch outside our borders that can attack at any moment with her horde of vampires. You'd really be fine with that?"

Iris shrugs and opens her arms up, showing her environment.

"I've got my own personalized bunker. If you lock me up, I'm probably just going to be happy watching from the sidelines! Oh, maybe I should get some popcorn?"

Can I just slap her? This selfish bitch! Our whole civilization is on the verge of war and she finds it funny!

"Iris, I'm not kidding, this is our pack you're talking about!"

"Our pack, Elena? More like your pack! Ever since Reagan dropped you here, you've been entitled to everything! Yes, I'll be fucking happy when someone finally gets rid of the eyesore that you are! My dad, Chris, Clark, even Eric! Since you arrived, you have done nothing but take what was mine, and disrupt other people's lives!"

"I'm fed up with your jealousy issues, Iris," I growl. "Yes, I was adopted into the pack, but that was it. Before I was stronger than you, my dad was stronger than yours. I'm sorry Xavier couldn't see anything but our strength, but if you wanted to change things, you should have stood up to him! If you wanted to be closer to Chris and if you wanted Eric to love you, you should have tried harder with both of them! And didn't Eric pick you when you tried? With all your schemes and lies, you're the one who disrupted everything! You can't blame me for everything when you never fought fairly for it!"

My words finally seem to hit her, as she takes a step back. Her sneer disappears, finally replaced by her hatred for me. Seems like playtime is over.

"Moon Goddess, I really hate you, Elena."

"Right back at ya."

We stare and glare at each other for a long time, until she rolls her eyes.

"Fine. I'll tell Chris."

I hesitate, but Levi replies before I can.

"Your brother doesn't want to see you, Iris, you know that."

"Well, then find a way, because I'm not going to tell anyone but Chris. You wanted an exchange? Well, there you go, I want to see my brother."

I frown, a bit confused.

"What are you planning, Iris?"

She clicks her tongue, annoyed.

"Oh, stop it, Elena. I may hate you, but Chris is my younger brother, and I haven't seen him in years. You said I should make an effort with him? Well, I'm starting now."

"Why didn't you ask for your freedom?" I ask, suspicious.

"With the shit show that's coming? Thanks, but no thanks, I'll stay here, you know, in my private bunker. Now, my brother."

I sigh and turn around, exchanging a look with Levi. Can we convince Chris, though? If he's been ignoring his sister's attempts to talk to him all this time…

We decide to go back. Surprisingly, it only takes a few minutes to convince Chris, but he's clearly unhappy about his sister's bargain. He insists that I come with him. Less than an hour later, we are back in Iris' cell. She stands up as soon as she sees her brother.

"Chris, I–"

"No, Iris, you listen to me," he says. "First, you tell Elena what she asked you. After that, we will talk. I don't trust you anymore, so if I doubt you're telling the truth, even one bit, I swear I'm leaving and you'll never see me again."

For the first time, Iris seems truly hurt by his words. She probably didn't expect Chris to act like this toward her. His spite seems to have hit a nerve. Her mighty attitude soon disappears, and she turns to me, clearly unhappy.

"Fine. What did you want to know?"

"What happened, the night Diego died. Everything you know."

She rolls her eyes, sitting on her bed, but with her brother in the room, she's a lot more docile and less arrogant.

"… I was there when they caught him. I'm not sure how blondie and Reagan kicked him out of the territory, but as soon as he stepped over, several Blood Moon wolves jumped on him. They dragged him farther away, so I followed secretly. I wasn't exactly overjoyed by this situation, as you can imagine."

I bet. It probably disrupted her evil plans a lot.

"It was quick, though. First, that bastard struggled a bit, but, well, your man didn't come alone, so he didn't have a chance to run. The Black blondie was furious, and wanted a duel with him, probably to make him suffer a long death."

"That fight never happened," I say. "Diego's body was fine; he was just shot in the head."

"Yeah, well, your boyfriend didn't see it coming either, from the face he made. His brother arrived."

I stay speechless for a few seconds. His brother?

"Liam?"

"No, not the brat, the King. He showed up out of nowhere. From the look on his face, your man didn't expect him. And just like that, the King took out a gun. The two brothers argued for a while. Your man wanted a fair fight or whatever, but the King said that he didn't deserve any chance. Something like he didn't have any pity for rapists. And just like that, he shot Diego right in the head."

I'm… I did not expect that at all.

Damian Black. Nora's husband killed Diego. Not to help Nathaniel, but because the King wouldn't allow a rapist on his territory. I suddenly remember Nora's past. She never really went as far as giving me details, but something like that happened to her; in her previous pack, someone attacked her.

No wonder the King was so cold-blooded as to kill Diego. For him, it wasn't a murder, it wasn't a crime. It was the execution of a criminal. Because I went through what Nora barely avoided, and Damian Black knew. And he wouldn't allow someone like that in Silver City. Did Nate tell his brother about what happened? There are so many ways Damian could have found out, back then. He was watching me because of my relationship with Nate, I bet he got a hold of my criminal record too.

"Shit," whispers Chris.

"Yeah, that doesn't make the situation better at all," sighs Levi.

Indeed, this is a problem. Nathaniel or Damian, either of the brothers killing Diego doesn't change anything. A member of the White Moon clan was killed by one of the Black brothers, that's all our pack members are going to see. This is such a mess! Even if he is the King, even if Diego was formerly banished, Damian Black had no right to execute him; he was part of another clan, not his.

We exchange looks, but this is a real situation. If we can't get the White Moon to change their opinion…

"Oh, please," suddenly says Iris with a dramatic sigh. "You guys are such idiots, aren't you?"

"Iris, you better have something smart and useful to say following that sentence," growls Levi, just as irritated as I am.

Chris glares at her too, but his sister just shrugs.

"There's one simple way to resolve this, isn't there? Tell them the truth."

I stay silent, unsure about what she means, and Levi and Chris look just as confused. Iris sneers.

"Just tell them the truth, Elena, what happened nine years ago. The real reason Diego and you fought. The White Moon will change their minds if they know what Diego did."

I slowly understand. That's right. I stayed silent about what had truly happened back then. Aside from a handful of people, no one knew that I stabbed Diego because he raped me, and that I lost a baby. I didn't want to talk about it, so I let people make their assumptions about the real reasons for the fight, and Clark was the only judge for it. I went to jail, Diego disappeared, and no one brought it up again. People thought we had always been an electric, unstable couple that suddenly crossed the line. For werewolves, especially alphas, it didn't seem so crazy.

However, it wasn't so simple. Iris is right. People would change their minds if they knew the truth about Diego. No one would cry or even mind the death of someone like him. Actually, they might even think it was justice. He committed the worst sin possible for a werewolf. The one thing our kind can never, ever forgive.

Killing a werewolf pup.

"I can't decide if it's a crazy idea, a genius idea, or the shittiest one ever."

I take a deep sigh. We have been debating Iris' suggestion for a while now, and this isn't getting any better. We're back at Clark's house with everyone, including Isabella and Orpheus. Daniel came back from work too, but Chris stayed behind with his sister to talk after Levi and I left.

"I'm positive the pack will be mad at Clark for keeping this whole thing quiet," says Orpheus. "It's too big."

"Agreed, but I think they have every right to be," announces Isabella, who has been glaring at Clark non-stop since we told her everything. "Really, Clark, what were you thinking?"

"It was my choice," I explain. "Back then, I was perturbed a lot, Isa. Losing my unborn child threw me into depression, and I was convicted too. I begged Clark and my parents to not tell the pack what had happened. I didn't want to hear about it anymore, and I thought if I was gone for a while, and Diego too, I would be forgotten."

Thinking back, it was also probably the only way for me to truly end my abusive relationship with him, by pretending nothing happened. I didn't care that I was convicted for attempted murder, compared to the loss I had suffered. As long as Diego was out of sight and far from me, I knew I'd be able to recover someday.

Isabella takes a deep sigh.

"I understand, Elena, but it was Clark's responsibility. Now, if we explain this to our people, they will accuse him of wronging you and allowing Diego back. Having him banished for good should have been the lightest punishment possible, but he was gone for only five years. People won't accept it, and they won't listen to his words to trust the Blood Moon after that."

"But they will listen to Elena."

We turn to Orpheus, who stands up.

"I know I would."

"Orpheus, no one will listen to me," I reply, surprised he would even suggest that. "I'm the girl who had a child with one of the Black brothers and left the pack who adopted her. Trust me, I'm not high on the list of the most trusted people right now."

"I don't think that's necessarily true, Elena," says Levi. "Most of our people are fine with the idea of mating with people from other packs now, even the Blood Moon. Since the Luna abolished the borders, it has become more and more common."

"No one will blame you for having Estelle, especially after what you went through," adds Bonnie.

"A lot of the fighters now are people you trained too! I bet they'd be happy to see you back!"

I chuckle at Ben's enthusiasm. The twins' words are very comforting to me, but I can't tell how realistic they are.

"I think it's worth trying. We need to ally with the Blood Moon officially, and no one will agree to it without a proper explanation," I admit.

I turn to Isabella and Clark. They are the ones to decide, as I know Orpheus is already agreeing with me. Isabella sighs.

"Will they believe you, though? It's coming out years later at a time like this," asks Bonnie.

"We have tons of proof if needed," replies Danny. "It went to court, plus we kept Elena's hospital bills and all."

"Clark?" I call to him.

He hasn't said a word in a while. Is he worried about the position this will put him in? He might lose all respect as the Alpha. My godfather suddenly stands up.

"It's fine, Elena. I would rather get it off my conscience. I was never comfortable with how things turned out, so it's high time I repair my mistakes and repay my debt to you. Isa is right. This pack had a duty to protect you, and we failed. I won't allow it twice."

I'm touched by his words. Back then, it did feel as if I was alone with my pain. It was convenient for everyone else to forget it all. He smiles at me and ruffles my hair.

"I knew you'd grow up to be a fine woman. Don't worry, I will handle this."

"I want to be there, to do it with you," I immediately insist.

"If you want."

After a few minutes, Clark calls most of the pack's adults over to the nearby park, the only place big enough to have all the werewolves attend comfortably. I wonder how fast the word spread about my return, because absolutely no one seems surprised to see me next to Clark and Orpheus.

As we discussed, Isabella and Clark do all the talking, and it's short anyway. About how full cooperation with the Blood Moon will be needed, and why Diego died. Everyone stays silent while the Alpha talks, but I can read shock and anger on a lot of faces.

"… We need to come to an agreement now," concludes Isabella.

"Clark, why didn't you tell us back then! We never liked Diego, but you should have told us the full story!" yells someone from the back.

"That's right! A rapist and a pup murderer? Clark, he could have attacked our other kids!" growls a woman.

"This was between him and me," I explain. "It was personal, I don't think Diego would have–"

"You can't say that for sure! A sociopath, a murderer! And the Alpha allowed him back!"

A lot of people start growling along but Clark doesn't flinch. He expected this, after Isabella's warning.

"Elena left because of you!"

"No, I had different reasons to leave!" I interrupt, annoyed. "Listen, we are not having Clark's trial now! He is your Alpha, and whatever he decided back then is between him and I!"

Some of them won't listen and keep yelling. It's frankly annoying to be facing such an undisciplined crowd. Werewolves are so damn stubborn.

"Stop it!" I yell, releasing all of my Alpha Aura.

Everyone shuts up as if a wave had hit them. I don't think I've ever used so much of my aura before, but here we are.

"This pack has enough issues as it is. Remember what happened just four years ago? All those that we lost? You want to avoid more deaths next time? Then stop acting so stubborn and listen, for once!"

A long silence follows my words. Some exchange glances and frowns, as if they were trying to reach a common ground. I take a deep breath and look sideways at Clark. My godfather smiles and nods.

"We will lose more people if we don't work as one with the Blood Moon clan," I explain.

"We are already on good terms with them, Elena!"

"I don't mean an alliance. I mean we need to fuse the White Moon pack with the Blood Moon pack."

I'm hit by a wave of protests. Some people are just speechless or hesitant, but some of them are completely against the idea.

"No fucking way! We are the White Moon clan! We won't become someone else's property!"

"Elena, what the hell! Is this Black's idea?"

"Shut up and listen!" I growl again. "It is my idea. Not Clark's or anyone else's. This isn't just about our turfs or our pack anymore. We have an army coming. An army of vampires, and a witch leading them. The same one that attacked us before!"

I undo my shirt, showing them my injury, still fresh.

"See that? I can't stand against her! We can't, okay? We are lucky enough to have a witch on our side. You think we won the previous fight? Well, listen up, we didn't! Sylviana, the witch of Silver City, saved our asses! Otherwise, what do you think would have happened?"

I catch my breath, looking at the crowd. I've managed to make them doubt. People are remembering, I know they can't have possibly forgotten. Not with the number of wounded people we had, or the ones we buried.

Next to me, Orpheus nods.

"Just try to remember the hell it was," he adds. "The water attacking us. Even with the Blood Moon helping us, it was a fucking nightmare!"

"Everyone lost a friend or a family member back then," says Isabella.

I know everyone in the pack is thinking about her son, Eric, who was among the victims. This is what we need to focus on. How many people we can save, what will be left after the fight, and what we could lose. I see a lot of them finally stop protesting, glancing at each other with worry.

"This won't be a regular fight," I declare. "There will be deaths. It's the sad truth, I won't lie to you. We will lose people. All I want is for us to lose as few as possible. I want the best outcome; I want us to win this fight.

We can't afford to lose, because if we do lose, it will be the end. Not only the end of our pack, but the end of everything we know and love. I don't care anymore about the packs, the borders. We are werewolves. We are the werewolves of Silver City, one large pack. I know I won't fear a witch, no matter how many vampires she brings, if I can stand with my people. My family, my friends, all of my kind, as one."

I let a bit of silence float after my words, hoping it will reach them.

"If we fuse with the Blood Moon clan, we will truly become one pack. All together, hundreds of wolves, able to mind-link as one body. The strongest clan this city has ever seen."

"… What about the other packs?" asks someone. "How do we know they will allow that too?"

"You know how loved and popular the Luna is," says Levi. "She's a Royal, people will rally to her. The Sapphire Moon and Jade Moon clans are already completely loyal to her. Most packs will follow her lead. We can follow Elena's."

Whoa, wait. When did I say anything about following me? I glare at Levi, wondering what the hell he is thinking, but I see him exchange glances with Clark and Danny instead. What are they planning?

"Clark will be leading," I warn them.

"No, Elena, you will," suddenly declares Clark, turning to me. "For this fight, we need you to act as the Alpha."

What the hell! I just decided I won't be an Alpha! I'm fine not being anyone's Alpha, why are they doing this to me now?

"You said it yourself, Elena, all the werewolves must act as one. We will need all the Alphas to act together to lead them. And no one is more capable of doing that than you."

I growl at Orpheus, annoyed that he is part of this freaking trap too.

"I am not fit to lead anyone!"

"You're a fighter, Elena, it's in your blood," says Daniel. "Your father was a Royal warrior, wasn't he? There is nothing more powerful than that."

I see the crowd start to whisper between themselves, surprised to hear about my parentage.

"Seriously, Daniel? Now?" I yell at him, furious.

"Don't blame him, Elena, we already discussed this."

"I am not going to fucking lead anyone! This is not–"

"Elena, you're an Alpha, and half-Royal. You're the best fighter of your generation, or any generation this pack has seen! And your mind-linking ability is way better than anyone else's too!"

This is a nightmare. How can they do this to me, in front of the whole damn pack! I never agreed to any of that shit! Would it have been too much to at least warn me? Did they do it on purpose, thinking I wouldn't be able to refuse?

"Elena is half-Royal?" asks someone from the crowd.

"Who freaking cares!" I yell. "Clark, I was gone from this pack for four years, who the hell do you think I am? I can't show up and start ordering people around! I am not Alpha material! I hate making decisions for others!"

My godfather turns to me, looking dead serious. I almost step back, feeling his all-out aura, but before I do, my wolf is growling right back at him, her instincts taking over.

"Elena, I'm ready to abandon my Alpha position right here and now for you to take it. You know this is what I've always wanted for you, and what you deserve."

"Clark, no. I've made my share of shitty choices, haven't I? You really think I would be able to–"

"You're good at protecting others, Elena. You make the decisions you make because you know when to attack, when to fight back, and when to retreat."

"This is insane," I mutter.

"This whole situation is insane, Elena," he continues, "but we have a war coming, and it's just as you said, we need the best chances. You're one of those chances. You came up with this idea, and I wholly support it. But now, you need to see it through to the end, and do what needs to be done."

"You fucking exile me for four years, and now you expect me to come back and save you all just because of my lineage?"

"Not just your lineage, Elena," replies Isabella. "Everyone here knows your skills. Despite what happened four years ago, everyone welcomed you back, didn't they? If we took back a jerk like Diego, what kind of pack are we if we don't take you back?"

"I never said I wanted to come back, Isa!" I growl. "I'm fine. I have my daughter, everything I need is not–"

I stop my sentence, realizing I'm wrong. The White Moon is, or was, my pack. I remember the feeling I had when I walked back in. The people I had missed. My friends, my family. I growl, frustrated as hell.

"You're the one we need, Elena," Clark sighs.

"I'm not. I don't know how to lead a pack. Even if I agreed to this absolutely shitty idea, I'm not in shape, I haven't fought in years and–"

"If I remember correctly, you killed dozens of vampires without even shifting into your wolf form," notes Orpheus.

"And while being pregnant," whispers Danny, avoiding my glare.

"You have time to get back in shape," says Clark. "What we need is for you to agree. If you do, everyone here will follow you into this union with the Blood Moon clan, Elena."

I glare at the little group, furious. I really hate the whole damn idea, especially since I'm well aware they would make me feel fucking guilty for abandoning them if I don't agree.

"Elena," whispers Isabella, "I know how crazy and selfish we may sound right now. But trust me, we talked it over. We truly believe this is the best shot we've got, and it's with you, honey. Maybe things should have gone differently for you, you should have gotten the Alpha position in a more normal and fair way, but here we are. We only have one chance, Elena. And I truly think it's you."

Chapter 33

"So, you agreed?"

"Heck no, Nate! They threw this at me, I was not prepared! I just… I said I'd think about it."

He's watching me walk in circles inside his apartment while he's carrying Estelle, who fell asleep in his arms. I just can't calm down since I left the gathering. Firstly, I'm still mad at Clark and the Lewis siblings for tricking me into this. Secondly, I'm still completely amazed that they even dared to come up with such an idea. I thought I was the crazy one for suggesting a fusion between the clans! Lastly, I'm supposed to be a pariah in that pack, and now I'm some sort of last-minute savior?

"It's a good idea, I think."

I immediately turn to him with a glare.

"Not you too!"

"Well, it does make sense," he continues. "Elena, you're not someone who can stand on the sidelines."

"Yes, but I was expecting to fight like any other wolf, not be some damn beacon for my former pack!"

He chuckles, walking to the sofa to sit down.

"As if you'd listen to anyone's orders, my sunshine. Your Alpha– I mean, Clark is right. You can certainly do this, and you should."

I shake my head. No, no. Not when I had just found who I am, who I want to be. This is madness. The whole point of putting the events with Diego into the light was to have the pack see the Blood Moon differently, not have Clark step down from his position and push it over to me!

I go to sit next to Nate on the sofa, suddenly tired from that whole mess. He puts a hand on my knee, gently caressing me.

"Don't think too much for now. You don't have to answer them now, Elena. You just confronted your former pack, that's enough for today. We need to talk to Damian and Nora about your idea too."

I nod, feeling a bit comforted by his words. He's right. I should take some time to consider it, see if I think I can shoulder this. I have no doubt Nora will agree to it though. She's always been keen on making any differences between the packs disappear, and she respects my opinion. I am not worried about my cousin-in-law either; almost everything Nora says he'll agree with anyway. And Nate agreed it's a good idea too.

"… We should make plans," he suddenly says.

I look at him, a bit surprised. What is he talking about? Nathaniel smiles and kisses Estelle's temple, laying her on the couch next to him before turning to me and taking my hand.

"You, Estelle, and me. I want us to have plans for when this whole mess is over."

"Nate, I'm not sure this is…"

"I don't want to live as if we are going to die, Elena. I want to have something to look forward to."

"I am not marrying you," I assert with a growl.

He laughs it off, but I know he's still holding on to that stupid idea. Well, he can forget about it. I don't want to get married, and certainly not to him. That jerk is not reliable at all. Moreover, he already got more than he was supposed to from me. I am not indulging him again. Well not for a few more years. As Danny said, he should suffer a bit for all the shit I went through.

"I'm talking about something else, Elena," he explains. "Like a trip, for example."

"A trip?"

That's probably the last thing I would have thought about at such a time, but Nate seems serious about it.

"We could go on a holiday, once this is all over. The three of us, somewhere far from Silver City. I want to see where Estelle was born and grew up in too."

It does sound good. Something we could look forward to. I want to imagine us, after all this madness, having fun together, somewhere safe and warm, and visiting our old house again… if there's anything left of it. That damn witch probably found it.

"To be honest, I miss the house a bit," I admit.

"How was it?"

I can't help but chuckle.

"When Sylviana took me there, it was just an old, abandoned house. But I liked it. It was made entirely of wood. It took us a while to clean it.

Sylviana used her powers to sweep away all the dead leaves, replace the rotten wood, and repel the plants that had started growing in or on it. I'm glad witches are so good at cleaning, but still, just the dust and dirt took ages to get rid of, since it was so fucking big. But it was worth it. It was the kind of old family house that has its own charms you uncover little by little, with large windows, a terrace, a big kitchen, a big bathroom. Ah, I really miss that place."

I can't help but smile, just thinking about it. Those four years there were really peaceful, just me and my daughter. Every day going by slowly, taking care of the house, hunting our food, and even growing vegetables in the little garden Sylviana made for us. There was a human village a few miles away, but we only made the trip once in a while. Whether they knew or their instincts sensed that we were werewolves, we were not welcome there. I just bought the groceries and left as soon as I was done.

Estelle played with me, or the pets she befriended, like the little rabbits she found and adopted, her bunnies. Maybe she can get to school in September. It would be good if she made some friends.

Will we still be here in September? It's only a few weeks away, but it feels so far away. I turn to Nate.

"So, a trip?"

He nods.

"Yeah, wherever you want. Just the three of us. We could even search for it. You know, the Blue Moon clan."

I stay speechless for a while. I had never thought about it. Going back to my roots, finding more about wherever Nora and I came from if there's anything left. Nathaniel is right, with the witch gone, we would be free to go and look for clues about our parents. We know so little about them. It feels like I never had time to stop and think about it, but it did cross my mind a few times. I could ask Nora about it, and even our long-lost cousin William.

"Maybe," I sigh. "Did Nora ever mention it?"

"Yes," he nods. "To Damian, at least. She's very curious about her mother. About Queen Diane too."

Nora is probably more at a loss than I am. After all, I was brought up by Reagan and adopted soon after by loving parents. My attachment to the White Moon is legitimate, as they retain so much of my childhood.

Nora is different. Her parents disappeared when she was a child, and though she was taken in by another pack, she never really felt any family love from them or even from her half-brother. Even if she has a family of her own now, she's probably the most curious one.

"I see," I simply reply.

Nathaniel smiles and leans in to give me a long kiss. It's a bit unexpected but it's nice as always… Well, not just nice. He caresses my arm too, in a gentle way. Though, with Stella next to us, we can't push it too far. We play nice and simply exchange long, hot kisses, warming up our lips and chuckling like teenagers in love.

After a while, we part, each with a smile on our lips.

"You have no idea how much I missed you," he whispers with a sigh.

I push him away with my feet. You damn idiot.

A few hours later, our baby girl wakes up, and we head to Nora's place to talk about my plan to fuse all the clans after a nice dinner. No one is really interested in the desserts, they are all listening with open ears, shocked by my words. All three Black brothers are there, plus Boyan and his siblings, as well as Isaac and Danny. Neal's wife is watching all the kids in the playroom next door. Only Sylviana refused to come; apparently, she's busy, but this is a werewolf matter anyway.

"So, the White Moon would agree to a fusion with the Blood Moon?" asks Tonia, doubtful.

"I convinced them."

"What Elena didn't say is that they want her to lead them," adds Nathaniel.

I roll my eyes. He didn't need to mention that part yet, but whatever. Nora's eyes are already full of excitement.

"Elena, this is awesome!" she exclaims.

"Really? I just told you they want to follow me into this crazy war, Nora. Me, of all people. I didn't think–"

But I stop talking as, around the table, none of them seem very surprised. Really? Nora glances at her husband, who starts talking.

"We have been in close talks with the Sapphire Moon and a few others recently," says Damian. "Elena, if the White Moon clan agrees to it too, we could have almost all of the werewolves clans of Silver City in."

I'm speechless. Already? How long have they been preparing for this? Nora blushes a bit, seeing my reaction.

"We had the same idea as you, so we started talking to the other Alphas these past few weeks, but it's nothing new, Elena. William insisted that I officially join the Sapphire Moon, and as of now, he has made me his successor. Since Damian and I are mates, the two packs are already aligned."

"I thought William Blue had a daughter?" I ask, confused.

"He does, but he doesn't want her to take over the Sapphire Moon clan. Rose will be the Luna for the Pearl Moon clan, her mother's pack."

All the math between the Sapphire, Pearl, and Black Moon relationships is way too complicated for me. However, I understand that Nora can basically become the Sapphire Moon's Luna anytime now, and through Damian, she is already the Blood Moon's Luna. The two biggest packs of Silver City are allied, and the next biggest and wealthiest one is the White Moon.

"What about the others? The Violet Moon, the Sea Moon wolves?"

This time, it's with Tonia that Nora exchanges a look. Right, Boyan's sister is going out with the Violet Moon Alpha, Lysandra Jones. That probably helps.

"Lysandra and Arthur are still reticent," she says, "but I'm pretty sure we can have them agree to a temporary fusion. After the war, they want their packs back, but they are fine with submitting to Damian and me until it's over. Same thing for the Red Moon."

Or whatever's left of them. Black should have banished those traitors four years ago when they turned on us with the Gold Moon clan. I'm trying to count, but those are all the main clans of Silver City. If the deal is done, Damian and Nora will be Alpha and Luna of 90% of the Silver City werewolf population. This is insane.

I'm getting chills. This is really to be an all-out fucking war.

"Our only missing piece was the White Moon clan, Elena," says Damian. "We couldn't talk to them until now, but if you agree to their terms…"

"I'll be a bridge between Nora and them. You want me to be the bridge between you and the White Moon, I get it," I sigh. "So, it all comes to this."

"I wasn't sure you could convince them, and I wasn't sure they would listen to you, so I was afraid it was too soon to ask you," admits Nora, a bit fidgety.

"Well, for once I was faster, I guess."

I stand up, pacing around again to think. Nate grabs my hand to stop me, pulling me to him.

"Elena, it all just happened today, but Sylviana said we have a few weeks, so you can think about it a bit longer"

I gently smile at my man and lean down for a quick peck on his lips. I turn to Nora, feeling a bit braver.

"Nora, there's something I have been thinking about for a while. With your power, do you think we could… officialize our relationship? When I talked to my pack, most of them were doubtful about my origins. If we had a way to make it official…"

"If this is about you having a bond with the Blood Moon clan, my sunshine, I'm pretty sure marrying me would–"

"Nathaniel Black, the answer is still no. And Nora is the one I need a bond with."

"Hey! Nate would be a bad husband, but I would make an awesome brother-in-law, Elena," says Liam with a cheeky smile.

"Thanks for the support, Liam," growls Nate.

Everyone laughs, breaking a bit of the heavy atmosphere that was floating around until just a moment ago. Nathaniel rolls his eyes and pulls me onto his lap. Nora smiles across the table.

"What did you have in mind, then?

"You know… just putting our family tree into the city records, things like that. And I want to take my real name, too.

She opens her mouth a bit, surprised.

"Elena Bluemoon?"

"No. I don't want to completely omit the White Moon part in me. From now on, I want to be Selena Whitewood, and have my relationship to you known. I think this is how I will find a middle ground between my two identities. I think this is what I would like better."

Nora nods, looking a bit emotional.

"I did almost the same," she says. "I registered as Eleanora Bluemoon, though everyone still knows me as Nora."

"Reagan is the one who saved Selena. She held on to my name for years, I think it's time I take it back."

"Damn, now you sound like a Royal," says Liam.

"I don't hear a Royal, I hear a warrior. You know what, Selena, I have been hearing about you being the best fighter for a while now, I want to see that."

I turn to Tonia, surprised. But then, I remember, that woman is the one who trained Nora, and is Boyan's sister. Moreover, she is the number two in the Violet Moon clan, known for its fierce fighters.

"Tonia," says Nate with a frown, but I stop him.

"Is that a challenge?" I ask.

Let's be honest, she woke up the wolf in me. Seeing a challenger, she just wants to go. Easy girl, we just finished healing a few hours ago.

"Mommy! You were so cool!"

Estelle runs to me, her little eyes sparkling. I smile and open up my arms, satisfied.

"Are you okay, Tonia?" I ask, while standing up with my baby girl in my arms.

She's still laying on the floor with a sour expression.

"Don't ask," she growls.

Truth be told, I can't really blame her. After she insisted on a fifth fight, I couldn't go easy on her, and went all out. Tonia is a very, very good fighter, I cannot lie about that, but she relies a bit too much on her strength and is stubborn. Once I analyzed her strengths and weaknesses properly, I found the key to beating her. She has great adaptability, though, and gave me quite a challenge. I'm sweating and a bit out of breath.

Our small audience is amazed. We picked one of the dojos near the Blood Moon's Headquarters, but after the first three days of watching Tonia and I fight for hours, only Liam, Nate, and Estelle are still here to watch, and some young ones from the Blood Moon and Purple Moon packs.

Damian is concerned about Nora's health, as she's been tired lately. The Luna is resting at her house, but it seems that, since we officially entered my new name into the city's registry yesterday, I've inherited a new nickname I didn't expect.

"White Luna! Can you show us how you did that move? The one with your leg and bam!"

I sigh at the sight of half a dozen young werewolves crowding around me with their eyes filled with expectations. That's right, they have been calling me the White Luna, while Nora somehow became the Black or Blood Luna. I still can't say how I feel about that.

"You little punks! Why don't you ask me!" growls Tonia while getting back up.

Seeing her come our way, the kids run away laughing. I can't help but chuckle too.

"They're cheeky, aren't they?"

"Tell me about it," she sighs. "The ones from the Violet clan are the worst, I swear. They are not afraid to tackle the older ones and have been groomed for fighting since they were pups. I often fight with Lysandra about their excitement. They think this damn war is going to be fun. Fun, for Moon Goddess' sake!"

I understand her concerns. It's hard to explain to the children what's at stake, and that they might be the first ones to die. I kiss my daughter's forehead and stare in the direction they left, Nate joining my side.

"Do you think we will be ready?" I ask.

"In all honesty, I don't know," replies Tonia. "If I knew how many vampires are coming or what kind of witch we will be dealing with, I could, but no. It's just as bad as it sounds, Elena. I am glad your plan with Nora is working fine and it's a good one, awesome even, but it really might not be enough."

Sadly, I know Tonia's pessimism is justified. We could really be wiped out in a few weeks' time.

I take a deep breath. I've trained enough. No matter how I look at it, I am in shape and ready. My injury's completely healed, thank Moon Goddess, even my fights with Tonia didn't cause any issues with my scar. It's ugly and it will remain, but it's healed. That's all I ask, and luckily, Nate doesn't seem to give a shit about it. I turn to him.

"You okay?" he asks.

"Sure," I say with a nod. "Nate, I want to change at your place and then go."

He seems a bit surprised, but he knows what I mean, and nods with a determined expression. I chat with Tonia a bit longer before we part, and Estelle bids her a shy goodbye too. It's funny how she bonded with her more easily than with Boyan, whom all the kids seem to love. Maybe she reminds her of Reagan?

I take a quick shower at Nate's place, and get dressed again in dark pants, a tank top, and a white leather jacket. I put my hair in a ponytail, almost ready for a fight. It's a different kind of fight that awaits me, though.

Nate drives us to the White Moon territory, and I'm nervous all the way there, despite chatting with Estelle. My daughter is excited to finally see the pack I grew up in, but I can't shake off that nervous feeling inside me. For some reason, I've always been so careful to keep her and Nate away from my clan; now that we're going there as a family, it's very strange and nerve-racking.

As previously planned, Nate carefully parks close to Clark's house, right after sunset, and we walk up to the clan's gathering point.

Everyone's here. A lot of people are glaring at Nathaniel, wary of the Black brother walking on our territory. He is a stranger, and a damn strong

Alpha. A lot of our people have shape-shifted already, either out of fear or just to feel safer. Maybe some want to show they don't trust him or his brothers either. However, since he's holding Estelle's hand, the most adorable little girl in the world with her floral white dress and cute ponytails, I can also see a lot of smiles and amazed eyes. Yeah, that's my baby, she looks just like me. I walk up to my godfather, who gives me a hug before his eyes land on Nathaniel. He sighs.

"If they had told me I would one day welcome one of the Black brothers on my territory…"

Nathaniel can't repress his smirk.

"Don't worry. I don't bite."

They both chuckle, and after a few seconds, finally shake hands, making everyone around relax a bit. As soon as they are done, Clark's eyes go down to Estelle.

"Hello, pretty lady!"

"Good evening, Mister Clark!"

"You know who I am?" he asks, surprised.

My daughter nods and blushes, a bit shy.

"Yes. Mommy explained to me that you are the White Moon clan Alpha and you are my mommy's godfather."

Clark's face brightens, visibly overjoyed with one sentence from the four-year-old. Damn, he should really get a wife and have some kids. He goes down on one knee, and rubs her head with a big smile.

"How did you make such a pretty girl! Even you were not as cute as this!"

"Thanks," I reply, unsure if that's a compliment or not.

On the side, Nathaniel laughs, and so do Orpheus and Isabella behind the Alpha.

"Well, I do have memories of you running around, dirtying your rompers, and calling out the boys for fights."

"Danny!"

My best friend just stepped out from the crowd, his mom, dad and siblings right behind him. While I quickly hug Danny, I notice Abigail is wiping some tears behind him. Ben sighs.

"Really, Mom?"

"I can't help it… Seeing our Elena where she is… after… you know, everything… It's making me so emotional…"

"Wipe your tears, honey, it's a joyous occasion," says Joseph behind her.

"Of course, I know, but… I can't help but see Elena like my own daughter, and… and…"

Abigail's words get lost in her handkerchief, and the twins take over to talk to her and try to help her control her emotions a little. While I'm so grateful for her kind words and thoughts, I do feel this is… somewhere between embarrassing and awkward. Joseph chuckles and takes this opportunity to step closer to me, giving me a big hug and whispering a few words in my ear.

"Selena Whitewood, you're the strongest, bravest she-wolf I have ever met in my life. You deserve all of this. You have the blood, the heart, and the guts of an Alpha. Never, ever forget that. We trust you, just like Ivy and Samuel believed in you. We really do."

I didn't expect to hear my parents' names after such a long time. I can't help but tear up a bit, and I'm glad I can hide it in his shoulder. Moon-Goddess-knows how much I miss them both. Joseph was close to my dad and hearing those words from him holds more value than if anyone else had said it.

We separate, and after a moment with each of their family members, I go back to where Clark stands. It's a bit weird, to be back to talk to my pack so soon, with Nathaniel and Estelle with me too. I take a deep breath, turning to the crowd. I thought Clark would say a few words to the crowd, but everyone remains silent. I guess I'm up.

For a few seconds, I stare at the entire audience. I look at those people I've known almost all my life, and I wonder, what right do I have to stand here? What do I tell them now? Can I say anything? Can I convey my feelings properly? Or will I just fail, lose their faith and have them regret picking me to lead them?

I take another deep breath. No. I am not, and I won't be, someone who backs off. Never. I am Selena Whitewood. I am a survivor, and a fighter. I'm someone's mother, someone's sunshine. I am a werewolf; I am just like them. These are my people.

"I… I was born in a place far from here," I declare, "a place I can't even remember. My first memories are with Reagan, right at the border of the White Moon clan. I remember my first meeting with you all. With Clark, with my parents, with my friends, with all of you. I was young, so I struggled with my identity. I grew up with parents who didn't look like me. With friends from a different background. I felt like I could never fit in, so I fought harder because I thought a strong werewolf was the only part of me you'd accept. I hated the word 'adopted' because it reminded me of something I didn't have. I wished my parents were my birth parents many, many times. I often wished I was more like the other kids. I wished I knew where I came from, though I never said it."

I take a deep breath, glancing at Nathaniel. He's gently smiling at me, his hands on Estelle's shoulders. I take a deep breath and turn to the crowd again.

"When you're a child, you don't know how to cope with your insecurities. I struggled with my identity. I made bad choices, because I was desperate to fit in, and rejected people who rejected me twice more. I couldn't see what I had, only what I was missing. I met… the wrong people, and lost sight of the ones I should have held close. I made poor choices."

I don't want to go on too long about Diego, not in front of my daughter, so I don't say his name. They will read between the lines.

"By doing that, I… I was hurting myself indirectly. It is sometimes easier to rebel against people who wish you good than to leave people who are intoxicating. It's sad, but it was my way of… punishing myself. No matter how many times my parents and the few friends I had left warned me, I… I didn't listen."

I hold back my tears, looking to my wolf for all the strength I need and solemnly put a hand on my tummy. I need them to understand, because I won't say it. I find Daniel's eyes in the crowd, and look at the pair of blue eyes to give myself some strength.

"I lost… a lot. I'll never get it back. I… I shut down, and I lost my family a second time. You all know what kind of place I went to. I don't know what you think I had done wrong for that, but the truth is, if I injured anyone, it was myself. Because I reacted too late and put myself in danger. I lost… what no girl or woman should ever lose. I lost my Angel."

I feel the tears slowly run down my cheek as I confess the truth. I take a moment and hear the audience's shock. Some women cover their mouths, some men are stuck between confusion and anger as they slowly come to understand.

I can feel the anger from behind me too. Nate's wolf is exuding a scary aura, but I ignore it, along with Clark's.

"When I came back to the pack, I was at the lowest point in my life. I had lost my family, a second time, a third time even. If it wasn't for Clark, and the Lewis family who helped me, I might have never come back from that darkness."

I manage to gather a smile for them, for Danny, and wake my wolf to finish.

"I got back on my feet, and I worked harder. I felt like I needed to prove myself, even harder than I used to. I was part of the White Moon clan. I truly accepted that when you didn't toss me aside despite my parents being gone, despite everything I had said and done. I really realized it then. Because the young ones were still looking up to me. Because the ones my age would still talk to me and count me in. Because the adults would invite me over, greet me, or just acknowledge me. Because everyone in this pack was fine with me being just me. Not Ivy and Samuel's daughter, not Clark's goddaughter. I was just Elena, your Elena from the White Moon clan."

A lot of people are nodding, some are even smiling to me with a tender look in their eyes. I can't help but smile back, a bittersweet smile.

"Just when… When I started getting used to that idea, things changed again. I… I fell in love with someone I wasn't supposed to. I met Nora Bluemoon, who was suddenly closer to me than anyone had ever been. Die… My ex came back. And the situation became a lot more complicated. I was conflicted again, between my identities, between my past and my future, between what I thought I owed to the White Moon and what I truly wanted."

I turn around and hold my hand out to Estelle, who takes it with a smile, walking a couple of steps to join me.

"If… I have disappointed people, I will apologize," I say, "but I won't apologize for making a new family of my own. I won't apologize for the beautiful baby I had, the man I love, or even for getting close to another pack. I love Nathaniel Black, but it doesn't make me less of a White Moon daughter. Eleanora Bluemoon is my blood cousin, but that doesn't make me less of a Whitewood. I am just building up my identity. Truthfully, that warrior part of me, the part I inherited from my father, is the only thing, perhaps, I have always felt confident in. I don't even really realize what it means to be half-human yet. I am gathering the pieces and constructing myself, piece by piece."

I take another deep breath, waiting a few seconds before breaking that solemn silence, through mind-linking this time, taking them all by surprise.

"I am Selena Whitewood and I want to keep that name. I don't want to forget the clan that raised me. No matter which pack my blood belongs to, what I know is that my heart sprouted right here, and you are the people my wolf's voice can reach out to. You are my pack, my people. I love every one of you. Even that bitch cousin of mine, yes. That's why I want to protect everyone here. I really do. But it won't be possible unless you all trust me, a hundred percent."

I turn to Clark, resolute.

"I, Selena Whitewood, claim the Alpha title of the White Moon pack, here and now."

After a long silence, all eyes are on Clark. My heart is beating like crazy in my chest, and my cheeks are burning. My godfather smiles, and finally, gets down on both knees.

"I, Clark Hamilton, fully acknowledge you, Selena Whitewood, as the sole rightful Alpha of the White Moon pack!"

A sudden wave of cheers, applause, and howls bursts all around us.

Chapter 34

"Elena… Elena, are you okay?"

I growl, a bit annoyed. Why does he have to ask so much? And my head hurts, too. Like, a lot. I frown and struggle to sort out my left from my right. I hear him chuckling.

"Elena…" he calls me, almost singing into my ear.

I can feel his beard on my back, and his breath right against my skin.

"Stop it," I grumble.

I kind of feel weird, but that feeling is familiar. Like, not the nice kind of familiar. A fucking hangover, and that headache that goes with it. I struggle, open my eyes, and sit up. I don't recognize this place. Where the hell is this? The bed is too fancy for my taste, and there's too much yellow. I'm not fond of yellow.

"Where are we?" I growl.

"I got us a room at a nearby hotel. You felt sick while I was trying to get us back to my place and kept asking me to stop the car."

"Oh, Moon Goddess…" I sigh, feeling some blurry memories come back. "I drank, didn't I?"

"Oh, yes," he laughs.

It's not funny! I haven't drunk or gotten wasted to that extent in years, what was I thinking? I vaguely remember everyone trying to party with me after I became Alpha, to celebrate, but I can't even count all the places I was taken to.

"Shit."

"It's not your fault, Elena, you really tried to stop," he says while getting off the bed. "Even Danny and Levi asked people to stop giving you drinks. You looked fine until you suddenly growled at them and asked me to take you home."

From the looks of it, I bet I didn't ask nicely. More like I probably whined or bossed him around. Damn it, I feel really bad now. Did I trouble anyone besides Nate? He pours me a big glass of orange juice and brings it to me with a pill. I take it gratefully. Moon Goddess, that feels good. I take a few seconds to enjoy that and silently apologize to my liver.

"Where's Estelle?"

"She slept at the Lewis'. Your friend Bonnie and her mother said they would take over to watch her when people started dragging you around. She's fine, Daniel texted me a few minutes ago to let me know she's still sleeping."

I grab my phone, only to see I got the same text from him.

"I'm such a bad mother," I whine. "I can't believe I didn't even look after her."

He chuckles, sitting to face me on the mattress.

"You've been taking care of her for four years, Sunshine. You can take a break for once."

I nod half-heartedly and drink some more juice. Truth is, I need to avoid his gaze.

What right does this idiot have to be so handsome so early in the morning? And half-naked again, of course. Not that I am going to complain though; that view is probably the best way to make me damn sober. Seriously, how could I drink so much?

"So? The man you love, huh?"

I almost spit out the damn juice. That idiot…! I'm as red as a beet, looking elsewhere, dead embarrassed. And it's too late to act like I didn't remember. I clumsily wipe off the juice from my chin. Crap… Why did I have to profess my love for him in front of the whole damn clan, anyway?

"Elena," he calls me with that naughty smile.

"Oh, shut up," I growl to hide my shame.

"My sunshine…"

Why does he have to stir me up on purpose! He takes the glass out of my hand, crawling closer to me on the bed. Oh, crap, I'm in real trouble.

"Elena, you said you love me."

"So w… what if I did…" I mumble.

He chuckles again and goes down to kiss my thighs. Holy crap, how can he cheat like that. I gasp and look away, trying not to give in. Crap, where the heck is he kissing… His lips go higher and higher, and I blush uncontrollably. That's…

Nathaniel keeps torturing me with that devilish mouth of his, and I bite my lip and close my eyes, unable to push him away. Moon Goddess, I forgot how good he can be at that too. I breathe louder and caress his hair, letting him play between my legs.

"Nate… Stop it…" I groan.

As if he'd listen. I take deep breaths, until he gets where he wants, and I can't help but cry louder. A fire burns underneath, where he's toying with me, and I lose all rational thought. It's just so good… Nathaniel intensifies his tongue movements, going faster, deeper, sucking a bit harder, and making me moan for real. I grip his hair, my legs trembling, and gasp and moan until I can't take it anymore. It bursts, exploding like fireworks and blowing my mind away.

All my extremities are tingling while I catch my breath. Damn it. I rest back on the cushions, and he leans over me with that annoying satisfied smile. Shit, why does he look happy like he's the one who just went to heaven and back.

"Marry me," he suddenly blurts out.

I roll my eyes.

"Nathaniel Black, are you thinking you can fucking buy me with a fucking orgasm?"

"… I could give you one any time you want," he says with a smile, "if we were married."

"You don't need to put a ring on me to do that!"

"We can skip the ring part if you want."

Moon Goddess, I am talking to a wall. I push him away, and stumble to the bathroom, hearing him laugh behind me. I let the cold water cascade over me, trying to get out of the post-coital daze. Damn it, he's good. So annoying. I take deep breaths, staying under the water for a long time.

What a crazy time to be alive… I just became the White Moon's Alpha, for real, and got myself drunk over it. Is this okay for an Alpha? I do remember seeing Clark drinking with everyone else.

I'm trying to figure out which bottle is the shampoo when I hear him sneak in behind me.

"This shower is busy, Mr. Black."

"It has enough space for two, apparently."

"Are you always going to have something smart and annoying to reply to everything I say?"

"Maybe. Or I can keep telling you I love you, if you'd rather."

Grr, he's so annoying. I ignore him and turn away, but he's faster than me at grabbing the other bottle. He pours a bit of it in his hand, and gently starts washing my hair for me. Mmh… I could get used to that.

"Let's leave Estelle with the Lewis', today. We can stay here, just the two of us, all day," he whispers.

"You're already tired of your daughter?"

"Never. But I would like a bit of alone time with her mom… with the woman I love."

I blush, and just when I'm about to hide it, he has me turn around and puts his arms around me, cornering me right there. His blue eyes are closer than I can bear, making me even redder. I really have no more defense against him.

Nathaniel smiles and softly kisses my lips. I miss a heartbeat and, slowly, answer him. I really need to work on my self-restraint with him. With the water still pouring over us, he keeps kissing me, leading this dance between our lips. It's a wet kiss, and somewhat exciting. I remember now, our second time was in the shower too. Maybe it's from the memory, but my body heats up even faster, and soon, I am the one craving for more. Our naked bodies against each other, our hands caressing our wet skin, his skillful fingers teasing me… It gets so hot, so humid in here. I need to hold on to his shoulder and the shower wall, because my legs are going numb as fast as I'm getting more and more aroused…

A couple of hours later, we are back on the bed, sweating, naked, and exhausted. Damn it. It's like we are back in the good old days, having sex over and over again like animals. My body is so exhausted, I just decide to keep lying there. Nate pulls something over me, a bathrobe, I think. I sigh.

"I hate you and your damn stamina."

"We can always work on improving yours," he chuckles, giving me a kiss.

Thanks for reminding me how I didn't train like him while raising our daughter. He is so fit, it's almost too much to bear. And I probably took on some weight too.

"I hate you," I grumble.

"Still no marriage?"

"No!"

"It's fine. I can wait until after the war, at least. Estelle will be so pretty in her little dress…"

Why is he imagining it already! I give him a kick.

"You're still not forgiven and nowhere near being forgiven enough, you jerk. I should have you on abstinence instead!"

For four years! That should teach him!

He frowns.

"I don't think I can resist you for more than a week, Elena. Fine, I promise I'll wait a bit longer for our wedding."

"You don't have a choice," I remind him.

He sighs, laying next to me after grabbing the other bathrobe.

For a long while, neither of us speak again. We just lay still on the bed, a bit sleepy, me resting and Nathaniel gently caressing my shoulder. He looks lost in his thoughts. The room is so quiet. It feels like the calm before the storm, and I don't want the storm to come any time soon.

Truth is, it might be our last weeks together. I'm scared. I'm scared I'll lose him, Estelle and everyone I love. I don't want to imagine, after the battle, all the corpses, and the silence. Even if I survive, who will I lose? Nathaniel will be on the front lines with me. Both of us might be among the first ones to die. Damian, too, or Liam or Sylviana. Even Danny, Levi, and Boyan. If we fall, Nora and the children will be next. Slowly, I recall all the faces of the people I love. So many faces, coming to my mind, haunting me. I buried my mother and father already. Eric and Reagan too. I don't want to lose anyone else.

A cold shiver runs down my spine, and the fear and sadness bring me to the verge of tears. I turn to Nathaniel, suddenly snuggling against his torso.

He puts an arm around me, the other in my hair, soothing me calmly. His smell helps me calm down a bit, but my throat is still tight, and I want to cry.

"What is it…?" he whispers.

"I'm just… a bit scared," I admit.

I hear him sigh shortly after, and he keeps caressing my hair and skin, gently. I try to calm down, letting his smell and skin surround me in a wave of warmth.

"Elena…"

"Hm…?"

"I want you to bite me."

"Really?" I growl. "Of all times, do you have to be feeling kinky now?"

He laughs.

"No, my sunshine, I meant… bite me, as if to mark me."

What the fucking hell.

I push him and sit away, completely taken by surprise.

"What did you just say?"

He sighs and sits up, facing me with a very serious expression.

"Elena, I want you to mark me as your mate. Your one, official mate."

"Nate, I don't understand."

"I know you don't trust me, and it will take a while longer to restore your faith in me because of how I ended things between us, of the mistakes I made before you came back."

"You mean all the hoes you slept with."

"Well, yeah," he replies, a bit nervously. "I know the fact that I had a fated mate bothers you too."

"I hope you're going somewhere with this, talking about the other women you slept with and the one bitch that left you."

I better never cross that one, because I swear I won't leave her leave in one piece if I do. Nathaniel nods again.

"Sorry, I'll… Let's leave that out. Anyway, what I meant to say is… I love you, Elena… Selena. I love you. Not because you bore my child, or because the sex together is great, or because of our past together. I love the woman Selena Whitewood. The strong, independent woman that doesn't let me get what I want, doesn't fear anyone, and is the most beautiful person I know. I even love how we fight and bicker, how you get grumpy and will pull away from me when you're upset, how jealous you get. I love how you're effortlessly sexy no matter what you do or wear, I love how you're both so strong and fragile. I love your fierce side, your caring side. I love your body, your skin, the taste of your lips, your amber eyes, your soft hair. But I love even more the woman inside. I'm crazy in love with you. I'll die if we part again, for whatever reason it is. I have one certainty, Selena. If I live or die in this war, I want it to be with you. With the one woman I chose to be in love with. I want your face to be the last thing I'll see if I die, and the first I'll see once it's over if we win. You're absolutely everything I want and will be satisfied with. I don't care who Moon Goddess said I had to be with. I don't give a damn about fated mates. I want the one woman that I chose myself. My second chance woman, my sunshine."

I… I'm sobbing already. How can he say such things… like that, just… taking me by surprise and not letting me prepare my heart beforehand?

He takes my hand, my shaking hand, looking at me right in the eyes.

"Selena, I know I want to spend whatever is left of my life with you. I don't want anyone else, I swear. That's why I want us to mate. I know a wedding is not something you'll rely on to trust me. But if you mark me, I'll be yours alone. I won't be able to mate with another woman ever. You don't even have to let me bite you if you want. I don't care, I can wait. What I want is for you to trust me. I'll do anything for that."

"Are you sure?" I ask with a trembling voice. "There is no changing your mind, Nate. Even if I grow old and smelly and very wrinkly."

"I know."

"I might get disfigured in the war. Lose a limb or be disabled. You'll be stuck with me all your life."

"I'm fine with that."

Damn it, why does he have to… to take me by surprise all the time? And with those kinds of big words, I don't even know how to react aside from my crying and my heart going crazy. I can become his mate? For real? His one and only mate? I had never imagined it. My marking on his neck… He had lost his fated mate. Whatever led me to think he wouldn't want to mate with anyone else? I see so many couples together without ever taking that one, scary step. For werewolves, marking each other is the most binding form of union. A wedding is something that can be ended by divorce. A werewolf's marking on their partner will never, ever go away no matter what. And he wants me to mark him?

"Selena, please."

"… Fine," I stutter, "but I want you to mark me too. I don't want it to be just one way."

He can't hide his surprise or his joy.

"Really? I can wait. I don't want to force you."

"After all those things you said?" I chuckle between my tears. "You think I'd ever find another idiot to love me like that?"

He laughs, and leans to kiss me.

"… I want to be the one and only very lucky idiot."

"No, Damian, you need to… No, not that either! Did you get the parmesan? Yes, exactly! Now you just cut a few pieces and put it on top. Slices, not chunks!"

I can't repress a laugh. Nate's been on the phone for over half an hour, trying to guide his brother who's making whatever crazy dish Nora is craving again. Apparently, the King's only weakness is his non-existent cooking skills to satisfy his wife, though I have to admit Nora's cravings are getting crazier every day. Moon Goddess, I wish I'd had that kind of pregnancy! With Estelle, I just felt sleepy all the time and unable to sleep when I was supposed to.

"Mommy? Can I put this one?"

"Try it, baby."

Estelle has gotten into puzzles lately, so we just bought this new one for her yesterday, but she picked a big one. We had to install it in the living room, and we are both on the floor, trying to make those five hundred pieces fit together somehow while chatting about her first weeks of school.

It was a bit last-minute, but Nate used his connections to get Estelle into a nearby school right in time for September. So far, she likes it. She even became friends with a deaf-mute girl one year older, who she "plays" sign language with. Her teacher is a nice, old lady, and they even have a little school farm where Estelle can see a rabbit every day.

While she tries to fit another piece of the puzzle, I turn to watch my man, visibly desperate on the phone. Despite his shirt, I can see the marking on Nate's neck, making me smile every time.

Nathaniel was right about one thing: I feel much closer to him now with that marking on both our necks. They finally went from pink, painful, and fresh to a proper scar. Truthfully, I didn't think I could like a scar so much. It's like I now have a special connection to him, something I can feel at all times, binding us together.

He feels my stare and turns to me with a smile as he hangs up and comes back to us.

"How are they doing?"

"I'm not sure. I can't guarantee she will get her almond butter and four cheese lasagna, but I do hope my brother doesn't burn it. When he hung up, I think I heard something about Nora trying to stab him with a spoon."

Estelle and I exchange a look before bursting out in laughter. It's just so funny to imagine the strongest Alpha of Silver City being subjected to his pregnant wife's crazy whims. It reminds us that Nora's delivery date is near though. I'm already glad that we finished the summer without any further incidents, but it won't last.

More and more, the vampires are coming closer. At night, our patrols in the north spot them from afar, and Sylviana says she can sense them trying to break the protections she put in place too. They are roaming around, but too afraid to come close. No sign of the Dark Witch though, which is scary. Since she attacked me, that woman hasn't appeared anywhere.

The good thing is that we didn't think we would have so much time left, and got ready as soon as we could. There were several Alpha gatherings between the few clans that had not yet fused.

The Sapphire Moon clan, the White Moon clan, and the Violet Moon clan were the last three. For a few weeks, Nora, the Black brothers, the Mura siblings, and I worked together to convince every pack to rally our cause. Truth is, I was surprised about how quickly my new position was accepted by other packs. The Sea Moon wolves even ended up rallying with my pack, unexpectedly. Arthur Seaver wasn't too fond of the Sapphire or Violet Moon, but their pack had a debt to Nora and I since the last battle, almost five years ago. Hence, after further discussions, he finally agreed to submit to me and use his Alpha position to lead his pack into the war.

The Rising Moon, after protesting a lot, wasn't given much choice. Every pack still resented them for their betrayal four years ago, and Damian Black made sure they would regret it if their Alpha didn't purely and simply renounce her position. When she was given a choice to fight against him or submit to him, she chose the option that would let her live.

Finally, once our cousin William Blue gave Nora the leadership of the Sapphire Moon as promised, only the stubborn Lysandra Jones was left. That was a very different battle, and one we didn't expect to last this long. The Violet Moon is the proudest pack, and despite Tonia being her partner, Lysandra refused to submit to Damian, Nora, or me until the very end.

This is the only issue we still have today. After many, many attempts to discuss this, Lysandra sort of agreed that she could potentially submit to Damian, but only when the Dark Witch would attack, not anytime before… which makes the situation more complicated, as we have to prepare a battle plan while continuously arguing with her.

"My sunshine, my little star, I have to go."

"Daddy? You're going to work?" asks Estelle, looking disappointed.

He gets on his knees and gives her a kiss on her forehead.

"Sorry, my princess, but your uncle Damian needs to stay home with Auntie Nora, so I need to take care of the company."

"With Uncle Isaac too?"

"Yes, exactly."

"Can I come with you?" she asks with that cute pout.

Damn, I need to intervene before Nate loses again against our baby girl's ultimate cuteness attack. I chuckle and caress her chubby cheek.

"We're going to see Auntie Sylviana and your Uncle Liam today, remember? You'll see Daddy tonight, baby."

"Okay, then…"

He smiles and hugs her once more, before giving me a long goodbye kiss.

I watch him leave with a light heart. Moon Goddess. I still can't believe this is my new daily life, with Nate and Estelle, in his penthouse. I wake up by his side, usually with a bit of delightful morning bed action, and let him make breakfast while I wake up our daughter, and all three of us eat together. Estelle goes to school, he goes to work, and I study or go to the White Moon territory for my Alpha duties. I still don't really know how we make it work, but with Nate, everything happens so naturally, it feels like I don't have to worry about anything but the war that's coming at us.

And it is coming. I'm satisfied with each day that we go through without incident, but my first worry in the morning is will it be today? I have never been patient, but Moon Goddess, this is utter torture.

Once again, I try to chase all the gloom away while getting ready. My little baby sunshine helps a lot with that too. She is happy with whatever it is we do, and today she is ecstatic about going to see Sylviana and Liam.

We arrive in the large garden, but as usual, I feel like I'm entering some wild, unique tropical forest. There's green everywhere, and flowers of all colors sprouting randomly here and there. The ivy is covering most of the house; I wouldn't even be able to tell what color her walls are. I can feel the wildlife too, notably the butterflies busy living their lives from one flower to another. Estelle immediately runs to play with them, excited. There is something really special about walking into a witch's lair. I can't quite describe it, but my instincts are never fully trusting. There's a tingling at the back of my mind that keeps me restless.

"Good morning."

Sylviana's pretty voice welcomes us, and Estelle runs into her flowery dress.

"Auntie Sylviana, good morning!"

"How are you, little star?"

"I'm fine! Mommy and I made a puzzle today!"

"Did you?" asks Sylviana, looking at me with a gentle smile.

"She loves it," I answer. "How are you, Syl?"

"A bit busy, as usual. Have you had breakfast yet? I was making waffles."

I suspect Liam is the main reason Sylviana always has some delicious food ready whenever we arrive. He comes out of the house behind her, greeting us and immediately playing with his niece. I'm surprised at how good Liam is with children; James and Estelle absolutely adore him.

"What's up, Selena?" he asks with his usual bratty attitude.

"The usual," I sigh. "You know, training, family time, waiting…"

He nods and lets Estelle follow Sylviana inside her house to talk with me, putting his hands in his pockets.

"I hate the wait too. I am not used to not doing anything."

"Your brother still makes you patrol at the border?"

"Every day, three or four times a day. He's as restless as us. Nora can give birth anytime now. It's making everyone crazy. To be honest…"

He sighs a bit, taking a glance at the house. From the kitchen's window, we can see Estelle and Sylviana chatting and smiling happily, playing with fruits.

Liam shakes his head, frowning.

"I feel like she isn't telling me everything," he says. "I mean, she never really does, but… About the witch, I feel like she has something she won't tell me."

"Sylviana's always a mystery to everyone, you know. She knew about my link to Nora, about my parents' death. She's different from us. Being a witch probably has its perks, but also some issues, I guess."

I wonder what it feels like, to be the only one of your own kind. I never stopped to really think about it. I've always lived surrounded by wolves. Silver City is this strange, somewhat functioning cohabitation between humans and werewolves. After all, both kinds have a lot in common. I'm living proof of how close they can be, actually. My hybrid status was never really an issue, whereas Sylviana doesn't seem to know any other witch. I know she said something about how she learned from her mother, but apart from her family, how did she grow up without ever interacting with other people her kind? She never mentioned any other witches.

I notice Liam seems to be lost deep in his thoughts too. I give him a little elbow bump.

"What is it?"

"I'm going to propose again, after the battle is over," he says.

I can't help but roll my eyes.

"What is it with you guys and weddings? Damian got engaged to a bitch and then to Nora when she was in a coma, Nate is asking every damn day. and now you too?"

Liam laughs.

"Hey, for the record, Sylviana and I have been together since way before you and Nate, okay? Also, this is my fifth time asking."

"Well," I sigh, "at least you're persistent. What's her excuse for saying no, by the way? I mean, I know I'm also making Nate wait, but…"

"Oh, that idiot brother of mine deserves to wait, I support you fully on that one."

"Thanks. But?"

"But," he says, "Sylviana says I should wait to be sure."

"Be sure of what?" I ask, confused.

"She thinks I'm too young, that I should at least wait until after the war. I think she's afraid, since she can't see past the war. She says there are too many futures pending."

"It's terrifying. If not even Sylviana can see what will happen in the war…"

Liam nods, scratching his head.

"Yep, tell me about it. Truth is, she's good about the past, but the future is always some blurry, changing sequence. I mean, that's what she says, maybe we're all going to die and she just won't say it."

"Thanks, Liam, a very heartwarming forecast."

"You're welcome. I bet it's going to be a downpour too, like in one of those super epic battle movie scenes."

"Against a Water Witch. Sounds awesome."

He realizes what a horrible situation that would be and makes a grimace.

"Okay, never mind that. Anyway, when will I get to call you sister-in-law?"

"No idea. I don't trust you to shut up, anyway, so I wouldn't tell you."

I leave him with his shocked expression and walk inside the house, hearing him shout behind me.

"That is so not nice, Selena! Really, I can't believe you don't trust me!"

I'm still laughing when I walk into the house to join my daughter and Sylviana, who are making some flower crowns together. Just like her garden, walking into Sylviana's house is like walking into an indoor garden. There are random plants in pots on about every piece of furniture available, some even hanging from the ceiling, and, especially for a werewolf, it smells so, so fresh and good, like a forest.

"Is it okay if she plucks out flowers?" I ask with a frown while taking a seat on the couch.

"Of course, I can always grow more," replies Sylviana with a smile. "Right, little princess?"

"Look, Mommy! Uncle Liam, can I make you one too?"

"I would love one!"

Half an hour later, Liam's head is covered in flowers, and Sylviana and I are watching him make some hot chocolate for his niece from the couch, laughing.

"I can't believe she is so big already," sighs Sylviana. "I still remember the day you gave birth to her."

"You're the first being she saw," I remind her. "No wonder she loves you so much."

"She still secretly calls me her fairy godmother," she whispers with a smile.

"Is that a compliment for a witch?"

"Of course! I even taught her a few tricks."

I can't help but frown a bit. What the heck did she possibly teach my daughter when I wasn't looking? I'll have to ask Estelle later. I love Sylviana, but sometimes she's a bit scary and unpredictable. I don't want a jungle to sprout in the middle of Estelle's bedroom or a butterfly invasion.

She chuckles, seeing my baffled expression.

"Liam told me you're making him wait," I whisper.

"The brothers and their attachment issues," she sighs.

"I know!"

"I love Liam, but he's still too young. And witches don't exactly make the best housewives."

"You do know Nora and Liam are the same age, right? And she's on her second pregnancy."

Sylviana laughs again, though quieter because Liam is listening, thinking we can't see his ears moving a bit or the glances he sends us from time to time.

"Nora matured faster, and she's found her fated mate. Liam and I… It's different. Sometimes, two stars don't align perfectly, but it still works."

"I think I know what you mean, but my parents were from different species too. And as a reminder, it saved my life."

She shakes her head, looking at Liam and Estelle fooling around with that lonely expression of hers.

"We'll see. After the war, things will be clearer, I hope. Oh, that reminds me, I need to make some more almond butter for Nora. Do you want some too?"

"Yeah, I guess!"

So this is where Nora's crazy infatuation with almond butter comes from. I'm about to follow Sylviana in the kitchen when I feel another wolf looking for me.

"Selena?"

"What is it, Levi?"

"Damn, this new link is kind of weird, I have a hard time getting a hang of it. Anyway, where are you? Everything okay?"

"At Sylviana's house, why?"

"Oh, the witch? Okay, um, well something happened here."

I freeze immediately, turning to Sylviana. She would have felt it if something had happened, right?

"Levi, what is it? What happened?"

"It's Iris. She disappeared."

"What the fuck do you mean she disappeared?"

"Her cell was open and empty, and we couldn't find her anywhere. We have two dozen wolves looking for her, but they've found absolutely no trace of her."

Fuck. How the hell did she break out of her cell? To go where?

"Elena, we know how she got out."

"What? How?"

"I just checked the CCTV. It's Chris. He opened her cell, and... he's missing too."

I can't believe it! I keep watching it over and over, but it's the same. The video in black and white, despite the poor quality, clearly shows Chris and Iris talking for a long time, before he opens her cell door, and they both flee out of the camera's range. I nervously bite my lip, annoyed.

Why the fuck would you do that, Chris? Why? Why now? My anger is so palpable, everyone is keeping a safe zone of a few steps away from me.

"How come no one was able to fucking track them?" I growl.

"I sent people, Elena, but they crossed the border right away, we had just noticed they were gone. By the time the clinic told me, and I told the patrol, they were already way ahead of us. I did send some people after them, but you don't want anyone stepping outside our territory, so…"

I sigh.

Our protective measures are made so that no one would get caught and killed outside of the protective barrier, but I didn't think anyone would be crazy enough to go past it and run away! I don't understand what could have happened. My cousins' whereabouts are unknown, and I hate it. I can see why Iris would escape and leave, but Chris? Did she persuade him? Despite him finally agreeing to talk with her, I didn't feel their relationship improved much. Why would he follow her? He was reluctant to go and see her again but still went. So, what happened?

"Do we send people after them?" asks Levi, the only non-alpha not terrorized by my fuming aura.

"No. I stand by my words, no one goes out."

We don't need more people getting killed by venturing outside. It may look like everything is peaceful, but I'm pretty sure some damn bloodsuckers are just waiting for our kind to step outside of Sylviana's protective barrier.

Next to me, Liam, who came along, takes out his phone with a frown, and lets Sylviana know about the events in a few sentences. When he hangs up, he looks annoyed.

"Yeah, no good at all. She can't do anything about people leaving, and more worrying, her barrier keeps vampires and witches from crossing over. Werewolves are free to go in and out though. And she did feel your cousins run outside a few minutes ago."

He scratches his head, looking at the screen.

"Sorry, Elena, but… your cousins are on their own."

Which means they could get killed at any minute! I take a deep breath. If they are not too far away yet, I still have a chance to mind-link them.

"*Chris? Chris! Iris!*"

I can feel both of them. It's faint, but I feel my cousins, in their wolf forms, far away from me. However, they either can't hear me or won't listen, as neither respond at all, no matter how much I try to call them. I keep forcing it, to the point I'm really growling, and other people in the room have to look down.

Then, I lose all contact. I can't feel them anymore. Either they are now really too far, or…

"Elena?" asks Liam, visibly worried.

"I need to talk to Nora and Damian," I growl. "Nate, too."

He nods and follows me outside of the building. We hurry. This is not good, and we need to sort this mess out quickly.

"Elena! What do we do?" asks Levi, coming out the doors behind us.

"Nothing!"

I climb behind Liam on his bike, and we ride out of the White Moon territory. Why do I have such a bad feeling about this? Something's wrong. Not just my cousin's sudden departure, but my werewolf instincts are going crazy.

Suddenly, Liam stops the bike, in the middle of several buildings, on the side of a large crossroad, taking off his helmet.

"Liam, what's wrong?"

"You don't smell that?" he asks.

Smell? Holy crap, he's right. I didn't notice because I had the helmet on, but the air reeks of blood! We both get off his bike, looking for the scent's origin. The smell is so strong, it's horrible, and even worse to imagine where it is coming from. We keep looking around until I have had enough. I try to find any nearby wolves to reach out to. We can't possibly be the only ones smelling that.

"*White Luna!*" several voices answer.

"*Do you smell that?*"

"*It's the river!*"

The river? The river runs from the north into our territory, crossing Silver City in the west to go down to the sea. I turn around and run towards the former Sea Moon wolves' territory, close to the seafront. Liam's right behind me, keeping up with my speed until we get there. Neither of us bothers to shape-shift; we are fast enough and unsure about the situation too. We finally stop, and Moon Goddess, the smell is even worse here. Both Liam and I cover our noses in the same movement.

"Mother Moon Goddess. Oh, that's so bad," gasps Liam.

No kidding. It's worse than bad, that's... A dozen werewolves and humans are just like us, staring in utter shock and disgust at the river, just a couple of feet beneath our level.

The water turned red and dark. So thick and red... The smell of blood covers any other smell, even that of the sea nearby, and it's reeking. Even worse, we quickly spot corpses floating by down the stream. Someone pukes on the other side of the river, not making it any better. I can't blame them, it's the most horrifying scene I've ever seen in my life. How many dead bodies does it take to fill a river with that amount of blood?

Liam and I both look upstream of the river; it's coming from the north.

"I think that's one nasty warning," mutters Liam, as shocked as I am.

"Grab them!" I yell to the men present.

Humans and werewolves look at me as if I was crazy, but as soon as they see me extend my arm towards the river, start obeying.

"Why are we getting them, exactly?" asks Liam, helping me pull the closest body we could grab out of the river.

"We need to know where they came from," I say, "and to see if they…"

I get my answer before I can finish my question. Liam, too, has a disgusted face. The poor man we grabbed and rolled over has his neck open wide, the flesh ripped open.

"If they were killed by vampires?" sighs Liam. "Yeah, guess they were."

"That can't be good," I growl.

I stand up, trying to look and think about what to do next, but I'm really clueless at this point. The men keep pulling the bodies out of the water, despite being grossed out by their state. Are those blood-suckers toying with us? Or getting ready for battle? Liam takes out his phone once again, calling Sylviana, but I need to get this across the quickest way possible.

"*Damian, Nora, Nate, we just found human corpses in the river.*"

"*What? Humans?*"

"*Yeah, a lot. I mean we found… five, no, six bodies so far, but judging by the amount of blood, there's at least four or five times that. It reeks, it's horrible. The river turned red.*"

"*Moon Goddess.*"

"*Your cousins flee Silver City, and now corpses in the river?*" says Nate. "*That's a lot for one day.*"

"*I know, it's not good, really not good.*"

"*I'm coming,*" says Damian.

"*Liam, what is Sylviana saying?*" asks Nora.

"*She's just as shocked. Blood in the river is not good for the Water Witch, so actually, the vampires might have done this without her consent.*"

"*What? I thought she controlled them?*"

"*Yeah, well, maybe she needs to work on her taming thing.*"

I can't believe he still manages to come up with some sarcasm in such a situation. We pull three more bodies out of the water by the time Sylviana and Damian arrive on the scene. The witch is absolutely horrified.

"Where is Estelle?" I ask.

"I left her with Nora," explains Sylviana. "By the Mother Earth, those poor people."

She sits next to the closest corpse, checking their injuries. The blood that immediately stains her hands and dress doesn't seem to worry her one bit. She keeps frowning and patting them here and there for a while.

"Sylviana?" asks Liam, making a disgusted face at whatever she is doing.

"Definitely a vampire attack," she says. "They didn't completely empty them of their blood though, which is odd considering the size of these bite marks. It's like they were in a rage, not hungry."

"Is this some sort of warning?" I ask.

She stays silent for a while, looking at the red river with an indecipherable look in her eyes.

"I think… she might be losing control over them. If they had attacked to feed themselves, they wouldn't have made such a mess of it. And if they had wanted to scare us, they wouldn't have left the bodies intact either."

"Nice thought of them," growled Liam, disgusted.

"What do you mean, losing control over them?"

"Maybe those vampires aren't willing to help her like the previous ones did."

"You're saying she's… forcing them?"

Sylviana sighs and gets up.

"A mind-control spell on so many vampires isn't realistic, but Water Witches are good at illusions. If she's controlling them in some sort of way, after all this time, maybe she has difficulties controlling how they hunt too. I'm not sure."

"Wait, illusions? How come you never told us about this?" asks Liam.

"I didn't think she was powerful enough for that. Each type of witch has their own set of skills that evolve depending on their own crafts, and I have never heard of a Water Witch attaining such a level. But I might need to reconsider now."

"Can you do something about it?"

I'm worried now. I don't remember hearing about any illusions while we were fighting five years ago! Did that damn witch improve so much? If we have to add this…

Sylviana doesn't seem worried, though.

"She won't be able to use it on us. Controlling the vampires must take everything she has already if they are uncooperative. I'm sure she won't be able to use illusions again, not on our people."

"What's your top skill?" asks Liam, curious.

Sylviana chuckles.

"That's a secret for now."

"What was that, then?" I ask. "They just… attacked those humans without reason?"

"They might have lost control, or she might have told them to feed without really measuring the mess they'd make."

I'm not sure calling it a mess is the appropriate language. This is a slaughter. Damian and I exchange a look, disgusted as more bodies float downstream. Crap, I don't want to spend my evening pulling damn bodies out of the river.

"I'll go upstream," I sigh. "If more bodies show up, I'd rather not have them go all the way through Silver City and freak everyone out. And the more we gather, the better idea we'll have of how many vampires are in her army."

"Good luck with that," replies Liam. "It's just so gross, I am not pulling another one of–"

"Liam, you stay with Sylviana and you help her check the bodies," growls Damian.

"What!"

But another growl from his older brother has him finally shutting up, and nodding despite his obvious disgust.

"*Luna, we caught a woman in the river!*"

"*I know, just get the body out of–*"

"*No, this one is alive!*"

They left one alive? I relay the information immediately to the Black brothers, including Nate who just arrived at the scene, and they are all as surprised as I am.

"Go," says Damian. "I'll coordinate with Lysandra to see if anything happened on their territory."

I nod, and both Nate and I turn around, taking his car to go back to the north. What a crazy day this is!

"How's your day going, my sunshine?" he sighs in the car.

"I did not expect to find dead humans in the river or to be faced with my cousins' little escapade," I growl.

Moreover, I'm ruining his car with my pants and shoes covered in blood and water, and my hands are no better. I'm in no mood to joke either, and everyone is shocked by my appearance when I arrive back to the former White Moon territory. My best friend shakes his head, seeing me arrive in front of the White Moon Clinic, as per the information I got meanwhile.

"You look like–"

"Please, Danny," I sigh, "Not today. You found one alive, you say?"

"Yeah," he says as we keep walking. "We took her to the ER right away, she was bleeding a lot, and having trouble breathing. A middle-aged female, human. She was still conscious when we brought her here."

He guides us inside the clinic to the room where a woman, sobbing loudly and visibly terrorized, is cornered on one end of the bed. She's still soaked despite the hospital gown they put her in, and very, very thin. She looks sick: her eyes too big for her face and her dark hair is a mess.

"Leave me alone, you dogs!" she yells at the closest nurse, which happens to be Daniel's mom, Abigail.

"Who are you," I ask her, holding her wrist as she's about to hit.

"Let me go! Let me go, I don't want to be near those dogs!!"

"Dogs?" I repeat, confused.

What the heck is wrong with that woman? Now that I notice it, she's only glaring, and apparently afraid, of the werewolves present. One of our nurses is human, and the only one she lets approach.

"You hate werewolves?" I ask.

"You're just talking dogs! I hate you! Let me go back to my master!"

"Your master… You're a vampire's property?" I suddenly realize, shocked.

"I only belong to my master! He's my everything!"

She keeps screaming, and it's so annoying, I have a hard time not slapping her. Nathaniel has to intervene to help the nurses put her in the shackles as I step back, letting them handle it while I think. Daniel and I exchange a look, shocked.

I had heard that vampires keep some humans like pets so they can toy with them and, most importantly, feed on them. To those humans, from what I had heard previously, the blood sucking thing is addicting, almost turning them into some creepy junkies. Now that I look at her, that woman has numerous bite marks on her neck and shoulders. The other bodies had their throats too damaged and ripped open to make a difference, but…

"What happened?" I ask her, once they had her shackled to her bed.

"I am not answering a filthy dog! You bit–"

Nathaniel is about to jump at her, but I hold his arm, and step forward, staring at that woman, and, without thinking, using all of my Alpha Aura. There is something strange happening with my wolf, too. She's… I don't know, it's like some warm halo around her presence, different from the usual feeling. I don't have the luxury to study that now though.

"Answer me!" I growl furiously.

Suddenly, the look in that woman's eyes changes from anger to fear. She looks at me like I'm some monster, a terrifying monster. She stutters a bit, shivering.

"I… My… master… attacked us…"

"Why? What happened?"

"The Master… he wasn't feeding… he was hungry… A lot of vampires were hungry… And the woman in the black dress was waiting…"

"The woman in the black dress?"

"Y… Yes. She came to the Masters a while ago, and… she did something to them… They don't like her… but they have to listen… So they didn't feed for a very long time, longer than they usually wait… and then, she told them to eat, and they attacked us… but it wasn't normal, they didn't control themselves… They killed… killed a lot of us."

"How did you make it? What about the bodies in the river?"

"We ran, because the woman in the dark dress said to kill us all. So… our masters tried not to, but they still attacked… They were hungry, it wasn't their fault…"

Moon Goddess, I'm going to be sick if I listen to more of their sick vampire shit. Daniel is a bit green, too, but Nathaniel steps next to me.

"How many vampires are there? Why do they listen to the witch?"

"She made them drink something… I'm not sure, but… The… The woman said she would give them a city, with new humans to eat… But our masters loved us, they loved us, they didn't want to change. So, the woman got mad, and she gave them this strange water to drink… After that, they couldn't disobey her, they became crazy… They didn't want to attack us… Oh, my poor master…"

Sylviana was right. The vampires aren't doing this of their own volition; she found a way to control them somehow. Moon Goddess, this is sickening enough as it is… Did she tell them to get rid of their humans so they would have no choice but to attack us? To get the ones in Silver City?

"How many? How many vampires are out there?" asks Nathaniel, angry.

The woman suddenly spits in his direction.

"Thousands! Thousands of our masters will gather and attack you! And get rid of you, dirty dogs! My master will come and find me!"

Chapter 35

"Babe, calm down."

"I am not calming down!" I yell. "That crazy bitch won't insult my man or my people here!"

I can't believe he stopped me! What does it matter if we keep that wretched thing alive? She's a total vamp junkie anyway! There is no coming back from that! But Nathaniel keeps getting in my way, trying to calm me down in the hospital corridor as Damian walks in.

"She is crazy, Selena, vampire slaves turn like that and you know it, alright. Let Damian handle it, okay?"

"You might want to take that back," says Liam, suddenly coming out of the room. "He lost it and killed her when she started threatening everyone."

Nathaniel rolls his eyes.

"Damn it."

"That's the Alpha temper for you," sighs Liam. "Anyway, Sylviana is still with the bodies we didn't burn, but I think this is bad. If what that crazy woman said is true…"

I know. She mentioned thousands of vampires. We don't have enough people to push away thousands of vampires. I hope she lied or exaggerated greatly, or else this is going to be a bloodbath.

"Sylviana says the timing is not good. If she let the vampires lose control like that and feed now, it means she felt Nora's power is changing."

"She will give birth soon," I grumble.

I take a deep breath and walk outside. I need a moment. A moment alone with my cousin. I can feel it, the tension in the air building up. It's coming anytime now.

"*Nora?*"

"*Selena, everything alright? Damian is on his way there.*"

I use our mind-link to tell her everything, wondering why Damian didn't tell her yet. As usual, he probably tried to spare Nora as much as he could. He's as overprotective as ever with his mate. I can't blame him, but Nora is strong, the only Luna I could rival with. When I'm done, she doesn't seem shocked or scared.

"*I see. Sylviana is probably right. I can feel my baby moving more than ever, I'm supposed to give birth within the next thirty days.*"

"*Nora, I'm going to stay here with the White Moon.*"

"*I understand.*"

"*We won't see each other until... after the war.*"

"*I know. I'm going to miss you so much, Selena... You have to survive, okay? You'll look after those idiot Black brothers for me, right? I'll join the fight if I can.*"

I chuckle.

"*You'll be busy giving birth, you idiot. Stay where you are. I'll handle it here. And, Nora?*"

"*Yes?*"

"*Look after our people. Danny, Estelle. If I don't survive, I'm counting on you, okay? You're the best Luna.*"

"*You're the fighter, Selena. I'm the healer. I'll take care of you after this. I'll be protecting you from where I am. Don't worry.*"

"*I love you, little sis.*"

"*I love you too, Selena.*"

I take a deep breath, holding back the tears the best I can. Not now, Selena Whitewood, you can cry later. Right now, they need the fighter.

Nathaniel joins me outside, putting his arms around me, his forehead against mine.

"Are you okay?" he asks.

"I have to be."

"I know. Many people are looking up to you. You're their Luna. But don't forget, I'm your mate. I'm here for you, okay? You don't need to push yourself, not in front of me, my sunshine."

I smile, and as if a door had been opened in my heart, I snuggle into his arms for a much-needed hug. I hear him sigh as he caresses my hair.

"We're going to be okay," he whispers.

"I know. I just want to be weak for one more day, and then I'll be the Luna they are all waiting for."

"I think they won't be disappointed. Do you know your aura is going… wild these days?"

I nod. Yeah, I've felt it too. Ever since Nathaniel and I solved our issues, or since I became an official Luna, I feel like all restraints broke loose around my wolf. Not only that, but it's almost like I can feel some strange halo around me too, something that seems to protect me in some way, I just don't know how yet.

"I want to see Estelle," I whisper.

I want to say goodbye to my daughter before this madness begins. I don't want her to be near when hell breaks loose, and I don't want to have regrets about not saying goodbye to her. I didn't get to say goodbye to my parents, twice. I'm not letting my daughter lose that as well.

Liam is the one to go and get my daughter from Nora's place, while I let Damian and Nate handle things around here, notably with the bodies. I need to be a mom, just for an hour or two.

"Mommy!" she says while jumping into my arms.

"Hi, baby star!"

I hold my daughter, while she tells me all about her game with her cousin, and her auntie Nora's baby moving in her belly. I decide to borrow Clark's house for a while to chat with her and let her have a hot chocolate in the quiet, far from the mess around the river.

After a while, I take a deep breath. It's been an hour. I need to tell her.

"My baby star, you are going to stay with your Auntie Nora for a while."

"Really? With Mommy and Daddy too?"

"No, baby. Mommy won't be there."

It's hard. It's hard to explain to my daughter that leaving her to my cousin is for her own safety while I'll be on the battlefront. I get up from my chair to go and kneel in front of her, getting to her level. She's still so small.

"Estelle, listen to me. Mommy and Daddy won't be able to stay with you for a while."

"Because the bad people will attack us?" she asks. "I heard Auntie Nora talk on the phone, and Auntie Sylviana too."

I nod, trying to think of how to explain war and death to a four-year-old.

"Yes. You know how Mommy is very strong? And Daddy too? Well, we will be protecting everyone. Your uncles, too."

"I can't stay with you?"

"No, my little star. Mommy needs to fight, and I can't fight if I am worried about my baby. So I need you to be a good girl and stay with Auntie Nora, okay?"

She starts sobbing, holding my hands with a distressed expression. Oh, Moon Goddess, I can't bear to see my baby girl crying.

"Estelle, Mommy will…"

"*Selena! My water just... My water just broke!*"

Moon Goddess. Now? Now, of all times? Crap… This is too soon!

I take a deep breath. I can feel Nora mind-linking everyone and the ruckus of all the voices talking at the same time. I still have a few minutes. Damn it, I didn't think it would happen so fast.

"Mommy will be here to protect you. Baby, I'll fight to protect you. Mommy loves you, Estelle. You remember in the forest? When you hid?"

"Y… Yes…" she cries.

"Well, it's the same, baby. Mommy needs you to be a good girl and hide with Auntie Nora."

"B… But… Mommy will be hurt again…"

She's looking at my shoulder, where I still have a hideous scar. I shake my head and caress her wet cheek. She's so cute even when she cries.

I hear Nathaniel behind me, and he comes next to me in silence, taking one of Estelle's hands.

"Mommy will be okay as long as you are safe, my baby star," I continue. "Mommy will do her best, fight the bad people, and come to find you again, okay?"

"Daddy will protect Mommy, okay?" says Nate. "I promise, my little star."

Estelle keeps crying loudly, looking at the two of us.

"I don't want you to go… to go fight… I… I want all of us to… to stay with Auntie… and together… I don't want Daddy and Mommy to go…"

Oh, crap… I'm starting to cry too. I was trying hard to hold it in, but I can't bear it. Estelle's sobbing is too much for me to handle. I lose it and hug her, standing up with my baby in my arms. I smell her, engrave her smile in my mind, the touch of her soft hair and chubby cheeks.

"I love you… I love you, my baby… I'll do my best and come back to you. Mommy will be alright."

I hear Nate whispering to her too, caressing her blond hair and trying to reassure her. After a few seconds, I put her in his arms, and undo my necklace for the first time in years, to give it to her.

"Mommy…"

"You keep Mommy's necklace, baby. You know how much Mommy loves it, so you take good care of it, okay? I love you, my little star, Mommy will come and find you soon, okay?"

"O… okay… Mommy… You have to come… with Daddy…" she replies, trying to talk despite her loud sobbing, her little hand on the sun pendant.

She continues crying in Nate's arms, who tries to soothe her, whispering into her ear.

"We love you, Estelle. Mommy and Daddy… We will come back for you. Daddy will protect Mommy, so don't you worry, okay? You're Daddy's little princess, don't ever forget. Forever, Daddy loves you and Mommy more than anything."

It's my first time seeing Nathaniel cry. He holds our baby for a long while, but it's never enough. He holds us together, a long hug, until it's time to part for real. I can't ignore the voices echoing in my mind anymore.

Liam walks into the room, looking sorry.

"Time to go, princess."

Estelle cries a lot when Nate hands her to her uncle. It's the hardest thing I've ever done. Watching my daughter go away, waving and crying loudly. Liam's bike disappears soon, and I crumble, falling on my knees to cry as loud as I fucking need to.

I feel Nate's arms around me. He doesn't say anything, just lets me cry. I just parted with my daughter once again. Maybe it was the last fucking time I saw her, hugged her. What will happen if I die? How will she cope? I can't bear the idea of not seeing her grow up. I already miss her so fucking much… I keep weeping, my mate rubbing my back.

"It's going to be alright," he whispers. "We will win and see her again. She will be fine…"

"I don't want to abandon her again."

"We are not abandoning our baby. We will be back. I won't let Estelle lose her mom."

I glare at him.

"You'd better survive this too," I growl.

He chuckles.

"I promise to do my best. I want more time with you and her, so much more time…"

Moon Goddess, we only had a few weeks to live as a family… Why does it have to be like this? If I die, or Nate dies… What will that all be for? I can't, I just can't imagine it.

Nathaniel gently kisses me, capturing my lips between my tears, gently caressing me. It's a salty kiss, a bitter one. I don't want it to end. I want to kiss him forever, enjoy this warmth until I die. My mate's taste on my lips, again and again. That would be a sweet poison to succumb to.

I lose my breath as our kiss gets a bit wilder, a bit more desperate. His lips go down my neck, making me gasp. I caress his skin, ripping his shirt without an ounce of regret. I just want to feel his skin against mine, one more minute, one last time. I caress his hair, feeling him grip mine, his breathing getting erratic too.

Our lips find each other again, our kiss resumes as if we needed each other more than air. I kiss him like crazy until my head spins, until I can't tell what's his from what's mine.

After a few seconds, we stop, out of breath. We put a bit of distance between our bodies before this gets out of hand, but my hands are still on his neck, his arms around me. He chuckles, kissing my forehead while I catch my breath.

"Let's continue after the war, okay?" I whisper.

"Sounds like a pretty good reason to stay alive."

I laugh. Damn right, it is. We kiss again, a well-behaved kiss, a loving one before parting. We need to go back to the madness of this world.

My head is aching from ignoring all the mind-linking from earlier. I sigh and push my hair back, focusing a bit.

"*Elena! Elena!*"

"*Levi, stop screaming. I hear you. Fill me in.*"

"*Finally! Some vampires are gathering outside the border! We are gathering too, but the King is gone, and–*"

"*The King is probably enjoying one last moment with his wife. He'll be back soon. How many vampires?*"

"*I would say about two or three hundred…*"

Damn, that's a lot already. I exchange a look with Nate. He's holding his ripped shirt. Yeah, I may have gone a bit overboard… Well, he'll have to stay half-naked then. He follows me outside as I take off my jacket. Time to get back to business.

"*Lysandra, show time!*"

"*On our way!*"

I mind-link all the Alphas except for Damian, as I can feel his wolf with Nora.

"*You're okay?*"

"*Selena! Sorry, it just happened so fast. I have contractions, the midwife is here with Tonia's grandma. Damian just left.*"

"*Don't worry, Nora. You stay safe and focus on delivering your baby, okay? I'll handle things here.*"

I take a deep breath and start running toward the north, my mate right behind me. I use my power to mind-link every wolf I can like we agreed, and I can feel Damian's voice echoing through mine. We gather everyone in the north, as planned, only leaving smaller packs to protect the other borders.

"*Seaver, it's now or never!*"

"*I know, I know…*"

I hope he won't be stubborn and just submit to Damian without a fuss. Nathaniel and I finally meet with the rest of the White Moon clan. Daniel comes to give me a quick hug. His brothers and father are all here, all in their wolf forms. Clark, Isabella, and all the warriors of the White Moon were the first to answer my call too.

The other packs start to arrive slowly, crossing the streets in small groups, most of them in their wolf forms. We wait and wait. We don't know when it will blow up. I try to follow Nora's state from afar, but her contractions amplify slowly. It's a strange atmosphere that has fallen on Silver City. The sun is setting already, and hundreds of wolves are slowly gathering, listening to the vampires' screeches from afar. I feel another wolf approaching and recognize William Blue's unusual black and white fur.

"*Ready?*"

"*It's now or never.*"

He probably left his wife behind to watch over Nora and the children; she's a good Luna but not much of a fighter.

Soon, Damian and Liam arrive, accompanied by Boyan, Tonia, and their older brother Neal, and most of the Blood Moon clan behind them. The King looks ready for a bloody fight. His dark and murderous aura gets everyone tensed up one level higher, and the crowd splits in two to let him through.

So am I. This bitch got me to part with my daughter twice. It won't happen ever again.

Chapter 36

This is it. The big fight we have been anticipating for weeks… Hundreds of wolves gather at the north border and, as the sun sets, the vampires slowly come creeping around. They hide in the shadows, avoiding the sunlight, their white faces clearly visible in the darkness surrounding them.

The wolves start growling. I channel my inner wolf, connecting to as many people as possible. I had never tried that before, but it feels incredible. I can feel every single wolf in our enlarged pack, like an invisible thread linking me to their hearts. There are hundreds of us, all connected to me and Damian Black. It's strange how the Alphas appear brighter, while my friends have more color. Is it because I know them well? The closest to me are Levi and Danny. Their wolves shine with a gold or bronze shade, something that warms me up.

The Black brothers are like dark shadows, each more terrifying than the other, even to our kind. All the wolves around are wary of them; the King and his brothers are easily identifiable no matter where they stand, even if they haven't shape-shifted yet.

Actually, as I look around, we are almost the last ones who have yet to take our wolf form. Aside from Nate, Liam, and Damian, only a handful of werewolves are standing on two feet. Among them, Lysandra Jones and Tonia are standing next to each other and talking while watching the forest, so softly I can't hear. Probably something private anyway.

Boyan too walks up to Daniel and I, looking more serious than ever.

"You okay?" he asks.

"Doing fine so far. How about you?"

"I just hope Nora and the kids stay safe," he says, looking determined.

I often forgot that, besides being her best friend, he is Nora's bodyguard. He's probably the first one, besides Damian, willing to defend her and her children… no matter the cost.

As I look around, there is still one person missing, one I can't mind-link though.

"What is Sylviana doing?" I ask Liam, a few steps away.

"She's still at the hospital. Don't worry, she'll be here in due time," he answers while glancing at the sunset.

I hope she does. I think the vampires will be hard to handle already, but if we have no defense against the witch either…

The fact that Chris and Iris' whereabouts are still unknown is bothering me. Why is this timing so perfect? Disappearing today, of all days? The one when Nora gives birth, the one when the battle happens? I can't shake off that feeling that something bad will happen. I hope it's just my instincts going crazy.

Just when my heartbeat and anxiety are about to blow through the roof, I feel a hand in mine. I don't even need to look.

"It's going to be okay," he whispers. "We're going to be back to our baby star by sunrise."

I nod.

Nathaniel's right about one thing at least: this will be over at dawn. The vampires are obviously waiting for the sun to go down and the sky to get dark. If this war lasts until the morning, we will have won.

Strangely, in this very moment, I miss Nora. She's like my other half, the power that completes mine completely. I can feel her, her aura linked to all of the wolves just like mine. It's pure white, not like my golden, shining light. It's similar, yet different, like the lights of the Sun and the Moon. I'm sure we would be invincible together. I have to make sure I can be strong enough for two as long as I can.

I try to channel my inner wolf as much as I can while this unbearable wait goes on. More and more vampires gather. I can't see them all, but we can feel them, like pests crawling and lurking in the shadows. There are a lot of them. I'm starting to wonder if this woman told the truth. If there are thousands…

Suddenly, I feel Nora's bond with the other wolves and I weaken. I can tell. Her labor is starting. I glance up, and sure enough, that barrier I was feeling is shaking too. The Royal's Aura is going down. Sylviana had poured her magic into that barrier, but whatever it is, it won't be enough.

The sun's almost set, and the enemies have gathered. My friends and I spread among the wolves, getting ready to fight. I exchange one final look with Nate.

"I love you."

"I love you too, my sunshine."

Once again, the barrier shakes. The vampires come closer, just a few feet away. All the wolves are growling.

"Wait until my signal," yells Damian.

Time to see if our weeks of preparation will pay off. All the wolves are waiting, ready to fight, but staying within the perimeter we marked while the vampires come closer. I don't see the witch! We need to find the witch and kill her as soon as we can! Sylviana hasn't arrived yet either, but the hospital is so close…

Suddenly, one of the vampires screeches, a horrible sound familiar to their race. A lot of wolves growl back, but as expected, no one disobeys the King.

As all of the other vampires screech in response to the first one, the warning becomes terribly clear. There's a fucking lot of them. I can't count them all, but one thousand or two is the minimum. Holy Moon Goddess. How many did that bitch of a witch gather?

"It's gonna be one fucking feast," sighs Liam before jumping into his black wolf appearance.

"They are not touching a hair on my children or my wife," growls Damian back.

That's it. Once they are done screeching, a handful of vampires start running, and dozens follow. No one on our side moves yet. We are all waiting, as Damian and I glare at the line of our border. Suddenly, Nora and Sylviana's protection disappears at once, and the vampires keep running, wide, scary smiles on their faces. Yeah, keep smiling, you monsters.

The first bomb explodes a couple of seconds later. One by one they go off, following the line we established and blowing up dozens of vampires each. Their limbs and blood is sprayed around, and some wolves step aside to avoid it. In a few seconds, the fifteen bombs we had planted exploded, killing maybe two or three hundred vampires at once. The ones who were running behind them slow down, and Damian's grin is terrifying.

"NOW!"

The King shape-shifts in a split second, the huge black wolf's appearance exhilarating everyone. All at once, the wolves start running, going past the ravaged line and jumping on the first lines of vampires. I start running too.

"The bombs! Can't believe we used the fucking Gold Moon's idea!"

"Liam, shut the fuck up and fight!"

Sure enough, I don't have time to squander any more time chatting with him about my idea. It's a fucking battle here. I jump on the first vampires I see, using my silver poles to beat the shit out of them. I want to use my weapons as much as I can before I shape-shift. I am the only one who can wield silver, the one thing both of our species fear.

Despite the ones we blew up, there's still way too many vampires waiting for us out there. We start holding a clear front against them. The best warriors target the groups of vampires, while the weaker ones of us attack the isolated ones.

I have to focus on fighting my own battles while keeping up with everything going on and directing the others with Damian when needed.

"The east! Guard the east! One just ran past us! Joe, get him!"

The betas are acting as the second line of defense, planted to kill any vampire that gets past the alphas and warriors. Levi and Joseph are the busiest, as the Lewis' are faster and right behind Lysandra, who's mostly playing around.

"Lysandra, just go for the kill! We don't have time for that!"

She growls but obeys, and her wolf starts making a slaughter of her surroundings. We made sure to keep the Alphas among us isolated, as we tend to get violent. Damian, Nate, and Liam are terrific too. I almost can't recognize them, it's a bloodbath in their area.

Unlike us, the vampires are uncoordinated and acting randomly, counting on their huge numbers. They are focused on one thing: entering Silver City, and probably killing Nora. We are not going to allow that.

I keep fighting, hitting every vampire I can, avoiding their bites and claws and kicking without distinction. My poles are covered in vampire blood, sticky and smelly, but I don't give a damn. I'm caught in that dance of death, I can't slow down or catch a break. It's a race against time, and it has just begun.

More and more vampires keep coming; I can feel some wolves struggling to keep up and soon, the first mortal bites. As soon as one of ours is in bad shape, two more wolves jump in to help them, but the situation is not so good. Except for our line of Alphas, most wolves are giving their all, and one second of inattention is fatal. I need to go on, I can't stop to mourn the dead, but I can feel it. The ties that were binding me to them, brutally cut off, or slowly growing thinner until they are no more. Shit.

I pour my rage into my fists and my will to fight. Our line of Alphas is merciless. Damian, Nate, William, Arthur, Lysandra, and I are not leaving them one second to rest. Around us, all the wolves are running around, catching any vampire they can and tearing them apart. The fight is getting so intense, all the soil is ploughed everywhere, leaving the mud to meld with the stench of the blood.

All this time, I'm trying to focus on the fight, but the deaths are crushing my heart, making it harder to breathe and to focus. I am a warrior, I need to get through this. I'll mourn the dead later! I take a deep breath and send two more vampires flying Liam's way with one blow. He's only too happy to jump and tear their throats open. I didn't think the Alphas would work so well together. Each one of us is holding their ground; we have barely moved a few steps since the beginning of the fight. Our line is doing a good job of thinning out their troops while acting as a barrier. We picked positions within a few feet of each other, so that only a few vampires can go past us, enough for the betas to deal with if they are not killed by the other wolves before that.

After a while, it becomes clear our plan is working, but I'm also aware this is only the beginning. The vampires just don't stop coming at us, as if there are an infinite number of them just waiting.

Also, the main players of this game haven't appeared yet, and I'm well aware everything will change then. What the heck is taking so long? Truth is, I've lost track of time. It's night time, that's all I can say. With the moon's shine and my wolf vision, I have no trouble seeing, but there is just too much going on all around. It's a blurry mess everywhere. I hear growling, screeches, and screams. Some wolves are wailing, crying for their lost loved ones. I'm lucky none of my loved ones are in difficulty yet, but I'm not prepared for it.

Suddenly, I can sense something's wrong on our west flank. Too many wolves are in pain at the same time!

"*William! What's going on there!*"

"*The water! She's here! The witch is–!*"

He's gone. I lose my breath. William's wolf is gone, completely gone, leaving a big void where I felt him just a second ago.

Oh Moon Goddess, I can't believe it, but I can't be wrong either. I know this feeling all too well. Just like Reagan… I keep mind-linking anyone I can in that area, trying to figure out what the fuck is going on. Their voices die one after the other. The witch is there. The water's attacking.

It's a fucking nightmare. I want to cry, but I can't. William died and now, there's nothing I can do about it. I need to settle this.

"Damian!"

"Stay where you are!"

"But–!"

"Stay where you are, Selena!"

I growl, pissed. I know it's our plan, but our people are dying on the west side! Suddenly, the earth starts shaking under our feet, and roots erupt from the ground, impaling nearby vampires before diving back into the soil. Sylviana! It was fucking high time!

I take a second to catch my breath as most vampires around us are being wiped out by the Earth Witch. Thank Moon Goddess. I didn't realize I was so exhausted, out of breath, and dirty. I'm covered in blood, vampire blood, and it stinks. Next to me, Liam shakes his head, catching his breath too.

Sylviana appears at my side. Instead of her usual flowery dresses, she is in jeans, barefoot in the mud with a simple top, quite a difference from her usual look. She looks exhausted already, a pearl of sweat on her neck. Is she draining so much energy already?

"Tell me you still got some fuel left?" I growl.

"I'll be fine," she nods. "I just… I'm not ready for this to happen."

While I'm lost trying to understand what she means by that, she agitates her hand, killing a nearby vampire.

"What now?" I ask.

"I need to confront her. She's probably controlling the Vampire King or Queen somehow. If I can stop her, we can stop them."

For the first time, I realize Sylviana looks really afraid. She's fearing that confrontation, it's obvious. She's looking towards the west with that worried look in her eyes.

"You can do it," I tell her, trying to share some of my inner strength with her.

She chuckles shyly.

"I hope you won't judge me too badly when you hear the truth."

"What? What truth?"

But before she can answer, new vampires attack us, and we both have to fight a new wave of vampires. Sylviana starts progressing toward the west, her butterfly, five times its usual size, following behind her.

I have to dodge a new attack, then riposte with a kick, and I slowly realize, the vampires are coming in larger numbers. Did they increase because the Water Witch is there? Or in response to Sylviana's powers? No matter which it is, the fight resumes, more savage than before. They are now coming at us by the dozen, and we all struggle to keep up the rhythm. It's one wave after another, and I have no idea what's going on elsewhere. I can't stop to focus on everyone. I try to push my wolf to its limit, spreading my mind-link like a web around me, catching as many wolves as I can and making sure to hold on.

I pour my aura and strength into our link, galvanizing our troops. I feel Damian Black, like a black monster scaring all the vampires and making a bloody slaughter around him. Liam is toying with them, tearing them to shreds and making a mess out of it. Nate is also being one scary Alpha, but with an unusual elegance to it. He takes them down, one by one, not showing one ounce of fatigue, and I'm proud of my man.

I try to feel the other Alphas. I can feel Lysandra, fighting like a lioness, and… and… Arthur Seaver. I can't… I can't feel him. I didn't even realize. Our link was so thin…

It means there's a big gap in the west. Whether the witch got him, or the vampires, I can't tell, but his wolf is nowhere to be found.

"*Damian! Nate!*"

The King knows too. He turns his head to me, nodding. The witch is in the west; now that we are sure, that's where we need to move. We break our former line, letting Lysandra Jones and all of the betas take our place to fight the new waves of vampires. I hope they will be able to hold on long enough. The Black brothers and I start running, but our run is cut short.

A few paces away, standing behind several lines of vampires, is a woman. Her blue-green eyes and human appearance can't be mistaken. She's dressed all in black, and looks younger than I had imagined, maybe about Clark or Reagan's age. We run to Sylviana's side, who stands facing her, though they are a few feet apart.

"So… Those are your little guard dogs. The sons of Black…"

Her voice is strangely hoarse, like she has been screaming for days. Next to me, Sylviana is fiercely staring at her, her fists closed.

"Enough, Nephera. You need to stop all of this, now."

The Water Witch chuckles.

"Nephera? Is that what you call me after all this time?"

We frown, confused. What the heck is she talking about? I exchange glances with the Black brothers, but even Liam doesn't seem to know what's going on. Suddenly, the Water Witch laughs loudly, staring at us like something funny is going on.

"Don't tell me? Sylviana, after all this time? You couldn't tell them? Really?"

What the fuck is she talking about? Sylviana looks utterly sad and sorry right now, making me fucking uneasy about whatever's going on. The Water Witch stops laughing, and sighs.

"Really, my little sister. You're as weak as ever."

You've got to be fucking kidding me.

I turn to Sylviana.

"She meant that metaphorically, right?" I ask, channeling the three brother's words echoing in my head into one question.

"We are half-sisters," confesses Sylviana, white as a sheet.

What? I did not see that one coming. Sisters. That Water Witch and Sylviana. Why did she hide this from us this whole time? Even Liam? He looks as confused and shocked as all of us. I would never have guessed. How many years apart are they anyway? Sylviana is Damian's age, give or take a few years, but that woman is much older. They don't even look alike, except for maybe their eyes? Damn it, what is going on?

The Water Witch sneers.

"That's right, we are," she says. "Witches, daughters of the same wretched mother. You didn't tell them anything, did you, Sylviana? Isn't that why you were Mom's favorite? Always the little werewolves' friend…"

"Nephera, you must stop this. Whatever Mom did to you, she–"

"What she did to me? You think this is only about our mother, Sylviana? Oh no, I'm going to destroy these packs and take this city. It was mine to begin with, wasn't it?"

"What the heck is that woman talking about?" I growl, glancing at Sylviana.

Just then, the Water Witch turns to me. It's odd that all the vampires stopped attacking when she started talking. It's almost like they froze up. Is she really controlling them all? It's like she's holding her dogs back.

"Your golden eyes. Aren't you Gabriel's precious daughter?"

I'm speechless. She knows my biological father? What the heck!

She looks at all of us, her eyes going slowly to Damian, Nathaniel, and Liam as an ugly smile appears on her face.

"Isn't that perfect. I already have four of you right here… Sylviana, did you do this on purpose? How thoughtful of you. Now you're going to watch while I make these dogs suffer."

For a second, a very scary thought crosses my mind, that maybe this was all part of their plan. It's wiped away as soon as I see Sylviana's horrified expression though, and how she steps forward in a protective stance.

"Nephera, enough!"

"Keep yelling and screaming all you want, Sylviana. I've been waiting for this for way too long, little sister. If you're going to hinder me again, I'll kill you too."

"Mom didn't want this, Nephera. She–"

But the Water Witch clicks her tongue before Sylviana finishes her sentence. She's obviously angrier now.

"Oh, I bet she was a great mother to you, wasn't she? Danica was so obsessed with protecting Diane and her children, what did she care about me!"

Danica? That name sounds familiar. I'm sure I've heard it before. Where have I heard about Danica…? I try to remember a witch named Danica… Oh, Moon Goddess!

"Danica," I repeat. "I know about Danica, the Fire Witch. Reagan told me about her; she was a friend of Queen Diane, the witch that was protecting the Blue Moon pack… Don't tell me you are Danica's… daughters?"

"That's right," says Nephera with that scary smile of hers on. "It all comes around, doesn't it? Diane's granddaughters, Danica's daughters, and… Judah's little bastards."

Judah, like Judah Black? Not only my birth father, but now theirs too? What the heck is going on? How does she know us all? The brothers start growling around me.

"*Why is she mentioning our father? Do we know her?*"

"*No idea.*"

Nephera sighs.

"Oh, well, since Sylviana didn't even bother to tell you the full story, I guess it's my chore? At least you'll know why you must die."

I don't care much about how she wants to kill me or why, but I am curious to how the fuck she knows both my dad and Nate's father, and also be Sylviana's sister. I feel like something's ringing like crazy in my head. Moreover, we could use a break, and buy some more time for Nora too.

"Let's go back many, many years ago," says Nephera. "You're a big girl now, you at least know who your grandmother was, Selena, don't you? The mighty, holy Queen Diane. The Alpha of your pack of Blue Moon wolves. I was born one year after her twins, Lilyan and Gabriel. Of course, the birth of a little Water Witch was nothing compared to the Moon

Goddess' reincarnation giving birth to twins. Even my own mother, Danica, didn't care much. Most witches don't have much of a maternal side, do they, Sylviana? So, when the younger sister of Diane left with some of the pack, to find a better location, she dumped me in with them!"

I remember that. Nora said that's how Cynthia, William's grandmother and our great-aunt, came to live and settle in Silver City with a part of the Blue Moon clan, about fifty years ago. Tragically, once she got here, Cynthia never could contact her older sister Diane again after that, and the Blue Moon clan became the Sapphire Moon here.

Damian and I exchange a look, agreeing silently to let her finish her little speech. He's probably mind-linking Nora to let her hear this too; I can feel her presence with us. I open my link to her, feeling her snow-white wolf. She's enduring the pain, for now, but her baby isn't born yet. We need more time…

"Imagine, the little witch I was, so young, suddenly coming to a big city like this one!" says Nephera. "My mother, Danica, had sent me so there would already be a witch at the destination, ready to protect Diane's precious children… I was supposed to help Cynthia establish communication with them too, but we knew that would take a few years before I was strong enough to do that."

Moon Goddess, so…

"*That's why they lost contact,*" suddenly says Nora's voice in my mind, echoing my own thoughts.

"*Yeah. She was probably the one who didn't do her part of the job, and why Cynthia could never reach Diane again.*"

"I wasn't really that interested in being Cynthia's little puppet. She was too busy taking care of the pack in Silver City, establishing themselves among the other clans, and so on. She was truly a workaholic. But me? I had all the time to grow up though, so I would wander around, learn about my power, and make some friends, both humans and werewolves. I made one friend, one werewolf boy I grew fond of, with my weak little girl's heart. Can you guess who that boy was?"

"Judah Black," I gasp.

The pieces of the puzzle are starting to fit into place slowly. Nora and I knew there was one part of the story that was missing, but I never would have imagined it was Nephera's, or that Sylviana had anything to do with our birth pack.

"Yes! The strong, fierce Judah Black. Of course, I knew him when he was only a young wolf, fighting to find his place in his pack. He was an alpha, but he wasn't that strong. So, little by little, I helped him… in my own way."

"You used your magic on him?" I ask, stunned.

Nephera gives me a little wink.

"I did. I mean, I was young, I thought it was innocent, a friend helping a friend. We grew up together, both getting stronger. I knew I was going to be this city's witch, and I was grooming my own Alpha to lead the werewolves!"

"*I don't like where this is going.*"

"*Damian, you knew?*"

"*No. None of this.*"

Nephera sighs, almost a bit too dramatically. She's like an actress, having fun on her own stage, making her show and taking pleasure in laying down her story. I take deep breaths, glancing around. The fight is still going on farther away, but here, she put everything on hold for her little speech's sake. I really hope this allows us to win some time; we'll need every minute we can get until dawn comes.

"Men are men," she sighed. "They are always hungrier for power. Judah was no different. He wanted to prove himself to everyone. To his pack leader, to his friends, to Silver City, to the whole world! I didn't see he was getting drunk on this."

"A witch's magic is not made to make someone stronger," said Sylviana. "There are side effects to a human or a wolf getting too much of it."

"That's right, Sylviana. Judah Black was a junkie, completely submitted to me and my magic. Honestly, when I understood that, I decided it was fine. By then, I was completely disinterested in the Blue, no, the Sapphire Moon pack who only wanted to use me. Instead, I wanted to make Judah and his pack mine. Being the witch of the Sapphire Moon would mean doing Cynthia's bidding, like my mom did with Diane, but I wanted to be my own witch, and make my own choices. Judah was giving me that. He was nothing without me. It was just another way of binding him to me."

"*That's fucking disgusting.*"

"*No wonder our father got so strong so fast. I remember our former pack kept talking about that, how it was unnatural.*"

"*Do you think the reason we are so strong too is because… I mean, he was our father…*"

"*I hope not.*"

"*Me too. I don't need him or that witch's magic.*"

While the brothers bicker through the mind-link, next to me Sylviana shakes her head.

"You shouldn't have done that, Nephera! You were using your magic for something wrong and corrupting his mind."

"I didn't corrupt him enough!" suddenly yells her sister. "He would have been mine, completely mine if it wasn't for that damn bitch!"

"Our mother! Our parents were fated mates!"

"He probably ditched the witch as soon as he could. So like our father..."

"Judah wanted everything from me," says Nephera, "but the one thing he didn't care about was my love for him. As soon as he had met that woman, it was over. This damn fated mate of his was robbing him from me!"

"Or the other way around," I growl. "You were desperately holding on to a man that wasn't yours. Black was wrong for using you, but you could have ended things anytime. You were the one with the power."

Nephera scoffs, glaring at me.

"You think it was that easy? I gave my childhood and my best years to that man, most of my magic for him to consume. Do you think it was easy to get over the first man I ever loved? The first person that ever showed me some affection? I was blind. Too blind to see the only thing Judah Black loved was power. Once I realized that, though it was too late, I did my best to get out of his life. I wanted to be the strong, independent witch I had always tried to be. I refused to give him my magic anymore, no matter how hard he was begging. He went crazy. You don't go sober from magic in a few days. He couldn't let go easily. But I really did try. I abandoned him, to forge a life of my own, leave him to his beloved mate, and move on. But everyone here knows there was nothing reasonable about Judah Black."

I glance at the brothers. From their growls, I would say they all agree. Nate and I never talked much about his father. I know he and Damian worked together to kill him, which I guess sums up about everything they shared other than a blood bond.

Now, I'm starting to think the "Mad King" may have become mad because of his own hunger for power, and the witch that let him taste too much of it. Nephera shakes her head, and her expression goes from an annoying smirk to a sour one.

"He learned I was with child. And that didn't sit well with him. He didn't need two witches, only one. So, he started planning to take my baby away from me. I knew Judah Black enough, I knew that man would have no remorse about killing me or stealing my daughter. I didn't trust Cynthia and the Sapphire Moon to help me, not after I had basically left them to serve another pack. So, I secretly left Silver City, pregnant and scared, trying to run away from him. I don't know if he did it on purpose, but around the same time, Judah drove away the vampires from Silver City."

"*That was right before Liam's birth...*" says Nate. "*One of them had bitten our pregnant mother, and our father was fighting them for years before he finally managed to send them away.*"

"*He sent them to Queen Diane's city though, according to William.*"

"*For now, I'm more interested in knowing how Nephera avoided the vampires, and how they got to our home city...*"

"I started running towards the north. I was hoping my mother would save me, help me find shelter, and protect me and my child. However, I couldn't outrun the vampires. They caught me way before I reached my destination."

I suddenly feel a cold shiver down my spine. Nephera looks at the closest vampires with a strange light in her eyes. I realize she hates them even more than she hates us, despite using them like she does. Those eyes… I know that expression, all too well. As if something was broken inside of her. Then, she slowly rolls up her long sleeves, and I gasp.

Bite marks. Hundreds of them, spread all over her skin. Now that I'm staring, even her hands are full of countless scars. If her dress wasn't covering her throat and neck, I bet there would be dozens there too. I feel so disgusted just looking at it. Next to me, Sylviana is shaken up too. I can't tell if she already knew, but she obviously feels sorry for what her sister went through.

"Vampires like to play with their food," says Nephera. "Truth is, most humans get used to the pain, until they aren't affected anymore and turn into junkies, addicted to that sensation. For werewolves, that bite is poisonous. For witches, however, it is just horribly, atrociously painful. We don't die from it, we just… suffer. It's like having razor blades plunging through your skin and pouring acid underneath. They bit me, over and over. I didn't die, but my body was filled with vampire venom. I lost my baby and all hope. I would have gladly died, but instead, I was left to endure weeks and weeks of utter torture."

I knew it. Nephera has the eyes of someone who lost a child. I can't even begin to imagine the hell that woman went through. The physical and emotional pain must have been impossible to handle with a sound mind…

"I kept trying to run away as soon as my magic could heal me. I always ran north, a bit farther every time, until I finally escaped those beasts long enough to reach the border."

I can already tell what happened next.

The border and its protective barrier. Diane put it up when she realized her sister wasn't returning to protect her children. It's like hearing Reagan's story all over again, except that this time, her story makes more sense as to why the barrier was up. The vampires were close because of Nephera.

"As it turns out," she says, "my mother's magic couldn't even recognize her own kin. She couldn't recognize her own daughter, coming back so many years later, not when my entire body was filled with vampire venom. The barrier Danica had put into place with Diane to protect the twins was keeping me outside. It couldn't even recognize me as a witch. Just a creature broken by vampires, reeking of them. I tried to break that damn barrier so many times!"

I'm starting to understand the tragic truth. Reagan and Nephera were trying to go back at the same time. Whether Nephera's venom was preventing it from opening for Reagan, or Reagan's jealousy was adding to the problem, both women were locked out, probably around the same time. If I think about the timing, that should be around my birth and Nora's too. That barrier must have been more cautious than ever to protect us.

"Every time I failed to enter, the vampires would catch me, and the cycle of pain and suffering would start all over again and again and again... Imagine that torture. Knowing your own mother is there, behind that barrier, but she doesn't recognize you, because she's busy protecting someone else's children. Her new daughter too."

She glances down at Sylviana. That's right, if they are half-sisters, it means Sylviana was born during that time as well... and she was originally from the same place as us.

So many things make sense now: how Sylviana knew about me and Nora, our connection, and our relationship to the Sapphire Moon and Blue Moon packs! No wonder she helped us so much; she kept watching over us all this time. But when we talked about it, she always remained so enigmatic! She never gave me any answers, aside from my birth parents' death.

"You were born in the same place as us?" I can't help but ask.

Sylviana slowly nods.

"I was. Just a few years before you and Nora. I was just a child back then. I barely remember Queen Diane, just the day she passed away. I remember your birth and Nora's though. Your parents were so nice to me."

"Oh yes, I bet you lived a great life there, Sylviana," says her sister, "just as great as the twins that our mother was so focused on protecting, and their children too. I had suffered so much, yet you were all living happy lives up there. My own mother had thrown me away for someone else's sake, and was leaving me to suffer at the hands of those vampires, while you were growing happily by her side."

"Mother had no idea, Nephera," Sylviana said. "Her barrier was just acting on its own, she couldn't have known it was you."

"Shut up!" she yells. "I don't want to hear a damn word about my mother and me. Danica was the worst! All because I was born first, you had a great life while I was sent to Silver City!"

"*Damn, someone has mommy issues.*"

"*Shut up, Liam. We need to talk about your girlfriend choices too.*"

"*I swear I had no idea...*"

"*Yeah, that's the problem.*"

I don't blame Liam. Sylviana kept the truth from all of us. Liam couldn't have known the truth, and neither could any of us. I turn to her, ignoring Nephera's fierce glare.

"That day… You know what happened? To our parents…"

Sylviana nods sadly.

"After Queen Diane's death, the barrier was weakened. Mother could barely hold it up, and the vampires were trying to get in too. She decided to keep it closed to everyone, but Princess Lilyan was worried about Reagan. They had to open it sometimes, but it was getting more dangerous every time… until Nora's birth."

"Reagan didn't know about Nora," I say, "and you pretended you didn't know about her either."

"Reagan really didn't, I think Princess Lilyan had just gotten pregnant when she saw her for the last time. I thought keeping your identities a secret was the best. The vampires were after the Royals. Royals have incredible power, and they wanted to get rid of them. They had found the perfect source of power to fight them and my mother's power, too."

"Me," sneered Nephera. "The more they abused me and drank my blood, the stronger they became, just like Judah Black. It was only a question of time before that damn barrier would break, wasn't it, Sylviana?

Our mother was getting old for a witch too. With Diane gone, she couldn't hold on much longer."

"She knew the vampires would attack the minute they could," said Sylviana. "Princess Lilyan tried to take over her mother's role in helping maintain the barrier, but the day Nora was born…"

Oh, Moon Goddess. It's the same as now. The witch does maintain the barrier, but the Luna is the one channeling the Moon Power. However, a Luna giving birth just can't possibly focus her power properly. Nora is experiencing the same thing as her own mother, Princess Lilyan, did more than twenty years ago!

"*Nora, you're hearing that?*"

"*Yes. I can't believe it. My birth was…*"

"*Don't you start saying shit about it being your fault.*"

She stays quiet, whether it's because of another contraction or because she doesn't want to say it. I'm choking up right now too. All those tragic events are unfolding under a new light now. Though I resent Sylviana for keeping quiet, I'm starting to understand why she did. She's on the verge of tears too, looking awfully sorry.

"The day Nora was born, Princess Lilyan and my mother just couldn't keep the barrier up for much longer. A few hours later, the vampires entered our city. They had been accumulating for months outside, there were too many of them. Princess Lilyan only had a few minutes with Nora. She was exhausted after the birth, so she asked my mother to pass her power to her daughter. I was with her until the end. I was holding Nora in my arms when Lilyan…"

She's crying for real now, and I feel my own tears coming too. I feel Nora's heart, echoing my own, breaking slowly as we both finally listen to the truth about our parents' death…

"Your parents, Selena, and my mother, they told us to run away. Gabriel told your mother to take you and go. Althea was a human, she couldn't fight. You were just two years old back then. Althea was the bravest woman I ever knew. She told you not to cry, soothed you, and ran with me. It was the most terrifying night of my life. We spent such a long time hiding, running, hiding again, desperate to find a way to escape. At some point, it became clear she was easier to track because she was human. She told me to run away, because she… she knew Nora and I would have died. So, I parted ways with her, and I used my limited powers to hide us as I could, and run, carrying Nora with me."

I can't believe it… Sylviana wouldn't have been older than ten years old back then. She managed to run away, carrying newborn Nora with her, saving both their lives!

Meanwhile, I don't know how, but according to Reagan, my mom and I managed to survive until the fight was over. How? Sylviana doesn't seem to know either.

"When I arrived at the scene," says Nephera, "everything was over. My home was burned to ashes. Mother had sacrificed herself, in a desperate attempt to save the twins' children. I hid from the remaining vampires, who were still fighting the survivors or feeding themselves, and crawled all the way to our source of magic there. I stayed for as long I could to replenish my magic, and while I did, I found something. The traces of another younger witch."

Her glare at Sylviana makes no mistake as to who she recognized.

"I couldn't believe my mother had another daughter while I was gone! I knew you were a young Earth Witch, I looked through my mother's things, the few she didn't burn to ashes. I tried using my magic to find you, the twins, or their children, but you were all gone!"

Reagan had probably taken me away prior to Nephera's arrival on site. She said she arrived shortly after the fight was over too. Thank Moon Goddess we left this hell before that crazy woman showed up.

"I was so furious," she continues. "I was finally back home, to the place I had left so many years ago, but only to find everything burnt, destroyed! After everything I went through, after all my suffering, my own mother had died to save someone else's child! She hadn't saved me when I endured the vampires' venom for weeks, but she killed herself for Lilyan and Gabriel Bluemoon! For their children to live! I resented those wretched twins even more than the vampires!"

Moon Goddess, that woman is… damaged. I can see the madness in her eyes. She's completely broken inside. She suddenly points a finger at Sylviana.

"And you! Knowing she replaced me with another daughter. No wonder she never cared about me for twenty years!"

Sylviana shakes her head frantically. I've never seen her so shaken up before, but for once, she looks her age. Her voice is so hoarse right now, I can barely recognize it.

"You're wrong! Nephera, our mother believed in you until the end," she says, sobbing erratically. "When everything happened, I went south. I knew that's where Mother had sent my older sister with Cynthia. I walked for days with Nora, hiding in human towns and trying to find Silver City, until I finally reached it many weeks later. But I couldn't find any trace of you or even a pack called Blue Moon. I didn't know they had been renamed the Sapphire Moon, I had never met any of them. I was young, I didn't know what to do. It had been over thirty years. Cynthia had died, there was no trace of my older sister or any witch being around, I just didn't know whom to ask without putting us at risk. All I knew was that I had to keep Nora's identity a secret. Vampires could still chase after us. I don't know if it was my fear as a child or my instincts that made me think that way…"

She was so young. I have no idea how I would have reacted if I had been left alone. I was lucky Reagan found me and brought me here. In a way, Sylviana had the same reasoning, but she was a child witch, no matter how mature she was, with little knowledge of the world and a newborn baby to take care of. It's already a miracle she got to Silver City at all, but basically anyone that could have helped her once she got here was gone… Nephera was gone. There was no way she knew what had happened to her older sister, they had never even actually met!

"Even as a witch," says Sylviana, "it was hard to take care of Nora, I was way too young. I used my powers to find what would be the best home for her. I knew I had to conceal her identity, so it didn't matter which pack it was, as long as she could grow up with her-kind, with werewolves, as if she had been born there. I knew werewolves care for their own, especially the pups. So I left her on a doorstep, with a note to ask those people to take care of her, with her name and birthday, trusting my magic would help me pick the best home for her."

"Holy fuck."

"She didn't find the best home for Nora. She found her actual biological father's home!"

"Moon Goddess," says Nora. *"Alec said I had appeared on their doorstep when I was a newborn. I thought… I thought my dad had brought me there for them to raise me without his wife knowing I was his!"*

"Turns out the guy, I mean, your father really didn't know. Sylviana's magic did the job, picking the house with your actual kin in it. This is crazy…"

"He probably realized later that you were his real daughter though, just like his wife. I wonder if he even knew that your biological mom had you."

I'm just as speechless. I can hear Nora's crying, I can't tell if it's sadness, relief over her father's truth, or due to her contraction pains. Her family's story, and Sylviana's, is even sadder than I thought.

Nephera doesn't seem sorry one bit though. She is looking at Sylviana with eyes of utter disgust.

"It took me a while to find them. First, I had to fight the vampires. Trust me, I enjoyed that the most. They are surprisingly weak to water magic, you know. So, once I had replenished my magic enough, hiding in our mother's lair, I decided to use those vermin the same way they had used me. I corrupted them slowly to my side, making their Vampire Queen my slave, poisoning her mind. She already hated the werewolves, it was almost too easy to persuade them to target the Royals that had escaped. I have never imagined that you would have brought the children back to Silver City. How ironic was that! I spent such a long time searching for you, I even thought you might have died."

I don't know much about magic and stuff, but Sylviana being an Earth Witch, I'll bet she surely wasn't the easiest to find in the forests from our birthplace and here. Between the time Nephera took to conquer the vampires and the time it took her to search for her sister and us, it probably saved us a few years.

"I had almost given up, you know, when I felt it. A wave of Moon Energy, an awakening to the Moon's power. So similar to Lilyan or Diane's signature aura. It came from the south. Never in a million years did I think you would have been able to reach Silver City, Sylviana."

Nora's power.

Nora's sudden awakening to her wolf was what guided Nephera right here. She went from a quiet girl to fully opening her Royal potential. Everyone in Silver City felt the Luna's slow rise… No wonder that witch felt something. Nephera sneered.

"You're more talented than I thought, Sylviana. You made sure I couldn't find her until she would be strong enough to fight me, didn't you!"

"What did you do?" I ask Sylviana.

"I put some sort of lock on Nora's mind," she admits. "I sealed her Royal power to a place deep inside her mind, where it wouldn't awake unless she had a strong stimulus."

"*Let me guess… like meeting her fated mate?*"

"*Holy Moon Goddess. Nora meeting Damian was the trigger? No wonder she went from a kitty to a tiger after that!*"

"It could have been the rape attempt too. She lost control when she was in the most danger. Or her first shape-shifting. Everyone felt her unique wolf's Royal Aura after that."

"I did feel something change after meeting Damian," admits Nora, *"but I– Ugh!"*

"Are you doing okay, Nora?"

"Yeah, I'll manage… Just… Please be safe."

Be safe, she says. I want to cry internally. There's no way she didn't feel William's passing, or all the others. And despite all the talking right now, this fight is still far from over, let's face it.

"I hoped Nora would be hidden until she was old enough to defend herself," continues Sylviana. "I stayed away from her, and secretly established myself, watching our surroundings. Since I was born, I had been told to watch out for people trying to attack the Royals, especially vampires. I met with Reagan on one of my trips to the outside a bit later. I was relieved you had survived, Selena, though I have no idea how that happened. But once again, I decided it would be better for me to stay away, and I knew Reagan was watching over you."

"You did a pretty good job of hiding them. I would never have found them if it wasn't for her child's awakening."

I was probably harder to find due to my human heritage too. My mom really protected me, even after her death. However, unlike Nora's seal or my human blood, Estelle was born without anything to hide her inner wolf, so as we feared, as soon as her inner puppy awakened, she became another target. I exchange a glance with Nate. Only a few minutes have passed, but it's enough for everyone to catch a little break. I don't feel any bit rested though; this is just too much information at once. Who knew we were still missing such a big part of the story, and all this time it was Sylviana's.

I need to keep her talking though. I don't care what that woman went through, she's still targeting us.

"The first attack was after Nora's awakening, right?" I ask.

Nephera turns her eyes to me, and I realize their color is changing. Like Sylviana, her eyes can change between several shades depending on her emotions. That woman is so thin too, and her skin so pale, it's like her big blue-gray eyes are the only color on her, making it even more obvious.

"When I realized you were in Silver City, I just… lost it. Of all places, in the city I should have been, I should have owned! It was painful to return, after all those years. I hated the idea of seeing Judah again, but as it turns out, that rotten man had already died, hadn't he?"

She glares at all three brothers, who growl together, warning her.

"Oh, your auras are so much like his… I was speechless, but it added to the pleasure of attacking this wretched place. I led the vampires, telling them I wanted the Royal, not even knowing there were two of you!"

No wonder the blood-suckers targeted Nora specifically back then.

"Yet, I couldn't enter. I attacked from afar, unsure about the whole situation. First, I didn't expect Silver City's packs to act altogether. But then, the real shock… The Earth Witch! Of all people, I sensed our family's blood's magic here, my own half-sister, suddenly protecting Silver City and running to the werewolves' side! Now that was a big surprise!"

I bet. She probably had forgotten about her half-sister entirely. I don't get how she recognized her sibling without even seeing her face to face, but I guess that's another witch thing I'll never understand.

"I admit, I lost that day. I left most of my vampires to die and ran away. I knew I couldn't win against you, Sylviana. You had the stronger element, you were younger, more powerful, and you had years to extend your protection over Silver City. I underestimated you, Lilyan's daughter, and those three. And you, Gabriel's daughter, the one I couldn't even detect. When I felt how strong you all were, and how the vampires couldn't match, I decided to turn away."

More like we kicked your ass and your damn vamps bad enough that you had to run away with your tail between your legs…

I glance at the brothers. They are growling, still tense. They know the fight can resume any minute now. I try to feel Nora, but she's overwhelmed by the pain. Moon Goddess, I hope her baby will at least be born without complications. We really don't need more problems…

Chapter 37

It feels a lot longer, but only a few minutes have passed since Nephera began her argument with Sylviana. I try to reach out to Nora, but she's too caught up in the pain now. Somehow, I think that baby number two is in a hurry to come out. I already love that kid.

"Once again, I had to be patient. I knew you'd protect Silver City for as long as you could, and Judah and the twins' little bastards too. I took my time, gathering even more vampires than before, after having their Vampire Queen acting like a puppet held by my strings. I didn't notice one of them was gone for some time, but once I felt another Royal print, I rushed there."

She killed Reagan but couldn't get to Estelle or kill me. Sylviana arrived right in time to save me and make her run away. Nephera shrugs.

"I didn't want to rush, anyway. I had an army almost ready, and I just wanted to destroy you all at once, along with Silver City. I waited patiently for this opportunity, until today. Now, finally, I'll take back what is mine, and get rid of all of you!"

I growl, pissed off. This woman went from a martyr to a villain, but I just can't listen to her bullshit any longer.

"So what?" I say. "Are we supposed to feel sorry for you now? Do you think you will feel better after this?"

Nephera immediately glares at me, not hiding her anger. A few steps away from us, I can hear the river going wild, the water raging, but I try to ignore it.

"You can never understand how I felt! My own mother abandoned me for someone else! She lived in comfort while I was left alone to grow in an unknown city! The only man I ever loved threw me away when he was done using me! And then, I lost my child to those wretched, abominations called vampires! How dare you tell me what can make me feel better or not!"

I step forward, mad enough to growl, barely keeping my wolf from jumping out. I'm tired of listening to this woman's rant.

"Yeah, cry me a river," I shout back. "You think you're a victim? What about all the people you deceived when you didn't help Cynthia reach out to her sister? The families you split just because you were a selfish brat!"

"How dare you!" she yells.

"You know what, it's about time someone gave you a reality check! You think you're the only victim out there? Well, sorry to say, you're not the only one who's lost their parents, or their child! I get you went through some shit, but you know what? You can suck it up! I lost my parents twice, my godmother, my baby, and that still didn't make me one hell of a heinous bitch like you! I know where I fucked up, and I made amends for that! I own my mistakes; I don't blame anyone else for them!"

I let my aura explode out as my anger reaches its peak on the last few words, but honestly, I'm fed up with this witch! Nephera isn't impressed. Instead, she looks more furious than ever, and suddenly, a wave comes from the river to her feet, and then gravitates around her hands. It's impressive, like watching some fantasy action movie. But this is very real, and I know she can do some harm with that damn water now floating around her.

"You think you can judge me?" she yells. "You know nothing! I never had anyone! My mother left me, I had no family, no friends, no one to rely on! You know what it's like, to lose everyone? To lose your only hope, your child? Judah Black, Queen Diane, her children, they all took everything from me!"

"Oh, yes, I know," I growl. "I also know what it's like to lose a child, and then have to abandon the other for her safety. I left my daughter alone in the woods, not knowing if I'd ever see her again, because of you! Maybe your mother wanted to protect you by sending you to Silver City, maybe she had bad reasons, but if you were so desperate to see her again, maybe you should have worked your ass off and helped Cynthia like you were supposed to!"

"*Selena...*"

I know Nate wants to comfort me, but right now, I just want to shut this crazy bitch up once and for all. I am so fed up with her blaming everyone but herself!

"You want to take it out on someone? Well, sorry, everybody you blamed is dead! The only guilty person now is yourself! Nora and I grew up without knowing our parents too! Damian and Nate killed their own father to save themselves from the monster he was! Who are you going to take it out on next, huh? It's your mistake, own it!"

Nephera's expression is ugly at that moment. Yeah, the truth hurts, bitch.

"You… You…!" she screams. "I'll get rid of all of you!"

I guess that's it for her arguments. She suddenly raises her water above her head, and we all get ready, knowing this is our signal. The fight is back on.

Damian, Nate, and I jump together to attack, but she launches her water attack as soon as we move. It's way bigger than what I had thought it'd be. I'm hit by a full wave, and feel my body thrown away, before something catches me. I choke a bit, but thank Moon Goddess I managed not to swallow any.

I realize I'm caught in some muddy roots, before Sylviana moves them again, creating several barriers between us and her sister. Nephera tries to attack again, but the roots sprouting in accelerated movements from the ground break her waves, transforming them into little splashes on us. For a minute, I think we might be able to take her down, until I remember she's not alone.

As soon as she attacked, all the nearby vampires resume fighting too. As soon as I am released from Sylviana's magic wood or whatever it is, I need to jump to avoid an attack. Those damn things! I don't know if they used her little speech to gather, but there's more and more of them around us. A lot more than before.

I need to jump, kick, throw a punch, run, and jump again to avoid the ones coming at me. I try to keep an eye on what's going on around, but I only catch a glimpse of Damian, surrounded too. They seem to have decided to attack the strongest of us in groups. I hear Liam growling furiously too, meaning he doesn't have time to play anymore. I use my silver bars again, managing to keep them off me, but I don't have a second to breathe.

The ground trembling dangerously and the sounds of waves crashing tells me the witch sisters are going hard at it too. When I think I'm about to be surrounded, another root suddenly sprouts out to impale several vampires or create another barrier. I appreciate the help, but I have no idea how Sylviana can keep it up.

This whole fight is insane. Wherever I look, there's mud, vines, roots, or vampires. Werewolves are growling somewhere behind me, and vampires are screeching from all sides too.

I have never seen so much violence on such a large scale. We just keep fighting, growling, trying to kill them one after another. I'm covered in blood and mud. Some managed to scratch me, but most of this blood is from the ones I killed. I try to rip their heads off, tear their throat open, or impale their heart. Those damn creatures are resistant, and if they are not killed properly, they can still move whatever's left of them. It's a horror movie. I can't help but scream when one of them suddenly scratches me deep on my back. Moon Goddess, that hurts!!

"*Selena!*"

"*Nate, no!*"

He must stay where he is! I keep fighting, but a few seconds later, I realize another wolf came to fight next to me. I kick away another vampire, avoid one's bite, and brutally smack its head before letting myself glance over.

"*Levi, you idiot! Don't help me!*"

"*Your back is bleeding, Selena! You can't protect your–!*"

Before he can finish his sentence, another vampire jumps at him, making him lose his focus on the mind-link. That idiot! He should be way behind, not on the front lines with us! I keep trying to tell him to fucking back off, but he won't listen!

I do feel the pain, but I can take it! I smack another vampire with my silver pole, and smash his head against the ground, when the earth violently shakes again. What the heck are they doing! I try to shift my position to get closer to Sylviana. The two witches are having an insane fight. I take half-a-second glances between two punches or kicks, but this is out of this world. Nephera is going all out against her sister, sending wave after wave, even shaping her water like ice picks to send them Sylviana's way!

Despite their several years difference, Sylviana is not letting herself be dominated. She is controlling so many roots and even some nearby tree branches so easily, I realize Nephera was right to be cautious of her. When she's experiencing difficulty, the ground will shake again, and a new crater emerges between her and her sister, putting some distance and destabilizing Nephera and the vampires around. The difference in strength is starting to show between them, but unfortunately, Nephera's weakness is compensated by the growing number of vampires.

I feel like we have been fighting for hours, but they just keep coming, more and more of them. The werewolves keep fighting back relentlessly, but I can feel everyone's injuries, and the wolves leaving us… I furiously growl, trying to gather all my strength. I throw my poles into the face of two nearby vampires, shift my balance to send my foot right into their head, right after a round kick, and send them flying farther away from me.

I growl ferociously and shape-shift, jumping into my wolf appearance as easily as putting on clothing. The vampires react strangely to my shifting. Some retreat, others hiss even more furiously at me. I guess my cream-white fur gave it away. I let out a warning growl, extending my aura like a halo around.

To my surprise, instead of reacting to my growl, a lot of vampires step back, terrified.

"*Selena, your eyes are glowing!*"

Glowing? What the hell is going on now! I feel my aura too, growing wilder like a burning sun in my core. What is that? I extend it again, to reach my friends, the entire pack, and this time, it's not a feeble mind-link but a strong connection I feel, like a solid chord. I can feel everyone, absolutely everyone. I feel like there's something else, tickling, some shadows I can't manage to connect to. Another code I need to crack, something I need to decipher with my aura. It's ringing in my mind, like a call I just don't know how to answer.

"*Selena!*"

"*For Moon Goddess' sake, Levi, go back! Please! You'll get yourself killed!*"

He won't be able to hold like that for long! There are just too many vampires here! Even the Black brothers and I just can't catch a break, and Levi is no match!

"*Don't worry about me!*"

He is doing okay so far, but one wrong move and he'll die! I just can't watch him and fight my own fights! I try to get closer to him, but the dance of the roots around is confusing me. I can't make any reckless position change without risking hitting one. Sylviana knows our positions, but she probably can't constantly watch out for us if we move too much! The only one who seems rather comfortable in this configuration is Liam. It's obvious he's got some experience in random environments or with Sylviana's power. He's like a fireball, jumping from one spot to another, easily adjusting to the roots' random appearances, even sometimes using them as support for jumping with all fangs out.

Damian and Nate are doing okay, judging by the bodies around them, but they have been careful not to move too much, facing the same issue as me. All of us have the same objective: get to Nephera while eliminating as many vampires as we can on the way, but I can feel the other wolves are suffering from our absence on the rest of the battlefield.

"You think you can win, Sylviana?" yells Nephera. "I can kill any of your little dogs anytime I want!"

"Nephera, please, stop this! You can still come back to Silver City! We don't have to fight, you're my older sister!"

"Your older sister that was left and abandoned while you had everything! You grew up with Mother, with friends! I had nothing! Nothing!"

They keep arguing, Sylviana begging her to stop again and again, but I can tell Nephera has gone mad being repair. It's not like Iris. My cousin was jealous to the core, but she could still hear us, be reasonable. She was smart enough, too smart. Nephera is just… She left all her feelings in one place and won't look at it again. She won't hear, she won't listen. She's so sure of her truth, nothing Sylviana will say can get to her. She spent years persuading herself she was right, that she was a victim and we deserved to die for making her life miserable. I can tell just by looking at her. She lives only for her revenge. That's all she has left.

"Selena!"

Sylviana's scream takes me by surprise. She made a mistake and, at the last second, I see one of Nephera's ice peaks flying my way. I try to dodge.

The damn thing scratches my other shoulder, but I throw myself on the ground and manage to avoid it. I'm lying on the mud, and that's all it takes for two vampires to jump on me. I'm on my tummy, I know I won't be able to defend myself in time. I try to roll over to at least manage to push them away with my legs, but even that is too late. I see their fangs, coming right at me when a brown silhouette covers me.

I scream internally. I can feel Levi's pain, the furious bites deep on his shoulder, on his neck.

"*Levi! Levi! Levi, move! Levi!*"

He can't hear me, I can't reach him. I see his body right above mine, but I feel this horrible hole, growing larger and larger as the pain sinks in, giving in to the darkness. No, Moon Goddess, no, no, no, not Levi, please, not him…

I want to cry, to scream, but this is a fight. One of my best friends' bodies is the only thing protecting me, but I feel the horrible movements coming from above, as the vampires keep biting and biting, killing him in a horrible, painful way. I want to scream in horror, I just can't bear it.

I push my feelings down and shift into position to jump out, grabbing the closest vampire and ripping its neck in one bite. One by one, I take down all the blood-suckers, those cursed creatures who were attacking him. I know it's useless, it's too late to save him, but I just attack, attack, and attack again, furiously, like some death machine. I'm blinded by fury.

I take all those monsters down, away from my friend. I'm choking up, crying, but I need to release my rage. I can feel Danny and his family, and they all felt him die too, and I'm even more furious and sad for them.

"Get to them! Kill them all, you useless vampires!" yells Nephera. "Get to their Luna's house!"

More vampires appear. Moon Goddess, is there no end to this? I growl menacingly as the anger gets to me. We are all here, all werewolves fighting to defend our turf, all connected, all standing, growling furiously. We are not letting them in.

The fight goes on and on, I don't know for how long. I'm tired, my injuries hurt, but I don't allow myself any rest or mistakes. I know my baby star's life is at stake, Nora's and her babies too. I am not letting those damn vampires or this wretched witch touch a strand of hair on them.

"*Nora, please tell me you're alright so far.*"

"*Yeah, yeah… The nurse says I'll be ready… soon. Just… give me a minute.*"

I can give her a lot of time as long as she gives birth to a healthy baby and is okay herself, or so I hope…

This hell here is far from over. I just can't see the end of the vampires no matter how many we kill. Hell, how many did she gather? We are stronger, as our bodies are conceived to kill vampires, our feral enemy, in the first place, but there is nothing we can do about the difference in numbers. They just keep coming. It's a freaking invasion.

Moreover, we suffer casualties too. With the way my aura changed earlier, I can now feel each wolf dying even more clearly, it's just overwhelming. If I wasn't focusing on my own fight, I'd be crumbling under the sadness. But I can't allow myself to be weak now. So many people are counting on us.

I keep fighting, still trying to make my way to Nephera. We need to kill her. She controls the vampires. I just don't get how she can control so many at once. I'm struggling to get past her vampires, and Sylviana and her are still busy exchanging water and soil all over the place. I have to be cautious of everything happening. Each emerging root can make me stumble, each water pick can injure me. I'm fine so far, but it only takes one miss.

"*Selena, we have a problem!*"

"*I just saw the Vampire Queen!*"

"*I saw her too!*"

What? What's going on? I rip another limb, bite another vampire, trying to sense where they are trying to mind-link me from. I can feel Damian, Liam, and Nate are hearing the sudden voices echoing too.

"*Wait, was that Iris?*"

"*Yeah, her lavender hair!*"

"*It's Iris!*"

"*What is she doing!*"

"*Watch out!*"

Holy shit, what? I try to sift through all the incoming information, holding onto the ones who saw this with their own eyes! This is like a hell jungle. My body has to be here fighting, but my mind is torn between my focus here and the mind-link. I try to jump on several vampires at once to get out of this crowd and catch one or two precious seconds to listen.

I look for the brothers, spread around me, dealing with the same issues. The vampires are gathered in bigger numbers around us. There are not many jumping on us at once, but almost as if those bastards were queuing and circling around us, making sure to contain me and the brothers. When the hell did those blood-suckers become smart enough to prepare such a strategy in the middle of a fight!

"*Damian, Nate, Liam, you heard that?*"

"*Yeah, go!*"

"*But...*"

"*We can't get to the witch this way, Selena, just go!*"

I decide to listen to him, though I feel bad for leaving the fight's main area. I jump to the side, biting another vampire's leg, dragging him with me in my run, and mowing some vampires as if I was reaping anyone standing in my way. I try to focus on the directions given by our wolves. Iris, why the hell would Iris be with the Vampire Queen! And what of Chris?

I try to help whoever I can on my way. I furiously attack a vampire that was gripping a wolf, break up a crowd of them, throw some bites to help whoever I can. Our line of defense is still doing okay, and I'm amazed by our betas. Lysandra is a monster by herself. No wonder the Purple Moon clan was famous for their warriors. I run past her; she almost seems to be having fun, taking down one vampire after another as if they are merely toys for her to play with.

I spot Tonia too, doing just as well. After all, she was one of the Blood Moon's fighting instructors. Her brother is more of a surprise, under his usual calm demeanor, he's another killing machine, and their family's giant size is good to intimidate the vampires too. Those siblings are worth two or three betas by themselves!

I keep running, but there are also the bodies… Those people I had felt dying, I get to see their corpses now, sadly covered in mud, while their friends are still fighting nearby. No one has time to close their eyes or cry for them, and it breaks my heart. I think I saw William too, my cousin's peculiar black and white fur, now dirtied with blood and mud, lying a few steps away, but I can't go see him now. I silently apologize, but this war is far from over…

I finally reach a little hill, where a lot of wolves are cornered by a humongous crowd of vampires. A few paces away, with four dead werewolves' bodies at her feet, I see the one who has to be the Vampire Queen. She's easy to recognize, her hair is completely white, her red eyes brighter than the rest and she is in some dark lace dress. Who the fuck wears a dress on a battlefield! Nephera and her are just so confident, it annoys me.

However, I have another problem: standing right next to her is Iris. My cousin looks different. I can't describe it, but her eyes look strange, almost… empty. Her hair is a hectic mess too and she's still in her outfit from when she left her cell. What happened to her? And where is Chris? I can't feel his wolf, did he run away?

I jump into the group of werewolves, resuming the fight right away. My sudden arrival breaks the vampires' cohesion, throwing them into disarray and allowing my peers to fight back. I bite again, use my claws to rip their white flesh until they can't move. My white fur isn't so white anymore, most of it has turned an ugly brown. I try to ignore the horrid smell of blood and ripped flesh, and help those guys fight off their assailants.

If only I could get to the Vampire Queen… I mean, my knowledge about vampire clans is rather limited, to say the least, but from Sylviana's words, she is the one controlling the vampires and their blood thirst. If we can take the Vampire Queen down, that will be half of the job done. The problem is, she is standing too far. Just like Nephera, she is standing out of my reach, out of any battle. Just watching whatever's going on. At least the witch is busy fighting Sylviana!

That damn Vampire Queen is just staring at the war zone, comfortably standing still, and Iris standing right by her side. I know this isn't good. My cousin is standing too close to her, and too confidently. Damn it!

"*Iris, what the heck are you doing?*"

I know I can still mind-link her. Iris was punished, but never banished from Silver City, she left on her own. It takes more than that to cut off ties.

"What is it, Elena? Are you surprised?" she says with a sneer, loud enough for me to hear despite the distance. "You didn't think I would stay put in my cell like a good girl, did you?"

"*I certainly didn't think you would be dumb enough to ally yourself with our worst enemy!*"

"Even vampires have their use, Elena," she replied with a blank voice.

What the hell is wrong with her? Something doesn't feel right about her, or about her answers. I know Iris too well, or at least I thought I did. This isn't the gentle Iris, or the wicked woman who was defying me from her cell.

"*Where is Chris!*"

She looks shaken up for a second, then she goes back to that strange look of emptiness, and suddenly, I realize. That's her problem. Chris.

"*Iris, what happened to Chris?*"

"What is it?" asks the Vampire Queen with a giggle. "Let me guess. Is she bothering you about that adorable little brother of yours?"

I don't like that. I don't like that at all. That bitch Vampire Queen looks way too amused, and Iris' face is even whiter than hers, if possible.

"*Iris, where is Chris!*"

"I should thank you again, Iris," purrs the Vampire Queen. "That wolf was such a nutritious meal."

No. No, no, no, Iris wouldn't have done that. She wouldn't have sold her own brother to vampires. It just can't be. They left together, why the hell did the two of them go to the vampires!

"I had to make an agreement with the vampires," said Iris, with a detached voice, "for them to trust me."

"You sold your own brother to them! You wretched woman! Iris, I swear you'll go to hell for this! I'll make you pay!"

"Oh, don't worry, this little girl was quite generous. She even told us where to find your precious Luna. You know, it saves us quite some time to know where to look!"

I stay speechless. Nora's house. She told them where Nora's house is! This means even if one vampire can get past our defenses, they can head straight there! They won't need to spread around Silver City to find her; one vampire gets in and it will be a race to catch him before he gets there! I just can't believe it. Even for Iris, this is the lowest of the low!

"I can't believe you! You damn traitor! You... Your own brother!"

"Get ready instead of yelling, you idiot."

What? I smash a vampire and get another off one of the werewolves' back. That was Iris' voice just now. What the heck? What is she preparing? I can't stop growling at her, so much my throat hurts, but that seems impossible. More and more vampires are crawling toward us, to the point even I am getting seriously in trouble. I get another deep bite, on my shoulder, but bite back and get that damn vampire off my back.

"You," says the Vampire Queen. "It can't be you're…"

I really don't have time to play her petty games! I bite a blood-sucker's head off and roll on the ground to avoid another one's attack, I can't stop to think.

"Bite her!" screams the Vampire Queen. "Bite that damn dog! The white female one!"

In seconds, I feel all red stares on me. That isn't good. They suddenly jump at me, and I have to retreat. What the hell! I have had a lot to endure until now, but a horde of vampires is not something I can handle on my own!

"Selena!"

I can hear Nate, worried, coming to my rescue. I sense him running to escape his opponents, running to me in utter panic.

"Nate, don't!"

However, I don't have time to mind-link right now. One of the vampires bites me violently, on my previously injured shoulder, making me internally scream in pain. Fuck, his damn fangs are deep in there, and I can't shake him off! I try biting, rolling over, but that blood-sucker has decided to stay glued to me! His sharp fangs lacerating my scar is driving me crazy with pain. Black dots obscure my vision, and I feel myself stagger, the pain making everything else numb…

"*Selena!*"

Suddenly, he lets go, and I see a black wolf overshadowing me, growling furiously at the nearby vampires. Nate…

I need a few seconds to regain my senses, but my shoulder is still painful as well. Damn, their fangs are worse than chainsaws! I don't even dare look at my bleeding shoulder, I need to get my head back into the fight, stand up… Nate's presence is the most comforting and reassuring thing I could hope for.

"*Come on, Sunshine, get up. I got you.*"

"*I know, I know…*"

I can't just sit and cry about the pain right now. I gather my strength, hoping my healing will speed things up a bit, because this is no state to be in for a fight. Nate hasn't been spared either. His ear is cut up, the blood has dried up on his fur already. His healing power probably could have done something about it if he wasn't missing a full chunk. He's got some cuts all around, and I can sense his left knee is painful, but no bite mark on him so far.

I try to forget the pain and resume the fight, jumping on one of the vampires that was threatening to attack my mate's open flank. With Nate by my side, I'm even more eager to fight and defend myself. We are together, with a handful of other wolves, trying to fight back the waves of vampires.

The presence of the Vampire Queen nearby doesn't help, All those damn blood-suckers are desperate to protect their leader. We take them down, one after another, but it's never-ending. I'm just amazed at their numbers. I understand that Nephera had years to gather them, but just how did she get so many? The human from earlier didn't lie, there are thousands of them.

"*Selena, any idea on how to get to that damn Vampire Queen?*"

"*Not yet. The plan for now is to survive, but I'm still working on the next step…*"

"*Watch your left, you idiot.*"

I'm surprised to hear Iris in my head again, but I jump just in time to avoid another bite. Did I just dream that, or is she really helping me? Why the hell…? I keep fighting, but I can't focus on too many things at once!

However, Iris keeps giving me instructions. All of them just turn out to be right, and slowly helps me get closer to the Vampire Queen. Which doesn't make her happy.

"Get her! Get that damn dog down!" screeches the Vampire Queen.

Feeling angsty now? I'm so going to get that damn Vampire Queen. I slowly progress, and as I keep running, fighting, biting, I realize my observation from earlier is true. The more focused I am on that golden, shiny aura of mine, the more the vampires are wary of me. I don't know if they actually sense my aura, but there's something they definitely don't like when I increase it, when I use more of my Alpha senses. It's hard to describe, like my halo can grow, expand, or heat up when I want. In any case, it makes them back off, reluctant to come near me. It's the same reaction as when they avoided the sunlight earlier.

"*Whatever you're doing, babe, continue, it's working!*"

It seems like it. I keep communicating with Nate to improve our tandem, but I also keep an ear open to Iris' random advice. What is she planning?

"That damn dog. She's resistant to vampire venom!" roars the Vampire Queen.

So that was it… Now that I think about it, I've received quite a dose since earlier, and I'm generally fine. It hurts like hell, but like a regular bite or claw injury, not like poison. Any wolf, though we resist it, would be at least sick after receiving so much, but for some reason, my healing ability makes me immune? And I was complaining about not healing fast like others…

I quickly share with Nora, but she's in the middle of her delivery. Our link is faint for the first time since we met. She's probably not in the right state to give a damn about her inner wolf right now.

Finally, despite her slowly stepping back, we are almost within the Vampire Queen's reach. If she didn't plan to fight at all, she might want to reconsider that. Her face is getting whiter, almost gray. She steps back, seeing me coming closer, looking scared for the first time. Just you wait, you blood-sucking bitch.

Suddenly, I see Nate jumping at her, a bit closer than me, and something in my gut warns me. Something bad is about to happen. It's too easy.

Everything slows down for a second. I see Nate's black fur, suspended in the air, and the Vampire Queen's arm moving. Something shines, and I see the blade before I scream. My instinct screams it's silver. I see the surprise in Nate's eyes, and the next second, my own scream resonates in the air.

Nate's blood splatters on me, and I see my mate fall on the ground. I don't hesitate, and run towards them, fangs all out, going for the kill. No vampire can stop me. I see the Vampire Queen's horrible smirk, as she raises her blade again, ready to pierce me, but no matter what, I won't stop. I'm avenging my mate.

I see the blade, a second away from my head, when something suddenly takes it out of my eyesight, and I feel a bump on my shoulder. The sound of flesh being ripped apart, and I bite violently into the Vampire Queen's throat, her eyes wide open in horror.

But she's not looking at me. Her eyes are on Iris, who grabbed her hand to impale herself on the blade, in her chest. My cousin has her mouth covered in blood as she gags out, and a sneer on her face.

"That was for Eric, you bitch."

Like an enraged animal, I keep biting deep, digging into the flesh until my mouth is full of blood, and the Vampire Queen stops moving under me. It was over in a few seconds. I didn't think… I keep biting, making sure the Queen is dead, but my eyes are on Iris.

I can't believe it. She slowly falls on her flank, in the mud, and her face is suddenly a few inches away from mine. Her eyes are open, but the light inside is almost gone. I try to hold on to the little bit of her inner wolf I still feel inside her.

"*Iris! Why…?*"

"*Chris' idea… For me… for… Eric… for Eric.*"

… She's gone. What? Chris' idea? What were they thinking…? I still can't believe it, but my cousin just sacrificed herself to help me kill the Vampire Queen, and I let go of my prey. Nate! I need to check on him.

Unlike my expectations, the vampires don't attack me as I run to him. Thank Moon Goddess, they let me through. The death of their Queen seems to have shocked them. They all start screaming, a horrible high-pitched sound, but I couldn't care less. I can't have anything slowing me down, I just run to Nate, lying on the ground. Oh, Moon Goddess, no, no.

"*Nate! Nate!*"

"*I'm fine.*"

I have another definition of fine! I'm trembling, shaking in despair, unable to accept this horrible sight. He's bleeding so much, and his arm… His arm is laying away from him, completely chopped off! Can I even fix this? Can we do something? I go to bend over him, about to shift back, but he growls.

"*Selena, don't you think about it!*"

"*I can heal you! If we kiss…*"

He growls even louder.

"*You can't fix that! Moreover, if you shift back, you'll expose yourself!*"

"*But, Nate...*"

I can't do anything about what I'm seeing! He's... in that kind of state...

"*Selena, no. Healing Damian from a gunshot put Nora in a coma for two years, and you're not Nora. You can't risk that now!*"

"*You'll bleed to death if I don't!*"

"*Selena, I won't. My healing will take over soon enough. It's okay.*"

"*Your arm is fucking chopped off, Nate!*"

"*I know. Don't worry about me. I'll be fine.*"

"*You... you're... losing... so much blood...*"

I start crying, whimpering, torn between healing my mate and the current fight. I look at the blood flowing, but his werewolf healing is indeed taking over. Slowly but surely, it's... closing off... Oh, thank Moon Goddess.

Around us, I feel the vampires gathering, targeting my injured mate. Do they want to avenge their Queen? I thought the fight would be over if we got rid of her! I growl angrily as a warning, and extend my aura to its limit, trying to keep them at bay. What do I do...? I can't leave Nate to them, he'll die. Even if his healing closes his injury, with the blood loss and missing limb, he'll be an easy target.

I need to do something, anything. I take deep breaths, slow my crying, and focus on my inner wolf. Come on, girl, what can we do? We are fighters. Fighters down to the bone, to our blood. I'm a damn Alpha fighter. I...

I sense something new. Another Royal Aura.

"*Nora?*"

I can almost hear it. A baby's crying.

"*He's born. Selena, it's a boy...*"

Yeah, I can feel him. My baby nephew, and his aura is so pure. Moon Goddess, I feel like crying again. I can't believe her son is here. During this madness. A baby is born. My new nephew.

I keep extending my aura. I feel the little newborn pup more intensely. It's like the appearance of another Royal is guiding me. I play with my aura, its heat, my eyes glowing like fire, piercing the vampires and somehow, terrifying them. I feel the baby, and so much more. Something else.

Nora's focusing on her healing. I sense our link growing back, stronger, her snow-white aura holding on tight to mine.

"*Selena, how is Nathaniel?*" she asks, worried.

"*He could use some healing.*"

I feel her power growing and expanding. Our auras are so similar yet different. Nora's is like fresh, pure snow, blown by a cold wind. I feel her, extending her strength, covering the battlefield. Our auras find each other, touch, blend into something even stronger. I guess we finally unlocked something between the two of us.

"*It's amazing,*" she says. "*I feel absolutely everyone's wolves so strongly, as if I can touch them.*"

"*I know, right? I'm starting to understand the Royal thing.*"

"*We're connected to every wolf. More than I thought. I think I can...*"

I feel her aura, somehow transmitting to Nate. What the… His injury is closing up even faster now! Amazed, I watch it close in accelerated motion, almost unreal. It takes a few more seconds before Nate tries to get up with my help, standing despite his missing limb. I'm amazed…

"*Nora! Are you alright?*"

"*Actually, yeah. I think your aura unlocked something in me. I don't use my own strength to heal others, but the Moon's power. It's not easy, but I think... I control it completely now.*"

Indeed, I can feel it. Nora's aura is slowly covering the whole battlefield, closing injuries and healing one wolf after another. She can't seem to do more than one at a time, but considering how far she is, it's still amazing.

I'm starting to feel hope again. Nate is standing by my side, and I know Nora will be on her way soon. We are far from safe, though. The vampires, seeing the werewolves get back on their feet one by one, are resuming the fight. Damn it, the Queen's death did almost nothing! I growl in warning.

"*Selena, go back.*"

"*But...*"

"*Don't worry about me, go back to my brothers. I'll follow.*"

I hate parting with Nate, but at least now I know he'll be alright, not just bleeding on the ground. The black wolf is still trying to find his new pace, the right balance. I help him, letting him use me as a crutch until he's stable enough. He growls and pushes me once he's fine enough to stand without me. I give him a lick on the cheek.

"*Love you.*"

"*I know, Sunshine. Go.*"

I growl a bit, frustrated, and run back to our former position. I can't babysit Nate for the rest of the fight, he'll hate it. He'll be fine, he'll be fine… I mind-link Damian, Liam, all the Alphas and Betas, telling those who have yet to know about the Vampire Queen's death. Of course, the Black brothers knew about Nate, and both thank me silently for protecting him, and Nora for accelerating his healing with her new enhanced power. I can sense Damian's worried about his wife, but Nora seems fine. She probably channeled some of the Moon's power for her own healing.

"*I'm coming,*" she says.

"*How's my nephew?*" asks Liam, excited.

"*He's adorable, of course. His brother's carbon copy.*"

"*Let's have a girl, next.*"

"*Damian!*"

I chuckle. It's crazy how he manages to bicker about having a third child in the middle of a battlefield. Even Liam didn't dare make any jokes yet.

"*Nate, are you okay?*"

"*Yeah, I just need to adjust to running on all three instead of… you know.*"

My heart hurts when I think about his arm. Maybe we can do something about it after the fight… I run back to the Black brothers, jumping on vampires on my way, trying to take down the ones I can, and catching a glimpse of the situation.

Our Alpha line is gone. With the brothers and I at the witch's position, Lysandra had no choice but to retreat all the way to where the betas are. We lost a lot of ground; they are almost at the border. Nora's intervention is helping maintain it for now, but we are running out of time. She won't be able to keep healing people once she gets into a fight herself, and I can feel she's on her way already. I can't believe her. She just delivered a baby and she's ready to join the fight. She's Silver City's Luna…

I tear apart another vampire, jump down, run, grab another one to pull it off one of our wolves, and kill it on the spot. I'm closing in on the brothers' position and trying to rekindle that feeling from before. I felt something else. My aura is different from Nora's. I can't feel that healing superpower she has. I'm not a healer.

I'm a warrior, a fighter. I wonder what that means… I'm stronger, immune to silver and vampire venom, but… if there's something more…

I keep running and heat up my aura, like before. This warmth I've been able to manipulate that's spreading to all the auras around me… it's not like Nora's healing aura. Mine is more like a lamplight, guiding them, grasping their wolf aura and holding on. Like charging them with some heat, more energy. We are all linked.

I push it even further. I can almost feel the glow the others see in me, as I keep testing that feeling, all those auras around me. So many auras.

It's… it's not just the werewolves. Thousands of auras. They are like mine, of the same, warm color… like the sunshine.

The sons and daughters of the Sun. The humans… Could it be? I keep running, stopping for a moment to fight another bunch of vampires, helping an injured wolf, and saving another right in time. My mind is everywhere. On the fight, with Nora, with Nate, with the brothers, with all those auras.

It's insane. I can feel the humans? Like Nora said, something unlocked in me. I try to hold on to them, to that strange feeling. I can't mind-link them, they are not wolves. How do I do this?

I keep growling, making my way to the heart of the battlefield. I know we can do this. There's a solution. Something more I can do, I can feel it. It's like a fire in my soul, something burning inside.

"*Nora, I can feel the humans!*"

"*What?*"

"*I know, it's crazy, but my aura... My aura reaches the humans of Silver City.*"

"*Can you talk to them? Tell them, 'Hey, we could use some help?'*"

"*I don't have a human channel and a werewolf channel, Liam! It's just... I feel connected to them, I just don't know how to use it.*"

It's true. It's like a tiny tunnel, something too small for me to send my inner words like I would do with a wolf. It's different, like another kind of link. They barely have any aura, and it's nothing like what us werewolves are used to. I feel like my aura is attached differently to the humans, but I can definitely feel them. If only I knew what to do with it.

"*I'm almost there!*" says Nora.

"*Me too!*"

"*You might want to hurry up, we are... Shit, Damian!*"

Liam's panicked wolf makes me jump and accelerate. Moon Goddess, not the King, not now! I can feel Damian, he just got injured, bad. His flank… Damn, his sharp pain almost wakes mine up, like my own injuries reopened violently.

"*Damian!*" screams Nora.

"*I'm... fine...*"

I would never have pictured him saying anything else. Even if he was dying, he wouldn't show his weakness. I hope Nora and I can get there fast. Nate too. I keep running to them, all of us gathering around Sylviana. She's the only one I can't reach through the mind-link, and aside from what Liam and Damian can relay to us, I have no idea how she's doing. We have yet to be drowned in waves of Nephera's magic, so I guess it means we are okay…

I desperately try to understand this strange bond to the humans, but I am not in the best situation for experiments. The situation is getting worse every minute now. Nora can't possibly heal every wolf, and we have already lost a lot.

The only thing is that all the vampires seem to be on the battlefield now, and I don't see any new waves coming. Did the Vampire Queen's death have some effect after all? I run into another close fight between two wolves and a handful of vampires to help.

"*Selena!*"

"*You okay, Ben?*"

"*Yeah, but… Levi…*"

I know. I've been trying not to think about all the dead. William, Levi, Chris… so many of our friends… I can't even stop to count them all. I want to cry, but I can't. We need to focus on the fight to avoid any more tragedy. We can mourn later, with those who survive.

Once I'm sure Ben and his friend are in a better position, I finally take back my position at Damian and Liam's side. I hadn't realized how much worse their situation has gotten. The vampires have aggregated around them, trying to overwhelm the brothers with their numbers. Damian seems to be getting rid of them easily like pests, but the King is injured. He has a few bite marks he hasn't even complained about, and more alarming, one large injury on his flank, the one we felt earlier. It's bleeding out, and the healing process has slowed down, most likely because of all the vampire venom he's been infected with. I hope Nora can do something about it as soon as she gets here.

Liam is in better shape, but not unscathed either. He's got cuts here and there, one leg limping a bit, and his tail is torn in an odd way. He still looks like he's eager to fight though. The brothers are keeping their position close to Sylviana, taking down any vampire that tries to get to her. Apparently, our witch took the central position in the fight, using her magic to control all of her immediate surroundings. Roots and branches appear in random positions to block most of Nephera's water attacks, or the nearby vampires.

This fight is so unreal. Elements of nature fighting one another, directed by the two women's movements. Sylviana's butterfly is way bigger than usual too, flying around her, though I have no idea what that thing is useful for. I think she's using it like a second pair of eyes, guiding her with her surroundings, because all this time, her power is acting everywhere while she's only looking at her sister.

Nephera is almost having fun. She's smiling like a creep, agitating her arms to throw one wave after another, leaving her younger sister no rest. Somehow, the fight looks more balanced than before. The witches are on the same level, but no attack seems to hit its direct target. Sylviana is being more passive than offensive.

"*Damian! Liam!*"

Next to me, Nora's white wolf just appeared, shining on the battlefield with her unique appearance. She immediately runs to help her mate, and I run to help Liam. The position is harder to hold than before. Because the number of wolves has lessened elsewhere, it feels like the vampires are focusing on us now. Damn, if only I could figure out this thing with my aura!

"How long do you think you can hold this for, Sylviana? I'm nowhere near done yet!" yells her sister, hysterical.

Sylviana doesn't answer. She's frowning, barely keeping up. Their elements are too different, her roots are struggling to block the waves and all the water spikes coming. Unlike Nephera, she has a lot of people to protect at the same time and can't just focus on her sister. The Water Witch is just acting randomly, hitting as many people as she can. She doesn't care about hitting the vampires, and those damn things still get up even if she hits them anyway!

I don't have time to help her, though. I'm focusing on my own fight, back to back with Liam. It's a fucking mess. Vampires crawling from all angles, and Nora can't heal anyone anymore while she's busy fighting. The fight is even more violent than before.

"*Nora!*"

"*I'm okay, I'm okay. I'm just... not in the best shape today.*"

No shit, she just gave birth minutes ago! I think she got scratched a bit, but she seems fine, and Damian is watching her like a hawk too. His own mate appearing on the battlefield gave him even more reason to fight harder. I try to sense my own, and Nate is near, almost here actually.

I roll back to avoid another vampire and bite him savagely. My aura, my aura. I try to take my friends out of my mind for a moment to focus on that strange bond with the humans. What can I do? I can't send them my thoughts or inner wolf's talk like I would for a wolf. They are humans!

"*Elena!*"

"*Nate!*"

My mate jumps next to me, but he immediately becomes one more target. Not my man, you damn blood-suckers! I growl and ferociously attack the enemy that was about to get him, taking them down in a fury.

Suddenly, I feel it. Like a spark. I growl louder, letting my anger grow.

"*Uh... Elena...?*"

My friends feel my furor, growing like a fire, a raging fire. My aura is burning up, ardent, and this time, it ignites. The vampires nearby suddenly screech, retreating, as if I was burning them. I let my anger guide me, and growl, attack, bite like a machine. I can even feel Nate and Liam backing away, unsure about my sudden state.

I'm just a big cloud of raging emotions right now. A raging sun, showing the way and burning high. The wolves can't feel it, they are stealing glances at me, confused by my sudden fit of rage and my aura going wild. But I feel it burst all the way to the humans I'm connected with. That's right. Silver City isn't just full of werewolves. Half of it is human. Half of my blood is human. Come and fight. Get angry at these vampires, get mad. I growl again, showing my fangs to those creatures who dare attack my territory. This is my city, you damn creatures. Our city.

Chapter 38

It's like something crawling under my skin, a spark, running through my veins and guiding my anger. I feel stronger, faster, fiercer. More dangerous, and my enemies know it too. I show my fangs and growl aggressively. The vampires around us are retreating, unsure, looking at me with fear in their eyes.

"*I don't know what you're doing, Selena, but please continue!*"

"*It seems to scare them. They won't approach you, Sunshine.*"

"*The humans are coming, too,*" I say.

"*What? The humans?*"

I'm sure of it. I can feel hundreds of them, moving to the northern border where we are. I hope somehow, it helps us get out of this mess and shift the balance in our favor. I never thought this would really turn into an all-out war, but after all, this is their city too. If we add the humans to our numbers, we might finally have an advantage.

"*I think you're doing it to our wolves too, everyone is... glowing.*"

I can tell. I'm communicating my aura all around me, spreading this fire to the other warriors. My rage is contagious. Is that the warrior side of my blood? Sharing my rage with them, making them eager to fight more. The fights are harsher and more violent than ever, like the werewolves have turned into complete animals, wild beasts.

We keep fighting, but another thing worries me. Sylviana is getting whiter, and the burn marks are extending on her body. This is not good news. Liam keeps glancing at her too.

"*She gonna be okay?*"

"*I don't know, she's been using a lot of her magic since earlier. I've never seen her use so much.*"

The witch is not sparing her efforts. We are surrounded by so much vegetation now, it's closer to a jungle than the muddy meadow it was a while ago. The water is raging too, flying all around and trying to get to us. Nephera keeps smiling evilly, like she's possessed.

"How long can you keep that up, little sister? You're burning so much magic for those pathetic dogs. But you're too young to use your powers fully, aren't you? You'll be exhausted before I'm done!"

With that, she sends another wave towards Liam. She seems to have understood their bond at some point, because she targets the youngest Black brother more than Nate or Damian. Liam is exceptionally agile and has been dodging her attacks for now, but the next mistake might get him killed. The vampires don't let him rest either. We need to find a way to stop her.

Suddenly, a gunshot resonates in the air, shocking everyone. The whole battlefield freezes. Everyone heard that. We are all waiting, our hearts beating like crazy, but I know. I smile internally, feeling a wave of adrenaline flowing through my veins. Another gunshot, and several others follow. Yes, that's it. We listen, and it goes on. Bang! Bang! Bang! The vampires start to screech and panic. All the wolves react to it, curious, anxious, trying to see what is going on.

"*Tell me that's good news?*"

"*What's going on at the back!*"

"*The humans! The humans have just come to help us! They have weapons, but they are only shooting at the blood-suckers!*"

"*Don't growl at them, you idiot! They're on our side!*"

"*I can't believe it!*"

"*Some are taking our injured!*"

"*Yeah, I saw them taking Joe!*"

Crap, Joe? Joseph Lewis got injured? I look for him, but thank Moon Goddess, he's alive, though he is moving farther away from me. I focus my mind-link and, with Nora, we relay the same orders in unison.

"*Cooperate with the humans! Give them space to shoot and let them take our injured away!*"

"*Make sure they don't get to the front lines and stay out of their shooting range!*"

Moon Goddess, this might be what we needed to win this fight! The arrival of the humans along with mine and Nora's auras fueling the battle give a newfound strength to the werewolves and the fight resumes in a better light.

However, our own battle is far from over. The Water Witch is not giving us any chance to approach her, and the vampires are resolute on defending her. It seems like she didn't just control the Vampire Queen; she must have made it so that they would protect her to the end! I try to keep up, find an opening, but Moon Goddess, she doesn't give us any rest.

Sylviana is losing ground too. I don't know why, but our witch is slowly starting to make mistakes. She's too busy trying to defend all of us. With me, Nora, and Nate back, she now has five people to protect from Nephera, who's just attacking blindly and trying to hurt us as much as she can. I'm worried about the quantity of water she's slowly gathering too. She controls it like tentacles, whipping it around and sending water spikes here and there. I dodge one at the last second, but it still grazes my shoulder. I growl back.

I need to get to her. I focus my aura on myself, making the glow even brighter and bigger. The vampires step back, afraid as if I was holding the sun itself in my hands. I growl furiously, jumping on one of them to kill them, and run past the others, trying to sprint to Nephera. Liam catches on to my move, and jumps right after me.

We are both determined to reach the witch, growling and speeding up. She sees us coming and for the first time, something that looks like fear appears in her eyes. She moves her water tentacles, trying to whip them our way, but we jump, roll, dodge, and do our best to keep going. Sylviana intervenes to protect us too as she sends a new salvo of water spikes, blocking it with a branch. Nephera steps back, frowning and panicking. We are almost there! I show my fangs, ready to bite. Anything I can do to take that damn witch down, I will! Liam is growling furiously right behind me too!

Suddenly, something breaks behind me, and I hear Liam's scream of pain in my head. Don't look, don't look, keep going! I finally jump over the witch, and for half a second, I see the fear in her eyes before I furiously bite down. I unleash the beast in me. I bite harder, like an animal, like a furious savage. It's not hard. I hate that woman, I hate her for what she did: how she hurt me, killed Reagan, and tried to hurt my baby! She screams loudly in my ears, and I'm suddenly pushed away by a wave, rolling in the mud before I brutally hit a tree.

"*Selena! Liam!*"

I hear Nate and Nora's screams, but it takes me a while to come back to my senses.

"It seems like the first time wasn't enough! You bitch! How much do you need me to tear you apart this time!"

I need to get up, get back on my feet, and get away from here. Come on, get up… It's like my whole body is numb. My head fucking hurts. It hurts… I open my eyes, growling a bit, fighting to stand.

A horrible wave of pain pierces me. I scream loudly because of the excruciating pain. I feel my scar being ripped open from my shoulder down, the flesh tearing under the pressure. I'm suffocating, I can't breathe when my whole body is screaming in utter pain.

"Shall we try going a bit lower? Hm? See if you can heal that!"

I scream again and that crazy bitch, whatever she does, it intensifies. I'm on the verge of passing out, but the sharp pain is what keeps me very much awake. I want to die. I want to die, anything but this horrible pain, I can't. I can't take it.

"*Selena!*"

Furious growls suddenly surround me, and whatever was torturing me suddenly stops. I want to faint, but my mate's smell calms me down. Oh, Moon Goddess.

"*Selena, hang on, hang on.*"

Something cold numbs my pain, and Nora's white fur is covering my vision. I can feel my cousin's aura, gently surrounding me, healing me. This is the best sensation ever, like some fresh, cold snow applied to my injury.

Nate is on top of me, guarding me like a furious dog, growling. I hear a fight going on nearby, but I can't see.

"*The witch…*"

"*It's okay, Sunshine, Damian and Liam are keeping her busy away from you. Just give us a minute to heal you.*"

"*Liam…*"

"*He… He's okay.*"

Why just okay? Can't Nora heal him too? I heard him getting injured before me. Did she just focus on me? Did Nora heal him already?

I try to find my inner wolf, reconquer my aura, and the glow comes back, helping me regain my strength. Moon Goddess… Nora steps away, and despite my sore and painful shoulder, I know I can go on like this. It's bearable. I growl a bit for Nate to give me some space and get back on my feet. We are in some sort of wooden trap, probably Sylviana's emergency solution to protect us from the vampires while Nora was healing me. Those blood-suckers have already gathered around to attack the minute they can though.

Behind them, I see the two black wolves, dancing around and trying to get to the Water Witch. Liam is badly injured, but fighting as hard as before. In fact, the right side of his head is covered in blood. His ear is ripped open, and I'm pretty sure his right eye is gone… Moon Goddess, what did that bitch do to him?

I growl, furious. At least I got her bad. She's full of blood too and a large injury is visible on her shoulder and neck, the exact same spot she hurt me twice. Karma bites back, bitch! Nora wants to heal me more, but we don't have that much time to lose. As long as I can stand, run, and fight, I'll be fine. I growl to have her and Nate step aside, and wait for Sylviana to open the cage. It was short, but that one-on-one with the witch makes me want to take her down even more. We need to end this damn fight!

Sylviana glances at us, and she sees that I'm up, but she doesn't open the cage yet. She seems to hesitate about something. Liam and Damian keep attacking, but with only two wolves and one witch, Nephera defends herself just fine. She just can't move as much because of her injury. I don't know who managed to bite her wrist too, but it's ugly, wide open, and bleeding. She's in a bad way!

"*Sylviana!*"

I growl after her, hoping she'll open that damn cage soon. She glances our way and turns to Nephera.

"Nephera, this needs to stop, now! Enough! You'll die if you continue!"

She's still trying to save her sister…?

Indeed, the Water Witch, despite her injuries, is starting to be covered in the characteristic burn marks that shows she is running out of magic, overusing it. I understand why she was wearing a black, long sleeve dress now, to hide her skin. But we have gotten close enough to rip several parts of her outfit, and everywhere we can see her skin, it's charcoal black.

However, despite her sister's warning, Nephera suddenly smirks.

"You think I care, Sylviana? As long as I take you down with me, I don't care! You think I'm weak? You think I can't beat you? I've had years to prepare!"

She suddenly calls her tentacles back. For a second, it looks like she's perfectly defenseless, and Damian and Liam are both about to jump. But Sylviana screams to warn them, and they both decide to jump back.

The next few seconds defies anything I had ever thought possible. Nephera's eyes suddenly turn completely blank, like a filter is covering them. The burn mark crawls up to her face, almost devouring her skin in black stripes. However, we have a bigger problem. A much, much bigger problem.

Behind her, a huge geyser of water erupts from the soil brutally. A cold shiver runs down my spine. That crazy witch just hijacked the river. A tower of water is standing behind her, like a waterfall ready to jump at us. This is nothing like her little water tentacles from before. The pressure and amount of water is terrifying. Even if it wasn't magic, this would be crazy dangerous already. If she uses that thing against any of us, we are dead.

I crawl back, realizing the cage is gone, and Nora, Nate, and I run back to Damian and Liam's side, unable to take our eyes off of that sight. It's a nightmare. Nephera is exerting her power to kill us. She moves her hands, and this damn column splits apart into six smaller ones, but still powerful as hell, like little geysers. She directs them to bend around her, looking like a spider's arms. But those arms are digging into the ground around her, just by the mere pressure of the water. Oh, Moon Goddess… If she attacks us with that, it will be like a water cannon hitting us directly.

"Liam…"

I'm surprised to hear Sylviana's voice now. She's looking at the tower, almost out of breath, looking more determined than ever. She ties her hair back and pulls her sleeves up, focused. The now one-eyed black wolf turns his head toward her.

"Promise me you'll do anything to stop my sister," she says.

He growls, confused.

"Promise me, Liam. Please. You need to protect them."

He stands there, growling, unhappy. I don't like what's going on. I don't like it at all. What is she hinting at? Sylviana looks at him, finally, looking angry.

"Liam Black. Promise me, now."

He hesitates, and finally, whines, lowering his head with a sad look.

"*Liam? Liam, what's going on?*" asks Nora, worried,

"*I don't know, I don't know! I…*"

He seems as lost as we are about Sylviana's attitude. Our Earth Witch nods and, looking resolute, suddenly drives her two hands into the mud.

"Get ready," she says. "Here we go."

Something starts rumbling under us. What the heck is going on? The ground keeps shaking, like an earthquake. We all crouch down by reflex, and I'm thankful to be on my four paws instead of two feet. It's too unstable! The nearby vampires all lose balance and fall in all directions. What is she doing? Preparing some giant root? Sylviana is frowning, a pearl of sweat on her temples, and like her sister, her burn marks spread alarmingly fast.

"*Sylviana!*"

"Don't… worry…" she mutters, her teeth clenched.

Suddenly, a giant form appears next to us, something twice the size of a human, made of roots and mud, with a vague humanoid shape. What the actual fuck…

"*What is that thing?*"

We are all thinking the same thing. She made a giant! A giant of mud, or whatever. It's a…

"*A golem!*"

I look down at Sylviana. She's confidently directing her creature, but like Nephera, her burn marks are spreading, fast. The two witches are running out of magic, and I don't know what comes after that, but I don't want to.

This will most likely be the final assault for everyone. Either Nephera manages to kill us with that thing, or we kill her first. Time to end this. I exchange a look with Nora.

"*It's now or never.*"

"*I know. But we must watch the timing.*"

"*I'll go in front, Nora, with Liam and Damian. You stay back with Nate; if Sylviana can protect you, maybe you can shape-shift in time to make Nephera stop.*"

She nods. This is such a reckless move at this point, but if the witches start attacking, with that giant water spider and this golem, we will only have a few seconds left for the last part of this plan to be put in motion. We only need five seconds. Five seconds for Nora to shape-shift back into her human form and scream with her Luna power for the witch to stop. I really hope this theory works.

It would be so much easier to carry out if it wasn't for all the vampires surrounding us. Those damn blood-suckers don't seem impressed by Sylviana's surprise golem; they are already screeching loudly and jumping back on their feet to attack us.

"*Nephera will target Nora first, she knows her Luna Power is the strongest. I'll be the decoy, but we have to move fast.*"

At least I managed to piss off that bitch enough to hope she'll focus on me instead of my cousin now. The large wound I inflicted on Nephera's shoulder and neck is still bleeding profusely, but it's hard to decipher her expression when her eyes have turned opaque, her iris and pupils hidden in a blue fog.

We are tensed up, waiting for the moment to attack. The vampires are crawling around us, ready to jump at us again. Moon Goddess, if Nora shape-shifts back at the wrong moment, her Luna Power doesn't work, or Nephera ignores her… So many things could go wrong with this plan, but it's our best shot. We gather next to the golem's feet. Sylviana nods, her green eyes went opaque too.

"Now!" she screams.

Everything gets set in motion at the same time. Damian starts running first, I'm right behind him. Nephera screams in anger, and the spider's legs start moving. Two of those water geysers are about to shift towards us, and I prepare to endure it, but an uproar above us catches the witch's attention first.

The golem is advancing towards her, and Nephera changes her attack at the last second to stop the giant. She steps back and agitates her arm, sending three of the spiders' legs against the golem. The pressure between the two strengths is making an awful rumble. The golem's head and hands are stopped by the water geysers, and for a second, it looks like one will have to give up. The giant of mud tries to fight back the water pressure, and both have to maintain full force not to give in. The struggle is happening right above our heads, and we are soon drenched by the downpour.

However, at least it's keeping three of Nephera's giant water streams busy. Damian and I accelerate, and I feel the others right behind us. Damian, Nate, Liam, and I need to stop her other "legs" long enough for Nora to get close, shape-shift, and yell for her to stop. We don't know how close or how loud she'll have to be, and I'm scared the ruckus around us will force my cousin to get too close to the witch. Nora will be in the most danger, and the vampires are rushing to stop our group too.

Suddenly, another water geyser moves, the fourth one, and Damian growls furiously, prepared to take it. It hits the Werewolf King full force, and I have to jump to the side to not be caught in it as well. The Black wolf struggles to keep standing for a second, his paws and claws digging into the mud. I can feel the full violence of the sudden hit. Nephera tries to increase the water pressure, to blow him away, but Damian won't give up. He remains there, blocking that geyser all by himself, shoulder first, and growling furiously. Moon Goddess, if even the King struggles this much…

I growl fiercely. Only two more of her "legs" to stop.

I'm now in front, but we are not there yet. Maybe a dozen feet between Nephera and us, but it feels like much, much more. The muddy ground and the downpour above us make it hard to run. Suddenly, I hear a furious growl on my right side, and Nate jumps in just in time to save me from a vampire's fangs.

"*Nate!*"

"*I'm fine! Keep going!*"

He fights off the vampires on my right flank, detaching himself from our group and growling furiously to defend us. I didn't notice the blood-suckers had already gathered around us! That was too fast! I lose a second watching Nate and, like an idiot, miss the sudden attack coming from the other side. I hear Liam's yell in my head, and the next second, I'm rolling in the mud, a vampire screeching above me. I growl furiously, defending myself and trying to kick him off me. The group of vampires have caught up on us, and I'm quickly surrounded. Liam intervenes to help me, his black fur suddenly covering my vision. He bites the vampire's arm off and pulls him away from me with infuriated growls to warn the others. Nora runs to catch up to me.

"*Selena! Are you okay?*"

"*Yeah, sor–!*"

I can't finish my sentence. I spot another vampire about to jump on Nora right behind her. I growl angrily and activate my aura again, brighter, before jumping on him. Damn it, I can't do everything at once! I finish that damn vampire off and use my aura to spread the message to humans and werewolves all at once.

"*This battle needs to end here and now!*"

I spread my anger to all our peers, calling our troops to rally. The vampires around us, once again scared and blinded by my glowing aura, retreat a bit.

Meanwhile, I feel all the wolves turning to our area, guided by my glow. Nora and I react together, and our combined auras are like a beacon, indicating to everyone where to gather on our side of the battlefield. In a few seconds, all the wolves not caught up in fights start running to our area, ready to end this. If the vampires reassemble, so will we. We need more wolves to fend off the vampires gathering to stop us. The humans can handle the frontier temporarily, or so I hope.

Moreover, Liam is still caught up in his fight on the side, a few steps away.

"*I'll be fine! Nora, Selena, go! Now!*"

I hate it, but if Liam and Nate don't stay behind to protect our flanks from the vampire attacks, we won't make it. I growl, frustrated, but my cousin and I resume running after exchanging a quick glance. We are only a few steps away, but there are still two of Nephera's water geysers to stop. Damn it, if she hits me or Nora with one of those…

While I'm wondering what to do, three familiar auras suddenly surge behind us. They detach themselves from the other approaching werewolves, quickly catching up to us. Nora and I recognize two of them at the same time.

"*Bobo! Tonia!*"

The Mura siblings are running fast to catch up with us. Just behind them, the third wolf, a white and brown male, breaks away from their duo and makes a sharp turn to go join Nate's side. He jumps in the fight to help my mate, and I suddenly realize it has to be Isaac, his best friend and Beta!

Tonia also decides to leave her brother to go and help Liam, whose missing eye has left him with many blind spots. Either way, I'm so glad those three came to help! Boyan and his humongous size is the best reinforcement we could hope for. The big brown wolf runs to get in front of us, like a big shield.

The trio's sudden appearance recalibrates the forces here. Our sides free of vampire attacks and Boyan running in front, we are almost at Nephera's position! I can feel all the werewolves gathering around us to fight back the vampires too, or whatever's left of them. For the first time, I feel more werewolves than vampires around us!

However, it's too soon to rejoice. Nephera's face makes an ugly grimace, and before we can react, her last two geysers move. Holy shit, if we take two from upfront…

I growl furiously, ready to take one, but it doesn't come. Instead, a wall of fur appears in front of me, and Nora screams in our heads.

"*Bobo!*"

Moon Goddess, this guy is… Boyan is not blocking one but two of the geysers, acting like a wall before us. No matter how big he is, he just can't block that much pressure by himself! We see him struggle and growl before us, and Nora and I exchange worried looks. Is he really going to handle it by himself? His huge paws are anchored in the mud, he's losing a bit of ground, sliding, but he's still standing. Can he really do this? Boyan growls furiously, and Nora and I don't dare move from behind him, waiting to see if he can hold it. I hear some of his bones breaking, it's horrible. Yet, he's still standing, making us hesitate. Should I replace him? But Nora can't go by herself.

"*Moon Goddess, Bobo.*"

We're hesitating for too long already. Can he really do this? Even the King is struggling just to handle one of those! No matter his size, if Bobo loses any more ground, falls, or gives up, we'll be the next ones she hits with those…

Just when I'm about to say something, another werewolf arrives like a bullet from behind.

"*Just go already, babe!*"

"*Danny!*"

I did not expect to see him jumping in the fight, but he immediately runs past us to go support his boyfriend. Daniel's thin figure can't handle one of those geysers, but he stands behind Boyan, pushing his other side to help the giant werewolf stand against the pressure. Boyan stops sliding and losing ground. My best friend is in a bad state too, his tawny fur is covered in blood and mud, but he growls at us.

"*What are you waiting for? Go!*"

I nod, and Nora and I both run past Boyan already. This is it. Nephera's water arms are all kept busy, she has nothing else to attack us with. Tonia, Liam, Nate, and Isaac are keeping the vampires busy, acting as a defensive circle around us. A hot shiver runs down my spine. This is it, this is it…

"*Nora! Whatever happens to me, stop her!*"

"*I know!*"

I see Nephera's face distorted by fear as I jump on her, all fangs out. She screams and tries to protect herself with her arms. We roll on the ground and fight for a few seconds, but I'm a werewolf. She's just a witch with no more power to fight me off. I finally pin her down to the ground, biting the previous injury again. I use all my weight on her, making sure that damn witch won't get up and do anything to Nora.

She struggles furiously, I feel she's trying to grab something. I try to change position to stop her, but I can't let go. My fangs are what keep her focused on me. Behind me, I feel my cousin shape-shifting back to her human form.

"*Selena!*"

A sharp pain pierces my flank. I scream internally, overwhelmed with the pain once again. Nephera has an ugly smirk, but I growl back, and bite her even deeper. I don't care. She stabs me again, with Moon-Goddess-knows-what, and the pain shocks my brain. Don't give up, don't give up… Those three seconds are like an eternity.

"STOP IT!"

Finally. Nora's scream freezes the whole area. All the vampires and werewolves close enough to have heard her voice are hit by her imperious command. None of them can move a muscle, her Luna's white aura is too strong. Nephera stops moving too, her eyes wide open in surprise. I'm the only one around able to ignore Nora's command. I see the witch frowning, struggling to fight my cousin's order and me, but I won't move, and Nora screams again.

"I said stop!"

Her voice carried even further the second time, stopping even more fights. Under me, Nephera's face is deformed by anger. Between my strength and Nora's voice, she's unable to move to defend herself. She can barely move her lips.

"You… rotten Royals…" she hisses. "Curse you and your damn blood. Little bastards… Cursed be Diane, her children… At least I'll take you with me!"

She fights Nora's command and I feel her move her wrist, turning the blade in my injury. Shit… I clench my fangs, enduring the pain.

"I hope you like silver, you little–"

I growl furiously, not intimidated by her.

"I may be a Royal, but my mother was human, you bitch. I don't give a shit about your silver!"

I furiously bite her throat, deeper. Her scream pierces my ears, but I keep going. I ignore the pain, the fatigue, the dizziness, and just keep biting, again and again. I need to end this. This madness has to stop. Everything she did, all the deaths, all the pain. It has to stop. I need to keep biting, ignore the pain, hold on, hold on for everyone's sake. I need to hold on until… until Nephera stops moving.

"Selena…"

My head is spinning. I feel someone's arms around me, pulling me back, and I finally let go. My legs give up under me. Is it over…?

The water sounds stop around us. The rain stops, leaving us drenched and exhausted. Moon Goddess… I lie next to my cousin, whose trembling hands are holding on to my fur. Nora cries silently, I don't know if she's exhausted or just overwhelmed. Nephera's body next to us makes horrible, erratic sounds. Her hissing breath is dying. I bit her throat so deep, she's drowning in her own blood.

Someone silently walks past us. Sylviana bends over her sister, crying. She's trembling, looking terribly sad. The witch sits next to her sister, taking Nephera's hand.

"I'm sorry… I'm so sorry, Nephera," she mutters.

I fight to not close my eyes and pass out. Nora and I silently watch the two witches, in a weird silence. Echoes of the ending battle are heard from some far away area, but here, it's a mausoleum. It's too quiet.

We stay a long time, listening to Sylviana's cries for her sister. She apologizes, over and over. Nephera's agony is horribly long and slow. I keep staring, like an invisible audience to this heart-wrenching scene. The black spots slowly retreat from the witch's skin, fading to white. Nephera's throat stops bleeding. For a second, the remains of my conscience are worried. She's healing. She's…

But Sylviana raises a little dagger, and ends it all.

Chapter 39

A long silence follows. There is always this strange numbness after a battle, as if what had happened was too much of a nightmare for anyone to process it. But no one is going to wake up, this wasn't a dream. There is no end to this, just that horrible feeling that, somehow, we need to move on.

Nora and I lay together for a long moment. I'm too tired to move, but too shaken up to collapse. I feel horrible.

After the witch's death, the word must have spread around quite quickly. The remaining battles, even from farther away, die down. Either the vampires all died or some ran away, I don't know, I don't care. I just feel the fights stopping, and this strange silence spreads wider on the battlefield. I feel Nora's aura, spreading like fresh snow around my injury, helping me heal. I hold on to that sensation, trying not to give in to the darkness that calls me. I feel so numb. I just want to lie there and sleep. But we can't…

Finally, Nora somehow manages to get up, and she walks away from me. I know exactly where she is going. My own mate is coming up to me. I shape-shift back, and soon feel Nate's fur against my skin as he lies down next to me. This contact is what finally frees me.

I start crying. I release all of my feelings, my pain, this bottomless despair. Moon Goddess, what happened to us? I'm even too scared to mind-link anyone, to find another one of my friends dead. I just curl up against my mate, looking for any bit of comfort I can grasp. I can't believe it. Levi… The reality that one of my best friends died hits me brutally. Chris, William, and so many more from my pack… Even Iris… I'm overwhelmed by the sadness. I know I need to pull myself together, but… I just need a minute. A minute to pour out the sadness filling my heart. I can't be a warrior right now. I'm just heartbroken.

Nate patiently waits for me to calm down in silence.

His presence is the one thing I need right now. To know my mate is here, my mate is fine. I selfishly hold onto that one thought. I take a deep breath, and struggle to get up. Even after this, there is so much to do.

It's a wreck around me. I spot Nora, a bit farther away, her hands on Damian's fur, looking concerned. Her white hair is glowing but, to my surprise, the tips are starting to turn back to their black color. Moon Goddess, the sunrise…?

I can't believe it. It's really dawn. Far behind the trees, the sky is starting to show some dark purple tones. It's just the beginning, but… I try to remember the whole fight, or how long Nora and I stayed lying down. It felt like eternity went by without us knowing. We really made this fight drag on until the last minute… No wonder we are all so exhausted, we fought for several hours straight.

"*Damn, I fucking love summer.*"

I chuckle nervously at Liam's words. He's standing, walking slowly to Damian's side. Nate and I walk up to them too.

"Are you okay…?"

"He has several broken bones," sighs Nora. "I'll do my best, but…"

"Nora, save it for other people. I'll heal this by myself."

I can tell she wants to save her mate first, but the King is right. There are a lot of people who need her healing aura more than Damian right now. I share some of my aura with Nora, giving her a bit more strength as she goes on to heal other people.

I walk up to Danny and Bobo, a bit farther, both wolves resting together on one side of the battlefield. They are both drenched, and Daniel is whimpering.

"*My poor babe...*"

"*I'm okay.*"

"*Okay? Babe, half of your bones are broken! It's gonna take ages to heal...*"

"*I'm okay.*"

I'm so glad they are fine. Those two were heroes tonight. Daniel is not a fighter at all, but he still stood with us, and jumped in to help Bobo. I'm proud of him. I sit next to Danny, caressing my best friend's fur. I can't help but cry a few more tears again, remembering Levi. My best friend sighs, putting his head on my lap.

"*Don't cry, if you cry... I'm gonna cry again too.*"

I nod, but I can't stop it. I don't even dare to go and see his body. I've rarely felt so helpless. I take deep breaths.

"Ahem... Excuse me."

I turn around, surprised to hear another voice. It's a human man, looking tired but standing, and handing me his shirt.

"It's just that, uh... I figured you might want to..."

Right, I'm still naked. I clumsily wipe my tears, get up, and thank him, grabbing the large piece of clothing. That guy is tall, his shirt covers me down to the middle of my thighs, it's good enough.

"You're the... sort of voice we heard, right?" he asks.

"Yeah. Thank you for coming."

"It's... We should have come sooner. We knew something was coming up, but you know, we thought it was werewolf business again. Then the word spread that the vampires were really getting... Anyway, we all heard your voice at the right time. We picked up whatever we had and decided to come. If we have a choice, we'd much rather pick the werewolves' side than vampires."

I chuckle nervously. No kidding. The vampires probably would have enjoyed a feast.

All around us, humans and werewolves are helping each other. Some rescue teams are still doing their best to take the victims to the nearby hospitals or give them first aid on the spot. I look around, feeling unsure.

There are so many victims. I start helping, like a robot. We decide to gather the dead together so everyone can find their loved ones, and help identify them. I see so many people I know... I have to stop several times to cry, pull myself together, find new bodies, gather them, and cry again. At some point, when I'm on the verge of tears again, someone pulls me away from the gathering of bodies.

"Hey, hey, come here."

Clark takes me away for a bit, and holds me in his arms, soothing me a bit. I didn't even notice my godfather was near me until then. I don't know where everyone is. I've just been going back and forth, helping whoever needed it and trying not to think.

"It's okay, it's okay," he whispers.

I just let go and cry again, sobbing loudly. I've been collecting so many bodies from our pack, I can't hold it anymore. People I grew up with, and some young ones I trained... How do we keep going after this? All of the clans have collapsed. Alphas, Betas, fighters... so many people have died. I mumble my worries to Clark, unsure if I make any sense with all the sobbing.

"Don't worry. We'll take it one step at a time. The pack will be okay. We will decide with the King what happens from now on…"

"Clark, Chris is… I think he… sacrificed himself."

"I heard what had happened with Iris. I think so too. That kid… He probably thought he wouldn't make it in this war. He also… He had some regrets about his sister. Chris was too good. He probably thought this would be the best way to help us. To help you."

I cry again, thinking about my cousins. I can't believe they did this. Even Iris redeemed herself, in a way.

"Xavier is…"

"I know."

I don't know when my uncle died. I didn't realize until I saw him among the victims.

Clark hugs me until I can calm down.

"Have you seen a doctor yet? Your back…"

"I'm okay," I sigh.

I know my back probably looks ugly at the moment. It's been stinging for a while, and I feel the fabric sticky with the blood. At least Nora healed my biggest injury for now. It's probably going to take a while before it stops being so painful every time I move my abdomen.

"You're really pale. Maybe you should– Hey, hey! Elena!"

I don't know what happened. I feel the earth move under me, and my legs become numb. Someone catches me before I fall to the ground. Voices gather around me.

"Okay, time out for you, babe."

I wake up on a couch. It takes me a moment to recognize Clark's house. It's full daylight too, I probably slept for a while. I'm feeling very weird, a bit… numb. Did they give me some drugs? I push away the blanket that was covering me, and struggle to sit up.

"Oh!"

In front of me, in the kitchen, Liam noticed me, and almost drops his sandwich to run to my side. He has a medical eye patch and a lot of bandages covering half of his head, but at least he looks fine.

"Selena? How are you feeling? Nate, she's awake!"

Liam gives up his spot to my mate, who comes down the stairs in his human form with jeans on, replacing Liam and crouching down next to me. I frown, seeing his bare shoulder. And no arm attached to it. Nate holds my hand, looking worried.

"Are you okay? Clark said you collapsed."

"Nate, your arm…"

He shakes his head.

"It was a small price to pay. Who cares about my arm. How are you feeling?"

"Like crap. I wish I'd forgotten… Do you have any news on Estelle? And everyone? How long was I passed out?"

"She's okay, all the kids are. They're still at Nora's house with William and Neal's wives. You just slept for a few hours, Sunshine, you can rest more. Nora is resting upstairs too, she tried to help everyone as much as she could, she's exhausted."

"Nate, what about the others? Your brother, Danny, Boyan?"

"Damian and Boyan were taken to the hospital, they needed some X-rays, but they'll be fine. Daniel and Tonia went with them to help the medical staff, the emergency room was overwhelmed. Clark lent us his house for you to rest."

I nod.

"What about Sylviana?"

"She went to her house, she said she needed to be alone for a while," replies Liam.

"We agreed to gather at Nora's house in a couple of hours."

"Okay."

Nate sighs and sits next to me on the couch. I'm only too happy to be able to cuddle with him for a bit. All the events from last night feel so… I don't know, impossible. Even while I'm resting like this, I can't get those images out of my head. Nate only has one arm to hug me with. Liam looks too tired to joke around, and I hear many people outside, doing whatever needs to be done.

I can't believe it's over. I'm still on edge, as if something was about to happen. My body is tired, but my mind won't relax. I thought I was a fighter, but after the fight is over, what am I supposed to be?

I miss Reagan. I know she would have found a way to get me back on my feet, whip me into finding the willpower to do something. It was already hard to have lost my mentor, but now… A part of me died with Levi. Losing my cousins, my uncle, too, it's like I barely have any roots anymore. Somehow, learning the truth about our parents' death didn't close any wounds, it just made the scars more meaningful for Nora and I. So, how do we move on from here?

"I love you," I whisper to Nate.

His fingers stroke my hair lovingly, and I feel his lips against my temple.

"I love you too, my sunshine."

I close my eyes, enjoying those words like the best medicine in the world. I'll be okay. I still have my family. I have my mate, my baby. I have Nora, Danny, Boyan. I still have a family, in my heart.

"Nate. I want to see Estelle."

"Okay. We can go now."

"Can I come with you?"

We both turn our heads. Nora just came down the stairs, her hair all over the place. My cousin got to take a shower and change into some new clothes. Somehow, seeing Nora as tired as I am makes me chuckle.

"Hi, Black Luna."

She pouts.

"Hi, White Luna," she replies. "How are you?"

"Right now, I'm jealous of your clothes. I'll go and take a shower before we go."

"I'll see if I can get us a car," says Nate.

Good, because I'm sure neither Nora or I are in any state to get there by foot.

I take a welcomed shower, putting the dirty shirt away, and freeing myself from all the dried blood and mud. I guess they just transported me to Clark's couch as I wasn't a priority, but I'm still one hell of a mess. My shoulder's scar looks worse than before, and I have some new ones on my abdomen and back. I guess Nora couldn't use too much of her power on me alone. My skin is dry as hell, and as I wash myself, I discover numerous bruises and little cuts underneath all the dirt.

As I get out of the shower and look at myself in the mirror, I don't recognize the woman staring at me. I have a bruise on my lower jaw, and some cuts above my eye. Looks like I went through hell and came back. I did. Somehow, I feel like I'm not the same woman I used to be. I've been through too much, and there's this feeling that I've lost something I'll never get back.

Once again, Levi's face comes to mind. It fucking hurts. A few tears escape me again. It's terrible to say, but his death hurts me more than any of the others. Levi literally died for me. He shouldn't have done that, but he died for me, and that thought is haunting me. I don't want to keep holding on to that.

I look at myself again in the mirror. I can't take it… I hurriedly investigate all the drawers and cupboards until I find what I need. I take a deep breath, and take one last look at my reflection.

When I come down the stairs, refreshed and with some clean clothes I borrowed from Isa, I'm feeling much better. Nathaniel and Nora give me surprised looks.

"Selena, your hair…"

I reply with a faint smile. My blonde hair is now freshly cut into a short bob, the rest of it in the trash bin upstairs.

I walk to my mate, and he gives me a little kiss, brushing my blonde hair.

"I like it."

"Thanks."

No one asks anything else, and we leave Clark's place.

Somehow, driving to the south makes me feel a lot better, like getting away from the battlefield clears a bit of my emotions. It's still way too fresh to forget the craziness we went through last night, but at last, it does finally feel like it's over.

When we park in front of Nora and Damian's house, the children are in the garden. To our surprise, Sylviana is with them. James and Estelle drop the flowers they were playing with to run to us.

"Mama!"

I get on my knees to welcome my baby with wide open arms. My little star runs into me and, the second I can hug her, I let out a nervous laugh of relief. Moon Goddess… She's alright. My baby is alright. It makes it all worth it.

"Mommy, your hair… It's like Rapunzel!"

I chuckle, and let her play with my hair, while Nate caresses her face and kisses her. She frowns when she sees her dad's arm. Nate put on a long-sleeved shirt to hide his bare shoulder, afraid she'd be scared.

"Daddy… What happened to your arm? And Mommy too, you look all hurt."

"Daddy and Mommy had to fight last night, little star."

"You beat the baddies?"

I exchange a glance with Sylviana, standing a few steps away. She has a very faint smile, looking at us. Her eyes aren't smiling at all. While Nate is talking to Estelle, she turns to Nora and hands her the newborn baby. Oh my gosh, Nora's baby.

We walk up to them, and James is already making a fuss, while his mother's attention is solely on her newborn. He's so small…

"Nora?"

Behind us, Tiffany Pearl-Blue just came out of the house, her daughter Rose right behind her. Moon Goddess, William's wife… From her expression, she already knows. Her eyes are red, but she looks very graceful. Nora turns to her with a sorry look, almost as if she's about to cry, but the young woman gives her a smile.

"It's okay, Nora. My husband is a hero. I'm already very grateful for how you are honoring him."

I don't know how she can hold in her emotions like that when William passed only a few hours ago, but my admiration for that woman is endless. Maybe she just doesn't want to show her sadness in front of her daughter, but even I have a hard time not tearing up, thinking about our cousin…

Nora turns to us, with her baby in her arms. The little boy already looks just like his older brother. His eyes are deep blue, and he has hints of black hair. He's awake, looking at Nora with big curious eyes. He's not even a day old.

"His name is William Black," whispers Nora, looking at him lovingly.

I chuckle. It's perfect. She then turns to Sylviana, who is standing on the side, looking at the baby with a faint smile on.

"Sylviana, do you want to be his godmother? He wouldn't be here if it wasn't for you."

However, the witch's expression changes into something sad. She shakes her head.

"Thank you, Nora, but… I can't."

"Why?"

"I'm dying," she whispers.

It has to be a nightmare.

We are all gathered in Nora's living room, trying to understand what the heck is going on. Liam is walking in circles like a lion trapped in a cage, while Sylviana is sitting, perfectly calm. I still don't understand.

"It can't be right," says Nora, translating my thoughts exactly.

Nothing makes sense about this. Damian and Nate, standing on the side, exchange looks. The King is carrying his newborn son, which he hasn't let go of since he came back from the hospital. Next to me, Danny keeps shaking his head, unwilling to believe it.

"Sylviana, there has to be something…"

"No, you can't do anything, Daniel. It's alright."

"It's not fucking alright!" yells Liam.

The baby starts crying, and Damian glares at him, but the youngest Black brother obviously doesn't care much at this moment. He's the most agitated, legitimately. He walks towards Sylviana, crazy.

"You can't tell me to fucking watch you die, Sylviana!"

"I'm sorry," replies the witch.

Moon Goddess. This situation makes no sense. We left the kids upstairs with Tiffany, Tonia, and Damian's Beta and his wife for now, but the situation here is unbelievable. I take a deep breath and turn to Sylviana.

"Sylviana, if we take you to the hospital–"

"It won't do anything, Selena. At best, it will buy me a few minutes. I don't want to die in a cold hospital room with machines keeping me alive until they can't. I'm fine if I can be with all of you."

"You look fine," whispers Nora. "How can you say you're–"

"My organs are failing, Nora. You can't see it, but I'm like a flower running out of sunshine and water. I've exhausted my magic way past what I had in that fight with Nephera. Even you can't save me, Nora. I condemned myself already."

"There has to be something we can do!"

Sylviana shakes her head. How can she be so fucking calm? She doesn't even look sick! Her skin is barely a bit paler than usual! If it was anyone but her, I wouldn't even be willing to believe it. Announcing that she's dying as we're talking with her!

I take a deep breath; I can't handle any more crying today. Next to me, Daniel stands up too, and walks to the kitchen, followed by Bobo.

"How long?" I ask.

"I–"

But before she finishes her sentence, Sylviana suddenly coughs up blood. Holy shit, this just got very real. Liam runs to her, completely shocked, but she calmly wipes it off, shaking her head.

"Not that long, apparently…"

Her eyes lose focus for a moment, and she needs to hold on to Liam and Nora not to fall. We jump off the couch, letting her lay down. Moon Goddess, she's really dying. Her face is getting whiter, and… I can feel she's fading away from us.

Sylviana is lying on the couch now, and Nora and I have given up, we are both sobbing, shocked. I feel Nate's hand on my shoulder. I'm trembling and I step back, holding onto him. Nora is on her knees next to Sylviana, looking desperate. We all are. Liam is standing next to her, unable to say a word.

Moon Goddess, none of this can be real. It doesn't feel real. A few minutes ago, everything was fine! Sylviana looks at us with that gentle smile of hers, and for a second, she has the eyes of someone very, very old. Nora takes her hand, my cousin's eyes filled with tears.

"It's fine, Nora. I had to do this. It had to be this way."

"I don't get it… What do you mean?"

Sylviana shakes her head.

"I wanted to save her. To allow my sister to finally have the peace she needed. She had been suffering for so long, and I couldn't do anything about it. I didn't want her to hurt anyone, or Silver City… I'm sorry."

"Why didn't you tell us?" asks Liam, desperate. "You could have–!"

"It wasn't about you, Liam. That hatred Nephera was carrying was a curse. Someone had to pay the price to break it, and I did. If only death could calm my sister down, then I'm glad I could do that for her, even if it cost me my own life."

"But–!"

She shakes her head and reaches out her hand. Liam falls on his knees, and she rubs his cheek gently.

"Liam, I had my mind set way before I even met you. You wouldn't have changed anything. I loved you, Liam, but my sister didn't deserve any of this. Silver City, our parents… Nephera was a victim too. She took the wrong path. Since I was born, I've felt sorry for my older sister, for what she had gone through. For our mother parting with her, and later, when I discovered what she had endured. I was born to protect Eleanora and Selena, Liam."

"You can't sacrifice your life for this! You can't…"

"It's not a sacrifice. Liam, I am so, so lucky I got to meet you, to have the life I wanted here. I even chose when and where I would die, love. If I die for the people I love, surrounded by my loved ones, I'm already so blessed. Not everyone gets to pick, but I do."

Hearing her last words, Liam suddenly breaks into tears. His head down against her hand, he completely loses it, sobbing loudly, his shoulders shaking from the utter pain. I can't even begin to imagine the hell he's going through…

"Eleanora, Selena?"

Nora and I step a bit closer. Sylviana gently smiles to us.

"I am so glad I got to see you both grow up and become Lunas. My mother was always too busy to take care of me, but Althea and Lilyan would always be there. You look like them so much, in so many ways... You're like little sisters to me. It was hard to watch you grow from afar."

"Sylviana..."

I already cried so much today... How is this happening? How can she even be smiling? I don't get it...

She caresses Nora's face with her other hand, while I'm standing there, helpless, sad beyond repair. I don't want to go through this, lose someone else today...

"It's okay... Everything will be okay."

For the first time, Sylviana lets out a tear, and her smile breaks a little. She's getting weaker. Her lips are losing their color, her cheeks too... Moon Goddess, no, no...

"Nora, you have to..."

"Liam, I can't heal that," sobs my cousin. "I... I'm sorry I can't..."

Damian walks up to her to hold her and comfort her.

I don't know if Sylviana doesn't have the strength to, but she just looks at us without adding a word. For a long while, we stay there, sobbing silently, waiting. Waiting.

It's... I close my eyes and take deep breaths. I know she wanted us with her, but... it's hard. I can even hear Danny crying from the kitchen. The house gets awfully quiet, and somehow, I know she's gone. Sylviana is gone.

Liam's crying gets even louder and more erratic, and Nora gently shifts her position to hug him. I can't deal with that. I turn and cry against Nate's shoulder, unable to hold back. Moon Goddess, why? Why Sylviana, of all people? She did nothing but protect us!

I can't take it. I can't stay here, with everyone crying around her body. I need some air. I run out of the house, into the garden, to take deep breaths. My head is spinning, but I'm just trying to calm down, calm down my frenetic sobs and breathe. Breathe, just breathe...

"Sunshine..."

Nate comes and hugs me, trying to comfort me. I'm so fucking tired. Tired of crying, tired of losing people. If it wasn't for my mate, my daughter, my family being here, I know I'd be a fucking mess. I'd collapse and crumble. I hear him sigh against my ear.

"It's been a fucking long day..."

I nod. When will this all be behind us? I feel like the end of the world is just taking forever.

"Boyan?"

We turn around and, standing at the entrance of Nora's house, Boyan is there, carrying Sylviana's body. What the fuck is going on now? He just walks out, looking determined. Daniel and Nora come out from the house behind him, both as confused as I am.

"What's he doing?" I ask.

"I don't know," sobs Danny. "He just said he had to do something, and he…"

Whatever it is, Boyan is walking away from us, and we need to get moving if we want to follow him wherever he's headed. Liam and Damian soon come out too, rushing behind us. It takes a while, but Boyan keeps walking, deaf to all our questions. Daniel is freaking out, and Liam doesn't even say anything, Damian almost has to support him…

Boyan takes us to the border, another part of the city. Where the hell are we? This is such a deserted part of our territory, why would he take Sylviana's body all the way here? He suddenly puts her down on the ground. This makes no sense. We all stare at each other, confused, but Boyan retreats, and opens his arms to push us to retreat too. What's going on?

Suddenly, something happens with Sylviana. Her butterfly! I had forgotten about her pet thing. It comes out of her chest, or maybe an inside pocket I didn't see. Is it supposed to survive its owner?

The butterfly flies above her, and I realize that thing is getting bigger. Much bigger. Before our shocked eyes, it grows until its wings are as wide as a human being. Some strange dust is coming out of it with each flap too, almost shining. Is that some witchcraft…? I exchange a look with Nora, but we are both lost.

"Look."

Nate points to the ground, and I realize the butterfly's dust is not simply falling, it's moving to some specific spots. The dust piling up is slowly starting to write some enigmatic scriptures on the ground. I have no idea what that writing is, but it's like gathering into shapes and circles around Sylviana's body and lighting up. Something strange is going on.

"Since when was that here…"

"Sylviana did this," suddenly says Boyan.

"And how the fuck do you know?" growls Liam.

"I just… remembered."

Boyan looks confused, like he's half-awake. Did she do something to him? How did he forget she did such a thing? I stare at the strange scene, and suddenly, the soil under Sylviana starts moving. It's trembling, like there's something underneath. What the heck is that!

"Step back," orders Damian, pulling Nora and Liam away from it.

Nate has me retreat too, and Daniel pushes Boyan. Every part of the soil that was touched or inside the strange scriptures is moving and suddenly, Sylviana's body starts being engulfed by it too.

"Sylviana!" yells Liam.

"Liam, no!"

Damian and Boyan both hold him back. Should we do something? I know Sylviana planned this, but… Slowly, the soil recovers her, digging under her and swallowing her in. Moon Goddess… Soon, her face is the last thing we see, and she disappears underneath the ground. I can't believe what just happened, but it's not over. The soil is still moving. No, it's shaking even more.

Something suddenly breaks out from the ground. A tree! A gigantic tree sprouts without warning, in accelerated motion, growing from a little twig into a majestic tree in front of our eyes. I… I'm speechless. The roots grow in all directions, while the tree keeps getting bigger, much bigger than a normal tree.

It suddenly stops, but for a long while, no one dares to say a word. It's… beautiful. It's a giant white oak. Its trunk is very pale, and I recognize some of the earlier scriptures imprinted into its bark. The leaves, thousands of them, are all an eerie green, almost shining. Somehow, I feel like I'm watching Sylviana when I look at this tree… It has her print all over it, I don't even know how. Moreover, I feel its magic, so mighty, pure, and powerful… It's spread all through the branches and beyond. I look down, but even the roots are overflowing with that magic, and I can feel it running underground too, extending further than what we see.

I turn to Nora, knowing we can both feel the same thing.

"It's a…"

"…a defensive barrier."

We nod along, convinced. So that's what Sylviana had been secretly preparing. Another barrier, for when she couldn't be here to hold on anymore.

She really knew all this time. She knew she wasn't going to make it. Maybe she had been lying all this time about being stronger than Nephera.

I don't know. She really did her best until the end, only thinking of protecting us.

I keep staring at that tree, and for a while, I feel a bit calmer. That's what she wanted. She did this for us… I nod and sigh, taking a step back into Nate's embrace.

For a long, long while, all of us stay here. I close my eyes.

I listen to the wind in the leaves, the familiar sounds of the city, and Liam's crying.

Epilogue

6 Months Later

"Moon Goddess, why does this have to be so fucking tight…"

I try to adjust it, but no matter what I do, my dress is barely letting me breathe. Why did my breasts have to get so big already? Like, seriously! This dress is a nightmare. I hear a chuckle behind me as Nora and Bonnie both come to my rescue, frowning and trying to adjust the lace on my back.

"I think we can make it a bit looser; it should be fine. We can find a shawl to cover your cleavage."

"Enjoy it, babe, it's the only wedding where the bridesmaids can be sexier than the bride!"

I roll my eyes and turn to Danny.

"Very funny, Daniel."

"Come on, I'm not the one who got pregnant two months before my wedding."

I sigh. I did not plan to get pregnant that fast! The Alpha compatibility is scary, I need to be careful in the future… I hear Nora chuckle.

"Can't you at least be on my side?" I sigh.

"Sorry, Elena, but… it's so cute! I know you and Nate were trying, but still…"

Well, I did insist a bit on giving Estelle a younger sibling. Nathaniel was the one who was against it. Not that he didn't want more kids, but my two previous pregnancies didn't turn out so great. Since he heard how much I struggled while I was pregnant with Estelle, he became so against it, we fought a lot on the matter. Thank Moon Goddess Estelle started asking for a younger sibling too, and he still can't say no to our baby star.

"I can't wait for you to be tired with baby number two," says Danny. "That way, I get to babysit Estelle all I want."

"You already see her twice a week!" I protest.

"You can babysit James if you want," says Nora. "Between all the work with the packs and Will who still doesn't sleep a full night, I feel like Boyan's been seeing my baby more than me."

I sigh. That's right, Silver City has changed a lot. With Arthur Seaver and William Blue gone, and so many werewolves dead, all the packs were at a loss for a while. Damian, Nora, Nate, and I had to work like crazy to get everything back on track, even with the humans. Once the funerals were over, we had to reorganize the packs.

While Damian is still of course the Werewolf King of Silver City, Nora and I have agreed to share the position of Silver City's Luna. After Clark gave me full control of the north and retired, Nora took over the south, including the now Alpha-less Sapphire and Sea Moon clans. The only two other clans remaining are the Pearl Moon and Violet Moon that Lysandra and Tiffany are still in charge of, and that's fine with us as it is.

"Thanks, but no thanks, Nora. Your baby is cute in pictures, but in the flesh? He's genetically linked with a chainsaw. Did you see the state of my rug? And Boyan's ear? His ear!"

Bonnie and I snort while Nora blushes, a bit embarrassed. James started shape-shifting last month, and pups chew everything, as we recently found out with poor Bobo.

"Sorry."

"Alright, we'll talk about the little monsters later. Daniel, are you ready or not?"

He smiles, perfect in his black tuxedo. I never thought I'd see Daniel Lewis wear a tuxedo! I've never seen him so elegant. Bonnie looks proud of him too, helping him adjust the bowtie.

"I think we should get going now," she says.

"Babe?" he says, giving me his arm.

I grab the flowers, and we leave the room.

Somehow, holding a wedding now was a bit of a crazy idea at first, but after thinking about it twice, everyone agreed it was the best way to signify new hope. Life goes on in Silver City. We survived. We lost people, but for those who remain, life can go on.

We arrive in front of the entrance and meet with the groomsmen. Nora is all too happy to find Damian. With a big smile, Ben takes his spot next to his sister, and all six of us wait for the music to start. I glance at my flowers. If only she could be here… and Levi…

"Hey."

Daniel caught my glance, and frowns.

"Chin up, young lady. Don't you dare think about unhappy things today. It's okay, babe. They would be happy for us."

"… I know."

I take a deep breath. That's right. Today is a wedding, a happy day. I smile at Daniel, and he kisses my cheek. I chuckle.

"Are you sure you shouldn't be going up with… your mom? Or your dad?"

"Babe, I want my best friend with me. All the way. You're my family."

Oh shit, he's going to make me cry.

"If you cry, I'll spank you right here."

I chuckle, and manage to hold it in. The music finally starts, and we walk in. It's a little, private wedding. Only close family and friends, not even thirty people inside. Daniel and I slowly walk up the aisle, all eyes on us.

I see Boyan, gorgeous in his white tuxedo, waiting nervously for us. I hear Daniel gasp. Yes, our Bobo is that handsome. We finally reach the altar, and Bobo gives me a hug before I go to the side, as the maid of honor, listening to the vows.

I love how they kept it simple. It's touching, very sweet with a hint of humor. They mention their first meeting in that club, Bobo's smooth dance moves, and even their love spats. I can't resist shedding a little tear, and I see Abigail in the same state on the front bench.

Finally, Estelle walks up, holding the rings, and Danny gives his goddaughter a little kiss. My daughter walks up to her dad and uncle on the other side. I wasn't sure Liam would show up, but apparently, they convinced him.

A lot of chuckles and a kiss later, they are pronounced husband and husband, and exchange a wild kiss that wouldn't have been allowed in church! A lot of cheers and a wave of applause take over the room and, after a few more hugs, I step to the side to let Danny and Boyan's families come and congratulate them.

A familiar arm surrounds me, and Nate gives my shoulder a quick kiss.

"Damn, Daniel managed to make me jealous again."

"Yeah, I think Boyan is definitely taken now, sorry?"

"Very funny… I was talking about our wedding, Miss Whitewood. When will I finally get to call you my wife?"

I chuckle and turn around to kiss him. Of course, he answers it, but I can tell my little distraction doesn't work. He frowns and steps back.

"Seriously, why won't you say yes?"

"Maybe because then I wouldn't get to hear you ask anymore…"

He smiles.

"Alright, I guess I can keep asking a bit more. I'll be patient until my new sunshine comes."

It's my turn to frown.

"Your new sunshine?"

Nate chuckles and puts a hand on my tummy.

"Yes. ***My Sunshine Baby***…"

The Silver City Series will end in

His Blazing Witch

About the Author

Jenny Fox is a French author, born in Paris in 1994.
She reads alone for the first time at 6 years old, Harry Potter and the Philosopher Stone, and writes her very first story at 9 years old. Her teacher reads it in front of the whole class, and from then on, she will never stop writing, from short stories to fanfiction.

His Blue Moon Princess is her first story to be entirely written in English, inspired by her experience overseas and her love for Fantasy Novels.

Follow her at **@AuthorJennyFox** on her Facebook Page.

Novels by Jenny Fox

THE SILVER CITY SERIES

His Blue Moon Princess

His Sunshine Baby

His Blazing Witch

*

THE DRAGON EMPIRE SAGA

The War God's Favorite

The White King's Favorite

The Wild Prince's Favorite (coming soon)

*

STAND-ALONE STORIES

Lady Dhampir

The Songbird's Love

A Love Cookie

Hera, Love & Revenge

*

THE FLOWER ROMANCE SERIES

The Fairy & The Thug

The Nymph & the Chef

The Vampire & The Secretary

The Demon & The Student

The Angel & The Soldier

CPSIA information can be obtained
at www.ICGtesting.com
Printed in the USA
BVHW051758260822
645581BV00003B/446

9 781838 109745